THE
SILENCE
OF
MURDER

THIS IS A BORZOI BOOK PUBLISHED BY ALFRED A. KNOPF

Visit us on the Web! www.randomhouse.com/teens

Educators and librarians, for a variety of teaching tools, visit us at
www.randomhouse.com/teachers

Library of Congress Cataloging-in-Publication Data
Mackall, Dandi Daley.
The silence of murder / Dandi Daley Mackall. — 1st ed.
    p. cm.
Summary: Sixteen-year-old Hope must defend her developmentally disabled brother (who has not spoken a word since he was nine) when he is accused of murdering a beloved high school baseball coach.
ISBN 978-0-375-86896-2 (trade) — ISBN 978-0-375-96896-9 (lib. bdg.) —
ISBN 978-0-375-89981-2 (ebook)
[1. Brothers and sisters—Fiction. 2. People with mental disabilities—Fiction. 3. Selective mutism—Fiction. 4. Trials (Murder)—Fiction. 5. Mystery and detective stories.] I. Title.
PZ7.M1905Sk 2011
[Fic]—dc22
2010035991

The text of this book is set in 11.5-point Goudy.

Printed in the United States of America
October 2011
10 9 8 7 6 5 4 3 2 1

First Edition

THE
SILENCE
OF
MURDER

DANDI DALEY MACKALL

Alfred A. Knopf
new York

To the memory of my dad,
Frank R. Daley, MD, who taught me to love words,
wit, and a good mystery. I have been blessed with
two fantastic parents, who gave me
a much better start to life than I deserved.

1

The first time Jeremy heard God sing, we were in the old Ford, rocking back and forth with the wind. Snow pounded at the window to get inside, where it wasn't much better than out there. I guess he was nine. I was seven, but I've always felt like the older sister, even though Jeremy was bigger.

I snuggled closer under his arm while we waited for Rita. She made us call her 'Rita' and not 'Mom' or 'Mommy' or 'Mother,' and that was fine with Jeremy and me. Pretty much anything that was fine with Jeremy was fine with me.

We'd been in the backseat long enough for frost to make a curtain on the car windshield and for Rita's half-drunk paper cup of coffee to ice some in its holder up front.

Jeremy had grown so still that I thought he might be asleep, or half frozen, either one being better than the teeth-chattering bone-chilling I had going on.

Then came the sound.

It filled the car. A single note that made it feel like all of the notes were put together in just the right way. I don't remember wondering where that note came from because my whole head was full of it and the hope that it wouldn't stop, not ever. And it went on so long I thought maybe I was getting my wish and that this was what people heard when they died, right before seeing that white tunnel light.

The note didn't so much end as it went into another note and then more of them. And there were words in the notes, but they were swallowed up in the meaning of that music-song so that I couldn't tell and didn't care which was which.

Then I saw this song was coming from my brother, and I started bawling like a baby. And bawling wasn't something you did in our house because Rita couldn't abide crying and believed whacking you was the way to make it stop.

Jeremy sang what must have been a whole entire song, because when he closed his mouth, it seemed right that the song was over.

When I could get words out, I turned so I could see my brother. "Jeremy," I whispered, "I never heard you sing before."

He smiled like someone had warmed him toasty all the way through and given him hot chocolate with marshmallows to top it off. "I never sang before."

"But that song? Where did you get it?"

"God," he answered, as simply as if he'd said, "Walmart."

I'd just heard that song, and even though it seemed to me that God made more sense than Walmart for an answer, I felt like I had to say otherwise. I was the "normal" sister, the one whose *needs* weren't officially *special*.

"Jeremy, God can't give you a song," I told him.

Jeremy raised his eyebrows a little and swayed the way he does. "Hope," he said, like he was older than Rita and I was just a little kid, "God didn't give it to me. He sang it. I just copied."

The door to the trailer flew open, and a man named Billy stepped out. Rita was breaking up with Billy, but I don't think he knew that. We'd stopped by his trailer on our way out of town so Rita could pick up her stuff, and maybe get some money off her ex-boyfriend, who didn't realize he was an ex. Billy stood there in plaid boxers, his belly hanging over the elastic like a rotten potato somebody'd tried to put a rubber band around. If I hadn't been so cold, I might have tried to get Jeremy to laugh.

Rita squeezed up beside the potato man. She tried to slip past him and out the door. But he took hold of her bag and grabbed one more kiss. She laughed, like this was a big game. Then she stepped down out of the trailer, wiping her mouth with the back of her hand.

I would have given everything I had, which I admit wasn't so very much, just to hear Jeremy and God's song again.

The tall heels of Rita's red knee-high patent-leather boots crunched the snow as she stepped to the car, arms out to her sides, like a tightrope walker trying to stay on the wire. She jerked open the driver's door, slid into place, and slammed the door hard enough to shake the car worse than the wind.

Without saying a word, she turned the key and pumped the pedal until the Ford caught. Then she stoked up the defrost and waited for the wipers to do their thing. I figured by the scowl on Rita's face that Billy hadn't forked over the "loan" she'd hoped for.

3

Jeremy leaned forward, his knobby fingers on the back of the seat. "Rita," he said, "I didn't know God could sing."

She struck like a rattler, but without the warning. The slap echoed off Jeremy's face, louder than the roar of the engine. "God don't sing!" she screamed.

That was the last time Jeremy ever spoke out loud.

Sometimes I think if I could have moved quicker, put myself in between my brother's soft cheek and Rita's hard hand, the whole world might have spun out different.

2

"Your Honor, I object!"

The prosecutor stands up so fast his chair screeches on the courtroom floor. He has on a silvery suit with a blue tie. If he weren't trying to kill my brother, I'd probably think he's handsome in a dull, paper-doll-cutout kind of way. Brown hair that doesn't move, even when he bangs the state's table. Brown eyes that make me think of bullets. I'm guessing that he's not even ten years older than Jeremy, the one sitting behind the defense table, the one on trial for murdering Coach Johnson with a baseball bat, the one this prosecutor would like to execute before he reaches the age of nineteen.

The prosecutor charges the witness box as if he's coming to get me. His squinty bullet eyes make me scoot back in the chair. "The witness's regrets about what she may or may not have done a decade ago are immaterial and irrelevant!" he shouts.

"Sit down, Mr. Keller," the judge says, like she's tired of

saying it because she's already said it a thousand times this week.

Maybe she has. This is my first day in her courtroom. Since I'm a witness in my brother's trial, they wouldn't let me attend until after I testified. So I can't say the whole truth and nothing but the truth about what's gone on in this courtroom without me.

"I'll allow it," the judge says. "Go ahead, Miss Long."

I smile up at her, even though she's not looking. I'm thinking there just might be a nice regular person under that black robe. I try to imagine what she has on under there and decide cutoffs and a T-shirt that reads GRATEFUL DEAD. That's what I remember seeing on the black shirt of one of Rita's girlfriends during her trial for solicitation, which is one fancy way of looking at that job. "Thank you, Judge," I tell her.

Raymond Munroe, attorney for the defense, smiles at me now, but it's a half smile, the kind a ninety-pound weakling might risk if a bully decided to walk on by instead of pounding him into the sand. Poor Raymond, our court-appointed attorney, looks more out of place than I do in this courtroom. He looked out of place in our house when he made Rita and me practice our testimonies. And he looked out of place when he stood up next to my brother in the Wayne County Courthouse and helped Jeremy plead "not guilty and not guilty by reason of insanity." Raymond's voice cracked.

I glance over at the table where Jeremy is sitting all by himself. He's in a constant state of motion—like a hummingbird—his hands patting the table, his knees bouncing, his arms twitching. He's not like this all the time, only when he gets upset. When Jeremy was little, his face was handsome. Then it took on angles, like his skull rebelled because it couldn't hold on to the thoughts Jeremy kept inside.

"Hope," Raymond says, looking at the jury instead of me, "have you always suspected there was something . . . well, let's say 'wrong' . . . with your brother?"

My brother is staring hard at me, his mouth slightly open, showing too much gum on top. I know Jeremy's waiting for me to tell the truth, the whole truth, and nothing but the truth because that's his way.

But it's not mine. And it hasn't been for a long time.

So even though I have never even once thought there was something "wrong" with my brother, I nod.

"You'll have to speak up," the judge says, leaning over her desk. You can tell she's not mad, though. "We can't record gestures," she explains. "Answer the question with words, please." She leans back in her big chair and waits for words.

"Sorry," I say, making sure not to look at my brother again. "Jeremy's always been different. I guess, like Raymond says, 'wrong.'"

I try to remember the way Raymond and I rehearsed this part of the testimony. This is not how it went. I remember that much.

I have a good memory, but it doesn't work with words. Just pictures. Like I can picture Raymond sitting at our sticky kitchen table, a pile of papers and a yellow pad in front of him. A full glass of Rita's too-sweet ice tea is sweating a water ring to the side of Raymond's notebook. Raymond's trying to tell me how to support his strategy, which is to convince the

7

jury that Jeremy's too crazy to be killed by the State of Ohio just because he murdered Mr. Johnson. Raymond wants to make sure we understand that Ohio can give the death penalty to anybody eighteen or over, unless they're really, really out of it.

I can picture Raymond, Rita, and me at that table as if we were still there. Jeremy's the same way. He notices details. He can tell when I'm getting a migraine headache even before I feel it, just by seeing the lines on my forehead change. Jeremy used to say God wired us alike, loaded us with the same film. That was before he stopped talking. Jeremy, I mean. But God too, I guess. At least to me.

Raymond's frowning at me, waiting for me to say what we practiced. I notice the shiny lining of his suit and his skinny black belt. I glimpse Jeremy swaying at his table, his skin drawn too tight over the angles and bones of his face. Two rows back sit three of my teachers from high school, not together but in a blur of other town faces, including T.J., a guy in my class and about the only friend I've got in this town. Behind T.J. a row of reporters lean into each other.

And I see Chase, Sheriff Wells's son, who stands out in this crowd, in any crowd. Even here, with life and death dangling from the courtroom rafters, his face—I notice every line in that face—makes it real hard for me to look back at Raymond.

Raymond clears his throat and glances at the jury, then at me again. "Would you mind giving us an example of how your brother is *different*?"

I do mind. I know exactly what Raymond wants me to say.

He wants me to tell the jury about something that happened when Jeremy was ten. That's what we rehearsed. Only I don't want to tell this story. I know it will hurt Jer.

But if *I* don't tell it, Rita will. And she'll get it all wrong, and Jeremy will hate that worse than having me tell it right.

Besides, it's important to tell it right. Because if I don't, if the jury doesn't understand Jeremy, then the State of Ohio will give my brother a shot that will put him to sleep forever. And even if they don't do that, they'll put him in a prison with grown men who will crush all the Jeremy out of him, or kill him trying.

3

"Hope, will you tell us about an incident that took place in Chicago when Jeremy was ten?" Raymond Attorney for the Defense asks. It's the exact question he made me answer half a dozen times at the kitchen table.

"I was eight, and Jeremy was ten," I begin. I close my eyes and remember. I can see Rita's hand reaching for something. I know it's her hand because she's wearing the big green ring she used to have. Jeremy's behind her, and I'm behind Jer. I have straggly blond hair and big blue ghost eyes, and I'm bundled into a quilted ski jacket a size too small. Steam rises from a loaf of bread. Plastic forks are piled at one end of a long, skinny table with a yellow-and-green-checked tablecloth.

"It was our first night in Chicago," I continue. "Rita decided we needed a change of scenery from Minneapolis, although the snow looked the same to me. She told us she'd always wanted to see the Windy City. Plus, there was this guy named Slater who was looking for us, and Rita didn't want him to find us. I kept thinking how Windy City was a real good name for this place because we could see snow blowing everywhere, like it wanted to get out of town fast as it could.

"Jeremy and I held hands and trailed behind Rita." I can see her in her pale pink wool coat and red high heels, but I don't bother telling the jury that. "We'd ridden all night on a bus from Minneapolis. Rita had struck up a conversation with a man who said he was a salesman."

Raymond steps in closer to the witness box. He glances at the clock, then at the judge, and finally back to me. "Get to the part where the police were called in."

That makes the prosecutor bounce up again. "Your Honor! He's leading the witness."

I can't imagine Raymond leading anybody, but the judge nods, agreeing with Mr. Keller. "Sustained." She turns to Raymond. "Just ask your question, Mr. Munroe."

I feel kind of sorry for Raymond because he looks like a kid who got his hand slapped for reaching where he shouldn't have.

"Would you tell us what happened when you arrived at the shelter?" Raymond asks.

I tell myself I need to cut to the chase. But thinking this reminds me that Chase, *the* Chase, is sitting in this very room, listening to and watching . . . me. And I have to talk about going to a shelter to get a meal.

I clear my throat. "There was a long line of people waiting to get their dinner for free. It was a good dinner too, with fresh bread and everything. Rita gave us plates and told us to fill them up. She and the salesman did the same thing. I think

I forgot to tell that part, that the salesman came with us from the bus station. He was the one who knew about the free-dinner place."

My mind is jumping ahead, and I see Jeremy's hand reaching for that bread. I remember being glad about that because my brother had started looking skinny as a shoelace.

"Please go on," Raymond urges.

I take in a deep breath and let out the rest of the story without taking in another. "Jeremy kept piling bread onto his plate, even when Rita tossed him a dirty look not to. And there were drumsticks too, and he piled those up. Then, instead of eating his own food, like he should have done, he walked around that room and handed it out."

"Handed it out?" Raymond repeats.

I nod, then remember about using words instead. "Yeah. He gave drumsticks to old men and little boys and other kids' mothers. And he gave bread to people right off his own plate, even if they already had some. When his plate was empty, he went back and filled it up again and then handed out the food all over again. It was like he couldn't stop giving it away."

"How did people react?" Raymond asks, right on cue.

"At first, people took the food without saying anything, just giving him a funny look. Then they got into it. They hollered, 'Over here! I can use some of that!' And Jeremy kept it up until there wasn't anything more to give out."

"And then what?" Raymond asks.

"And then he took off his shoes."

"His shoes?" Raymond looks all surprised when he turns to the jury. But he knows what's coming, which is why he wanted me to tell this story.

12

"He took off his brand-new snow boots, and he gave them to a kid who wore beat-up tennis shoes. Then he took off his socks, and he gave those away too."

"Where was your mother during all this?" Raymond asks. As if he doesn't know.

"Rita was yelling at him to stop. She kept saying she paid good money for those boots, although it was really Slater who did, and I'm not so sure the money was all that good."

"And what did your brother do when your mother yelled for him to stop?" Raymond asks.

I answer just like we practiced. "It was like Jeremy didn't hear her. He gave his coat to a red-haired girl with a long braid down her back. He unbuttoned his shirt. Rita took hold of his hand, but he kept going, unbuttoning with his other hand. So she smacked him."

"Smacked him?" Raymond says, like he's never heard of such a thing in his whole life.

"Just the back of his head," I explain. "But it didn't stop him. He gave the shirt off his back. And he kept going. He was down to his boxers when security got him. I don't like to think what might have happened next if they hadn't stopped him when they did." I deliver that line exactly like Raymond and I practiced it.

But I feel like a traitor bringing up this story this way. I can't look at Jeremy, but I can imagine the look he's giving me. I've seen it enough to know. Not mad. Disappointed. Like he thought I'd understood that day and now he sees I didn't and it's too bad—for me, not for him—that I don't.

The truth is, when the security officers stopped him, Jeremy didn't look crazy. I don't think a single person in that

13

room thought he was crazy. They'd all grown quiet by then. All except me. I shouted for them to get their hands off my brother.

Then this little boy walked up to Jeremy and held out his own jacket for Jer to put on, and Jeremy did. And then a very large woman took something out of a grocery bag, and it turned out to be shoes exactly Jeremy's size. And not only did she give him those shoes, she put them on his feet. But not before a little girl ran up and gave my brother her own white socks that had little yarn balls on the back of them so they wouldn't fall down. Somebody else came up with a pair of jeans for my brother. One of the security people helped Jeremy get those jeans over his new shoes because by then guards had his arms behind his back.

When we left that place, people said goodbye and waved. And Jeremy was better off than when we'd come in.

We all were.

I feel sick inside my bones. My whole life I've fought anybody who said Jeremy was crazy, or treated him like there was something wrong with him. And now I've done that and worse, here in front of everybody and after swearing about it with my hand on the Bible.

"It's getting late," the judge says. "We'll adjourn until nine o'clock tomorrow morning." She turns to the jury and gives them orders not to talk to each other or anyone else about this case. Then she bangs her gavel on her desk. We all stand up to go home.

Only not Jeremy.

4

I stumble down from the witness box because I have to get to Jeremy fast. He and Raymond are standing up at the defense table, and an officer is heading for Jer. I don't know what the rules are here, but I need to talk to my brother.

"Jeremy?" I rush over to him before anybody can stop me, but the table is between us. I can't touch him. I want to hug him, to feel his stiff arms fold around me, to have his chin on my head. "I'm sorry. I had to tell it that way." I want to shout to Jer that I don't believe he's crazy, but I can't. Raymond told me I can't ever say that to anybody, especially not in court.

"You need to leave, Hope," Raymond says. He's tossing papers and files into his briefcase.

I ignore him. It's Jeremy I want. "Jeremy, you have to tell them you didn't do it. Write it out. Please? Just write down what happened." He can write. Until this . . . until Coach died . . . Jeremy wrote notes all the time, in beautiful, pointy, swirling letters, his own brand of calligraphy.

Jeremy turns and gives me a sad, disappointed smile filled with forgiveness. Bile spouts from my belly to my throat, but I gulp it back down. His eyes widen as the officer slaps on handcuffs. His wrists are bruised, and his forearms have blue-and-yellow fingerprints. I'd be horrified if I didn't know firsthand how easily my brother bruises. It was Rita's curse when Jeremy was young because the world could see her temper spelled out on Jeremy's skin in purple and blue. She made him wear sweatshirts and jeans, even in Oklahoma summers. Most of the bruises came from Jeremy's clumsiness, though. I used to call them nature's decorations.

"Wait!" I beg. "Please let me talk to him."

I watch my brother's hands, his long, knotted fingers twisting frantically in the cuffs.

"Settle down, son," says the officer of the court, a burly man with tiny wire-rimmed glasses. Except for his soft eyes, he looks like the bald bouncer Rita fell for in Arizona, right after she quit her waitress job. "Come along now."

Jeremy's wrists spin faster and wilder. The metal cuffs clink together. He stares over his shoulder at me, intense, desperate.

"Take it easy, Jer," I urge, angry at myself for making him worse, for upsetting him, for calling him crazy in front of God and everybody.

Then I get it. He's not trying to wrestle out of the cuffs. He's doing charades, mimicking the motion of turning a lid on a jar. Jeremy wants one of his jars. He collects empty jars, and he wants—*needs*—one now.

"I'll try, Jeremy. I promise. And I'll take good care of your jars. Okay?"

His hands stop twisting. His body goes limp.

The officer takes him by one arm. "There's a good boy," he says, leading him away. "Time to go."

I stare after Jeremy for a solid minute after he disappears behind a side door. I don't want to think what's on the other side, where Jeremy will spend one more night.

I wheel on Raymond. "This is wrong, Raymond. He didn't do it."

Raymond doesn't look up from his overstuffed briefcase. "Hope, we've been all through this. Your mother and I settled on a trial strategy."

"But you pled not guilty by reason of insanity *and* not guilty?" I sat through as many of Raymond and Rita's trial talks as they'd let me. I'd wanted them to come out and say Jeremy didn't do it, but they wouldn't listen to me. Rita is convinced Jeremy did it but didn't mean to, so she was all about the insanity plea. Then Raymond told us that in Ohio, you can plead both things, "not guilty" and "not guilty by reason of insanity." So that's what we did. He said it was like covering your bases, like telling the jury: "My client didn't do it, but if he did, he was insane and didn't know what he was doing."

Raymond sighs like he's losing patience with me. "Yes. We pled NG and NGRI, not guilty and not guilty by reason of insanity. At the insanity hearing, Jeremy was deemed capable of standing trial and helping in his own defense. Hope, I thought you understood that."

"I did! But if they've already said he's *not* insane in that insanity hearing, why are you trying to make out like he's crazy now?"

"One has nothing to do with the other," Raymond explains. "That hearing was separate from this trial. The jury wasn't there. Here, in this court, we can still go for not guilty by reason of insanity."

"But what about proving he didn't do it? Period! Why aren't you doing that?" I'm shouting now, but I can't help it.

Raymond glances around, then whispers, "Because there's no evidence for that."

That shuts me up. No evidence, except the evidence piling up *against* my brother. I haven't been allowed in the courtroom before now because I had to testify, but I've read the newspaper articles about the state's witnesses, who claim they saw Jeremy running from the barn with a bloody bat, *his* bloody bat.

I sense someone behind me before he speaks. "I'm sorry. You need to clear the courtroom." Sheriff Matthew Wells has the gravelly voice of an old-time Wild West sheriff.

I turn to face him. He's about Rita's age, tall with a beer gut. The sleeves of his light brown shirt are rolled up to the elbow, showing a purple tattoo of a star, or maybe a badge. His black hair has a circular dent where his hat must belong when he's not in court. There's a gun in his holster. "Need to move along, folks."

"Of course," Raymond says. "Sorry, Sheriff." He snaps his briefcase shut and looks over at me. "Hope, I'll see you tonight, all right?"

I nod. But that sick feeling in my stomach comes back. Raymond wants to prepare me for tomorrow. More testimony, including the prosecutor's cross-examination. How do you rehearse for that?

"Miss?" Sheriff Wells touches my arm, and I automatically pull away. "You really do need to leave now."

I hear footsteps and wonder if he's called in reinforcements. A posse? A SWAT team?

But it's only T.J., coming to my rescue. "She was just trying to talk to her brother's lawyer, Sheriff." Thomas James Bowers is a couple of inches shorter than I am, about half the size of the sheriff. Everything else about T.J. is too long—his nose, his jaw, his hair, which flops over sturdy rectangular glasses. He swore he'd stick with me through this whole trial, and he has.

"She can talk to her brother's lawyer outside the courtroom," Sheriff Wells snaps.

Shouts flood the courtroom as the main doors open and Raymond exits. He's swarmed by reporters. Before the doors close again, I see Raymond duck, like he's dodging tomatoes.

"Let's go, Hope," T.J. says. "I got us a ride home."

I nod, grateful. Rita dropped us off this morning, but she's not coming back for us. I don't feel much like walking seven blocks to the station to catch a bus back to Grain, especially since buses don't leave that often.

Following T.J. to the big doors that swallowed up Raymond, I feel Sheriff Wells's gaze on my back. It's the same invisible shove Rita uses to make sure I do what she tells me to.

As soon as I step out into the hall, cameras click. I keep my head down and rush through the courthouse. Half a dozen reporters follow me, shouting questions: "Hope, why won't your brother speak?" "Did you know he did it?" "What did he—?"

I try to block out their voices and focus on the clatter of

our footsteps on the hard floors, the echo that reaches the high ceiling and bounces off marble walls. I make it to the front doors and am amazed how dark it is outside. And the temperature must have dropped twenty degrees. August should be dry-bones hot, and usually is around here, but the gray clouds and west winds are promising rain.

I stop on the top step of the courthouse and glance around for T.J. He must have gotten lost in the crowd of reporters. A couple of them close in on me. One has beautiful red hair, which she pushes behind her shoulders while signaling to the cameraman beside her. "Hope, Mo Pento, WTSN. Can you tell us if you think—?"

I push past her. My head feels like it's floating off my shoulders. I think I might vomit. *How'd you like that, WTSN?*

A horn honks. A blue Stratus is parked at the foot of the steps. A window lowers, and Chase Wells peers out. Green eyes, sun-blond hair. He doesn't look a thing like his dad. Everything about him screams East Coast, from his khaki pants to his navy polo shirt. Chase is not just cute; he's beautiful.

I feel a hand on my back. "Sorry." T.J. guides me down a step or two. "They had me trapped back there. You okay?"

"Where are we going, T.J.?" I shout because it's too loud out here. Reporters are crowding in again. I smell sweat and perfume and cigarettes.

"There he is!" T.J. exclaims, pushing too hard from behind. I have to struggle to keep from falling down the steps.

"There *who* is?" I know he's trying to help—he always tries to help. But I think I should have made a run for it on my own. I could have been at the bus station by now.

Chase's car is still at the bottom of the steps. He honks his horn again and shoves the back door open. T.J. waves at him and keeps pushing toward the car.

I stop short on the bottom step. "Wait. Who did you—?"

"I—uh—I talked Chase into giving us a ride back to Grain." He takes the last two steps down, but I don't follow him. "Hope?"

I shake my head.

T.J. tosses a smile to Chase and whispers up to me, "You know Chase. He plays ball with me." He lowers his voice. "His dad's the *sheriff*?"

Do I know Chase Wells? I've watched him for two summers and thought about him in between.

"Hope?" That reporter with the hair sticks a microphone in my face. "Can you tell us why your brother—?"

I reach for T.J.'s hand. We make a dash for the car, dive into the backseat, and shut the door as Chase Wells takes off, tires squealing like they're in pain.

5

The second Chase pulls away from the courthouse, I know I've made a big mistake. I have to get out of this car. "Listen, we . . . I can walk to the bus station from here. Thanks."

T.J. elbows me and makes a face. We're in the backseat, being chauffeured.

Chase doesn't slow down. "That's okay. I'm headed to Grain anyhow. I can drop you guys off."

"Thanks again, man. I didn't know who else to ask. Dad's stuck at work." T.J. fastens his seat belt and nudges me to do the same.

"I really want to walk," I insist. There's an edge to my voice, like metal on metal. I reach for the door handle.

"You want to walk fifteen miles?" T.J. says, trying to make a joke of it.

"I get it," Chase says. He lets up on the gas. "Sorry about that."

But it's not speed that terrifies me. It's definitely not his · driving, which could never be worse than Rita's after half a bottle of vodka. It's him. Chase Wells. The guy I've worshipped from afar—or at least watched from behind my bedroom curtains—as he's jogged by every summer morning, regular as sunrise.

"My dad's always on me about driving too fast," he admits.

Dad. As in *Sheriff Dad.* I didn't hear the sheriff testify, but Raymond said he did a lot of damage to our side. So what am I doing in a car with his son? What was T.J. thinking?

"Pretty sure you two know each other from Panther games," T.J. says, reaching across me to fasten my seat belt. I let him. His voice is thin, with that tinny laugh he gets when he's nervous. "Hope, Chase. Chase, Hope."

I'm thinking Chase knows my name. He just heard me swear *on a Bible* that I'm Hope Leslie Long.

As for him, there's not a human being in Grain who doesn't know who Chase Wells is. I've sneaked peeks at him while waiting for Jeremy to collect bats and balls for Coach Johnson at games and practices. Chase was hard to miss, with Bree Daniels hanging all over him, and guys like Steve and Michael and half a dozen of their crowd cheering him on.

Chase glances at us in the rearview mirror. Smiles. His eyes are framed, deep-set, the color of green sea glass, like the smooth, translucent chunks in my desk drawer at home.

I collect sea glass, or at least I used to. It's how I met T.J.

I stare out my window and remember a rainy day just like this one, when T.J. and I first got together. It was about three years ago, a month after I'd started school at Grain. T.J.

brought in some pieces of sea glass he'd found by Lake Erie, near Cleveland. He used them for a science project. I knew all about sea glass because Jeremy and I used to walk the Chicago shoreline hunting for it. We called the pieces mermaid tears. T.J. had reds that came from the lanterns of old shipwrecks. And pink from Depression-era glass. Broken pieces of history worn smooth by years of violent waves and rough sand. I had to gather all my courage to go up to T.J. after class and ask him about his collection. When I told him I made jewelry out of sea glass, he wanted to see it. Before long, he started bringing me pieces to work with. He still brings me some now and then, even though I've stopped making jewelry.

"Seriously, man," T.J. calls up to the rearview mirror, "we appreciate the rescue. That was pretty crazy back there. I actually used to want to be a reporter. Not now. Huh-uh." He elbows me again.

"Yeah. Thanks." I settle into the seat and stare out the window again. Tiny drops of rain speckle the windshield, but Chase hasn't turned on his wipers. A splat of rain trickles down the glass, shaking and splitting into streaks. The car smells like oranges, unless that's the way Chase Wells smells.

"Not a problem," Chase mumbles.

"So, now I guess we're even," T.J. says.

I frown over at him because I don't understand.

"I told you how I convinced Coach to give Chase a shot pitching the Lodi game, didn't I?" T.J. explains. He lets out his tin chuckle again. "If it hadn't been for me, Chase would still be stuck on second base. Right, Chase?"

"Mmm-hmm," Chase answers, without a glance in the mirror.

24

I want T.J. to stop talking. I'm still not sure why he pushed Coach into letting Chase pitch that game. It's not like he and Chase are buddies or anything. I used to think it was because T.J. thought Chase might be his ticket to the "cool guys." If that was it, it hasn't worked out.

I tune in to the whir and whistle of the wheels on black-top, the steady splatter and patter of rain picking up.

"Hope?" Chase says, breaking our silence with my name. "I've been wanting to tell you that I'm sorry for what you're going through—you and Jeremy. Your family."

He's sorry? What am I supposed to do with that? I shrug.

"I know my dad—well, he's not the most sensitive law enforcement officer in the world."

I can think of a million comebacks. If it weren't for Sheriff Wells, Jeremy might not be where he is right now, behind bars, on trial for murder. I'll never forget the way the sheriff barged into our house and arrested my brother.

We turn onto a one-lane road I've never been on. The only sounds are the rain tapping gently on the roof, a rumble of thunder, and the hum of the windshield wipers starting up. We pass a dozen black-and-white cows huddled under a tree in spite of the threat of lightning.

Our silence has turned uncomfortable, awkward. I wish T.J. hadn't asked Chase for a ride.

I sneak a glance at Chase in the rearview, and he catches me. Before I can look away, he grins.

"You don't talk much, do you, Hope?" he says.

"More than Jeremy," I answer before I can stop myself. I want the words back. It feels wrong to talk about my brother with the son of the enemy. Besides, people like Chase Wells don't get Jeremy. They don't get me either. Whenever we move somewhere, it's almost funny how popular I am right off. From day one, guys try to sit by me in class. The cool girls invite me to eat with them. They think I'm like them because I look like them—blond hair, blue eyes, pimple-free heart-shaped face, and a figure that made me self-conscious in elementary school because I developed earlier than everyone else.

But I'm not one of them, and it only takes a couple of weeks for them to figure that out.

"So, Chase, bet you miss Boston, right?" T.J. asks, changing the subject with the grace of a hippopotamus.

"I don't know. Maybe I miss Mom and Barry sometimes. But after three summers, Grain's home too, I guess."

"You play ball there too, don't you?" T.J. says. "Must be where you learned that wicked curve. I wish you'd teach me that one."

We come up over the crest of a long hill, and an Amish buggy appears in front of us. "Look out!" I scream. Chase slams his brakes, then swears and swerves to pass. I look back and see a mother and three little boys. "You can't drive like that around here." I keep staring out the back window to make sure they're all right.

"Man." He's breathing heavy. "I know. I'm sorry." He slows to about ten miles an hour.

"That's the worst part of driving around here," T.J. says.

"No kidding," Chase agrees. "I love seeing the buggies, but I'm always scared I'm going to hit one, especially at night. Aren't you guys?"

"Yep," T.J. answers.

Taking his eyes off the road, Chase turns back to look at me. He's waiting for me to answer.

"Hope doesn't drive," T.J. says.

"You mean she doesn't drive at night?"

"Hope doesn't drive, period," T.J. explains.

"Why not?"

I answer for myself this time. "Rita doesn't want to share the Ford."

"Ah," Chase says. "I get that. I thought it would be tough sharing the Stratus with Dad, but it's worked out. He's got the squad car. And in a pinch, he can borrow one of the impounded cars at the police lockup."

"Cool," T.J. mutters.

"The what?" I smooth my skirt and wish I were wearing jeans. Raymond picked out my court clothes—white shirt, gray skirt.

"Impounded," T.J. explains. "You know. Cars they lock up from drug busts or three-strike drunk drivers."

Chase continues, "The sheriff's office really isn't supposed to use the vehicles, but Dad's deputy, Dave Rogers, took me for a spin in a silver BMW they found drugs in last summer. I don't think my dad would take anything out for a joy ride, though. He's not exactly into joy."

"He looked pretty happy watching you pitch for the Panthers at that Lodi game," T.J. says.

I'm not so sure I'd call it *happy*. Chase's dad screamed at Coach and shouted to Chase for every play. I remember I didn't know whether to be embarrassed for Chase or jealous. I

27

played T-ball one summer, and Rita didn't attend a single game. She's never come to Panther games either, except for the big Wooster-Grain game. Everybody in both counties goes to that one. At least they used to . . . until this summer.

"Dad definitely gets into it," Chase admits.

T.J. leans forward. "Man, can you imagine what he'd do if he watched you pitch the Wooster game? He played in that game 'back in the day,' right?"

"Yeah. Still, I don't get why everybody around here makes such a big deal over that one game."

"Are you kidding?" T.J. grips the seat in front of him. "Wooster and Grain have hated each other since, like, forever! It's the biggest summer-league rivalry in the state. The *Cleveland Plain Dealer* covers the game. Even people who don't like baseball come for the fireworks, and the picnics and tailgate parties. You know what I'm talking about. There's nothing like the Wooster-Grain game. I was almost relieved when Coach said you'd be starting pitcher. Too much pressure for me. The whole state would have turned out for that game if—"

He stops short of saying "if Jeremy hadn't knocked off Coach," but the words are there, invisible, in the air of the car. We hear them.

In silence, we cross the railroad tracks, where I don't think trains have passed in years, and enter Grain, population 1,947, give or take. Cornfields flank the blacktop on the left all the way to the Dairy Maid, a tiny white shack with a single serving window. BEAT WOOSTER! is still printed on the side window in big black letters. Half a dozen girls are eating ice cream cones while they sit on—not at—the wooden tables outside. As we pass, Bree Daniels looks up. Her gaze follows us, her expression unchanged.

"I think you may have some explaining to do," T.J. says when we're past.

Chase turns around to look behind us. There's something about his jawline and the way it hits his chin. Boys from Grain don't have faces like this. "Bree and I aren't talking anymore. I just wish we'd broken up two days earlier than we did."

"How come?" T.J. asks. This time *I* elbow *him*.

"Then I wouldn't have this to remember her by." He lifts the short sleeve of his shirt and leans forward to show us the back of his shoulder, tanned and muscled. I can see something tiny and green moving with his skin. I think it's a four-leaf clover.

"Lucky," I mutter.

"Lucky I didn't get the idiotic clover tattooed on my forehead, I guess." He lowers his sleeve. "She got one on her ankle. I have a feeling she's regretting it too. It was a dumb impulse. We were at her cousin's house, and he does tattoos on the side. One minute we're looking at patterns. The next we've got these clovers drilled into our skin forever. One second of stupid, a lifetime of tattoo."

My throat burns, like it's being tattooed. Because I'm thinking that life is like that. In one single moment, things can change forever—like Rita's hand smacking Jeremy's cheek and mine not lifting to stop hers. Like the bat picked up and swung, and Coach Johnson's life leaving his body forever.

29

I need to get out of here. "Listen, Chase. Thanks for the ride and all. You can let us out now. I can walk from here."

"That's okay. I'll take you home. I know where it is. I run by there every morning. T.J., want me to drop you off first? Unless you're going home with Hope?"

T.J. turns to me, his bushy eyebrows raised. I shake my head. I just want to get home and be by myself. "Just let me out at the intersection." He points to West Elm, his street.

Chase pulls over, and T.J. climbs out, thanking our driver two more times, then leaning into the back before shutting the door. "I'll call you about tomorrow."

I nod. "Thanks, T.J." Amazing how much thanksgiving is going on in this car.

In dead silence, with me still in the backseat, Chase drives through town and turns onto my block. I should feel embarrassed by the house we're renting. It's pretty awful. But I guess I'm past being embarrassed. Having a brother on trial for murder will do that to you.

"Uh-oh." Chase takes his foot off the gas.

"What?" I look up to see a blue van with *WTSN* on the side. It's parked in front of my house.

6

I don't say anything, but I'm grateful when Chase drives past my house. I slump down in the backseat as he passes the minicrowd hanging out on our front lawn. "Stay down," he commands.

After they arrested Jer, it was like this for a week or two, but they've mostly left Rita and me alone since then. "If you let me off at the next block, I can circle back and go in through the kitchen."

Chase stops where I tell him to, and I get out. "Thanks, Chase," I say through the window. Only I mean it this time. Maybe he's not Jeremy's and my enemy just because his dad is. I suppose I'm the last person who ought to judge a kid by his parent.

He nods and drives off. I watch his car until it turns the corner—I'm not sure why I do that. Then I hightail it through Old Man Galloway's yard and backtrack to my house.

I guess I haven't walked through our backyard in a

while—that, or Jack Beanstalk sprinkled seeds out here last night. Some of the weeds are almost as tall as I am. I pick up the beer cans, empty potato chip bags, and candy wrappers on my way through, then dump everything into the smelly trash bin by the back door.

The second I step inside, I'm smothered by a blanket of humidity. The after-rain freshness hasn't touched this house, where a musty onion smell hangs in the air. It takes a few seconds for my nostril cells to die so that I can breathe again.

Heavy metal blares from the bedroom radio, and canned laughter cackles from the TV in the living room, where lights and shadows battle.

I make it as far as the hallway when Rita steps out of her bedroom. She's wearing a denim skirt that's too tight and too short, but I'd never say so to her face. Her red checkered shirt is unbuttoned for maximum display. There's never been the slightest question of where I got my own cleavage. Other than that, we don't look a thing alike. We're about the same height, five six, but I don't think Rita has ever been thin like me. Her eyes are big and brown. Her hair is bleached blond now, frizzy and overpermed, but she's a natural brunette. The dark roots have grown a couple of inches out from her scalp. I can tell she's heading off to waitress at the Colonial Café because she's caught up her hair in a rhinestone clip—a safety pin snapped around a haystack.

She squints up the hall at me. "Where the devil have you been?" In other families, like T.J.'s, mothers greet their kids with "Hi, honey. How was your day?" This is Rita's version.

"I've been in court." Suddenly I'm dying of thirst. I head back to the kitchen.

"I know that," she snaps, following me.

"And you didn't drive me home, so—"

"I know that too. What I want to know is why that TV van is parked out front. What did you say in that courtroom?"

"I said Jeremy was crazy. Isn't that what you wanted me to say?" I open the fridge. Nothing to drink but beer and out-of-date milk.

"You better have said that." She checks her watch. "Raymond called and wants you at his place at seven."

I step back so I can see the pear-shaped kitchen clock that hangs above the toaster. It's six-fifteen. The sooner I get out of this prep-school skirt and blouse, the better. I need my jeans. I head for my room, which is just off the living room. Jeremy's bedroom separates Rita's and mine. "Can you drop me off on your way to work?" I ask.

"No. I'm leaving now. I was supposed to be there at six. I hate this shift." She says this like it's my fault she's working tonight. It probably is. If I didn't have to get coached by Raymond, Rita would likely make me work for her.

Coached by Raymond. I don't even want to think the word *coached*. Suddenly a picture pops into my head of Coach Johnson straightening Jeremy's Panther hat before a game, as if my brother would be stepping up to the batter's box and had to look just right. Jeremy's tongue is hanging out, like a puppy that's been patted on the head.

I shake my head to get rid of that image. As if my brain is an Etch A Sketch, the tiny gray crystals of Jeremy and Coach together break up and slide down. But they're both still on my mind.

Rita hasn't left yet. I trail back to the living room, where she's reapplying dark red lipstick, making a fish face in the mirror. "Rita," I ask, leaning on the back of the sofa, "what was he like?"

"Who?"

We're six feet apart, a body's length. Coach was about six feet tall. "Coach Johnson. What was he like?"

She shoves a pack of cigarettes into her purse. "You saw him more than I did."

"But you and Coach went to high school together, right? What was he like then?"

Still not looking at me, she stands on one foot and slaps a two-inch-heeled sandal onto her other foot. "He was like every high school boy—girl-crazy. And not a one of them knew what to do with a girl when they got one." She sticks her other foot into a sandal and stares at her red-tipped toes. "Jay Jay wasn't quite like the rest, though. He was all right."

This is a lot for Rita to say about any male. I try to imagine both of them at my age, but I can't see it.

"It was a long time ago." She grabs her purse off the back of the chair and opens the front door. "The TV van's gone." I can't tell if she's disappointed or relieved. She takes our umbrella and closes the door behind her.

By the time I grab a sandwich and change into jeans, I have to leave for Raymond's. I know where his house is, even though I've never been inside. All of our other meetings with Raymond have been at our house, or in his tiny law office on Main, next to the Subway shop.

Since Rita took the umbrella, I have to hope the rain holds off for now, and that Raymond can drive me home when we're done. The shortest route is straight up Main

Street, but I don't take that. Instead, I circle the back lot behind the IGA and go across the street to the thrift store, behind the post office, through the bank drive-through to the sidewalk by St. Stephen's Catholic Church, then across the damp grass of the practice field behind the high school, where Ann, who used to be kind of a friend at school, told me couples go to make out.

From here, it's about a ten-minute walk. It gives me time to think. And to plan. Since day one, Raymond and Rita have gone with the insanity plea for Jeremy. I went along because it scared me to think about what would happen to Jeremy if the jury found him guilty. Raymond's lined up doctors to talk about what's wrong with Jer, and I'm supposed to help with the "human side." But I hated telling those stories in court. My brother isn't insane. He's innocent.

So far, the rain is holding off, sticking to the air like it's afraid to hit earth. A girl younger than me is mowing her lawn with a push mower. She's wearing a tank top and shorts and listening to her iPod. When she looks up and sees me, she wheels the mower around and cuts a strip through her lawn all the way to her front porch.

Seconds later, a car pulls beside me. The driver gawks like I'm a traffic accident, then drives away. At the next intersection, an Amish buggy crosses. I close my eyes and listen to the clip-clop of the horse's hooves on pavement, the squeaky jiggle of the buggy. I'd trade places with any of the four kids piled into the back of the buggy, or the mother driving. I could disappear into the black dress and white bonnet, the sensible shoes, and the sensible family.

Raymond's house is set on a hill, back from the road. It's a brick one-story, really nice by Grain standards. Flower beds flank both sides of the walk. He must take a lot of real cases, not just freebies for the state, "pro bono," like ours.

I ring the doorbell, and the door is opened by a tall woman with thin brown hair and a big belly under a spandex top and cotton sweats. Raymond is going to be a daddy.

"You must be Hope." She stands on tiptoes to gaze out at the road. "Isn't your mother coming in with you?"

"No."

She motions for me to step in, so I do. Her smile makes her pretty. She puts one arm around her belly, like she's protecting her child. "Come and sit down. Ray will be out in a minute."

I take off my soggy sneakers and wish I'd worn socks.

"You don't have to do that, Hope," Mrs. Munroe says.

"It's okay." I take a whiff of the house and wish Jeremy were here to breathe Munroe air. There's nothing stale or musty here, just a hint of vanilla and maybe lemon. The white carpet looks new, and it makes me nervous to walk on it, even in bare feet. The furniture matches, and the only mess is on the dining room table, where papers are spread out all over.

"Becca, is that Hope?" Raymond comes out of the hall-way, wiping his face with a little towel. He tosses it into a room I'm guessing is the bathroom. "Hey, Hope. We better get down to business. We have a lot to cover."

"If you'll excuse me," Mrs. Munroe says to both of us, "I think I'll go lie down for a while."

Raymond stops in his tracks. "Are you okay? Are you nauseous?"

"I'm just tired, Ray. Offer Hope something to drink, will you?" She smiles at me.

"I'm good, thanks." I feel as if I'm watching one of those TV family shows, where people are nice to each other even though they're related.

She kisses Raymond on the forehead and disappears down the hall. He watches her go before settling us at the table.

Soon as we sit, he gets serious. "What happened after court adjourned today can't happen again, Hope." He doesn't raise his voice or sound mad, but I know he means business. I think Raymond Munroe might make a good dad. "You and your mother, and Jeremy and I, have to present a united front, whether court is in session or out."

"I know, and I'm sorry. But . . . but I don't agree with you and Rita about Jeremy."

"I realize that, Hope. But even if we have differences, we have to appear as though we're on the same team." He reaches into his briefcase like this discussion is over.

"Please, Raymond? Could I just say something?"

He sighs. I think he's going to say no, but he puts down his pen. "Two minutes. That's all I can give you. We have to prepare the rest of your testimony *and* your cross."

My heart thumps, and my head feels dizzy. This is my chance, and I know it. "Jeremy didn't murder Coach Johnson. He liked Coach. I think he may have loved him. And anyway, Jeremy couldn't kill anybody, even if he hated them. And he's never hated a living soul. You don't know Jer like I do."

"Trials aren't about what happened. They're about what either side can prove. You haven't been in court to hear the prosecution's case, Hope," Raymond says.

"You wouldn't let me," I protest.

"The judge wouldn't let you. When you're done testifying, you might be allowed in the courtroom as a spectator. But that's not the point. The point is, you didn't hear the evidence that the prosecution has against Jeremy. And evidence is all the jury can consider."

"Then we need to get our own evidence!" I insist.

"What evidence? Keller put Sarah McCray on the stand, the woman who discovered the body. She came to the barn a little after eight that morning, and Jeremy almost knocked her over running away. He got blood on her, Hope. John Johnson's blood."

I try not to picture this. "He was scared. That's why he was running away."

"He was carrying the murder weapon," Raymond continues. "She saw the bat in his hands."

I know these facts. I read the papers. "There's an explanation. I'm sure there is."

Raymond shakes his head. "Jeremy certainly hasn't given it. He won't talk to me."

"He doesn't talk!"

Raymond doesn't lose his cool, even with me shouting. "All right. He hasn't written. He could write the explanation."

"Maybe he's scared! Maybe he . . . he saw it happen. He saw who did it, and he's afraid to say."

"His are the only fingerprints on the bat. And Mrs. McCray would have seen if somebody else had been there."

I'm breathing hard. If I cried, ever, I'd be crying now. "He didn't do it. Jeremy didn't do it."

"I'm not saying he did." Raymond's voice is softer, less lawyerly. "I'm just telling you what the jury's heard up to now. The prosecution's case is strong. I'm the only lawyer your brother has, and I have to look out for his best interest. Right now, that means going after the insanity plea as hard as I can. If I don't, and if the jury finds him guilty . . ."

Raymond doesn't finish his sentence . . . because he doesn't have to.

7

Raymond sits up straight and pulls over a file from the stack on the table. "So, are you ready to get down to some serious work?"

I nod. I want to keep trying to convince Raymond that Jeremy couldn't murder anybody, but I'm all out of arguments. I wish Jeremy had somebody smarter for a sister.

"Okay." He's already jotting things on his yellow notepad. "Tomorrow, I have to let Dr. Brown, the psychiatrist, testify before I recall you. I don't like breaking up your testimony, but I don't have a choice. Dr. Brown is testifying in a big case in New York and has to get back. She's good, though. She won't take long, and we need her to explain Jeremy's condition to the jury."

People have been trying to explain Jeremy for as long as I can remember. I keep this thought to myself. "Then maybe you don't need me again?" I'd give almost anything not to have to get back up on the witness stand.

Raymond smiles at me. "I need your testimony, Hope. You give a human face to the clinical analysis."

I nod.

"Good," he says, shuffling papers. "We should still be able to finish your direct testimony with no problem. I want you to tell the jury about Jeremy and his empty jars."

I've already agreed to this, but I don't like it. Everybody else thinks it's weird that my brother collects empty jars, but I don't. I tell Raymond a bunch of stories, like how Jer always carries a couple of jars in his backpack and sometimes gets them out and opens and closes them. Then I tell him about the time we were in the IGA and Jeremy loaded up his backpack with Mason jars, then threw a fit when I took the jars out and put them back on the shelf.

"Good," Raymond says, scribbling notes. "You can tell that one—just like that, Hope. What else?"

It feels like I'm tattling on my brother, but I keep going. "Most of the time, he uses regular jars that are empty. He peels off the labels. I have to wash them fast, when he's not looking, before he puts them in his pack or squirrels them under his bed. They can really stink if I don't."

"What does he do with all those jars?" Raymond asks, still writing.

I don't know if he's asked for real or for practice, but I answer anyway. "He saves them. Sooner or later, they end up on the shelves in his bedroom. I've never counted, but he probably has a couple hundred in every shape and size."

"Keep talking, Hope."

I have so many memories of Jeremy and his jars. It's hard

to settle on a single story. "Sometimes, if a jar of mayonnaise is almost empty, he'll dump out what's left—usually into the wastebasket, but not always."

I remember a day about four years ago. I can almost see Jeremy in his jeans and a gray sweatshirt I got him at the Salvation Army thrift store. His whole body is wound tight, and his eyes bulge. He's in the kitchen, with the refrigerator door open. At his feet is a pile of long, sliced dill pickles swimming in a sea of yellow-green pickle juice.

"Once," I begin, "Jeremy came running into the house, dashed to his room, then darted out again. He was pacing the kitchen floor and refused to stop long enough to write me what was wrong. For whatever reason—and we never know the reason—Jeremy needed a jar. A fresh jar. Before I could stop him, he took out a giant jar of pickles and dumped the whole thing onto the floor. I just stood there, staring, while he tucked that jar into his chest like a football and ran back to his room, closing the door behind him. He didn't come out the rest of the night."

"What did you do?" Raymond asks.

"I cleaned up the kitchen. The next day I took a lot of flak from Rita for eating a whole jar of newly bought pickles."

We keep talking about the jars. I tell Raymond about the elderly neighbors we had in Oklahoma who saved their empty jars for Jeremy, no questions asked. They even washed the jars out first. I bring up every jar story I can remember, including the time Jeremy went through the garbage to get a mustard jar. That jar sat in his room for weeks before I found it.

Raymond settles on the pickles, the mayo, and the mustard.

He makes me tell him each story two more times, prepping me on what to cut and what to draw out. Finally, he puts down his pen and squeezes the bridge of his nose. "Hope, tomorrow the prosecution gets to cross-examine you. I've got to warn you that Prosecutor Keller won't go easy on you just because you're a young girl."

"I didn't expect he would."

"You didn't see him in action all month, Hope. He's a pit bull at getting what he wants out of witnesses. He's even tough on his own witnesses."

"Well, he can't get anything out of me. There's nothing to get."

"Don't kid yourself, Hope. He's earned his nickname, Killer Keller. Keller has been at this a long time, a lot longer than I have anyway."

"I think you're doing great, Raymond," I say, although I don't have any idea how he's doing.

Raymond looks grateful. "So, we better start preparing you for the state's cross-examination. Remember that Keller can only take side doors if we open them. Let's get started."

Footsteps patter up the hallway, and Mrs. Munroe scurries into the bathroom. She tries to shut the door, but I can hear her hurling.

"Honey?" Raymond gets up so fast his chair tips. "I'm sorry, Hope. I'll be right back." He joins his wife, and they close the bathroom door, but I can still hear them—her puking, him murmuring to her. If I listen to her, I'm in danger of hurling too. Whenever Jeremy has the flu, I throw up worse than him.

I turn back to the table, where Raymond has every last folder out of his briefcase. Thumbing through loose papers, I spin a couple of the folders so they face me. One is labeled "Cases—Precedents." Another says "Crime Scene."

I slide the crime scene folder over and open it. The top photo is of a woman in the stable. I recognize her. It's Mrs. McCray, but it looks like a much older version of the woman who let Jeremy ride her old pinto. She kept two horses at the Johnson Stable, an expensive bay gelding for dressage and the old mare Jeremy fell in love with, Sugar. Coach taught Jer how to ride on that horse. Sometimes I'd come by the barn and see Jeremy riding that spotted horse bareback through the pasture, his backpack of jars clinking like angel chimes.

In the crime scene photo, Mrs. McCray looks like she's seen a ghost, or worse. Her back is to the sun, which peeks through gray morning clouds and lights the barn entrance. Her arms are wrapped around her like she's keeping herself from splitting into pieces. She's the one who found Coach dead in front of her bay's stall. She's the one Jeremy bumped into.

I glance back at the hallway. The bathroom door is still shut. I hear dry-heaving.

I slide Mrs. McCray to the side to see what's underneath . . . and there's Jeremy. I guess this is what they call a mug shot—Jeremy looking forward and to both sides. In each shot, he's smiling for the camera. The photos look like every school picture Jeremy ever posed for—that same goofy grin he'd get when the photographer told him to say "cheese."

Shoving Jeremy's mug shots to the side, I take a look at

the next photograph. It's Coach Johnson, lying on his side, curled up like a baby inside its mother's womb. His hands are drawn over his ears, like he doesn't want to hear his own cry. A circle of darkness pools beneath his head and shoulders. If I didn't know better, I'd think it was a shadow. I know better.

How can a single blow do that?

I can almost hear the horses screaming, a rumbling thunder, life bubbling out into sticky dark pools. I can smell manure and blood mixed with sweat and flies and fear.

The person on the ground isn't just "the victim" anymore. Tears are trickling like early rain down my cheeks, but I don't know how they got there because I don't cry. This is Coach Johnson, the nice man who gave Jeremy a job mucking stalls at his stable and paid him twice what he should have paid, the kind coach who made Jeremy feel part of the team, who gave Jer a Panther uniform that he would have worn every day, all day, if I'd let him.

I can't stop staring. Coach is not so much a dead person as he is a person without life. I take in all the details of this picture—sawdust and a dark pool of blood, a hoofprint partially covered by Coach's foot, a cell phone inches from his hip, fallen from his pocket. Coach—faceless, lifeless John Johnson.

My brother could not have done this.

The toilet flushes, and the bathroom door opens. I shove the photos back into the folder and push the file away from me.

"Sorry, Hope," Raymond says, returning to the table.

"Is she okay?" I ask.

Raymond runs his fingers through his hair and looks about twelve years old. "The doctor says not to worry about the nausea, even though it's late in her pregnancy. But I can't help it."

"You'll make a good dad," I tell him.

"You think so?" he asks, like it matters what I think.

"I do."

We go at it for another thirty minutes. Raymond does his best to prepare me for cross-examination. But when it's time to go, I'm pretty sure I'm a whole lot less prepared than your average Boy Scout.

Raymond follows me to the door, where I put on my shoes. It's raining pretty good now. "Isn't Rita here yet?" he asks.

"I'm meeting her." I don't add that I'll be meeting her at home, though, and not out on the street.

Raymond frowns. "Are you sure you don't need me to give you a lift?" He tosses a nervous glance down the hall. I can tell he's worried about his wife.

"Nope. But thanks."

"Here. Take an umbrella. That's the least I can do." He hands me a giant black umbrella, leaving three just like it in a tall white can by the door.

"Thanks, Raymond. I'll see you in court."

"You'll do fine, Hope!" he calls after me. But I know neither of us believes him.

8

When I crawl into bed, I'm too tired to sleep. In every other apartment where we've lived, I slept on the couch. This is the only bedroom I've ever had. It's the smallest room in the house, but I'm not complaining. I should paint the walls, but one wall has a cracked wallpaper mural of a green forest, and I love it, even though it curls at every seam. I keep the room picked up, except for books I've checked out of the library, books I almost never finish. I jump to the end after a few chapters and then lose interest. Near one wall, half a dozen books are spread out in tepees that mark my quitter pages. But I'm too tired to read.

I close my eyes, and my mind fills with images from the courtroom. I can see Jeremy, wearing a suit that could never fit right. And Chase, leaning forward, elbows on his knees, his green eyes staring up at me.

Other images of Chase flip through my brain too. The tighter I shut my eyes, the faster they go—Chase driving, the back of his head, his golden hair thick but not coarse, his broad shoulders and strong back. Chase, his neck craned to see something out the rear window. His arms are muscled without being gross, the arms of a runner.

I can see each line and curve of Chase's classic features, the angle of his chin when I thanked him for the ride. Thinking about him makes me feel ... what? Content? Peaceful? Maybe a moment, just one moment, of good?

Then I stop. Because mixed in with the joy of that picture of Chase Wells is the mug shot of Jeremy. And the crime scene photo of Coach Johnson.

And I wonder what kind of a person can feel even a piece of good in the middle of so much bad.

When I wake up at six the next morning, my first thought is of Chase. I guess I really can't help myself. I roll out of bed and head for the window, where I always watch for him. Dust and dirt cling to the windowpanes. Sunrise is officially past, but I have time to get a cup of instant coffee.

I take up my lookout post again. And before I finish my coffee, Chase comes running up the street like somebody's after him. He's tan and fit in his running shorts and looks more like a California surfer now than a Boston preppy. I can see the muscles of his legs twist and tighten as he gets closer.

This is the moment when every other morning I duck into the shadow of my musty curtains. But today I stay where I am, watching, willing Chase to look this way.

"Morning, Hopeless."

Rita startles me so bad I spill coffee on my T-shirt.

"Hopeless" is her little joke. Hope Leslie. Hope-Les. Hopeless. Funny as ever.

"What are you looking at?" she asks.

I turn back to the window, but Chase has already passed. He's halfway up the street.

Raymond leads off with his expert witness, who couldn't look less like a psychiatrist if she tried. If I didn't know she came in on an airplane this morning, I'd swear she left her Harley and biker jacket, size extra large, parked out back. Her hair is shaved so close to her head I can see her skull from where I sit. The only doctorly things about her are the thick black glasses, and even they are strapped to her head like she's off to play ball instead of testify in another case.

Raymond starts out slow, getting her to list all her college and doctor degrees. I guess the jury has to believe her, since she swore on the Bible and all, but if I were Raymond, I would have made her bring in her framed diplomas to prove what she's saying about being so smart.

RAYMOND: Please tell the court your current position and title.

DR. BROWN: I'm senior advisor for NORD, based currently in New York.

RAYMOND: Please explain NORD, Dr. Brown.

DR. BROWN: The National Organization for Rare Disorders is an American nonprofit group that provides support and advocacy for people with rare diseases. I meet with individuals all across the United States and help in any way I can.

RAYMOND: Were you able, from your experience and expertise, to discover what might be Jeremy Long's particular disability?

PROSECUTOR KELLER: Objection! Lack of foundation.

JUDGE: Overruled. Answer the question, Dr. Brown.

DR. BROWN: I can't state it unequivocally, but the boy certainly has a disability along the spectrum of autism. He has impaired social skills, yet high-functioning splinter skills—which is to say, he has overall developmental delays and lacks certain ordinary skills, such as dressing himself appropriately and interacting appropriately in social situations, yet he excels at writing and organizational endeavors. This, coupled with certain repetitive gestures, would lead one to suspect a diagnosis of Asperger's syndrome. I personally believe the boy may also be suffering from Landau-Kleffner syndrome. One of the symptoms of the disease is the inability to verbalize language. It's often misdiagnosed as pure autism because the patient tends to rock back and forth, or side to side, and focus in unusual ways. And there are often tantrums associated with the disorder.

RAYMOND: Tantrums. I see. When a person has one of these tantrums, is he aware—in your opinion—of what he's doing while he's doing it? And again, I'm only asking for your expert opinion here.

DR. BROWN: I would say that, in general, a person is a victim of his own tantrum. Tantrums are not malicious. Toddlers have tantrums. We're all familiar with the behavior; most of us outgrow it. Some do not. However, no one *wants* to have a tantrum.

RAYMOND: You say you can't be one hundred percent certain of the diagnosis. Is there any diagnosis you can testify about with absolute certainty before the court today?

DR. BROWN: Yes. Jeremy definitely suffers from SM.

RAYMOND: SM?

DR. BROWN: Selective mutism. He is able to speak, but he chooses not to.

RAYMOND: Tell us more about this selective mutism, if you will.

DR. BROWN: Of course. Let us start by defining our terms, shall we? A mute is one who cannot talk; a selective mute elects not to talk. Originally identified in 1877 as aphasia voluntaria, selective mutism presents itself most frequently in children around the age of five but can develop at any age. Over the past two decades, more and more American children have decided to stop talking. Due to the lack of funding and research for this disorder, it is a daunting task for those of us in the field to determine whether the child is simply shy, extremely shy, or if something more serious underlies the behavior—drugs administered to, or by, the mother during pregnancy; early childhood trauma; displaced hostility. One hypothesis suggests that the absence of speech results from biological deficiencies combined with psychological and social abnormalities. We may never know with absolute certainty, although future funding would help us find the answers we need to help children like Jeremy.

RAYMOND: Thank you so much for enlightening us, Dr. Brown. We appreciate your taking time out of your busy schedule. I have no more questions for the witness, Your Honor.

Prosecutor Keller is scribbling so much in his notepad that all of the rest of us, including Dr. Brown, have to wait for him to get up and take his turn. When he does stand and head for the witness box, he's frowning, like he has no more idea than I do what the expert psychiatrist really said.

KELLER: Hello, Dr. Brown. I have a few questions I hope you'll help me with. I admit that I'm not familiar with Landau-Kleffner syndrome, but I've done a bit of research on Asperger's and on selective mutism. Perhaps you could help us understand the nature of these tantrums you talk about. Would it be correct to say that many individuals with selective mutism—the one diagnosis you're certain of—have tantrums?

DR. BROWN: Of course. As I explained, there are cross symptoms with L-K, SM, Asperger's, and autism—the focus, the mannerisms, and, yes, the occasional tantrum.

KELLER: I see. And is temper generally associated with the tantrums?

DR. BROWN: That's correct. We believe that in selective mutism especially, the frustration of self-imposed silence fosters a temper, and thus the tantrums.

KELLER: I see. And how many of these selective mutes, in a sudden burst of insanity, have murdered another person?

RAYMOND: I object!

JUDGE: Overruled.

DR. BROWN: Well, no one that I know of.

KELLER: No one has given in to the insanity and committed murder, in spite of himself?

DR. BROWN: You can't equate selective mutism or Asperger's or autism with insanity.

KELLER: I can't? Ah. So let me be sure I'm understanding you correctly, Doctor. You're saying that just because someone is selectively mute, or has Asperger's or autism, we should not assume he is insane. Have I got that right?

DR. BROWN: Yes, technically, but—

KELLER: Thank you, Doctor. By the way, Dr. Brown, how long has the defendant been a patient of yours?

DR. BROWN: What? No. He's not my patient.

KELLER: Oh? I'm sorry. You must have interviewed him, then?

DR. BROWN: That's right. I was able to meet with Jeremy Long this morning.

KELLER: I see. For how many hours?

DR. BROWN: Well . . . we had to be in court. I suppose I was with Jeremy under an hour.

KELLER: Under an hour? And you were able to get him to tell you enough about himself to diagnose him? You must be quite an expert psychiatrist.

DR. BROWN: He didn't actually tell me about himself, per se, of course. By definition, selective mutes don't answer questions. I was, however, able to observe the boy and—

KELLER: Observe him? Like the jury is doing now? Only . . . for a much shorter length of time?

DR. BROWN: Well, I wouldn't say—

KELLER: That's all right, Doctor. I think I've gotten all the information you're able to give. No more questions for the witness.

9

It's afternoon before I'm called back up to the witness stand. I guess swearing must have lasted overnight because I don't have to do it again. My palms are so sweaty they slip when I grab the wooden railing.

I try to get Jeremy to look at me as I take my seat. He's wearing another suit I've never seen, and I figure Raymond must have bought it for him. It's a nice suit, gray and brand-new. I'm grateful, but Jer looks like he's playing dress-up in it. His hair is cut short and close, which looks neat and everything, but makes his ears stick out. He won't look at me. And then I remember I promised him I'd see if I could get him an empty jar, and I didn't even try.

"Good afternoon, Hope," Raymond says.

"Afternoon." My voice sounds thin, like a little girl's. I clear my throat.

"I won't take very long today, Hope. Just a few more questions for you. The court has heard expert testimony concerning Jeremy's mental condition. I just want you to tell the court about your brother in your own words. Is that all right with you?"

"Yes."

"Good. Hope, can you tell us if Jeremy has had any hobbies like other boys his age?"

This is how we practiced getting into the glass-jar stories, so I tell the first one. Then I wait for Raymond to ask me about Jeremy dumping all the pickles on the kitchen floor so he could have the jar, and I tell that one, glad that Rita's not allowed in the courtroom until after she testifies.

When I'm done, Raymond smiles at me. I think he winks, but it might be a twitch. "Thank you, Hope." He turns to the judge. "That's all, Your Honor."

I'd like to get up and follow Raymond, but the prosecutor is already out of his chair and heading for me.

"Good day," he says. He unbuttons his jacket and walks so close I think I smell the sweat that's left dark circles around his armpits. It's hot in the courtroom, even with the fans going. "My name is Mr. Keller. Can I call you Hope?"

"Okay."

"Good. Thank you." I keep thinking how Raymond called him a pit bull. And I guess he was kind of hard on the doctor. Still, I don't see him as a pit bull. Not yet anyway. On the other hand, people who get bitten by pit bulls are always saying how the dogs were so sweet until that minute before the bite.

"I just have a few questions for you, Hope," Mr. Keller begins. "Then we'll let you get out of here and go home."

I wish he could say that to my brother.

Raymond warned me to keep my answers short and not volunteer information not asked. So I wait to be asked. Only Keller is flipping through his notes. My knee starts bobbing all by itself, and my heart is pounding so loud I wonder if the prosecutor can hear it. I look past him to the crowd of reporters in the back row, to the jurors on my left, to Jeremy on my right. T.J., wearing a red T-shirt with a gold dragon on it, is sitting as close to the front as he could get. Then my gaze passes over the gallery in the little balcony, and I see him. Chase. He's sitting in the front row, leaning forward, his hands on the rail.

And instantly, I feel better.

I don't know why Chase shows up every day, but T.J. says he's been here for the whole trial. A lot of Grain citizens have. Maybe they come for the same reason rubberneckers gawk at highway accidents.

"Hope," Mr. Keller says, turning his side to me so he can smile at the jury, "what was your brother's relationship with Mr. Johnson like?"

Raymond jumps up. "Objection! The witness isn't qualified to answer. She isn't an expert in relationships."

Raymond's right about that.

But the judge disagrees. "Overruled. Proceed, Mr. Keller."

He turns to me this time. "Why don't you just tell us from your own observations how your brother got along with the deceased?"

"They got along fine."

"Could you explain your answer for the court, please?"

I'm trying to keep my answers short, like Raymond said, but I can't see how it would hurt for the jury to know how much Jeremy liked Coach. "Coach Johnson gave Jeremy a real good job at the stable. Jer mucked the stalls and all, but he got to ride and brush the horses too. He loved his job. And the pay was great."

"Did they see one another outside the stable?"

"On the ball field," I answer quickly, eager to make the jury understand how much Coach meant to Jeremy. "Coach let Jeremy be his assistant for the summer games. Jeremy was the first one to show up on the ball diamond and the last to leave. He was in charge of the bats and balls, the game equipment."

Keller looks like he wants to ask another question, but I'm not done yet. "Plus," I add quickly, "Coach gave Jeremy a Panther uniform. Jeremy loved that uniform. He would have worn it every day if I'd let him. And—" But I stop myself just in time because I was going to say how Jeremy carried his bat with him to the barn every single morning.

Mr. Keller nods, like he's taking it all in. "Did Coach Johnson ever give Jeremy a bat?"

I bite my lip so hard it hurts. I try to glance at Raymond because we didn't practice for this question, but the prosecutor's standing in my way.

"Do you need me to repeat the question?" Keller asks.

"No. I mean, yes. Coach gave Jeremy his bat."

"Thank you. Now, Hope, I'd like to go back to the day of the murder."

I wouldn't. It's the last day I'd like to go back to.

"I'm hoping you can help us fill in a few time gaps," Prosecutor Keller says. "Where were you on the morning of June eleventh?"

"Asleep. In my bed."

He nods, like he knew this already. "Did you see your brother that morning? Before the police knocked on your door, that is?"

"No." I add quickly, "But I saw Jeremy when I went to bed the night before. He was in his bed sound asleep."

"Okay. Let's talk about the next day. What woke you that morning?"

"Pounding on the door. The front door. It woke Rita and me both up."

"But not Jeremy?"

I shrug, then remember I'm supposed to use words. "I wouldn't know about that."

"Of course," he says, like he agrees with me. "So what did you do when you heard this pounding on the door?"

"I answered it."

"Go on, please, Hope."

The facts. Just the facts. Raymond's coaching throbs in my head, along with a headache that better not turn into a migraine. "Sheriff Wells was standing there, with a couple of others behind him. He asked me where Jeremy was, and I told him Jeremy was asleep."

Keller nods for me to continue, waving one arm while he takes a couple of steps toward the jury.

"Sheriff Wells started to come in, but that's when Rita took over."

"That would be your mother and the defendant's mother, yes?"

"Yes. Rita shoved in front of me and stood in the doorway so they couldn't get in. 'What do you want with Jeremy?' she shouted." I figure it's okay to leave out some of the four-letter words Rita used. "'We need to talk with him. There's been an accident, Rita,' Sheriff said.

"So Rita asked what kind of accident. And the sheriff told her that Coach Johnson had been found murdered.

"Rita gasped, and tears filled up her eyes. I thought she was going to pass out, so I took hold of her. But she shook me off and glared back at the sheriff and told him to stay right where he was unless he had a search warrant. He said he was waiting on one right now, and she said he would just have to wait then, wouldn't he.

"Then she slammed the door right in Sheriff Wells's face and told me to go and check on Jeremy while she kept an eye on the police. So I ran to Jer's room and knocked and hollered and knocked. Only he didn't come. And I got so scared that I went in anyway." I stop then because my mind is flashing back to my brother, sitting on the floor, in the corner, in nothing but his boxers, rocking back and forth and staring at the wall as if he were watching a movie, which I suppose he was in a way.

Keller turns to me, and his voice is soft. "I know this isn't easy for you, Hope, but would you please tell the court what you saw when you entered Jeremy's room?"

I take a deep breath. "I saw Jeremy, but I'm not sure he saw me. He wouldn't look at me, so I sat down on the floor with him and tried to hold him. I sat there with him until Sheriff Wells got his warrant and barged into the room."

"What happened next?"

"They tore up his room. They searched under the bed and took photos of everything, including me and Jeremy. Then they searched his closet."

"And what did they find in your brother's closet?"

I know this whole courtroom, except for me, has probably already heard exactly what they found. They've probably seen pictures. Maybe they've even seen it for themselves. "A bat."

"Was it a wooden bat?" Keller asks.

I nod. "Yes."

"And even though most of the Panthers use metal bats for the league, what kind of bat did Jeremy own? What kind of bat had Coach given him?"

"A Louisville Slugger."

Keller bows his head. "Metal or wooden?"

"Wooden," I admit.

Keller is silent for at least a minute, probably letting that answer soak in. I wish I knew if the jurors were picturing everything in their heads the way I am. I hope not.

"Hope," Keller asks at last, "do you love your brother?"

"Yes!" I exclaim, looking directly at Jeremy now. He gazes up at me, the touch of a grin on his bony face. "I love Jeremy more than anybody in the whole world."

"I'll bet you'd do just about anything for him, wouldn't you?"

I lock gazes with Jeremy and will him to take this in.

"I would do anything in the world for my brother. He's the most important thing in my life."

"I can see that," Keller says, like he understands. "Let's go back to your earlier testimony, if you don't mind."

I'm grateful to go back, to go anywhere that's not June eleventh.

"When did Jeremy start collecting jars? Can you remember?"

"I'm not sure. Maybe when he was nine."

"And were you upset by your brother's troubling hobby?"

"I wasn't, but Rita was. If I missed a jar under his bed, it could smell up the whole room pretty quick."

Keller wrinkles his nose as if he can smell sour mustard right now. "Empty jars . . . You have to admit it's a pretty unusual hobby."

"No. I don't admit that at all. People collect all sorts of things."

"Like . . . ?"

"Like stamps and spoons and bells, for example. Like sea glass." I finger my necklace. I made it out of a tiny, smooth piece of glass T.J. gave me two years ago.

"True," Keller mutters, agreeing with me.

"Or even Barbie dolls. People pay hundreds of dollars for old Barbies, don't they? If you ask me, I'd say *that's* crazy."

Keller laughs a little, and so do a couple of the jurors. I'm thinking my testimony today is going better than it did yesterday.

"What do you admire most about your brother, Hope?"

I can't believe it's the prosecution asking me this. Raymond should have asked this a long time ago. "A lot of things." I smile at Jeremy. He's smiling back at me, and I see the old Jeremy peeking out. "My brother is the kindest person I know. He loves the little things, like watching ants carry bits of food on a trail, or hearing people laugh, or seeing the sun go down every single evening. He gets excited when an acorn falls from a branch and lands at his feet, or a leaf spins in the air. He calls them God-gifts. That's what he writes on his pad for me when he sees a butterfly or a deer, or whenever he makes out a cool shape in a sky full of clouds."

"Jeremy dropped out of school in the eighth grade, didn't he?" Keller asks.

"That was more Rita's doing than Jeremy's. Jer never caused any trouble, except with teachers who were too lazy to read his writing instead of getting the answers out of his mouth. Have you seen Jeremy's handwriting?"

"No, I haven't," Keller says, as if he'd really like to.

"It's beautiful. Jer's own brand of calligraphy."

"Why do *you* think your brother can't talk, Hope?"

"He *can* talk. I know because I heard him when we were younger. He just stopped one day. That's all. But he doesn't really need to talk because he communicates just fine—with his notes and his gestures. Jeremy can say more with his eyes than most people can in a whole speech."

Keller laughs. "I know exactly what you mean. We lawyers hear a lot of those speeches. We even give a few ourselves." He gets some chuckles from the spectators. "Do you have anything else you want to tell us about your brother, Hope, before I let you go?"

Raymond was wrong about this guy. I think Keller *gets* Jeremy. Maybe *he* should have been Jeremy's lawyer. "Thanks," I tell him. "There are a lot of things I could tell you about my brother. Jeremy is trustworthy. He took good care of the team equipment. And he was so responsible at the stable—he never missed a day of work or complained about the messiest stalls or anything. He has a sense of humor, and . . . and he loves me. I'd do anything for Jer, and he'd do anything for me. I know that."

Keller smiles at me. "Sounds like a normal brother to me." He turns from me and repeats this to the jury. "Absolutely and completely normal."

And that's when I see what he's done. What *I've* done. What I've done to Jeremy. "No! Wait! I didn't mean—!"

"I have no more questions for the witness, Your Honor."

"But—!"

"You may step down now, Miss Long," says the judge. "The court will take a short recess." She bangs her gavel. All I can think is that it sounds like a hammer, the hammer that nails Jeremy's coffin shut.

And it's all my fault.

10

I don't know how long I sit in the witness chair while the courtroom clears. Finally, T.J. comes up and gets me. He leads me through the courtroom. The second we step into the hallway, reporters start shouting my name: "Hope, over here, honey!" "Ms. Long!"

I stare at them, their faces blurred, their words nothing more than static. I don't know whether to run through the mob or find a corner and curl myself into it and rock like Jeremy did that morning.

T.J. jerks me back into the courtroom and slams the doors shut. "There's got to be another way out of here." He glances at the little door that swallows my brother every day when he leaves the courtroom. "Besides that one," T.J. mutters.

Together, as if somebody's pointing a gun at us, we back farther into the courtroom. T.J.'s head swivels in every direction. Then he shouts, "Chase!" He's staring up into the gallery. I look too and see Chase, still sitting in his balcony seat. "You know another way out of here?" T.J. hollers up.

For a second, Chase doesn't answer. Then he pushes himself out of his seat, and I think he's going to leave without answering T.J. Slowly, he points to the side stairs that lead to the gallery.

T.J. takes my hand, and we climb to where Chase is, in the small balcony area, where it's even hotter and stickier than the witness stand. The gallery smells like sweat, smoke, and furniture polish.

None of us says a word as Chase leads the way, threading through the wooden fold-down chairs, pushing up each seat so we can get past. He stops at a skinny door. There's a big silver alarm on the doorpost. He takes out his pocketknife and does something to the alarm. His back is to me, so I don't see what he does. But he knows what he's doing. He's obviously done it before, somewhere. He turns around and sticks the knife back into his pocket. "We're going down the fire escape. Are you both good with that?"

I nod. Then I remember T.J.'s afraid of heights. If Jer and I sit on the top bleacher at a practice, T.J. won't come up. "You don't have to," I tell him.

"I'm fine," he says, but the pupils of his eyes are too big, and his voice too high.

I don't let go of his hand as we follow Chase, taking each black metal step, clang-clanging with every move on the rickety ladder. I expect to descend into a pool of reporters and spectators, who will swallow me whole.

But nobody's there when we reach the bottom. I glance back at T.J., asking, without words, if he's okay. He nods, his face cloud white, his glasses crooked. I squeeze his hand before letting go.

"I'm parked back here," Chase says. We haven't asked for a ride, but we follow him. The sun has already set, leaving the sky a mess of gray.

We get into the backseat like before, and Chase starts the car. He eases around the side of the courthouse, then away from the throng of people forming on the courthouse lawn.

When we're safely away, T.J. and Chase exchange words in low tones, but all I hear are empty voices. My mind is back in the courthouse, on the witness stand, going over all the things I should have said . . . and all the things I shouldn't have.

We're halfway to Grain before I try to speak. Even then, I'm scared I won't be able to hold back the tears that are so hot and thick they're clinging to my throat. "I can't believe I did that to Jeremy. I should have let those reporters tear me apart, piece by piece. I deserve it."

"Don't beat yourself up, Hope," T.J. says. We're sitting as far apart as possible. I'm gripping the door handle.

"You didn't say anything wrong," Chase whispers, so soft I'm not sure he really said it.

"Are you kidding?" I'm too loud, but my heart is pounding in my ears. "Raymond and I practiced, but not for that. Not for *those* questions. That prosecutor, Keller, he tricked me. He got me to say exactly what he wanted, that my brother is strange, but not insane. I'll never forgive myself if I—"

Nobody except Jeremy has ever seen me cry. I cover my face and try not to let out the sobs that rack my body. But I can't control anything. I hear the animal noises coming from me as if they're from someone, or something, else. T.J. reaches out his hand, but I don't take it. "I thought I was doing so great," I say between sobs. "I wanted the jury to know Jer the way I do. Then they'd have to see that he couldn't murder anybody. But all I did was make them see he's not insane."

"It's not up to you, Hope," T.J. says, sliding his fingers through his slicked-back hair. "And anyway, you did better than that fancy psychiatrist."

I know T.J. is trying to help. But it's not helping. My head's pounding, and I feel like I'm going to throw up. This is no time for a migraine attack.

"Hope?" Chase's voice is soft, but firm. He expects me to answer.

"What?"

"Did you say anything in court that you don't believe?"

"No!"

"Do you believe your brother's crazy?"

"Of course I don't!"

"Well, then, you couldn't say anything except what you did, could you? Not under oath."

I don't answer.

"What the jury saw today was a sister who loves her brother. That's it. Jeremy's attorney can still make a solid case for insanity."

"But Jer's not insane." The fire has gone out of my voice. Out of me.

"Okay," Chase says, not looking back at us, not glancing in the rearview. "But isn't that the best outcome of the trial? If they find Jeremy insane, they'll just send him to some kind of mental facility, right? And if he's okay, they'll see that and let him go eventually."

"He's right, Hope," T.J. whispers.

I'm shaking my head. "Jeremy wouldn't survive in a mental hospital. He needs to be with me. He needs me. We need each other."

"Great," Chase mutters. "That TV woman is there again."

When I look up, I can't believe we're in front of my house. The blue van is parked in the same spot as yesterday. "I can't face them. Not after what I did today. I don't even want to face Rita."

Chase does a one-eighty and heads north. "Where do you want to go?"

"We can go to my house," T.J. offers.

In a few minutes, we're walking up to the Bowers's two-story white house. There's not much of a front yard, but what there is looks like a green carpet. Impatiens hang in baskets from the front porch, and black-eyed Susans form gold-and-brown clumps big as bushes against the house.

T.J. goes in first. "Hey! Anybody home?"

His mother comes downstairs carrying a laundry basket. "That you, Tommy?" T.J.'s real name is Thomas James, but his mom is the only one who calls him Tommy. When she sees Chase and me, she balances the basket on her hip and pushes thin strands of brown hair out of her freckled face. "Well, how are you, Hope? Good to see you too, Chase." If she's surprised to see him, she doesn't show it.

I'm surprised he's still here, and I'm pretty sure I'm showing it. He tried dropping us off, but T.J. wouldn't have it. Chase is hanging back, close to the door, like he's ready to bolt first chance he gets.

T.J. takes the laundry basket from his mom. "We need

someplace to hide out for a while. Reporters are all over Hope's lawn."

"What a shame." She shakes her head, then smiles at me. "You know you're always welcome here, Hope." I thank her, sure that she means it. Her smile passes to Chase, who reaches for the doorknob. "You too, son. Say, are you kids hungry? I'd be happy to make you something to eat. Plenty of time before I have to get ready for the night shift." Mrs. Bowers has worked at the Oh-Boy cookie factory longer than any other employee, so she could have the day shift if she wanted. But T.J. says she started working nights the year they adopted him so somebody would be home all the time. She got used to the hours, and now she can't imagine working days.

"I'm not hungry, Mrs. Bowers," I tell her. "But thanks."

"I should be going," Chase says. His eyes dart around the living room. He looks like he's scared the house is about to blow up. He probably never hangs out with people like me and T.J.

"Don't go, man." T.J. nods to the basket he's holding. "Let me run this down to the basement. I'll meet you in the kitchen. Hope, get us something to drink, whatever's in the fridge." He slants his eyes at me, like he and I have some kind of secret that explains why he's making sure Chase sticks around.

I don't get it. But a lot of times I don't get T.J. "Sure," I say to his back as he heads toward the basement. Then I start for the kitchen.

Chase stays where he is a second, then follows me.

I love the Bowers's kitchen. It's the biggest room in the house. T.J.'s dad built all the cupboards, plus a cooking island in the center. Chase slides into the small corner booth, also built by Mr. Bowers. They have a dining room, but I've never seen them use it.

I pour three glasses of OJ and join Chase in the booth, taking the other end of the L. "You really don't have to stick around," I tell him.

Chase is fiddling with the salt and pepper shakers. He shrugs without looking up.

After a minute, I can't stand the silence. "I'll go see if T.J. needs any help." I make my way to the basement and find T.J. pulling clothes out of the dryer. "T.J., what's going on?"

He glances back at me. "Sorry this is taking so long. I'll be up in a minute."

"No. I mean, why are you trying to keep Chase around? It's weird."

T.J. sets down the clothes basket and walks over to me. "Hope, he can help us."

"Help us what?"

"Look," he says, like he's explaining a tough algebra problem to me. "Chase is an insider. He's going to know more than we do about your brother's trial."

"So?"

"So we can use him." T.J. grins and touches his glasses. "Why else would I want to hang out with Chase Wells?"

I can think of a couple of reasons, like becoming popular by association, like being part of Chase's crowd. But I keep my thoughts to myself.

T.J. puts his hands on my shoulders. "Hope, trust me. Okay?"

I take a breath of basement air filled with mildew and dust. If I can't trust T.J., who can I trust? "Okay."

He nods toward the stairs. "Go back up. I'll be there in a minute."

Chase is sitting exactly where I left him. I scoot into the booth. "T.J. will be right up."

Neither of us says anything else until T.J. gets back. "You guys sure you're not hungry?" He opens the fridge and takes out bologna, cheese, mustard, and bread. Who keeps bread in the fridge? "Bologna sandwich? I'm having one. Well, actually two."

"No thanks." Chase and I say this at the same time, exchange glances, then stare at the flowered tablecloth.

A sandwich in each hand, T.J. scoots in on my side, forcing me closer to Chase. The smell of bologna and mustard makes me think of Jeremy. "Jer likes bologna sandwiches," I say, more to myself than to them. "Not as much as peanut butter." I turn to Chase. "What do you think they're feeding him in jail?"

"I don't really know," Chase says. "I can find out . . . if you want."

Do I? Do I want to know? Chase could find out. Maybe this is what T.J. meant about Chase being able to help us. "All I know is that Jeremy has got to be going crazy locked up in a cell." I glance up because I didn't mean to say "crazy."

"They have to take good care of him, Hope," T.J. says. But he doesn't know. He doesn't know Jeremy either, not really. He's nice to Jer, but he never seems at ease around him. Most people are like that.

"Was Jeremy always like . . . like he is now?" Chase asks.

I frown at him and wonder if he really wants to know or if he's trying to change the subject. Or if he's working for his dad, the sheriff.

"Never mind," he says quickly. "None of my business. I just . . . I don't know. Seeing him in court every day, I wondered."

"So why *are* you in court every day?" The question's out before I can stop myself.

"You sound like my dad," Chase says. "He'd just as soon I never set foot in the courthouse."

"Yeah?" T.J. sounds surprised. "I thought he'd want you to be there. You know? So you two could talk over the case and how the trial's going and everything?"

"Yeah, right," Chase mutters. "I don't know. I've never been to a trial before. There wasn't anything else to do, so I went. I guess once I started going, I got hooked." The whole time, he's been staring at his fingernails. Now he looks up at me. "Sorry. I didn't mean to get personal, about Jeremy. You don't have to talk about him if you don't want to."

But the thing is, I do want to talk about Jer. Pretty much every thought I have goes back to my brother, so talking about anything else feels like a lie. "Jeremy has always been *special*. I know people say *special* so they don't have to say *different*. But for me, it means something wonderful, like full of wonder. That's what Jer's always been. My brother could sit for hours and listen to birds sing, but he couldn't sit for two minutes in most of his classes."

Chase smiles. "He likes birds?"

"He loves their songs. But I think what Jeremy loves most is when birds and man-made things get along."

72

Chase narrows his eyes. "You lost me."

"Like birds on telephone wires, the way crows and jays seem so comfortable on wire made by people. Or gulls hanging out at shopping malls in Cleveland because of those white stone roofs that look like a beach, but that it works out because people leave food for the birds."

"Only birds?" Chase asks.

"He loves our cat," T.J. says. Then, as if he's just realized his cat's not around, he says, "Speaking of which, I better see where Whiskers got off to." He slides out of the booth and heads for the door. "Be right back."

There's a minute of awkward silence with T.J. gone. I hear him in the backyard calling his cat. Finally, Chase breaks the silence. "I like dogs. Mom's husband number two had a cat when he moved in, and he got a dog for Trey and me the only Christmas we had with them. Trey was my stepbrother . . . for maybe a year. How about you? Any pets?"

I shake my head. "Jeremy and I begged Rita for a pet, but we've never had one, except a puppy I can barely remember. Rita said we called it Puppy. Apparently, we were exceptionally original and bright toddlers." He makes a low laughing sound that helps me breathe easier. "Puppy ran away, or got run over, or maybe found a family who'd give him a better name. When we moved here, there was a cat in the house we're renting, but Rita called animal control on it."

T.J. stumbles into the kitchen with his cat draped across both arms. Whiskers weighs more than a poodle. "She was eating the neighbor's dog food again." He sets the cat down and slides back into the booth.

Chase's cell rings. He checks the number. "It's my dad."

He glances at T.J. and me. "Do you guys mind not talking for a minute?" He puts the phone to his ear. "Hey, Dad. What's up?"

It's impossible not to eavesdrop, although we can only hear Chase's end of the conversation:

"Just hanging out with friends."

. . .

"Yeah, I did." He rolls his eyes. "Easy, Dad. Dial it down, okay? The way those reporters went after her, *you* should have given her a bodyguard. Somebody had to do something. I just—"

. . .

"Will you listen?" Chase's eyes are dark slits. "I said I—"

. . .

"I can't come home now."

. . .

"Because I'm in the middle of something." He holds the phone away from his ear.

I can hear his dad yelling, but I can't make out the words. I don't think I want to.

Chase puts the phone back to his ear. When he gets a word in, he doesn't raise his voice, but I get the feeling it's taking everything he has not to. "Sorry. You're right, Dad. I should have told you." He listens for half a minute, the only sound his heavy breathing as his chest rises and falls. "All right," he says. He flips his cell shut and squeezes it so hard his knuckles turn white. Then, without taking his eyes off the phone, he whips it across the kitchen floor.

11

Whiskers darts out of the kitchen. I can't blame her. T.J. and I exchange wide-eyed gazes. Neither of us says a word. Then T.J. gets up and retrieves the phone from across the room. "Still in one piece," he offers.

Chase rubs the back of his neck and looks kind of sheepish. "Guess that's one good thing, huh? Sorry about that. So now you've seen the famous Wells temper for yourselves. I'm really sorry . . . and embarrassed. It's just . . . Sheriff Matthew Wells isn't the easiest person in the world to live with, even for the summer."

"Wish you'd stayed in Boston?" T.J. asks, sitting down again.

"Not really. There are a lot of things I like about Grain."

"For instance?" I ask, glad the anger has gone back inside, where we can't see it.

"I love hitching posts, for one thing. And the Amish buggies. Nobody back at Andover believed me when I told them about the hitching posts everywhere—at the post office, the dollar store, even the car wash."

"Jeremy rolls down the car window whenever we pass a buggy, just so he can hear the clip-clop. I love it too. I really didn't want to move to Ohio. But when I saw those buggies tied out behind the thrift store the first day we got here, I changed my mind."

"Let's see. What else? I like that Dalmatian statue in front of the firehouse," Chase says. "No idea why."

I can't believe he said that. "Jer and I used to walk out of our way to church so he could pet that concrete Dalmatian."

Chase grins. "My dad is always on me about being too much of a city boy to be a real Panther. Guess this proves I'm not so different from you Grain guys after all."

"Yeah, right," T.J. mutters. He laughs, but it doesn't sound real.

"Come on," Chase says. "I'm into birds, cats, dogs, hitching posts, and buggies. And fire station Dalmatians. What more does a guy need to be a real Panther?" He looks at me to back him up. "Right, Hope?"

"Maybe," I admit.

Chase turns to T.J. "See? Even Hope agrees I'm a regular Panther."

T.J. still won't go for it. "Yeah? Well, she must not have seen you at batting practice. None of the *regular* Panthers work that hard at it."

T.J.'s got a point. I have seen Chase at practice. Jeremy and I watched him at the batting cages too. Talk about intense.

"I have to work hard," Chase answers. "I don't have your natural swing."

"I don't know about that," T.J. says, obviously pleased.

"Do you play sports, Hope?" Chase asks.

T.J. laughs. I glare at him. "Sorry," he says. "I didn't mean you *couldn't* play sports. You'd probably be great, if you ever stuck with anything long enough."

It's true, the part about not sticking with things. "So I'm a born quitter," I admit.

"I find that hard to believe," Chase says.

I stare over at him, wondering why he'd find that hard to believe.

"And regardless," he continues, "I still say I'm no different from you two, or anybody else in Grain."

I tilt my head, sizing him up. "I'll bet you're a morning showerer."

"I shower in the morning, after my run."

"But you'd shower in the morning even if you didn't run," I guess.

"Yeah. Is that important?"

"It is where we come from. Right, T.J.?" He nods, agreeing with me. "White-collar workers shower in the morning because they can," I explain. "Blue-collars shower at night because they have to. They need to get the dirt and grime of the mine or factory off. I'm a night showerer by birth."

Chase narrows his eyes at me. I couldn't look away if I wanted to. "Hope Long, you may be the most interesting person I've ever met."

I have nothing to say to that. Neither does T.J. Nobody

has ever told me I was interesting, much less the most interesting person they've met. Maybe it's a line he hands out. If it is, it's a good one. Without thinking, I tug the rubber band out of my hair and free the ponytail Raymond wanted me to wear in court. My hair follicles tingle, thankful for the freedom.

Mrs. Bowers shuffles into the kitchen, a giant purse over one arm. "I'm sorry I have to leave." She sets her purse down in the middle of the floor and reaches into a cupboard. "You children have to try these." She brings down a box of cookies and takes out a plate. "They just came off the line last week— Monster Nuts and Chips." She dumps the whole box onto the plate and sets it in front of us.

"Thanks, Mrs. Bowers." I take one, even though I don't like nuts. "That's really nice of you."

"It is," Chase agrees, taking a big bite. "It's great."

T.J. keeps staring at the table. "Bye, Mom. Thanks. See you in the morning." His voice is strained. His fingers clench and unclench.

The second his mother leaves, T.J. springs to his feet, grabs the plate of cookies, and takes them to the counter, where he puts every cookie back into the box.

"T.J.? Are you okay?" I've never seen him like this.

For a second, he doesn't answer. Then, without looking at me, he says, "I'm tired. It's pretty late. I don't think the TV van will still be at your house."

I glance at the clock, amazed it's almost ten. "I didn't realize it was so late." I scoot out of the booth. "I've got to go. Thanks for letting us come over."

78

He nods, still not looking at me.

"I'll drop you off," Chase says, moving for the door. "Bye, T.J."

T.J. doesn't return the goodbye. Something's going on, and I don't know what.

When we're outside, I turn to Chase. "What was that back there?"

He doesn't answer until we're in the car, pulling away. "I guess T.J. knows how to hold a grudge."

"What are you talking about?"

"He didn't tell you? It was stupid. At the last practice, Mrs. Bowers showed up with cookies—you know, from the factory? She said it was to get us ready for the big game with Wooster. People were bringing us all kinds of things, like we were headed for the Olympics. Anyway, soon as she left, one of the guys broke out laughing. We were all dead tired from practice. Before we knew it, we were all laughing—the cookies really are pretty bad. Then Coach said, 'Let's save the cookies and give them to the Wooster team. All's fair in love and war.' That did it. Everybody cut loose. I kind of thought T.J. joined in, but I guess I was wrong. We didn't mean anything by it."

I feel bad for T.J. He loves his family, and so do I in a way. More than once, I've shown up on the Bowers's doorstep after a bad fight with Rita. They always welcome me, feed me, and ask no questions. But I guess I'm not that surprised that T.J. didn't tell me about what happened with his mom and the team. We're both pretty private. We know what subjects to stay away from. We don't talk about Rita. Or Jeremy, really.

But T.J. is always there when I need him. And it's just good to have somebody to eat lunch with at school and do homework with sometimes. T.J. gets A's, and he deserves them. He works hard. I'm fine with B's, but he's always up for helping me if I want to shoot for more.

Chase punches the radio on and station-hops until there's loud music pouring out of the front and back speakers. I don't know the songs, but I'm grateful to have music blaring in my head, drowning out thought. This is Rita's kind of music. I'm not about to tell Chase, but my kind of music is way different. I love old songs from the forties, especially the ones written during the war, when people pined for each other—"I'll Be Seeing You," Billie Holiday's "Lover Man." The Andrews Sisters. I used to try to get Jeremy to jitterbug with me, but he was too stiff to jive.

Chase's phone rings.

"Guess your cell really is okay," I say.

He glances at the number, then shuts it off. "I think Dad needs a cooling-off period."

"He's really mad, isn't he?"

Chase shrugs. "He'll get over it. He has to control everything. Guess it's part of the package when you have a cop for a father." He passes a semi, and I can see a little boy on the seat next to the driver.

"At least you have a father." I say this in my head, but it comes out in words too. My mind drifts back to my imaginary father. Every time things got tough with Rita, I'd imagine leaving with my dad. We'd take Jeremy and go live somewhere far away.

"Where is your dad, Hope?" Chase asks. "Unless you don't want to talk about him."

I never talk about him. There's not much to talk about. "He died when I was three. Sometimes I think I remember him, his face, and his eyes. He was tall and thin. I can almost picture him wearing a red baseball cap. But I might have imagined the memory. I do that sometimes."

"How did he die?" Chase has slowed so much that the semi passes us back.

"He was run over. He drove a truck for a living, and it was a truck that ran him over." I have a picture of this in my mind, but I know I've imagined that one.

"You think Jeremy remembers him?"

"Maybe. But he wasn't Jeremy's father. We didn't have the same dad. Rita used to tell Jeremy that he didn't have a father. I guess it was true, in a way. We sure never saw him. But Jeremy believed her literally. He was so excited the first time somebody at church told him God was his father. He came right home and asked Rita where she and God met and fell in love."

"That could sure screw up a kid," Chase observes.

"Maybe. Jeremy would disagree, though." For some reason, I think of that night when Jer and I sat in that old car and Jer's song, or God's song, filled the air.

We ride in an easy quiet until we're at my house. I thank him for the ride, then run up the sidewalk, wondering why I told him so much about me.

The front door swings open and Rita steps out in her white slip, a beer in one hand. She's the only person I know who wears slips, although I've never seen her wear them under anything.

"Where in red-hot blazes have you been?"

I glance back, willing Chase to be gone. The car pulls away from the curb and drives off.

"Was that Chase Wells? Matt's boy?" She downs the rest of her beer, shaking the can to be sure she hasn't missed a drop.

"Don't start, Rita." I shove past her into the house.

She trails in after me. "Mmm . . . mmm. He's a lot better-looking than his old man, that's for sure. What were you doing with him?"

"Nothing. He just gave me a ride home." I kick off my shoes. "We didn't do anything."

"Well, you can take it from your mama—you'd better do a little something with him if you want to keep him coming around."

Only Rita would be upset because I hadn't done anything.

I try to get to my room, but she's not finished with me. She lights a cigarette and takes a deep drag. "I've been trying to reach you all day."

I pull out my cell and see that it's turned off. "Sorry, Rita. You have to turn off cell phones in the courthouse. I guess I forgot to turn it back on."

"I guess I forgot to turn it back on," she repeats, mocking me in the whine of a six-year-old. Her words slur into each other. "Don't you lie to me!"

I have to be careful around Rita when she's like this. I need to get away from her. "All right." I try to walk around her to get to my room, but she blocks me with her cigarette hand.

"Did I say you could leave?" she cries.

I stop, turn to face her, then wait. "What, Rita?"

"The sheriff called here looking for you," she says.

"Sheriff Wells? Why?"

"Looking for his boy."

I think about Chase heading home. Maybe I should call him, warn him.

"Four times! That's how much . . . how many . . . times he called." Rita sniffs, then swipes her nose with the back of her cigarette hand. "He said you and his boy were together."

"Is that a crime now?"

"Don't get smart with me!" She takes a step forward. Automatically, I take a step back.

She comes at me, but stumbles. Ashes break from her cigarette. "I'm still your mother, you know!"

"I know," I mutter.

She squints as if trying to see through me. "What happened in court today?"

"Why?"

"Because Raymond called and said things went lousy."

A rush of guilt sweeps over me. My stomach feels like I swallowed lead. "What else did he say?"

"He said I'm going to have to testify because you screwed up. What did you say anyway?"

She's gotten to me. Even though she's drunk enough to pass out, Rita's still got the upper hand. And once again, I feel like everything in the world is my fault. "I'm sorry. I tried, Rita. I really tried."

"Tried? All you had to do was tell them Jeremy's insane. And you couldn't even pull that one off?"

"But he's *not* insane!" I take another step back so I can lean on the couch, brace myself against it.

"Not this again!" She slams against the end table. Something falls off, but neither of us makes a move to pick it up. "Get your head out of the clouds, girl! How do you explain that bloody bat in his closet? He was there! That McCray woman saw him running from the barn, swinging that—"

"Maybe he was scared! Did you think of that?"

"He was scared all right. Scared he'd go to jail and—"

"No! Rita, listen to me. Anybody could have used Jeremy's bat. He always left it right inside the barn door. Everybody knew that. Maybe somebody's trying to frame him."

Rita lets out an ugly "Ha!" Then she takes a long puff on her cigarette stub and grinds it out on her beer can. "Framed? Right . . . just like in the movies. So, Sherlock Hopeless, whodunit? Who's framing your poor, innocent brother?"

"I don't know. Anybody on his baseball team could have done it. Any one of them could have taken Jeremy's bat. Or somebody from the stable? One of the boarders, maybe."

Rita's shaking her head, but I don't care. I've gone over this a million times. Nobody will listen to me. So even a falling-down-drunk Rita is better than nothing. "What about Coach's wife? Mrs. Johnson might have—"

"Are we talking about bedfast, cancer-stricken Caroline Johnson?" Rita asks.

"Maybe she's not as sick as she pretends. Did anybody think of that? She hated her husband." Out of all the people I know who might have murdered Coach Johnson, his wife is the most likely. I saw her go off on Coach one time before a

84

game. She was scarier than Rita. "Don't they claim it's almost always the spouse who does the murder?"

These aren't new thoughts for me. For the first month after Jeremy was arrested, I went over and over all of this with Raymond because Rita refused to talk to me about it. Well, now she's too drunk to run away. She can just hear me out. "Jeremy didn't murder anybody. If you knew him at all, you'd know that. You and Raymond aren't even trying to prove somebody else could have done it!"

Rita points at me, her lips curled into a snarl. "You listen to me!" Her finger stabs the air with each word. "Thanks to you, Raymond says he has to call me to testify now. I'm going to have to clean up the mess you made and get that jury back to believing Jeremy's insanity plea."

"But he's not—!"

"Don't say it!" Rita screams. "We are not proving that boy innocent, because he isn't! You think I don't know my own son? He probably didn't know what he was doing, but he did it. And we're proving he's insane so they don't execute him for what he did. You get that through your empty head, hear? So don't be talking around town about how normal your brother is, because he isn't and he never has been!"

"You're wrong, Rita. My brother is innocent, and I'm going to prove it."

"You?" Rita laughs. "You and T.J. and that sheriff's boy, I suppose? That's what the sheriff tried to tell me. And I told him he didn't have to worry. You'd give up on your own sooner or later—sooner, most likely. I don't know why I'm wasting my breath."

I can't take any more of this. Rita knows exactly how to shut me down. I run past her to my room and slam the door. My whole life this is how it's been. I hate the arguing. It's so much easier just to let Rita have her way.

Only not this time. For Jeremy's sake, not this time.

12

I stay in my room until I hear Rita leave the house. The lingering toxic aroma of cheap perfume tells me she has a date and won't be back until morning.

Part of me wants to pray, to talk to God the way Jeremy does. Wouldn't God know who killed Coach, if he's keeping an eye on everybody? So I ask—not out loud but inside my head, the way Jer does it: *God, who did it? Who really murdered Coach Johnson?*

Nothing.

Okay. I'm not so sure how this works anymore.

For a minute, my mind is a blank. Then, slowly, I remember a cozy night years ago. Jeremy and I are sitting on his bed, and I'm reading from a kids' book of fairy tales. Only I'm too little to read the words, so I'm just telling the stories and Jeremy's filling in the parts I forget. He could talk then. We look so normal, both of us in snowflake pj's. This could be the best memory I have of childhood. Of Jeremy.

This is the Jer I want back home. I can't let them take him away. Not to prison. Not to a mental hospital. Home. Jeremy belongs at home, with me. I'm all he has. *I* have to find out who really killed Coach.

Unsure where to start, I go to my closet to search for something to write on. A shoe box tumbles from the top shelf, and sea glass rains down on my head. I sit on the floor and put back each piece—a pale green chip from an old railroad insulator, a red piece from a railroad lantern, a chunk of orange carnival glass T.J. said came from one of Lake Erie's famed shipwrecks. Each piece is smooth from over a hundred years of being knocked about in the waves.

I put the box back and keep hunting through the closet until I find a notebook without much writing in it. It was my American history notebook, and I gave up taking notes after the midterm, when all the questions came directly from the book. I still got a B-minus. I tear out my history notes, leaving paper pieces like tiny teeth on the left side of each page.

I settle onto my bed with the notebook. At the top of the first page, I write: SUSPECTS. The blank paper staring at me is almost enough to make me shut the notebook and throw it back into my closet. But then I see Jeremy at the defense table, wringing his hands and looking up at the ceiling as if he could read the outcome of the trial there.

A vagrant. That's my first suspect, listed on the pale blue line of notebook paper. I don't want the murderer to be anyone I know. Why couldn't some crazy homeless guy have been sleeping in the barn when Coach walked in and surprised him? Maybe the man didn't even know what he was doing until it was too late.

The police said nobody had seen an unknown person hanging around the barn, but maybe they were wrong. When I asked Raymond about the possibility of a stranger being the murderer, he told me the police had ruled it out because Jeremy's fingerprints were the only ones on the bat. Supposedly, the police canvassed the area for transients anyway and came up empty. In Grain, Ohio, a person who doesn't belong gets spotted fast and turned over for gossip before the sun sets.

I move on. I want a long list of suspects, especially since the prosecution has a short list. A list of one—my brother.

The Panthers. Any boy on the team could have murdered Coach. They all knew where Jeremy parked his bat. They knew where Coach would be that early on a game day, especially *that* game day. Why aren't *they* suspects? A little voice in my head answers: *Because they weren't spotted running from the scene of the crime with the murder weapon.* I ignore the voice and write down as many names as I can remember:

Austin—first baseman, a freshman
Tyler—catcher, new to the team, nice to Jeremy
Greg—second base, good hitter, quiet
Kid on 3rd who yells at umpires—has a temper
David and Manny—outfielders

I can't come up with the rest of the team, and I want to know their last names, especially the third baseman with a temper. What I need is a team roster. I know that Coach used to post a game roster on the park bulletin board on game day, but I think he passed them out to the team too.

I search for an old team roster in Jer's room but come up

empty. Frustrated, I drop to the floor and lean against Jeremy's bed. Leaving space in my notebook for other players' names, I move on with my suspect list:

Caroline Johnson. Coach's wife has to be my number one suspect. She used to teach at the high school with Coach. T.J. had her for one class and hated her, the only teacher he never got along with, as far as I know. Married people have a bottomless pit of motives to kill each other. Money, for one. No money, for another. Since they never had kids, Caroline would get everything if Coach died. I have no idea what "everything" is. I do know that the stable was really Caroline's. Coach had an office there, but he only started getting involved with the horses after she got sick.

Jealousy—that's another good marriage motive. Maybe Coach had an affair? I'm not sure I'd blame him after seeing the way she yelled at him that day at the game. Or maybe Caroline had an affair and Coach found out about it?

Or anger. I've seen her temper in action.

It was a little over a year ago, back before she got really sick. Coach called a practice before a Saturday home game. I don't remember which team we were playing. Jeremy and I were the first ones to get there. Jer was laying out bats and balls when Coach drove up. I don't think he saw us, because the minute he stepped out of his car, his wife drove up in her car. I could hear her screaming at him before she even shut off her engine.

"You think you can get away from me that easily?" she shouted.

"Caroline, please." Coach was harder to hear because he was trying to calm her down. It wasn't working.

90

"*I'm* the one who's sick! *Me!* I'm the one with cancer! I won't stand for it!"

Coach said something else I couldn't make out.

Then she exploded. "No! I hate this entire business! And I hate you! I'm not putting up with this. You're going to be sorry you were ever born!" Or something like that. She climbed back into her car and roared off. Coach had to jump out of the way or she'd have run him over.

Through the whole quarrel, Jeremy kept setting out the baseball equipment. I never knew if he'd heard the yelling or not.

And me? I acted like I hadn't heard a word. It's what I do—I smooth things over. I put the whole incident out of my mind . . . until now.

I never found out what Coach and his wife had been arguing about that day. But I heard what I heard, and I saw what I saw—Caroline Johnson's rage.

Maybe Caroline Johnson didn't plan to murder her husband. Maybe she just lost her temper and snapped. One lucky, or unlucky, blow.

Rita's voice in my head is laughing, mocking me.

I don't think the police ever investigated Caroline Johnson because she's supposedly an invalid, confined to her bed and all, or maybe to a wheelchair. But what if she's faking?

On the suspect page by her name, I write: *Caroline . . . a fake? . . . money problems? . . . affair?*

The phone rings. I figure it's T.J., apologizing for being so weird about the cookies at his house. Maybe I can ask him to fill in the names of the Panther players and tell me more about Caroline Johnson as a teacher. "Hello?" I flip on the living room lamp.

A muffled voice says something I can't make out. It's not T.J.

"Excuse me? Who is this?"

I hear breathing. Definitely breathing. Somebody's there. "Hello?"

Static hits the line, then a click. And the dial tone buzzes.

I hang up. Probably a wrong number. Or a prank. When Jeremy was first arrested, we got some pretty nasty phone calls.

I try to get back into my list of suspects and motives, but it's no use. A headache is starting at the back of my neck, creeping up like electric fingers climbing the back of my skull. I close my eyes and hear branches scratching the roof.

The phone rings again. I jump, like an idiot, then pick up after the second ring. "Hello?"

No answer. I think I hear breathing again. The line is clear as ice.

"Hey, if this is some kind of sick joke, it's not funny." I hang up, hard.

The house is too dark, so I walk from room to room, turning on all the lights. I'm never scared in the house by myself. I've stayed home alone more nights than I can count. And usually, I really like it.

But tonight feels different. I wish Jeremy were here.

The phone rings again, and my heart jumps like it's been shocked with heart paddles. We don't have an answering machine, so the phone keeps ringing and ringing and ringing.

Finally, I can't stand it any longer. I grab the receiver. "What? What do you want?"

A second of silence passes, and then a voice: "I'm watching you. Leave it alone." I think that's what he—or she—says. The voice is so muffled and faint that I'm not sure of the words.

"What did you say?" I demand.

Click. And nobody's there.

13

now, I'm sure it's kids. It has to be. I was at a sleepover once, the only one I've ever been to—the girl's mother made her invite every girl in her class—and they spent most of the night dialing numbers out of the phone book and saying stuff like "I saw what you did," "I know what you're up to," and "I'm watching you."

But no matter what I tell myself, I keep imagining men in black hoodies surrounding the house, peering into the windows, hiding in the bathroom, the kitchen, the bedroom.

I'm calling T.J. I don't care if it is late.

T.J. answers on the third ring, and I tell him about the calls.

"Okay," he says, like he's the officer in charge. "Don't answer the phone. Lock the doors, and we'll be right over."

"We?"

"Chase and me."

"Wait . . . what's Chase doing—?"

T.J.'s already on the move. I hear something thud to the floor and imagine him dropping his shoe. "Chase forgot his wallet. He came back for it. He's right here."

"Aren't you mad at him, T.J.? You sure acted mad before."

"Nah. We're cool. Can you run over to Hope's with me?" T.J. says this last part away from the phone.

"Wait! T.J.?" I don't understand what's going on.

"I was talking to Chase," T.J. says, sounding out of breath. "We'll be right there." He hangs up.

Chase Wells is coming here? Into this house? Jogging by is one thing. Coming inside is another.

I glance at the kitchen wall clock and try to guess how long it will take them to drive over. Not that long. I race around the house, picking up after Rita—the lacy bra strung over the easy chair, an empty beer bottle on the coffee table, one black heel in the kitchen, another in the hallway, shot glasses on the counter.

Before I get a chance to change out of the skirt and blouse I wore to court, there's a knock at the door. I sniff under each armpit. Nothing bad. Then I open the door.

T.J. looks like he just woke up on the wrong side of the bed. Chase, still in jeans and a gray shirt, could step directly onto the cover of one of Rita's celebrity magazines.

"I'll have a look around," T.J. says, pushing past me. He's only been here a few times, but he acts like he owns the place, or maybe like he's got a warrant to search it.

Chase, of course, has never been here, and I wonder if he's ever seen a house like ours close-up. The confetti carpet is worn to the paper-thin padding in spots, and furniture is arranged to hide the worst rug stains, most of which were here before we were. Furniture too. Except the TV. Rita always has a great television.

Suddenly I realize Chase is waiting for me to invite him in. I step back so he can enter. He ducks, as if our doorway is too low for him. "You didn't have to come over here. I didn't know . . . I mean, I thought just T.J. would . . ."

"T.J. said you sounded pretty strung on the phone. What did they say? Was it kids? Could you tell?"

I try to call up the voice in my head. "I don't know. It could have been anybody. Mostly, they just breathed." I try to laugh it off, but even I can hear how fake my laugh sounds.

"And you don't have caller ID?" he asks, taking a couple more steps in.

I'm embarrassed to admit that we don't. We're probably the last people in America not to have it.

I'll kill T.J. for bringing Chase here. What was he thinking?

T.J. reappears. "Clear! Nobody's hiding in the kitchen or the bathroom. I didn't hit the bedrooms, though."

"I didn't say somebody was hiding," I snap. Chase must think I'm an idiot. "I'm sorry you guys had to drive all the way over here for nothing. I really don't need a babysitter."

"Babysitter, huh?" Chase perches on the arm of the couch and crosses his long legs at the ankles. "I always wanted to be a babysitter."

"You did not," I say.

"Seriously. I did. I didn't have little brothers or sisters. I always thought it might be cool to hang out with somebody else's. But nobody ever wanted a guy babysitter where I came from."

"So what did you do instead?" T.J. asks this like he's not really mad at Chase anymore.

"What did I do? Instead of babysitting, you mean?" Chase says. "Nothing."

"What are you saying? You've never had a job? Even an after-school job?" T.J. frowns like he can't believe this.

Chase shrugs. "Sad, but true."

I'm coming down on T.J.'s side on this one. I've had so many jobs the child labor people should have arrested Rita.

Chase turns to me. "You're a workingwoman, aren't you? I've seen you at that café on Main Street, the Colonial."

"You have?" I don't get it. I'd have remembered if he'd ever been my customer. He hasn't been. Panic strikes when I imagine Rita waiting on him, hitting on him.

"Driving by," he explains. "I've seen you through that front window?"

I didn't think Chase Wells even knew who I was. I try to picture him cruising Main Street, turning his head to see me.

Behind us, paying no attention to us, T.J. plops onto the couch. A tiny puff of dust billows up.

"Haven't seen you there lately, though," Chase says. "Did you quit?"

I'm still standing just inside the door, not sure what to do with myself. "What? No. I haven't quit working at the Colonial. Bob—the owner—has been pretty cool about the trial and Jer and everything. But customers stare and whisper. Some of them ask questions about Jeremy. Rita can handle them, but I can't. So I work in back most of the time."

I can't keep standing here, arms folded across my chest, like I used to do in fifth grade to hide my "early development."

97

"Want something to drink?" I shoot past them to the kitchen and inhale the scent of leather and Ivory soap Chase brought in.

He follows me. "Water would be great."

"Got any Coke?" T.J. hollers in from the living room.

I open the fridge and find three brands of beer on the top shelf, but no Coke. No juice. No bottled water. No ice cubes in the freezer, just an empty plastic ice cube tray.

I run the tap water and get down two glasses. Chase pulls back a chair and sits at the kitchen table. The chair legs squeal on the linoleum. I call out to T.J. to come in for his water.

Setting down the two glasses, I spot a Snickers wrapper and Rita's overflowing ashtray on the plastic checkered table-cloth. I sweep both items off the table and dump them into the garbage. Tiny flecks of ash float up, along with the stench of stale cigarettes.

"Sorry, T.J.," I tell him as he takes a seat across from Chase. "No Coke."

"That's okay," he answers. "Hate to ask, but I'm starving."

I watched him eat two bologna sandwiches an hour ago. He eats more than anybody I've ever met, but you wouldn't know it to look at him. "Sure. Chase?" My brain cycles through the slim possibilities for food in this house.

"Maybe. If it wouldn't be too much trouble," Chase answers.

"No trouble," I lie. I ferret through the fridge, then the cupboard. *No lunch meat. Crackers? No cheese. No cookies.* "I make a killer peanut butter sandwich."

"Prove it," Chase challenges.

"Yeah," T.J. agrees.

I laugh . . . until I picture my brother sitting at this table taking a giant bite of a peanut butter sandwich. "That's the one thing I make sure we never run out of—peanut butter. Jeremy would live on the stuff if I let him."

Before I can get the bread out, Chase is up and searching through our gross fridge. He comes out with the grape jelly, Jer's favorite.

"Know your way around the kitchen, I see," T.J. observes.

"I've had lots of practice finding my way around strange kitchens. Every time Mom remarries, it's off to a new house." He finds our silverware drawer on the second try, takes out a knife, and spreads jelly after I do the peanut butter. "Is this really all your brother likes?" Chase asks. "Peanut butter sandwiches? And bologna. How about hot dogs?"

"He loves hot dogs too." In my head, I can see Jeremy at a baseball game. He's wearing a White Sox cap and biting into a ballpark frank. "We got to go to a White Sox game once. Rita was dating some guy who'd just gotten out of prison. Anyway, he took Jeremy and me to a game, and Jer ate six hot dogs and got so sick that he threw them all up . . . and all over the ex-con."

Chase laughs.

"You never told me that," T.J. says.

"I haven't thought about it in years," I say, sounding too defensive. T.J. hasn't told me much about his past either, but I don't bring that up. It's nice having the three of us get along like this. Still, it feels a little like we're balancing on a seesaw. One shift could send the whole thing crashing down.

"Dad and I love going into Cleveland for Indians games," T.J. says. "We've made it to the home opener every year for as long as I can remember."

"My dad's never taken me to a major-league game," Chase admits, picking up his sandwich and slapping on more peanut butter. "He keeps promising to, but he never does. He and Mom used to fight all the time about Dad's promises. They fought about a lot of things. I guess they fought over me a lot. Never *for* me, just over me."

I'm not sure what to say. Even though I knew his parents were divorced, I've always pictured Chase Wells as having the perfect life, in Boston or in Grain.

"Voilà!" he says, lifting his four-inch-thick peanut butter masterpiece like it's a baseball trophy.

T.J. applauds. "I want *his* sandwich."

"Don't worry. I made you two." I pull the stepping stool up to the table and sit on it. Although I made myself a sandwich too, I'm not hungry. I let it sit in front of me while Chase and T.J. eat.

T.J. wipes his mouth with the back of his hand, smudging peanut butter to his chin. Then he nods at Chase. "Go ahead and ask her."

Chase almost chokes on his sandwich.

I glance from one to the other. "What? Ask me what?"

Chase shakes his head and won't look at me.

T.J. takes over. "Chase wanted to know what's really wrong with Jeremy. I told him I didn't know anything he didn't and he should ask you."

Chase's cheeks have turned pink. "You don't need to

answer that if you don't want to. I wasn't being nosy, but I didn't understand much of the expert testimony in court. And I wondered, when you said it would be a terrible thing if they put Jeremy in a mental hospital, why you said that. Why would it be so hard on him if he has something wrong with him that they could fix, or help? You'd be able to visit him, right?" He stops. "I'm sorry. It's none of my business. I didn't mean to bother *you* with it, Hope. I just thought T.J. could help me understand."

T.J. and I never talk about Jeremy. Usually, I hate it when people ask me what's wrong with my brother. But I don't know now. I want Chase to understand, and T.J. too. I don't want to be the only one who understands Jeremy well enough to believe he didn't do what they say he did.

"Jeremy was born with a neurological disorder. Probably Asperger's syndrome, although he's had all the standard labels pasted on him at one time or another: learning disabled, ADHD, autistic. One counselor at a school in Chicago was sure Jer had epilepsy because of his tantrum fits. And, yeah, selective mutism, which is a no-brainer since we know Jeremy selected to be mute."

"So he's been tested before all this, like in a hospital?" Chase sets down his sandwich and leans in, catching every word.

"Jeremy's been tested and retested. Every time he got a new teacher, they'd call Rita in and ask her about him. Then they'd send him to the school psychologist—those people have some big problems of their own, if you ask me. Then *they'd* give up and send Jer on to some doctor, or hospital, or specialist."

"And nobody knows why he won't talk?" Chase asks, almost like he can't quite believe this.

I understand where he's coming from. "At first, Rita thought he was just being stubborn. She'd get so mad at Jeremy." I stop talking because I'm remembering times when I had to get between Rita and my brother. I remember one time when I shoved a drunk Rita out of the way so Jeremy could escape to the bathroom and lock himself in until she got over it, or fell asleep.

But if I'm honest, there are other pictures stored inside my mind too. Rita sitting on the floor with Jeremy, holding up word cards the speech therapist gave her. Rita all excited over a new "herbologist" or "naturalist" she heard about, who could cure what didn't come out of Jeremy's mouth by being more picky about what went into his mouth.

I get up and run myself a glass of water. It tastes as cloudy as it looks and smells like iron. Then I sit back down.

"I don't remember any of that stuff going on when you and Jeremy moved to Grain," T.J. says.

"By the time we moved here, Rita was so tired of the whole rigmarole that she'd started telling new schools Jeremy had been in an accident and *couldn't* talk. She just didn't want to go through all those tests again. I guess Jer's language arts teacher, Ms. Graham, tried to teach him sign language our first year here. It didn't take, though. Jeremy likes to write notes. You should see his handwriting."

"So that's it?" Chase asks. He hasn't taken another bite of his sandwich since we've been talking about Jeremy. T.J. has finished both of his. "There's really nothing else wrong with him?"

"Nope. Not with Jer," I answer. "Nothing except the fact that people have a hard time understanding unique."

"Unique." Chase mutters this, so I can't tell if it's a question or not.

I know he doesn't get what I'm saying, and I'm not sure how to say it any better. I want him—them—to *get* Jeremy. I struggle for a minute over how to explain the Jeremy I love, what makes him who he is. And then I know.

Leaving our dirty dishes, I get up from the table. "Come with me."

14

Standing outside Jeremy's bedroom, my hand wrapped around the doorknob, I know one thing. Chase and T.J. are about to get a true glimpse of Jeremy Long. What I don't know is how they'll react. Slowly, I turn the knob and open the door.

This time, it's T.J. who hangs back and Chase who goes in first. He stares up and around, in a full circle, as if awed by a starry sky. His gaze passes over the baseball bedspread I found at Goodwill in Oklahoma. My brother loves that spread. Most days since he's been gone, I've come in and smoothed out the wrinkles. The only piece of furniture in the room besides this single bed is an old dresser I painted blue to match the bedspread. Above the dresser hangs one of Jeremy's drawings—a circle divided into sixteen pie pieces, each meticulously colored in with a different color. This is Jeremy's art. My brother has made me dozens, maybe hundreds, of these pictures, each with a different color scheme, but all the exact same design. I've saved every one of them.

But Chase isn't looking at the dresser or the color wheel. He's staring at Jeremy's glass jars. Three walls are lined with shelves. The last owner or renter must have filled these shelves with books—most people would.

But not Jeremy.

"These are the jars you talked about in court," Chase whispers, as if afraid of disturbing the row after row of emptiness. His eyes widen as his gaze shifts from one wall to the next. "How many does he have?"

"I've never counted them."

"It's pretty amazing, isn't it?" He says this like he's able to admire the collection, to respect my brother. "It must have taken him a long time to do this."

"He'd have more if a box of the jars hadn't been left back in Chicago one time. Not a pleasant experience for any of us," I admit. An image flashes through my mind—Jeremy throwing glasses and plates in our new kitchen, Rita the one hiding under the table for once.

T.J. clears his throat. It startles me, and I turn to see him still standing in the doorway, his arms straight out from his sides, like he's holding on to the doorframe. He nods at the baseball curtains I got when I found the spread. "He really loves baseball, huh?"

I sit on the edge of the bed. "At least that's something you guys can understand. You've probably been baseball-crazy since you were little boys."

"Got that right," T.J. agrees. "Dad took me to my first Wooster-Grain game when I was six weeks old."

I wait for Chase to say something like that, but he doesn't. "I don't know. I like to play, but I can't say I've ever been *crazy* about baseball."

I'm surprised. He always looks so serious about it at practices, dedicated even.

"Hold on a minute," T.J. says, venturing into the room with us. "You play here in the summer, and you're on a team in Boston too, right?"

"That was Husband Number Two's idea. When I started playing, I guess I was pretty good, like it was natural for me. All of a sudden, my dad started calling me after games to see if we won and how I did. Then he began calling before games too, to give me last-minute tips and advice."

"And that was a good thing?" T.J. asks.

"Yeah. Before baseball, Dad almost never called me. And when he did, we didn't have anything to talk about. After I got into baseball, we could talk for an hour on the phone. And things weren't as awkward when I came to visit him. We had baseball, you know?"

"I know what you mean," T.J. agrees. "My dad and I can talk baseball for hours. He can talk about grass and weeds for hours too, but I don't stick around."

Chase frowns, like he's trying to understand, so I explain. "T.J.'s dad works for TruGreen lawn care."

"Ah." Chase nods. Then he takes another long look at Jeremy's jars, tracing the shelves all the way around the room. He gets it. I can see he does.

T.J.'s already back to baseball. "Your dad played ball in high school, didn't he? Did he play with Coach?"

I'm watching the lines of Chase's forehead, and I don't think he's enjoying all of T.J.'s questions. But he answers anyway. "Dad played in high school, but he lived in Wooster. So he and Coach were rivals. I'm not sure either one of them ever got over it. I don't think Coach appreciated Dad's postgame advice after our Panther games."

"Still," T.J. says, "Coach was going to let *you* start against Wooster. Your dad must have been pumped to see you pitch in the biggest game of the year."

Chase doesn't look at either of us. "You could say that. He practically ordered everybody in his office to go to the game. He even bought fireworks to set off when we scored against Wooster."

I'm beginning to think it was a mistake to show them Jer's room. Somehow we've ended up talking about the day of the murder, the game that wasn't played. I think I hate baseball.

"What's this?" T.J.'s picked up something off Jeremy's dresser. He reads out loud: "Suspects. A vagrant. The Panth—"

"Give me that!" I tear across the room and grab my suspect list out of his hands. I don't remember leaving my notebook on Jer's dresser, but I must have.

"What was that?" T.J. asks, standing on his toes to try to read over my shoulder.

"None of your business." I clutch the notebook to my chest, feeling stupid, like I've been caught at something.

T.J. won't let it go. "You're trying to solve the murder. That's it, isn't it? I knew it. You've got a list of suspects and—"

I wheel on him. "Well, why wouldn't I try to figure out who the real killer is? I'm the only one who believes, who *knows*, it wasn't Jeremy. Who else is going to—?"

"It's cool, Hope," T.J. says. "I've been expecting you to do this. I think you need to try. I want to help." He glances down at his feet. "I've just been waiting for you to ask."

I narrow my eyes, studying him. I know he wants to help me. But I'm pretty sure he's believed Jeremy is guilty all along—I've never asked. Still, T.J. has always been there for me when I really needed him. I glance back at Chase. His face is a blank. I have no idea what he's thinking.

Then, as if he's planned all of this, scripted it even, T.J. crosses the room and sits next to Chase on the bed. "You can help too, Chase, if you'll do it."

Chase stiffens. "No."

"Think about it at least, man," T.J. urges. "You have an inside track to what's going on in the trial, to evidence . . . to your dad. Hope needs us."

I know T.J. is doing this for me. I can't even look at Chase. "T.J., don't."

"What?" T.J. asks.

I stare at him. "Why would *he* want to help Jeremy?"

"It's not that," Chase says. "I just . . . I mean . . . I wouldn't be any help."

"But you would!" T.J. insists.

Chase shakes his head. "My dad barely talks to me, T.J."

"I don't care," T.J. says. "Besides, you owe me, man."

Chase's forehead wrinkles. "I thought two rides from the courthouse squared us."

"Not by a long shot." T.J. waits a minute, then adds, "And you know it."

They exchange a weird look. I am definitely missing

something. There's more to this than T.J. convincing Coach to let Chase pitch. I can tell that much.

T.J. gets to his feet and turns to me. "Chase is in. Tell us what we can do."

I don't know what's going on between them, but I don't want any part of it. "T.J., drop it. Chase doesn't want to help."

"It's not that," Chase says. "I mean, I'd be glad to help, if I could. But—"

"See? He's in," T.J. insists. "Go on, Hope. What do you need?"

I glance at Chase, and I know he's not "in." He'll probably take off as soon as he can. And that's fine. But what if T.J.'s right? What if Chase knows something that could help Jer? Something he heard from his dad or got out of the trial? It's possible. So, embarrassed or not, I might as well get what I can out of him while he's here. For Jeremy's sake.

"Okay. I know you need to go," I tell him. "But if you could help me with just one thing, that's all I'll ask. I'd really like to get my hands on a roster. Do either of you have a team roster?"

"Why?" Chase frowns at me, and I wish I'd waited until he left. T.J. probably has one. "Why do you want a roster?"

"Well, maybe I don't need a roster exactly. I just need to know the names of all the players on the Panthers. And anything else about them, especially how they got along with Coach."

"For your suspect list," T.J. says. "Right. I can give you the names of everybody on the team." He reaches for my notebook, and I let him take it. He starts filling in my list of names.

Chase stands up. "You don't really need me for this."

"Sit back down, man," T.J. says, still writing. "You know more about some of these guys than I do."

"Are you serious?" Chase asks. "You live here. They go to school with you, don't they?"

"That doesn't mean they hang out with me. They don't. They hang out with you."

I get the feeling it costs T.J. something to admit this. I'm grateful.

Chase sits on the edge of the bed and rubs his hands together as if he's warming himself by a bonfire. "Give me a name. I'll tell you what I know."

Fifteen minutes later, my suspect list has doubled.

"I have to tell you, Hope," Chase says when we're finished with the Panther list, "everybody on the Panthers really liked Coach."

"So did Jeremy," I add.

"So did Jeremy," he agrees.

T.J. has been sitting cross-legged on the floor, but he gets up. "They liked him. Maybe. But maybe not."

"What do you mean, T.J.?" I ask.

When he looks at me, his face is hard, his mouth a razor-thin line. "Coach wasn't perfect."

I'm a little stunned at the change in T.J. I know he was angry about Coach making fun of his mom, but I wonder if there's something else going on. After another minute, I ask him again, "What do you mean?"

He's quiet for so long that I don't think he's going to answer me. Then he does. "It's just . . . everybody talks about

Coach Johnson like he's this saint or something. Just because people are dead doesn't mean you forget all the bad stuff they did. He wasn't perfect. That's all I'm saying. So maybe everybody *didn't* like him."

I want to ask more, but I don't. I just say, "Good point," and let it go at that.

"Okay." Chase frowns, like he doesn't understand either. "Nobody's perfect. I'm just saying that I don't think the Panthers make great suspects."

I hate to agree with him, but I do. "I had to start somewhere. But I think the best possibility is Caroline Johnson, Coach's wife."

"You underlined her," T.J. says, sitting down again. He taps the end of the pen on the list. The *click, click* reminds me of Jeremy, the way he can drive me crazy with constant clicking whenever he has a pen in his hand.

Chase turns to me. "Did you underline her name because you really think she murdered her husband?"

"Lots of wives do, you know."

"That's true," T.J. says. "Spouses are the number one suspect in any murder. One-third of female homicide victims were killed by their husbands or boyfriends. Some say fifty-three percent of murders were done by spouses, but most of them got off."

I don't know where he comes up with this stuff, but I'll take it. Over half of victims are killed by their spouses? I wonder if Raymond knows this.

"Okay," Chase says. "But could Mrs. Johnson even get to the barn? Or swing a bat?"

"Why not? Maybe she's faking it. You don't know. Has anybody even looked into her?" I know I sound defensive. But I want them to believe somebody else did it. I want Chase to believe it.

T.J. keeps clicking his pen and staring at the notebook. The *click, click, click* is the only sound in the room.

Then Chase sits up and leans in so he can see my suspect list. "You know . . . and this is pretty random . . . I've always thought there was something wrong about that woman."

"You did?" I can't believe it. "You do? Tell me. Us."

"I don't know exactly. I've only seen her a few times when Coach had us over to his house."

"He had you over to his house?" T.J. interrupts.

"Just a couple of times. Me and Austin and Greg and some others."

"Figures," T.J. mutters.

"Go on," I urge, wishing T.J. would quit interrupting.

"I can't explain it," Chase continues. "She was friendly enough and said the right things. But there was just something about her I didn't like."

"Jeremy too!" I slap my knee, then tug my skirt down. I'm not used to wearing skirts, and I sure haven't been thinking about this one. "Jer's a great judge of character. He's always stayed away from Coach's wife, and he wouldn't tell me why."

"That fits," Chase says.

"What? What fits?" I ask.

He tilts his head at me. "That's right. . . . You weren't in the courtroom for her testimony, were you?"

I shake my head. "I didn't think she testified. I thought they said she couldn't make it to court."

"That's what I thought too," T.J. agrees.

"She didn't. Not in person," Chase explains. "But Keller was allowed to read her testimony into the record."

"Is that fair?" I ask. "Keller gets to read whatever Caroline wants to say, and Raymond doesn't even get a chance to make her take it back?"

"Jeremy's lawyer asked her questions too," Chase says. "Only not very many."

"Wouldn't he have the right to subpoena her to appear in court?" T.J. asks. "I'll bet Raymond could make her testify."

"Well, he might not want to put her on the stand," Chase says.

"Why?" I demand. "What did she say?" This is the first I've heard about any of this.

"Mostly, it was how great her husband was. She gave an account of the day of the murder, how Coach left the house early, and how my dad's deputy went to the house to give her the news."

I can tell he's leaving out things. "What did she say about Jeremy?"

Chase bites his bottom lip, then comes out with it. "It was pretty bad, Hope."

"Tell me."

"She said she was afraid of him. I guess Jeremy went to the house a couple of times with Coach. I don't know what happened, but she told Coach not to let him in the house again. She made your brother sound dangerous."

"Dangerous? Jeremy?" I can't stay sitting down, so I pace Jeremy's floor. "Jeremy's right about her. I don't trust that woman." I keep thinking about what I saw that day in the ballpark when she went off on Coach.

I start to tell them more about that argument, but the phone rings. I quit pacing and stare out to the living room, where the phone is ringing and ringing.

"Aren't you going to answer it?" T.J. asks.

Ring! Ring! Ring! It sounds angry.

"Want me to get it?" T.J. makes a move toward the phone.

"Wait!" I cry over the scream of the phone. "It could be Rita." The last thing I need is Rita making a scene because I have two guys over when she's not here.

I walk to the phone, but I can't pick it up. I'm too afraid.

Footsteps come behind me. I think it's T.J. until I see Chase reach down and pick up the receiver. The silence is like a slap, scarier somehow than the ringing. Chase holds the receiver to my ear and leans in. When I don't say anything, he does: "This is the Long residence."

I recognize the quiet that floats on the other end of the line. I know the breathing.

"Is anybody there?" Chase shouts into the phone.

There's no answer. Of course.

"Listen to me, whoever this is. Stop calling here! I'm telling the sheriff, and we'll be listening and tracing your number. Do you understand me?" His voice is getting louder and louder. "You better! This ends right now. Do you hear me? Answer me!" When nobody does, Chase lets loose a string of cusswords that would make even Rita blush. Then he slams down the phone and stares at it, like it could jump back up and knock us both down.

"Way to go, Chase!" T.J. shouts, clapping. "Didn't think you had it in you."

Chase looks at me as if he forgot T.J. and I were here. "Hope, I'm sorry. I guess I lost it."

"Kind of," I agree.

"It's just . . . I hate cowards," Chase explains, staring at the phone again. "But I should have let you handle it."

"I wasn't exactly handling it," I admit.

"If you're okay, I should go," he says. I nod. He pats his pocket, probably making sure he doesn't leave his wallet again.

"I can stay if you want," T.J. says.

"I'll be okay." I wouldn't mind having T.J. stick around. But I don't want him to have to walk home. "Besides, who would call back after a phone . . . uh, conversation . . . like that one, right?"

"Yeah. Okay." T.J. squeezes my arm. "I'll take off, then. Dad's got to be home by now, wondering where I am." He glances at Chase. "He's probably called *your* dad to get the posse out looking for me." He laughs at his own joke.

"That's all we both need," Chase says, moving toward the door.

I follow them outside. Chase stops on the step. T.J.'s already halfway to the car. "Thanks, T.J.!" I call after him. Softer, I say, "You too, Chase." I feel like I need to say more. He's gotten dragged into my mess all day long. But I stare up into those green eyes, and I can't say anything.

"Jeremy's lucky to have a sister like you," he says.

As he walks off, I think that out of all the things he could

115

have said, this is the best. It's the only thing I've ever cared about—being a good sister to Jer.

I watch them drive away under a sliver of moon. They're still in sight when my cell phone rings. Only a handful of people have my cell number, so I answer it.

"It's me." The voice belongs to T.J., but the number doesn't. "I'm on Chase's cell. Mine's dead. I just wanted to make sure we're on for driving lessons after church tomorrow." T.J. is determined to help me get my driver's license. He's been giving me lessons Sunday afternoons for about a month. I've been doing it because it helps keep my mind off Jeremy, even if it only lasts an hour.

"I don't know, T.J. Driving doesn't seem that important anymore."

"But I want to run some ideas by you. Like surveillance on Mrs. Johnson. A couple of other things too. We can talk about the case."

I can't say no. I'm too grateful that he's taking Jeremy's case seriously. It makes me feel like it's not *all* up to me. "Okay. I'm not going to church, though. Can you come by for me?"

"I'll be around about noon, okay?"

"Okay. Thanks again, T.J. See you tomorrow." Chase's car is still in view when I sign off. What did people do before cells?

I turn to go back inside. And that's when I see it. An old white pickup truck, headlights off, creeps from the shadows and inches up the street. I step back as it passes my house and keeps going. At the corner, it turns right, just like Chase did. Then it speeds off, disappearing into the darkness . . . just like Chase.

15

While I shower and get ready for bed, I try to explain away that old white pickup. The driver might have forgotten to turn on the lights. It definitely went the same direction Chase did, but there are only two choices at that corner—straight or a right turn. It might have been going anywhere.

I know I'm being paranoid because of the crank calls, but I can't shake the idea that somebody was following Chase and T.J.

What if they didn't make it home? I grab my cell and hit T.J.'s number. The call goes directly to voice mail, and I remember he said his phone was dead. So I return the call from T.J. on Chase's phone. It goes straight to voice mail too.

This isn't good. What if the pickup ran them off the road? *Think. Think!* Maybe Chase is home already, and he's turned off his ringer because he doesn't want to wake his dad. That makes sense. I could text him. As fast as I can, I type: R U OK? Not much of a message, but I send it and wait. My stomach's cramping as I hold my cell in both hands and stare at it.

Finally, I hear the double beep. **Fine. U?**

I let out a big sigh. Now I feel stupid. He probably thinks I'm flirting with him . . . and that I'm really bad at it. I text: **Good.**

I have got to stop seeing bad guys everywhere.

By the time I climb into bed, I'm tired enough for sleep to come, but it doesn't. Twice I think I hear somebody inside the house. I call out to Rita, but nobody answers, except the old house creaking, the refrigerator roaring, and the branches scratching my bedroom window.

After double-checking the front and back doors, I get back in bed and burrow under the sheets. I close my eyes, but I can't stop imagining things. I picture someone sneaking in through Jeremy's window, and I can't remember if I locked that window. But I don't want to go check. Outside, there's a faint rattle of an engine creeping by, but not passing, the house. It could be the white pickup. I know it's ridiculous to think like this, but I can't help it.

For the first time in ages, I actually wish Rita would come home.

The second I wake up, I have the feeling someone is watching me. I stumble out of bed. My window faces west, but I can tell the sun is up.

I yawn, stretch, and check the clock. It's late, and I've already missed Chase running by. I wish he wouldn't run the same time on weekends that he does weekdays.

Thinking about Chase changes my mood. It shouldn't, not with Jeremy still in jail. But as I gaze out the window at the deserted shack across the street, images of Chase from last night flash through my mind: Chase on the edge of the couch, legs outstretched; Chase in my kitchen, spreading grape jelly and laughing about something; Chase in the middle of Jeremy's room, staring wide-eyed at Jer's jar collection. But his expression isn't just gawking. There's awe on his face. He's truly amazed.

I walk over to my closet and open the door. The wood is splintered, the latch never worked, and the closet isn't deep enough for most hangers. Jeans, khakis, and shorts are folded on the top shelf, along with other junk. A few shirts and T-shirts hang on kid hangers. I haven't been shopping since before Jeremy was arrested. If he were here, we'd be going to church, and I'd wear either the khaki pants or a long, funky, crocheted black skirt that's not at all churchy.

But I'm not going. I've only gone to church once since Jeremy was arrested. It felt like everyone was staring at me, even if they weren't. I do miss it, though, especially the songs. Jeremy says God sings everywhere, but it's easier to hear in church.

I settle on denim capris I've only worn once and a sleeveless white shirt with big buttons and just a tiny spot that I didn't see until I got it home from Goodwill.

About five in the morning, I heard Rita come in. You'd have had to be dead not to hear her. She was Happy-Singing-Drunk Rita. She pounded on my bedroom door until I got up to unhook her necklace for her. She was Rita in White—white feather collar rimming a white cardigan, the tiny buttons straining to hold her in. Rita the Chatterer: "Hope,

Hope, Hope," she said, taking my face in her hands. "You're a pretty girl. Did you know that? Don't ever let anybody say you're not, hear? My girl. My own little girl."

I'm hoping she sleeps until noon. I grab my bag and ease out of my room.

"Where do you think you're going?" Rita's standing in the middle of the hallway. Her slip is on inside out, and her bleached hair looks like something made a nest out of it. When she eyes me up and down, her mascara-clumped lashes make tiny window shades for her bloodshot eyes. "Is it Sunday?"

I nod, hoping she'll think I'm off to church.

Rita groans, turns her back on me, and staggers to her bedroom.

Just when I think I'll make a clean getaway, she glances over her shoulder. "Hey. What was that old truck doing last night?"

My blood stops running through my veins and turns to ice. "What truck, Rita?"

"A white pickup parked across the street. Somebody around here buy that old thing? I don't want carbon monoxide polluting our air." She coughs, like it's the truck and not the thousands of cigarettes she's smoked. "Some pervert was sitting in there too, watching me come home."

"Who?" I demand. "What did he look like?"

Rita frowns. "How should I know? I'm the one who asked you, remember?"

It had to be the same truck I saw follow Chase's car.

"What's the matter with you?" Rita scratches her belly, and her slip makes a *zip, zip* sound.

"Rita, I saw that truck"—I almost say "following Chase and T.J."—"last night, in front of our house."

"Probably just some loser with no life watching people who have lives." She yawns.

"And somebody kept calling here and then hanging up."

Rita lets out a dry laugh. "Let me get this straight. You think somebody's out to get us, right? That it? Somebody who murdered Coach and is so scared Detective Hopeless will uncover the truth that they're . . . what? Parking across the street? Calling and hanging up?"

When she says it like that, it does sound pretty dumb.

She yawns again, so big that her face is nothing but an open mouth. Then she shuffles back to her bedroom.

I grab a cup of instant coffee and go outside to wait for T.J. I don't want to think about the pickup or the phone calls. It's August hot, and there's no shade on the front step. I squint across the street at the empty lot, where they tore down a condemned house, leaving rubble and trash. Shards of glass catch the morning light and toss it into the air in glittering patterns of delicate color. It makes me think of Jeremy and the way he finds beauty everywhere—twigs floating in mud puddles, snowflake mountains on windowsills, crow's-feet wrinkles at the eyes of old men, pudgy toes on babies, and dandelions, frail and feathered and ready to be blown bald.

Far off, I hear a couple of lost geese honking. Closer in, a woodpecker competes with the cry of a mourning dove. I want them to smother the breathing on the other end of the phone, to cover up the chug of the white pickup truck, and to drown out Rita's voice in my head.

121

A horn honks. I stand up, expecting to see T.J.'s dad's '81 Chevy, but it's the Stratus Chase drives. He gets out of the car and stands beside it. "T.J. couldn't make it."

I take a couple of steps toward him. "Why didn't he call me?"

"He said your cell was off, and he was afraid to wake Rita. So he called me."

Once again, Chase is dragged into the mixed-up life of Hope Long. I'm totally embarrassed—again—but I have to admit I don't mind seeing Chase.

"T.J. shouldn't have called you. I'm sorry, Chase. Thanks for letting me know, though."

Chase meets me the rest of the way up the sidewalk. I don't think I realized how tall he is, more than a head taller than me. I'm used to looking down at T.J., not up like this. "He had to help his dad finish some big lawn job in Ashland, I guess."

"Well, thanks again." I'm not sure whether to go back in or wait until he leaves.

"Anyway," Chase says, "he felt pretty bad about you missing your driving lesson and all. So I thought maybe I could stand in for him?"

"Wait. Did T.J. put you up to this?"

Chase grins, showing straight white teeth. "No. But I got the feeling he thinks you can use all the lessons you can get. I figure this will square me with T.J. for good."

"You must have owed him big-time." I wait for Chase to fill in the blanks.

"Okay," he says at last. "But don't tell T.J. I told you. In the Lodi game last year, he didn't just talk Coach into letting me pitch. He pretended he hurt his arm so Coach would have to put me in."

"Why would he do that? I didn't think you guys were that tight. It doesn't even sound like something he'd do."

Chase seems to be studying our cracked sidewalk. Then he says, "T.J. overheard my dad and me arguing in the locker room. Dad thought I wasn't working hard enough and that was why I wasn't getting to pitch. It was a pretty big blowup. T.J. walked in on it."

Now things are starting to make more sense. T.J.'s probably never fought with his dad. He would have wanted to fix things for Chase, no matter who he was.

"It was T.J.'s idea," Chase says. "But I went along with it. I threw a horrible couple of innings, but it got my foot in the door. He's right. I do owe him."

"And teaching me to drive lets you off the hook?"

He nods again. "Not just off the hook . . . but out of the house. To be honest, I'm grateful for an excuse to get away from my dad for a while. But listen, Hope, if you don't want to, that's fine. If this is, like, your and T.J.'s thing, I don't want to get in the way of that. I make it a rule never to mess up a relationship."

For a second, I don't know what he means. Then I get it. "T.J. and me? We're friends. It's not a 'relationship.' Not like you mean anyway." I laugh a little, picturing last Sunday's driving lesson, when T.J. vowed he was quitting. "I'm a terrible driver. I wouldn't be surprised if T.J. made up the whole story about helping his dad so he didn't have to go through another driving lesson with me."

"I doubt that."

"I'm just kidding, except for the part about me being a terrible driver. I don't think I've gotten any better either." I glance at his car. It's reflecting sunlight so bright I have to squint. Did he wash it overnight? "Even if I agreed to let you waste your time trying to teach me to drive, I couldn't do that to your dad's car."

"Yeah, you could," he says, dangling the keys in front of me. "I'll have you driving by midday." His smile fades. "And there's something I want to talk to you about anyway."

He heads for the car, and I follow him. "What?"

"Later," he says. "It's about the trial."

"The trial?" I can't believe he's the one bringing up Jer's trial. Good ol' T.J. His crazy plan might be paying off already. "What about the trial?"

"Not yet," he says, motioning for me to get in the other side. "I promise. Drive first, talk later."

16

When Chase and I get to the high school, we're the only car in the parking lot. T.J. and I picked this spot because there's nothing you can hit here, except a big tree a few yards to the east, and the school, of course, but it's half a football field away. Good thing. My driving performance has never been worse. Chase makes me more nervous than T.J. does, even though he doesn't scream at me.

"Give it some more gas," Chase says, watching my feet. "Gas. That's the one on your right."

"Gotcha." I press the pedal, and the car lurches forward, so I slam on the brakes with both feet.

"You really haven't driven, like, at all, have you?" he says.

"I told you I haven't."

He laughs and makes me circle the lot until I'm dizzy. Then he has me change directions and drive in more circles "to unwind."

I'm not sure how long we do this—longer than T.J. and I

usually last—but eventually I'm not horrible. I can flick on the turn signal and make the car turn, and I can stop without dashing our heads through the windshield.

"Not bad," Chase says. "Let's take a break. Pull up under that tree on the edge of the lot."

It's the one shady spot in sight. "Are you sure? I could hit the tree, you know."

"Are you kidding? I promised I'd have you driving by mid-day, and I never break a promise."

I remember what he said about his dad breaking promises. Apparently, promises are big deals to him. If Rita makes a promise—to quit smoking or drinking or whatever—I don't even pay attention.

When I pull up exactly where I'm supposed to, Chase gives me a thumbs-up. Then he reaches into the backseat and brings out a cooler. "I'm hungry. How about you?"

We set up on a wool blanket by the big tree. Chase hands me a peanut butter sandwich and an ice-cold bottle of root beer. It feels like a real picnic. Jer and I used to go on picnics when we lived in Oklahoma. I can't remember why we stopped.

"I love root beer." I take a deep swig from the bottle and try to think of the last time I had one.

"Told you we were alike," he says. "I even took my shower last night instead of this morning."

I laugh. "Doesn't count. It was already morning when you left my house."

"You're right."

While we eat our sandwiches, we talk about schools, his

126

and mine. He asks about Jeremy, and I tell him about the time we let them keep Jer in a hospital, on a mental ward, overnight. "It took Jer a month to get over it. Rita thought it would do him some good. I knew better, but I went along." I fight off the images of my brother the day we brought him home—Jeremy without his energy, sitting in a heap wherever I parked him.

Chase talks about running, the "high" he gets running hard, alone.

Before I realize it, I've eaten my whole sandwich. "I still can't believe you made sandwiches. What if I hadn't come along for the lesson?"

"I'd have eaten both sandwiches," he answers. "I needed to stay out of the house until my dad left for work. He and I can use a little distance." He wads up his napkin and wipes his mouth.

"It's my fault, isn't it? Did your dad find out you were with T.J. and me last night?"

"Don't worry about it. It's a cop thing. He doesn't like the idea of relatives of the defense fraternizing with relatives of the prosecution."

"Fraternizing?" I can't help grinning at that one. "I'm not sure I've ever fraternized before. Is this it?"

"Apparently so. Yes."

I lean against the tree and let the bark dig into my shoulders. I don't mind.

Chase pitches his trash into the cooler and leans back next to me. The tree trunk is big enough so our arms don't touch, but I feel him there. "Okay. Let's talk," he says.

I know what he means. I've been waiting for him to tell me what he said he would, *promised* he would, about the trial. "So, tell me."

"I've been doing a lot of thinking about your brother's case," he begins. A leaf falls, spinning in front of us until it brushes the grass and tumbles to a stop. He scoots around to face me. "Okay. Hear me out on this, Hope. I think we need to keep in mind that it's not up to us, to you, to prove who really murdered Coach."

Disappointment begins as a slow burn in my chest, rising up through vessels and veins. I thought Chase understood. He doesn't. Fine. I'll do it with T.J., or I'll do it myself. I wasn't counting on *his* help anyway.

As if he's reading my mind, he holds up one finger. "Hang on. I know that's what you want, to prove somebody else murdered Coach. But it can't be easy to prove murder. I mean, even if you know who did it, it's a whole different thing proving it. I don't think even you could pull that off, Hope. But here's the good part. You don't have to. All you have to do is create reasonable doubt. And people doubt just about everything. *That's* what I've been thinking."

I want to nail the person who killed Coach and let Jeremy take the blame. But I can tell Chase has done a lot of thinking about this. And I'm not stupid. I've heard of reasonable doubt. "Go on."

"Doubt," he repeats. "That's all you need. How hard can it be to get a couple of people on that jury to doubt?"

I turn "doubt" over in my head. "Doubt. Like getting them to believe somebody else *might* have killed Coach?"

"Exactly. Or even just that Jeremy might not have. You give them a reason. Then they have *reason*able doubt." Chase is now kneeling in front of me, almost begging me to understand. "You can make them doubt, Hope." His eyes are intense, green as mermaid tears.

My heart quivers because I think he's right. Doubt is so much easier than proof. "Okay. I'll make them doubt." I breathe deeply, taking in clean air, sunshine . . . and hope. "I just don't know where to start, Chase."

"Hey, you two!"

Across the school lawn, I see T.J. waving his arms like he's flagging down fire trucks. Automatically, I scoot farther away from Chase. He gets off his knees and sits down. My stomach lurches, and I feel guilty, which is silly because there's nothing to feel guilty about. "Hey, T.J.!" I call.

He jogs toward us. I take the trash out of Chase's cooler and walk it over to the garbage can. Then I wait for T.J. "Sorry I forgot to turn on my cell this morning," I say when he's close enough to hear.

"Not sorry enough," he answers.

"Huh?"

"It's still off. I tried to call you again." He glances over at Chase, then back to me.

"Oops. I don't deserve the title of Cell Owner." I hand him my root beer bottle, with a couple of sips left.

He downs it. "So, how was the driving lesson? I'm guessing that's what's going on. Sully, down at the site, said he saw you two here. I figured the driving show must be happening without me." He pulls out that tin laugh again.

"Yeah. I'm giving it a try," I say, sounding really stupid.

Chase gets to his feet. "Got to say you were right about Hope's driving disability."

"Says you." I snatch the keys off the picnic blanket. "Wanna see if I've improved, T.J.?" I don't know why I'm so nervous, but all I can think is that I don't want to stand here with the two of them.

"Maybe later. I've only got"—T.J. glances at his watch—"twenty minutes before I have to get back. Dad needs to finish the job by tomorrow."

"Sure. I understand." I want to offer him a sandwich, include him in the picnic. But we're out of food.

T.J. sits on the picnic blanket as if he's put it there himself. "I've been working on the suspect list."

Chase and I join him, sitting on either side. "That's great, T.J.," I say. "We were just talking about the case. I'm really glad you're here. Chase has an excellent idea about strategy. Tell him, Chase."

T.J. frowns over at Chase.

"I'm sure you've already thought of it," Chase begins. He glances at me, then gives T.J. a shortened version of "reasonable doubt."

"You're right," T.J. says when Chase is finished. "I should've thought of that myself."

"But we still have to get clues or evidence, don't we?" I ask. "We have to have something that will make the jury doubt. Or at least make them suspect somebody else did it."

T.J. sits up, straightens his glasses, and takes over. "Means, motive, and opportunity. That's what we have to work with.

That's what I wanted to talk to you about." He sounds so logical. I wait for him to explain. "Stay with me. Means is the bat. That's a given. Coach was killed with Jeremy's bat. But almost anybody could have used it."

"Right!" I agree. "Everybody knew he left his bat inside the barn door when he went to the barn."

"Opportunity and motive," T.J. continues. "They're a little tougher, depending on which suspect we want the jury to doubt."

"I still vote for his wife," I say. "I know we don't have any proof or anything. But you should have heard her yelling at Coach."

Chase nods.

"Okay," T.J. continues. "But we're going to need a better motive than an overheard argument, especially since you're not even sure what the argument was about."

I try to think. "Rita told me she never thought Coach and his wife were happy together."

"Still not much to go on," Chase says.

"Yeah," T.J. admits. "But if Rita knew they weren't happy, other people probably did too. We can ask around." T.J. scribbles in his notepad, a pocket-sized black one.

I feel my blood pumping through me faster. "What about opportunity? Coach's wife was supposed to be in her house, right? That's not far from the barn."

When I glance at Chase, a stray wave of his hair blows across his forehead. He doesn't brush it back. "If you could prove that Caroline Johnson can walk, it wouldn't be a stretch to believe she could walk to the barn." Chase squints at T.J. "Have you ever seen her when you've been at the barn?"

I frown at T.J. I didn't think he ever went to the barn. He's scared of horses.

T.J. pulls a weed from the ground and begins tearing it into tiny pieces. "I don't go there anymore."

"When did you ever?" I ask. "I thought you didn't like horses."

He shrugs. "I hung out there sometimes. And I like horses, sort of."

"Yeah. Right," I say. I know he doesn't like horses. If I had to guess, I'd bet he hung out at the barn to be around Coach, not horses.

"Why are you making such a big deal out of it?" T.J. asks.

"You're right. No big deal," Chase says. "I just saw you there a few times when I was on my run, so I thought I'd ask."

"Wait. You run out there?" I've pictured Chase running through the streets of Grain every morning, not out in the country.

"Every day except game day," Chase says. "You know what Coach says—said—about saving your energy for the field."

"Too bad," T.J. says. "You might have seen the killer that day."

"Don't think I haven't thought about that," Chase says.

Me too. If I'd gone to the barn with Jer that morning, or if T.J. had wandered over there, or if Chase had run past . . . "We need to focus on what we can do *now*." I get to my feet and try to think. *Means, motive, opportunity.* "You know, anybody could have been there. The jury *should* doubt. It's crazy *not* to have reasonable doubt." Brushing grass and leaves from

132

my pants, I stare down at T.J. and Chase. "It only took a second to kill Coach. One swing of the bat, one moment where somebody lost control. *Anybody* could have done it, don't you think?"

Neither of them says anything for a minute. T.J. won't look at me. Chase looks like he's going to throw up. I wonder if we're all picturing the same thing—that one swing of the bat. "Okay, then," I say, trying to sound more confident than I feel. "Let's show the jury. Let's make them doubt. And I think we have the best shot at getting that doubt if we go with Coach's wife. If we can prove she can walk, that she's not as sick as everybody thinks she is, that would be enough for doubt, don't you think? Raymond could get the jury to have reasonable doubt with that." I spot a gum wrapper on the other side of the tree, and I dash over to get it. Then I see a crumpled beer can, and I pick that up and throw it all into the rusty trash can. The words *reasonable doubt* swirl in my head. I really think we're onto something.

When I come back to the tree, Chase is grinning. T.J. has his nose in his notebook.

"What?" I ask.

"Does she always do that?" Chase asks T.J.

"Hmm?" T.J. doesn't look up.

"What?" I ask, confused. "Do what?"

"Hope," Chase explains, "in the middle of all this, you still pick up other people's trash. And you don't even realize you're doing it."

I glance down at my hands, but I've already thrown whatever it was away.

"It's not the first time I've seen you pick up litter," he

133

continues, still grinning. "And candy wrappers, and even cigarette butts."

"Really?" I never even thought about it. "Sorry."

He shakes his head. "Don't be."

We're staring at each other, neither of us looking away.

"Man!" T.J. springs into action. "I've got to run."

"Want me to drive you?" Chase volunteers. I feel a twinge of sadness that my driving lesson must be over.

T.J. walks backward toward the school building. "No. I'm good. Hope, you working tonight?"

"Yeah!" I shout because he's halfway to the school.

"I'll stop by the Colonial if I get done in time!" T.J. pivots and takes off running.

For some reason, Chase's keys are in my hand. "How about one more time around?"

"You're on."

I'm about to shift the car into drive when I spot something white creeping along Chestnut, the street that runs beside the high school. It's a pickup truck, and it's about a block away. "Chase! There it is!" I scream.

"There *what* is?"

Then, without thinking, I slam the car into gear and hit the gas.

17

All I can think about is catching up with that white pickup truck. The car lunges forward. The truck turns the corner.

"Hope!" Chase screams. "Brake! Hit the—!"

A branch slaps the windshield. I see the pointy green edges of leaves, the crooked knots on the branch.

Thump! Scritch! There's a whine of bark on metal. Then the car shoots across the grass and rolls to a stop.

"You want to tell me what that was about?" Chase shouts.

"I can't believe I let him get away," I mutter, as out of breath as if I chased him on foot.

"Who?" Chase demands.

"The white pickup truck." I'm a little dizzy. A wave of nausea floats through me.

"What pickup truck? Where was it?"

"Didn't you see it?" I point across the lot to the empty street. "It was right there."

"But why chase it?"

I start at the beginning and tell him about the truck following him and not turning on its lights. About Rita seeing somebody watching the house from a pickup parked on our street. "I think it's the same person who's been calling the house."

He looks away, where the truck was only minutes earlier. "There are a lot of trucks around here. Are you sure—?"

"How can I be sure? That's why I wanted to follow it." I should have known he wouldn't believe me.

"Okay. Calm down. Maybe you scared him off." He runs his fingers through his hair. "You sure scared *me*."

"I'm sorry." Then I remember the thud. The scrape. "Chase, what did I do to your car?" I pop open the door and struggle to get out of the driver's seat. At first, I don't see anything. Then I take a step back. "Oh man!" On the roof of the car is a scratch at least a foot long. "Look what I did! I'll . . . I'll get it fixed. I'll buy you a new one." *With what?* I can't believe I did this to his car, to his dad's car, the sheriff's car.

Chase walks up and puts his hand on my head. "Settle down. It's okay. Really, it is."

I throw off his hand and stand on tiptoes to inspect the scratch. It's worse than I thought. The cut is wider, a crooked silver snake across the top of this beautiful blue car. "Your dad already hates me."

"No he doesn't."

"He told you not to hang out with me. He'll probably put us both in jail."

"Hey, at least we'll go down together, right?"

Warm tears press against my throat, choking off air. I'm as close to crying as I get. "This isn't funny."

Chase's lips twist in a feeble attempt to kill his grin. "Okay. It isn't funny. But it isn't tragic either. Come on. It's just the roof. And it's just paint . . . mostly." He walks over to the car. He's so tall he can reach the roof easily. His finger runs along the scrape, as if he's petting the snake. "I can fix this."

"No you can't. Can you?" A spark of hope rises, and I snuff it out. "You're just saying that."

He leans against the car. "I mean it. I've even got the right color paint."

"How—?"

"Last summer I scratched the rear door." He moves to the passenger-side back door. "Bet you never noticed this."

I follow him, but I can't see anything from where I'm standing. "Are you telling me the truth?"

"I scraped a stop sign making a turn after a party and a six-pack. I knew my dad would kill me—I already had one DUI— so I got the right paint and fixed it before he noticed. Your scratch isn't even as deep as that one was."

My heart pounds a little softer. I'm not crazy about taking driving lessons from a guy with DUIs, but still. "You're not just saying that to make me feel better?"

"We can fix it right now, before Dad has a chance to see it, if you want to. He won't be home." Chase opens the driver's door. "Only, if it's all the same to you, I'll drive."

A few minutes later, Chase pulls the car into the garage behind his dad's house. It's a small garage, with barely enough room for one car. We get out, and I look around. Shelves are loaded with paints and stains, all neatly arranged by color and size.

"Found it!" Chase hollers from the back of the garage.

"I'm not surprised. Everything is so neat and orderly in here." There's not a single tool on the ground or slung onto a bench. Hammers hang with hammers, all according to size. Shovels and rakes line one wall.

Chase pulls out brushes and rags from a wooden worktable. It's obvious he's done this before. "Sheriff Matthew Wells is big on organization."

I watch him fill the scratch and begin the paint process, but the fumes make me cough.

"Go on in," Chase says. "The back door's unlocked."

"I'm okay," I say, but I cough between the words.

"Go. The garage is really too small for paint jobs. I'll be in pretty soon. Make yourself at home. Water and soda in the fridge, all arranged alphabetically. Just kidding. Sort of."

"You sure it's okay?" I'm wheezing a little now. A doctor once told me I might have asthma, but that was before we moved to Ohio. Still, I wouldn't mind getting out of here.

"I mean it, Hope. Go!"

I feel funny letting myself in through the back door of the sheriff's house. It's a neat brick ranch, with white shutters.

Inside, it smells like evergreen. The off-white carpet is totally clean. No newspapers or magazines strewn on this couch. Not even a jacket folded over the back of a chair. The giant brick fireplace takes up one whole wall, and there's not a speck of ash to be seen. On the entry wall is a picture of the Andover baseball team. I pick out Chase right away, the cutest guy on the team.

Crossing the kitchen to find a drink, I can't get past the refrigerator magnets. Our fridge has one magnet that holds one of Jeremy's color-wheel pictures because I put it up there myself. This fridge has magnets with ball-game schedules and chore responsibilities, plus Chase's past achievements. On one side are report cards, all of them with A's or A-pluses. On the other side, blue ribbons from baseball and track events.

Would Rita have kept things like this if I'd won first prizes and gotten all A's? I remember one time in second grade—no, third grade—when a math team I was on won a prize. Our mothers got to come to our classroom and sit in the front row. Rita came. She got there late, but she was there. I'd totally forgotten about that.

I peek outside. Chase is still hovering over the car.

I shouldn't, but I'm dying to see Chase's bedroom. What posters would he have on his walls? What books? What bed-spread? Maybe he has pictures of Boston girls on his dresser.

I wander down the hall and see three doors feeding into the hallway. I pass one room, the bathroom. The next room has white walls and a big bed in the center. There's nothing on either dresser, and the shades are pulled down. This has to be Sheriff Wells's room.

I tiptoe into the only other room in sight and know instantly that it belongs to Chase. It's almost as tidy as his dad's room—bed made, clothes picked up, shades drawn even, but at half-mast, not all the way. On the nightstand is a framed picture of a beautiful woman with blond hair and

Chase's eyes, green as emeralds. His mother. Except for some loose change, the photograph is the only thing on the little table.

I glance around the room, taking in an autographed base-ball in a plastic holder on his dresser, a phone charger, and a paperback book I can't make out. There aren't any posters on his walls, but there are photographs of the Cleveland Indians and a team picture of the Red Sox.

I should leave. On the way out of Chase's room, I take one more peek into his dad's. The only halfway messy thing is the built-in desk. File folders line the back of the desktop, and even those stand at attention, like books on a library shelf.

I wonder if Jeremy's case file is in there. I check the window that faces the garage and see Chase with some kind of blow-dryer thing still hard at work on the car.

I have to see Jeremy's file, if there is one. I go back to the line of folders that stretches from one edge of the pine desk to the other. I don't have time to go through all of them.

I'm willing to bet that these files are arranged alphabeti-cally. I thumb through, and I'm right. But there's no "L." No "Jeremy Long."

Then I get another idea. The victim.

It only takes a second to find the file labeled "Johnson." Quickly, I pull out the folder and open it. There are piles of court documents, copies of arrest and search warrants, forms and petitions.

And then I see the photos, lots more crime scene photos than I saw at Raymond's house, maybe four or five times more. I wonder if Raymond has more pictures than the ones I saw.

The photo on top is the same one I saw at Raymond's—Coach Johnson, bloody and curled into a ball on the floor of the stable. Or maybe it's not exactly the same photo. I go to the next photo in the file, and it's also like the one I saw at Raymond's, only different too. More complete somehow. But I can't put my finger on it. In a dozen photos, Coach is lying in the exact same spot. Junk from his pockets mixes with the straw and sawdust—cell phone, a receipt or something wedged under one shoulder, a ticket or stub.

A door slams.

I shut the folder and cram it back with the others, hoping I have it in the right place. "I'm coming, Chase! Right out!"

I tear out of the bedroom, straightening my shirt and trying to look normal. "Sorry, I—"

I stop. It's not Chase standing there, frowning at me, looking like he'd shoot me if he had a gun handy. It's Sheriff Matthew Wells. "What do you think you're doing here?"

18

Sheriff Wells is even bigger in his own house. "I said, what are you doing here?"

I open my mouth, but only a squeak comes out. All I can think of is what Chase said about the famous Wells temper. I try again. "I . . . The back door was open."

"So you just came on in?" He takes a step toward me. "What were you looking for? Answer me!"

"Hope?" Chase appears from the kitchen. His gaze darts from me to his dad. "Dad? What are you doing home already?"

"All right, what's going on here?" Sheriff Wells turns on his son. "You tell me right now what you two are doing snooping around—!"

"Snooping around?" Chase glances over at me. I shrug. Then he smiles at his dad. "Come on, Dad. Snooping around? We were just getting something to drink." As if to prove it, he walks to the fridge and gets two bottles of spring water. Then he comes over to me and hands me one.

"This is where you come to get water?" his dad asks.

"I'm sorry." Chase frowns. "I didn't know I wasn't supposed to bring friends over to the house."

"*Friends?*"·He shoots me a look that clearly states I'm no friend of his.

"Dad, please?"

I recognize something in Chase's eyes as he talks to his dad. It's the way he tries to please him, not just make peace with him like I do Rita. Chase still wants to please his father, and that makes me sad. I gave up trying to please Rita a long time ago. Maybe I'm not sure if I'm sorry for Chase still hanging on, or sorry for me having let go.

What I do know is that I don't want to make things worse for Chase. "Sheriff Wells," I begin, "this isn't Chase's fault. It's all me." Chase starts to object, but I keep going. "I wanted to find you."

"You wanted to find *me?*" He's not buying this. Not yet anyway.

I nod. "I guess I should have called, but I wasn't thinking straight." He's staring holes through me, but I press on. "Somebody's been stalking me, and I—"

"Stalking you?" Now he looks like he can't decide whether to laugh me out of the house or force me out at gunpoint.

"I know it sounds crazy," I admit. He nods in agreement. "But it's true. Somebody's been following me, watching me. And there have been phone calls too."

"Phone calls?"

"Yeah. Heavy breathing. Hang-ups. That kind of thing."

Sheriff Wells glares at his son. "What do you know about this?"

Before he can answer, I jump in. "I've told Chase most of

it. I think he got tired of me and went out to the garage for something. That's when you came in."

"What does your mother say about all this?" asks the sheriff, some of the fire drained from his eyes.

"I haven't told her everything, but she's seen the pickup."

"The pickup?"

"A white pickup truck. Rita saw it parked on our street, and I've seen it a couple of times. It's pretty scary. And I think that's why it shows up everywhere. Somebody's trying to scare me."

"Why would anybody try to scare you?" Sheriff Wells asks, like I'm lying.

I shrug. "Maybe because I'm the only one who knows my brother didn't murder Coach Johnson. The only one besides the murderer anyway."

The fire shoots back into his eyes. "Are you insane?"

"No, sir," I answer. He scares me to death, but I won't let him see it.

Sheriff Wells squints at Chase. "Did *you* see this mysterious white pickup?"

"Not exactly," Chase admits. "But I believe Hope."

His dad reaches behind his neck and twists his head, exactly the way Chase does sometimes. "Do you have any idea how many white pickups there are in this town?"

"No, sir," I answer.

"Or kids who make crank calls?"

"Dad," Chase reasons, "could you just look into it, please? Maybe one of the patrol cars could drive by Hope's house at night."

"That's a great idea," I chime in.

"You think so, do you?" Sheriff Wells says, glaring at me.

"Absolutely. And I appreciate it. Thanks." I turn to Chase. "It was a long walk over here. Would you mind giving me a ride to work?"

"Not a problem," Chase says, following me out.

I smile back at Sheriff Wells. "I'll be looking for that patrol car tonight. Thanks again."

Once we're outside, Chase whispers, "You were great in there!" He cranes his neck around so he's staring into my face. "I never saw *anyone* stand up to my dad the way you did."

"I did, didn't I?" I'm every bit as amazed as he is. I don't stand up to people.

"I wish I had it on film. Did you see his face when you told him you'd look for that patrol car tonight? You, Hope Long, are one brave lady."

We walk the rest of the way to the car without speaking. My head is filled with what Chase said. *You, Hope Long, are one brave lady.* I have never been brave, not in my entire life. Only right now, for this one instant, as the car backs out of the driveway and onto the street, I feel brave. With Chase beside me, I feel so brave that I think I could reach up and stop Rita's hand from touching Jeremy's cheek.

Chase drops me off at the Colonial, and I head back to report in to Bob. The booths along one wall are full. So are two of the eight tables. I ignore the stares as I traipse through.

Bob's pouring coffee behind the counter. Three of the four gray vinyl stools are taken.

"Hey, Hope!" he calls. "Thanks for coming in." Bob

Adams looks like a happy-go-lucky butcher instead of a restaurant owner. I can't remember if I've ever seen him without his full-length white apron. Under the apron are jeans that are too big or too small—I can never decide which. So much of the material is taken up by the front of him that the back of him gets shortchanged. When he bends over to get clean glasses, the unlucky customer behind him sees a lot more than he bargained for.

"Looks like you got some sun, Hope," Bob observes.

Maybe I did. Or maybe my face is red from embarrassment. I hate people gawking at me.

"I need you at the tables this afternoon, I'm afraid," Bob says. "Sorry. I thought Rita was coming in."

"That's okay." We're lucky to have this job. I know he would let me hide in the kitchen if he could. Rita calls in sick all the time, or just doesn't come in, and still Bob doesn't fire her.

I put on an apron and backtrack to table four. Two little boys are shooting straw papers at each other while their mothers whisper to a woman behind them. I clear my throat, and the chubby mom with short brown hair wheels around.

"Oh, I'm sorry." Her face gives it away that the whispers were about me. "Um . . . we'll just have fries. *French* fries."

"*French* fries? Not Spanish fries?" I ask, going for humor because humor translates into tips, nine times out of ten. "Or English fries?"

"No. Just French fries," she answers, without cracking a smile.

Behind me, a chair squeaks, followed by footsteps. I turn

to see a well-dressed woman in her forties. I recognize her from church, but I can't think of her name. I brace myself for whatever she's going to say.

She leans forward and gives me a hug. "How are you holding up, Hope?"

It's about the last question I expected. "Hanging in there, I guess."

"Well, good for you," she says. "I want you to know that we're praying for you and for your brother. For your mother too. Tell Jeremy we miss him, will you? Give him our love?"

"I will," I manage.

"Tell him God hasn't forgotten him," she says. "But I'm sure Jeremy knows that if anybody does."

"Thank you." I want her to hug me again. I'd hug her back this time.

Things get crazy busy for a couple of hours. After supper, the restaurant finally calms down. About an hour later, it empties out totally, and I can retreat to the kitchen. I would rather wash a thousand dishes than talk to one more human.

As if sensing what I feel, Bob walks to the front door and turns over the CLOSED sign. Then he joins me at the sink. "Tough, isn't it?" he says.

"Yep." I hand him the dish towel, and he starts drying glasses I've washed and set to air-dry.

"How's your mother doing with everything?" Bob asks this like he's twelve and has a crush on the homecoming queen.

"Rita? She's just Rita, I guess."

Bob has a dishwasher, but he doesn't like to run the extra load at night. So when there's time, we do the leftover dishes by hand. I switch to the scrub brush and start in on the plates. "Bob, how well did you know Coach Johnson?"

"John? Pretty well when we were in school. We weren't close or anything. And we didn't get any closer over the years, I guess. I'm not sure why."

"Did you go to school with him and my mother?"

"Sure did. Your mom was really something." The angles of his face soften when he says this.

"Did Mr. Johnson think Rita was really something?" I dump in more green liquid soap and run the hot water.

"We all did. John was no exception. Heck, even Matt had an eye for your mother."

"Matt? Sheriff Wells? And Rita?" I can't picture it, not now, not then. I shut off the water before the suds overflow.

"Uh-huh. She had those Wooster boys going too." Bob takes a plate from me, holding it in one hand with the edge of the towel and wiping swift circles with the other end. "You should have seen her, Hope. She was a looker, I'll tell you. And the only girl in that whole school who knew how to flirt, I suspect."

I'd love to ask him more about Rita and Sheriff, or Rita and Coach, but I don't because I'm pretty sure Bob had a crush on Rita in school. I believe he still does. I can tell by the way he always asks about her and the look in his eyes when he says her name.

We're quiet for a few plates. Then he says, "I'm pretty nervous about testifying in court." He takes another plate to dry. "You know that lawyer's calling me as a character witness, don't you?"

"Yeah. Thanks, Bob. You'll do great." But I have to admit that I just don't get Raymond's trial strategy. First, he tries to prove Jer's crazy. Then he calls witnesses to show what a good character my brother is? Raymond says he wants the jurors to like and trust Jeremy, but he still has to get in enough stories so the jury can call Jeremy insane if they need to. I guess it's all part of that "kitchen sink" defense, as in throwing in everything but the kitchen sink. I don't think I'd make a very good lawyer.

I'm not sure what I would be good at. It's not that I've never wanted to be anything. Maybe I've thought about being too many things. I wanted to be a dancer once, but you can't make a living at it. Well, at least I'm pretty sure I couldn't make it pay. When I was little, I wanted to be a teacher, but that was just because I liked my first-grade teacher so much. I like art. My sea glass creations are pretty good, and I'm not that bad at drawing. But the things I try to draw never look as good on paper as they do in my head. I think I'd like photography.

Bob and I start in on pots and pans.

"I hear Rita has to testify too," Bob says, pulling my thoughts back to dishwater. I hand him the broiler pan.

I start to explain about how it's my fault Rita has to take the stand, but there's a loud knock at the main door.

Bob ignores it. We closed at eight-thirty instead of nine, but Bob's used to closing when he feels like it. The knock gets louder. "They'll give up pretty soon," he says.

But they don't. They switch to the window and tap, banging with something metal, probably car keys.

"Go away!" Bob shouts. "Dang fools are going to scratch

my window." I've seen Bob's temper blow a couple of times. Once, he threw a customer out—and I mean threw him. I don't want to see that temper now.

The scratch-tapping continues.

"I'm warning you!" Bob hollers through clenched teeth. "Stop doing that right now!"

But apparently, the wannabe customer has never seen Angry Bob. Bob flings the towel down, unties his apron, and throws it to the floor. "That's it! I warned him!" He strides to the door in four giant steps.

I peek around the corner and see Bob grab the doorknob and yank the door open.

A young guy in a white shirt and black pants almost falls on his face. He scrambles to keep hold of the camera he's tucked under one arm. "I thought you were open until nine," he says. "Is that girl still here, the Long girl?"

Bob pokes the guy in the chest and keeps his finger there, drawn like a gun. "There's a CLOSED sign on that door. Can you read, Mr. Ace Reporter?"

"Easy, fella," says the reporter. "I just want to ask her some—"

"What's your name?" Bob demands.

"Why?"

"Because I'm going to sue you, your publisher, and the pony you rode in on. Now get out of here!" He shoves the man backward and slams the door so hard the glass rattles.

19

When I leave the restaurant a little before nine, I head north to walk home. A car starts up, and I turn to see Chase's Stratus parked under the streetlight a few feet away. Surprised, I wave and wait for the car to pull up alongside the curb. Tiny bugs swirl in the headlight beams.

"Not stalking you, I promise," Chase says out his window. "I drove by a couple of times and saw you in there. Thought you ought to have a ride home."

Nobody's dragged Chase here. Not this time. He's here because he wants to be. I feel my grin stretch too wide. My teeth aren't perfectly straight and white like his. "Thanks." I jog around the front of the car and happen to glance up. The sky has cleared, and the stars are so bright I can't look away.

Chase sticks his head out the window. "You okay?"

I move around to the door and get in. "Sorry. It's the stars. They're amazing tonight."

"I didn't notice." He puts the car in gear.

"You didn't notice? How could you not notice?" A picture flashes to my mind—Jeremy and me lying on our backs, trying to count the stars. "Jer and I used to spend hours picking out constellations."

"You can do that?"

"Yeah. . . . Can't you?"

He shakes his head. "We live too close to the city in Boston. I've seen a lot of stars here in the summers—don't get me wrong. I just can't pick out the shapes everybody talks about."

Nobody should go through life without knowing how to find the Bears—the Big and Little Dippers. Or Leo the Lion? Or Draco the Dragon! I snap my seat belt. "Drive," I command.

"Where to?"

"To the greatest show on earth." I direct Chase to Jeremy's and my secret stargazing spot, an Amish pasture on the edge of Grain, where lights are not allowed unless they come from the sky.

When we get there, I spread out the picnic blanket and lie down on my back. Chase sits next to me. It was so hot in the Colonial that my shirt clung to me like plastic wrap. Now a breeze rustles the grass and fans us. Bullfrogs croak from a creek I can't see but know is there, even in August droughts. A chorus of crickets gets louder, then softer, then louder, like someone's messing with the volume control. Somewhere far away, a horse whinnies, and another one answers. "Jeremy loves it here."

"I can see why," Chase says, his head tilted up to take in the sky. "The greatest show on earth."

I inhale clover and damp grass. The sky is cloudless, and the moon barely the tip of a fingernail, so the stars pop in the sky, crystals on black velvet. "Isn't it the most beautiful thing you've ever seen?"

Chase eases himself onto his back and gazes up. "It is."

"Look!" I point toward a row of trees, where lightning bugs flash on and off. "They're signaling, looking for mates."

"Seriously?"

"It's the boy who flashes first. If the girl likes him, she flashes back." I glance at his face, rich in shadows. He's grinning up at me. "What are you smiling about?" I can just imagine what I look like after a hard shift and dish duty at the Colonial.

"I don't know. I guess . . . I wish I'd gotten to know you when I first started coming to Grain. You and Jeremy. And T.J. Maybe I wouldn't have been so lonely."

"Right. You made more friends in Grain in three minutes than I have in three years."

"And all they talk about is each other, or themselves."

"Don't you and your dad talk?"

"Dad? Dad's not much of a talker. The first summer I was here, he hardly said two words to me. I'd gotten into some trouble at home, in Boston, mostly vandalism, petty stuff. Mom thought Dad could straighten me out, I guess. But he was so used to living by himself he had no idea what to say to another person in his house, especially a kid."

"And then you got baseball," I say, remembering what he told T.J. and me.

"And then we got baseball."

We're lying on our backs and staring up at a sky full of stars that seem close enough to touch. "Jeremy told me that a long time ago people believed stars were holes into heaven, peeks behind a black curtain."

"Peeks into heaven," Chase muses. "I like that. Jeremy told you that?"

"Wrote it," I explain. But I can tell Chase still doesn't understand. "You're wondering how the same guy who writes amazing notes and knows what people used to believe about stars can fail half of his school classes and freak out if somebody tries to take one of his empty jars from him."

Chase shrugs, but I know I'm right about what he's thinking. "It's okay," I tell him. "Jer's impossible to figure out. 'A contradiction in human terms.' That's how the Asperger's specialist described kids like Jeremy."

We're silent as the stars for a couple of minutes. Then Chase asks, "Where will you go from here, Hope?" It makes me think he's been lying here thinking about me. I'm not used to that. "Where will you go to college? What do you want to study?"

I love that Chase assumes I'm going to college. Rita assumes I'm not. But I am. I will. "Maybe photography?"

"Cool. I'd like to see some of your pictures sometime."

"I don't have a camera," I admit. "I've bought a few of those throwaways, but I don't usually get the pictures developed." That's the trick of those instant cameras. Cheap camera, expensive developing.

We talk a little about photography and college. Chase knows a lot about lighting and shutter speeds. His mother's first husband after Sheriff Wells was a Walmart photographer who took pictures of families and portraits of kids.

"What about you?" I ask, suddenly aware that our shoulders are touching. I try to focus. "Where will you go to school? I'll bet you could be anything you want." I try to imagine what that would feel like.

"Princeton. Barry pulled quite a few strings to get me in. That's where he went. I think Barry gives the school so much money they'd let his cat in if he asked."

I have no trouble picturing Chase at an Ivy League school. "What will you study?"

"No idea."

"You could always paint cars and repair scratches for a living. Maybe you could own your own car-repair garage and call it Chase Cars, or Car Chase, or—"

"Very funny." Before I see what's coming, he's rolled over and pinned me to the ground. "Why don't you laugh about it?" Without letting go of my wrists, he manages to tickle me.

I squirm and try to kick free, but he's too strong. I can't budge. Laughing, I shout, "I give! I take it back!"

For a second, Chase stops, but he doesn't get off. Our bodies are millimeters apart, his thighs trapping mine. His face, brushed with moon shadows, is suspended above mine.

Then he eases off me and stares up at the stars. I hear his breathing, heavy and strained, and my own heart beating to his rhythm.

After a minute I point to the sky. "You can see Draco the Dragon right there. I don't think I've ever seen the whole constellation so clearly—all four stars of its head and that long tail."

"Where?" Chase tilts his head closer to mine. "I can never see these things."

Hoping against hope that my hand isn't shaking and my deodorant still works, I lift my arm and point. "See the Big Dipper there? Start at the tip and follow it over to—"

He clasps my wrist and holds it for a second, then slides his fingers down the length of my arm. Currents race through every inch of skin and bone. In one movement, he rolls onto his side. I feel his leg next to mine, pressing. His other hand reaches across so that he's above me, his head touching mine. Our breath is one. His chest rises with mine. Slowly, so that I can see every move, he lowers his face. . . .

And he kisses me.

I don't close my eyes. I always thought I would, if anybody ever kissed me. But I don't. Why would I want to miss even a second of this? With my eyes open, I can see Chase's skin, a shock of his hair that falls over my forehead. I can see stars above us, shining outside like I'm shining inside.

When he stops, when *we* stop, I whisper, "I'm not sure what to say now." I can't get over the tiny shivers in my arms and the way my heart shudders. "What do people say after they kiss?"

"Haven't you kissed anyone before, Hope?" Chase winds a strand of my straight, straight hair and turns it into a blond curl around his index finger.

"Not like that."

He grins. "You could have fooled me."

"I wouldn't want to."

"You wouldn't, would you?" He touches his forehead to mine for an instant, then pulls back. "You know, every other girl I've been with pretends to be more experienced than she really is. Don't ask me why."

"I won't. But I can't imagine why anybody would pretend that."

"That's because you don't pretend. You're real, Hope. Maybe the most real person I've ever known."

I laugh a little, embarrassed. "You need to get to know my brother."

"Tell me more about him."

I gaze up at the stars, and I think of all the times Jeremy and I have stared at the sky. "Nobody sees things like Jeremy," I begin. "I'll bet he sees more sunrises than most people. But you'd think he'd never seen one before, if you sat with him during a sunrise."

Chase laughs, but I can tell he's not making fun, so I laugh a little too. "Jeremy says that every morning God says to the universe, 'Do it again!'"

Chase is quiet for a spell. He stares at the sky. "There! I can see Draco the Dragon."

"See? It was there all the time. You just never looked."

He turns his gaze on me. "Like you."

"Me?"

"I didn't want to get involved in all this. Believe me. You have no idea. T.J. asked for that ride at the courthouse. Then, before I knew what hit me, there *you* were." He kisses me softly on my forehead. "I better take you home, Hope."

The ride to my house is too short. I'm thinking that tonight might have been the best night I've ever had. Only I feel guilty thinking that because Jeremy is locked up in a cell, where not even the moon can find him. "Will you be in court tomorrow?" I ask when we turn onto my street.

"Sure," he answers, pulling over. "I'm your ride."

"Good. And I want to start finding out everything we can about Caroline Johnson. We have to come up with something, some kind of evidence to give the jury reasonable doubt. So maybe we—"

"Hope?" Chase has stopped in front of my house. He's staring up the sidewalk.

I turn to see T.J. sitting on my front step. "What's he doing there?" I mutter.

"I'm not sure, but I don't think he knows you guys are just friends. You better go."

I'm already halfway out of the car. I can't imagine why T.J. would be here at this hour.

Chase drives off. I turn to wave. He waves back. Then I walk up the sidewalk to my friend. "Hey, T.J."

"Hey." He waits until I sit on the step next to him. He takes off his glasses, then puts them on again. "I stopped by the Colonial to see if you needed a ride. You'd already left."

"Thanks. Yeah. Bob closed early. Chase was driving by."

T.J. glances at his watch, although I doubt he can see the time. It's pretty dark on our street.

I know he's wondering where we've been. "I ended up showing him where Jer and I go sometimes. Did you know he'd never seen Draco before? I don't think I could stand living in a city again." I'm talking too much. Too fast. "So, what's up?"

He shrugs. He still hasn't looked at me. "I don't know. I had an idea, about figuring out motive and opportunity, maybe proving . . . well, at least raising reasonable doubt, about the murder."

"Great! Go on. I want to hear it."

He fidgets for his notebook and takes it out. "I got the idea from a Raymond Chandler story we read in English. I want to build a model of the crime scene, exactly to scale. You know? It might help us visualize where Coach was, where the murderer was, if somebody could have sneaked up on him, or if it had to be somebody he trusted, like his wife. I'd build a model of the barn and put in stalls and everything."

The hairs on the back of my neck are standing up.

"What?" T.J. puts his notebook back into his pocket. "You think it's a dumb idea."

"No! T.J., it's a great idea! A fantastic idea."

"Yeah?"

"Only why do it with a model? Let's re-create the crime scene, but for real." I stand up, so psyched my knees are quivering. "T.J., let's go to the barn. Right now. I want to see the crime scene."

20

I take T.J.'s elbow to pull him up, but he stays planted on the step. "You want to go to the barn? Now?" he asks.

"Now's the perfect time!" I insist. "Nobody will be there. We can look around."

"For what?"

I'm starting to get irritated. "Clues, evidence, whatever."

"Hope, it's been months. They don't even keep horses there now. We're not going to discover anything the police didn't already find and take away."

Of course he's right. But something inside me is telling me that I have to go there. "Please, T.J.? I need more before I can bring Raymond in on all this. There's got to be something everybody's missing. Not a clue, maybe. But something." I make myself picture the crime scene photos I saw at Raymond's and at the sheriff's house—Coach curled on the ground, shadowed in blood. But it doesn't feel real, more like something I saw in a bad movie. "I have to see the real scene of the crime, and I need you to take me there."

T.J. stares up at me, hard. "*Me*, not Chase?"

"You." The truth is, Chase would probably say no. And even if he agreed to go, there's his dad to think about. "Just you."

A minute later we're jostling in T.J.'s dad's old Chevy on our way to the barn, my mind bouncing worse than the Chevy's worn tires. "Wouldn't it be great if we caught Mrs. Johnson running around out there when nobody's looking? We should have a camera. 'Cause if she really is faking, don't you think that would be enough for people to believe she *might* have gone to the barn that day? That she might have gotten angry enough at her husband to kill him, even if she hadn't planned on it?"

"Maybe." T.J. doesn't sound convinced.

"What do you mean *maybe*? I told you how she blew up at the park that day. She's got a temper. I'll swear to that. If she'd had a gun that morning, I think she might have used it."

"I'm not saying she doesn't have a temper. I had her in class, remember? She could be scary."

"So?" I know T.J. well enough to sense he's still holding back on making Caroline Johnson our prime suspect. I know he thinks Jer did it.

He shrugs. "I don't know. Her fingerprints weren't on the bat, for one thing. Just Jeremy's."

"So . . ." I'm thinking out loud now. "Maybe she wore gloves." Soon as I say it, something clicks in my brain. "That's it! She wore gloves."

"Okay."

"Why hasn't anybody talked about that? Maybe there

weren't any fingerprints except Jeremy's because the killer wore gloves."

"It's possible," T.J. admits. "But aren't we going for spur-of-the-moment? Like she lost her temper and struck him? So she wouldn't have had her gloves with her."

"What about Jeremy's batting gloves? Why couldn't she have grabbed those when she grabbed the bat?"

T.J. looks confused. "Did Jeremy have his gloves at the barn?"

"I don't know. Maybe."

"Jeremy carried that bat everywhere," T.J. says, glancing in the rearview, "but I don't remember him wearing his gloves that much."

Once again, I feel this slim hope slipping away from me. "Okay. So I can't swear he had the batting gloves at the barn, but I haven't seen them around the house either. And I don't remember the police taking them."

"You could be right, Hope. But we can't sound like we're guessing. Keep it simple. Logical. Otherwise, you won't even get past Jeremy's lawyer. Like you said, he's the first one we have to convince." He takes a deep breath and lets it out. "Okay. How about this? Caroline Johnson may have murdered her husband. She's not as sick as she lets on. She has a bad temper. She would have used Jeremy's bat. She would have worn gloves—we don't say which gloves because we don't have to. That should be enough to plant doubt in the jury's mind." He turns to me. "So maybe we don't need to see the crime scene?"

I don't answer.

"Hope, do you have to put yourself through this?"

Do I? Do I really want to see where Coach was murdered? I know how my mind works. My brain will soak in dozens of images I'll never be able to erase. Part of me wants to tell T.J. to turn around. What could we get out of the crime scene so long after the crime anyway?

But another part of me knows I have to go there. Nothing will make sense until I do. "I have to see it for myself, T.J."

He shakes his head and keeps driving. We stop before we reach the barn. He pulls the car off the gravel road, but keeps the engine running. We're about half a mile from the barn and house. "This isn't a good idea, Hope. It's too dangerous."

"Nobody's there, remember?"

"What about Caroline Johnson? If you're right and she did murder her husband, she's not going to want us snooping around."

"She's not going to know. But you don't have to come. I mean it." I unbuckle my seat belt. I don't need a partner. I don't need anybody. It's Jeremy and me, the way it's always been, and that's fine with me. "Thanks for driving me out here. I'll just walk home when I'm done."

I get out of the car and start walking toward the barn.

Behind me, I hear the engine shut off and a car door open and close. Then T.J. calls up, "Will you wait until I get the flashlights?"

Purple clouds race across the sky now, making shadows dance on the path. We walk past an Amish pasture, where hay is stacked in crisscrossed bundles, lined in straight rows like nature's soldiers ready to attack. The only sound is the *crunch, crunch* of gravel under our feet.

When the path dips, we run straight into a cloud of tiny bugs. As if they've been waiting all night for us, they swarm, landing on our heads, arms, and legs. I swat wildly at them, smashing a few on my arms, brushing them off my face.

T.J. grabs my hand and takes off. "Run!"

I run. I'm an arm's length behind him, trying to catch up. His grip is tight. The bug cloud thins and finally drifts away behind us.

We slow down. I take my hand back and stop to catch my breath. My side aches.

"Are you okay?" T.J. asks, circling back for me.

"What *was* that back there?" My voice comes in spurts.

"Bugs. I've seen them like that a couple of times out here in the mornings. Once I saw Chase running like he was on fire, with a cloud of those things after him. There's a bog down that hill, where the bugs hang out. They're the same kind of bugs that helped the Cleveland Indians beat the Yankees in a play-off game a few years ago. It was all over the news."

"They're wicked."

He brushes my hair with his hand. I don't want to think that he's brushing out bugs. If I were going to give up this crime scene trip and go home to bed, this would be the moment to do it.

We start walking again. "So why *do* you come by the barn?" I don't think he ever answered that. "Or why did you?"

"I wanted to get used to horses. I don't like being afraid of things." He pauses a minute. "And I guess I used to like to talk to Coach."

It's what I thought. "Chase mentioned something about you and Coach having problems, something about your mom and the cookies?"

"It wasn't a big deal," he says, but it comes out too quickly. "It was mostly the guys. But Coach shouldn't have laughed. They took their cue from him. Anyway, it's over. Forget it."

We're at the last stand of sheltering trees. The barn is out in the open about a hundred feet away, with the house another hundred feet beyond that.

"Let's do it," I whisper.

We run, crouched like we're dodging bullets. When we reach the entrance to the barn, we both just stand there, looking in.

T.J. breaks the spell. "Last chance to turn back."

I stare into the barn, toward the stalls, the place where they found Coach's body. There's no crime scene tape anywhere, no chalk-line drawing of the body. "I'm sorry, T.J. You don't have to come in. Really. But I do. I have to try to understand. I have to do that much for Jeremy."

"All right. But we better get going before the sun comes up. There's a light on in the Johnson house. For all we know, that woman could be calling the police right now."

I glance behind us toward the house. He's right. I see the light through the window. But I can't worry about that now. I take a few steps into the barn. My eyes adjust to the dark, and I point to a spot just inside the door where a stall forms a right angle with the wall. "That's where Jeremy put his bat when he came to the barn. If he'd brought his gloves, he would have dropped those there too."

"Keep going."

I stare at the exact spot where Jeremy would have left his bat. "He parked his bat there because it scared the horses. Then he'd get down to business and haul manure or groom the horses. He loved it here." I'm picturing everything in my mind as I talk. "He even loved cleaning out the stalls. Coach taught him how to brush the horses, and Jer was really good with them." I smile over at T.J. and can tell he's listening. "Coach paid him a salary. Jeremy was so proud of that, even though Rita got all the checks."

I take a few steps deeper inside the barn and inhale the scents of sawdust, manure, and horse. The smells are strong, even after so much time, but mold and must are mixed in with them. "Did you know Coach taught Jeremy how to ride?"

T.J. nods.

"He learned fast too." I can almost see Jeremy riding Sugar, Mrs. McCray's old pinto, bareback. Jeremy's mouth is open, probably catching all kinds of bugs. His green backpack of empty jars bounces on his back. It was a miracle none of his jars ever broke that way.

I feel myself getting choked up. I have to stop it. This isn't why I came here.

We move toward the last stall, the one Coach was found lying outside of. The whole barn feels eerie, as if ghost horses have taken the place of the former boarders.

"Whose horse was in that stall the morning . . . ?" T.J.'s voice fades.

"Lancer, Mrs. McCray's show horse. She boarded two horses here—Sugar, the old pinto Jeremy rode, and Lancer, a bay gelding she rode for dressage."

We're standing in front of the stall. For all I know, my feet are in the exact place where Coach was lying. I should have come sooner, when things were fresh, when I might have seen something. I turn on my flashlight and shine it on the floor.

"What are you looking for, Hope?"

I point the beam of light on the sawdust. There are feces now—mice, rats. I can almost hear the squeals of frightened horses, the thump of the bat, Coach's cry.

"Hope, are you okay?" T.J. grabs me by the shoulders. "You look like you're going to faint."

"I'm okay," I whisper. I try to focus on Jeremy again. "Jeremy would have been so excited—that's why he got up early that morning. He put on his Panther uniform, like he did every game day, and wore it to the barn, even though he knew he'd be mucking out stalls. He'd have his backpack of jars too."

"You need to hurry, Hope." T.J. glances over his shoulder.

"I know. But I have to think it through, the whole thing. Because I can feel it. I'm missing something." I turn back and stare at the sawdust beneath my feet. I can see the shadow of blood there, but I know it's in my head. "Jeremy would have looked around for Coach. They said he rode Sugar that morning. Maybe when he didn't see Coach, he decided to go for a ride." I look over at T.J. "That makes sense, doesn't it?"

He shifts his weight from one foot to the other.

I keep going. "Normally, Jer would never ride before he

finished chores. I guess he might have wanted to ride so bad that he went ahead. Coach wouldn't have minded." This part of my story is shaky, and I know it. Why would he ride that morning, on a game day? Why would he ride without doing his chores? "Maybe Coach told Jeremy to go riding, and he'd clean the stalls himself."

"Okay. Move on, Hope," T.J. urges.

"And that's when Caroline saw her opening," I continue, visualizing her hobbling to the stable. "Opportunity. Means. She sees Jeremy take off on Sugar, and that is her cue. So she comes to the barn, brings her own gloves or puts on Jeremy's, picks up the bat, and—"

"Can we go now, Hope? Please?"

But the images are running through my mind. "She hits him. She hits him with the bat. His knees buckle, and he goes down."

"Stop it, Hope."

But I can't stop. Because I can see it. I can see Coach. The blood. Stuff flying from his pockets. The life going out of him.

"Please—!" T.J. begs, shaking me by the shoulders. I barely feel it.

"She drops the bat. Maybe she's horrified at what she did. One instant. That's all it took. And everything changed. She gets back to her house and climbs in bed, pulling the covers over her head, and shutting her eyes to block out what she's done. Jeremy finishes his ride and returns to the barn. He looks for Coach, because he doesn't speak so he can't call for him. When he sees his boss, his coach, his friend, lying in a pool of blood, Jeremy runs to him. He cradles him and rocks

168

him. But Jeremy knows he's dead. Maybe he knows he'll be blamed. Maybe not. Maybe he's so shocked he picks up the bat and holds on to it until he gets home. Or maybe he sees the killer and, scared to death, runs for home. But that's when he bumps into Sarah McCray." I can picture all of these things as if they're in my memory instead of my imagination.

Only why now? This is the question that pounds in my head. "Why would Caroline Johnson choose that morning to kill her husband? What happened? Did she find out something about him? Did they argue? What about? If we knew that—"

T.J. takes hold of my hand. "Hope," he whispers, "you have to stop this." He leads me away, up the stallway. I let him. But I can't get the crime scene photos out of my head.

I spin around to face him. "What did Coach have on him?"

He frowns. "I—I don't know."

"But you heard some of the testimony. Things fell out of his pockets. What? What was lying on the ground beside him? Surely they showed that stuff in court. It's evidence, right?"

He scratches his head. "A cell phone, I think. Keys maybe? A stub of something, like a ticket maybe?"

"A ticket to what?"

"How should I know? What are you getting at, Hope?"

"I don't know, not yet. Just tell me. What else?"

"Gum? Or gum wrappers? What does it matter?"

I can't answer that, but I know it matters. I just know it. I want Raymond's picture side by side with the ones I saw at Sheriff Wells's. Something was in one of those photos that wasn't in the other ones. But what? What was it and where did it go?

"Come on," T.J. says. "We're getting out of here."

"Not until I find what I'm looking for."

"What are you looking for?"

"I don't know. But I'm not leaving here until I find it." Near the door, where T.J. has practically dragged me, there's a little room with a glass window. I was in there once when I was looking for Jeremy. "That's Coach's office, isn't it?"

"I hope you're not thinking what I think you're thinking."

"T.J., we have to search that office."

21

"I can't believe we're doing this," T.J. mutters for the thirteenth time as he watches me try to work the lock to Coach's office. "We are so getting out of here after this."

"Fine. I want to leave as much as you do."

"I doubt it."

I don't have a bobby pin or a credit card, like people use to open locks in movies, but I have a horseshoe nail I found on the stable floor. It's flat and thin enough to poke into the lock and twist. Finally, the lock clicks. "I did it!" The knob turns, and I'm in.

"Great," T.J. says. "Now what?"

"Now we search."

"Search for what?"

"Clues," I answer, stepping inside. "A divorce letter or a journal would be great. Maybe some hate notes from his wife. I don't know." The police must have searched Coach's office, but it doesn't look ransacked. I'm guessing Sheriff Wells didn't waste his time looking into anything or anybody, except Jeremy. The only two pieces of furniture in the room, besides several chairs, are a big desk and a tall metal filing cabinet. "You take the files, and I'll take the desk. Deal?"

"Are you sure we shouldn't be wearing gloves?" T.J. asks, stepping over a pile of trash on the floor. "What about our fingerprints?"

"Nobody cares about our fingerprints. They're done with this office."

T.J. mumbles something, but I can't make it out.

Coach's desk looks like it hasn't been touched in months. Even the papers on it are dusty. Mouse droppings form a trail across the glass-slab surface of the desk. There's a framed photograph of Coach and his wife on their wedding day. I pick it up and dust it off. "They don't look that happy to me," I observe. "And it's their wedding day."

"I'll bet she was hard to live with," T.J. mutters.

"How come?"

"You didn't have her for English. Trust me. She was hard to take for fifty minutes a day. I can't imagine having her twenty-four/seven."

I shine the light on the faces in the wedding picture. Their expressions are relaxed rather than excited. "Comfortable. That's what I'd call them. Not in love, but comfortable."

I set down the photograph. Just above the desk are two pieces of paper pinned to the wall. Color wheels. Right away, I know they're Jeremy's. I would have sworn on a stack of Bibles that nobody except Rita and me ever got one of Jer's drawings. He must have liked Coach a lot. This extra loss for

Jeremy makes my throat burn—as if my brother hadn't already lost enough.

The file cabinet rattles. "Man, look at this!" T.J. calls.

"What?" I start to go over and see.

"This whole drawer is filled with baseball trophies."

I return to the desk. In the middle drawer, I find a photograph of Jeremy sitting on Sugar and another one of Jer grinning in his Panther uniform. It might have been taken the first day Coach let him suit up. Coach must have taken it himself. Looking at it makes me sad. I put it back.

"Find something?" T.J. asks.

"Nothing."

Under the photos, there's a pile of long, skinny strips of paper, like you'd use to write a grocery list. I pick them up and see they're all printed with numbers from one to ten, with a blank after each number. I know they're team rosters because Jeremy brought some home. I hold one of the rosters and imagine how excited Jer would have been to see his name written on there. Guys and their sports.

I open the bigger drawer on the right. There's only one thing in it, a framed letter. I take it out and shine the flashlight on it. "T.J., you've got to see this." It's typed on New York Yankees stationery, and it's addressed to John S. Johnson. "Is this what I think it is?"

T.J.'s already reading over my shoulder. "Wow! That's the real deal, Hope. They were asking him to play for the Yankees. Coach never said a word about this, not to me anyway—not that that's saying much. He might have told Chase and the others."

"I can't believe he didn't talk about it all the time." I put the letter back and close the drawer.

"Some of the guys used to ask him about when he played ball, but he'd say, 'The past is in the past. And any man who has to live in his isn't doing what he ought to in the present.'" He does a lousy imitation of Coach's voice.

"I don't know," I say, thinking out loud. "It might be kind of nice to have a past you'd want to live in again."

In the bottom desk drawer, I find a stack of old high school yearbooks. I bring them out and stick the flashlight between my teeth so I can thumb through. I flip pages and pages of kids who look too old to be in high school.

I'm leafing through the last yearbook when I see a picture of Rita in a cheerleading uniform. She's trim, at least thirty pounds thinner than now, with the same giant boobs. No wonder every guy in the tricounty area had a thing for her. There's some writing on the bottom of the picture. I take the flashlight and get a better look. It says: "To my Jay Jay—Hugs and kisses . . . and so much more! Love, Rita."

I close the book and put it back where I found it. Rita was a tease. A flirt—that's what Bob said. She probably wrote that in every panting guy's yearbook.

I know we have to leave. T.J.'s on the last drawer of the file cabinet. But I haven't checked the piles on top of the desk. I shine the flashlight around. Coach had sticky notes to remind him to do everything: "Turn off lights." "Buy feed." "Call Max." But none of the notes sound threatening or suspicious.

There's a small pile of rosters to one side of the desk. I

shine the flashlight in that direction. These rosters are filled in, held together by a rubber band. I fan through them. They're dated, and they seem to be in order too. The top one is for June eleventh, the day Coach was murdered. My stomach knots, and I take a few short breaths. It almost feels like I shouldn't be holding this—was it one of the last things Coach touched?—but I can't help myself.

I move the light down the row of names. They're all familiar now, part of my suspect list. Only the top name is crossed out. I hold the roster closer, shining my flashlight directly on it. "Chase Wells" is crossed out, and "T. J. Bowers" is penned in. I check the date again. It's definitely the right day, the right game, Wooster versus Grain at home.

"T.J.?"

"Hmmm?"

"Didn't you say Chase was going to be the starting pitcher for that Wooster game?"

"Yeah. Why?"

"Look at this." I show him the roster with his name written in as starter. "What does it mean?"

"I don't know. Maybe Coach came to his senses?" He laughs a little, but it's a fake laugh. "It's weird, though. I wonder when he did it." He stares at the roster, at his scribbled name, as if it's a code he's trying to decipher. "I admit I was pretty surprised when Coach said he was going to start Chase. He's good—I don't mean that. He may even be a better pitcher than I am. But he can't bat worth a hoot. Dad said he thought Chase's dad had something to do with Chase getting to start that game."

"Really? I thought Sheriff Wells and Coach didn't like each other." I remember what Chase said about Coach not appreciating the sheriff's after-game criticism.

"You got that right. Manny—you know him, center fielder for the Panthers—he said he heard Coach and the sheriff really getting into it after practice. Maybe Sheriff Wells won the argument, but Coach changed his mind later? Who knows?" He turns away. "It doesn't matter anymore anyway. Can we get out of here now?"

"Not yet, T.J." I start to take the roster with me so I can show Chase. But I change my mind. What good would it do for him to know that Coach didn't choose him after all? It sure wouldn't help for Chase's dad to know. At least now his dad gets to think Chase was going to pitch.

"Hope, maybe there's something here." T.J. is still at the files.

I tuck the roster at the bottom of the stack. Then I join T.J. at the file cabinet. "What did you find?"

"Loan applications. Some went through. Some got denied. There are a bunch of unpaid medical bills here too. Maybe Coach really did have money troubles."

"Maybe his wife did."

I stare at the papers in T.J.'s hands. He pulls out another file full of forms.

"T.J., we have to take these with us. I want Raymond to see them."

"You can't just take them," T.J. protests. "That's theft. Besides, they can't be evidence unless the police find them. Tell Raymond they're here and let him worry about it." He shines his flashlight on his watch. "*Now* can we go?"

"All right. Just let me finish with the desk. One drawer left."

"Hope," he whines.

I pull at the tiny drawer on the left side of the desk, but it's stuck.

"Hope?"

"One minute." I yank hard, and it comes out. The whole drawer is filled with canceled checks. I look through them. Everything seems pretty normal—electric, gas, groceries, feed store—until I see four checks, dated December, January, February, and March, each for a thousand dollars . . . and all made out to Rita Long.

22

"T.J., why would Coach Johnson pay out that kind of money to Rita?" We're walking away from the barn so fast that I'm straining to catch my breath. Our footsteps and my heavy breathing sound out of place in the stillness around us.

T.J. sticks out his arm like a school-patrol fifth grader and stops me cold. "Wait," he whispers, looking both ways before letting us cross the open barnyard. "Okay. Now!"

We tiptoe-trot, zigzagging like we're dodging gunfire again. When we slow down, camouflaged by the tree-branch shadows, I ask him again. "Tell me! Why would Coach give Rita so much money?"

"I don't know, Hope. You said Jeremy was a great stable hand."

"Not *that* great! Nobody's that great." A dozen possible reasons for those checks fly through my head, none of them good. Was Rita having an affair with Coach Johnson? Her Jay Jay? She'd been staying out all night. Even the night before Coach's murder, Rita hadn't come home until after dawn.

T.J. takes my hand. "Don't turn around, but we're being watched."

Immediately, I imagine that white pickup truck. I glance over my shoulder, expecting to see it, but I don't see anything.

"I said, don't look." His grip tightens. It hurts a little, but I'm too scared to care.

"Is it the stalker?" I whisper, making my eyes focus straight ahead.

"It's Caroline Johnson," he whispers back. "We should have gotten out of there before she spotted us."

I whirl around before he can stop me. In a lighted window of the old farmhouse, I make out the shadow of a woman in a dress, or maybe a nightgown. "She's standing up! T.J., did you see—?"

He yanks me back around, jerks me up beside him, and keeps me there, one arm around my waist. He's about ten times stronger than he looks. "Don't let her see your face."

I fall into step and do what T.J. says, but I know it's too late. She's seen us, and she's seen us seeing her. She knows that we know. Everybody else believes poor Mrs. Johnson is bedridden, that she needs help getting in and out of her wheelchair. But we've seen her. "She can walk. Coach's wife could have walked to the barn, T.J. She could have murdered her husband."

"Yeah, but who's going to believe we saw her?" he says, speeding up. His dad's car is in sight now. "And who are we going to tell?"

"We can tell Chase. And he can tell his dad."

"I can see that," T.J. says, his voice filled with a sarcasm I didn't know he had. "'Dad, when Hope and T.J. were breaking into Coach's office after ransacking the crime scene, they happened to see Caroline Johnson standing on her own two feet. So that proves she murdered her husband, right?' I'm sure the sheriff will run straight over and arrest her—after patting *us* on the back for breaking and entering."

I hate sarcasm. But I have to agree we'd be in a lot more trouble than Caroline Johnson if we told what we saw. And she knows it.

We reach the car and get in fast. T.J. starts the engine, then turns to me. "We'll figure something out." He backs up and wheels the car around without turning on the headlights. "Hope, what if Caroline knew about the money Coach was giving Rita?"

My brain hasn't even gotten that far. "Do you think she did? Of course she did. She had to know, didn't she? I mean, with him not making all that much money, and her not making any, and a thousand dollars going out each month? You can't hide a thing like that. She would have known."

"Uh-huh. And that would give her motive. I don't know if she knew about her husband and Rita, or the money, but it's got to be good enough for reasonable doubt." The car hits a rut, and I remember to fasten my seat belt. T.J. still hasn't turned on his headlights. I know he's trying to get out without anybody seeing us.

"Plus," I say, gripping the dash, "we've got those rejected loans. They give her a motive for killing her husband—money."

"And the canceled checks," T.J. adds. "All great stuff for giving her motive."

"Motive, which is something Jeremy never had. Raymond has to get Caroline back on the stand and ask her about the money. Just asking her about it should give the jury reasonable doubt."

T.J. is quiet for a minute. Then he glances over at me. "Only . . . only that means everybody will know about the money he paid to Rita. They'll say things about Coach and Rita, whether they're true or not, Hope."

"Do you think I care if the world discovers Rita and Coach were having an affair, or worse? The only thing I care about is getting my brother out of jail."

T.J. still hasn't turned on the headlights. He quits talking and keeps taking peeks in the rearview mirror. I turn around and stare out the back window. Far behind us, about the length of a football field, I see two headlights, white eyes watching us through the darkness.

"T.J.!" Panic rises like bile in my throat.

"I know." He touches my knee, then puts his hand back on the steering wheel. I don't understand how he's staying on this road without headlights. He must really be familiar with this part of Grain. The road winds one way, then the other, with no warning. He takes a turn, and for an instant there are no lights behind us. Then they pop up again. "Who'd be following us this time of night? If Mrs. Johnson called the police, they'd just arrest us and get it over with."

"It's the white pickup truck," I mutter. When he frowns at me, I explain as fast as I can.

"Why didn't you tell me somebody was following you?"

Because I told Chase. "I should have. What can we do now?"

He rolls down his window. A rush of humid air floods the car, bringing in clover and dust and a faint scent of skunk. "I'm pretty sure there's a path up on the left," he shouts above the wind. "I think we can lose him if I can find— There it is!"

He brakes, and we swerve left. Weeds slap the sides of the car. There's a blur of fence, barbed wire. The car skids at a ditch and stops.

I look behind us in time to see a pickup speed by our turnoff. "He's gone. You did it! You lost him."

T.J. leans his forehead on the steering wheel. "I think I'm turning in my license." He looks over at me. "Was it the pickup?"

"You didn't see it?" My heart is clawing to get out of my chest. "It was definitely a pickup. I couldn't tell the color, but it had to be the same one. Why would anybody do that?"

In almost a whisper, he says what I've already figured out. "Because somebody doesn't want us investigating Coach's murder."

Rita's car is gone when T.J. pulls up in front of my house. He insists on walking me to the door and checking inside before he leaves. We're both so tired we can barely stand up. "See you in court," he says, glancing at his watch. "In a couple of hours." He starts down the sidewalk but turns back, hands in his pockets. "My dad needs the car again today. I asked Chase to give us a ride to court."

"Okay." I try to pretend like it doesn't matter one way or the other. Then I race inside, and the first thing I do is text Chase. I can't text everything I want to, but I get in the general outline of the night, knowing he won't get the message for a couple of hours anyway.

Two minutes later, my cell rings. "Chase?"

"Hope, what did you do? Tell me I didn't read your text right."

I tell him about the loans, the checks, seeing Coach's wife standing up, and about the white pickup truck. When I stop, he doesn't say anything. "Chase? Don't be mad. I had to do it. I needed to see the crime scene for myself."

The silence is too long. Finally, he says, "I thought . . . I was going to tell you I couldn't help you, that we shouldn't see each other anymore."

Something burns a hole in my chest. I don't want it to matter. I don't want *him* to matter.

"But I can't," he says.

"Can't see me anymore?" I ask.

"Can't stop seeing you."

Neither of us says anything, and I picture our breaths traveling from cell tower to cell tower and back.

"Start over, Hope. At the beginning. Tell me everything."

I do. I go into more detail this time.

When I'm done, he says, "Those checks? Hope, what do you think they mean?"

That's what it comes back to—the checks made out to Rita. "I don't know," I tell him. "But as soon as Rita steps in the door, you can bet I'm going to find out."

23

An hour later, Rita still hasn't come home. I pace the living room, trying to come up with an explanation for those thousand-dollar checks. If Rita did have an affair with Coach, who's she seeing now? I never ask. I never want to know.

I have to do something, so I search Jeremy's room for his batting gloves. Then I check Rita's room for her old high school yearbooks.

Zilch. Nothing.

After another restless hour, I stretch out on the couch to see if I can catch a few minutes' sleep. But when I shut my eyes, I see Caroline Johnson standing at the window, watching. Or I see Coach Johnson curled up on the barn floor.

A few minutes before six, I can't wait a second longer. I have to call Raymond and tell him about the new evidence.

The phone rings and rings until the answering machine picks up. While I'm waiting for the beep, I try to figure out how to word what I want to say.

But before I can leave my message, Raymond answers. "Hello?"

"Raymond?" The machine finishes telling me to leave a message, then squawks out a beep. "Raymond, I'm sorry if I woke you up."

"Hope?"

"Yeah. Listen, I have to tell you some stuff, but I don't want to tell you how I got the information."

"Just a minute." He sounds like he's underwater. I hear the receiver clunk. A minute later Raymond is back. "This better be good, Hope."

I fill him in as much as I can without telling him about breaking and entering the crime scene and Coach's office.

"Wait now," he says. "How did you . . . ? No. Never mind." His sigh carries over the phone wires. "What does your mother say about the checks?"

"I haven't asked her yet." I don't add that I haven't had a chance to ask because she's stayed out all night.

"Well, it might not matter."

"Are you kidding?" I shout. "Raymond, how could that not matter? Don't tell me I broke into Coach's office for nothing!"

"I didn't hear that," Raymond says, not shocked or surprised, like he's already figured out that much. "I don't know about the checks, Hope. But the other things, the loan apps and the bills, nobody's said anything about Coach's finances. Where there's debt, there's motive. How many loan refusals were there?"

"I'm not sure. Three or four, at least. T.J. could tell you."

"T.J.?"

Rats! I shouldn't have brought him into it. Such a long silence follows that I'm not sure if Raymond is still on the line. "Raymond?"

"Hmmm? Sorry. I'm thinking. . . ." More silence. "Okay. I'll level with you, Hope. Your testimony didn't help our insanity plea any."

"I'm sorry, Raymond." I get a flashback of that second in court when I realized I'd walked right into the prosecution's trap. Keller looked at me like I'd single-handedly won him his ticket to Washington, D.C., and bigger fish to fry. I can see his nose hair in his left nostril, the bead of sweat on his curled upper lip.

"It's not just your testimony," Raymond continues. "My *expert* witness didn't do much for us either. Insanity is a hard sell around here. People are too practical."

"Too insane, if you ask me."

"Could be," he admits.

"So what do we do?"

"I think I'm starting to agree with you, to tell the truth," Raymond says.

"Really?" I'm not sure what I expected. Maybe that this was going to be a much harder sell to Raymond. "That's great!"

Raymond keeps going, and I think he's talking to himself more than to me. But I don't mind. "We need to begin creating doubt, give the jury a few reasons to find Jeremy not guilty." He sighs. "Thank God for the double plea—not guilty by reason of insanity, and not guilty."

Maybe Raymond is right. Maybe that really is something

to thank God for. I haven't done much thanking lately. I have a feeling that even in jail, Jeremy isn't forgetting to thank God. I can almost hear him: *God, thanks for these bars that make cool shadows. And thanks for my roommate, Bubba, and the pretty tattoos on his arms . . . and legs, and shoulders, and head.*

"Hope, did you hear me?"

"What?"

"I said, I'm going to issue a subpoena to have Caroline Johnson testify in person. If there's an objection, the judge will have to rule. We could establish motive. And that's more than Keller has done with Jeremy. They haven't even suggested a motive."

"Yes! Raymond, would it help if you had two people who've seen Mrs. Johnson standing on her own and staring out her window?"

"Not if those circumstances would put the two people in prison for breaking and entering."

"Got it. It will be so great to watch her squirm on the witness stand, though." Sometime during our conversation, the phone cord got wrapped around my arm. I work on unwrapping it now. "Don't forget to ask her if she can get out of the wheelchair on her own. And ask about money. And the loans. And those canceled checks to Rita."

"Easy, Hope," he interrupts. "I don't even know if the court will allow this. And if they do, we could be too late. Trial is winding down, whether we want it to or not. My witness list isn't that long."

"What about Rita? What about her testimony? Are you still going to make her tell all those stories about Jeremy, the ones that make him sound crazy?" I hate those stories. Rita tells them to strangers in bars and grocery stores: about the winter Jeremy wandered off without his shoes or coat and ended up with frostbite; about the time he walked up to the screen at the movie theater and punched a hole in it; or the day he grabbed a kid in his stroller and ran and ran until the police stopped him—Jeremy had seen the mother hit the little boy, slap him on the cheek.

"I'll put Rita on hold and see if we still need her," Raymond says.

"Great!" I'm glad Rita's not testifying.

"There are a lot of variables here, Hope. I might not get permission to bring in Mrs. Johnson. And if I do put her on the stand, she may not be a good witness for us."

"I know. Chase told me she's not a big fan of my brother."

"Chase? Chase Wells?"

"Y-yeah." I shouldn't have brought him into it either.

"Well, it's true. Mrs. Johnson did some damage," Raymond admits.

"Why would she say she was scared of Jeremy? People ignore my brother. They don't understand him. They're uneasy around him. But they're not afraid of him."

"Maybe she's not scared of him," Raymond says. "Maybe she just wants the jury to be scared of him."

All right, Raymond! It's the first time I've felt that Raymond believes Jer might be innocent. "You have to get the jury to see through that woman," I tell him. I think about her dark figure watching T.J. and me leave the barn. "Um . . . you know those two people who saw her standing at her window?"

"I do. I know one of them rather well." Raymond's voice has a little smile to it.

"Well, they saw her tonight. . . . And I'm pretty sure she saw them too."

"Hope!"

"Plus, if Mrs. Johnson owns a white pickup truck, or knows somebody who has one, it would explain a lot of things."

"Do I want to know about this pickup truck?" Raymond asks.

Whether he wants to know or not, I tell him. And I tell him about the phone calls.

"I don't like this," Raymond says. I've been so afraid he wouldn't believe me. Instead, I'm pretty sure he sounds . . . worried. "Have you told anybody about this?"

"I told Sheriff Wells, and he said he'd drive by the house at night, even though I know he didn't take me seriously."

"You need to call him, or dial 911, if anything like that happens again. I mean it, Hope. Or call me."

I like having Raymond worry about me. A giant yawn comes up from nowhere, making me exhale into the phone.

"See if you can get some sleep," Raymond says. "I need to get going on that petition to the court."

"Good luck, Raymond." I yawn again.

Before I can hang up, Raymond shouts, "Hope! You be careful, okay?"

In spite of everything, I feel myself smile. "Thanks, Raymond."

24

"The defense would like to call Andrew Petersen."

"Andrew Petersen!"

Chase, T.J., and I are in the back row of the courtroom. Raymond said it's ok for me to be here now that I've testified, as long as the prosecutor doesn't object, which he hasn't yet, and which is why I'm lying low. On the drive over here, I sat in the front with Chase, leaving nowhere for T.J. except the backseat. Since T.J. didn't say more than two words to either one of us the whole drive, I figure he doesn't like riding in the backseat by himself. But I don't have the energy to make sure everybody's happy. I have to focus on the trial.

The problem is, I don't understand how trials work because I slept through most of eighth-grade civics and government classes. Leaning toward Chase, I whisper, "Who's Petersen and why is Raymond making him testify?"

"Petersen testified for the prosecution and claimed he saw Jeremy twice that morning—once galloping through the fields on that spotted horse."

"Sugar."

"Right," T.J. throws in. "I was here for that part of the prosecution's case too."

I watch Petersen stroll across the courtroom. He's tall, balding, and maybe fifty or sixty years old, wearing glasses and a black suit with a red tie. "So why would Raymond want him testifying again?"

T.J. and Chase exchange weird looks. Then Chase whispers, "Petersen claims he saw Jeremy carrying a bat and running away from the barn."

I look over at Jeremy. He's sitting up straight, his gaze on the judge.

I make myself listen to every word of the testimony as Raymond leads Mr. Petersen through the events of his morning, including what he ate for breakfast—instant oatmeal, wheat toast with fake butter, OJ, and coffee. He tells us where he found his morning paper—in the bushes—how loud the neighbors' dogs are, and when he saw Jeremy. He's a horrible storyteller, wasting time trying to recall details nobody on earth could care about.

"I've called that newspaper office to complain," he drones, "seven times. Or was it eight? I remember the sixth time clearly because it was after the Fourth of July and those kids down the street were still shooting off their firecrackers. Then I found my newspaper on the roof, saw it right up there when—"

Finally, Raymond retakes control and interrupts the winding, windy trail of Mr. Petersen's thoughts. "Mr. Petersen, how do you know Jeremy Long, the defendant?"

"Everybody knows the Batter," he answers. That's the horrible name the *Cleveland Plain Dealer* gave to Coach Johnson's murderer. CNN picked it up.

Raymond moves closer to the jury. "I meant *before* everybody became familiar with the defendant. When did you first come to know Jeremy?"

Petersen's face wrinkles, and he looks like he's pouting or about to cry. "I don't understand."

"Let me clarify," Raymond says, smiling. But I'm thinking Raymond may be a better lawyer than he looks. "When did you and the defendant first meet?"

Petersen frowns. "I . . . I never met him."

"No?" Raymond looks surprised. "But you'd seen him around? You knew what he looked like? Before the murder?"

"No," Mr. Petersen admits.

Raymond looks puzzled and turns to the jury for his next question. "Then how did you know that the boy you saw running with a bat was Jeremy Long?"

"I didn't. Not at first, leastwise."

"So what you saw was *a* boy running with a bat and *a* boy riding a horse?" Raymond keeps going, leading Petersen on a trail that ends up with the man admitting he didn't know who Jeremy was until the newspapers told him. And he hadn't been wearing his glasses.

When Petersen is so confused he'd have trouble identifying himself, Raymond moves in for the kill. "So, you didn't really know who the boy was running. And you didn't report this alarming incident because, although you believed the bat was bloody after the papers reported it, at the time you assumed it was a muddy bat. Have I got that right?"

"Yeah. I guess," Mr. Petersen admits.

Raymond smiles up at the judge. "Then, Your Honor, I have no more questions for this witness."

Mr. Petersen hurries out of the witness box and out of the courtroom. The whole question-and-answer routine took a lot longer than things take on TV court shows. Twice it looked like Juror Number Seven fell asleep.

But not Jeremy. I could tell my brother was tuned in, listening to the testimony, absorbing it. If Jeremy is focused on something, he's smart, really smart. It's just when he loses interest that he drifts into his own, much more fascinating world.

The judge announces a short recess, and when we get back, Raymond calls Bob Adams to the stand. Bob is a few rows up from us, but he glances back as he steps over people to get out of his row. I smile at him, relaxing a little because I know Bob likes Jeremy. That's why Raymond wanted him to testify about Jeremy's character. When we first moved to Grain, Bob hired Rita on the spot. When I began standing in for Rita, mostly because she wanted to sleep in or just didn't feel like working, Bob wasn't crazy about the idea. But when he saw how hard I worked—a lot harder than Rita—he came around. He came around with Jeremy too.

Bob swears on the Bible to tell the truth, then makes his way to the witness box, where he balances himself on the edge of the wooden seat, like he may need to get away quick. I might not have recognized Bob outside of the restaurant if I'd seen him dressed like this—gray suit, blue tie, leather shoes, and no apron. I try to remember if I've ever seen Bob outside of the Colonial Café, and I don't think I have. He clears his throat. His hair is slicked back, and he looks as nervous and out of place as a cat in a courtroom full of rocking chairs.

Raymond has Bob identify himself, and then he starts asking Bob about Jeremy.

"I've always thought Jeremy was a great kid," Bob answers. "A little different maybe, squirrelly, you know, what with not talking and all. But nice. Real nice."

Bob gives examples of nice, like when Jeremy would come by the Colonial and jump right in to help wash dishes for no reason and no money. Or the time Jeremy picked black-eyed Susans and put a glass full of flowers on every table in the Colonial.

I'm thinking Bob's done a good job talking about my brother. Jeremy comes off as different, just in case we still need the insane version of the plea, but nice and regular too.

Raymond announces that he's finished with the witness, and Bob starts to get up to leave.

"I have a few questions for the witness," Prosecutor Keller says from behind his table. He stands and buttons the middle button of his light gray suit.

The judge nods, and Bob sits back down.

Keller is all smiles, which makes me nervous. "Mr. Adams, wasn't there a time when Jeremy caused some disturbance in your restaurant?"

"That . . . that was nothing," Bob answers, but he shifts his sizable weight in the witness seat and loosens his tie. I know what's coming, and I'm sure Bob does too.

I glance at Jeremy, and he's staring at Bob like he'd trade places with him if he could, just so Bob wouldn't have to be on that witness stand any longer.

"You say it was nothing? Really?" Keller turns his wrinkled-up, surprised look on the jury. I've come to hate that look. "Didn't someone call the police? Didn't Sheriff Wells have to restore order?"

I glare at the sheriff. I know he had to be the one who told Keller about this.

"It all got blown out of proportion," Bob answers.

It really did. It shouldn't have been such a big deal, and it wasn't Jeremy's fault anyway. He lost his temper, but only because some jerk at school told him that Rita served horse and dog meat at the café. Jer loves animals, so he got upset.

"Mr. Adams," Keller insists, "I remind you that you're under oath. Please tell the court what transpired about a year ago on August second, when Sheriff Wells was called to your establishment."

Bob glances over at Jeremy, then back to Keller. "Well, Jeremy came storming into the restaurant at lunchtime. It was a Saturday, and we were busy. He ran from one table to the next, over to the booths, and down the short-order counter, peering at every plate."

"Go ahead, please," Keller urges.

"If a customer had a hamburger, say, well, Jeremy grabbed the plate and tossed the whole thing into the garbage. It all happened so fast. I guess some kids in one of the booths tried to hang on to their plates, and Jeremy got a little carried away. But it was them kids at his school that done it. They messed with Jeremy's head, telling him his mother was serving horse-meat and dogs."

A ripple of restrained laughter flicks across the courtroom. I can't believe anybody thinks this is funny.

"Mr. Adams, tell us about the plates," Keller urges.

Bob stares at his pudgy hands. "He broke most of them," he mutters.

"Speak up, please," Keller says, "so the jury can hear you."

"He broke them!" Bob shouts, staring Keller straight in the eyes. "Jeremy broke them plates and a dozen others, okay? But that busybody Mrs. Rouse had no call to phone the sheriff. We didn't need the police. We could have handled it."

"It's a shame you couldn't have been in the barn to handle things the day of the murder," Keller says.

Raymond stands up and pounds the table. "Your Honor! I object!"

But the judge is already on it. "Mr. Keller, save your comments for your closing. I'm watching you."

"Sorry, Your Honor," he says, clearly not one bit sorry. He turns to Bob and smiles. "Mr. Adams, Bob, you like Jeremy Long, the defendant, do you not?"

Bob looks at Jeremy again. "I like Jeremy fine," he says, still obviously upset at Keller.

"Would it be fair to say that you like Jeremy's mother too?" Keller presses.

My stomach twists. I'm not sure why, but I know something bad is coming.

"What are you saying?" Bob demands.

"Just that I believe you like Jeremy and his mother."

Raymond stands up, but only halfway, like he's not quite sure of this one. "Your Honor, I object to this line of questioning."

"Goes to motive for testifying, Your Honor," Keller explains.

"Overruled. Answer the question, Mr. Adams."

"Fine. I like Rita and Jeremy. So what?"

"Could we say that, at least in the case of the defendant's mother, Rita Long, you more than like her?" He sounds like a second grader teasing a kid with a crush.

"Your Honor!" Raymond complains, starting to stand again.

The judge raises her hand to stop him. "Move along, Mr. Keller."

This is what I'm thinking—move along.

"Isn't it true that you and Mrs. Long are lovers? That you—"

"I object!" Raymond screams. I have never seen him this angry.

I object too. But I have to admit that I'm not surprised. I knew Rita was seeing somebody. I should have guessed it was Bob, if I guessed about it at all. I knew Bob liked her. I've just never seen the "like" coming back from Rita's side.

"Mr. Keller, that's enough." This is as firm as I've heard the judge, and it makes me like her even more.

"All right," Keller says. "Just one more question, Mr. Adams, and then I can let you go. Where were you the night before Coach Johnson was murdered?"

"Home." Bob stares at his hands again, and I get a sick feeling about where this is going. Rita and I are the only alibi

Jeremy has, and I was asleep until the sheriff woke me up pounding on the door.

"You were 'home alone,' as they say?" Keller asks.

I want to smack that grin off his face.

"No," Bob answers, barely above a whisper.

Keller acts amazed. "Really? Who was with—?"

Bob doesn't wait for the question. "Rita! Okay? Rita Long was with me."

"Ah," Keller says, as if everything is finally all cleared up. "I see. Um . . . excuse me for asking, but all night?"

"Yes. I went into work at six-fifteen, like I do every morning."

"And Jeremy's mother was still there?"

Bob nods.

"For the record, Mr. Adams, will you please answer the question aloud?" the judge asks.

"Sorry, Your Honor. Yes. Rita was there when I left at six-fifteen."

The spectators break into murmurs, and the judge bangs her gavel and asks for order.

I don't know what to think or how to feel. I try to figure out how bad this is for Jeremy, but I can't. So Rita slept with Bob? So she wasn't home to make sure Jeremy was in his bedroom all night. That one would have been pretty hard to prove anyway—what with the bloody bat and Jeremy's bloody uniform. And it's not like Rita would have checked in on Jer even if she had been home all night.

Chase looks over at me, like he wants to see how I'm taking it.

There's a tap-clapping noise at the front of the courtroom. I can't see where it's coming from, but I have a good idea. A chair squeaks and somebody slaps a table. Every other noise stops. The slap sounds again and again.

"Mr. Munroe, can you please control your client?" asks the judge.

I lean to the left until I can see between two reporters' heads and get a view of my brother. Jeremy is swaying back and forth. His hands fly above his head like frightened birds.

"Mr. Long," says the judge, "you must settle down, or I'll need to have you removed from court. Do you understand?"

Jeremy's hands twist in the air, clenching and unclenching as he moves faster and faster. Raymond puts a hand on his shoulder, and Jeremy shakes it off like Raymond's hand is made of fire.

From where I sit, in the back, my brother's face is split in shadows. He is Jekyll and Hyde, light and darkness.

I don't want the jury to see him like this.

I don't want Chase and T.J. to see him like this.

I don't want *me* to see him like this. And in that fraction of a second, I wonder. *Did he do it?*

25

I make Chase drive me straight home after court. It's probably the quietest car ride any three teens have ever taken. I'm saving every word I have for Rita. I can't believe she didn't tell Raymond, or me, about her affair with Bob. What did she have to worry about, her reputation?

Chase pulls the car next to the curb in front of my house, and I see the light of the television glowing from the living room. "Want me to come in with you?" he offers.

"Yeah," T.J. says. "*I* could come in with you."

"No. Thanks. This is between Rita and me."

When I walk in, I see Rita in her white slip, kicking back on the couch. Her feet, crossed at the ankles, are propped up on the coffee table. It's four-thirty in the afternoon, but she's got a beer in one hand and two empties on the table.

"Hey!" she calls, all cheery. "You ought to watch this. Dr. Phil's about to let this loser have it right between the eyes." Her speech is slurred already, making me wonder what she had before the beers.

I charge the TV, shut it off, and stand in front of the screen.

"Hey!" she whines. "I was watching that." Under her makeup, Rita is a child, with pouty lips and fuzzy slippers.

"Why didn't you tell me you were sleeping with Bob?"

"What?"

"Bob! You know, as in our boss, Bob?"

She frowns and sets down the beer. No coaster. I've told her to use coasters. Our table looks like a bad version of the solar system, with the planets out of whack. "How did you—?"

"He testified in court, Rita."

"About us?" Her forehead wrinkles form a V as she tries to grasp this. "Why would Bob—?"

"Because things come out when you're on the witness stand, Rita. The truth comes out. I don't care what you do with your life. Not anymore. Not for a long time. But it made it look like you and Bob were lying to protect Jeremy—and all you ended up doing was making Jeremy look more guilty!"

"Hold on a minute." She's coming out of her drunken state. Angry Rita is hardening in front of me. "What's one thing got to do with the other? And what's any of it got to do with you?"

"Jeremy is my brother!" I shout. "I know he couldn't have murdered Coach Johnson, and I'm trying to prove it, but you—!"

"Don't tell me you haven't given up on that yet." She falls back onto the couch and turns on the TV with the remote.

I slam the TV off again. "Rita! Don't you care what happens to Jeremy?"

She sits up straight. "Of course I care! He may be a legal

adult, but he's still my boy. I borne him. And I don't want him to go to prison. I want him safe, in a mental home, where people can look after him and he won't get into no more trouble. That's what I want!"

I feel like throwing the TV at her. How can she be so cold?

Rita shoots me a look I've seen a million times. Lips pressed together and shifted sideways, her head tilted, eyes full of disgust. If I had just one picture of my mother in my head, this would be the expression on her face, a look that says, "I'm sick to death of you. You're too stupid to talk to. Get out of my way."

"We're done here, Hopeless." She takes a gulp of beer and drains the can. "Get me another one of these from the fridge."

Here's where I would give in, do what she says so that things wouldn't get uglier, so that nobody would get hurt. Here's where I always make peace by giving up, by giving in.

Only not this time. "Rita." My voice is calm. I see her flinch at the sound of it, surprised maybe? "Why was Coach Johnson paying you off?"

Her body stiffens, and she scoots to the edge of the cushion. At last, I have her attention. "I don't know what you're talking about."

"Really? You and Jay Jay? Are you saying he wasn't writing you checks?"

She tucks her feet under her and smooths her slip over her flabby thighs. "I had him pay me Jeremy's salary for working in the barn. So what? Jeremy wouldn't know what to do with a check."

"A check for a thousand dollars? Every month?"

"Where did you—?"

"Were you and Coach, 'Jay Jay,' having an affair, Rita?"

"Shut up!" Rita screams. "This is none of your business!"

"Was it *your* business? Was Coach paying you to keep quiet?"

"You little—!" The words squeeze through her teeth, greased by spit.

"Was he afraid his wife would find out? You were blackmailing him, weren't you!"

"You don't know what you're talking about!" she screams.

I have never seen Rita so angry, and that's saying something. But I'm not backing down. This is too important. "Is that why you're so eager to send Jeremy away to a mental hospital?"

Quick as a flash, Rita picks up the remote and flings it at me. I dodge, but it catches my cheekbone before crashing into the TV. The remote breaks into pieces. Batteries fly. The screen looks chipped. She gasps. "Hope, are you all right? Are you hurt?"

"You're pathetic, Rita!" I feel something trickling down my cheek. I touch it, and my finger comes away red. I don't care. I can't feel anything. My body's shaking. "You'd send your own son away to keep your ugly little secrets from getting out! You'd help them convict Jeremy of murder just so you wouldn't have to be tried for blackmail?"

Rita stands up, and I think she's going to fly across the coffee table and tackle me. But I don't move. I don't care.

Instead, she shakes her finger at me. "I would send my own son away so he wouldn't kill anybody ever again!"

"He didn't kill anybody!"

203

Her eyes narrow, and I know I'm about to get the worst of this argument, the worst of everything. "Hope, he did it. I know without a doubt that your brother murdered Jay Jay."

I want to yell again. I want her to throw something else at me. I don't want this.

She continues, her voice calm, "I saw him washing that bat of his in the bathroom sink the morning of the murder."

Her words take the rest of the fire out of me, out of both of us. I want to call her a liar, but I'm doused, drowning in her words.

Rita is quiet now. The whole house has turned silent. "I saw him, Hope. I came home that morning and tried to go back to sleep. I thought you and Jeremy must be in bed still. But I couldn't sleep, so I got up and went to the bathroom. I opened the door, and there he was. He was trying to wash blood off his bat."

"What did you do?"

"I looked at him. He stared back at me with his wide, panicked eyes, like he was begging me for something I couldn't give him. I closed the door."

"You—?"

"I know. I should have asked him right then and there what he done. But I figured he'd clubbed some animal—not a dog or a cat, but a squirrel or a gopher. And I didn't want to deal with it." She stares past me, at the blank TV screen. "I didn't think he'd . . . he'd . . . used that bat on a . . . a person."

I've been backing away from her, stumbling toward the door. Images of the crime scene flash through my head. They bring pain, as if they're mounted on arrows. Coach, bloody, curled on the stable floor. Jeremy curled in the corner of his bedroom.

My back slams into the door. I reach behind me, frantically feeling for the doorknob. I have to get out of here.

Rita is shouting at me, but I can't hear her. A buzzing in my head drowns her out.

I'm outside. I take off running. One foot, the other foot. I used to read a book to Jeremy when we were little. Dr. Seuss. *One foot. Two feet.* I can't remember how it goes. *Left foot? Right foot?*

I keep running. I want the pain in my chest to hurt more. To explode.

My run ends in front of an old church that's been turned into an antiques store. If it were still a church, could I pray? Would it help? A dozen signs are posted on the big front door: DON'T TOUCH ANYTHING! IF YOU BREAK IT, YOU BUY IT. NO CHECKS, NO CHARGE. CASH ONLY. NO RUNNING. NO EATING.

I shove the door and go in. I've been here before. Every inch of this place holds a table, or chair, or dresser, or picture frame, or statue, or trinket. The smell of dust and must mixes with lemon and varnish.

"May I help you?"

May she? May anybody?

God? I ask in my heart. *May you help me?* Is it a question? A plea? An antique prayer?

I shake my head, then walk to a wooden banister and climb the stairs to the loft. It's been transformed from a choir loft to period rooms. Dresses from the 1920s hang on a rack in front of the open room. Inside, there are helmets and uniforms

205

from every war. Did their original owners kill people? Did they have sisters at home who would have died for them? Who believed they were heroes, no matter what they'd done?

I sit on an army trunk tucked in front of a Japanese silk-screen room divider that splits the space in half, the West and the Orient. A bayonet hangs on the wall to the left, rifles and pistols in a glass case against the opposite wall.

I want out. Out of my own century and into this one, the past. I don't want the present, and I don't want the future. "I can't do this." I say it out loud, even though there's nobody to hear except God and me. I can't prove Jeremy didn't kill Coach Johnson. All I've done is wreck his chances for being found insane.

Rita was helping Jeremy more than I was.

26

"Hope? Hope!"

The shout jars me back to the present. I get up from the
army trunk, walk to the balcony railing, and peer down. I
know it's Chase even before I see him. I turn away and slink
back to the war room. I don't want to see him. I don't want to
see anybody.

But Chase must have spotted me. "Hope?" I hear his footsteps on the stairs. He barges into the past, my room, shattering the quiet here.

"Go away."

"Hope, listen. . . ."

I shake my head.

"What did you do to your face?" He touches my cheek.

It doesn't hurt. I can't feel it. Maybe I'll never feel anything again. I brush away his finger.

He sits down beside me on the trunk. "Talk to me."

"Go home, Chase. Leave me alone." I stare at the floor,

the wooden slats that let light peek through from below. Choirs used to sing here.

"What happened?"

I shake my head. "It's over. I'm done."

"You don't mean that. What about Jeremy? He needs you. And now you've got Caroline Johnson coming to court and reasonable doubt and—"

"Wait. How did you know I was here?"

"Rita," he answers.

"Rita?"

"She called me, Hope. How else did you think I knew to come looking for you? She's worried about you. She was afraid you might do something stupid."

This isn't making sense. "Wait. Rita called you?"

He smiles and nods. "Surprised me too. I don't think I was her first choice. But she *is* worried about you. So am I. You can't give up. I think things are looking better for Jeremy than they ever have."

"No. They're not." I shake my head and lower my voice. "Rita saw Jeremy that morning. Chase, he was trying to wash his bat." I can see it in my head—Jeremy trying to get the bat into the sink, water and blood splashing, and that look, the wide-eyed look of being caught in the act. "Why would he do that if he hadn't . . . ?" But I can't finish.

"First of all, whatever Rita saw, Jeremy washing the bat, might never come out in court."

"If Rita has to testify, Keller will get it out of her." My hand hurts, and I raise it to see why. My fingernails have left deep marks on my palm from the fist I must have been making.

"Rita might surprise you. She kept it from you this long. My money's on her keeping what she saw out of court."

Chase is right. Rita's stronger than I am, a better match for the prosecutor. "Still . . . it doesn't change what she saw." I make the fist again. I want it to hurt.

"What did she see?" Chase asks. "Jeremy cleaning his bat? So what? Who knows why he was doing it? Even you don't know how his mind works all the time. Maybe he loved his bat so much that he couldn't stand to have it dirty. Or maybe he was trying to cover up for somebody, to protect somebody."

"Like who? Caroline Johnson? They didn't even like each other."

Chase shrugs. "Okay. So maybe he wasn't trying to cover up for anybody. Maybe he just couldn't stand having Coach's blood on his bat."

That rings true to me. "Jeremy hates the sight of blood. Once when I got a nosebleed, I grabbed the nearest thing, a dish towel, to stop it. Jeremy made me throw it away, outside of our apartment."

"See?" Chase says, like I've proved him right. "Maybe that was why he tried to wash the bat. Or not. We don't know, Hope, and we probably never will know. But it doesn't prove anything. That's all I'm saying. What Rita told you hasn't changed anything. We've still got reasonable doubt. Jeremy still doesn't have a motive for killing Coach, and Caroline Johnson still does. After Bob's testimony, the jury could even believe that *he* had a motive."

"Bob? Why would he have a motive to kill Coach?" I can't imagine Bob hurting anybody, not really.

"Who knows?" Chase takes off one running shoe and dumps out a tiny pebble. He's not wearing socks, and his shoes aren't tied. "But if your mother was having some kind of love triangle thing going with Coach and Bob, that would give Bob a motive. I'm not saying he did it, just that he has a motive."

"And Jeremy doesn't." Relief, mixed with guilt, rushes over me. It's hot, blazing hot, up in this loft. "Jeremy doesn't have a motive."

"And," Chase continues, the lines of his face deep and intense, as if he's willing me to believe, "juries don't like to convict without a motive, no matter what the law says about not needing to prove one. My dad's always told me that people on a jury have to understand why someone would kill. That's just human nature, and jurors are human."

I close my eyes. A picture comes to my mind of Jeremy about eight months ago, standing on top of a hill, ready to ride his sled. He's the perfect image of innocence. It's nighttime, and the stars are out in full force. I remember thinking that he looked close enough to heaven to touch it. And I thought about the song I'd heard in the car that day, a decade ago, the God song Jeremy "copied." I'd give almost anything to hear that song now.

"Jeremy couldn't have done it," I say quietly. I feel grief, a deep sorrow at having even for a minute believed that my brother could have committed murder. "I was ready to quit on him," I admit, too ashamed to look at Chase.

He wipes away whatever is on my cheek—blood, tears. "I doubt it."

I frown up at him.

He shakes his head. "Not a chance. The Hope I know would never quit on Jeremy. I've seen the way you love your brother."

"But—"

He puts his finger to my lips to stop words from coming out. Then he draws his fingertip across my bottom lip.

I still feel his touch on my mouth, even after his finger is gone. Slowly, he leans in and presses his lips to mine, moving softly across the spot where his finger was. The heaviness in my body lifts until I feel like I'm floating. Around us, army uniforms, guns, and helmets watch as decades melt into each other, bringing us into the timeless group of lovers.

"You up there! What's going on?" Mrs. Gance, the owner, shouts, and stomps one foot, like we're mice to be scared back into the walls.

Chase and I break apart. He walks to the railing and calls down, "Sorry, ma'am! We were kissing."

"Chase!" I whisper, but it makes me grin.

"In my store?" Mrs. Gance sounds horrified. "Well, you two can just skedaddle, you hear me? No kissing in my store!"

"Sorry," Chase says, running back to me and grabbing my hand to pull me up. "We must have missed that sign on the way in."

We thunder down the stairs and out the door. The sun is setting, and a flock of geese aim for it, honking. We stand on the sidewalk, facing each other. I'm pretty sure Chase is about to kiss me again. And if he doesn't make the move, I will. We kiss again. I've closed my eyes without thinking about it, and I don't want them closed, so I open them.

T.J. is standing there. "What is this, some kind of joke?"

I shove Chase away, so hard he nearly bumps into T.J. "T.J.? Wh-what are you doing here?"

"Rita called me. She said you were going to do something crazy." He glares at Chase, his brown eyes tiny dots filled with hate. "I guess she was right." He turns his hate on me. "I just don't understand why she had to bother me with it."

"Let's go sit somewhere and talk, okay? I was upset . . . about the case, and Jeremy, and something Rita said that—"

"I don't care." T.J. shakes his head.

"Come on, T.J.," Chase says, his voice calm. "We need to talk about this."

"Talk? *I'm* the one who made you help out Hope in the first place. You didn't even want to." He stabs the air at both of us. "I sure didn't mean this! But I should have known. You are such a phony! You're no better than all the rest of them. Your dad. Coach. Coach's wife. And now Hope? Everybody treats you—and guys like you—like you're kings. So what am I? Some cockroach? Just because I don't have your money? Because I'm not *cool?*"

"T.J., what do you—?" Chase tries.

"I'll bet you and Coach got a lot of laughs out of me and my family, didn't you?"

"If this is about the cookies," Chase begins, "I said I was sorry. I don't know what else I can say. And as for Hope and me, I'm sorry you—"

"Right!" T.J. is screaming now. Two boys on bikes cross to the other side of the street, staring at us. "You're sorry. So that fixes everything, then, doesn't it? Do whatever you want, then

212

say you're sorry? Well, it doesn't work that way! Some things you can't take back! They're done. Over. But they're not, not really. And you can't take them back!"

I glance at Chase, who looks stunned to silence.

"T.J., calm down," I plead. "I'm sorry you're hurt, but you're scaring me. Can't we talk?" I move toward him, but he steps backward.

"No! We *can't* talk. Don't expect me to do handstands for you anymore either. I'm done! I'm done with the whole trial. And I hope your brother—!" He stops, choking on his own words. Then he turns and runs away, dashing into the street without looking.

"T.J.!" I scream.

A car slams its brakes and swerves to miss him. T.J. barely glances at it. The driver honks his horn, then takes off, tires squealing.

I watch my friend disappear behind a row of houses.

27

I keep staring long after T.J.'s out of sight. "Chase, we have to go after him."

"That's not a good idea, Hope." He takes my hand. "Not now anyway. Give him time." He starts walking toward my street, and I let myself be drawn along with him.

"Why did he act like that?" I've never seen T.J. so upset, even when guys at school teased him or messed up his locker.

"I told you he didn't think of you as just a friend," Chase says softly.

"But it's more than that. Do you think he's really finished helping Jeremy?" I glance up at Chase, and he shrugs. "What did he mean about not being able to take things back?"

Chase doesn't answer for a minute. Then, without looking at me, without slowing down, he asks, "Hope, how well do you know T.J.?"

"How well do I know him?" The question takes me by surprise. "T.J. was my first friend when we moved here. After the popular kids realized I wasn't one of them, I didn't have anybody at school. I don't think I'd even noticed T.J.—and we had three classes together—until he brought in sea glass for a science project. I love sea glass. I used to make necklaces and earrings out of it. He walked me home that day, to see the glass I'd brought with me from Chicago. After that, he'd bring me a few pieces, and we'd hang out together. We went on walks, or we went cricking—you know, trolling creeks for fossils or cool rocks. It was nice to have somebody to talk to at school. I've eaten every lunch in the cafeteria with T.J. for the last three years."

"But how well do you really know him, Hope? And think about it before you answer."

"Why are you asking me this?" My stomach is twisting. I don't want to answer Chase's question. How well *do* I know T.J.? We don't talk the way Chase and I do. After three years, I still don't know how he really feels about being labeled one of the weird kids at school. He never tells me anything personal—like about the team making fun of his mom, about Coach joining in. He never said a word about going to the barn, not even when he knew I was trying to get a timeline fix on how Coach spent mornings at the stable.

On the other hand, how open have I been with T.J.? I never talk to him about Jeremy or Rita or what it's like for me not having a dad, moving all the time. "What are you getting at, Chase?"

"I'm not getting at anything. It's just . . . Well, if you need another suspect for reasonable doubt, I nominate that guy."

"You can't be serious!"

Chase's phone rings, cutting me off. He checks the number, then swears under his breath. "I have to answer this." He turns away slightly, and into the phone says, "Hey, Dad." He glances over at me. "Yes, she is." He holds the phone away from his ear while his dad screams at him. When the yelling lets up, Chase puts the phone to his ear and says, "Okay. I'll be right home."

He hangs up and stares into space a second, and then smiles over at me, like he's apologizing. "Sorry I have to go like this, Hope. My dad is on the edge. I don't want to push him over."

He takes the time to walk me home first. When we're a block away, he asks, "You okay?"

"I'm pretty confused . . . but I'm not going to do anything stupid, if that's what you mean." I squeeze his hand, loving the feel of his fingers wrapped around my palm. "Thanks for finding me, Chase."

"My pleasure." He stops in front of my house. "And don't worry about T.J. He's a big boy. He can take care of himself. You've got enough on your mind with Jeremy. He's the one who needs you now. And he's lucky to have you." He leans down and kisses me goodbye. "Call me if you need me."

A glow from inside the house spills over the lawn. It flashes on and off as the TV images change. I guess we didn't break the television. There's no sign of Rita, but her car is here. The last thing I want to do is talk to her.

So I do something I haven't done in way too long. I dig out the lawn mower. It starts on the first try, although I don't know how much gas I've got.

Mowing our lawn is tough going because of the weeds. But once I make a clean swipe the length of the front yard, it feels great looking back and seeing what I've done. Maybe that's why I like mowing. That, plus the fact that it gives me time to think. Mostly, my thoughts keep bouncing back to the way my hand felt in Chase's, the way his finger felt on my lip, the way his lips felt on mine. I can almost feel him here with me as I walk back and forth across the grass, bringing order to the chaos of our lawn.

Then, just like that, my mind flashes back to T.J. outside the antiques store. His hair is wild, his eyes too deep into his skull, like somebody pitched them there too hard. I don't want this image of T.J. in my head. I try to picture him in his Panther jersey at a ball game. I can see Jer in his uniform and T.J. in his, but I don't have a single memory of Jeremy and T.J. together. Why is that? T.J.'s never been mean or rude to Jer, like some of the guys were. But he and Jeremy have never been friends either. I accepted that. Maybe I shouldn't have.

My mind spirals down to Jeremy, and a whole tangled ball of nerve endings shoots through my brain. *Jeremy.* I miss him. I miss walking into his room and plopping onto his bed so I could tell him everything about my day at school while he placed one of his jars on a shelf. I miss "talking" with Jeremy. He'd write his calligraphy almost as fast as I could talk. Sometimes we'd sit outside, each of us with a notebook, and we'd write miniletters to each other, exchanging them, then writing again. My handwriting always looked like somebody was elbowing me, but Jeremy's was perfect, each letter a piece of art.

I haven't seen a note from Jeremy in weeks. They let me visit him in jail twice, with a plate of glass between us and two phones, which didn't help much because Jeremy wouldn't pick his up. I tried writing notes and holding them to the glass window: "Jer, pick up the phone!" "Are you OK?" "Write me!" Jeremy smiled at me and touched the glass with both hands. But he wouldn't write.

By the time I finish mowing, it's pretty dark, but I go ahead and weed anyway. My eyes are used to the dark. I've caught Rita peeking out from the living room window a couple of times and from the back door once. I act like I don't see her.

I'm almost finished outside when the front door opens and Rita steps out. She's wearing too-tight blue jeans and a peasant blouse tugged down over both shoulders.

She stops when she gets to me. I'm kneeling by the sidewalk, and I brace myself for Rita's attack. But she gazes around the yard and says, "It looks real nice, don't it, Hope? Real, real nice."

I stare after her, still waiting for the punch line. It doesn't come.

When I go inside, my arms and shoulders cry out for a long, hot bubble bath. I start the water, then remember to close the shades and curtains. I'm struggling with the living room curtains when I catch sight of something white across the street. It's the pickup truck.

How long has it been there? Was someone watching me while I mowed? I shiver, thinking about it, picturing it. What if they were waiting for Rita to leave?

Fast as I can, I lock the doors. Then I edge toward the window and peer out.

Nothing moves.

No cars drive by.

If the pickup is still there, I can't see it. But I didn't imagine that truck.

I hear the bathtub water running and dash in to shut it off before it overflows.

911. I need to dial 911. I race through the living room looking for my cell. I don't know what I did with it. I don't have time to look.

Heart pounding, I run to the house phone. I reach for it, and the phone rings. I jump back.

Ring! Ring! Ring!

I watch as my arm stretches down and my fingers wrap around the receiver. I lift it to my ear, but I don't speak. I don't breathe.

Someone's there. There's a rustling noise. I think I hear an engine, a car. Then he—or she—says, "I'm watching you." The voice is calm, firm, as sexless as it is faceless.

"Who are—?"

"Quit poking around where you don't belong. Leave . . . it . . . alone." The line goes dead.

I stand there, receiver to my ear, until it buzzes. I drop the phone back onto the holder.

Almost instantly, it rings again. I stare at it.

Ring, ring, ring. It won't quit.

I jerk the phone off its hook. "Stop it! Stop calling here! You leave *me* alone!"

"Hope? What's wrong? Did they call again?"

It's Chase. I burst into tears.

"Hope, is Rita there with you?"

I shake my head. "No."

"Hang on. I'll be right over." There's a click, then nothing but the scream of the dial tone.

28

I curl up on the couch, pulling the afghan blanket around me. And I wait. Pipes creak. The fridge roars. Branches scratch the roof. Each noise is louder than the one before.

Outside, I hear a car drive up. A car door slam. Footsteps running up the walk. A knock. A banging at the door. It gets louder and louder.

"Hope! It's me! Open up!"

I fling the blanket to the floor and rush to the door. The lock won't turn. My hands are shaking. Finally, I yank the door open and throw myself into Chase's arms.

Without a word, he picks me up and carries me to the couch. He has to go back to the door and lock it.

"Chase?" I call.

"I'm here." He kneels beside the couch and wraps me in the blanket. "You're shivering." He rubs the blanket, warming my arms and legs. "Tell me what happened."

"The truck was outside." I start to sit up. "It might still be there!"

He eases me back down. "It's okay. I didn't see it out there. Go on."

"The phone . . . rang. They said to stop poking around, or something like that." I can't finish because that scratchy, breathless voice is in my head, telling me to let it go or leave it alone.

Chase sits on the couch and holds my head in his lap. He strokes my hair, and I wonder if this is what children feel like when their parents take care of them when they're sick or frightened. I think it might be.

"Hope?" His voice is as soothing as his fingers on my hairline. "Talk to me. Tell me again what the caller said."

I tell him. It's easier now. I'm safe.

When I finish, Chase lets out a breath, like he's been holding it during my account. "Did the person on the phone sound like a man?"

"Yes. At least, I think so. I guess it could have been a woman. It didn't even sound human. But I thought it was a man."

"It's got to be the same person who's stalking you," Chase says, "the guy in that pickup. I wish I'd seen him."

"You believe me, don't you?"

"Of course I believe you," he answers quickly. "I'd just like to be able to tell my dad that I saw it too, with my own eyes."

"I knew he didn't believe me."

"I'm not sure he would have believed me either, to tell the truth. I doubt if he even sent that patrol car over here to watch out for you."

A shiver passes through me, shaking my whole body.

"You need something hot to drink." He stands up, gently

settling my head on the arm of the couch. "Do you have any tea without caffeine?"

"I don't know." Since the trial, I haven't gone to the grocery store regularly. I haven't felt much like eating. My clothes are baggy, and I haven't even cared. I start to get up to search the cupboards for tea bags.

Chase eases me back onto the couch and tucks the blanket around me. "Stay where you are, and that's an order."

I listen to cupboards open and close while my mind tries to fight off the images racing through my head—blood, bats, a dark figure behind the wheel of a white pickup. The pictures won't stop until Chase comes back into the room.

"Here. Hot chocolate." He sets a steaming mug on the coffee table, but not before finding a coaster.

"We have hot chocolate?" I inhale the warmth. I'm so cold, even though I know it's hot outside.

"But no marshmallows." He helps roll me to a sitting-up position. I'm still wrapped in the blanket, swaddled. I wriggle my hands out and reach for the cup, but a stabbing pain knifes the top of my head and forces me to sit back.

"What's the matter?" Chase asks.

"It's okay. I think I'm getting a migraine." This time, I'm pretty sure it's coming. I haven't had a real one in a couple of months, but this sure feels like the beginning of the bad.

"Can you take anything for it? Can I get you something?"

I try to smile at him. "You didn't see any aspirin in the cupboard, did you?"

"I've got aspirin. Wait here." He races out of the house and is back in seconds. "Dad always keeps some in the glove compartment." He opens the little plastic bottle and taps two pills into my palm. Then he caps the bottle and shoves it into his pocket.

I know these won't do any good, but they can't hurt. Chase brings me a glass of water from the kitchen and watches me swallow the pills. Then he hands me the mug of hot chocolate and sits beside me.

I take a sip of the chocolate because he went to all that trouble, but if this is a real migraine, I shouldn't put anything into my stomach because it will come right back up sooner or later. Still, it feels great to hold heat in my clammy hands. "Nobody has ever taken care of me like this." Steam from the cup floats away with my breath.

"Seriously?"

"Seriously."

He puts his arm around me. "Then that's a shame because you deserve to be taken care of."

We sit like this, and Chase talks to me about his dad, his mom, and his life in Boston. I listen, tuned in to the sound of his voice more than the words. I have to close my eyes because the light digs into my skull like an invisible hatchet. My hair follicles prickle. The roots are needles sticking into my scalp. And yet, I have never felt more at home in my own home than I do right now.

When I wake up, I'm on the couch, the blanket tucked around me and a pillow under my head. There's a note on the pillow. I have to squint to read it. My eyes are still blurry from the headache.

Had to leave. Sorry. Call me if you need me.

I need him. But I don't call. Instead, I go back to sleep and dream of him.

I don't know how much time has passed when I wake up to the door slamming. I sit up so fast that my head takes a minute to catch up with the rest of me.

Rita bursts through the room, a cloud of smoke floating in with her. "What are you doing up? Did you sleep out here?"

"Rita, somebody was outside." Light filters in. It's morning.

"What?" She drops some things in the kitchen and drifts back into the room.

I shed the blanket. "And I got another one of those phone calls. Only this time—"

"Just hang up. I told you that's how you handle prank calls. Hang up hard." She yawns. "I'm going to bed. Are you going to court today?"

It's no use talking to her. She doesn't believe me. But Chase does. And that's all I need now. "Yeah, Rita. I'm going to court."

Raymond has good news when Chase and I get to the courthouse. He's been granted his subpoena for Caroline Johnson to appear before the court—just like T.J. said would happen. I wish T.J. could hear it too. I text him the news. He doesn't text me back.

It will take a couple of days to make it happen, but Caroline

Johnson will have to sit in the same seat I did and answer Raymond's questions, whether she wants to or not.

In the meantime, Raymond puts everybody who ever liked my brother on the stand to testify as character witnesses. As I listen to their accounts of Jeremy, I hope Jer is taking in all the kind words people are saying about him, from the woman at the IGA and the post office person to the first teacher Jeremy had here.

Chase and I sit through every testimony for the next three days. I can't stop looking for T.J., expecting him to walk through the courtroom doors and take his seat with us. But he doesn't show. It's like he's disappeared, like he was never there in the first place.

We still sit toward the back, surrounded by reporters. People greet Chase as if they've known him all their lives, but only a few speak to me.

On the day I'm sure Caroline Johnson will show up, she doesn't, and Raymond has to call more character witnesses. He even recalls Sarah McCray, the woman who found Coach dead. Chase and I watch her take the stand, and I feel a dull thud on the side of my head. I close my eyes and touch the spot, hoping the migraine isn't coming back.

"You okay?" Chase whispers.

"I think I'm getting a headache."

He digs into his backpack. The security people searched it by hand before letting us come in. Chase brings out his little bottle of aspirin. "I brought it just in case," he says. He shakes out two pills and hands them to me. "Here. Can you take them without water?"

I never have, but I toss them into my mouth and swallow. They scratch going down.

Raymond has Mrs. McCray identify herself again. After thanking her for returning to court, he begins the real questions. "Mrs. McCray, do you like Jeremy Long, the defendant?"

Mrs. McCray smiles at Jer. I watch my brother's feet kick the floor, faster and faster. He doesn't look at Mrs. McCray. "I've always liked Jeremy very much. He is such a polite, sweet boy."

"And you let him ride your horse, Sugar, isn't that right?" Raymond asks.

"I did."

"You must have trusted Jeremy to allow him to handle your horse," Raymond observes, facing the jury.

"That's right. I don't let just anybody ride my horses. A few of the children in town like to visit the horses and would like to ride mine. But horses are sensitive creatures. I can't just let anybody ride."

"And yet, you allowed Jeremy Long to ride your horse?" Raymond continues.

"Yes. I knew John would teach Jeremy what he needed to do to get along with my Sugar."

"John, as in John Johnson, correct?"

"Yes."

I look over at Jeremy. From where I'm sitting, it doesn't look like he's paying much attention to the testimony. He's swaying, and his fingers are playing something on the table. He could just be listening to his own music inside his head . . . or he could be starting to get upset about something.

I see the judge glance his way, but Jer doesn't see it. Neither does Raymond.

"Mrs. McCray," Raymond says, "I'm sorry to make you think back to the day of the murder, but I do have a question I need to ask." She nods and grips the chair with both hands. "When you first saw the body and realized John Johnson had been killed, murdered, even after Jeremy had bumped into you with that bat, was your first thought that Jeremy killed Mr. Johnson?"

"No! Not at all."

"Were you frightened? Didn't you fear that Jeremy might come back with his bat and go after you next?" Raymond asks.

"Certainly not! That sweet boy? How could I have had such thoughts?"

I feel like running up to the witness stand and hugging Mrs. McCray. I crane my neck to get a better look at Jeremy. I want to know if he heard her. But I see right away that he didn't. Jeremy's arms are raised, and he's swaying. He's closed his eyes. It's too bright in here for him, at least when he's like this—more agitated than usual. There are too many sounds—buzzing in the walls, screeches from chairs, murmurs from the gallery, where people are starting to watch Jeremy instead of Mrs. McCray.

He's getting worse. His hands twist. With his eyes shut, I know he's imagining an empty jar in his fingers, one hand screwing the lid on tight. It's been too long for him, too long without his jars. They calm him.

"Mr. Munroe, will you please restrain your client?" the judge asks.

Raymond turns around. His eyes double in size when he sees Jeremy jerking back and forth, arms raised, his fingers working an imaginary jar. The motion looks weirder if you don't know that's what he's doing, pretending he has his jar.

Raymond rushes to Jeremy and whispers fast to him. He touches my brother's arm, but Jeremy jerks away. He makes a tiny squeal, the sound of an animal caught in a trap.

"Mr. Munroe," the judge says, "if you can't get your client under control, I'll have to ask that he be removed from the proceedings."

Raymond can't help my brother.

I turn to Chase. "Give me the aspirin."

"It's too soon, Hope."

"Give it to me!" I'm loud enough that people around us turn to stare.

Chase gets the bottle out of his pack. "You shouldn't—"

I yank the bottle out of his grip. "Open your hand."

"What?"

"Just do it!"

He opens his hand, and I dump the entire bottle into his palm. Several pills fall to the floor.

Jeremy's noise gets louder. He doesn't speak, but there's nothing wrong with his vocal cords.

"Mr. Munroe?" the judge demands.

I'm on my feet, bottle in hand, sliding through the rows of spectators, not stopping until I reach the defense table.

People are talking now, and the judge bangs her gavel to stop them. Or me. "Order in the court! Mr. Munroe, do you want to tell the court what's going on at your table?"

I know any other judge in the world might have thrown me and Jeremy and even Raymond out by now. So I turn to her, picturing that Grateful Dead T-shirt under her robe. "Your Honor, I'm his . . . his helper?"

"His helper?" she repeats.

I elbow Raymond until he gets it. "Um . . . my assistant. In a manner of speaking."

"Uh-huh." The judge's eyebrows arch up to her forehead.

I reach across the table to give Jeremy the bottle. I don't know if he realizes I'm here.

"Just a minute," the judge warns. "May I ask what it is you're trying to pass to the defendant?"

"I object, Your Honor!" Keller stands up as if he's been asleep and has to make up for lost time.

"To what?" the judge asks.

It takes him a second to answer. "To the disruption to the proceedings, Your Honor. This is totally out of order."

"I'll take care of my own court, thank you, Mr. Keller. You may sit down." She turns to me. "Will the attorney for the defense's *assistant* please approach the bench, with whatever that is you're trying to hand over to the defendant?"

I glance at Jeremy. He's looking at me now. He sees the bottle. His eyes are wide open. He reaches for it.

"Ms. Long?" the judge calls.

"Yes, ma'am. Your Honor." I head for the bench. Behind me, Jeremy starts up with the animal noise. It's louder now, filled with pain. I run the rest of the way to the judge and hand her the bottle. "Please," I beg. "He needs to hold this bottle." I can imagine what's running through her mind. *Is he addicted to aspirin?*

Jeremy whimpers. Then from deep in his throat comes a scream. Not a regular, mouth-open scream, but a throat scream, filled with guts and stomach and insides. The whole courtroom goes silent, making the growl sound louder.

"Your Honor, I object," Keller says, sounding a little bit scared, I think.

"To an empty aspirin bottle, Mr. Keller? I don't remember anything on the books about that one." The judge shoves the bottle back into my hand and waves me off. "Go, girl!"

I run back to the table and put the bottle into Jeremy's hand. His eyes flick open, and the sound cuts off as clean as if somebody shut off the sound track. I hand him the cap to the bottle. He stares from the bottle to the cap. He breathes more easily as he clutches the bottle to his chest.

"It's plastic, Jer," I explain. "I don't know how long they'll let you keep it. But if they give it back to me, I'll put it on the shelf with the rest of them. I'll try to bring you another one too. I'm sorry I didn't bring you one before."

I breathe in the scent of my brother. He smells like mint toothpaste or mouthwash, and sweat. He's back. The real Jeremy is back. The good Dr. Jekyll.

I risk glancing at the jury as I turn to go. They're all wide awake now. What are they thinking? What are they saying about Jeremy?

I take my seat next to Chase, but my gaze is fixed on my

brother. He sweeps the bottle in the air above him, and with his other hand holding the cap, he brings them together and caps the bottle, as if capturing a rainbow no one else can see. The act itself transforms my brother's face into something angelic. I want the jurors to see this change, this face. But I don't think they're watching. They're listening to the testimony that's started up again.

I listen too. But I keep one eye on Jeremy.

I glance at the jurors, and I catch Juror Number Three looking at me. I smile, then nod at Jeremy. She doesn't look at my brother, but she gives me a tiny smile—I'm almost sure of it.

The instant court is adjourned, I'm out of my seat and heading for my brother. Nobody stops me until I'm almost there. One of the officers of the court puts out his arm. "I'm sorry, miss. I can't let you get closer. They're taking him back now."

I shout over the guard's arm. "Jeremy! I know you didn't do it. Everybody can see that. You could never kill anybody. *I* could, if I got mad enough long enough." I can imagine an instant of hate exploding out of my hands in a black smoke of anger. "Or Rita. We've both seen that temper of hers. It's not a very big leap to imagine Rita doing it."

Jeremy stops fidgeting with the bottle and glares at me. The angelic look disappears from his face.

"But not you," I say quickly, finishing my thought. "I can picture almost anybody I know losing his temper and in a single instant doing something he'd regret. But I can't picture you doing it." I lean in and lower my voice. "And I know you're not crazy. I'd sooner believe the whole world is crazy than believe you were crazy for one minute."

"We have to go." The guard steps away from me and takes one of Jeremy's arms, with a second guard holding Jer's other arm. He goes with them without a struggle, his back straight, his chin held high, like he's been invited to visit royalty.

29

After court, Chase drops me off in front of my house. As soon as he drives away, I feel someone watching me. My skin tingles, and for a second I can't move from the sidewalk. I glance around for the pickup truck I know I'll see, but it's starting to get dark, and I can't make out forms across the street.

Then I see him. T.J. He's standing in the neighbor's yard, leaning against a tree, staring at me.

"T.J., you scared me half to death!" I start toward him, but I'm struck with a mixture of sadness, loss, and something else . . . fear. I stop a few feet away from him. "I've missed you."

He doesn't say anything. He just keeps staring, his mouth hard, his eyes invisible behind those glasses.

"I look for you every day in court," I say, my voice sounding thin and false, even though I'm telling the truth. "I can't believe you stopped coming."

"I've been there." He doesn't budge. I don't think his lips

moved. If I didn't know better, I'd think somebody else had spoken, not T.J.

"I didn't see you."

"I saw you. You and Chase."

"But how—?"

"From the gallery." His voice isn't angry or hurt, but something worse. It's cold as death.

I don't know what to say to him. "Well, I wish you'd come sit with us."

I think he laughs, but his face doesn't change expression. The word *us* hangs in the air. "We've been friends a long time, T.J."

He takes a step toward me. It's all I can do not to run away. "Have we?"

I watch him walk off. And this time, nothing in me wants to run after him.

Finally, it's the day we've been waiting for—Caroline Johnson is called to the witness stand. Reporters are on the edge of their chairs. Nobody on the jury looks the least bit sleepy.

The double doors open, and as if she's been waiting her whole life for this grand entrance, Caroline Johnson is wheeled into the courtroom. It's a thousand degrees in this room, but she's wearing a tailored business suit, solid navy or maybe black, and she has a plaid blanket folded over her lap, topped off by a box of tissues.

Seeing her makes me think of T.J. He was trying so hard to help me find something against this woman. The morning after we searched the crime scene, T.J. texted me that he wished he could get a look at Mrs. Johnson's shoes. He'd seen some TV show where they proved a guy was lying about being stuck in a wheelchair because the bottoms of his shoes were all scuffed up. I try to get a glimpse of Mrs. Johnson's shoes as she's wheeled in, but her feet rest on little footrests.

I want to wipe out my last conversations with T.J. I want to forget the way I felt the last time I saw him. I just want to hold on to how much he tried to help me, how much he's always tried to help me.

Instead of making Caroline Johnson walk to the witness chair, which I totally believe she could do, they have a ramp in place so she can be wheeled right up and into the box. Raymond smiles at her, and she sort of smiles back, but it looks more like a wince. I can't help analyzing every movement, wondering if she's for real. On the one hand, she's taken the time to paint her fingernails and put on lipstick. On the other hand, if she is faking, then she should get an Academy Award because even I'm starting to feel a little sorry for her.

I try to bring back the image of Caroline Johnson screaming at her husband in the ball field parking lot. How does *that* Caroline fit with the withered woman in front of me? I want the jury to see *that* Caroline Johnson, not this one.

RAYMOND: First of all, Mrs. Johnson, I'd like to express how sorry I am for your loss.

MRS. J.: Thank you. (*She pops a tissue out of the box and dabs one eye.*)

RAYMOND: And I'd like to say how grateful we are that you've made this effort to appear before the court. If there's anything you need, please let us know.

Mrs. J.: Thank you. I'm all right. (*She takes a whiff of her asthma inhaler before going on.*) I want to do all I can to make sure justice is served. That's what John would have wanted.

I whisper to Chase, "Right. And it only took a court order to get her here."

Raymond: Mrs. Johnson, did you and your husband ever argue?

Mrs. J.: What couple do you know who don't argue once in a while? We were married for fifteen years.

Raymond: I suppose you're right about that. And they say that the number one reason for arguments in marriage is money. Did you and your husband argue about money?

Mrs. J.: After I got sick, I left the finances up to John.

Raymond: At this time, I'd like to offer as exhibit G an acknowledged copy of a letter from First National Bank, denying Mr. and Mrs. Johnson's loan application three months prior to the murder. (*Turning to the witness*) Mrs. Johnson, is this your signature on the application?

Mrs. J.: Yes.

Raymond: Would it be fair to say that your illness and the decline of your stable business, which Mr. Johnson tried to maintain, put a strain on your finances?

Mrs. J.: I suppose.

Raymond: And isn't it true that you—or your husband—made several applications for loans, and that you were turned down by at least three banks?

KELLER: Your Honor, I object to this whole line of questioning.

JUDGE: Overruled. The witness is directed to answer the question.

MRS. J.: We tried to get a loan, yes.

RAYMOND: Thank you. Now, Mrs. Johnson, can you explain why, especially in light of your financial constraints, your husband would pay out one thousand dollars a month to Rita Long?

MRS. J.: That's absurd!

KELLER: Your Honor! Objection! Facts not in evidence and prejudicial. I ask that the question be stricken from the record.

JUDGE: Sustained. The jury is instructed to disregard counsel's question.

RAYMOND: Mrs. Johnson, are you familiar with Rita Long, the defendant's mother?

MRS. J.: I know who she is. She and John went to high school together for a couple of years. Neither of us had anything to do with her after she moved back to town.

RAYMOND: So you're saying that you knew nothing of a relationship between them?

KELLER: Your Honor! I object!

JUDGE: Sustained. Move along, Mr. Munroe.

RAYMOND: Mrs. Johnson, did your husband have a life insurance policy on you?

MRS. J.: He had a small policy with his teachers insurance plan, I believe, although I can't see what—

RAYMOND: Thank you. And do you have a life insurance policy on your husband?

MRS. J.: I . . . I suppose. John took care of those things.

RAYMOND: Perhaps this will refresh your memory. (*He hands her a document, explains that it's exhibit K, and opens to the last page.*) That is your signature, is it not?

MRS. J.: Yes.

RAYMOND: Would you please read the death benefit on John Johnson's life insurance policy, the amount that goes to you, his spouse, in the event of his death?

MRS. J.: Five . . . five hundred thousand dollars.

It's all I can do to keep from shouting, "Go, Raymond!" I admit I wasn't crazy about Raymond bringing up Rita like that, but it's clear that I have seriously underestimated Raymond Munroe, Attorney for the Defense. He leads Caroline Johnson through a series of questions and answers about her husband and Jeremy. Even she has to admit how much they liked each other. I whisper to Chase, "I'm so glad Raymond got her on the stand. Everybody has to see that she did it, or at least that she could have done it."

Chase isn't bubbling over like I am. "Don't be too sure. Keller will get another crack at her when Raymond's done."

This is something I hadn't thought about, and it doesn't seem fair. Keller already had his turn when she was *his* witness, even though she only testified on paper. Raymond finishes his questions, and I still think he nailed it. But Chase is right. Keller stands up the second Raymond announces that he's out of questions.

KELLER: Mrs. Johnson, on behalf of the court, I'd like to apologize for putting you through this today. You've been most gracious to come to court and help us finish up the trial.

May I get you anything? I'm sure the judge would consider a short recess.

MRS. J.: No. Thank you. I'm here to help.

KELLER: I'd like to revisit your husband's relationship with the defendant. Can you describe it for us?

MRS. J.: Of course. John felt sorry for the boy. Well, I suppose one has to, doesn't one?

KELLER: So he spent time with the defendant and gave him a job?

MRS. J.: John was always generous to a fault. He taught the boy how to care for horses and taught him to ride, not that John had that kind of time. After the cancer made me an invalid, John had to do his own job and mine. He took over the stable. He let Jeremy muck the stalls, and he undoubtedly paid the boy much more than the task merited.

KELLER: And what about Jeremy and the Panthers, your husband's baseball team?

MRS. J.: Again, John's heart was too big for his own good. Jeremy couldn't play on the team, of course, so John let him carry the clipboard and equipment bag. John even gave him a uniform.

KELLER: Forgive me for making you relive this one more time, but I need to talk about Jeremy's bat. Do you know where the defendant got his bat?

MRS. J.: From my husband. John bought it for the boy. And it wasn't cheap. All the other boys wanted aluminum bats. But John said Jeremy wanted a *real* bat, a wooden one. I never liked seeing Jeremy with that bat of his. I knew it was trouble from the minute I—

RAYMOND: Objection!

JUDGE: Sustained. Just answer the questions, Mrs. Johnson. Proceed.

KELLER: Did you ever see the defendant with his bat?

MRS. J.: All the time! He carried that bat with him everywhere. He scared a couple of our broodmares with it. John wheeled me to the barn from time to time so I could be around the horses. That was before this last bout with the cancer.

KELLER: And you saw Jeremy in the barn? With a bat?

MRS. J.: Yes. I'm the one who insisted he leave the bat at the entrance the minute he stepped inside the barn.

She breaks up, and Keller hands her one of her tissues. I think her crocodile tears are a crock. I stare at the jury and hope they got the part about her knowing exactly where the bat was kept.

KELLER: After you stopped going to the barn, did you see the defendant again?

MRS. J.: John brought him by the house, but . . .

KELLER: Please go on, Mrs. Johnson.

MRS. J.: But that boy always made me nervous. Anxious.

KELLER: Anxious? How so?

MRS. J.: He brought that bat into our house, for one thing.

KELLER: Tell the court about the last time you allowed the defendant into your home.

MRS. J.: Jeremy had supposedly gotten a splinter in his finger from one of the spades or pitchforks in the barn. John brought him to the house so he could get a pair of tweezers. He needed more light to see the splinter, so they used the bathroom. On the way out, they stopped by the bedroom so John could check on me and explain. I tried to put the boy at ease and asked him questions about the horses, yes-or-no questions. But he got more and more agitated. He started swinging that bat. He swung it around and around, harder and faster, until I was frightened. He ended up breaking my bureau mirror, my grandmother's mirror. John said it was an accident, but I don't know.

KELLER: What do you mean?

MRS. J.: I thought then—in fact, I was sure—that Jeremy had swung his bat into my mirror on purpose. He knew what he was doing, all right.

After Keller sits down, Raymond stands up and tries to get in some last words about how much Jeremy and Coach liked each other. But it doesn't help. He can't erase Caroline Johnson's words. They're stuck in our heads, and nothing is going to drive them out: *He knew what he was doing, all right.*

I'm so angry when court adjourns that my stomach aches and my whole head feels like it's on fire. "That woman is evil!" I tell Chase as we watch his dad and a deputy wheel her out of the courtroom. "She made my brother sound like a bat-waving, mirror-breaking, weapon-swinging maniac."

"I know."

"And I guarantee she knew about those checks to Rita and maybe what Coach was paying Rita for."

"You don't know what those checks were for, Hope."

"*She* knew. I know she did. Give me ten minutes alone in

that house, and I'll bet I could find more canceled checks and who knows what all." We're at Chase's car in the parking lot, and I wait for him to unlock the doors. Across the street, in front of the courthouse, an ambulance drives up. Sheriff Wells pushes Mrs. Johnson's wheelchair into the back of the ambulance. "Chase, what's that about?"

"Didn't you hear them when they were wheeling her out? Dad and Keller are taking her to the doctor to have her checked out after the 'ordeal.' It's all for show, if you ask me."

"Wait a minute." I hadn't heard one word of that conversation. I'd been too wound up to hear anything. "Are you telling me she's going to the doctor, and your dad *and* the prosecutor are taking her?"

"That's what they said." He climbs behind the wheel and unlocks my door. "Why?"

I slide into the seat next to him. "Don't you see what that means? Chase, not only will she be out of the house now, but your dad will be out of the way too!"

Chase rests his forehead on the steering wheel. "Hope, no. Please?"

I buckle up. "We have to do it, Chase. It's our last chance to prove that Caroline Johnson is a dirty rotten liar."

30

Twenty minutes later Chase pulls up at Caroline Johnson's house. We don't have time to park far away like T.J. and I did when we searched the barn and Coach's office, so Chase cruises behind the house and parks around back.

As we make our way to the front porch, I'm still fuming. "Jeremy never liked that woman. And he's an excellent judge of character."

"So you've said. On numerous occasions." Chase tries the front doorknob. "Locked. I think we should leave, Hope."

"So *you've* said on numerous occasions."

He doesn't smile.

"Please, Chase? Maybe there's a key hidden around here." I check under a pot sitting on the front porch, under the planters along the sidewalks, and all around the porch swing. Chase doesn't help. He's definitely getting restless. I don't know how much longer I can keep him here.

"Let's try the other door," I suggest. I jog to the back of the house. The screen door is locked too. Chase comes up behind me. I rattle the screen. "Can't we yank it open? Or cut the screen?"

"Not unless you want to end up in jail." He steps in front of me and takes his car keys out of his pocket. "Here. It's just a fall latch."

I watch while he jimmies the latch and pulls open the door in one smooth move. "Where did you learn to do that?"

His mouth twists like somebody snapped a rubber band over his lips. Then he says, "I told you I ran with the wrong crowd in Boston. Enough said?" He says this like he's mad at me.

"Enough said." I shove in front of him and try the doorknob. It turns. I push the door until I can squeeze through. A strong odor hangs in the air—a mix of bacon grease, burned cookies, and sickness. Or maybe death. I don't move from the doorway.

"Are you sure you want to go through with this?" Chase asks, making it clear he doesn't.

I turn and face him. It's dark inside the house. Outside, the sun has stopped shining for the day. "I have to, for Jeremy. But you don't. You could wait in the car."

He sighs. "Do you even know what you're looking for?"

"One of those checks to Rita maybe? A divorce paper? Or a journal, where Coach's wife tells how she did it? Or a copy of a contract she gave to a contract killer?" I smile up at him, willing him to smile back.

He doesn't. But with one finger, he pushes back a strand of my hair that's sprung loose. "Well, we better hurry. They could bring her home any minute."

I squeeze his arm and hope that he can read how grateful I am that he's staying with me.

I'm afraid to turn on lights. Chase opens the back door wider so the remaining light of dusk sneaks in with us. I've never been inside this house before. The floor creaks with every step. The air is too moist, like in our house.

After a second, my eyes adjust to the shades of gray, and details sharpen, coming into focus as if I'm turning the lens of an expensive camera. I try to take it in: white lace on end tables that flank a light green sofa, doilies under lamps and vases, lacy curtains. The whole house is frilly. You'd think two old women lived here. On the walls and on the hall table are pictures of Caroline with her horses. Over the couch hangs a giant painting of a little girl holding the reins of a pony in one hand and a blue ribbon in the other. The kid has to be Caroline.

I bump into a table and hear something wobble. There are breakables all over this place. No wonder they never had kids. Children wouldn't last two minutes in this house. "Chase?" I whisper. My heart thumps because I can't see him.

"In the kitchen," he calls out in a normal voice. Why not? If anybody's here, they've already heard us.

I stumble over a recliner with the footrest still up, then make it to the kitchen. "Find anything?"

"I don't know. But I don't think she's bedfast like she claims. She'd have to get around pretty well to keep some of this stuff on top shelves."

"She probably has a housekeeper."

"True. How about you? Anything?"

"Way too many pictures of Caroline." I open a cupboard

246

by the fridge. I try to imagine how the murder might have taken place. "She pretends she can't get out of that wheelchair, but she can. So maybe she got up early that morning. She could have had a blowout argument with her husband—about money, or about those checks to Rita, or a million other things married people argue over. She makes her way to the barn. Jeremy's bat was there, so she grabbed it." I'm picturing the whole thing: Caroline in a cotton nightgown, pink flowers and white lace. She's screaming at her husband. She sees the bat, lunges for it, and—

"Hope, we have to finish up and get out of here."

Chase is right. I need evidence. "I'll take the den we passed when we came in. You take the bedroom. Check the bottoms of her shoes!" I cross back through the living room to the den, or study.

Before I reach the desk, Chase cries, "They're back!"

I hear gravel crunch in the driveway. The sound of a car engine is drowned out by brakes. The engine cuts off.

"Great," Chase mutters.

Please! I'm not sure if it's a prayer or a wish. I grab Chase's hand and pull him to the back door.

"What are you doing?" He tries to tug his hand away, but I hold on.

"Quiet!" I stumble and bump into the couch. It hurts my hip, but I keep going until we're outside. I shut the door, then the screen. Reaching up, I straighten a lock of Chase's hair, then smooth my own. "Let me do the talking."

"Why? Hope, what—?"

I shush him and wait.

A car door slams. And another.

247

Part of me wants to run and hide. But Chase's car sits six feet away in plain sight. I hear their footsteps on the front porch. A blend of voices. The front door being unlocked. Opened. They're inside.

I haven't let go of Chase's hand. With another wordless prayer, the kind I may have inherited from Jeremy, I reach up and knock on the screen door, hard.

"Hope?" Chase whispers.

I ignore him and keep banging on the door, my heart thudding against my chest with every knock. "Hello? Anybody home?" I open the screen and bang even harder on the door, shouting, "Yoo-hoo! Mrs. Johnson?"

I hear footsteps storm through the house toward us. The back door opens, and Sheriff Wells frowns down at us. "What in blue Hades are you two doing here?"

Chase opens his mouth to speak, but I beat him to it. "Sheriff Wells? I was starting to think nobody was home."

He ignores me. "Answer me, Chase! What are you doing here?"

"Don't be mad, Dad. We just—"

"We just wanted to ask Mrs. Johnson a couple of questions." Somehow, my voice is strong, friendly even.

"You what?" Sheriff Wells shouts. He glances back over his shoulder, then lowers his voice. "I can't believe you're this stupid."

Chase flinches.

"We didn't mean to cause anybody trouble," I say reasonably. "It's just that Mrs. Johnson said some things in court today that hurt Jeremy, and I thought if I could just talk to her for a minute—"

Sheriff Wells glares at me. "You want to ask her questions? Hasn't your family done enough?"

"Dad!" Chase steps in front of me, like he thinks his dad might come after me. I wouldn't be surprised. He looks mad enough to spit nails.

The sheriff takes a deep breath, sucking in anger through his teeth. "Look, miss, I have nothing against you. But you better leave this poor woman alone."

"Poor woman?" I'd like to tell him what I really think about this *poor woman*.

He turns to me, and if looks could kill, the sheriff would be on trial for murder. "I just came from the doctor with her. Mrs. Johnson isn't expected to live out the year. So you can tell your brother's lawyer that she won't be around long enough to collect that insurance money, much less spend it."

In spite of everything, and even though I don't want to, I feel sad for her. I wonder how long she's known.

The sheriff straight-arms Chase in the shoulder, knocking him back a step. Then he turns to me. His bushy eyebrows meet above his nose, and his upper lip curls to show teeth. "You kids leave it alone, you hear? *Leave it alone!*"

"We hear, Dad," Chase says. He takes my hand and tugs me toward the car.

I let him. I let him because suddenly cold fear is slicing through me like sharp knives.

We drive a long way in silence, leaving the barn and the Johnson house behind us. A couple of times, I glance over at Chase, but it's like he doesn't even know I'm in the car with him. That's how far away he seems. His forehead is wrinkled, and every now and then he rolls his lips over his teeth and makes a weird noise, almost like he's fighting himself. I'd give a lot to know what's going on inside his head, but I'm afraid to ask.

Finally, Chase speaks without looking at me. "My dad's right, you know."

"Right about what?"

"She didn't do it."

"Mrs. Johnson? Of course she did it! We just didn't have time to—"

But he's shaking his head and won't let me finish. "To what? Find some kind of smoking gun? The police already have the weapon. And that woman, no matter how nasty she is to your brother, didn't kill anybody. She's dying, Hope. You heard what they said."

"Maybe she's *not* dying. Maybe she paid the doctor to—"

"Don't even go there. This isn't some big conspiracy, with the doctors and my dad and Mrs. Johnson all in on it together."

"I didn't say it was. But she's the one with a motive—the only one with a motive."

"The only one? How about Rita? Or Bob? Or T.J.?"

I don't know why he's so angry. "I can't believe any of them would have killed Coach and let Jeremy be blamed for it."

"Fine. If you can't believe it, then I guess it isn't true." His sarcasm stings. "So get Jeremy's attorney to use Mrs. Johnson for reasonable doubt, but I'm telling you nobody's going to believe she did it for the insurance money. Why would she?

You heard my dad. She won't be around to spend any of it. And all you're doing is ruining the little time she has left. But don't listen to me. You won't listen to anybody anyway."

My throat burns. I don't know what I did to make him so angry, why he's changed on me all of a sudden. "Why are you doing this?" My voice sounds like I've swallowed sand.

"Enough is enough, Hope. Dad's right. We've done enough."

"I haven't done enough until I get Jeremy out of prison!"

"Don't shout at me."

I hadn't realized I was shouting. I take a deep breath. I hate this. We've been so close, so together in everything. "Chase, what is it? Is it your dad? Are you afraid of what he'll do when you both get home?"

"Yeah, I am." He glares over at me, and for a second he doesn't look like Chase. His green eyes are black. He has his father's mouth. "He's really mad, Hope. And maybe he's got good reason. I don't know what he'll do this time. Just be glad you don't have to go home to him."

"Right. Because I have it so much better going home to Rita."

"You don't understand how good you've got it having a mother who doesn't care, instead of too many parents who care too much."

That hurts. I know Rita doesn't care, but it stings to hear Chase say it. I sting back. "Fine. I didn't realize you were so scared of Sheriff Daddy. Just take me home."

"That's what I'm doing."

We don't speak until he pulls up in front of my house.

I pop the seat belt before he comes to a stop. I'm so mad that I'm fighting tears. "Thanks for the ride," I mutter.

"Don't mention it."

"I won't. Don't worry." I slam the door and stomp up the sidewalk.

Then I wheel around. "I was doing all right taking care of Jeremy on my own. I don't need you, or T.J., or anybody else to help me now! It's always been just me and Jeremy. I should have known better than to—" A lump fills my throat and blocks the words. So I turn and run into the house, slamming the door behind me.

Once inside, I can't stop shaking. I collapse to the floor and cover my head with my hands, letting my hair make a tent around my face, shutting me off from everything and everyone.

31

A noise makes me look up. A sob, or a sniffle. Rita's sprawled on the floor, leaning against the couch. In her lap is a shoe box, and in front of her, spread out in a semicircle, are photographs. She holds one up and cocks her head to the side. I don't think she knows I'm here. At first I think she must be drunk, but I don't see a glass or a bottle.

My mother is crying. She is, in fact, sobbing.

"Rita? What happened?"

She doesn't answer.

I move in closer. She's holding a baby picture, taken at a hospital. The baby wearing a white pointy cap and wrapped in a white blanket looks like every other baby I've seen in hospital photos. Only somehow I know it's Jeremy.

I sit beside her and finger through the photos scattered on the carpet. Half a dozen look like the one she's holding, Jeremy a couple of minutes old. But there are other pictures of Jeremy—outside on a lawn somewhere, in the back of a faded car, in a building with other kids his size, no older than two. I've never seen these pictures. Where did she get them? How did she manage to hold on to them? *Why* did she?

"He's my boy," she says, not looking at me. "My own little boy."

I don't know what to say. This isn't the Rita I know. It makes me think of what Chase said about me: *The Hope I know . . .* , something about how the Hope he knew wouldn't give up on Jeremy. And the Chase I just left in the car, was he the Chase I know? The sickly Caroline Johnson on the stand, was she the same woman who screamed her hate at her husband? The T.J. who ran away without looking back, who scared me, was he the same T.J. who brought me mermaid tears and ate lunch with me at school every day?

I pick through the pictures of Jeremy. This is the Jeremy I know, sweet, innocent.

Are we different people every single moment of our lives?

"I have to testify for Jeremy," Rita says, not taking her eyes off a photo of a much younger Rita and her son.

"What? Why?"

"I'm Raymond's star witness."

"Wait. Did Raymond call and tell you he wants you to testify?"

"Yep. Saved the best till last." She leans back and takes a deep breath that turns into a cough.

I think I may hurl. Rita's going to testify? And she's the last person the jury will hear from? I don't understand why Raymond would do this, even with his stupid kitchen-sink strategy . . . unless Caroline Johnson really did that much damage.

"Rita, did you and Raymond rehearse what you're going to say?"

She wipes her eyes with the back of her hand, the same hand that's holding the photograph of Jer and her. "I got to get to Raymond's."

I call Bob and ask him to drive her. Rita isn't drunk. She hasn't been drinking. But she's shaking, shaken and stirred. I don't trust her behind the wheel of a car.

I volunteer to cover for them at the restaurant, but Bob says he doesn't need me. In twenty minutes, I have Rita dressed and ready.

"Don't you leave the house again!" she calls to me on her way to Bob's car. "Not like you ever do anything I say," she mutters. Then she's gone.

I put away the pictures of Jeremy. With Rita gone, the house turns up its noise volume—a hum from the fan becomes a roar; water leaking in the toilet, a waterfall; and the fridge groans like it's being tortured. I lock the doors and windows, trying not to think about the stalker. What if he knows I'm alone, really alone now? No Rita, no T.J., and no Chase.

Exhausted, I lie down on my squeaky mattress, and my thoughts go to Chase. I miss him already—not just his help, but him. I miss his slow smile, like he's grinning against his better judgment. And the way his voice gets deeper when he's trying to explain about his life in Boston. Raising my hand, I think about how his large fingers feel interlocked with my small ones.

What have I done?

Chase has been so good to me. Did I really accuse him of caving to his "daddy"? He didn't have to help me in the first place. But he did, even when his dad tried to keep him away from me.

I need to apologize. If I never see him again, he has to know how grateful I am for everything he's done. I don't think I could have made it this far without him.

Since the last person I called was Chase, I take out my cell and hit Send. His phone goes directly to voice mail. No way I can say what I want to say on a recorder. I hang up. In a few minutes, I try again. And again. I don't know how many times I dial Chase over the next hour. Finally, I give up and decide I can, at least, text him. He'll have to read that, and I can delete before sending if I screw it up. I punch in: I'm sorry. Hope. Then I change it to: I'm sorry! Hopeless.

I send it and wait, staring at the screen until it goes blank. I picture Chase hearing the beep. He glances at the number, sees it's me, and . . .

No answer.

I try again: Please, Chase. Can't we talk?

I send it and go back to waiting. Jeremy and I used to text each other before Jer lost his cell. Our exchanges were as fast as phone calls.

I'm not giving up. Chase said it himself. The Hope he knows is no quitter. I send another text: Meet me tonight? Now? I don't want him to come to my house, and I sure don't want to go to his. So I keep typing: At school? Driving practice? He'll know what I mean. He'll remember that day when we were so close we read each other's thoughts, when he didn't get mad at me, even after I wrecked his car.

I wait for a reply. While I'm at it, I should text T.J. too.

We were friends for a long time. I stare at the screen, trying to think of a message for him. But I can't.

My phone beeps. It's Chase. I have a message: OK.

It takes me five minutes to change into jeans and brush my hair. I'm as nervous as if it's our first date. I try to tell myself not to get my hopes up. He's agreed to talk. Nothing else.

I hurry outside and up the walk in the direction of the school. It's muggy out, and a cloud of gnats hovers around me. I shoo them away and keep going.

Behind me a car starts up. Headlights pop on and shine through me, turning my shadow into a jagged ghost.

Coincidence. But I walk a little faster.

The car creeps along behind me. I want it to speed up. I want the lights to vanish when I turn onto Walnut Street. But the headlights stay with me, like two giant flashlights keeping me in their sights. I walk faster. It's all I can do not to break into a run.

The car pulls up beside me, keeping pace with me. Then I hear a voice: "Hope?"

"Chase! How did you—?"

"Get in." He's ducking low from the driver's side so we can see each other.

I climb in, my heart still jittery, maybe more so. Then I scoot as close as I can get to him. "Chase, I'm sorry. I'm so sorry."

"I know. Me too." He reaches out an arm, and I fall into him.

I close my eyes and let myself soak up everything about

this moment, his strong arms around me, my head on his chest, rising and falling with his breath. I want to dissolve into him, to lose myself in Chase Wells.

Suddenly I pull away so I can see his face. "Were you out here the whole time?"

"Yeah. As soon as Dad finished yelling at me—which only happened because he had to go in to work—I came over here. I was pretty sure he was never going to have a patrol car on your street, so I thought I'd better keep an eye on things myself, in case that pickup came back."

"You've been guarding me? Even after I said those horrible things to you?" I snuggle closer.

"I admit I was pretty mad when I drove away, but not mad enough to leave you for the stalker." He grins down at me. I want to freeze that look, the dimples, the warmth.

"Nice to know you wouldn't throw me to the stalker in a fit of anger." I stretch up and kiss him, then pull back. "Why didn't you answer your phone?"

"You called me? Sorry. Dad played the big-bad-father card before he stormed out. I'm grounded—yeah, right—and phoneless. He made me turn in my cell. I'll get it back. Don't worry."

"Wait a minute. He took your cell?"

"Yeah. I'm surprised he didn't take the keys to the car, my driver's license, and—"

"But you're here." Something's wrong. Really wrong.

He squints at me. "Don't look so worried. I haven't been grounded since I was ten. He'll get over it."

"But how did you know to come and meet me?"

"Meet you? What do you mean?"

My mind is spinning, trying to piece together the messages. "I sent you a text. We're supposed to be meeting at the school parking lot."

"Didn't get the message, Hope. I didn't have the phone. I just saw you leave because I was guarding the—"

"But you answered. You texted me back and said okay."

Chase's face changes. Even his eyes seem to darken. He takes me by the shoulders and eases me back into the passenger seat. "Hope, that wasn't me."

Neither of us says a word until I can't stand the silence. "Chase, if you didn't send the message . . ." But I can't finish it.

So he does. "My dad did." He stares at his hands. "I was afraid of that."

"But why would he do that? Why would he tell me to meet you at the school?"

Chase still won't look at me. "I don't know."

He's hanging over the steering wheel as if his bones have dissolved from his body. He knows something. When we drove away from the Johnson place, I sensed something wasn't right with him. "Chase," I whisper, "you have to tell me what's going on."

Finally, he looks at me. "I think my dad is the stalker."

"What? That's crazy! Your dad is the sheriff! Why would he stalk me?"

Chase is shaking his head. "He's not. He didn't. Not really. Not *stalk*. I'm sure he didn't mean to hurt you, Hope. He just wanted to scare you."

"Well, he did that all right! But it doesn't make sense. Why would he—?"

"He wanted us to stop investigating. Dad's a control freak,

Hope. I knew he didn't like me blowing him off and seeing you anyway. But I didn't start figuring things out until this afternoon, after we saw him at Caroline Johnson's. I've never seen him that desperate. There was something in his eyes." He puts his hand on my head and strokes my hair. "He's not a stalker, Hope. He probably just didn't know what else to do— and I'm not defending him. Believe me, if I'd known he was the one calling you, I would have made him stop. He kept telling me to leave it alone, and—"

"That's it! *Leave it alone!*" Those words have been circling like a tornado in my brain. "Chase, that's what the stalker said on the phone, and it's what your dad said this afternoon." The pieces click together. I should have figured it out before now. "Could your dad get a pickup from that police impound?"

Chase nods. "He can drive anything on that lot, and nobody knows or cares."

I don't know whether to be relieved that the stalker is the sheriff . . . or terrified that the sheriff is the stalker. "So why did he want me to show up at the school lot tonight?"

Chase's lips tighten. He sticks the key into the ignition. "I don't know, but we're going to find out."

Chase drives through the fast-food parking lot to come in behind the school. He stops just inside the fence, too far away for us to see much. "I know he's out there, watching."

I scan the field, imagining myself walking across the parking lot, calling Chase's name, no answer but the wind, a warm August breeze. I'd get closer and closer to the tree. Maybe I'd sit there, waiting. And then what? What would he have done?

A flash of white shines from behind the big oak, the one I scraped. "Chase, there! Behind the tree."

"I see him." He swears under his breath. His eyes narrow to black slits. "I've spent half my life trying to be like him, trying to be who he wanted me to be. Perfect son. Perfect student. Perfect pitcher. Not anymore."

"Chase? What are you going to do? Chase!"

He doesn't answer me. He backs the car up, then eases it all the way around the lot until the truck is in full view. Without a glance at me, he floors the accelerator. The car squeals and shoots forward, back tires skidding, then righting to aim us directly at the pickup.

I scream. We're going to ram into that truck. "Chase!"

Inches away, he slams the brakes. I catch myself, hands braced on the dashboard. The car swerves. I feel a *thunk*. I open my eyes and see that we've bashed in the door of the white pickup truck, pinning it to the tree.

Sheriff Wells swears so loud I hear the words, the hate, through our closed windows. Chase jumps out of the car, leaving the driver's door open. He waits, legs spread, hands on hips, while his dad struggles to get out of the truck. But the driver's door is blocked by our car, and the passenger's door is smashed against the tree. He kneels at his window and lets out a string of cussing.

Midway through cursing the day Chase was born, the sheriff stops. I think he notices me in the car for the first time. His glare raises the tiny hairs at the base of my neck. Nobody has ever looked at me with so much hate before. I want to curl up in a ball on the floor of the car.

"Are you done?" Chase asks his father. He takes the ground between them in three strides until he's face to face with his dad, still trapped inside the cab. My Chase is strong and fearless, and he's not backing down a single step.

I want to be with him. He's standing up to his dad for me. I open the car door and start to get out, but my seat belt yanks me back. Fumbling with it, I manage to get free and step outside. Without glancing at the sheriff, I walk around the car to stand beside Chase. He and his dad are inches apart, locked in a stare-down.

"I asked you if you're finished." Chase's voice is hard, controlled.

"Finished?" Sheriff says, shifting his weight from one knee to the other, still caged inside the truck. His head has to bow to keep from hitting the ceiling. He rolls down the truck's window, but it won't go past halfway.

"Finished stalking Hope?" Chase says.

"I wasn't stalking anybody." Sheriff Wells turns to me. "I was just trying to get you to stop nosing around in things you had no business in. You should have left it alone. Then I wouldn't have had to—"

"Stalk me?" I finish his sentence. "How could you do that? You're supposed to be . . . I don't know . . . a protector. Not a stalker." I feel Chase's hand wrap around mine.

"You're really something, Dad," Chase says.

"You don't understand. You're just kids! You are nothing but a child, Chase!" Sheriff Wells shouts. He turns to me. "Look. I know you want to get your brother off, but you're out of your league. You're just going to make the jury send Jeremy to prison, instead of a mental hospital, where he belongs."

"You have no right to say where my brother belongs!" I shout. "You don't know Jeremy. And you don't know me."

"What were you going to do if I hadn't shown up, Dad?" Chase demands. "What would have happened tonight if Hope had come here alone, like you planned? Huh? Answer me!"

"Quit yelling!" Sheriff Wells shouts back. "Don't talk crazy. I'd never do anything to the girl. I figured she'd show and you wouldn't, and that would be the end of it. She'd think you stood her up, that you were done with her for good, which is what you should be."

"I'm done, all right," Chase says. "Only not with her. With you."

32

Rita is sound asleep when I get back home. I want to wake her up and tell her what happened. I want her to know that it wasn't just kids trying to scare me. It was Sheriff Matthew Wells, someone who should be looking out for kids like me, for kids like Jeremy.

I open her bedroom door and start to go in when I realize I'm about to wake up my mother for a mother-daughter talk. It's ridiculous. I can't explain why I want to talk to Rita after so many years of not talking to her.

I shake off the notion, step back out of her room, and close the door. I need sleep. So does she. I want her to be the best witness for Jeremy she can be tomorrow.

In the morning, Rita tries on every outfit in her closet as if she's going for an audition. She settles on a peach blouse and a straight black skirt that's a little small for her, but not too bad. This is definitely the most courtworthy outfit in her closet. After trying her hair up, then down, she compromises, pulling the top part back and letting the rest hang in bright yellow waves. She looks pretty good . . . until she adds giant hoop earrings I can't talk her out of wearing.

"How about you let me wear one of those necklaces you used to make?" Rita asks. "The ones with those little stones from the lake?"

I'm amazed she even knows about my mermaid tears. "Sure, Rita. Hang on." I find a necklace with a piece of sea glass a little darker than Rita's blouse, and I put it on her.

Rita fingers the necklace. "That's real nice. Real nice, Hope."

I ride with her to the courthouse. She checks herself out in the rearview mirror at least a dozen times, nearly ramming into the back of a police car at the courthouse intersection. "Good luck, Rita," I tell her as she steps out of the car.

"Don't you worry none, Hopeless. Rita has everything under control."

Chase is already there. I slide in next to him, in the seat I've sat in ever since I testified. I can't believe it could all be over today, except for the closing arguments from the lawyers. Rita takes a seat in the first row, behind the defense table. Jeremy is already restless, his hands flying over the table's imaginary keyboard. It's too early for him to be this nervous.

I watch as Jeremy takes something from his pocket. The aspirin bottle? I can't believe they let him keep it. But it's not the same bottle I gave him. It's bigger, a different shape. Somebody has given my brother an empty bottle. I'm so grateful that I thank God for every drop of kindness left in the world, this being one of those drops.

Rita swears on the Bible, her voice loud and dramatic, like

she's kicking off her audition. She takes her seat and crosses her legs.

Jerking his tie to one side, Raymond gets up from his seat behind the defense table. He walks right up to the witness box. "Good morning, Mrs. Long," Raymond says.

Rita gives him her biggest, fakest smile, but maybe the jury won't know it's fake. "Good morning, Mr. Munroe," she says.

Raymond starts out kind of slow . . . and dull and boring. He walks Rita through her life, or parts of it, growing up in Grain and then moving back here with me and Jeremy three years ago. She tells the court about her parents being dead and about how she works at the Colonial Café. To hear Rita tell this, you'd think she was one of those heroic and stoic single mothers who fight off the world in order to raise their children.

Then Raymond zeroes in on Jeremy.

RAYMOND: When did you first notice there was something, well, wrong with your son?

RITA: I knew right away. A mother knows these things. He just wasn't right, that's all.

RAYMOND: Go on.

RITA: Well, the older he got, the more *insane-like* he got. When he went to school, them teachers didn't know what to do with him. I'd get these phone calls from the principal that Jeremy wasn't paying attention. He didn't talk. He didn't get on with the other kids. Well, it hasn't been easy raising two kids anyhow, all by myself. And then I get this one, who's messed up in his head.

RAYMOND: How old was Jeremy when he quit talking?

RITA: Six or seven, I guess. Or maybe more like nine. I'm not
    sure. But that ought to tell you all you need to know about
    Jeremy. The boy can talk—all the doctors agree on that
    one. He just *won't* talk.

I want to stand up and scream at both of them. Raymond
and I agreed to stop making my brother out as insane and start
showing he wasn't the only one who could have killed Coach.
Raymond is supposed to be creating doubt, the reasonable
kind of doubt, like that Caroline Johnson might have done it.

Clearly, Raymond and Rita have been plotting strategy
without me. They've shut me out, just like before. And it's
not fair. Rita conspires with Bob, with Coach Johnson, with
Raymond—with everybody except me.

Furious, I whisper to Chase, "Why are they doing this?
They're trying to make Jeremy look crazy again."

He whispers back, "I think they have to, Hope. Raymond
probably didn't like Caroline Johnson's testimony. Maybe he's
afraid she made Jeremy look too guilty. I think he's just covering all his bases."

I don't want Chase to be right.

I listen to a couple more Crazy Jeremy stories that I can
tell Rita and Raymond have cooked up together. And then
Rita, sounding too confident, launches off on her own. I
cringe when I hear her start the next story, and I'm pretty sure
Raymond has no idea what's coming.

RITA: Okay. Here's another one. Jeremy has always been real
    big on God and church—not that that makes you crazy

necessarily, if you know what I mean. Even as a baby, he loved those hymns and them big brick churches.

RAYMOND: Uh-huh.

RITA: I've never been much of a churchgoer, so the church bus would come by for the kids on a Sunday morning. This was when we were living in Chicago, I think. Yeah, that's it. Well, anyways, Jeremy came home from one of those Sunday school meetings all excited. He still wouldn't talk, but he wrote in great big letters on his notebook paper: "How did you and God meet?" "What?" I asked him. He wrote again: "How did you and God meet and fall in love?" Well, come to find out, their lesson that day was on God the Father. Some teacher had told him God was his father. I've always told the boy he don't have no father. Well, it's easier that way for him. So that kid was all excited thinking he'd found out who his father was. God! And he wanted to know how I met his father. That boy. Another time, he—

RAYMOND: Mrs. Long, let's get back to Jeremy and the deceased. Did Jeremy like John Johnson?

RITA: He liked him fine. He loved going to ball games. He even loved shoveling sh—uh, manure out of them stalls. You'd have thought he had the most important job in the world.

RAYMOND: And you can't think of a single logical reason why Jeremy would want John Johnson dead?

RITA: Of course not.

RAYMOND: Thank you.

Rita starts to get up, but Prosecutor Keller is on his feet and heading straight for her. I shiver remembering the look on

Keller's face the second I realized he'd led me right into his trap. I pray Rita doesn't have a trap waiting for her.

KELLER: Good day, Ms. Long. I won't keep you, I promise. Just a few questions to clear up a couple of matters.

RITA: You go right ahead.

KELLER: Let me see if I have this straight. You told your son that he didn't have a father?

RITA: It was easier than going through the whole story with him, you know? He wouldn't have understood.

KELLER: But, of course, Jeremy does have a father?

RITA: Sure. I'm no Virgin Mary, if that's what you mean. But he might as well not have had one, for all the good it did him.

KELLER: I'd like to explore that a bit. Tell me about Jeremy's father, if you—

RAYMOND: I object! Jeremy's heritage is irrelevant and immaterial.

JUDGE: Mr. Keller?

KELLER: I believe I can prove it is highly relevant, Your Honor. If you'll allow me to make the connection, I'm confident the court will agree. Besides, the witness has opened the door. She brought up the subject of Jeremy's father.

RITA: I did no such thing!

JUDGE: The witness will refrain from comments unless directed to answer. Mr. Munroe, I'm afraid Mr. Keller has a point. Your witness opened the door. But, Mr. Keller, make your point quickly and move along, understood? Now, Mrs. Long, please answer the question.

RITA: What question? I can't remember the question.

KELLER: That's all right. Let me rephrase. In fact, let's back up just a bit. You said you went to high school in Grain, isn't that right?

RITA: Part of high school.

KELLER: Why did you leave?

RITA: I felt like it.

KELLER: I see. You left in the middle of your sophomore year. Is that correct?

RITA: I suppose.

KELLER: Either you did or you didn't. Which is it, Ms. Long?

RITA: Fine. I left during my sophomore year. Are you happy?

KELLER: Were you dating anyone at the time?

RITA: Do I have to answer this?

RAYMOND: I object to this line of questioning!

JUDGE: Mr. Keller, the court asked you to move along with this line of questioning. Move along. I'll overrule the objection, but the clock is ticking, Mr. Keller. Mrs. Long, answer the question.

RITA: Yeah, I was dating. So what? Maybe you didn't date in high school, but the rest of us did. And last time I looked, it wasn't a crime.

KELLER: You and John Johnson were in high school at the same time, isn't that true?

RITA: So were a lot of other people in this town.

KELLER: But John—I think you called him Jay Jay—and you, you liked each other. You dated, went steady, whatever they were calling it then?

I am in the middle of a train wreck. I'm tied to the railroad tracks, and the train is coming fast. Rita feels it too. She's

270

acting all cocky, but I see through that act to her fear. I can count on one hand the number of times I've seen her scared, and this is one of those times. I glance over at Jeremy and see that he's full-on watching this happen. His empty bottle sits on the defense table, as if he's forgotten about it. He is watching Rita, and he's not breathing.

Something bad, very bad, is coming.

33

KELLER: Ms. Long, I'll ask you again. Were you and John Johnson in an exclusive dating relationship in high school?

RITA: Yeah. So what? That was a long time ago, in case you don't know that. I dated a lot.

KELLER: But that year, were you in an exclusive relationship with the deceased, John Johnson? Or did you sleep around?

RAYMOND: I object!

RITA: So do I!

JUDGE: Overruled. But, Mr. Keller, I'm pulling in your chain. Get to it.

KELLER: I'm sorry, Your Honor. Ms. Long, I don't know how else to ask this. And I apologize if the question embarrasses you. Were you Jay Jay's girlfriend? Did you sleep with him?

RITA: Yes. Okay. Yes, I was his girlfriend. And I did sleep with him, but I didn't sleep around. Just him. You can ask anybody.

KELLER: Thank you. I have. Let's change the subject for a minute.

RITA: Good idea.

KELLER: You ran away from Grain how long ago?

RITA: About twenty years. I couldn't take it here anymore.

KELLER: And yet, here you are. You came back. Why was that?

I'm getting a sick feeling in my stomach. I think I know where this is going. How could I have been stupid enough not to guess it before now?

Rita is rattling on, like she does when she gets nervous. Raymond has to have told her what he told me: Keep your answers short. Stay on point. Don't offer up information not asked for. But she won't stop talking, and I know where it's going to get her, to get Jeremy.

"I think my parents were too old to be parents, God rest their souls." Rita crosses herself, but she's never been Catholic. I think she does it wrong. "They're both dead now, so I suppose that's why I came back. I could still have a fresh start here. I figured I could get a job waitressing."

Keller moves in closer, the predator creeping toward his prey. "About twenty years?" He nods, as if calculating, counting on invisible fingers. He turns and looks at Jeremy. "How old is your son, Ms. Long?"

Jeremy doesn't flinch.

Keller wheels back around to Rita. "Ms. Long, how old is your son?"

Rita stares at the ceiling, then spits it out: "Almost nineteen."

Keller's lip curls up—a grin? a snarl? "Were you pregnant when you left Grain and dropped out of school?"

Rita turns to the judge. "He can't ask me that, can he?"

The judge looks like she feels sorry for Rita.

Raymond's slow on the draw, but he jumps up. "Objection!"

Keller smiles at the judge. "Goes to motive, Your Honor."

Does it? Does it go to motive?

I lean way forward so I can see Jeremy's face more clearly. He's staring at Rita. His eyes are still and deep. He knows. I can see that. Jeremy knows exactly what's coming.

"Overruled," says the judge. "Please answer the question."

"I was pregnant," Rita says softly, not looking at Keller.

"Was the child Jay Jay's?" Keller asks. "Is Jeremy the son of John Johnson?"

The courtroom goes crazy. Everybody's talking at once. The judge bangs her gavel and threatens to clear the courtroom if we don't shut up.

"Do you need me to repeat the question?" Keller shouts. "You're under oath, ma'am."

"I know that!" Rita snaps. "And I don't see what any of this has to do with anything. Yes! Jay Jay was Jeremy's father. Okay? Is that what you wanted? But Jeremy didn't know it."

I haven't taken my eyes off my brother. Rita is wrong. He did know. I can read my brother better than anyone on earth. Jeremy knew that John Johnson was his father. I don't know how or when he discovered it, but I can see the truth in his eyes. There's not a hint of surprise on his face.

Why didn't he tell me, write me a long note in his delicate calligraphy? I thought Jeremy told me everything. How could he have kept this enormous secret from me? I will myself to quit staring at my brother. When I look back to Rita, she's wringing her hands in a way I've never seen her do before. I hate her for keeping this secret, but I almost feel sorry for her too.

Keller isn't finished. "Are you positive John Johnson was Jeremy's father?"

Rita acts insulted. "I told you! I didn't sleep around in high school. I think I ought to know who the father of my baby was."

How many times have I asked her about Jer's father? I try to picture the two of them together, Rita and Jay Jay. But I can't. He was quiet, patient, good-natured. I don't think I ever saw him say more than a couple of words to Rita. She never talked about him. On the other hand, I have a dozen memories of Jeremy and Coach together. Jeremy and his father: in the barn, at the ballpark, with the horses.

I try to listen to what else Keller will make Rita say.

KELLER: Did you and Jay Jay pick up where you left off when you returned to Grain?

RITA: No!

KELLER: But he gave Jeremy a job, didn't he? And he took the boy under his wing, let him help out at ball games. Weren't the two of you having an affair?

RITA: We were not having an affair!

KELLER: But Mr. Johnson gave you money. Isn't that right?

RITA: So what? He should have been giving me child support all those years. It was the least he could do to try to make up for that.

KELLER: How much was he paying you?

RITA: Oh, he was real generous at first. Helped us with the

security deposit on that little house we rent. And he helped with rent.

KELLER: At first? You said he was generous at first? When was that?

RITA: When I first told him Jeremy was his son.

KELLER: And when was that?

RITA: Right after we moved here. So about three years ago.

KELLER: Not before then?

RITA: That's what I said. I'd started a new life for myself, and it didn't include a husband and father. I didn't need him trailing after me. No way I was going to get stuck in this town my whole life.

KELLER: But things changed when you moved back and told him Jeremy was his son? He paid you money, helped with the bills . . . at first?

RITA: Yeah. Then he stopped, refused to pay me a penny.

KELLER: When did he stop giving you money?

RITA: Last spring.

KELLER: Why did he quit paying?

RITA: He said he didn't have it. He said he had hospital bills and responsibilities. What did he think *we* were? We were his responsibilities too.

KELLER: Is that what Jeremy thought?

RITA: Jeremy? He never knew about Jay Jay or the money.

KELLER: I find that hard to believe. Didn't Jay Jay want to tell Jeremy he was his father?

RITA: Huh-uh. He was the one who didn't want Jeremy to know. I didn't care either way.

KELLER: Why? Why would John, Jay Jay, want to keep Jeremy a secret?

RITA: Because of his wife having the cancer and all. She couldn't have children, he said. He didn't want her to know that he already had one.

KELLER: But you told Jeremy anyway, didn't you?

RITA: No! I didn't tell him nothing. Jeremy didn't know.

KELLER: Ms. Long, when was the last time you saw John Johnson alive?

It seems like a full minute of silence passes. I think the courtroom is holding its breath.

KELLER: Your Honor, will you please instruct the witness to answer the question?

JUDGE: Mrs. Long, please answer the question.

RITA: I don't remember.

KELLER: I'll ask you again. If you lie, you'll be subject to a charge of perjury. Do you understand? One more time. When was the last time you saw the deceased?

RITA: That morning. The morning of the murder. I stopped by the stable.

I cannot breathe. Rita didn't say anything to me about seeing Coach then or any other time. "What time was this?" Keller presses.

"Just after seven," Rita mumbles.

"Please speak up," Keller asks, but there's no politeness in his voice. "What time was it, and how do you remember the time?"

Rita squeezes her lips together so hard it looks like she doesn't have teeth. "It was seven-oh-seven, and I know

277

because they said so on the radio right before I shut off the engine, okay? Station seventy-point-seven at seven-oh-seven. AM radio in the AM."

"Where exactly did you find Mr. Johnson that morning?" Keller asks. I get the feeling that he knows the answer to every question before Rita opens her mouth.

"I told you. In . . . the barn." Rita cocks her head at him, then looks down.

"Was Jeremy with you?" Keller asks.

"No!" Rita snaps. "I was going home from Bob's, but I decided to stop by the barn and talk to Jay Jay face to face about the money he owed me."

"So you argued?" Keller asks.

Rita squirms in her seat. "He owed me child support. I had that coming. I just wanted what was rightly mine. He had no right to stop paying. Jeremy was his son, his flesh and blood! And we needed the money. I could have asked twice what I did. But I didn't."

"I understand," Keller says, like he's suddenly on Rita's side. "You and Jeremy deserved that money, and he was cutting you off."

"Exactly!" Rita sits up straighter.

"When you told Jay Jay that you and Jeremy deserved that money, were you loud?" Keller asks.

"Yeah. You ever argue without being loud?" Rita challenges.

"Precisely where did this argument take place?" Keller asks.

"Near one of the back stalls. I had heels on, and I remember that I had to watch where I was stepping and walk way to the back because Jay Jay wouldn't come up front and talk."

"So if someone had been in the stable, for example, they would have heard you?" Keller asks.

"They'd have heard us. But nobody was there," Rita says.

"You're wrong about that." Keller turns and points at Jeremy. "Your son was there."

Rita gasps. She shakes her head. "No. That can't be. He never . . . He didn't . . ."

Raymond jumps to his feet and objects all over the place. He yells phrases like "facts out of evidence" and "move for a mistrial" and other things I can't hear because everybody is shouting. I don't have any idea how Keller knows what he does about Jeremy finding out Coach was his dad that morning, but I recognize truth when I hear it. And that's truth. Jeremy knew. He didn't know before that morning, so he must have heard Rita screaming it. That's why he doesn't want to see me, why he won't write to me. He couldn't keep that secret if he did.

The judge is angrier than I've ever seen her. She pounds her gavel and orders the courtroom cleared.

I watch Rita staring at Jeremy. Tears stream down her face. Mascara streaks her cheeks like tribal paint. Over and over again, she mutters, "I'm sorry, Jeremy. I'm so sorry. I didn't know. I just didn't know."

Chase and I are ushered out of the courtroom like everybody else. The second we're outside, I dash around the corner and hurl. I vomit again and again until nothing else is in me.

Rita, how could you?

I don't know what will happen in the courtroom, or what it will mean. But I do know this for sure. My mother has just given the jury the one thing they didn't have—motive.

34

Chase drives me around and tries to talk me down, but I'm too angry. It's all so unbelievable, even for Rita. "All that time," I say, to myself as much as to Chase, "she knew who Jeremy's father was, and she didn't tell him? I don't care if Coach wanted Jeremy to know or not. *Jeremy* wanted to know! Didn't that count for anything?"

"You really didn't have any idea, did you?" Chase says. Mostly, he's let me rant and has just been circling Grain while I blow off steam.

I glare at him. "Are you kidding? There's no way I would have kept it secret if I'd known."

"Maybe your mother was trying to do what she thought was best for Jeremy."

"Rita?" I let out a one-note laugh that has no laughter in it. "She did what she thought was best for Rita. It's what she always does." I think about those pictures of Jeremy in Coach's desk, Jer's special color wheels pinned up on the wall in his office. "They might have had a relationship, Chase. A shot at a father-and-son relationship, if Rita had told Jeremy the truth."

Chase sighs. "I don't know. Father-son relationships are overrated, if you ask me."

"You don't mean that. I've missed my father my whole life, and I never got to know him in the first place."

He reaches across the seat and puts his hand on the back of my neck. "Ready to go home?"

Rita is waiting for me when I walk in. "Don't start, Hope," she warns the minute I close the door.

I stare at her. Her hair is a mess. She's in that same white slip. And she's drinking, not bothering with a glass. She tilts her head back and gulps. I watch the whiskey travel down her throat, making waves in her neck.

"How could you do that to Jeremy?" My voice is quiet, but I'm screaming inside.

She shakes her head, coughs, then chokes out her answer. "I didn't do nothing to that boy."

"True enough," I admit. "You didn't tell him he had a great father, who really cared about him."

"Jay Jay didn't want the kid to know!" Rita screams.

"Since when do you care what anyone else wants?" The anger is bubbling up now. "You didn't tell Jeremy because you were afraid Coach would stop giving you money. Was he paying to keep you quiet? That's blackmail, Rita."

"That's not the way it was." She sprawls on the couch, the bottle cradled between her knees. "He didn't want his wife to find out."

"So you took advantage of that. You made him pay you to keep your mouth shut." I can see on her face that I'm right.

"You don't understand," she moans.

"And when *Jay Jay* stopped paying, why didn't you tell Jer then? He would have been so happy, Rita. Now he won't ever have that, the feeling that he has a father who loves him. You should have told him."

"Jeremy was all right. He was already spending lots of time with Jay Jay. I thought I could change Jay Jay's mind. I thought I could get him to start paying up again." She shoves her hair out of her face and takes another drink.

"That's what you were doing the day he was murdered? Trying to get more money out of him? What happened, Rita? What really happened that morning?"

"Get away from me." She says this because I've slipped in front of her, eased onto the coffee table so we're face to face.

"Tell me the truth. Did you lose your temper?" I've seen Rita lose her temper. I've felt her temper. "You did, didn't you?" I can see it in my mind—Rita exploding in front of Coach, grabbing the bat, swinging it. "You killed him. And you're letting Jeremy take the blame." Pieces fall together when I say this. "Is that why you didn't tell anybody, even Raymond, that you went to the stable that morning? That you talked to Coach? That you—?"

"Shut up! I didn't—!"

But it's making sense now. "Jeremy saw you. He saw you kill Coach. And he's trying to protect you! He's covering up for *you*! *That's* why he wouldn't see me. He knows I'd get the truth out of him."

"You're as crazy as he is." Rita shoves me, but I won't give an inch. "Why would I kill Jay Jay?"

"How should I know why you do anything? Maybe you couldn't stand Jeremy having another parent, a *good* parent, in his life. Maybe you killed him for that."

"Don't be a fool." She takes another swig, a big one this time.

"You couldn't stand for Jeremy to have a real parent, someone who was kind to him. Was it like that with *my* father, Rita? Were you glad when my father got killed too?" Those dreamlike images of my father shoot through my brain, too fast for me to tell whether they're real or imagined. "Two fathers, two sudden deaths. Quite a coincidence . . . Or was it? Was it, Rita?"

She shrugs. "You're talking crazy."

"Rita, did you kill my father too?"

Rita raises her arm and aims the back of her hand toward me. I brace myself for a slap, but I don't budge. She lowers her arm. "You don't know what you're talking about."

"I remember."

"You were three years old. You don't remember nothing."

"He was wearing a baseball cap. A red cap. And it was sunny."

That makes her look up at me. "How did you . . . ?"

"Tell me what really happened."

"He was run over by a truck. How many times do I have to tell you?"

This is what she's told me every time I've asked. But it's not good enough now. I'm standing up to her. I want answers, real answers. "Why? How did it happen? Why would he be in the street? Did he run out in front of the truck?" I pause because the image is there. My father. Me. And Rita. Rita, her arms outstretched. Then I say it, what I think I've wanted to ask her my whole life. "Did you push him?"

Again, I think she's going to hit me, but I don't care. I don't flinch, or duck, or scoot back to break the impact. "Did you kill him? Did you push my father in front of that truck because you were tired of him? Because *he* wouldn't pay you anymore? Rita! Did you kill him too?"

"You crazy little—!" Her teeth are clenched. Her eyes are watering. She stands up, weaving from side to side. Then she leans forward and gets in my face. I smell her stale breath, the liquor like vomit in her mouth. "If anybody killed your father, it was you."

I start to yell back at her, but I stop. I remember something—an image in black and white. They're never in black and white. It's blurry too. I think it must be cloudy, but then the day clears, and it's sunny. I can see a tall, thin man in a baseball cap. The red cap is the only color in the scene. I'm looking up at him, and he seems like the tallest person in the world—in my world, at least. I walk away, laughing. The ground is dry and lumpy, and it's hard to walk without trip-ping. The picture is joined by other images, one after the other, fast, like animation, a jagged film. A shaggy puppy dances around my feet, then dashes ahead of me. I laugh and run after it. There's a curb, and I spread my arms to step down from the grass to the pavement. Cars are parked there, but I follow the puppy and go between them. Someone's yelling at me from behind. It's a game, so I keep going, chasing Puppy. I hear footsteps behind me and more shouts from Daddy, who lets me call him Daddy and wants Jeremy to do the same. I hear thunder from the street and screeching that makes me stop so I can cover my ears. The next thing I know, I am lifted off the ground, as if an angel has flown by and picked me up. Only instead of carrying me, the angel tosses me like a football. I land hard, and it hurts. I cry and scream because I'm scared now. People run at me, past me, into the street. The truck driver stumbles out of his cab. I see his face, looking like he's just seen that angel and doesn't know what to make of it. "I tried to stop! I tried to stop!" He says this over and over. And Rita is screaming, and I want her to quit, but she won't. She keeps screaming and screaming and never stops.

I gasp for air. I'm sitting in the living room, staring at the empty couch. I am light-headed, and I think I'm going to be sick again.

Rita is right. I caused my father's death.

What's wrong with us? Are we all killers? Murderers? Is Rita? Is Jeremy?

Am I?

35

After the weekend, the prosecution takes two days to sum up its case and for Keller to give his closing argument. Chase and I sit through all the explanations. Keller brings in his whole team and puts on a grand finale. A short, chubby lab guy uses four-color art to reexplain diagrams of the blood evidence found at the scene and on the bat, in spite of whatever Jer did to wash it off. A gorgeous assistant prosecutor, with long black hair and a body that three of the jurors can't stop staring at, sets up a miniature stable, complete with horses and a baseball bat, just to show the jury who stood where and what the prosecution has been claiming all along took place, that Jeremy Long willfully bludgeoned to death his father, John Johnson.

Life is as miserable out of court as it is in court. Rita and I aren't speaking, which isn't such a big loss. I've tried to put myself in her shoes and imagine what it might do to a person to see her husband crushed by a truck. She's apologized for blurting out something she kept to herself all these years. In her own way, I guess, Rita has tried to take back what she said about me killing my father.

But T.J. was right. Some things you can't take back.

And sometimes you can't go back to the way things were. I saw T.J. again. He was standing on the sidewalk outside my house when I left for work Saturday morning. We stared at each other for a minute or two. He didn't scare me this time, but I still found nothing to say to him. Finally, I kept walking, passing him without looking back.

"Hope?"

I stopped but I didn't turn around. I waited, wanting him to say more. I yearned to hear the old T.J. and know he was still there. But he didn't say anything else. So, after a few seconds, I walked off again. I didn't stop until I got all the way to the Colonial. And when I looked back, I saw that T.J. hadn't followed me.

But the worst is that something's happening between Chase and me, and I don't know what it is, unless he can sense that I killed my own father. Of course I haven't told him. When he's dropped me off after court, I haven't asked him to stay, and he hasn't asked me to go with him. Maybe we're both just too tired.

I've thought about my father and what happened the day he was killed. I've gone over and over it enough to be as depressed as I've ever been. Then I started writing about everything to Jeremy. I wrote *for* him too, still in my chicken-scratch penmanship, pretending I was writing his fancy, swirling letters. We argued. "Jeremy," I said, "I killed my own father!" And Jer said back, "You were three, Hope." And I said, "But if I hadn't run into the road, he wouldn't have run after me. It was my fault!" "You were three," Jeremy replied. "How much fault could you have had in you? You didn't mean to hurt anybody." We argued more, and finally Jeremy got in the last word: "Fault, schmalt. You're forgiven because God says so. He's got your back. He's your father too, you know." So even though he wasn't really there, my brother got me through the worst of it.

Still, it's not something I want to tell Chase. Could that explain the distance I feel growing between us?

Chase and I text at night—he's positive Rita isn't the murderer. I think he's wrong, but I don't want to fight him. I'm pretty sure neither of us wants to risk arguing. So we guard our words. We're careful with each other. If I've moved away from Chase, he's moved away from me, too. Maybe it's just that we both know the trial is almost over and things will never be the same.

More than anything, I want to talk to Jeremy. I want to tell him about my father, about what I remember. I want to talk to Jer about Coach. My brother lost his father, and he's had to grieve all by himself.

The night before Raymond's closing, I can't sleep. As I pace the living room, an August moon pushes its way inside the house so I don't need to turn on lights. I miss Jeremy so much that it hurts my chest, my arms, my throat. I didn't know missing could do that.

I wander into Jeremy's room. The moonlight is even brighter here when I open the curtains all the way. I gaze around the room. This is the room of a little boy—baseball curtains, comic books, and his jars. The only poster is pinned to his door, one he made himself. It says: BEYOND HERE, THERE BE DRAGONS. Jeremy told me that's what mapmakers used to write on unknown spaces on maps so travelers would know where they shouldn't go.

Jeremy has been gone from this room for so long, but it still smells like him, like late-season grass and cherry Kool-Aid. I crumple to the floor, then lie on my back and peer up at his shelves of jars. Tomorrow that jury may decide whether or not my brother will ever come home. I want to pray. I know that's what Jeremy's doing. Only he never calls it praying. He just talks to God in his head. He doesn't have to write. Maybe that makes it easier for him to talk to God than to talk to people.

It's not that easy for me, but I close my eyes and try:

Dear God, this is me, Hope, talking to you in my head like Jeremy does. I guess I've clammed up on you like Jer has with the rest of us. Maybe we both got slapped somewhere along the way. You know he didn't do this. You must have seen who actually did. If it's Rita, then I don't know what to say about that. Look, I know Jeremy hears you—you loaned him your song that once. I'm not asking for a whole song—but maybe just a note or two would be good. Thank you. Love, Hope.

Feeling a little better, I sit up too fast and bang my head on Jeremy's bottom shelf. I spin around in time to see Jeremy's glass jars wobble. One jar tips in slow motion and topples off the shelf before I can catch it.

Crash! The jar shatters into pieces that skid across the wood floor. I'm horrified. Jeremy would freak out if he saw this.

I drop to all fours and scramble to pick up the lid. It's

289

rimmed with broken glass, and my finger slices across it, mingling blood with jagged shards. The bottom of the jar lies upside down at my feet. I can make out writing there, something scrawled on the glass in black marker. Carefully, I examine the bottom of the jar. It says: **9:23 a.m., May 4.** The date is there too, faded and harder to read. But I make it out—it's three years ago, about the time Rita moved us to Ohio.

I'm stumped. Was Jeremy dating the time he got his jars? I guess it makes as much sense as anything else in this room. I think I may have seen him scribbling on the bottom of a jar a couple of times. Since he's always been so private about his collection, I never paid much attention.

I start to clean up the mess when I see a piece of paper wedged underneath the lid of the broken jar. I pull it out and unfold it, careful not to drip blood from my cut finger onto the paper. The writing is Jeremy's tight, controlled calligraphy, the only thing controlled in his life. I hold the slip of paper up to the moonlight. It says: **Air on the day Rita smiled and Yellow Cat purred.**

Yellow Cat. The old yellow cat that was living in this house before we rented it, the cat Rita made us turn over to the animal control people.

Why would Jeremy write that?

I pick up another jar, a tall, skinny one that once held olives for Rita's martinis. I remember the night—about a year ago?—when Rita caught Jeremy dumping out an almost full jar of olives. He needed a jar, and we were all out of empties. If Rita hadn't been so drunk, I think she would have killed him. I hid him under my bed until she got over it.

My mind is already flashing images at the speed of light.

Jeremy, his arms raised above his head, like thin branches against a black sky. While his bony fingers clasp a lid in one hand, an empty jar in the other, he sweeps the sky like he's catching fireflies . . . or maybe stars. Then, with angel eyes and a devilish grin, he twists the lid on tight, like the earth might stop spinning if he didn't do it right.

On the bottom of this olive jar is a date, close to a year and a half ago, and the time: 10:22 p.m. I open the jar and turn over the lid. I knew it. There's a piece of paper stuck there, under the lid. I can't unfold it fast enough. It reads: **Air on a perfect starry night, sprinkled with Hope's laughter.**

Air? That's it. Air. My brother didn't collect empty jars. He collected air. Did this jar contain the air from one of our stargazing nights a year and a half ago? Had Jeremy trapped that night in an olive jar, saved that moment? I can almost feel a chill in the air and those stars loosed in his room, mingling with atoms of Kool-Aid and grass.

I look around at the dozens and dozens and dozens of glass jars filled with Jeremy's collectible moments. *Air.* My mind is a slide show on speed: Jeremy, his jar sweeping air above his head as he rides that pinto around the pasture; air captured as the church choir sings "Amazing Grace"; air gathered from the top of a slide when I took him to the park. Jeremy taking a canning jar from a store in Salina, Kansas, and running straight to the middle of a wheat field. Did he capture the scent of grain and the feel of dust and sunshine? In Chicago, Jeremy grabbing jars from the fridge and dumping their contents on the floor . . . to fill the jars with memories.

How long has he been collecting air? When did he start? I try to remember.

There's a system to the jars. If I know my brother at all, he's ordered this world of glass and air. Where I'm standing, the jars are three years old. I want to know when he started. I follow the shelf all the way back to the door. First shelf, first jar, a peanut butter jar. I turn it over and check the bottom. It's hard to make out, but I can read the month, February, and the year—a decade ago, the year my brother stopped talking. I remember we came home to our shack in Minneapolis, and Jeremy scooped out the last drop of peanut butter, eating it right from the jar and not giving me any. I thought he was mad on account of Rita hitting him for no reason.

I know I shouldn't open this jar. I have no right. Jeremy has saved the air of that day for over ten years. He wouldn't want that day to show up in his room now. But I can't help myself. I can't keep my fingers from turning the lid, from lifting it off, from stripping the yellowed paper away from the lid, from unfolding the secret message: **Air from the day Jeremy Long stopped talking.**

"Jeremy, Jeremy, Jeremy." I hug the jar and slide to the floor, where I rock back and forth. Tears blur the air swirling in Jeremy's bedroom. How could I have missed it? I should have known the jars meant more than empty glass.

I survey the walls of shelves, all full except for one, the bottom shelf across the room, where half a dozen jars have started a new row. The last row? My heart speeds up. Jeremy was collecting jars, collecting air, right up to the day of the murder. He always had his pack with him and empty jars in the pack. Did he collect air that morning?

I get to my feet so fast that I almost drop the jar I'm

holding. I set the peanut butter jar back down, right where it was. Then I hurry to the other side of the room, to the shelf farthest away from the beginning shelf. I want the end, the last jar.

There are four jars dated the morning of the murder. I want to rip off the lids to the jars right now and see what Jeremy collected that morning. Did he save air when he learned Coach was his father? He would have. He wouldn't have let that moment escape. Did he keep collecting air as things kept happening? He couldn't stop the events, but he could capture them. Four jars. Four jars with the date of the murder, and the last one has a dark smear on the side of the lid. A smear of dried blood.

I have to know. I put one hand on the first lid. I am set, ready to turn, to release that air and see what he wrote.

But I can't. What if this is evidence now? It might prove beyond a reasonable doubt that Jeremy knew Coach Johnson was his father. It might prove he was there. What if this is bad evidence, *incriminating* evidence?

Slowly, I let go of the lid. I know Jeremy didn't murder Coach. I know it without a shadow of a doubt. But I think he saw it happen. And I believe what he saw might be captured in these jars of air. Did he see who murdered his father?

Was it his mother?

I am holding living witnesses, air particles that were there the day of the murder. These jars could prove that my brother is innocent.

I don't remember Raymond's number, so I have to look it up in the phone book. It's past midnight.

Mrs. Munroe answers. "Yes?"

"I'm sorry to call so late, but it's an emergency. Could I speak to Raymond, please?"

"Just a minute, Hope. I'll get him."

It's way more than a minute before I hear Raymond on the phone. "Hope, what's wrong?"

"I'm sorry. I didn't mean to wake you up, but—"

"You didn't," Raymond says. "I've been working on my closing argument. I think we're going to have to stick with the insanity plea."

"No!"

"I know you don't want to go that way, but you heard Keller's closing, didn't you? I'm afraid your mother gave them the missing piece, motive. Coach was Jeremy's father, a father who refused to acknowledge him. No, I'm sorry, Hope, but—"

"But I have something to show you, Raymond! Something the jury has to see. I think it will prove Jeremy didn't kill Coach, and I think it will prove who did."

"Hope, it's too late to—"

"Just hear me out, Raymond. Please?" I can tell he thinks I'm making it up. There's a silence over the phone. Then Raymond sighs. "Okay. But make it fast, Hope. I have to close tomorrow, no matter what."

I tell Raymond about the jars, the air, the dates, everything. I read him the notes from the three jars I opened, one accidentally, two on purpose. And I tell him about the four jars, the murder jars.

He doesn't say anything until I'm done. Finally, he says, so soft-like that I barely hear him, "Imagine that boy collecting air like that, seeing moments and saving them."

I'm proud of Jer for that. "I know."

Then Raymond's tone changes, from awe to something else. Fear? "Hope, what do the jars from the murder date say? Read me the notes."

"I didn't open them, Raymond. I don't think I should. Do you? Won't Keller say that I did it myself? That I made it up to save Jeremy? This way, I can prove I didn't write the notes. I didn't even know what was in them. And the jars, they could do tests on them, right? They could tell they haven't been opened?"

"Wait. Hope. You haven't opened the jars?"

"Not the ones from *that* day."

"Hope, what if one of the jars, the jar with the blood, says: **The day I killed my dad**? Did you think about that?"

I swallow hard. I know Raymond doesn't mean to hurt me. If Jeremy killed his dad, that's exactly how he'd have labeled that jar. "It won't say that. He didn't do it, Raymond. It will be okay. I know Jeremy didn't do it." What I don't want to add is that I think I know who did. I can almost see Rita's name on that note: **The day Rita killed my dad.** Rita's done a lot of bad in her life, but she's the only mother I've ever had.

"Hope, even if those jars clear your brother, I can't use them. I don't even know if I could get any of this before the judge. Trial practice precludes introduction of new and unsubstantiated evidence in a closing argument."

"Raymond, you're smart. You're smart enough to get these jars in. You have to give Jeremy's jars a chance to save him. Please?"

"I don't know. . . ." But I can tell he's thinking.

"You can do it, Raymond. I have faith in you."

295

There's a long silence, but I can hear Raymond breathing, thinking. "Maybe I can't introduce the jars," Raymond says slowly, ". . . but maybe you can."

"Huh?"

"Why not? The prosecutors took two days for their show-and-tell. Keller brought in half his office for their closing. Why couldn't the judge let me have my one assistant?"

"Raymond, do you think it would work? I'm not that great talking, even just to one person, you know? And I'm horrible when I have to speak in front of my class at school." I close my eyes and try to imagine standing up in that courtroom and talking to the jury in front of all those people. It's horrifying.

But Jeremy's in that courtroom. And Jer needs me more than he's ever needed anybody. "If that's what it takes, I'll do it."

"Good. I'll give it a shot if you will," Raymond says.

Raymond and I stay on the phone and talk about the best way to show the jars to the jury and to re-create the crime with them. I scribble notes and ask Raymond questions until I can't think of any more.

Finally, Raymond says, "Hope, we better hang up now. I have a closing to finish, and you have a demonstration to prepare. So, see you in court?"

"See you in court."

I stay up the rest of the night, working on what I'm going to say to the jury. Pulling out my old school note cards, I write something for each jar. I try saying everything out loud over and over.

When I notice the moonlight has switched to sunlight, I jump into the shower and smile to myself, remembering what I told Chase about morning versus night showerers. I guess this shower counts for both.

Rita's still out cold, so I'm on my own for wardrobe selection. I end up picking out the gray skirt and white blouse I wore the first day I testified in court, but adding a wide black belt and my favorite sea glass necklace. The glass is green, shaped like a tear.

When I check myself in the mirror, I still don't look much like a lawyer's assistant, but I'll have to do. I'm all Jeremy's got.

36

I wait until the last minute to wake Rita. She stumbles out of her bedroom, looking like death warmed over. She's sober, but that's about all I can say in her favor. We don't speak to each other, except for me trying to hurry her up. I put ten jars into my backpack, wrapping them in towels. She doesn't even ask what I'm doing, or why I'm taking a backpack to court. Would she try to stop me if she knew?

It takes me twenty minutes to pass through the courthouse turnstile because the guard insists on searching my pack. It isn't easy to convince her that the jars don't have anything deadly in them. Rita doesn't wait for me.

"Where've you been?" Raymond asks as soon as he sees me. He must have been pacing because he's worked up a sweat.

We only have ten minutes to iron out our plan, and Raymond spends most of it on how to convince the judge that the jars are our way of re-creating the crime scene. That's his "legal premise" for bringing in the jars and me.

"I have a bad feeling about this," Raymond says as we enter the courtroom. His feeling is contagious. The room smells like stale pond water and cigars, although it's against the law to smoke in here. Heads turn when Raymond and I walk by the rows. We set off low conversations, tiny buzzes, like bumblebees in our wake.

I'm relieved to see Chase is already here, sitting in the front row, right behind the defense table. As we pass that row, I risk a glance at him. His hair, uncombed, makes him look wildly handsome. His head is in his hands, so I can't see much of his face, but enough to tell he hasn't shaved. I try to catch his eye as we walk toward the judge, but he doesn't look up.

I can't think about Chase now. I can't worry about anything except Jeremy.

My brother is already sitting behind the table, looking like his skin won't hold him, like everything he's knotted up inside is fixing to bust out.

The courtroom grows silent as Raymond and I stand in front of the judge. It's a packed house. I scan the back row, and there's T.J., sitting with his mom. He nods at me, and I nod back. I'm not sure if I'm glad to see him or not. I think I'm a different person than I was when we were best friends. Is it possible to change so fast? All I know is that the old Hope wouldn't be standing here, fighting for a chance to speak in front of everybody. But I am.

Prosecutor Keller strolls up, shoving between Raymond and me so he's closer to the judge than I am. I watch Keller's eyebrows arch up and down, like a couple of woolly worms doing calisthenics. Raymond talks fast. Keller interrupts. Raymond talks louder, waving his arms almost like Jeremy.

"Your Honor, this is ludicrous," Keller says. I think he also says something about Raymond trying to bring elephants into the courtroom, but I'm having trouble focusing. I want to go sit down with Chase and Jeremy. "The defense's entire request is absurd."

"Absurd?" Raymond shouts back. "Absurd is you bringing in half your staff for your high-tech show-and-tell performance and then having the unmitigated gall to accuse *us* of wanting to put on a circus!"

"Mr. Munroe makes a good point, Mr. Keller," the judge observes calmly.

"All I'm asking, Your Honor, is to be allowed one assistant and a few glass jars for demonstration and re-creation," Raymond finishes.

"With glass jars?" Keller mocks.

"Unopened jars," Raymond explains. "And the prosecution is welcome to test each jar for fingerprints and age to ensure they've not been opened by the defense or the defense's assistant, if—"

"Ridiculous!" Keller throws back his head in a fake laugh.

"If it's so ridiculous, then you have nothing to worry about," Raymond says.

"Worry? Who says I'm worried?" Keller snorts. "I just don't want to waste the court's time with a—"

"That'll do," says the judge. "I'll be the *judge* of what wastes the court's time. I've heard enough." She takes her time leaning back in her chair. "I'll allow the defense's request." She turns to Raymond, who is beaming like he's won a gold medal. "But, Mr. Munroe, let me remind you that I'm paying close attention. Be careful out there. And tell your *assistant* to do the same."

I smile up at her, but she doesn't smile back.

It doesn't take long for the trial to officially start up again. This time it's Raymond's turn to talk to the jury. He starts off his closing argument by recalling the nice things people said under oath about Jeremy. I'd like to listen, but I can't. I block out everything except Jeremy and his jars. As quietly as I can, with my back to the jury, I put my backpack up on the defense table and start taking out jars. One by one, I set them in front of me, straightening them, arranging each jar in chronological order. I have notes that go with each jar, if the judge lets me get that far. So I set out all my notes.

Only then do I let myself look at Jeremy. Jer isn't looking at me. He's staring at the jars, his eyes soft, his mouth open, lips turned up slightly, like he's just run into old friends he hasn't seen for years and missed something awful. When I'm all finished lining up the jars, I take Raymond's seat next to Jer.

Raymond is still repeating testimony of the character witnesses, but the jury isn't looking at him. They're watching me. Me and Jeremy. Raymond must see this too, because he stops suddenly. Then he says, "I could go on and on and tell you what you've already heard, but I don't want to do that. Instead, I've brought with me my assistant. I think you'll remember her from when she testified before you in court: Hope Long, Jeremy's sister. I'd like Hope to walk you through what we believe really happened on the day John Johnson was murdered." He comes over and waits for me to get up so he can sit down.

My knees wobble when I stand. Something that doesn't belong in my throat is pounding there. I cough a couple of times as I step around the table and face the jury on the other side of the courtroom. "You guys may be wondering why I brought these empty jars to court this morning," I begin. "These are just a few of over a hundred glass jars my brother has on shelves that go all the way around his room. Jeremy collects them. You already heard that in court." I hate my voice. It's weak and shaky, but I make myself keep going, like I rehearsed. "Collecting empty jars is a weird hobby, but so's collecting stamps or aluminum foil, or string, or Barbies, or glass fairies, or sea glass, right? My whole life, I thought these were empty jars, that Jeremy was collecting the jars themselves. But I found out different last night when I accidentally knocked into a shelf full of these jars. One fell off and broke." I glance at Jeremy. "I'm sorry about that, Jer."

"Louder, Hope," Raymond whispers.

Out of the corner of my eye, I glimpse Keller, itching to stand up and object. I clear my throat and try to speak louder. "Anyway, that's when I discovered that these jars aren't empty at all. And that's why I brought these here—to demonstrate and re-create that day of June eleventh, when somebody murdered John Johnson." Raymond told me to work those words in, so now I have. "See, each jar is labeled on the bottom with a time and a date." I hold up the first two jars, one in each hand, and walk them over to the jury and back. "There are labels on the inside, on bits of paper tucked under the lids, so you can't see them. That's what I discovered when I broke that jar last night. And I discovered something else too. My brother didn't collect empty jars. He collected air. Air and moments and memories."

I let that one sink in while I set down the two jars. "I brought a few jars from different years so you could get an idea of how Jeremy stored things, all in perfect order. Some days, he collected moments that meant a lot to the whole nation or world, like this one, dated **November 4, 2008.** I can read the date on the bottom of the jar, but I can't see the inside label unless I take off the lid, which I don't want to do, if it's all the same to you. I'm pretty sure the label will read something like **Obama is elected president.**"

I pick up a Mason jar, and it strikes me that the glass is the color of Chase's eyes early in the morning. "The date on this one is five years ago, July second. I have no idea what's in here. But if Jeremy doesn't mind, I'd like to find out the same time you do, just to give us a better idea how this all works."

I glance back at Jeremy. He doesn't give me a go-ahead nod, but he doesn't freak out either. I take that as a yes and twist the lid. It takes muscle, and for a second I'm afraid I won't be able to get it off. Then it gives. As I lift that ridged silver lid, I imagine a whoosh of air in my face, and I blink.

"Yep. There's a piece of paper wedged in here." Fingers trembling, I dig out the note and read it, my voice breaking: **Air of a sunlit afternoon in Enid, Oklahoma, when Hope and I write funny notes.**

I bite my lip hard enough to keep back tears. I have no

idea which afternoon that was or why it meant enough to my brother to save. "I can do another jar like this, if you want," I say to the judge. "But I'd rather skip to these last ones. They're all dated June eleventh, the day of the murder."

"Why don't you move on to that day, then, Hope?" The judge widens her eyes at the jury, then turns back to me. "I think the jury understands the collection."

I'm relieved, but I can't remember what's supposed to come next. "Um . . . could you hold on just a minute, please?" I thumb through the note cards I've made up until I get to the right one. "Okay. Got it."

Raymond leans up and whispers, "Talk to the jury, Hope."

"Right." I step closer to the jurors and begin at the beginning. "That morning of June eleventh, Coach Johnson got up early. It was a cloudy morning, but nobody expected rain. He walked to the ballpark, like he did every game day, so he could post the team roster for the day's game." My mind flashes me a picture—not of Coach or the ballpark, but of the roster again, the one I saw in Coach's office, the one with *Chase Wells* crossed out and *T. J. Bowers* written in. I make myself keep going. "Then he went to the barn to do chores. He might have started mucking stalls before Jeremy arrived, just to help him out. We'll never know that."

I go back to the defense table because I need the right jar. "I think that brings us to this next jar. The date is the morning of the murder, and the time is seven-ten a.m." I take the jar over to the jury box and walk it along the rail while each juror leans forward and studies the date, written with black marker on the bottom of the jar. Juror Number Three pulls her glasses out of her purse and puts them on. Juror Number Eight waves me away as soon as I get to him.

"Seven-ten in the morning," I repeat. "That means the air in this jar was collected by Jeremy a few minutes after Rita got to the barn. Remember how Rita was so sure she got there at seven minutes after seven? Seven-oh-seven."

I study the lid of this jar that I think may have held grape jelly once. "I haven't opened this jar before," I tell the jury. "But I'm going to do it right now." I twist the lid in one turn and pick out the label from the underside of the lid. My heart is jumping in my chest, making my hands shake. I can barely unfold the jagged paper. I read: **A fortress of gray clouds as I walk to the barn on game day.** My heart stops thundering. I try not to show how relieved I am, but I shoot up a Jeremy-style prayer of thanks.

"We know that Jeremy got up really early too because he always did. He couldn't wait to put on his Panther uniform. Jer loved game day. He was so excited about the game that he must have stopped to write this note and collect air on his walk to the barn.

"Jeremy makes it to the barn and parks his bat, like always, and maybe his batting gloves—we don't know for sure. He starts to look for Coach, but he hears voices. Arguing. Screaming—at least Rita was. Maybe he'd seen Rita's car, and maybe he hadn't. It doesn't matter. He walks toward the shouting, but Jeremy hates arguing, so he stops, maybe hides.

"And that's when Jeremy hears something he never thought he'd hear. His own mother shouts, 'Jeremy is your son! You better pay up.' Or something like that. Those words

305

would ring in Jeremy's ears. *Your son. Jeremy is your son. Coach's son!* Can you imagine what went through Jeremy's mind? He had a father, the best father in the whole world. Coach was already the best man in Jeremy's world. Now he had a father who was kind and good to him, who loved him."

I can't look at Jeremy. I won't look at Jeremy. He'll make me stop. Or he'll cry, and I'll want to stop.

"So what does Jeremy do next? He does not want to hear his parents argue. He wants to let those words play in his head: *Jeremy is your son.* So he races out of the barn, grabbing his pack with his jars in it—he has to record this day, this moment of all moments. He stumbles to the pasture, and there's old Sugar. He's ridden her bareback with the halter a dozen times before. So he jumps on that old pinto and rides. Beside himself with joy, he circles the pasture on Sugar— people saw him. Pretty soon, the old horse slows down and goes back to grazing, with Jeremy on her back.

"Maybe that's when Jer gets off the horse. Maybe he rolls in the grass, or twirls in the pasture, or dances a jig—who knows? Having a dad feels too good to be true."

I walk back to the defense table and take up the next jar, a honey jar, dimpled on the sides. "This is a day that Jeremy Long . . . Jeremy Johnson . . . never wants to forget. His world has changed in one moment. He has a dad. A daddy. And he already loves John Johnson. So he takes out this honey jar from his backpack. He writes the date on the bottom of the jar with his special pen that writes on glass, the pen he always carries with him. And he writes the time, 7:44 a.m."

I walk the jar over to the jury, showing them the flat bottom with the date and time in black calligraphy. "Can't you see him, waving the jar high above his head and snapping on the lid, capturing the glorious air on the day he found out he had a father, a kind and loving father?"

I pop open the jar. I'm dizzy, woozy with the air in this jar, or the lack of it in the courtroom. I wish I'd read the note first. I unfold the note and read it to the jury. "It says, **Air on my first Father's Day.**" Tears try to squeeze up my throat. My mouth fills with them, and I have to swallow so hard it hurts.

I go back to the table and trade jars, choosing the next one in line. I've already read the time written on the bottom of this one. "This next jar is labeled only three minutes later, three minutes after the last jar filled with air of a special 'Father's Day.'" I show the date and time to the jury. "I think there was too much joy in Jeremy for only one jar. So he had to use another." I'm pretty sure this note will be filled with more hallelujahs about having a dad, but I open it anyway. The courtroom has gone quiet, not even a cough. I read the note out loud: **Chase runs toward the sun on my Father's Day.**

I stare at the slip of paper in my hand, Jeremy's tight calligraphy still dancing on the paper. I read it again, to myself this time.

But Chase didn't run that day.

I don't understand. I try to catch Chase's attention, but his head is down. My stomach cramps. Tiny claws pinch my insides. How could Jeremy have seen Chase if he didn't run that day? Chase said he didn't run on game days.

"Hope," Raymond whispers, loud enough for me to hear, "open the last jar."

I don't move.

"You want me to do it?" Raymond asks, reaching for it. When I don't answer, he picks up the jar and stands. Numb, I watch as he turns the jar upside down and faces the jury. "This jar is dated the same day, June eleventh, the day of the murder. The time written on the bottom is 8:01." Raymond turns to me, frowning. "That's right before Mrs. McCray came into the barn and found John Johnson dead." Slowly, he rolls the jar in his hands until it's right side up. He walks toward the jury, his hand on the lid of the final jar.

I can't let him do it. I run after him. "No! Don't!" Grabbing the jar from his hands, I beg him. "Please? Please, Raymond. I'll read it."

He nods and sits back down.

I hold the jar gently, the glass cool in my hand. At last, I turn to my brother. I'm still afraid he'll shout at me with his eyes, scream for me to stop. But he's not even looking at me. Instead, he's gazing up, smiling, taking deep breaths of the air I've released into the courtroom, his father's air. He closes his eyes and inhales so long I half expect him to float away.

I move in closer to the jury and hold up the jar so the jurors can see the lid, the dark red dried in the ridges of the rim. "You can see this is blood that—"

Keller objects, and the judge sustains.

But I know they've seen it, the blood. "Jeremy has been happier than he's ever been in his life. A father. A loving father. With that air tucked away in his jars, he goes back to the barn. We may never know what he planned to do. Maybe he'd just watch John Johnson in a new light from now on. Maybe he'd hug his father and draw him pictures to tape to his refrigerator. Maybe my brother would have spoken, called him Daddy.

"But Jeremy never gets the chance. Instead, when he walks into the barn, he doesn't see his father. He searches the stalls for him. Then Jer spots him, his father, lying in a muddy red pool of sawdust and blood. Does he scream? Does he cry? Whatever else he does, he runs to his father and kneels beside him. The blood soaks into his uniform. He hugs this man who has been his father for less than an hour. Hugs and rocks him.

"And then what does he do? Jeremy Long does the only thing that's ever put order in his world. He takes out his last jar, writes the date and time on the bottom: **June 11, 8:01 a.m.** And he captures this air." I open the jar and think I feel a rush of stale air, scented with blood and death. Behind me, Jeremy moans as the death air mixes with the Father's Day air, with the air of game day, with Chase running, and with a father's breath leaving his body. Then I pull out the slip of paper tucked away inside the lid, and I read it: **Air of blood and my dead father.**

I'm not the only one crying in this room. I hear sniffles from the spectators. In a blur, I see T.J., and he's standing up, crying. And Rita, in the very back row. Sobbing.

But I have to finish. I don't want to. But it's the only way left. "Poor Jeremy. There he is—no father. Only a mother, a mother he last saw arguing with the man lying on the ground. A mother Jeremy loves, no matter what she's done. He has to protect her. He stands up, grabs the bloody bat, and races home, where he'll try to hide the bat . . . to save his mother."

These are the words I rehearsed all night. I couldn't let

myself think of what might happen to Rita because of them, because of my words. I believed those words. I'm not sure Raymond did, but I did.

Only now, they don't sound right. They don't ring true in this courtroom. *The truth, the whole truth, and nothing but the truth.*

I have to keep going. "My brother didn't kill John Johnson. He was protecting someone he thought did, someone he loves." As I say this, I'm meaning for them to understand that Rita did it, that Jeremy didn't. This is what I've rehearsed, what I've believed. And yet, something nags at me inside. The air I'm breathing swirls in my head, making me dizzy—death, fathers, sons, baseball, and Chase running. Why was he running toward the sun, away from the barn? He said he hadn't gone near the barn that morning. Why would he lie?

"She's right!" Rita stands up at the back of the courtroom. "I did it. It was me!"

37

The courtroom goes crazy. The judge bangs her gavel and tries to get order.

I stare back at Rita, and I know that this is the best thing she's ever done. And in that same instant, I also know she's not telling the truth. Rita's best moment, and it's a lie.

Because of Chase. Because he lied about being there.

Because I keep seeing Chase's name crossed out. Because I can't get the crime scene photos out of my head. A crumpled long strip of paper beside the body in at least one crime photo. I've seen those long, narrow papers before. And then I see them again, in my mind, on Coach's desk, in his drawer. Rosters. And I see the name crossed off: *Chase Wells*.

Not wanting to see the truth I know I'll see, I turn and look at Chase. He's staring back this time, and the truth is all there on his face, his gorgeous face, and in those eyes. "Why?" I whisper it, but it feels louder than the commotion going on all around me. I think everybody in the courtroom may be going crazy, declared insane, everybody except Jeremy.

But it feels like Chase and I are the only ones here. We're three feet apart, separated by a table, a railing, and people passing between us. But all I see is Chase. Chase and the dozens of images in my head of us together.

"I'm so sorry," he says. "I never meant for Jeremy to be blamed."

Behind us, Sheriff Wells's booming voice rises over the courtroom. "You better adjourn this trial, Judge! This whole thing's out of order. You want me to take the kid's mother into custody?"

"Hope," Chase continues, as if I'm the only one here, "you have to know I wouldn't have let Jeremy go to prison. I'd have—"

The sheriff wheels around and is on Chase in two strides. "Shut up! Don't say another word!"

Chase flinches as if he's been slapped. "You knew, didn't you?"

I don't know which face shows more pain, Chase's or his father's.

"That's why you tried to scare Hope off the case, to keep us apart." Without taking his gaze from his dad's face, Chase says, "You knew all along that Jeremy didn't kill Coach . . . and that I did."

His words take away what's left of my breath.

"I said, shut up!" Sheriff Wells cries. His face is cartoon red, like faces in those animated shows Jeremy loves to watch. "I told you not to try to dig up trouble, but you wouldn't listen. Everything would have been okay if you'd just listened to me! I had it all under control."

Crime scene photos are flashing through my brain. I knew all along something was wrong with them. And now I see it. The photos of Coach with the stuff from his pockets spread out on the ground—the picture I saw in the sheriff's crime scene file had a long strip of paper that wasn't in Raymond's photo. I didn't know what the paper was then, but I do now. The roster. Probably the roster Coach had posted at the ballpark that day . . . with Chase's name crossed out, just like it had been on Coach's copy, the one he kept on his desk. That roster wasn't in the photo they gave Raymond . . . because Sheriff Wells took it away. He must have seen it and figured out everything right then and there.

Chase turns his back on his dad and stares at me. "I am so sorry. I didn't mean to. I didn't—please, Hope?"

I don't know what he wants from me. Arguments leap like flames around us, but they don't reach me. My head shakes back and forth as I stare at Chase, my Chase. I'm piecing together the lies. I still feel the air, full around us, slicing apart, then coming together, like air through vents. "I don't understand."

"We're not saying another word!" Sheriff Wells shouts.

"I am." Keeping his gaze on me, Chase grips the rail and gets to his feet. His voice is loud enough for the judge and everyone else to hear him. The crowd quiets as if their volume has been turned off, like the night crickets Chase and I listened to a million years ago.

Still looking only at me, he says, "I didn't mean to do it.

You have to believe me. And I didn't plan for Jeremy to get arrested for the murder. I wouldn't have let them send Jeremy to prison. I just thought—or at least I convinced myself at first—he'd be better off wherever they put mental patients, and I wouldn't have to go to jail for something I didn't mean to do."

I hurt inside, in places I didn't know I had. I'm aware of people moving around Chase, talking to him. I think they're reading him his rights, like on television. Somebody's handcuffing the sheriff, then Chase. The judge is talking to Chase, and he's listening to her. T.J. has pushed his way in closer, and his lips are moving. But the words are floating over me, like this air, circling above me but not letting me breathe it in.

"I didn't plan it, not any of it," Chase continues. "I think, with time, I could have convinced myself I didn't really do it, not even the murder—if I hadn't spent time with you, Hope, if I hadn't gotten to know Jeremy through you."

"Why?" I can't ask the things I really want to ask. *Was it all a lie? Was I totally and completely fooled? Were you spying on me the whole time? Did you ever care about me? Is everything hope-less?*

Chase takes in a big breath of air, Jeremy's air. "I went out for my jog, like I always do . . . even on game days." He looks down before admitting, "I always check the roster on game day. Only I couldn't believe it. Coach had scratched out my name and put T.J. in as starting pitcher. I wasn't even on the roster. I'd told Dad I was starting pitcher. He'd rounded up his buddies to come and watch me pitch. He'd bought fireworks.

I'd never seen him so proud of me. For weeks, it was all he could talk about—his son was going to pitch in the biggest game in all Ohio, to hear him tell it. Coach Johnson had promised me I could pitch. And I wasn't even going to play?"

"All this over a stupid game!" Sheriff Wells shouts.

Chase glances back at his dad. "Couldn't disappoint you, could I, Dad? I couldn't let you down. *I* keep my promises."

"You're a fool," Sheriff Wells mutters, but he looks broken, not angry.

"I know. I'm a screwup, okay? Don't you think I know that better than anybody? I just couldn't stand to see that look, the look you give me when I've disappointed you . . . again."

Chase turns back to me, as if I'm the one he's explaining everything to, not the judge, not his dad, not the court reporter taking down every word. "I knew there had to be a mistake. I yanked down the roster and ran to the barn. Coach was always in the stable early. I found him in the back stall, brushing one of the horses. He didn't want to come out, and when he did, he seemed tired. The sun was peeking through the clouds, making an orange glow inside the barn.

"'What is it, Chase?' he asked, like I was just another inconvenience to him. That's me. Mr. Inconvenience.

"I shook the roster at him. 'What's with this?' I demanded, trying to control my temper. I was already breathing hard from the run. All the way to the barn, I'd been imagining the scene when Dad would show up at the park and discover I wasn't pitching. I'd gone over it in my head, over and over.

"'That looks like the roster I put up this morning, Chase,' Coach said. But he knew what I meant.

"'I'm supposed to be the starting pitcher. You promised I could start the game this afternoon!' I was shouting.

"He shook his head. 'Maybe your dad promised you that. *I* didn't. I thought you could get your swing under control, but you're not there yet. This is a big game, Chase. You ought to know that by now. I want to beat Wooster.' He was so calm. And the calmer he got, the angrier I got, like I had to turn up the heat so he'd understand how important this was.

"'So you're pitching T.J.?' I screamed. 'You've got to be kidding! He doesn't even have a curveball.'

"'Chase, you've got a lot of talent,' Coach admitted, 'and I think you're going to be a strong pitcher. But pitchers bat in our league. You know that. And your swing has been way off.'

"I told him how hard I'd been practicing. I told him over and over.

"'That's good,' he said. 'You keep it up, and we'll see.' Just like that.

"'No! You can see *now*!' I told him. I'd spotted Jeremy's bat leaning against the wall when I came in. I ran and got it. His gloves were there, so I put those on too. I took a couple of practice cuts and ran back to Coach. He was heading into the stall. 'Wait! I want you to see. I've evened out the swing like you told me. I have, Coach!'

"'It's over, Chase,' he said.

"But he'd promised. He'd *promised* me!

"'Go on home and tell your dad, son. It's about time he learned how to lose too.' Then he turned his back on me. He was breaking his promise. He shouldn't have done that. I was counting on that game. My dad was counting on it. Everybody would be there. He couldn't take that away from me.

"Something went off inside me. It felt like an explosion. I swung the bat. Just like I'd been doing in the batting cages. One swing. I only wanted to show him. That's all. He dropped to his knees, like he was praying. Then he toppled to the ground. I stared down at him. Blood poured out of his nose, his mouth. So much blood.

"I dropped the bat, and I ran. I ran fast so the whole mess got farther and farther away from me. I couldn't believe what I'd done. Had I really killed him? It wasn't possible. It was too horrible to be real. So maybe I hadn't done it. When you run far enough, fast enough, all thoughts leave your head. It's a running high. You can imagine things. Maybe I'd imagined this.

"I was all the way home before I realized I was still wearing the batting gloves. Nobody was there. I put my shoes and shorts and the gloves into a garbage bag and set it out with our trash. Then I waited for Dad to get home and arrest me.

"Only it didn't happen. I got a phone call from one of the team mothers—all the players on the team got it." Chase makes a move toward me, and the guard closes in, stopping him. "I didn't even know they'd arrested Jeremy until that afternoon. I thought they'd let him go the next day. Then the next. Then it was weeks.

"At first I figured they'd see right off it wasn't Jeremy. How could they find evidence when he didn't do it? When they didn't let Jeremy go, I convinced myself that he'd get off. Dad kept telling me the jury would just put Jeremy in a kind of home, that he'd be happy there."

I remember all the questions Chase asked me about Jeremy and how surprised he'd been when I told him why a mental hospital would kill my brother. He'd wanted to believe Jeremy could live happily ever after in one of those places.

As Chase has been talking, I've pictured everything—Chase arguing with Coach, Chase picking up the bat, swinging. . . . But I've pictured other moments too—Chase wrapping me in a blanket, bringing me hot chocolate; Chase, his arms around me, his hand lifting my chin, his lips brushing mine.

I have two hearts. One is jumping for joy because I know my brother can come home. Everyone will know he's not guilty, not crazy. But the other heart is broken, shattered in pieces because I think I loved Chase. "Why did you pretend to help me, to care?"

"I wasn't pretending, Hope. Do you think I wanted to get involved? I tried to quit, to keep away from you . . . but I couldn't. I wanted to help you, to be with you. Then when you talked about Jeremy, I wanted to help you get him off. Remember? Reasonable doubt?"

I want to believe him. And I don't want to believe him. I want the truth, but it's trapped in between horrible facts, out of reach, like air in a bottle. "Was everything a lie? You? Me? Us?"

"No!" he shouts. "God, no!"

God hangs over the courtroom, echoing in the air.

"Hope?" the judge says. And for a minute, I think it's a question: *Hope?* I burst into tears, sobs that shake the earth. I have to lean on the defense table or I'll fall to the floor and never get up.

Things happen fast. Reporters are shouting questions. The judge pounds her gavel. Keller agrees with Raymond about releasing Jeremy. One of the officers takes Chase by the elbow. Another one struggles with Chase's father. T.J. and his mother come up, both offering help, friendship.

Something touches my shoulder. I know that touch. It's my brother. His stiff fingers press something cool and hard into my palm. It's the aspirin bottle. He's printed on the side in tiny, curled letters: *Hope's tears—Psalm 56:8.* When I smile up at him, he wipes the tears from my cheek.

Rita edges in close, closer than she's been for a long, long time. I look up at Jeremy. He's smiling at her, the lines in his face soft with relief that his mother didn't kill his father.

Rita starts to say something to me, but she stops and turns back to Jeremy.

And then I hear it. It has been ten years since I heard that sound, but I recognize it as clearly as if I'd been listening to it just this morning. I close my eyes and take in the single note that swallows every other noise in the courtroom. It drowns out shame and anger and lies. Then it slides into more notes that mingle with the words blowing around us, in the air, filling the room.

I open my eyes and see that Chase isn't looking at me anymore. He's staring at Jeremy because that song, of course, is coming from Jeremy's mouth. From his heart. His soul.

When my brother stops singing, the courtroom stays silent. We look from Jeremy to one another. Nothing will ever be the same for anyone in this room. I think we all know that.

When we finally leave the courthouse—Raymond, Rita, Jeremy, and me—the air outside has changed. We stop on the top step and breathe in the moment, clear as sunshine, right as rain, and true as song.

Epilogue

"Hope! Hope!"

I don't answer right away. It's Saturday morning, nearly eight months since Jeremy started talking again, and I still get a rush hearing my brother say my name. I make him say it again. Then I join him on the front lawn. Our dog, a black-and-white mutt we rescued from the shelter, trots over to greet me, then races back to Jer. Jeremy named the puppy Maple, but only he knows why.

Outside, a white fog hangs over the budding treetops. A car door slams, and I see Raymond getting out of his car, followed by his wife and daughter. Jer and I run to meet them. "How's my Christy?" I ask, checking to see if the baby's grown hair yet. She's dressed in pink so we'll know she's a girl anyway. Her whole name is Christina Hope Munroe. Raymond says you can't have too many Hopes.

"Want to hold her, Jeremy?" Becca Munroe offers up her prize.

My brother shakes his head. He loves that baby, but he's afraid to hold her. "We sing tomorrow," he says, grinning.

"I know," Becca says. She and Jer sing in the choir, and tomorrow is their Easter cantata.

I glance back at the house, and Rita waves from the window. She won't come outside. Hangover. At least being drunk embarrasses her now. She and Bob spend a lot of time together, and not just at the Colonial or at night. They went to the zoo last week, and they took Jeremy with them. Rita was sober for almost three weeks after the trial. Maybe she will be again.

"So," Raymond says, picking up Maple and scratching his ears, "did you get enrolled at Wayne County okay?"

"Yep. Thanks." Raymond tried to get me to apply to Ohio State, but I'm not ready to leave Jeremy. I'm going to commute with T.J. to Wayne County Community College for now. Raymond wants me to major in prelaw. I might. But right now I'm leaning toward being a private investigator. Anything's possible.

I still think about Chase. At the weirdest moments, a picture will flash to my mind, and I'll see his green eyes, tanned face, and that smile—and I'll miss him so much it hurts. He's in a juvenile facility, where he'll be for a long, long time. I haven't seen him or spoken to him. I wrote him once, but I didn't mail it. He could be in prison the rest of his life.

Jeremy tears into the house and comes back with a quart pickle jar I washed for him over a month ago. He writes the date on the bottom of the jar, then folds a slip of paper and tucks it under the lid. I don't ask what he's written. I think I can guess.

The fog moves in, rushing to get a part in my brother's memory. As Jeremy raises his arms, I can't take my eyes off him. In the instant he sweeps the air, his face changes from gawky—too much gum, too big ears—to handsome and wise with secret knowledge. And in that instant, he captures in his jar the fog of spring and the promise of hope.

You have collected
all my tears in your bottle.
Psalm 56:8 (New Living Translation)

Acknowledgments

I love acknowledgments, although mine should really be called "Thanksgivings"!

A million thanks to Allison Wortche, my gifted editor, whose sensitivity and insights have strengthened this book, and whose gracious spirit makes the work fun. I'm so grateful to Alfred A. Knopf Books, a house I've admired my whole life, for welcoming me into their family.

As for Anna J. Webman, my magnificent agent, thanks for taking such great care of me. I'm proud to be part of Curtis Brown Ltd.

For such an intricate mystery, I needed help! Thank you to the experts who answered all my questions and often came up with better ideas than I did:

- Patrick G. Lazzaro, prosecuting attorney, Cleveland, Ohio, and former administrative judge in Ohio (we must do this again!)
- Rick Acker, deputy attorney general in the California Department of Justice
- Assistant prosecutor, Ashland County, Ohio

And on the home front, thanks to my amazing family for letting me steal so much material from your lives. I hope you realize how very thankful I am for all of you.

About the Author

Dandi Daley Mackall is the award-winning author of many books for children and adults. She visits countless schools, conducts writing assemblies and workshops across the United States, and presents keynote addresses at conferences and young author events. She is also a frequent guest on radio talk shows and has made dozens of appearances on TV.

Dandi lives in rural Ohio with her husband, three children, and their horses, dogs, and cats.

SilenceofMurder.com
DandiBooks.com

PORTRAITS of LIBRARY SERVICE to PEOPLE with DISABILITIES

PORTRAITS OF LIBRARY SERVICE TO PEOPLE WITH DISABILITIES

EUNICE G. LOVEJOY

G.K. HALL & CO. • BOSTON, MASSACHUSETTS

Portraits of Library Service
to People with Disabilities

Eunice G. Lovejoy

Copyright 1990 by
G. K. Hall & Co.
70 Lincoln Street
Boston, MA 02111

Printed on acid-free paper and bound in
The United States of America.

Library of Congress Cataloging-in-Publication Data

Lovejoy, Eunice G.
        Portraits of library service to people with
    disabilities/ Eunice G. Lovejoy
            p. cm. -- (Professional librarian series)
    ISBN 0-8161-1922-8. -- ISBN 0-8161-1923-6 (pbk.)
        1. Libraries and the handicapped--United States
--Case studies. 2. Handicapped--United States--
Books and reading--Case studies. 3. Handicapped--
Information services--United States--Case studies.
4. Public libraries--United States--Case studies.
I. Title. II. Series.
Z711.92.H3L68 1989
027.6'63--dc20   89-19829
                                            CIP

Contents

Foreword vii

Acknowledgments ix

Introduction: Why Another Book on Library Service to People
    with Disabilities? 1

Part 1: Service on Wheels

Chapter 1: Washington County Free Library, Hagerstown,
    Maryland 11

Chapter 2: Bloomington Public Library, Bloomington, Illinois
    19

Part 2: Emphasis on Outreach

Chapter 3: Public Library of Cincinnati and Hamilton County,
    Cincinnati, Ohio 27

Chapter 4: Hennepin County Library, Minnetonka, Minnesota
    43

Chapter 5: District of Columbia Public Library, Washington,
    D.C. 57

Chapter 6: Tampa-Hillsborough County Public Library System,
    Tampa, Florida 69

Part 3: Special Needs Centers

Chapter 7: Tucson Public Library, Tucson, Arizona 81

Chapter 8: Phoenix Public Library, Phoenix, Arizona 87

Chapter 9: Montgomery County Department of Public Libraries, Bethesda, Maryland 101

Chapter 10: Duluth Public Library, Duluth, Minnesota 113

Chapter 11: Broward County Library, Fort Lauderdale, Florida 119

Part 4: Mainstreamed Service

Chapter 12: Monroe County Library System, Monroe, Michigan 131

Chapter 13: Fitchburg Public Library, Fitchburg, Massachusetts 139

Chapter 14: Prince George's County Memorial Library System, Hyattsville, Maryland 147

Chapter 15: Queens Borough Public Library, Jamaica, New York 157

Chapter 16: Skokie Public Library, Skokie, Illinois 169

Chapter 17: Memphis-Shelby County Public Library and Information Center, Memphis, Tennessee 181

Part 5: Regional Libraries for the Blind and Physically Handicapped

Chapter 18: Kansas State Library, Division for the Blind and Physically Handicapped, Emporia, Kansas 197

Chapter 19: Alabama Public Library Service, Regional Library for the Blind and Physically Handicapped, Birmingham, Alabama 209

Chapter 20: Conclusion 221

Appendix A: ALA Decade of Disabled Persons Committee Checklist 225

Appendix B: Glossary and Resource Directory 229

Appendix C: Samples of Library Forms, Brochures, and Other Materials 253

Foreword

Eunice Lovejoy has been an ardent advocate of people with disabilities for several decades. She came to my attention during the mid-1970s at a meeting on library services for the deaf at Gallaudet University, where her energy and concern for practical library programs reaching out to *all* persons was amazing. In more recent years she has put that energy into her newsletter, *FOCUS: Library Service to Older Adults, People with Disabilities,* which reaches about 1,000 librarians around the country. *FOCUS* is full of practical tips, bibliographic sources, and concerns about library services for people with disabilities.

Ms. Lovejoy has brought the same enthusiasm to the visits that resulted in this book. She asked for nominations of libraries with outstanding programs of service to people with disabilities; she reviewed the nominations and made site visits; and she submitted each chapter for review by the local library staff after the visit. The result is a practical guide to how libraries are successfully serving persons with disabilities.

In a rapidly aging society, people with disabilities make up an increasing proportion of the population. Persons with disabilities do not want special services or library outreach; they want a restructuring of library facilities, programs, and services that will make the library accessible to all. Eunice Lovejoy has taken this into account, visiting public libraries and centers for library services for the blind and physically handicapped nationwide.

Libraries with ongoing programs for persons with disabilities will find the book helpful because it gives a basis for comparison with other programs. Libraries considering such services will find practical suggestions, illustrations of promotional materials, and descriptions of typical problems that will be most helpful. Library science professors (this one included) will find in Ms. Lovejoy's book a very good way to move students from the theories and philosophies of library services into the practicalities of real, day-to-day library operations.

Kieth C. Wright
University of North Carolina at
Greensboro

Acknowledgments

Thanks first to Dr. Frederick A. Thorpe, whose consolation gift when I was not chosen as a recipient of the Frederick A. Thorpe Traveling Fellowship Award in 1986 encouraged me to pursue this project.

Thanks to the librarians who took the time to recommend what they felt were outstanding programs for people with disabilities.

Thanks to an even larger group of people who spent hours answering my questions and showing me their services, reading a draft of their chapter, suggesting changes that more accurately reflected what they were doing, and graciously answering even more questions.

I talked to many people at each library I visited. Here I have listed only the names of the people who met with me initially and usually arranged for me to talk to other staff. They are, in chronological order:

- Coy Hunsucker, head of the exceptional children's department, Public Library of Cincinnati and Hamilton County, Cincinnati, Ohio.

- Judith Lessee, developmental disabilities specialist, Tucson Public Library, Tucson, Arizona.

- Mary Roatch, supervisor, special needs center, Phoenix Public Library, Phoenix, Arizona.

- Caroline Longmoor, librarian, Kansas State Library, Division for the Blind and Physically Handicapped, Emporia, Kansas.

- Ann Eccles, head of outreach service, Hennepin County Library, Minnetonka, Minnesota.

- Randy Vogt, coordinator, handicapped access center, Duluth Public Library, Duluth, Minnesota.

- Liene Sorenson, manager, Skokie accessible library services, Skokie Public Library, Skokie, Illinois.

- Neil Kelley, extension librarian, Bloomington Public Library, Bloomington, Illinois.

- Pat Wilson, bookmobile supervisor, Washington County Free Library, Hagerstown, Maryland.

- Grace Lyons, librarian, library for the blind and physically handicapped, District of Columbia Public Library, Washington, D.C.

- Virginia Wygant, librarian to the homebound, Montgomery County Department of Public Libraries, Bethesda, Maryland.

- Honore Francois, coordinator of extension and special services, Prince George's County Memorial Library System, Hyattsville, Maryland.

- Eileen Gellman, library assistant, library services to persons with disabilities, Queens Borough Public Library, Jamaica, New York.

- Elizabeth Watson, coordinator of children's and extension services, Fitchburg Public Library, Fitchburg, Massachusetts.

- Bernard Margolis, director, Monroe County Library System, Monroe, Michigan.

- Jean Hofacket, coordinator of special services, Memphis-Shelby County Public Library and Information Center, Memphis, Tennessee.

- Fara Zaleski, acting head, Alabama Public Library Service, Regional Library for the Blind and Physically Handicapped, Birmingham, Alabama.

- Jeannette Martin, special services librarian, Tampa-Hillsborough County Public Library System, Tampa, Florida.

- Joanne Block, head, talking book library, Broward County Library, Fort Lauderdale, Florida.

Thanks finally to my husband Albert, who shared the driving as we crisscrossed the country and provided companionship between library visits, who did a share of the editing, and who encouraged me to persevere.

Introduction

Why Another Book on Library Service to People with Disabilities?

In 1957 the American Foundation for the Blind in New York City had published Francis St. John's *Survey of Library Services for the Blind*. Twenty years later Maryalls G. Strom brought together a collection of articles from professional journals in *Library Services to the Blind and Physically Handicapped*. Both of these books, however, were for the most part limited to a single disability group.

Ruth A. Vellaman's *Serving Physically Disabled People: An Information Handbook for All Libraries* was the first comprehensive book about library service to people with a range of disabilities. It came on the heels of the civil rights movement for disabled people and responded to the concerns librarians should have been feeling with the passage of two pieces of federal legislation. Section 504 of the Rehabilitation Act of 1973 stated that any agency receiving federal funds directly or indirectly should provide access to its programs for people with disabilities. The Education for All Handicapped Children Act, passed in 1975, promoted the mainstreaming of children with disabilities.

Vellaman's book was followed in 1979 by Kieth C. Wright's *Library and Information Services for Handicapped Individuals*, which is different in organization but similar in content. Both were written by library school professors, and both cover legal background, attitudinal barriers, and descriptions of disabilities. Both books show librarians how they can make their services accessible to people with disabilities. Judith F. Davie coauthored Wright's revision of his book, which was published in 1983. In that year Libraries Unlimited published *Improving Library Service to Physically Disabled Persons: A Self-Evaluation Checklist* by two more library school professors, William L. Needham and Gerald Jahoda. This self-assessment tool-- which can be used in public libraries, in school libraries and media centers, and in academic and special libraries--helps library administrators identify weaknesses in facilities, services, resources, staffing, funding, and external relations. It then offers suggestions for improvements in these areas.

Other books published in the United States during the early to mid-1980s include:

Mainstreaming Library Service for Disabled People by Emmett A. Davis and Catherine A. Davis (1980).

Meeting the Needs of the Handicapped: A Resource for Teachers and Librarians, edited by Carol H. Thomas and James L. Thomas (1980).

The Mainstreamed Library: Issues, Ideas, Innovations, edited by Barbara H. Baskin and Karen H. Harris (1980).

Speaking Out: Personal and Professional Views on Library Service for Blind and Physically Handicapped Individuals, compiled and edited by Leslie Eldridge (1982).

Library Services for the Handicapped Adult, edited by James L. Thomas and Carol H. Thomas (1982).

Library Services to Developmentally Disabled Children and Adults, edited by Linda Lucas (1982).

Librarians Serving Disabled Children and Young People by Henry C. Dequin (1983).

The Disabled Child in the Library: Moving into the Mainstream by Linda Lucas and Marilyn H. Karrenbrock (1983)

That All May Read: Library Service for Blind and Physically Handicapped People (1983).

Library Service to the Deaf and Hearing Impaired by Phyllis I. Dalton (1985).

R Is for Reading: Library Service to Blind and Physically Handicapped Children, compiled and edited by Leslie Eldridge (1985).

This wealth of books, along with the articles appearing in professional journals, should provide librarians with more than adequate motivation and skills for implementation. The bibliography *Library Service for the Blind and Physically Handicapped in the United States*, prepared by the National Library Service for the Blind and Physically Handicapped, lists almost 800 items.[1] Add to this the influx since 1966 of Library Services and Construction Act (LSCA) funds for services to disabled people and workshops at the national, state, and local levels. The person with disabilities should expect excellent library services.

PROCEDURES AND LIBRARY VISITS

The International Year of Disabled Persons was observed in 1981. During that twelve-month period, the American Library Association (ALA) promoted services and collected information about what libraries were doing. In her report in the *ALA Yearbook, 1983*, Phyllis Dalton, chairperson of ALA's Decade of Disabled Persons Committee, showed that a wide variety of efforts were being made to meet the library needs of persons with disabilities.[2] Yet with all that has been written in books and articles, no one to my knowledge has taken a detailed look at actual programs of service for people with disabilities. It is with that gap in mind that I placed the following item in the January 1987 issue of *FOCUS: Library Service to Older Adults, People with Disabilities* which I publish: I need your help.[3]

> For years I've had this dream of visiting libraries across the country which have outstanding programs for people with disabilities, and writing a book about them. 1987 is the year! I've decided to do it and I definitely need your help!
>
> I'm looking for libraries--public, school, academic, and even special--that give people with disabilities optimum access to materials and programs available to other people in their

3

communities. Obviously I can't visit every library but would like to find a selection that we can point to with pride and say, in the sixth year of the International Decade of Disabled Persons, this shows what some libraries in the U.S. and Canada are doing. You can do it too!

I'll spend the first half of the year "narrowing the field." During the summer my husband and I will "tent-camp" our way from library to library. The hard work will come in the fall-- writing about the experience and finding a publisher.

Because I believe that the people who are often doing the most don't have the time or inclination to write about it, I'd like to be their voice. Please send me your suggestions of libraries I shouldn't miss.

FOCUS reaches approximately 900 libraries in the United States and Canada, through either individual subscriptions or subscriptions with the right to reproduce and distribute to libraries in a system or state. I also sent copies of this item to key people (state librarians, library consultants, or regional librarians for the blind and physically handicapped) in state library agencies that do not subscribe to *FOCUS*, to five publishers (to test the waters), to the executive director of the American Association of School Librarians, and to the U.S. Department of Education. Recommendations came from state librarians, regional librarians for the blind and physically handicapped, state consultants, a publisher, and a U.S. Department of Education staff member. Several librarians wrote and invited me to visit their own programs, which they felt were outstanding. I heard from no school libraries or libraries in Canada. One academic library was recommended, but its director felt his library's services for students with disabilities were far from outstanding.

During March, April, and May I wrote to the libraries that had been recommended, asking for written materials to help me determine whether I should include a visit to them on my summer schedule. Several libraries were excluded because their programs were too new (e.g., a recently funded LSCA project), too limited in scope, or similar to the services of another library I planned to visit. My trial visit was to the Public Library of Cincinnati and Hamilton County, a library with a long history of serving people with disabilities. I hoped to spend two days and requested appointments with staff and a sample of users. When a one-day schedule was set up for me without users, I recognized that it was probably unrealistic to expect librarians to recruit users to meet with me. By early June I had made appointments to visit sixteen libraries in June, July, and August.

Although I prepared a list of subjects to cover, the interviews did not follow a prearranged format. I tried to keep in mind the items in the checklist from the brochure prepared by the ALA's Decade of Disabled Persons Committee (see Appendix A). If I had received information on the library's program before my visit, I was able to pinpoint my questions and so shorten the visit. Several librarians arranged for me to go with staff on the bookmobile or van and participate in the delivery of library materials or programs. At other places I talked with key staff about their individual responsibilities. Sometimes I met the library director or assistant director; in one case I saw a board member. Sometimes I spoke only to the person who was giving direct service.

I sent a draft of the appropriate chapter to each contact person and asked him or her to read it and make corrections if necessary. In many cases other staff and administrators reviewed the material. Sometimes it was necessary for me to follow up for further clarification. My last contacts with the librarians were in early 1988.

This is not a scholarly publication. Rather, I have attempted to give a complete picture of the people providing services and their modus operandi at the time of my visit. My credentials are twenty-eight years as a practicing librarian. I spent ten of these years as a consultant for services to the handicapped at the State Library of Ohio and six more years as a free-lance consultant. I have had many opportunities to visit library programs throughout the United States.

THE FINISHED PRODUCT

The division of services into categories--service on wheels, emphasis on outreach, special needs centers, mainstreamed service, and regional libraries for the blind and physically handicapped--is my attempt to identify the predominant characteristic of a particular library's services to people with disabilities. The reader will soon be aware that there is much overlap. The Tampa-Hillsborough County Public Library System, which is shown as emphasizing outreach, has a subregional library for the blind and physically handicapped. So do the Prince George's County Memorial Library System, which is essentially a mainstreamed service, and Broward County Library, where service is offered through a special needs center.

Because the library experience of readers will vary considerably, I have included in Appendix B a combination glossary and resource directory for more information about materials, equipment, and programs mentioned in this book. I have not attempted to be consistent in my use of library terminology. The people who use libraries are variously called patrons, users, clients, readers, and customers. The building that houses the administrative offices or is in the center of the city may be the central library or the main library, or it may have a some other name. Job titles vary from library to library. Large type and large print are used interchangeably. Some libraries use the terms TDD and telecommunications device for the deaf, while TTY (the teletypewriter that serves the same purpose), is used by others. I have tried to use the terminology of the library I am writing about.

I do not pretend that this is a complete picture of library service offered to persons with disabilities in the United States. It may not represent the best that exists, although I believe that in some cases it does. I do feel that it represents the most current forms that service has taken. I hope these portraits will make individuals with disabilities and disability groups aware of the services libraries offer and will inspire them to ask more of their local libraries. I hope this book will encourage librarians, library administrators, and boards to compare their programs with those described here and learn from the experiences of other libraries. And I hope that *Portraits to Library Service for People with Disabilities* will offer library school students a picture of the real world.

Notes

1. *That All May Read: Library Service for Blind and Physically Handicapped People* (Washington, D.C.: National Library Service

for the Blind and Physcially Handicapped, Library of Congress, 1983), 431-84.

2. Phyllis Dalton, "Focus on Service to the Disabled," in *ALA Yearbook 1983*, 69-71.

3. "I Need Your Help," *FOCUS: Library Service to Older Adults, People with Disabilities*, no. 1 (1987):1.

PART 1

SERVICE ON WHEELS

Bookmobile service has gone through many changes over the past eight decades during which wheels have carried library service beyond the physical boundaries of the library building. Bookmobiles went to rural areas until country dwellers became as mobile as city dwellers. Bookmobiles stopped at schools until schools became less dependent on public library services. Owing to the emphasis on reaching nonusers in the sixties and seventies, bookmobiles were visible in urban areas. As fuel costs skyrocketed in the late 1970s, however, many libraries phased out bookmobile service.

Bookmobiles, or some modification of the conventional bookmobile, such as a delivery van, should be used to serve people with disabilities who find it impractical to come to a library, even if it is wheelchair accessible. There is currently renewed interest in bookmobile service. Evidence of this is the increase in attendance at the State Library of Ohio's Bookmobile Conference from 50 people in 1985 to 150 attendees representing libraries throughout the United States and Canada in 1987. At the 1987 conference guidelines were developed that were to be tested throughout the year and evaluated and adopted at the 1988 conference. The two libraries described in this section illustrate the changing emphases in bookmobile service.

The Washington County Free Library in Hagerstown, Maryland, and the Bloomington Public Library in Illinois are alike in many ways, even though the former serves the whole county and the latter serves a city. Although located in physically accessible buildings, both libraries provide mobile service for people who cannot go to the library. Both leave deposit collections at nursing homes and other sites; both provide service to homebound individuals, with staff making the delivery in one case and volunteers in the other; both depend on an outside agency, at least partially, for large print books; and both offer programs to people who cannot go to the library. The people-oriented staffs are willing to bend the rules when that is necessary to meet the needs of people with disabilities.

The Washington County Free Library, however, provides service to the deaf community, while the Bloomington Public Library is involved in promoting the talking book program. In this and in other important respects, they are different.

Chapter 1

Washington County Free Library, Hagerstown, Maryland

Washington County Free Library, founded in 1901, was one of the first county libraries in the country. When it was four years old, the library sent a Concord wagon fitted with bookshelves and drawn by two horses to call on isolated farms. The world's first bookmobile service was created.

CHANGES IN BOOKMOBILE SERVICE

The service I visited in early August was quite different from its eighty-two-year-old antecedent. Pat Wilson, bookmobile supervisor, scheduled a full day for looking at these changes: a program at a nursing home, visits to several shut-ins, a picnic in the city park where I could talk with all the staff, and an ice cream social at Goodwill Industries.

Ms. Wilson was an outreach librarian at Boston Public Library before she went to the Washington County Free Library in 1981 to coordinate the delivery van service This servive had been established several years earlier with an LSCA grant. Ms. Wilson hired Cynthia Rowe as her assistant.

The original delivery van, purchased with LSCA funds, carried bookshelves on wheels (not a library truck but something much bigger and less manageable) that could be taken off the van on a lift and rolled into each nursing home or luncheon site. Ms. Wilson and Ms. Rowe would fill the shelves with books and, with great difficulty, push them from room to room in the nursing homes. Because so few people wanted books, Ms. Wilson asked the activity directors to designate a space where books could be left. It became the responsibility of the activity director, or a volunteer to get the books to individuals who could not go to the book area. Ms. Wilson promised that the library would leave whatever they wanted. Each month the library leaves sixty to seventy-five books, including large print, regular print, a few paperback romances, and whatever else the people want.

The library communicates well with the activity directors and lunch site coordinators. Ms. Wilson was to have met with them shortly after my visit to elicit their suggestions for improving the service and to remind them of the importance of updating readers' interest files and channeling the names of new readers to the library. (The library keeps a list of readers' names and their interests but no record of what books have been sent to them.)

When the library bought two new bookmobiles in 1985, the delivery van service was consolidated with the bookmobile service. Ms. Wilson became head of the department and responsibilities for other staff were rearranged as well. Jeff Phillips continues as the library assistant responsible for maintenance of the bookmobiles. He drives the larger one to the rural areas and schools. Diane Sharpe, another library assistant from the bookmobile part of the merger was assigned responsibility for the shut-in service as well as for office routines. David Poffenberger has retired from the bookmobile department but comes back to substitute for Mr. Phillips. Ms. Rowe is now in charge of programming for children in day-care centers and for adults. All staff members drive the bookmobiles, help readers, and check out books.

The library purchased its bookmobiles from Thomas Built Buses of High Point, North Carolina. One is approximately twenty-two feet long and goes to schools and rural communities. The other is fifteen feet long and goes to nursing homes, homes of shut-ins, sheltered workshops, group homes, correctional centers, and nutrition sites for senior citizens.

OUTREACH PROGRAMMING

Ms. Wilson and Ms. Rowe became heavily involved in taking programs to the sites where they delivered books each month. When interest in the film programs they provided declined, they started inviting people with special skills, such as quilting, to make presentations. Ms. Rowe baked and decorated cakes and made homemade ice cream to serve after the programs. (Now they solicit food from local grocery stores and the ice cream factory.) As they added more places to their route--twenty nursing homes and luncheon sites for senior citizens per month now--they could not continue monthly programs. They have reduced their schedule to three or four programs a year at each place.

The program at the Ravenwood Nursing Home, which we visited, featured slides of wedding gowns from the nineteenth and twentieth centuries (one of BiFolkal Productions' "Slideas") and a movie about a wedding in a Persian village, borrowed from the Enoch Pratt Free Library in Baltimore. Thirty-five people from the home and nearby apartments came for the event, which ended with the serving of wedding cake provided by a local baker, tea, coffee, and conversation.

Several days before each program the library sends the activity director or nutrition-site coordinator a poster advertising the coming attraction.

The ice cream social at Goodwill Industries was for people with developmental disablities working in the sheltered workshop. It followed the showing of several short 16mm films and bingo.

At Ravenwood, the semiannual programs are held in the lunchroom. The bookmobile stops once a month for people to choose reading materials. The bookmobile staff members show films once a month at the Potomac Center, a state institution for developmentally disabled persons, and show films and leave books at a private residential site, the Anita Lynne Home.

SHUT-IN SERVICE

I went with Ms. Sharpe to the homes of several of the fifty-five shut-ins she visits. She normally goes alone in the smaller bookmobile once a month or whenever readers call. She is scheduled to use the bookmobile in time slots on the first Tuesdays and Thursdays and the second Wednesdays and Thursdays of each month. She preselects a bag of books, based on each person's interests, and the reader is free to choose or reject these selections. She stamps the date due on the slips ahead of time so that the clerical routines do not distract her attention from the person she is visiting. If she is taking special requests, she checks these out before her visit. She limits her visit with each person to thirty minutes. That is not easy to hold to because everyone has things he or she wants to share with her--a new craft project or conversation about a pet or a neighbor. Several of her readers in wheelchairs like to come on the bookmobile where there are more books to choose from once they overcome their fear of the lift.

Ms. Sharpe does not visit these shut-ins alone. Another staff member is with her so that one can work the lift from the inside of the bookmobile while the other stands on the lift and steadies the wheelchair.

Ms. Sharpe keeps a 3-by-5-inch card for each reader. The card has the person's name, address, telephone number, birth date, date when service began, and notes about his or her reading interests. She refers to these cards when she selects books, but she does not keep records of what a person has read. She calls readers before she goes to visit them and sends each one a birthday card. No overdue fines are charged here or at the other sites served by the smaller bookmobile.

The bookmobile department is involved in a small way with the talking book service. When readers can no longer use printed materials, members of the staff refer them to the Maryland State Library for the Blind and Physically Handicapped in Baltimore, offer to go to their homes to help when the talking book machine arrives, and call occasionally to see whether the service is satisfactory.

BEHIND THE SCENES

Ms. Wilson makes a monthly narrative and statistical report to the library director. She involves staff in planning, both informally and at monthly staff meetings. (Ms. Wilson wrote to me in December 1987, saying that she had just completed a bookmobile manual that included information about all the sites served by the bookmobile, forms, schedules, office procedures, and types of programs. This was compiled with input from the staff.)

The bookmobile department spends $24,000-$25,000 each year for books and $1,000 for records. It has standing orders with G. K. Hall and Curley for large print books but needs so many that Ms. Wilson borrows 150-200 books every six months from the Maryland State Library for the Blind and Physically Handicapped.

The bookmobile department has continual publicity about its service, and the bookmobiles themselves are very visible as they roll about the county. A folder was prepared for the hospital to give to new patients, but it elicited only one call. Ms. Wilson sent churches an announcement for their bulletins. One church gave her a list of shut-ins. Ms. Sharpe called each person, but no one wanted library service. Staff members are working on a new brochure about the shut-in service and will send it to community agencies with a letter asking for publicity in agency newsletters.

In the near future Ms. Wilson hopes the library will be computerized so her department will no longer have to use its McBee keysort cards for circulation records. She would like a system that would enable staff to respond when users ask, "Do I have any more books out?" Because the bookmobile department's circulation is as high as that of any other department, Ms. Wilson feels a responsibility to give input as the library administration shops for a computer system. She has visited several libraries where this technology is being applied in bookmobile departments. As a long-term goal the department will continue to try to reach more shut-ins and will evaluate and improve its services to institutions and nutrition sites.

SERVICE TO THE DEAF COMMUNITY

Jan Viands, the library's deaf services coordinator, is not part of the bookmobile department. Like Ms. Wilson she reports to the director. I did not get to meet her, but I did learn about her work from the bookmobile staff. The library received an LSCA grant in

1982 for materials and equipment. They purchased two telecommunication devices for the deaf (TDDs). One is on the main floor of the library for patrons to use, and the other is at Ms. Viands's desk in a nonpublic area of the library to receive incoming calls.

The TDD number is publicized on bibliographies that feature books, films, and videocassettes purchased with grant money. Some of them are: "Coping with Deafness or Hearing Loss," "Learn to Sign," "Signed Stories and Books for Children," and "Working with the Deaf and Hearing Impaired." A brochure called "For the Deaf and Hearing Impaired" describes all the services, including learning kits for deaf or hearing impaired children and interpreter services provided by Ms. Viands. With other interested persons Ms. Viands has formed a deaf awareness group in the county. That group is trying to raise funds for additional equipment and to get volunteers to operate the TDD for longer hours. Ms. Rowe said that she taught the sign language alphabet and some simple signs to kindergartners and Boy Scouts and gave out copies of the brochure entitled "Sign Language Manual Alphabet," prepared by Ms. Viands.

BUILDING ACCESS

It is a stated policy of the Washington County Free Library to provide service to people with disabilities. The twenty-three-year-old building was made accessible ten years ago. People in wheelchairs use it frequently.

The Western Maryland Room, which contains historical and genealogical materials, has presented some problems. This room is on the mezzanine and can be reached only by the staff elevator or a stairway. The head of adult services said that the department keeps statistics on the use of the elevator, but often they don't catch people until they are halfway up the stairs.

I learned about a blind man who comes to the library each month to have staff read a magazine to him. Also, I happened to pick up an issue of *Handi-rap,* published by the Disabled Citizens Coordinator's Office in Washington County and read that the reference section of the Washington County Free Library houses a collection of materials owned by the Washington County Children's

Council. This collection includes information on children with special needs, for which the council had prepared a free bibliography. This library is working with the community to meet the needs of people with disabilities.

Chapter 2

Bloomington Public Library,
Bloomington, Illinois

It was recommended that I visit the Bloomington Public Library because it does an exceptional job of reaching out to blind and physically handicapped persons in Bloomington in cooperation with its subregional library. I soon discovered that Neil Kelley, extension librarian, has been an enthusiastic advocate of the talking book service since he became involved with it five years earlier.

EXTENSION SERVICES

In January 1985 the library board adopted the mission statement, goals, and objectives formulated by a planning process committee of twelve citizen members. The extension services department is involved in meeting two of the objectives: to make service accessible to residents, regardless of their ability to come to the library, and to identify community needs and respond to them. A brochure entitled "Let the Library Come to You" describes the extension services department, which takes services to people in the community who cannot use traditional library services. (See Appendix C.) The department uses a bookmobile, deposit collections, and homebound service as the delivery modes.

BOOKMOBILE SERVICE

Mr. Kelley and I headed for Westminster Village, the only retirement center served by the bookmobile, in a 1979 Gertenslager bookmobile. (Other retirement centers and nursing homes have deposit collections.) The bookmobile was stocked with paperback books, records, large print books, children's books, travel books, comic books, and current fiction acquired through the McNaughton plan. The bookmobile goes to twenty-four other places every other week. Most of these are family stops, so they are scheduled in the late afternoon and early evening when parents are home from work and children are home from school.

When Westminster Village opened, the residents immediately filled the bookshelves in the community room with books from their own collections. The bookmobile supplements this library by bringing current materials.

We stopped at Westminster Village for an hour, and a steady stream of people came to the bookmobile. A woman who couldn't climb the steps knocked at the door. She is a regular patron, and Mr. Kelley had some books ready for her. Some people borrowed books for friends who weren't able to come.

The extension program was expanding to deliver bookmobile service on evenings and Saturdays to four unserved townships contiguous to Bloomington and to use books-by-mail for residents in outlying areas. In March 1988 the residents of these townships were asked to tax themselves 1.5 mills per $100 of property assessment if they wished to continue the service by contract with the Bloomington Public Library. The one-year experimental period was funded by the Illinois State Library with an LSCA grant.

Although the library had been using UTLAS (University of Toronto Library Automated Service) since January 1986, automation had not yet reached the extension services at the time of my visit. The bookmobile was using a Regiscope charging system. Mr. Kelley said that he anticipated having a computer on board the bookmobile by the spring of 1988.

DEPOSIT COLLECTIONS AND HOMEBOUND SERVICE

Nursing homes, retirement homes, and senior centers are served by deposit collections. Extension staff members take minilibraries of 50 to 300 titles to twenty-one places, including day-care centers and the jail. These are left for three-month periods and then picked up and replaced by new collections. The library provides book cards and Gaylord boxes where volunteers or residents can leave a record of borrowed materials. The department has its own simple method of keeping records of the deposit collections. It uses a two-letter code for each site. This is put on the book card, thus providing a future record of which sites have had which books. Until mail rates went up several years ago, homebound readers were served by a books-by-mail program. Now they receive personal service, except when winter weather makes driving hazardous; then books are mailed once more. Mr. Kelley selects all the materials for fifteen homebound readers and takes care of their special requests. He puts the books in double plastic bags, donated by a local bank, and someone on his staff checks them out. Two volunteers come to the library for the bags, deliver the books to the readers, and visit a bit. One long-time volunteer is now a library board member but chose to continue her homebound visits. Mr. Kelley's wife is the second volunteer, and she substitutes for the first. Service is publicized by word of mouth, contact with social service agencies, and distribution of a brochure. A year ago Mr. Kelley sent a two-page letter to every church in town, hoping to recruit new readers, but there was no response.

THE TALKING BOOK PROGRAM

Mr. Kelley is a firm believer in the talking book program. In Illinois the books produced by the National Library Service for the Blind and Physically Handicapped are circulated from the headquarters of the state's eighteen library systems. The systems act as subregional libraries for the blind and physically handicapped. The Bloomington Public Library is part of the Corn Belt Library System and received a collection of 1,500 talking books from the subregional library in 1982. Initially Mr. Kelley selected books for many of the talking book readers in his service area and phoned requests for books not in his collection to the Corn Belt library. The service has grown to such an extent that he can no longer handle direct service. In five years he signed up 150 people, from a preschool child to people close to 100 years of age. Now he publicizes the service, sets it up, and acts as a troubleshooter.

Mr. Kelley puts information about the talking book program in the hands of doctors, optometrists, social service agencies, and the county health department. People often have to be talked into taking the service. On the one hand it has a certain stigma because it may be viewed as a handout. On the other hand people can't believe it is free; they expect there to be some catch to it. Word of mouth is the best publicity. One woman has signed up four of her friends.

People generally call to inquire about the service, and Mr. Kelley gives them the option of coming to the library or having him go to their home. (Ninety percent choose the latter.) He tries to discover their interests in the telephone conversation so he can take one or two books in each format--hard disk, flexible disk, and cassette--when he delivers the machine. He asks the person to have a friend or family member with him or her so he can train two people at one time. He prefers going to people's homes because they are more comfortable there and are not distracted by the strangeness of a new place. A visit takes about an hour. Mr. Kelley unpacks the machine, demonstrates it, and explains the service, which now comes by mail from the Corn Belt subregional library. Readers can choose to receive selections made by the computer based on their interests, to receive requests only, or to use a combination of the two. Although readers can call the Corn Belt library's toll-free number, Mr. Kelley acts as a liaison and encourages them to call if they are having problems.

Mr. Kelley has introduced talking book service to nursing homes by suggesting that the activity directors schedule listening hours while people do quiet things like puzzles or crafts. When an individual becomes interested, Mr. Kelley offers direct service. Many people start with a magazine, which may be a continuation of a subscription they had to give up when they lost their sight. Eventually they turn to books. One 45-year-old man had never read anything but westerns until he discovered talking books. Then he wanted almost everything listed in *Talking Book Topics.* Over a period of time the man requested 2,500 books.

PROGRAMS

While I was at Bloomington, I went with Mr. Kelley and Vince Sampson, his assistant, for an afternoon presentation of a BiFolkal program at a residence for senior citizens. The library has these programs four or five times a year at centers that do not have activity directors. The program was called "Remembering Summertime." Mr. Sampson played taped music reminiscent of summertimes past as the residents came into the social room of the home. Mr. Sampson read several poems from the BiFolkal kit and showed slides with recorded commentary. Then they passed around scratch-and-sniff cards, baseball cards, a small flag like the ones distributed at Fourth of July parades, mosquito netting, and a nose clip for swimmers. These items prompted people to talk about the past. Both the Bloomington Public Library and the neighboring Normal Public Library have purchased BiFolkal materials and jointly publicize their availability to people of all ages.

EXTENSION STAFF

Mr. Kelley, as head of the extension service, reports to the library director, as do the children's librarian, the adult services librarian, the circulation librarian, the technical services librarian, and the assistant to the director. Saul Amdarsky, the director, recently left to head the Kalamazoo, Michigan public library, and staff were anticipating the announcement of the new director while I was in Bloomington. (Matthew Kubiac was chosen.)

The extension services staff must be flexible. Mr. Kelley hires individuals who get along with all kinds of people and who are extroverts. He is assisted by two full-time people, Vince Sampson, whose skills as a magician are an asset in bookmobile programming, and Dwayne Hoskins, a college student at Illinois Wesleyan University, who does the evening bookmobile runs. Debbie Suttle, a part-time clerk, helps with the experimental project.

MATERIALS

Extension services uses its own collection of materials, except for special requests, which are filled from the library's regular collection. The 1986-87 budget for materials was $24,000. The service buys no large print but borrows around 1,000 books on extended loan from the Corn Belt Library System headquarters. A staff member in the long-term-care section of the local hospital also goes to the system headquarters to borrow large print books. The Bloomington library has a collection of large print books for its walk-in patrons. Extension services has some, but not enough, commercial spoken word books. Mr. Kelley applied for LSCA money to buy a collection to serve as a bridge for people not yet eligible for the Library of Congress talking book service. He was turned down but will reapply and will try to get funds from other sources. The department also has collections of high interest low reading level materials and BiFolkal kits.

OTHER SERVICES

While extension services is primarily responsible for serving people with disabilities, the rest of the library is also responsive to their needs. A power-assisted door with a push button was recently installed in the front entrance as part of a $20,000 LSCA grant. Accessible restrooms, water fountain, and telephone; an elevator; and parking spaces close to the library help make the library accessible to people with physical disabilities. The computer terminals can be used by people in wheelchairs. Sign language classes were offered in the city at the instigation of a concerned advocate for deaf people, but there has been little opportunity for the staff to practice their skills because deaf people rarely use the library. The library has books on signing and will be getting some videotapes on library usage, produced by the Illinois School for the Deaf. In addition to its books the library circulates sculpture, art prints, videotapes, folders of pamphlets, college catalogs, records, cassettes, and magazines. A wealth of bibliographies and guides to library service encourages people to use the library.

PART 2

EMPHASIS ON OUTREACH

Outreach is one of those words that can be used to mean what you want it to mean. One library administrator called outreach peripheral activities. The *Library Outreach Reporter,* a bimonthly newsletter initiated in 1987, reports on topics such as services to people with disabilities, programs for older people, literacy programs, and ethnic library service. Its emphasis is consistent with New York State's definition of outreach in its Coordinated Outreach Service grants. Grants have been appropriated since 1981 for services for people who are educationally disadvantaged, for members of ethnic or minority groups in need of special services, for unemployed people in need of job placement assistance, for people living in areas underserved by a library, and for those who are blind, physically handicapped, aged, or confined in institutions. Based on this view of outreach, librarians reach out into the community to attract nontraditional library users.

In this section I am using outreach in a more limited sense, to mean the delivery of service to patrons beyond the library building. This seems to be the focus of the four libraries discussed in this section. All of these libraries serve metropolitan areas and have strong outreach programs. All have bookmobiles, but they use them in different ways. Service to homebound individuals is provided by volunteers and by mail in the Hennepin County Library in Minnesota, by staff in the District of Columbia Public Library, and by mail in the Public Library of Cincinnati and Hamilton County in Ohio and the Tampa-Hillsborough County Public Library System in Florida. All the libraries deliver collections of library materials to nursing homes and other sites from where it is difficult, if not impossible, for people to go to the library. The District of Columbia Public Library devotes more time to programs for adults, and the Cincinnati library to programs for children; both Hennepin County and Tampa do some programming for people who are unable to attend programs at the library. Cincinnati's exceptional children's department has been a model for service to children with disabilities.

Two of the libraries operate regional libraries for the blind and physically handicapped: Cincinnati for half a state, and the District of Columbia for the nation's capital. The Tampa library has a subregional library for the blind and physically handicapped that serves the residents of Hillsborough County.

The District of Columbia Public Library has the nation's first librarian to the deaf community and a well-developed service. Hennepin County and Tampa have TDDs at several locations in their systems, and Cincinnati has a TDD at the main library. Hennepin County interprets some of its programs for deaf adults and children.

Services to people with disabilities in Hennepin County are primarily the responsibility of the outreach section. Cincinnati's services are clustered in three departments: exceptional children, institutions/books-by-mail/bookmobile, and the library for the blind and physically handicapped. Most of the services for people with disabilities in the District of Columbia Public Library are provided through the library for the blind and physically handicapped. In Tampa the special services branch has this responsibility.

Chapter 3

Public Library of Cincinnati and Hamilton County, Cincinnati, Ohio

Coy Hunsucker and I were at the Frost Elementary School in Cincinnati, Ohio, waiting for a group of children with multiple handicaps to return to their homeroom. Ms. Hunsucker, head of the exceptional children's department of the Public Library of Cincinnati and Hamilton County, was preparing to create a bit of magic as she introduced several dozen books to the class.

Ms. Hunsucker takes Benny, a bashful puppet, along on many of her library visits. Benny hides in her canvas book bag with an assortment of books that are preselected for the particular group she is visiting. After Benny overcomes his shyness, he comes out to talk to the children, asks Ms. Hunsucker to read a favorite story, and encourages the group to participate in the conversation, finger plays, or songs.

Earlier we had visited a class of hearing impaired children who use several forms of communication: cued speech, lip reading, and sign language. Teachers and parents were there to help with the interpretation, and Ms. Hunsucker communicated by speaking slowly and signing.

Our last visit was to another school where a class of learning disabled students received Ms. Hunsucker enthusiastically and competed for the opportunity to help carry bags of books to her car. Normally she leaves books for the children to read until she returns the following month, but this was her last visit of the school year.

SERVICE TO EXCEPTIONAL CHILDREN

Each month during the school year Ms. Hunsucker and two other staff members (one professional librarian and one paraprofessional who has been in the department over twelve years) visit approximately sixty-five classes in forty-two schools in Hamilton County. These classes contain children who are educable or trainable mentally handicapped, multiple handicapped, visually impaired, emotionally disturbed, or severely behavior disordered. (This last group is a growing one.) Staff members also make year-round visits to read stories and leave books with twelve groups of children in seven hospitals and disability centers. These groups include autistic, deaf, and multiple handicapped preschoolers and young people with cerebral palsy. The librarians also take collections of books to young people in four centers for socially maladjusted youth and visit six schools and institutions for profoundly handicapped and hearing impaired children.

Although some of the agencies are in session the entire year, library staff make fewer visits during the summer. Instead they offer programs in parks, playgrounds, and church-related centers. Puppet shows, story hours, and enrichment programs in branch libraries, primarily for but not limited to gifted and accelerated children, keep the staff extremely busy from June through August.

All of this is accomplished with the help of a full-time clerical person and a part-time person with a learning disability who shelves books and does other clerical tasks. Preparation for a visit takes several days. Each librarian collects books for his or her visit and chooses stories to read or tell. The library assistant prepares the collection for circulation, keeps records of what is taken, and marks the appointment calendar to show when everything is ready.

The visits last twenty to thirty minutes each, and the books are introduced in the manner most appropriate to the particular group. For example, with developmentally disabled children between the ages of six and eight, the librarian reads at least two stories and has a special treat between the stories, such as a pop-up book, a song from a book in the collection, or a flannel board story.

To keep up with the schedule, some staff go for visits every day, traveling in a library van or using their own cars with the library reimbursing them 22.5 cents per mile. In spite of the number of children the staff works with, this is a very personal service. The same staff member visits the same place each time and makes an effort to remember the names of the children. The children get to know the library lady or man and find it hard to accept a new face when it is occasionally necessary to send a substitute. At the beginning of the school year the librarians go to the school office and identify themselves. After that the formality of school visits is reduced to a wave as they go by the office.

The service to homebound children is minimal now. Privacy laws have slowed the referral process; area boards of education cannot give the library the names of the children in their programs. The contact person in the special education office must tell the home tutors, who tell the parents about the service. Then the request for service comes back to Ms. Hunsucker through the same channels. Even a flyer directed to the home tutors has not produced referrals. Personal contact between the librarian and the child's family is the magic element.

History of Exceptional Service

Exceptional service will soon celebrate its thirtieth anniversary. It was begun in 1959 when Eulalie Ross, the coordinator of library services for children, appealed to the library director and the library board for a children's librarian to devote full time to exploring the needs of exceptional children and giving them service tailored to those needs. Hilda Limper, a children's librarian in the system, was hired, and she worked alone for eight years. In preparation for her responsibility, Ms. Limper did extensive reading, followed by course work on the exceptional child at Syracuse University and a week each observing at the Lexington School for the Deaf in New York City, New York's Library for the Blind, and Children's Memorial Hospital in Boston. Back in Cincinnati she became familiar with the resources for exceptional children locally and spent time at agencies, hospitals, and schools in Cincinnati and Hamilton County.

In 1966 the program became a two-year demonstration project on library service to exceptional children sponsored by the ALA, Children's Services Division, Committee on Service to Exceptional

Children, and funded through the State Library of Ohio with LSCA funds. Four additional persons were hired at that time: Coy Hunsucker, another librarian, a paraprofessional assistant, and a clerical assistant. Dr. Michael Hirt, research psychologist at Kent State University in Ohio, worked on the research aspects of the project, and a committee representing ALA served as advisors. "Reaching Out: The Library and the Exceptional Child," a film produced by Connecticut Films, Inc., in 1968, disseminated the results of the project nationwide. An article in *Top of the News* in January 1970 generated further interest.[1]

The objectives of the project were to demonstrate how ALA's 1964 *Standards for Children's Services in Public Libraries* could be applied to exceptional children. In a brochure produced by the project, these are stated as: "(a) to make a varied collection of books and other library material available; (2) to give guidance to children in their choice of books; (3) to . . . cultivate the enjoyment of reading. A further objective is to compile lists of suitable books and suggestions for techniques to increase use and value of library materials."[2] The project was successful and grew from the 52 classes and groups serving 466 children in October 1968 to 200 groups serving 2,509 children in 1987. This growth occurred in spite of the loss of one professional staff member and half of a clerical position when federal funding came to an end. Ms. Hunsucker became head of the department in 1974.

In its early days the program was well publicized in the local media, and Hilda Limper called, wrote letters, and visited principals, teachers, directors of hospitals, and key agency staff.

The Service Today

Now the exceptional children's department does not advertise for new sites but keeps a waiting list of places that hear about the service and request it. The librarians go back to the same schools and agencies each year, making contacts as early as August if the schools have not called them first to set up a schedule. They work closely with the teachers who often call with special requests. Ms. Hunsucker and first assistant Mark Kelso are generous with their time and frequently speak to librarians and university classes (library science and education) about the program or about motivating children to read. The department also advises parents and teachers in their choice of reading materials for children.

The department is now housed in a nonpublic area of the beautiful, newly renovated, and expanded main library. Its collection of over 16,000 items includes books for the developing reader who needs basic materials, the nonreader who will never be able to read, the reluctant reader who needs books with appealing formats and low reading levels, and the average reader. These are supplemented by books for adolescents on contemporary topics, books about handicapping conditions, and stories about children with special needs. The collection also includes stories in sign language, pop-up books, pictures for augmenting programs, puppets, realia, stuffed animals, flannel board stories, and puppet stages. Pamphlets on the needs of the children served by the department and on subjects of interest to the children and periodicals about handicapped children and of interest to children and young adults are also part of the department's library. The newest collection is a file of materials for use in the summer enrichment program for gifted and talented young people.

All three librarians are involved in book selection. They go to the library's book selection room where they can examine new books before purchasing them. They indicate which ones they'd like, and Ms. Hunsucker reviews all choices and makes the final decisions. Currently the department spends approximately $17,000 annually for books and other materials. There is no petty cash for expendable items like play putty or flour and salt for play dough, so Ms. Hunsucker purchases these with her own money and is reimbursed by the library later.

Publications

Based on the program's experience with children with special needs, the department has compiled lists of books for specific groups and has suggested techniques to increase children's appreciation and enjoyment of library materials. One of the first bibliographies, and perhaps the most popular, was "Books for Mentally Retarded Children." It has been revised twice and was issued as two bibliographies in 1986: "Books for Developmentally Handicapped Children" and "Books for Severe and Profoundly Developmentally Handicapped Children." The "High Interest Low Vocabulary Reading List" is being revised for the second time, and "Dealing with Difficulties" is in its first revision. Ms. Hunsucker is developing three new booklets with the following tentative titles: "Feelings and Emotions for Younger Children," "Books about Handicapped Children," and "Books in Large Print for Children" (in the intermediate grades). Ms. Hunsucker is a frequent speaker at workshops and conferences for librarians where she shares the techniques developed over almost thirty years. She also shares them through articles such as those listed in the bibliography of this chapter.

Planning and Evaluation

Seven years ago Ms. Hunsucker had to hire her first professional staff member. Mark Kelso was a children's librarian in a branch, and Ms. Hunsucker knew by observing him that he would fit into the department. She introduced him to the work by taking him to the places he would be visiting. The service is flexible; when assignments do not work out, Ms. Hunsucker is willing to change the schedule. When staff come up with a new idea, her philosophy is to try it and see what happens.

There has been no formal evaluation of the service since the demonstration period, but Ms. Hunsucker measures its success by the responses of the children and the teachers. If the children can catch the excitement of reading, she feels the librarians have done their job well. Some teachers are very enthusiastic, as I observed when I visited; others take the exceptional children's department for granted. Teachers transferring from one school to another frequently request library service if library staff members are not already visiting their school. The fact that other librarians seek out Ms. Hunsucker's advice is an additional measure of the effectiveness of this program. Her ambition is to have more staff who can go to other groups in the community, including groups of adults.

The exceptional children's department is responsible to Paul Hudson, deputy librarian for main library services. He is in charge of two other special service departments: the library for the blind and physically handicapped, which was formerly housed in a warehouse building approximately six blocks from the main library, and institutions/books-by-mail/bookmobile, previously located in two separate library branches.

INSTITUTIONS/BOOKS-BY-MAIL/
BOOKMOBILE

Keith Kuhn, head of institutions/books-by-mail/bookmobile, took me on a tour of his department, which is close to the exceptional children's department. With its relocation in the main library, institutions/books-by-mail formally merged with the bookmobile department. There has been close cooperation between the two since 1982. Most of the community stops for the bookmobile were phased out from 1979 to 1985. The service to homebound adults, established in 1969 with an LSCA grant, was replaced by books-by-mail in 1979. The merger of all three services was a logical progression of events.

In 1987 the department offered the following services:

- Deposit collections and/or personal service to individuals in 116 nursing homes and retirement centers.

- Collections in five correctional institutions.

- Free books-by-mail service to persons confined to their homes.

- Large print books and juvenile collections to branches as requested.

- Several bookmobile stops in areas not served by branches and stops at schools and centers for mentally handicapped and hearing impaired people and an orphanage.

- Juvenile collections to schools.

The service budgeted $48,000 for adult materials and $66,500 for children's items in 1987. Walking through the large stack area that has already expanded into another department's stack space since the move to the main library in 1982, I saw children's books; adult fiction, color coded to make Gothics, mysteries, westerns, and other genre easier to shelve; adult nonfiction; popular magazines, like *Ladies Home Journal, McCall's,* and *National Geographic*; craft and gerontology books for use by activity directors in nursing homes and retirement centers; paperbacks and picture books for adults; large print books and magazines (the department has standing orders with G. K. Hall, Ulverscroft, Thorndike, ISIS, Walker Large Print, and Curley for two to three copies of their books and is starting to order children's books); BiFolkal kits for activity directors to use in programming; musical cassettes; and records. The librarians go to the book selection room once a week to select new books. They receive four copies of best-sellers, selected by the deputy librarian. The department has its own adult, juvenile, and large print card catalog and shelf list.

Circulation statistics show that the collection is well used. Of the 31,787 items circulated in April 1987, 29,556 were books. Nursing homes, retirement centers, and senior centers used 5,472 regular print books, 3,356 large print, and 2,231 nonprint items. (Nonprint circulation is high because each slide in a BiFolkal kit counts as one circulated item.) Circulation at community stops not served by branches totaled 1,818 and that at schools was 15,826. Books-by-mail readers received 426 regular print and 275 large print books and magazines; 2,300 large print books and 83 juvenile books went to the branches.

Staff

The department is staffed by eleven full-time people and four part-time shelvers. Two of the staff, the head and the first assistant, are professionals. Except for two librarian Is (paraprofessionals) and three library assistant IIIs (between clerical and paraprofessional), the rest are Library Assistant IIs (clerical). Generally staff members are promoted from within the system. In interviewing potential employees Mr. Kuhn emphasizes the special service aspect of the work and talks to candidates about situations that may make them uncomfortable. He goes along with new staff members on their first visits into the community. The drivers for the van and bookmobile are employees of a separate department, facilities services. The institutions/books-by-mail/ bookmobile department sends its monthly schedule to the supervisor of facilities services, who assigns drivers.

Service to Institutions

The internal procedures have changed little since the institutions/homebound service was established. The department keeps a profile sheet and record of what each person has read. The profile sheet for large print readers requesting books through the branches lists the name, address, and phone number of the reader; the date service began; the name of the branch; the reader's card number; and the number and type of large print books the reader wants. Staff keep records of books read on 3-by-5-inch slips for all except sporadic readers. They also keep profile sheets for the institutions.

Preparation for trips on a three to four week schedule is continuous. The trip box, a wooden box with 3-by-5-inch cards for each institution and for each individual in the institution who gets personalized service, is the circulation file. After staff select books from the shelves, library assistants place the cards for each book in front of the appropriate 3-by-5-inch card and secure them with a rubber band. They pack the books in green canvas bags and tag each bag with the name of the institution, the individual, or both. A staff member and the driver deliver the books, but someone must be on hand to receive them. If no one is available, a brightly colored bookmark with a Sorry We Missed You message is placed in the door.

The calendar for May 11, 1987, showed a van scheduled for the West Hills area. On that trip it delivered books to individuals at Crestview Nursing Home, Harrison House Nursing Home, Hillebrand Nursing Home, Hilltop Nursing Home, Judson Village, Summit Nursing Home, Three Rivers Nursing Home, and West Hills Nursing Home, and it left book collections at Judson Village and West Park. Whenever the staff member returns to the library, he or she processes notes from the trip--requests, changes in patron profile information, new patrons, problems. A library assistant types and files the reader records (3-by-5-inch author/title slips) of the books delivered on the trip. The slips are arranged alphabetically, first by the name of the institution and then by the patron's last name; these slips are referred to when future selections are made. The department does not charge overdue fines.

Mr. Kuhn said that there has been considerable growth in the service to institutions in the past year because of the local development of retirement communities. The department has been adding one to three institutions each month. To keep up with this development, Mr. Kuhn and Tania Moorman, first assistant, watch the media and look for listings of new homes in the yellow pages of the telephone directory. They then call the administrators, who assign library contact persons. Some places want only collections. Some want both collections and delivery to individuals. Some have a library committee or a librarian in residence.

The Cincinnati library does not have contracts with the institutions. However, if there is evidence that no one is taking responsibility for the collection, the department withdraws it. The institutions service distributes a yearly calendar to each institution and circles the appropriate delivery dates. A department representative publicizes the service at the annual Senior Expo, which is sponsored by the Cincinnati Council on Aging, and at fairs in local neighborhoods.

Books-by-Mail

A single staff member is responsible for books-by-mail, which replaced the homebound service when gasoline prices skyrocketed in the late seventies. The library administration felt the homebound service was so labor-intensive that its cost could not be justified. Books-by-mail service is available to anyone without good access to library service. The person does not have to have a disability, nor is certification of eligibility required. The books-by-mail brochure states that the service can be used by any adult who cannot travel to a public library because of ill health or a physical handicap or any adult who has no transportation to the public library. The library's public relations department publicizes this service.

The department buys two copies of each paperback title for its basic books-by-mail collection and places blue dots on the spines to identify them. Each year it produces an annotated catalog that, consistent with library policy in response to local community concern about obscenity, identifies books of an explicit nature with an *A*--for adults only. The department also produces an annual catalog of large print books from which readers can make choices.

Guide Post, accompanied by flyers listing current books, is also sent to books-by-mail readers and readers in institutions. *Guide Post* is published by the library ten times a year. It gives library news and descriptions of both fiction and nonfiction of general interest, children's books, large print books, books for exceptional children, books from the library for the blind and physically handicapped, videocassettes, audiocassettes, records, and compact discs from the library's total collection. If books-by-mail readers want a title or information on a subject not listed in any of these, the staff will try to locate it, just as they would for any other reader.

The books-by-mail service is free. The library pays the postage both ways, except for large print books, which can be mailed as free reading matter for the blind. Staff members mail regular books in jiffy bags and enclose another jiffy bag, preaddressed to the library, with return postage on it. Large print patrons return books in the same envelope in which they receive them and place the preaddressed mailing label marked Free over the old label. Readers can call in their requests or can use an order form supplied by the library. Books are checked out for thirty-five days.

Large Print Books

The institutions/books-by-mail/bookmobile department is the major purchaser of large print books in the library. Patrons who want titles that are not in the browsing collection in the public area of the main library are directed to the special services desk, where a staff member will make a call to the department to see if the titles are available. One staff member in the department prepares short annotations for a large print catalog and the *Guide Post*. The annual catalog is typeset in 16-point type, upper and lower case, black print on white paper. Titles are arranged by subject categories--historical adventure, suspense, general fiction, Gothic, and the like. They are also arranged alphabetically by author. Again an *A* indicates books for adults only.

The department is planning a major public relations campaign for large print materials, feeling that they have been a well-kept secret. Even though there has been a dramatic increase in circulation (9 percent in the past year), much of that comes from the institutions.

Other Services

The adult centers for developmentally disabled people are served by monthly bookmobile stops. The bookmobile also goes to St. Rita's School for the Deaf and to St. Aloysius, an orphanage.

The BiFolkal kits are popular with activity directors. These are publicized through a brochure prepared by the public relations department.

As to the future, Mr. Kuhn would like more staff, computerization of the department's records, and more programming. Staff do a few book talks now, and a poetry program is quite successful. This department and the exceptional children's department are jointly planning puppet shows at selected bookmobile stops during the summer.

LIBRARY FOR THE BLIND AND PHYSICALLY HANDICAPPED

The third part of Cincinnati and Hamilton County Public Library's special services is the library for the blind and physically handicapped. This is in fact the oldest department. The library for the blind and physically handicapped mails books and magazines recorded on discs and cassettes and in braille to approximately 6,000 eligible readers in thirty-three counties in the southern half of Ohio. It employs a staff of seventeen: one professional librarian (Carol Heideman, regional librarian); eight clerks, including one who is blind; and eight part-time shelvers. Sixty-eight percent of its funding comes from the State Library of Ohio. An automated system, developed in cooperation with IBM, enables the library to match readers' interests with the collection. As soon as a book is returned, another is sent in its place. This is called the return and exchange service. Priority is given to filling the patron's requests for specific books; however, if no requested titles are available, the computer makes a selection. Readers also have the option of request only, by which they receive only the books they request from catalogs produced by the National Library Service for the Blind and Physically Handicapped. The third option is will-call service. Where the library sends books only when the reader calls with a request. The department communicates with readers through a newsletter, published twelve times a year, and a toll-free telephone line.

How do persons in Hamilton County benefit from having a regional library so close by? Readers have easier access to talking books. If they run out of books delivered through the usual mail channels, they can go to the downtown library or call the regional library, which will send books for them to pick up at their local branch library. The local radio reading service, which broadcasts the *Cincinnati Magazine*, the Sunday edition of the *Cincinnati Enquirer* and the *Catholic Telegraph* (all local publications), sends taped recordings of these to the library. The library in turn makes copies for interested readers. The library arranges for volunteers to record League of Women Voters information about candidates before each election. The librarian belongs to local consumer groups, such as the American Council for the Blind and the National Federation of the Blind. In fact Ms. Heideman was named Sighted Person of the Year in 1986 by the Ohio chapter of the National Federation of the Blind. A consumer advisory committee meets with the two regional libraries in Ohio; a Hamilton County woman, Debbie Kendrick, formerly chaired that group.

SPECIAL SERVICES DESK

When special services were brought together under one roof, a special services desk was established on the second floor in a public access area of the main library. It has a browsing collection of books for children and adults in braille, on disc, and on cassette; catalogs of materials available from the regional library; a braille dictionary, and the *Talking World Book.* Also in the area are a disc player, a cassette player, a radio reading service receiver, and a battery-operated TDD that is kept in the desk drawer. The desk is staffed half-time by the regional library staff and the rest of the time by the institutions/books-by-mail/bookmobile staff. Both Paul Hudson, deputy director and head of the main library, and Carol Heideman expressed disappointment that it has been used so little. It was planned as a private place where users with problems could be sent. Yet it is so private that staff on duty do not have direct access to the public catalog and are hampered in their information-giving role. The electrical outlets in the carrels are inoperative and the equipment cannot be used. The collection is too small for browsing. It is hard to get to, even when a staff member gives directions. Ms. Heideman reported that its greatest hour of effectiveness was during Bookfest, an annual event, when several thousand school children toured the library and had the opportunity to talk to a regional library employee who is blind.

ACCESSIBILITY

The main library meets the standards for access to people in wheelchairs. Although it has parking space for only a few staff members, Mr. Hudson assured me that it was convenient to public transportation lines. Accessibility was a primary concern during the construction of the main library addition and all new branch libraries. People unable to use the older inaccessible branches are served in an accessible building or through books-by-mail. For many years the administration has shown sensitivity to the information needs of people with disabilities and has purchased books about disability issues. These have been featured in displays and bibliographies. In 1987, the library received two important awards. The Cincinnati chapter of the National Association of the Physically Handicapped, and Total Living Concepts, an accessibility advocacy group, recognized the library's services to people with disabilities.

UNMET NEEDS

I asked Mr. Hudson what he felt still needed to be done. Although he has no long-range plan in mind, he would like to initiate some service for the deaf community. The TDD at the information desk is rarely used (except by one staff member who is deaf), even though there was newspaper publicity when it was installed and it is listed in the TDD directory. The library has sent staff members to sign language classes, but there has been no opportunity for them to practice their skills at the library. Mr. Hudson suggested that the library offer story hours for deaf children. The Public Library of Cincinnati and Hamilton County has served people with disabilities for over fifty years. Once it makes the decision to commit the resources and to extend service to another segment of the population, I'm sure it will meet with success.

Notes

1. Hilda K. Limper, Michael Hirt, and Elaine Tillman, "Library Service to Exceptional Children," *Top of the News* 26 (January 1970):193-204.

2. "Demonstration of Library Services to Exceptional Children" (Cincinnati, Ohio: Public Library, n.d.), 2.

References

A Decade of Service, 1930-1940. Cincinnati, Ohio: Public Library of Cincinnati and Hamilton County, 1941.

"Demonstration of Library Services to Exceptional Children." Cincinnati, Ohio: Public Library, n.d., 2.

Hunsucker, Coy K. "Library Service to Children with Special Needs." April 1985. Mimeo.

_____. "Library Service to Developmentally Handicapped Children." November 20, 1985. Mimeo.

_____. "Library Service to Learning Disabled Children." April 1985. Mimeo.

_____. "Public Library Service to Blind and Physically Handicapped Children." *HRLSD Journal* 2 (Fall 1976):3-5.

Limper, Hilda K., and Michael Hirt. "A Demonstration of Library Services to Exceptional Children." Mimeo.

Limper, Hilda K., Michael Hirt, and Elaine Tillman. "Library Service to Exceptional Children." *Top of the News* 26 (January 1970):193-204.

_____. "Work with Exceptional Children." October 1968. Mimeo.

Smith, Claudine. "Special Library Services for Ohioans' Special Needs." *Wonderful World of Ohio Magazine* 33 (October 1969):34-37.

Chapter 4

Hennepin County Library, Minnetonka, Minnesota

My appointment was with Ann Eccles, head of the outreach service of the Hennepin County Library. While I waited in the administrative offices, in the Ridgedale Library in Minnetonka, Minnesota, I read a wall plaque stating that in July 1986 the National Association of Counties had awarded the library its County Achievement Award for Putting People First.

The Hennepin County Library serves all of Hennepin County except Minneapolis on the eastern edge of the county. This represents roughly one-twelfth of a total area of 611 square miles. Most of the library's funding comes from property taxes and other taxes levied by county government. The system has twenty-two community libraries (the last opening in October 1987) and three area libraries. Several contiguous community libraries now form clusters. The area libraries have larger collections and offer more services. Ridgedale area library has an impressive collection: books; periodicals; records; compact discs; videocassettes; audiocassettes; 8-, super 8-, and 16-mm films; filmstrips; slides; art prints; maps; pamphlets; computer software; microfiche; and microfilm. It also houses a collection for adult new readers, consumer information, telephone books, and large print materials.

Online database searching at no charge for a maximum of fifteen articles is offered at the three area libraries. Children's and adult nonfiction have been shelved together since the mid-seventies. Easy nonfiction and fiction for children is in the children's room. An active Friends group has purchased Apple computers for many of the libraries. The information desk is staffed by professionally trained librarians. The library catalog has been computerized since the early 1970s. The printed catalog was discontinued in 1986. How to use the catalog is explained in a readable, easy-to-understand, four-page brochure. Small conference rooms are used by adult new readers and their tutors. The library and all but four branches meet the standards for access to persons with disabilities.

STAFF TRAINING

Ms. Eccles arranged for me to talk to Marilyn Lustig from the materials selection section. Ms. Lustig serves on the eight-member Staff Development and Training Committee, made up of both professionals and nonprofessionals. A workshop held by the MELSA Task Force on Service to the Disabled inspired her to plan an Awareness Workshop for Special Populations for the Hennepin County Library staff. (MELSA is the Metropolitan Library Service Agency, an organization of libraries in the seven-county Minneapolis-St. Paul area.)

The same two-and-a-half-hour workshop was presented eight times to different staff members during October and November 1986 to increase the staff's racial and cultural awareness and sensitivity to disabled persons. A member of the committee hosted and introduced each session. The workshops began with "Sensitivity to the Disabled," a videotape produced by Library Video Network in Baltimore, Maryland. Sharon Rendack, a library staff member with postpolio syndrome and a counseling background, led participants in a fifteen-minute session of imagining what it would be like to have a disability. A panel of two people representing agencies in the community or persons with disabilities (including a hearing impaired library staff member) spoke for ten minutes each and then led open discussion. The panel was different for each of the sessions.

After a break participants viewed "Eye of the Storm," a film about racial and cultural awareness, and an affirmative action representative of the county concluded each workshop by leading fifteen minutes of discussion. The library administration strongly recommended that staff attend one session of the workshop and

250-300 did, more than half the total staff. The committee gave supervisors a page of guidelines for follow-up sessions, and some supervisors later held discussion sessions with their staff.

PROGRAMMING

Hennepin County Library is heavily involved in programming. Through MELSA the library contracts with a local community college theatre group called Theatre in a Trunk to perform plays during the summer. Twenty performances are also taken to nursing homes. Several are interpreted for hearing impaired people, as are mainstreamed story hours for children. Programs on how to use the library are presented to senior citizens, teenagers, and other groups. Community librarians serve people in group homes in their areas by giving tours of the library and special programs. The library has its own television studio and offers programs for adults and children on cable TV on a regular basis. The Southdale-Hennepin Area Library has a media lab with two darkrooms and audiovisual equipment that the public can use.

SERVICE TO DEAF PERSONS

Hearing impaired persons have access to the library through TDDs at two of the three area libraries. Messages are forwarded to community libraries as necessary. A brochure for hearing impaired persons, published in 1982, lists library materials and services and explains how the library's TDD service works. The library purchases closed-captioned videocassettes when this is an option. Its video catalog lists these items.

THE OUTREACH SECTION

Although people with disabilities can use many of the services and resources of the Hennepin County Library, the outreach section has primary responsibility for serving them. Ann Eccles became supervisor of the section in August 1986, following seventeen years of experience in the system. She was most recently head of the Wayzata Library, part of an experimental four-library cluster. The outreach section, which is part of the collection/special services division, includes the bookmobile, the deposit collections, the homebound program, the volunteer office, and corrections (service to jails and other correctional institutions). Responsibility as liaison with the Friends groups was added when Ms. Eccles became head. Ms. Eccles and a secretary are the only full-time employees in the section, and part-time people are assigned to individual segments of the section's operation.

Shortly after Ms. Eccles began her job, she had to start long-range planning as part of the library system's five-year plan. Everyone in the section participated and saw how their work fitted into the total picture. Ms. Eccles anticipates a major change in the bookmobile service. It currently has half-day community stops four days a week, and goes to four or five residences for senior citizens on alternate Fridays, making stops of thirty to forty-five minutes at each place. The bookmobile librarian is investigating alternatives, possibly a mobile service with more emphasis on nursing homes and day-care centers.

Deposit Collection Sites

Nancy Nyberg, the deposit collections librarian, works twenty hours a week in this service. For the past two years the library has served sixty nursing homes, senior centers, and senior apartments. Outreach coordinates what is essentially a service from all the libraries in the system. It tries to pair libraries with deposit collection sites in their immediate community, but it is not always able to do so because the nursing homes tend to be concentrated in the southern part of the county. A librarian at each library selects books for one or more sites from that library's collection, which includes large print materials. The collections are boxed and sent to outreach by Friday afternoon for delivery by library truck to the homes the following week. The secretary at outreach checks to see that all collections are ready for delivery. Every other month each site receives a new collection in exchange for the books it has. The books that are being returned are brought back to outreach first and sent back to the community library the following day.

Although no overdue fines are charged, the library's computerized circulation system does generate overdue notices, which are mailed to the person responsible for the collection at each site. This individual may be an activities director, a resident, or a volunteer selected and trained by the library. The library provides carts for the books if no area has been set aside for shelving the collection. The checkout system at the sites is quite loose and varies according to the whim of the deposit collection "librarian." The size of the collection depends on the number and interests of the residents. Ideally the librarian at each community library calls the site to see if there are special requests. Sometimes the site calls the community library or outreach with requests; if a book is needed between regular deliveries, the deposit collections librarian will mail it.

To request a deposit collection, the site usually contacts the outreach section. The deposit collection librarian visits the site to meet the staff, tour the facility, and collect relevant information. She recommends sites to the outreach librarian, who consults with the appropriate division manager for assignment to a library. After approval, she and the librarian selecting the deposit collection from the community library meet with the activity director to determine the size and types of materials that should be sent. There is no written agreement, although Ms. Eccles feels there should be some form outlining the responsibilities of the library and the site and the conditions for terminating service. Whenever service has been terminated in the past, it has been a joint decision by both parties.

Ms. Eccles suggests that community library staff also offer book talks at deposit collection sites, but it is up to the local library to take the initiative for any programs.

Service to Homebound Persons

Materials sent to Hennepin County residents confined to the home temporarily or permanently because of illness, physical handicap, disability, the weather, or lack of transportation may be delivered by mail or a volunteer. A brochure describes both services, and an application form lets people specify their choice of delivery as well as the option of receiving service through the Minnesota Regional

Library for the Blind and Physically Handicapped at Faribault. Homebound readers are recruited primarily by word of mouth (e.g., a satisfied reader tells a friend.) Application forms are available at all branch libraries. Articles about the service appear in local newspapers, and outreach has worked with the Jewish Family Service and the Hennepin County Social Service Department to publicize it.

Becky Mobarry, a half-time library assistant, is responsible for mailing books to homebound readers. This is the preferred service because readers can be more independent when using it. With the help of clerks and volunteers, Ms. Mobarry sends approximately 400 books a month to 250 people. She chooses books from a collection of paperbacks and books leased from Baker and Taylor. There are thirty new titles every month. However, her readers have access to anything in the Hennepin County library collection. She has a computer terminal in her office through which she can request books from other libraries in the system or can have a book that is out of the library sent to her when it is returned. She can also request books from libraries outside the system, but mailing time makes this impractical. She checks books out for six weeks, using the automated circulation system, and mails them in a canvas zip bag that can hold up to twelve paperback books or four to six hardcover books. The library supplies stamps clipped inside a book for return postage. Readers call or put a note in the return package if they want more books.

New readers can apply for service by using the library's application form or they can call outreach. If they do not already have a library card, a fact that can be checked in the computer, Ms. Mobarry gets the necessary information and assigns the reader a number. For persons who want the mail service, she asks their permission to keep a record of the books they read.

The outreach section has a personal computer, and every day Ms. Mobarry gives the secretary who operates it a stack of slips for books she has mailed out, each having the date, reader's name, author, and title of the book. On Friday of each week the outreach secretary gives her a list of books each reader has had, arranged alphabetically by title. As she chooses books for readers, she checks this list to avoid sending a reader a book he or she has already had.

The list also alerts her to readers she has not heard from recently. She encourages readers to send in requests, and she sends the library's current annotated book list to avid readers. She sends the library's large print catalog to the thirty or forty large print readers. Ms. Mobarry encourages everyone to read reviews of new books in magazines and newspapers. She refers readers who require talking books to the Minnesota Regional Library for the Blind and Physically Handicapped or offers to send them audiotapes from the Hennepin County library's collection. Readers who receive books by mail receive overdue reminder notices, but no fines are charged.

In March 1987 Ms. Mobarry sent a survey form to the 225 people who were then receiving books by mail; 145 readers responded. Most were satisfied with the service. The most radical change they suggested was that they receive a monthly list of books. Ms. Mobarry sent all readers an annotated list of books in May 1987 and plans to continue this service on a quarterly or semiannual basis. Such a mailing always generates extra requests.

The Volunteer Office

Among her many duties Cathy Hoffman, volunteer coordinator, finds and trains the more than sixty volunteers who take books to homebound people who choose that option. She says that a notice in the library nearest to the person to be served is the best recruiting method. This service requires a low investment of time, and library users often want to give something back to the library that has given so much to them. Ms. Hoffman first interviews the volunteer applicant by phone and then sees them face to face. She gives the volunteer a packet of material about library service. She calls the homebound person to set up an appointment for the volunteer's first visit, at which time the volunteer will work out a schedule for future visits. Frequency varies--once a week, every other week, or every third week--in order to fit the library's loan period. The volunteer can select books from any library. Ms. Hoffman's role after placing the volunteer is one of troubleshooting and record keeping. The volunteer gives her a quarterly record of the hours spent on the assignment, and Ms. Hoffman checks to see how things are going. Seventy to eighty readers are visited by volunteers.

When Ms. Hoffman conducted a survey of readers served by volunteers, she learned that some volunteers had not been in touch with readers for two or three months and that some readers no longer lived in Hennepin County's service area.

Ms. Hoffman also recruits, places, and helps to train seventy volunteers who are responsible for the collections the library places in nursing homes and other sites. She recruits and places sixty volunteers who work in libraries in the system on a regular basis and another thirty who help with special projects occasionally. An additional 200 people are involved in twenty-two Friends of the Library groups. They are affiliated with community libraries and raise money through book sales for computers, puppets, and so on. While recruiting with notices in libraries has been her most successful method, Ms. Hoffman also advertises for volunteers in the newspaper, through the volunteer organizations to which she belongs, and through the Retired Senior Volunteer Program (RSVP). After she recruits and places a volunteer, she provides support when needed. A large part of her job involves keeping records of volunteers' hours. Volunteers worked almost 14,000 hours the year before I visited; Ms. Hoffman is grateful that the outreach section can now keep her records on computer.

Ms. Hoffman is also responsible for recognizing volunteers during National Volunteer Week at the end of April. Traditionally this has been done with a personal letter signed by the library director, a commendation from the library board, and a gift of a notepad and poster produced by the library's public information office. The library hosts an event with entertainment, refreshments, and brief speeches and gives a small gift to long-term volunteers. The 1986 budget for volunteer recognition was $1,250. In addition to this some individual libraries recognize their own volunteers. Ms. Hoffman, who has been at the library for a year, would like to put more life into recognition and is developing a proposal for a library-related event to promote the volunteers' bond with the library. I asked if the library insured its volunteers. Ms. Hoffman said that in Hennepin County volunteers as well as library employees are covered by workers' compensation. Her philosophy is that the best insurance is a well-run program.

One of the special projects for which Ms. Hoffman was recruiting volunteers was a month-long promotion of library service to visually and hearing impaired patrons. She was collecting materials and equipment (a radio reading service receiver, talking book equipment, and a slide show called "More Than Meets the Eye" from the National Library Service for the Blind and Physically Handicapped) for a display at the three area libraries in September 1987. At times when the library is busiest, volunteers will be stationed at display tables to talk to friends, care givers, and relatives of people with disabilities.

Publications

The outreach section is responsible for two publications: *Outreach News*, a quarterly newsletter with news of interest to outreach patrons, and an *Activity Resource Directory*, a biannual listing of program resources in the Twin Cities metropolitan area, which was originally developed as a service to sites with deposit collections and now sells for $4.00. (Ms. Eccles wrote in December 1987 that *Outreach News* and the *Grapevine*, the newsletter of Friends of the Library groups, are being merged into a new publication.) Outreach works with the system's public information office to produce its publications and all public information materials.

A *Catalog of Large Print Books*, which listed 4,173 titles in the 1986 edition, is produced by the technical services division and distributed by the outreach section. The library charges $16 for the large print catalog, but copies are loaned to each homebound large print reader and placed in each deposit collection site and library branch. Some libraries have copies that circulate for a week.

Listings in the *Catalog of Large Print Books* are arranged alphabetically by author, title, and subject. The introductory section mentions other agencies that provide materials to readers who need to use large print. These are the communications center in the Minnesota State Services for the Blind and Visually Handicapped, which has equipment, textbooks, and job-related materials, and the Minnesota Regional Library for the Blind and Physically Handicapped, with its talking book collection. The catalog will be revised in 1989-90, and a supplement was issued between the two editions. In July 1987 the library system had 4,800 titles. In the Ridgedale library are eight sections, six shelves to a section, filled with large print books. Large print is publicized by short lists of books by popular authors (e.g., ten to fifteen westerns). The library has also publicized the catalog as a potential Christmas gift.

PROGRAM RESOURCES

In addition to the occasional book talks that Hennepin County Library staff members give at deposit collection sites and the publication of the *Activity Resource Directory*, outreach has a complete collection of BiFolkal and Slideas kits, which it lends to the sites it serves. These are booked through the outreach office and delivered to the community library closest to the site. These program kits can be borrowed for three days to three weeks. They are publicized in twice-a-year mailings to deposit collection sites in *Outreach Newsletter*, which is sent to all sites, homebound patrons, all libraries in the system, and a selected mailing list. When the section looked at the statistics on BiFolkal kit use, it discovered that deposit collection sites accounted for only 20-25 percent of the circulation and that the kits were being used by as many groups outside Hennepin County as inside. Until recently Hennepin County was the only library in the metropolitan area that had the kits.

PLANNING AND EVALUATION

Staff are involved in planning for outreach. Ms. Eccles meets with individual staff members once a month and with the group every four to six weeks. Topics for discussion range from the five-year plan to accommodating a volunteer who has epilepsy. In the latter case a social worker/nurse came as a resource person. A professional staff committee of the library meets quarterly to discuss library issues. After a meeting in May 1987 it made a recommendation to the director to establish a task force on library service to seniors. This was approved and Ms. Eccles is the chairperson.

Ms. Eccles measures the success of outreach by the enthusiasm of her staff and by unsolicited testimonials from readers. She keeps circulation statistics, feeling that increased use is another measure of success. She is gratified by the support of the community librarians who have volunteered to take additional deposit collection sites in order to serve so more places and people.

CONCERNS OF OTHER STAFF

When I corresponded with Ms. Eccles before my visit, I asked whether it would be possible for me to talk to two people at Hennepin County library whom I knew by reputation. One was Emmett Davis, author with his sister, Catherine Davis, of *Mainstreaming Library Service for Disabled People*, a book about integrating people with all kinds of information-gathering styles under the roof of the library. The other was Sanford Berman, head of the catalog department, who is known internationally for his appeal for a sense of ethics and accuracy in cataloging.

Mr. Davis worked in succession as a clerk in a small branch, as a bookmobile driver in the outreach section, in the Southdale library, and in the cataloging department. He then moved out of the library to the Hennepin County Department of Human Services and is also working as library director of a parent self-help group (A Chance to Grow) dedicated to rehabilitating brain injured children and adults. Started in the late 1970s, A Chance to Grow recognized the importance of having consumer health information in order to open up home-based treatment and residential options. In 1986 the group founded the Josephine Kretch Brain Injury Resource Library. With private grants and donations, it has enlarged the collection. Under Mr. Davis's direction A Chance to Grow has developed kits of materials for loan to librarians, teachers, and other professionals who serve parents. The organization has also prepared a bibliography and computer-generated sheets of information, usually two pages long with a short summary of a topic and a list of relevant books and materials. Mr. Davis strongly believes in library service to the whole community. The focus of much of his work is to encourage other libraries to build their own collections of current materials on topics relating to brain injury and to encourage families to seek help from public libraries. He envisions a future when the Kretch library, responding to a call from a family member of a brain-injured child, can make a conference call for information to the family member's local library; all three would be involved in negotiating the request for information.

More than half of Mr. Davis's book shows how important cataloging can be in eliminating negative stereotypes of people with disabilities. He compared the standard subject headings used by most libraries (Sears and the Library of Congress) with Hennepin County library's and made suggestions for further changes. For example, he suggested changing the Library of Congress and the Hennepin County heading Learning Disabilities to Learning Differences.

I was interested in talking to Mr. Berman about the impact of Davis's book on Hennepin County cataloging. Mr. Berman said that because Mr. Davis focused on the area in preparing for his book, many of Mr. Berman's suggestions were already in effect by the time the book was published. When a group or individual is critical of some area of the catalog, Mr. Berman initiates a thorough study of the subject and makes changes in the subject headings. Mr. Berman said that, while he had never had positive or negative feedback about the changes, he would welcome an advisory group of disabled people to monitor the library's disability-related services and make recommendations. He listens a lot, watches television, reads special interest newspapers and publications from the alternative press to become aware of new concepts and new terminology.

LIBRARY POLICY

The Hennepin County library board has issued policy statements on the following topics that affect service to people with disabilities: services to groups and individuals with restricted library access (reflected in outreach services); fine exemption for disabled persons (defining disabled people as people who are prevented by a permanent disability from access to or normal use of a library or library materials); and staff treatment of users and other staff. (Staff are expected to be friendly and courteous to the public and cooperative and courteous to other staff at all times.) A statement in the 1987 Hennepin County library brochure listing summer hours reads: "Hennepin County provides equal access to employment, programs, and services without regard to race, color, creed, religion, age, sex, handicap, marital status, affectional preference, public assistance, criminal record, or national origin. As required by Section 504 of the Rehabilitation Act of 1973, Hennepin County provides a procedure to resolve complaints of discrimination on the basis of handicap. If you believe you have been discriminated against, contact the Affirmative Action Programs Department, A-303 Government Center, Minneapolis, Minnesota 55487 (348-4096)." The library administration is committed to implementing this policy.

Note

1. Emmett Davis and Catherine Davis, *Mainstreaming Library Service for Disabled People* (Metuchen, N.J.: The Scarecrow Press, 1980).

Chapter 5

District of Columbia Public Library, Washington, D.C.

The Martin Luther King Memorial Library, a completely accessible building ten blocks from our nation's Capitol, is the service center for the District of Columbia Public Library's outreach program to people with disabilities. In February 1973 Grace Lyons, previously librarian at King's Park Psychiatric Center on Long Island, New York, was hired to develop special services. Prior to that time blind and physically handicapped readers using braille and talking books had been served directly by the Library of Congress's Division for the Blind and Physically Handicapped. Ms. Lyons inherited the Library of Congress files for those readers and set up the District of Columbia Regional Library for the Blind and Physically Handicapped.

Institutions and homebound people had been served by the extension department. They came under Ms. Lyon's umbrella when special services opened on April 11, 1973. Twelve years later a senior mobile service, which attempts to meet the needs of some of Washington's 107,000 elderly citizens, became part of this department, now called the library for the blind and physically handicapped. A separate position of librarian for the deaf community was created in 1976. Alice Hagemeyer, already a member of the public library's cataloging staff and deaf herself, has filled that position since its beginning.

I have known Grace Lyons and Alice Hagemeyer for years and have observed the work they are doing. Nonetheless, my visit gave me an opportunity to learn more about the structure of their programs.

LIBRARY FOR THE BLIND AND PHYSICALLY HANDICAPPED

When Ms. Lyons came to the District of Columbia Public Library, she started with a staff of twenty-six people. Training and communication were top priorities. Ms. Lyons developed a series of forms to help with both processes. Everyone on her present staff, reduced to ten people, can handle all the forms, so that the department's work flows smoothly even when some staff are absent. (See Appendix C for a sample.) Ms. Lyons gave me the opportunity to talk to key staff members and the coordinator of the volunteer taping service, allowing me to have an in-depth exposure to operations.

Talking Book Service

Edith Lewis, readers' advisor, came to the department in 1978 after the bookmobile service where she had worked for many years was discontinued. She selects books for 250-350 of the library's 2,044 registered talking book readers and makes sure that the others receive their mail and telephone requests. She calls newly registered readers to see whether they have problems with or suggestions about the service. In a folder that contains basic information about the reader (the reader information sheet in Appendix C), she keeps records of the books she mails to each person. She also compiles statistics on books circulated through the library's manual system.

Ms. Lewis helps the thirty to forty readers who come to the library to borrow braille and talking books each week and those who come to select large print books from the library system's main collection. Branch librarians and the head of the library's popular library division also use this collection. The librarians borrow up to fifty books at a time. (The District of Columbia Public Library's coordinator of adult services orders large print books and has standing orders with G. K. Hall, Thorndike, and all major large print publishers.)

Ms. Lewis is assisted in her work by James Hawkins, Ms. Lyons' administrative assistant, and Martin Colbert, a stock person. Ruth Aford, the tape technician, duplicates copies of the master tapes for talking books whenever the demand is greater than the supply. She duplicates and checks the quality of all tapes produced by volunteers, working closely with the volunteer coordinator. She also keeps an inventory of talking book equipment inventory.

Donald Hailes has been the regional library's outreach worker since 1975. He is responsible for home delivery of talking book equipment and for teaching people how to use talking book machines, a task that may take from one to one-and-a-half hours per user. Mr. Hales makes a follow-up visit after service is initiated if he suspects a reader may need extra help. Once a year or on request he makes a presentation about the regional library's services to organizations that provide other services to disabled people, institutions served by the department, and senior citizen centers. He picks up damaged equipment and takes it to the Telephone Pioneers at Silver Spring, Maryland, to be repaired or to the National Library Service for the Blind and Physically Handicapped in Washington, D.C. , if it is beyond repair. Mr. Hailes feels that his contact with readers and institutions is very important because he represents the Library of Congress.

Volunteer Readers for the Blind

William Bradford is a volunteer who coordinates fifty to sixty volunteers to supplement the service provided by the National Library Service. Mr. Bradford joined the Washington Volunteer Readers for the Blind (WVRB), with a current membership of 160, soon after it was incorporated as a nonprofit organization in 1978. When I met him he had been volunteer coordinator for four or five years. The group was established by Ms. Lyons and Martin Brounstein to meet the demand from disabled students and employees in the Washington metropolitan area for materials not already available in recorded form (e.g., memos and sections from the *Federal Regulations*). Now WVRB records sixteen periodicals, including the American Association for the Advancement of Science's *Bulletin on Science and Technology for the Handicapped,*

Handicapped Americans Reports, HEATH Resources Center publications, the *New York Times Book Review*, the *Occupational Outlook Handbook*, *American Rehabilitation*, *Journal of Rehabilitation*, the *Washingtonian Magazine*, and five publications of interest to senior citizens.

Copies of these recordings are lent to other libraries for the blind and physically handicapped as well as to local readers. Although there is a recording booth in the regional library, Mr. Bradford says most volunteers would rather work in their own homes. WVRB has membership dues ($10 a year for individuals; $100 a year for organizations) that enable the organization to buy equipment for volunteers who do not have their own. Members have also raised funds for an IBM-PC/XT computer and a printer that help Mr. Bradford keep track of the volunteers' skills, assignments, and progress toward meeting deadlines. About half the volunteers are retired people who have time to handle rush jobs. Several volunteers do in-person reading, but generally, people who want this service are referred to other organizations in the city. At the open house each April, Ms. Lyons, Mr. Bradford, and WVRB board members recognize and present awards to outstanding volunteers for their participation. There is also an annual WVRB dinner in October.

Service to Institutions

Vernon Hardy has been in charge of coordinating library services to institutions for thirteen years. He leaves collections of regular print, large print, and talking books and magazines with playback equipment at eighty-five institutions: hospitals, homes for the elderly, nutrition sites, agencies for the disabled, rehabilitation centers, group living homes, and senior citizen centers. He estimates that the library serves 95 percent of the nursing homes in the District of Columbia. The library distributes flyers for this as well as other services, but most new agencies hear of the service through their counterparts already being served. Mr. Hardy is the person who sets up service with new institutions. If the agency uses talking book equipment, he asks the agency director and the library's contact person in the agency to sign a contract with the regional library. (This is a Library of Congress requirement.)

Every thirty to sixty days Mr. Hardy, with Arthur Smith's help, packs sixty to sixty-five books in large brown boxes and delivers them. He keeps a list of the books he delivers in the file folder for each institution and a running count of the books. Every six months he makes an extended visit to determine whether changes in the service are necessary (e.g., more large print books? fewer romances?). He checks equipment to see if it is functioning properly and does an inventory. If he has time, he visits individuals in the institution to see whether they are satisfied with the talking book service. He refers any talking book problems to Ms. Lewis. If there are other problems, such as excessive loss of books or equipment, Mr Hardy confers with Ms. Lyons who decides whether the service should be discontinued.

Arthur Smith has been in charge of the homebound service since the department was created. He delivers library materials to most of his ninety patrons every month, but he visits a few voracious readers every week. Persons eligible for the service are those who have been unable to visit their local library or use a bookmobile for at least six months because of a physical disability. They range in age from thirty-five to ninety-eight. Brochures describing the service are distributed to hospitals, churches, and senior residences. Other library staff refer readers to him. Mr. Smith calls to make an appointment for his first visit, gets some notion of the reader's interests, and visits within a week, taking some books along. He has access to any books in the system. He keeps statistics on the number of books circulated to each person but keeps a record only of what avid readers have actually had. Homebound visits prompt some reference work, which Mr. Smith handles through the mail. He also handles the deposit collections for one-third to one-half of the nursing homes.

Senior Mobile Service

Wanda Cox is in charge of the senior mobile service. She started her library career as a cataloger, but her undergraduate degree in family and community development and her minor in recreation stand her in good stead in her present job. She and Maurice Smith, the driver/clerk, take the bookmobile to fifteen sites, which house 3,000-4,000 people, every two weeks. Ms. Cox plans and delivers programs. Mr. Smith checks out regular and large print books, LP recordings of spoken words and classical music, and talking books and magazines for those certified for the Library of Congress program.

Ms. Cox has the resources of the District of Columbia area to draw upon as she develops programs for the fifteen sites. Planning starts a good three months in advance, and she misses no opportunity to ask people she meets about their interests and to evaluate their potential for presenting a program. Ms. Cox has drafted a retired children's librarian, now in her eighties, to do storytelling. Photographs of the District of Columbia in the early 1900s from the library's Washingtonian Collection are a surefire way to prompt discussion and reminiscence. On several occasions photographs taken before urban renewal changed the local neighborhood sparked hours of discussion. One group wanted to do a Christmas play. Ms. Cox couldn't find an appropriate one in the library, so the group wrote its own. They took it out into the community after a successful run at the housing site.

Programs like those may interest one kind of audience; slides from local art galleries may attract another. Many programs cannot be used with equal success at every site. Some audiences are regular bookmobile users. Others have never been readers. Still others are frail and heavily medicated. Ms. Cox's goal is not to educate but to provide a little something extra in people's lives.

Some programs are failures. Ms. Cox is honest in saying to people, "This isn't working. What would you like to talk about?" Sometimes it's the little things that lead to success, such as using a handheld mike in a reading group with hard-of-hearing people. At other times she has no control over the situation. (Ms. Lyons wrote in December 1987 that the library had received a National Council on the Aging/ National Endowment for the Humanities grant and would start a six-month "Silver Editions" program in January 1988. Using scholars and selected resources that meet the guidelines of the two sponsoring groups, ten programs were to be presented in ten sites for seniors.)

The bookmobile for the senior mobile service makes two-hour visits twice daily. Sometimes Ms. Cox plans her programs for the first hour; sometimes the second. If many people at the site are readers, she stays on the bookmobile the first hour to help with book selection and to answer reference questions. The bookmobile has a lift, and people are comfortable using it. If they aren't in a wheelchair already, she borrows one from the site--they are always available--and rides on the lift with the person while Mr. Smith operates the controls from inside. Ms. Cox says people are used to lifts because many of the buses they ride have them.

Readers using the senior mobile service bookmobile generally read fewer large print than regular print books. Nonfiction, especially biography and history, is popular. Ms. Cox orders the regular print materials for the service. The bookmobile uses a very basic circulation system with book cards and pockets.

In addition to the bookmobile the library has three vans for the delivery of other services. To avoid congestion from commuter traffic, trips are normally scheduled between 9:30 A.M. and 4:00 P.M.

Other Services

As librarian Ms. Lyons is responsible for the entire department. Because there is no children's librarian, she also works with the schools. With the staff, she plans an annual Christmas party especially for the children, but adults come and enjoy it, too. Around 250 children from twelve special schools are invited; approximately 100-125 come. After a program of stories and carol singing, the children are given Touch Toys, tactile toys made by a local volunteer group called Touch Toys, and refreshments are served by WVRB volunteers.

The library celebrates each anniversary of its beginning. On its fourteenth birthday it had an all-day open house featuring Touch Toys and Sculpture to Touch, an exhibit of art from all over the country, organized by the Sculptors Group of the Washington New Arts Center. Stories were told that could be enriched by the sculpture. Volunteers are also honored at these birthday parties.

Ms. Lyons does not have a secretary, but several times a year she produces a newsletter on her large print typewriter. It contains much more than news of the library. It is a source of information about local and national resources for people with disabilities. The public area of the library for the blind and physically handicapped also has a wealth of information: brochures about community services, talking book and braille catalogs, *Talking Book Topics, Braille Book Reviews*, a browsing collection of braille and talking books, and large print books.

In the hallway outside the library, enlarged photographs of previous anniversary celebrations are on display. The stacks are on the floor above the library, but master copies of tapes are kept near the tape technician's area. The library has a sizable reference collection of books and periodicals covering library service, death, group dynamics, retirement, aging, disabilities, education, service delivery, children's services, recreation, living aids, travel guides, and biographies.

Present and Future

The library is under the jurisdiction of the supervisor of branches and extension, who in turn reports to the assistant director of the District of Columbia Public Library.

In 1987, the library for the blind and physically handicapped circulated 158,199 items, and staff made 583 visits to homebound persons, 766 visits to individuals using the talking book service, and 730 visits to institutions. The bookmobile made 372 visits to senior homes, 2,781 people came on the bookmobile, and 7,551 attended programs. The statistics show that use is increasing each year.

As for the future, Ms. Lyon's short- and long-range goals as listed in her annual report are publication of a timely newsletter, a cumulated and monthly updated large print book catalog and a cumulated commercial recording catalog, updating of WVRB production quality to qualify for inclusion in the National Library Service distribution, and automation of her entire department's operation to eliminate overlapping paperwork and to free staff for work in programs. She was planning three workshops for 1988: one for institution services contact persons, a workshop on computer access for readers, and a workshop on senior institution services based on Brooklyn Public Library's SAGE program, which employs senior citizens to plan and implement programs.

LIBRARIAN FOR THE DEAF COMMUNITY

Deborah Gilson, one of Alice Hagemeyer's volunteers, talked to me. Ms. Gilson is finishing a college degree in English and volunteers twenty to forty hours a week. Alice Hagemeyer worked in the District of Columbia Public Library's catalog department for seventeen years before she went to the University of Maryland for her master's degree in library science. Since she became librarian for the deaf community in 1976, she has been the profession's most vocal advocate for library and information services for deaf and hard-of-hearing people. Even before the position was created, she was responsible for the first Deaf Awareness Week at the Martin Luther King Memorial Library in December 1974. On that occasion the lobby of the library had demonstrations of flashing light alarm clocks, a light signal doorbell, and devices to warn parents when a baby is crying. Some library staff volunteered to teach miniclasses in sign language. A brief questionnaire was distributed to give people a better understanding of the problems of deaf people. Ms. Hagemeyer promoted this event nationwide until it expanded into Deaf Action Week, then into Deaf Heritage Week. Her two booklets, *The Public Library Talks to You*, for deaf persons, and *Deaf Awareness Handbook for Public Librarians* are both unique contributions to library service.

Ms. Hagemeyer developed an idea to bridge the communications gap between hearing and nonhearing library staff and users at the District of Columbia Public Library and has expanded it for application throughout the United States. *The Red Notebook* is a compendium of information about deaf people, deafness, and services (including library services) to deaf people. It contains suggestions for celebrating Deaf Heritage Week, a directory of agencies serving the deaf community, information about TDDs and other communication aids, examples of deaf folklore, an so on. It has a loose-leaf format so subscribers can add or delete materials to make it of maximum usefulness in their community. Each September subscribers receive an update.

Ms. Hagemayer was instrumental in forming a Library Services for the Deaf group within the American Library Association in 1976. She has spoken to librarians at state and national conferences and workshops throughout the United States and is equally involved with deaf organizations like the National Association of the Deaf and SHHH (Self Help for Hard of Hearing People).

I knew all this before I talked to Ms. Gilson but was not sure of Ms. Hagemeyer's role at the District of Columbia Public Library. She works in the library services and programs office on the fourth floor of the Martin Luther King Memorial Library and shares a section of a large room with community information services, the duplicating unit, the library for the arts, and the public information office. Like other staff in this office Ms. Hagemeyer is concerned with communicating to the community the knowledge and information that can be found in libraries.

Ms. Hagemeyer feels that deaf people have the right to the services of a full-time librarian. It is her job to see that the library system is adapted to meet their various library and information needs. She has a TDD in her office so deaf people can call the library and she can call them. She handles a multiplicity of reference questions through the TDD. She also handles reference questions on deafness or about the deaf community that may come from the library staff or walk-in patrons, and has a good reference collection on this subject in her office. She publicizes the library's resources on deafness and the language, culture, and history of deaf people. She is the library resource person on the deaf community at meetings of both deaf and hearing groups. She visits schools, colleges, universities, and government agencies by invitation and introduces both hearing and deaf people to library services, especially *The Red Notebook*.

Ms. Hagemeyer arranges for a series of eight sign language classes to be given at library branches once a year and arranges for library programs to be interpreted when that is requested. She plans activities for National Library Week and Deaf Heritage Week. She publicizes library services in local publications and in the library's special newsletter, *CROSSROADS, Library and Information Services to the Deaf Community*, which is mailed to 150 subscribers of *The Red Notebook* in the District of Columbia. She met with groups of deaf students in Gallaudet University's adult basic education class (taught at the Martin Luther King Memorial Library in the summer of 1987) to introduce them to library materials.

FRIENDS OF LIBRARIES FOR DEAF ACTION

In January 1986 Ms. Hagemeyer formed a nonprofit organization, Friends of Libraries for Deaf Action (FOLDA), which has the following goals: "(1) to improve library and information services to the deaf community, (2) to encourage the entrance of people into the profession of library science and other related professions, and (3) to both improve the deaf community's awareness of their rights and potential as well as to alert the public of the strengths and needs of their deaf fellow citizens."[1] FOLDA is a group of volunteers, both deaf and hearing, who interpret and teach sign language classes at public libraries, help in fund raising, prepare supplements to the *Red Notebook*, and generally extend Ms. Hagemeyer's efforts. The group publishes an international edition of *CROSSROADS*.

In Ms. Hagemeyer's office is a UNI-PTC, a minicomputer with the capability of communicating with TDDs as well as with other computers. This new technology, purchased with LSCA funds, enables Ms. Hagemeyer to communicate with many more people. She also has a TV decoder for display or loan on request and a portable TDD that people can use at the library's public telephones. Because many deaf people in the Washington area do not own TDDs, they come to the library to use one.

I wondered why Ms. Hagemeyer is not a part of the library for the blind and physically handicapped. This has been considered but currently there is little communication between the two areas. They are separated physically and philosophically. The library for the blind and physically handicapped is a special services center. It appeared to me that the office of the librarian for the deaf community promotes mainstreaming. When I suggested this later to Ms. Hagemeyer, she said she promotes the use of the library by all groups within the deaf community. This includes deaf people who are legally blind or homebound and can use the services of the library for the blind and physically handicapped. In the District of Columbia Public Library the two paths of service to disabled people operate successfully side by side.

Note
1. Friends of Libraries for Deaf Action," *Crossroads* 1, international ed. (July 1986):1.

References
Hagemeyer, Alice. *Deaf Awareness Handbook for Public Librarians.* Washington, D.C.: District of Columbia Public Library, 1976.

_____. "Library Service to Deaf and Hard of Hearing Persons." (Mimeo presented at the Statewide Workshop on Library Services to Deaf and Hard of Hearing People, Columbus, Ohio, September 25, 1981.)

_____. "Library Service to the Deaf and Outreach Programs for the Deaf." *Illinois Libraries* 63 (September 1981):530-34.

_____. *The Public Library Talks to You.* Washington, D.C.: Gallaudet College, 1975.

"Library Celebrates with Art to Touch." *News* (National Library Service for the Blind and Physically Handicapped) 18, no. 3 (July-September 1987):8-9.

The Red Notebook. Washington, D.C.: Friends of Libraries for Deaf Action.

Chapter 6

Tampa-Hillsborough County Public Library System, Tampa, Florida

The special services branch at the Tampa-Hillsborough County Public Library System is in a nonpublic service area on the third floor of the central library building annex. The annex is connected to the main building by a covered walkway, which runs along the side of the auditorium between the two buildings. The whole complex covers a city block in downtown Tampa.

SPECIAL SERVICES BRANCH

The special services branch is over ten years old. Jeannette Martin, its head since 1983, works under the supervisor of branches and participates in the monthly meetings of the branch librarians. The supervisor of branches reports to John Adams, director of libraries.

Ms. Martin is responsible for five areas of service: bookmobile, books-by-van, books-by-mail, talking books, and programming on her staff are one library services specialist, two library assistants III, and one library assistant I. Recently a library page was added. The page relieves other staff of shelving responsibilities. Ms. Martin hopes she has set a precedent by hiring a young woman who is hearing impaired for this position.

Bookmobile Service

A single midget bookmobile primarily serves sites where at least 60 percent of the population is over sixty-five. It goes to mobile home parks, congregate living facilities for retired people, and apartment complexes. (Because of mechanical problems with the bookmobile, the schedule to serve forty-five locations every three weeks was disrupted for a total of three months in 1986-87. In December 1987 bids were to go out for a replacement.) The bookmobile is stocked with best-sellers, large print books, older fiction and nonfiction, Spanish materials, and paperback books. Readers may request materials not on its shelves. Because the bookmobile does not have a wheelchair lift, Myra Libman-Silverman, who is both clerk and driver (a library assistant III), carries books to those who cannot climb steps.

Books-by-Van

Ms. Libman-Silverman drives the bookmobile all day on Tuesdays and Wednesdays and on Thursday and Friday mornings. On Mondays and Thursday afternoons she delivers packages of books in boxes and plastic grocery sacks to forty-three sites using the library van. Every four weeks, books-by-van goes to convalescent centers, boarding homes, hospitals, homes for developmentally disabled people, a juvenile detention center, correctional institutions, alcohol and drug abuse centers, and temporary shelters. Library service is one of the many options nursing homes can choose to get a superior rating by the state accreditation board, a factor that could account for the high number of facilities using the books-by-van service.

Ms. Martin selects the materials and keeps reading records for the voracious readers. Ms. Libman-Silverman has personal contact with the readers as she delivers the materials, and she checks with the person in charge of each site to see whether new people are interested in library service. When readers can no longer use regular print materials, she introduces them to large print or talking books. Once every other month she takes books to Sun Terrace Health Care, a retirement community about thirty miles from the central library.

I went with Ms. Libman-Silverman to several old houses that had been converted into boarding homes for six to ten developmentally disabled people who share a common social room. Our visits were brief. We simply said hello, left one lot of books, and picked up another. Occasionally we chatted with residents who needed a listening ear. At a larger nursing home (250 or so residents) we talked with the activity director, who had ordered recorded copies of the Bible in Spanish, English, and Italian from the Bible Alliance in Sarasota, Florida. He had also created a tape of German music for a German patient and was working on a tape of truck-driving songs for a former truck driver. He promotes the use of talking books by individuals who are not able to participate in group activities. He encourages people to come to the activities area for books, but if they are not able to, he takes books to them.

Books-by-Mail

Suzanne Bell, a library services specialist, manages the books-by-mail service, which has been in operation since the 1970s. The eligibility statement in the brochure says: "Who is eligible? Adult residents of Hillsborough County who are confined to their home because of age, chronic illness, or physical disability." People hear of this service through satisfied users, and approximately thirty people ar served currently. They have a choice of large type or regular type. Those requesting large type must be certified by a doctor, nurse, optometrist, social worker, counselor, teacher, or other qualified person. Regular type readers can receive hardback or paperback books. The application form lists twelve interest categories, and readers can specify other subjects or favorite authors. Readers can also request specific titles by phone. Ms. Bell selects the books from the special services collection, keeps records of her selections for each reader, and sends a maximum of twelve books once a month. Materials are mailed in reusable zippered canvas bags, and instructions for returning them, postage prepaid, are mailed with the first shipment.

Talking Book Service

Leigh Myers, a library assistant III, is responsible for the daily operation of the talking book service and is assisted by Marti Wilkins, a library assistant II, who works half a day in the talking book service and the other half in other areas of special services.

Eleven hundred talking book readers from Hillsborough County use this subregional library.

When the library gets a request for service, Ms. Myers sends out the fact sheet that special services has developed and the application form from the Florida Regional Library for the Blind and Physically Handicapped. All applications go to the regional library in Daytona Beach, where reader information is put on its computer, machines are mailed to the new user, and procedures are initiated for mailing magazines and braille materials. The regional library then returns a copy of the application form to special services, and Ms. Wilkins sends a package of talking book catalogs and order forms to the reader. Books are mailed from the subregional library. Six years ago Ms. Myers used to call all the new readers to make sure they had received the machine and knew how to use it. As the volume of readers has increased, she has not been able to continue this service; now she calls only when she anticipates problems. She does visit a few homes of readers who are alone and have no one to help them use the machines.

In the past Ms. Myers sent flyers about the subregional library service to optometrists, doctors, and nursing home activity directors. However, the increased volume of service without a corresponding increase in staff has made an aggressive publicity campaign impractical. The Tampa subregional library has been able to offer twenty-four hour turnaround service, even with its high volume of readers and with the majority of its collection housed in another building. Ninety percent of the readers send in requests; Ms. Myers selects for the remaining 10 percent based on individual interests. As she processes the new books the library receives from the National Library Service for the Blind and Physically Handicapped, she writes descriptive headings on the book labels to match the interest categories checked by the readers. This makes it easier for her to go to the shelves and select books, a task she does each morning. Records of the books an individual has had and has requested are kept manually on forms used in many libraries for the blind and physically handicapped. The library took its first steps in 1987 to prepare for computerization. In 1988 it was to receive an IBM personal computer from the regional library. Record keeping will eventually be accomplished with the Reader Enrollment and

Delivery System (READS) developed by the National Library Service for the Blind and Physically Handicapped.

Ms. Myers and Ms. Wilkins have a supply of talking book machine parts and have taught themselves to do minor repairs of talking book machines and cassettes. Ms. Myers has even trained volunteers and can instruct readers by telephone on how to repair their machines. If that fails, she mails out a replacement machine and asks the reader to return the defective one. The part-time library page inspects all cassettes to ensure that the correct tapes are in each container and are properly rewound. (For the latter task she uses a high-speed rewinder capable of checking six tapes at a time.) When a piece of string has been attached to the container to indicate that the patron is having a problem with the tape, the tape is repaired or replaced. If the tape is not defective, Ms. Myers returns it to the reader with a note to call her if it continues giving problems; often the machine or the reader may be the problem. This personal attention to readers' concerns is the hallmark of the talking book service.

For the second time in two years Ms. Myers sent a reader survey to all 1,110 readers in the spring of 1987. (See Appendix C.) Twenty-nine percent (315 people) responded after a follow-up contact. Of the 315 respondents, 70 percent (222) use the service at least once a month, and 16 percent (49) have received talking books for ten years or more. Sixty-nine percent (218) contact the library by telephone. Only 3 percent (10) make contact in person. Many people would prefer to visit the library in person, but transportation for 30 percent (96), the downtown location for 18 percent (58), and parking for 20 percent (63) are problems. Ninety-four percent (295) of the readers use cassettes. Eight-six percent (272) rated the service excellent. Twenty percent (63) had suggestions for improving the service. Ms. Myers prepared a summary of the survey responses, with comments on the readers' suggestions. She has offered to send the survey to readers who fill out a request form found in the special services department newsletter, *Tampa Talks.*

Ms Myers has developed a reference file of materials to answer information questions from readers. She photocopies information for them, reads it over the phone, or orders copies of catalogs to be sent to them.

Programs

When she became head of the special services branch, Ms. Martin, with Ms. Bell's help, presented programs at twenty-two places each month. After eight months it became apparent that book deliveries were suffering. There wasn't time to do both, so programming was reduced until more staff could be hired to share the work. (One new position was added on January 1, 1988.) Ms. Martin now leads book discussions at two bookmobile sites where people are quite interested in reading. Initially she used a standard book talk format, giving everyone the same book to read. She now varies that by having participants read different books by the same author. She gives an overview of the author's life, people give their impressions of the books they have read, and the group looks at similarities and differences between books, thereby savoring the full flavor of the author's writing. Other library staff lead discussions from time to time. When readers are not able to use regular print materials, Ms. Martin goes to her staff for help in finding the books in large print or talking books. Eight to sixteen people attend each of the programs.

MATERIALS

Like in other large library systems Tampa has wrestled with the problem of how best to handle the purchase of large type books. The branches used to buy their own, but Ms. Martin says that inadequate book budgets limited the number they could purchase. The library administration decided that all large type books for branches should be purchased by special services. The branches sent their large type books to special services, and staff there selected and sent the branches rotating collections of 100 books. When I was there, special services had standing orders with the major large print publishers. Ms. Martin ordered multiple copies of titles she anticipated would be used by books-by-mail, books-by-van, the bookmobile, and the branches. Each branch gets forty large type books each month, keeping them for three, six, or nine months, depending upon the branch's size and readership. Before collections are sent to the branches, they are sent to technical services for bar coding and entering into the computer.

Tampa-Hillsborough Public Library System has approval plans whereby 222 publishers send copies of their new books. Biweekly book examination and ordering sessions are conducted by the young adult/adult materials coordinator. Each library department or branch is allocated a budget measured by points. Department and branch heads examine the books, look at photocopied reviews, consider other information prepared by the coordinator (e.g., location of books in the same series), and mark the number of copies (reference or circulating) they would like on the order sheet for each book. The coordinator also prepares quarterly replacement lists from which replacement copies can be ordered. Ms. Martin and Ms. Bell work together in placing orders for their branch.

PUBLIC RELATIONS

Special services does not have an advisory group, but in the summer of 1986, Ms. Martin invited users of her branch's services to become part of the Special Friends of Special Services. Some branches already have a Friends group, and there is a Friends group for the system. Invitations went to users through *Tampa Talks*. A meeting was held in the Seminole branch library. More than twenty people, some of them in wheelchairs, were there. The meeting provided an opportunity for users to get to know each other and the staff. It also gave the staff feedback; users talked about what they liked and didn't like about the service. One complaint was that some people couldn't read *Tampa Talks* because it was printed on colored paper. Since that time Ms. Martin has used black ink on white paper for copies sent to persons with visual impairments. The experience was a positive one for branch staff, too, who learned to interact with people with disabilities through firsthand experience. The branch librarian learned, to her embarrassment, that she didn't know anything about escorting blind persons.

Special services maintains contact with local organizations such as the Deaf Service Center, Florida Council of the Blind, West Central Florida Area Agency on Aging, Tampa Light House, and the Sun City Lions Club. Staff members have participated in the

Senior Expo, a countywide extravaganza. Ms. Martin has a weekly program on the WUSF Radio Reading Service. She prerecords a thirty-minute segment, during which she reads interesting and relevant items from newsletters of other libraries for the blind and physically handicapped and speaks about new talking books, services of local agencies, or other information of interest to listeners.

PLANS FOR THE FUTURE

Ms. Martin has big plans for special services. In her office is a floor plan for a proposed special services branch in the suburbs. It seems that people do not like to come downtown. She worked hard and persistently for an additional staff member and a new bookmobile, goals finally to have been achieved in 1988. Some day she would like to have a children's librarian. Ms. Martin and Ms. Bell were planning to produce a catalog of large type books for books-by-mail readers and a catalog of regular print and paperback books. Ms. Martin hoped to have Ms. Bell prepare *Tampa Talks* once a quarter. A little farther down the road she would like to interest local Lions Clubs in sponsoring a project to produce program kits for use in congregate living facilities.

At times Ms. Martin feels that her staff are stretched too thin to provide the service she would like to offer people with disabilities. The figures speak for themselves: 36,167 books circulated through the bookmobile in 1986-87, even though it was out of service for three months, 2,219 books mailed to homebound readers, 14,985 items delivered through books-by-van, and 37,963 talking books mailed out.

ACCESSIBILITY

What about the person with disabilities who doesn't qualify for or need special services? The central library is theoretically accessible. Designated parking is located at the back of the building, with an accessible entrance and elevators within the library. Even though it is hard to find one's way around the library, a dozen or so people go to the special services branch each month. There are tentative plans to join the buildings and provide indoor parking in the 1990s. The newer branches are accessible. The older ones are not, but the county is providing funds to make them accessible. Since the county assumed responsibility for the library in 1984, it has been on a much sounder financial basis than when it was jointly funded by Hillsborough County and the city of Tampa.

OTHER SERVICES

The fine arts/AV department in the central library has 16-mm films, audiocassettes, and videotapes. The business, science, and technology department has a strong collection of books about disabilities. The humanities department has a large collection of large type books and a TDD that the Deaf Service Center in Tampa publicizes.

In Hillsborough County, special services is the primary link between people with disabilities and the library. Ms. Martin speaks to staff groups in the central library about the services her branch offers and has a ready-made opportunity to make branch librarians aware of special services at their monthly meetings. New professional staff visit her branch as part of their library orientation.

PART 3

SPECIAL NEEDS CENTERS

Special needs centers in libraries can be viewed as the places where people with disabilities are most likely to have their library and information needs met. The libraries for the blind and physically handicapped represent the earliest form of this service. A subregional library for the blind and physically handicapped is the principal focus of the centers at the Montgomery County Department of Libraries in Bethesda, Maryland, and the Broward County Division of Libraries in Fort Lauderdale, Florida.

The special needs center at the Tucson Public Library is primarily a collection of materials with special indexes to make these materials easier to use. Montgomery County and the Phoenix Public Library have strong collections of materials about and for people with disabilities. Duluth Public Library, Montgomery County, and Phoenix use computers to make information more readily accessible. The Phoenix service has been set up purposely as a model for other libraries to follow in developing services to people with disabilities.

In all five libraries a distinctly identified physical area, ranging in size from the equivalent of a small room to a whole floor of a library, has been set aside to house materials and equipment for people with disabilities and to provide direct service to them. The special needs center may or may not be involved in outreach activities, such as service to nursing homes and homebound people, but the person in charge is generally viewed as being responsible, systemwide, for library service to people with disabilities, even when this service is offered through other branches and departments.

Chapter 7

Tucson Public Library, Tucson, Arizona

The appearance of the Tucson Public Library's main library, both inside and out, is of a structure that has seen better days. Like many of the buildings in the downtown area of the city, it is scheduled for replacement in the near future.

SPECIAL NEEDS SERVICE

The special needs room has a sizable collection of books, pamphlets, and newsletters relating to disabilities. Large print books occupy even more space. Also available are fiction about people with disabilities and a handful of signed English books and twin-vision books. No one is on duty, but help is available at the nearby circulation desk or reference desk.

During my visit a gentleman was using the Visualtek, an electronic aid that magnifies print up to sixty times on a television screen. He is the only regular user of this equipment; he takes the bus some distance across town for this purpose. I learned later that a smaller Voyager magnifier was moved to the library branch nearest his home. Several street people were dozing at the wheelchair-accessible study table in spite of a long list of prohibitions, including No Napping, posted on the front door of the library. A lighted reading desk for wheelchair users is also available.

When I met Judith Lessee, developmental disabilities specialist, she gave me the history of the service. Following a needs assessment study of the Tucson Public Library and the Arizona Training

Program at Tucson by a library consultant from Florida, the library received a two-year LSCA grant to develop library services for people with developmental disabilities. Ms. Lessee was hired in 1978 to establish a special needs collection. Although the grant specified that services were to be given only to people with mental retardation, Ms. Lessee chose to expand the scope to the federal definition of a developmental disability: a severe, chronic disability, attributable to a mental or physical impairment, manifested before age 22, likely to continue indefinitely, results in substantial functional limitations in certain specific areas and reflects the person's need for lifelong, individually planned services.[1] The special needs service eventually included all disabilities with less emphasis on mental illness than on other areas because it alone is a subspecialty with a sizable volume of literature.

Ms. Lessee feels that people with disabilities need a good resource person. She functions as that resource person and has developed a collection and promoted it in the community. It has been difficult to acquire many of the materials reviewed in periodicals in the disability area and requested by agency staff because they are not available through library brokers. The purchasing department must alter its procedures. Still, these materials represent some of the most useful acquisitions.

COMMUNITY CONTACTS

Ms. Lessee has spoken to community groups and has set up exhibits in shopping malls, and at information and referral resource fairs, very special arts festivals, and conferences of organizations such as the National Society for Autistic Children. She participated as a volunteer with the Junior League's "Kids on the Block" program, which featured a troupe of puppets representing children with disabilities. She has held sensitivity workshops for library staff and conducted annual developmental disabilities media festivals for the public from 1979 until 1983. She developed *For All of Us (A Resource Guide Especially for People Who Work with the Differently Able)*, now available as ERIC Document 249 732.[2] Her free bimonthly newsletter, *People to People,* created to promote library use, listed new materials in the special needs collection and programs and services across the country for people with disabilities. Its mailing list grew from 300 to 1,200 and circulated far beyond the library's service area. A brochure listing resources of the special needs service included a form for requesting *People to People.* (*People to People* was discontinued in 1986 because of budget cuts.)

In Ms. Lessee's office, which is reached through a labyrinth behind the reference area, is a collection of developmental toys and games, posters for display in the room with the special needs collection and at exhibits, several of Hal's Pals (dolls with disabilities), and a collection of audiocassettes and microfiche that she promotes and circulates. She has some aids for deaf persons-- she uses these for demonstration purposes--and a collection of free and inexpensive materials that she distributes at exhibits and gives to people in response to their requests for information.

ACCESS TO THE COLLECTION

Even though Ms. Lessee has had clerical help for only a short period, she has developed a card catalog for the collection and a key to it, which she calls the special needs Rosetta stone. The catalog cards are color coded: green for audiovisuals (sound filmstrips, videocassettes, slide-tape programs, and microfiche) available through the reference desk; purple for books; red for materials that help develop community living skills; orange for magazines, which are kept in the periodicals room in the library annex; black for Spanish language materials; yellow for uncataloged materials, kept in alphabetical order by title in file boxes on the shelves; blue for materials in the vertical file, which include newspaper clippings, photocopies of articles, and equipment catalogs; and white for chapters from a book, with the call number, author, and title of the book shown on the card. Ms. Lessee has developed her own subject heading list, which is used in the vertical file as well as in the card catalog.

Along with changes in administrators have been changes in the service. Originally it was part of extension service, which included the bookmobile, jail, and homebound services. There is no longer an extension service. Now Ms. Lessee is directly responsible to a library supervisor at the main library. She works half-time at the information desk and divides her other twenty hours between the general reference vertical and citation files and special needs. She has a budget of $6,000 a year for books, magazines, media, and vertical file materials. She subjects the collection to an annual weeding in an effort to keep materials current, recognizing the dangers of giving out-of-date information in an area that is always changing.

FIRST DIBS

Although publication of *People to People* was discontinued, Ms. Lessee has been responsible for creating a successor independent of the library. In 1984 a group met to form First DIBS (Disability Information Brokerage System), a resource-sharing network for individuals and agencies serving people with disabilities in the Tucson area. It has since become an information clearinghouse throughout Arizona. In July 1986 First DIBS published its first bimonthly newsletter, called *First DIBS*, which continued in the tradition of *People to People*. It lists new books, media, magazine articles, and organizations and includes a special feature in each issue. A page called "FYI" includes a potpourri of information: for example, job openings, meetings, free and inexpensive materials.

One hundred and twenty individuals and agencies are members of First DIBS. Anyone interested in disability information on the local, state, or national level can join. In addition to publishing a newsletter, the organization compiles an up-to-date directory of members each month, sponsors community workshops, and provides disability information and resources to members on request. Membership is $15 a year. One-hour, brown-bag luncheon meetings are held each month at noon in a different agency (including the library). The library gives Ms. Lessee time off to attend meetings and to develop workshops. First DIBS, in cooperation with the library, has been able to give the community a high-quality disability information service.

OTHER SERVICES

A staff member is available at every branch of the Tucson Public Library to help readers sign up for the talking book service. At the main library, Ms. Lessee refers people to State Services for the Blind. A TDD is at the circulation desk of the main library and at one branch, and a closed-captioned decoder is at the same branch. The main library, an old Carnegie building soon to be replaced, is accessible by means of a long ramp leading to the front door. There is parking for handicapped people behind the building. The bathrooms, water fountain, and public telephone have been modified. The building has three floors and no elevator, but staff will assist patrons. Ms. Lessee says all the branches are accessible.

After I visited the library, I read an article, "The Use of Library Roles in Planning at the Tucson Public Library," by Liz Rodriguez Miller, which says that staff identified as one of their three goals in 1981, "to maintain the highest level of service for the maximum number of users; to provide specially designed and delivered programs and services to institutionalized, physically disabled, ethnic minorities, illiterate, economically disadvantaged, urban, and rural populations".[3] A letter from Ms. Lessee in late 1987 indicated that institutionalized, physically disabled had been eliminated from the library's current long-range plan.

Along with the minutes of the January 1988 meeting of First DIBS, I received a notice that there was no longer to be a special needs collection. Its pamphlets have been filed in the general vertical file, its books are everywhere on the library's three floors, and its posters and games have been distributed among community agencies. Ms. Lessee left the Tucson Public Library, but she is still very much involved with First DIBS.

Notes

1. Rehabilitation, Comprehensive Services, and Developmental Disabilities Act of 1978.

2. *For All of Us (A Resource Guide Especially for People Who Work with the Differently Able)*, (Tucson, Ariz.: Tucson Public Library, October 1984).

3. Liz Rodriguez Miller, "The Use of Library Roles in Planning at the Tucson Public Library," *Public Libraries* 26 (Summer 1987):69-71.

Chapter 8

Phoenix Public Library,
Phoenix, Arizona

The Phoenix Public Library is located in the downtown area of the city. The special needs center is marked with a large sign. I found Mary Roatch, supervisor of the center, already engaged in animated discussion with a volunteer about some project for the day. The atmosphere of the special needs center is symbolized by the logo on its brochure--a circle within a circle, illustrating Edwin Markham's poem, "He drew a circle and shut me out . . . we drew a circle and took him in."

SPECIAL NEEDS CENTER

The special needs center serves three target groups: (1) people with disabilities (blind and visually handicapped, speech and hearing impaired, physically and mentally handicapped people; (2) their families; and (3) staff from the organizations that serve them. The center occupies 1,500 square feet of space in a very visible location on the first floor of the central library. Ms. Roatch says that the center acts as an advocate simply by virtue of its location. Everyone goes by, from school groups to individuals on their way to another part of the library. Just seeing the center reminds people of a friend or relative who could use its services.

The center is completely accessible, with a wheelchair ramp leading to the library's front door, which opens automatically, restrooms and drinking fountains close by, and elevators to all floors of the building. Parking is near the entrance of the building, and access by public transportation is good. Dial-a-Ride is another option for the center's users. In the center itself are a telephone and a TDD unit. As we walked through the center, Ms. Roatch pointed out the ways in which each segment of the collection met particular needs.

A Walk through the Center

A wheelchair carrel is directly to the right and past the entrance to the area. Its desk surface can be raised or lowered to accommodate a wheelchair. The lighting is good, and there are electrical outlets for tape recorders or print magnifiers. Although the staff encourage independence on the part of people in wheelchairs, they help when necessary by bringing catalog drawers to the carrel, by helping with catalog searches, or by making arrangements with other departments to bring material to the carrel. The library is in the process of automating its card catalog, and soon the center will have computer terminals that will give access to the entire collection.

The only collection of large print books in the central library for children and adults is in the special needs center. The center has many standing orders but supplements these with orders for individual titles, especially biographies and other nonfiction. Older people enjoy the classics for young people--the oversized books published in the 1960s by Keith Jennison--and Ms. Roatch doesn't intend to get rid of them until they are replaced by easier-to-handle editions. The center even has a few large print titles in Spanish but not enough to meet the demand from Phoenix's Spanish-speaking population. It also has a collection of large print magazines for adults and children.

The center is a division of the library, like arts and humanities, and has its own reference collection. One of the staff always covers the reference desk. The collection is used to answer information and referral questions from any of the target groups or from other divisions or branches of the library. The reference collection contains statistical data, educational directories, consumer information, and subscription services such as the *Handicapped Requirements Handbook* (published by the Federal Programs Advisory Service) and *The System: Accessible Design and Product*

Information System (published by Barrier Free Environments) that are updated continually. Arizona laws, the *Red Notebook* (published by Friends of Libraries for Deaf Action), sources of financial aid, and the *Reference Circulars* published by the National Library Service for the Blind and Physically Handicapped are also on the reference shelves.

The vertical file contains some of the gems of the collection. The center has developed its own subject heading list, taking a topic and subdividing it by the disability group (e.g., DOGS--BLIND; DOGS--DEAF). Part of the file contains a collection of equipment catalogs, for which Ms. Roatch has developed a location index by company name, commercial name of the product, and kind of product. This file is updated frequently so that the catalogs will be current.

The files also contain a braille copy of a proposal to the Regional Transit Authority for a merged system of service in the Phoenix area. People who are blind are greatly affected by changes in bus routes and schedules. A volunteer entered the report into the center's Apple IIe computer, which translated it into grade II braille.

Next to the files are visual aids: a Visualtek (a video print enlarger) and a portable lighted magnifier that can be moved to any part of the library to accommodate readers using materials in other departments. A Sun Sounds Radio Reading Service receiver and talking book equipment are on hand for demonstration. The center has a small collection of talking books that eligible readers can use to try out the service. Readers already enrolled in the program can take a break in their daily routine and come to the library to read.

A collection of basic adult books (for grade K-3 reading level, grade 3-5, and tutors) was moved from the former social sciences section to the special needs center. The library has recently received an LSCA grant for enriching these holdings and for working with literacy programs in the valley, the area surrounding Phoenix.

Collection Development

To build the collection of the special needs center, Ms. Roatch pulled books from different sections of the library. Books on rehabilitation, employment, accessibility, toys, travel, setup of services, parenting, and sign language and biographies of disabled people are among the materials used by the three target groups. Subjects run the gamut of the Dewey Decimal classification system.

Ms. Roach realized that conventional selection tools such as *Library Journal* and *Publisher's Weekly* would not help her identify the resources for keeping the collection up to date, so the center now subscribes to over eighty periodicals and over sixty national newsletters in the disability area. Before she places them on a revolving display stand, Ms. Roach goes through them to identify materials to purchase. Back issues are kept in the magazine storage area two floors below.

There are sixty advocacy groups in the Phoenix area, and the special needs center receives their newsletters, too. The current issues are kept in notebooks; back issues go to a work-storage area on the mezzanine. The agencies publicize the special needs center in these newsletters, and the newsletters are a source of information for center patrons. The center maintains an alphabetical index to the file, which gives the title of the newsletter, address, deadline for getting information to the editor, telephone number, name of the organization, and contact person.

Materials in nonprint format include a small collection of braille books and magazines for short-term loan, print/braille books that blind parents and sighted children can read together, a VersaBraille tape dictionary, an audio dictionary, and pieces of sculpture for lending to visually impaired persons. Students at Arizona State University created a tactile model of the center that can be used to orient blind users to it.

Audiovisuals

While I was at the center, "The Joy of Signing" was being shown on a television set in front of several comfortable chairs. This is part of the center's collection of videocassettes housed in the audiovisual department. It was being broadcast through the library's closed circuit channel. Among the videotapes purchased by the center are "Abilities and Disabilities," a five-cassette set of interviews with twenty-nine successful local people who are disabled; "Selecting Toys for Disabled Children," a signed tape; "Giving Birth to Independence," a four-cassette tape to help parents learn to meet the demands of having a handicapped child; and "Exploding the Myth," a tape about developmental disabilities. Many of the tapes are produced by local groups. The sign language tapes are especially useful to students in a college interpreter training program, as are tapes produced by the San Francisco Public Library, called "American Culture: The Deaf Perspective."

These tapes, like the large collection of closed-captioned videotapes, can be borrowed from the library's audiovisual department. The special needs center has developed a procedure allowing deaf persons to borrow one of five videocassette recorder/decoder units. The person must first get a permanent library card from the library registration desk and then fill out a certification of deafness form at one of five agencies in Phoenix. The third step is to bring these two documents to the special needs center and sign a borrower's agreement form that outlines the responsibilities of the person using the equipment. A special needs center staff member puts the center's symbol on the library card, and the person goes to the audiovisual department for service. The tapes can be borrowed for one week and the recorder/decoder for three weeks.

At the information center in the special needs center a wall rack contains dozens of giveaway brochures from local agencies. Agencies also contribute to the bulletin board where announcements of meetings and workshops and a print copy of the current "Dial-a-News," a local service for TDD users, are posted.

The Toybrary collection is kept in a nearby alcove. When Head Start programs were phased out in the late seventies, their toys were offered to the library. Initially the toys were put in the branches, often ending up in a back room or on an out-of-the-way shelf. When the special needs center was established, the toys were brought back to the central library. Ms. Roatch began to work with local agencies serving parents of disabled children. Parents and agency staff came to the center to enroll in the Toybrary, receive a listing of the toys, and borrow their first toys. They could return the toys to the library branch nearest them and borrow toys through the branch after that. Each of the nine branches and the agencies working with disabled children has a copy of a catalog, which describes the toys, classifies them by the skill they help the child develop (e.g., fine motor, spatial relationships), and lists them by order number.

But the catalog has no pictures of the toys, a shortcoming that limits agency staff as they advise parents. In the spring of 1986 Ms. Roatch presented the idea of a Toybrary catalog with pictures to local Kiwanians, just when the Kiwanis had a national program to help libraries develop toy libraries. The clubs took on the challenge, solicited funds to produce sixty copies of a catalog that members have helped with from beginning to end. Ms. Roatch feels that this fourteen-month project is a good example of what community groups can do to help libraries. The catalogs are distributed to the nine branch libraries and to the agencies.

Ms. Roatch prepared a detailed selection policy for the special needs center that was approved by the library administration in June 1986. The total budget for large print books (both reference and circulating copies), periodicals, newsletters, toys, audiotapes and videotapes was $16,300 in 1986-87.

The Computer Workplace

Probably the most unusual and well-publicized service offered by the special needs center is its computer workplace for people with disabilities, which is separated from the rest of the center by see-through panels. In 1981 the local school district lent (and eventually gave) the library a Kurzweil Reading Machine (KRM), a computer that converts printed text to synthetic speech. The library introduced it to the public by offering a training program for blind readers. To further publicize the KRM, it offered workshops a year later on interfacing the KRM with other computers. Stimulated by the potential for library service, Ms. Roatch wanted to learn more. She visited the Veterans Administration's Western Blind Regional Rehabilitation Center at Palo Alto, California, and a private firm, Telesensory Systems, which produces electronic visual aids. She came home and convinced the library administration that it needed to seek federal funding to make a wider range of new technology available to disabled readers. Since then both LSCA funds and Community Block grants have enabled the library to develop the computer workplace for people with disabilities.

The workplace has VersaBraille, a paperless brailler with which braille can be entered on a cassette tape and read back on a keyboard simulating braille cells. It can also be used to put data into the computer or to read data from the computer.

The Apple IIe computers with Echo speech synthesizers make it possible for users to hear the screen being read. BEX, a talking word processing program, enables a blind person to edit the text. BEX also translates computer code into grade II braille and vice versa, makes the Apple keyboard into a braille writing keyboard, and produces many sizes of large print on the screen monitor.

The workplace also has a Cranmer Modified Perkins brailler, which produces hard-copy braille, a letter-quality inkprint Diablo printer, and a MacIntosh computer with a dot matrix Imagewriter printer to produce large type text. One of the Apple computers has a DP-10 large screen monitor that readers with limited vision can use. Blind readers have access to bulletin boards and information systems by using the VersaBraille or the ProTerm talking terminal program in the Apple IIe computers.

(After I visited the special needs center but before the end of 1987, a local Kiwanis Club donated an IBM PC-XT computer with SynPhonix synthetic speech and Screen-Talk voice access software and an Epson dot matrix printer.)

Ms. Roatch demonstrated how print material can be read by the KRM, sent in computer code to the Apple IIe computer for it to be translated into grade II braille, and sent to the Cranmer brailler to produce hard-copy braille. In reverse a student can write a paper using the VersaBraille or Apple IIe with the talking word processing program and have it printed out for a sighted person to read. If the user chooses, he or she can have the KRM read the paper back in synthetic speech.

Training for the electronic communications training program is held from Monday through Friday from nine to five, the hours the center is staffed. Staff and several volunteers who are blind teach on a one-to-one basis. When students can use the computers independently, they are certified as independent users and allowed to use the center in the evenings and on weekends when no library staff are there. Since it was established, 110 people have been trained at the computer workplace.

HISTORY

How did this program get started? In 1980 the library began to hear more about library access for people with disabilities. A library services to the handicapped committee was formed and Mary Roatch, who was social sciences librarian at the time, was the chair. The committee included representatives from the literature and language, audiovisual, and fine arts sections and from three branches (Cholla, Saguaro, and Century). Before the library received federal Community Development funds for a TDD and LSCA funds for a Visualtek and nine lighted magnifiers (Gaylord Master Lens), service to disabled people at the central library consisted of telephone reference, large print books, and information about talking books. To make the best use of what they had, the committee first recommended that the Visualtek be kept with the humanities collection, the TDD in interlibrary loan, and all but one of the magnifiers at the branches. The new equipment was used infrequently so the committee revised its approach. The Visualtek was moved close to the social sciences section, along with a demonstration collection of talking books, a Sun Sounds Radio Reading Service receiver, and a collection of large print books. A librarian in the social sciences section had to learn to use the equipment and teach others.

The committee then planned the Handicapped Awareness Fair, held on a Saturday in February 1981. Services for disabled people in the community had booths around the lobby of the library. Sun Sounds Radio Reading Service broadcast live. The crowd was entertained by mimes, signed story telling and singing, and puppet shows. Demonstrations of signed and telecaptioned television, magnifiers, TDDs, and the latest equipment appealed to adults with disabilities. Ms. Roatch said it was the first time the lobby had been noisy since the library opened in its present location in 1952. Over 2,000 people were there. The community was excited about the idea of library service for people with disabilities.

Soon after this the library sections were reorganized. Social sciences merged with several other sections and moved one floor down. Arts and humanities moved in where social sciences had been. The committee wondered what would happen to its beginning services to the handicapped. Ms. Roatch masterminded the plan, which today is the special needs center. With LSCA and Community Development grants from 1983 to 1985, the library has been able to create a prototype of a comprehensive, centralized library service for people with disabilities.

GUIDES TO SERVICE AND COLLECTION

The center staff are creating guides that will enhance the service and its collection. Technology and the handicapped is the subject of one of its subject bibliographies, which lists books, magazines, and relevant headings in the vertical file. The center orders everything it can on technological aids for disabled people. Staff produce and update three other subject bibliographies annually: "Toys and Play," "Manual Communication," and "Employment and the Handicapped."

A guide to library services and materials for the deaf community highlights the TDD (used by staff to answer incoming information questions and by the public to make outgoing calls) and closed-captioned video. It lists educational videocassettes that can be used in the center and computer software (two finger-spelling programs). Under "Books/Bibliographies," the guide notes that the library publishes a bibliography of books on deafness, which is updated periodically, and "Manual Communication," a comprehensive bibliography of all the center's books on sign language, which is updated annually. Titles of magazines and newsletters focusing on deafness and hearing impairments are listed. Under "Special Programs" are notes about the celebration of National Better Hearing and Speech Month in May with the Read Out, Speak Out, Sign Out Festival (held at the library for three years and continued outside with the cooperation of other agencies) and about Deaf Heritage Week activities at the library during December. The guide also mentions the availability of demonstrations and tours of the library and center for special groups and classes. Finally there is the announcement that center staff can communicate by sign language-- three of them do.

"New Arrivals" are lists of new books on specific subjects. As new books come to the center, staff review them and enter the author, title, and call number on a 3-by-5-inch slip that is put behind the appropriate subject card. When four to six slips are accumulated, the center produces a "New Arrival" list on the subject and sends copies to all interested agencies. Some agencies want all the lists. The center also produces a large print catalog that is distributed to the Phoenix Public Library branches and other libraries in the county.

PROGRAMMING

The special needs center has also been involved in programming inside and outside the library. A sampling follows:

- May 1984: "Mental Retardation: A Family Perspective," in cooperation with the Arizona Department of Economic Security, Division of Developmental Disabilities, Parent Involvement Program.

- September 1984: "Come Play With Us: Toys for Children with Special Needs," in cooperation with the Arizona Department of Economic Security, Division of Developmental Disabilities.

- April 1985: "Serving Special Populations in Your Library," a workshop for Arizona librarians.

- September 1985: "Communication: The Key to Low Vision Services in Arizona," a two-day seminar in cooperation with the American Foundation for the Blind and the Arizona Department of Economic Security, State Services for the Blind and Visually Impaired, attended by professionals and doctors in the field of low vision.

- November 1985: "Technology Awareness Workshop," with Alan Crafton of Telesensory Systems, attended by ninety blind consumers, resource teachers of the visually handicapped, rehabilitation counselors, and employers.

- December 1985: "Deaf Awareness Week--Closed-Captioned Video Services for the Deaf," for the deaf community.

- January 1986: "Sensitivity to the Wheelchair Patron," two workshops for Phoenix Public Library staff; Large Type Week Author Program with Eleanor Godley, author of *Easy Cookery in Big Print.*

- March 1986: "Sensitivity to Handicapped Library Users," two sessions for library staff.

- March 1987: World of Work Job Fair at Phoenix Day School for the Deaf.

In 1986 Ms. Roatch taught classes offering credit through Northern Arizona University extension service for teachers of visually impaired persons and vocational rehabilitation staff from the Arizona Department of Economic Security.

STAFFING

Staffing for the center has come gradually. At first Ms. Roatch had only a half-time library assistant. As of June 1987 she had a full-time library assistant, a part-time library technical assistant, and a part-time library clerk who is hearing impaired. Ms. Roatch has been able to find sensitive, outgoing, enthusiastic persons, who handle themselves in a professional manner. They are self-starters who have teaching skills and can train students to use the computers.

Since its beginning the center has been staffed only from nine to five, Monday through Friday. Ms. Roatch was happy that a consumer group had recently gone to the city council and demanded that the special needs center be open longer hours. As a result, beginning in the fall of 1987, staff would be available all the hours the library is open. The addition of staff will enable the center to operate with a full-time supervisor, library assistant, and library technical assistant, a part-time library assistant and library technical assistant, and two part-time library clerks.

The office that Ms. Roatch shares with three staff members is a short distance from the special needs center. This is where staff retreat to order books, compile statistics, plan programs, write reports, and perform other behind-the-scenes activities. Although removed from the center, the office has telephone communication to it.

EVALUATION

Ms. Roatch issues a weekly narrative report to her supervisor, the central library administrator. On April 23, 1987, she reported that a staff person from the city of Phoenix personnel department had been trained to use the center's Braille-Edit word processing program to type test materials on the personnel department's Apple computer. The personnel department then gave the diskette to the center staff to have the material translated to grade II braille and produced as hard copy for a blind person applying for a job. The center also made its copier/enlarger available to the personnel department to enlarge tests for low-vision applicants.

The center's monthly statistical report for May 1987 showed that 2,017 people had attended two programs where the center was featured (a Lions Club breakfast and the Reach Out, Speak Out, Sign Out Festival), and 211 people had been to the center for demonstrations or tours. During the month patrons had used the computers for 270.5 hours. Of the books checked out, 1,029 were large type, 215 were nonfiction, and 23 were basic education materials. Twenty-five toys circulated. Also 51 items were hand-charged for short-term loan (braille, audiocassette tapes, videotapes, etc.).

I asked Ms. Roatch if anything had gone wrong as the program was developing. She felt that things had progressed amazingly well. She has had good advice from consumers and from persons already involved with the technology and has been able to purchase equipment as it was being developed. Naturally she wants more. A tractor-fed braille embosser is next on the wish list, and Ms. Roatch has her antennas out for sources of funding.

OUTREACH ACTIVITIES

While I was at the Phoenix Public Library, Ms. Roatch arranged for me to meet staff members involved in outreach activities. The bookmobile department serves nursing homes through a van.

Collapsible book trucks are loaded with cartons of books and pushed from room to room. One branch, whose librarian works very closely with the community, offers library service to homebound persons. A book storage warehouse has standing orders for large print titles that are supplied to the bookmobile department and sent to the branches as rotating collections.

I spent a day and a half at the special needs center and could have used a week to good advantage. There was so much to see and read and talk about. The history of the center is well documented. Thick notebooks crammed with reports, publicity items, publications, and photographs tell the complete story.

Ms. Roatch received the first Annual Outreach Services Award of the Arizona State Library Association in 1981 and has been asked to speak at American Library Association meetings and to librarians in Canada and Georgia. She has served as a consultant to numerous public libraries that hope to replicate the special needs center. This program has been recognized by the U.S. Department of Education and is included in *Check This Out: Library Program Models,* published in July 1987.

References

Roatch, Mary A. "Computers in the Public Library Assist Blind Users to Read and Write." *Interface* 9, no. 4 (Summer 1987):7-8.

_____. "Kurzweil-Plus: Good Technology for Disabled People at the Phoenix Public Library." *American Libraries* 15 (November 1984):699.

_____. "Your Computer and the Disabled." Mimeo presented for panel discussion at the American Library Association Conference, June 25, 1984.

_____. "Special Needs Technology in the Public Library." In *Fifth Annual Microcomputers in Education Conference--Tomorrow's Technology.* Edited by Donna Craighead. Rockville, Md.: Computer Science Press, 1985, 286-97.

U.S. Department of Education. *Check This Out: Library Program Models.* Washington, D.C.: GPO, July 1987.

Chapter 9

Montgomery County Department of Public Libraries, Bethesda, Maryland

The special needs library of the Montgomery County Department of Public Libraries is located in the same building as the Davis Community Library in Bethesda, Maryland, on the lower level. It is one of the twenty-three branch, regional, and community libraries in the system. A large sign identifies the separate ground-level entrance.

This library is spacious. It houses a library for the blind and physically handicapped that serves all the talking book readers in Montgomery County, the Charlotte Clark collection for people with special needs, a microcomputer room for adults and children with disabilities, homebound service, services for deaf and hard-of-hearing individuals, a job information center, and materials to support all these activities. There are a large meeting room, two smaller meetings rooms, accessible restrooms, and offices for key staff. The Davis Community Library can be reached by an elevator. The center is staffed by five professional librarians (two work half-time), the equivalent of four library assistants (two work half-time), and a page.

Martha Spencer was head of the library when I was there. (She has since retired; Devin Liner was appointed her successor in March 1988.) However, I talked with Virginia Wygant, librarian to the homebound, and Sue Nichols, children's librarian.

The information desk is a busy place and draws upon all the resources of the library. Each professional staff member is scheduled to spend at least one-forth of his or her time at the information desk and must know about all the services. Requests for talking books and information come to it as well as requests for a sympathetic ear. Staff call on appropriate social agencies in emergency situations, such as when a lonely woman was contemplating suicide. Professional staff members view it as their responsibility to make referrals to other agencies; the library resources cannot answer all needs.

The Davis Community Library and the special needs library are accessible to people in wheelchairs, but they are located on a very busy thoroughfare. Both the metro bus and ride-on buses go by the library. Westbound persons can ride to the end of the line and back to the library on the south side of the street for no extra fare if they let the driver know of their destination.

THE SPECIAL NEEDS LIBRARY

The special needs library, which opened in January 1986, brought together services already established at separate locations. The concept of a special needs library grew out of a plan developed by an ad hoc citizens' planning committee formed in 1982 to develop a long-range plan for the Montgomery County public libraries. Its ten members included Alice Hagemeyer, librarian for the deaf in the District of Columbia Public Library.[1]

Library for the Blind and Physically Handicapped

The library for the blind and physically handicapped is one of two subregionals in Maryland. (Talking book readers in other counties except Prince George's, which has the other subregional library, are served by the Maryland Regional Library for the Blind and Physically Handicapped in Baltimore.) People who apply for the talking book service can come to the library to get a machine, have a messenger deliver it to the library nearest their home, or have staff mail it to their home. Readers can come in for talking books or call in and have the staff mail out the records and cassettes. The Montgomery County public libraries have a computerized circulation system; the circulation system for the talking book service was to have been automated within the next year after my visit.

The number of people coming in for talking books has increased since the subregional library became part of the special needs library. Families make an outing of a library visit. (While there, sighted family members can borrow print materials from the Paris Community Library.) Once a month the Talking Book Club, which attracts twelve to twenty members, meets in the large conference room at the library. Ms. Wygant said that author Tom Clancy was scheduled to speak to the club in November 1987.

Homebound Service

Homebound service was founded fifteen years ago under a one-year LSCA grant. Any adult in Montgomery County who is unable to get around is eligible for the service. Ms. Wygant delivers books to over ninety people on a demand basis. She drives a county-owned car, visits people by geographic area, and takes enough material to last the average reader four to six weeks. She advises her patrons to call and make an appointment several days before they run out of books. She visits some people every two to three months and some every two to three weeks, depending on the number of books they read. She has great freedom in her work and visits as many people as she can handle, spending fifteen to thirty minutes with each one. When she was hired thirteen years ago, the visit was a very important part of the service. Now her visits are briefer so she can accommodate more people. Recently she recruited two retired librarians as volunteers to visit several readers.

In a folder for each patron, Ms. Wygant keeps a record of the author, title, and call number of the books she delivers. During my visit, she anticipated that the special needs library would soon have software for its IBM computer that would make it easier for her to keep these records. She and the volunteers are free to choose books from any library in the system and can also borrow them through interlibrary loan. Bethesda Regional Library is invaluable as a source of materials because it has a collection of older fiction by authors such as Thomas Costain and D. E. Stevenson, popular choices of her readers.

Ms. Wygant is responsible for purchasing large print books for the entire library system. While all branches have some, the collection in the special needs library is the largest in the system. It supplies forty nursing homes with twenty to thirty books each month. Two days a week a driver from mobile services comes to the special needs library to pick up six or seven collections and deliver them to the nursing homes. A contact person at each home has another collection of books ready to be returned to the library. The library also provides frequently changed (every three to six months) deposit collections of large print books to other library branches. As in several libraries I visited, the Montgomery County public library administration has been attempting to find the most satisfactory arrangement for large print books. These books have alternately been the responsibility of the branches and the subregional library.

Charlotte Clark Room

The Charlotte Clark Room, named in honor of Montgomery County Department of Public Library's first coordinator of children's services, was established under a grant that provided for a full-time children's librarian and a collection of toys and books for children with disabilities, their parents, and teachers. From its beginning in 1972 until May 1986 Janice Andrew was responsible for the collection and three microcomputers--an IBM PC/XT and two TRS-80s--that were added in the early 1980s. After Ms. Andrew retired, her position was divided into two half-time positions. Susan Nichols, a children's librarian at one of the branches who developed a program for deaf children over ten years ago, was hired to work with parents and children. Fran Kaplan is responsible for the microcomputers and the job information center, which focuses on specialized information for disabled job seekers.

At first glance the Charlotte Clark Room looks no different than a children's room in a small library. On closer examination you see that materials have been chosen carefully to meet the needs of children with disabilities. The books for young children have very clear pictures. The stories for children through age five are realistic rather than imaginative. There is a collection of beginning reader books for young people reading at first and second grade levels and easy reading books for those at third grade reading level. There are also books on crafts, sports, science, and biographies written below the fourth grade level. Most of the recently published books in the Montgomery County system, written for parents of children with disabilities, are duplicated in this collection. Ms. Nichols has reorganized the toy collection with the help of a volunteer. She cataloged each toy, assigned a number based on the level of skill required to use the toy, and put a bar code on it so that the toy could be checked out through the library's computerized circulation system. Ms. Nichols has even developed a collection of fiction about children with special needs by asking for extra copies from the branch libraries.

While I was there, several parents came in to choose toys or books for their children. The collection is more likely to be used by parents, who are referred by the schools, than by teachers. Parents bring older children with developmental disabilities to use the high interest-low vocabulary books, or the young people come to borrow them on their own. Ms. Nichols gets referrals from other librarians who recommend special needs library services, but she must remind librarians periodically that these services are available. She talked to the children's librarians in the system at their spring 1987 meeting. As a parent of a child with a learning disability, Ms. Nichols feels she can be empathetic with parents. She is involved in two parent support groups and occasionally attends meetings of other groups. Her outreach efforts are limited by the time she spends on the job, especially when 25 percent of that time is spent at the information desk.

The Microcomputer Room

The microcomputer room was inspired by a nationwide search for inventors who are making personal computers adaptive to the special needs of persons with disabilities. The applied physics lab of Johns Hopkins University, the Tandy Corporation, and the National Science Foundation sponsored this effort. The library service was established in the Charlotte Clark Room in 1982 with a $30,000 LSCA grant. Initially the library staff developed a two-week training program to prepare volunteers to instruct people at the terminals of two TRS-80 model III microcomputers with modems to access outside information utilities, such as the Source and CompuServe, and a seed collection of software. A simple query to the Maryland Computer Service led it to donate a Votrax speech synthesizer. An IBM PC/XT has been purchased more recently, and the library expects to acquire additional adaptive devices in the near future. Now Ms. Kaplan schedules appointments to coincide with the twenty hours she is scheduled to work and instructs individuals with a variety of disabilities in the use of word processing and educational software. Most of her patrons are learning disabled.

Ms. Kaplan is also responsible for the job information center, one of five in the system. The one in the special needs library has been developed to meet the needs of people with disabilities. It has a volunteer/employment job bulletin with current information about opportunities, catalogs from colleges with supportive programs for students with disabilities, and a vertical file with materials on education, employment, and support agencies for disabled people (e.g., materials from the HEATH Resource Center). It also has brochures, newsletters, and books on careers, education, job hunting, disability employment issues, skills, small businesses, literacy, and tests.

Librarian for Deaf and Hard-of-Hearing Individuals

Susan Cohen was hired as full-time librarian for deaf and hard-of-hearing individuals in 1984. She was born deaf, received an oral education, and learned to sign when she was in college. Since she can lip-read and speak very well, she also spends 25 percent of her time at the information desk. Her primary responsibility is not just to bring deaf and hard-of-hearing people to the special needs library, but also to sensitize library staff and the community to the needs and contributions of deaf people. She also promotes the use of other library resources by deaf and hard-of-hearing persons.

Ms. Cohen spent her first year at the library visiting parent groups, schools, sign language classes, deaf and hard-of-hearing clubs, and agencies serving deaf and hard-of-hearing people. She went with an interpreter to meetings of the Metropolitan Washington Library Council, represented the library, and thus raised the participants' consciousness of deaf people. She has been responsible for the installation of audio-loops in the meeting rooms at five of the libraries.

Two of the system libraries had TDDs for years, but they were rarely used except to relay messages. Ms. Cohen has promoted their use. Now six TDDs are in regional and community libraries as well as in the special needs library. Staff at these libraries can relay messages to the smaller libraries. The TDDs can be used by the public to make outgoing calls and by the library to receive incoming telephone reference calls. Closed-captioned videotapes are available at the four regional libraries, and the special needs library lends two telecaption adapters. Telecaption adapters will soon be circulated out of the four regional libraries, the service to the aging office, and the detention center library.

Ms. Cohen worked with the auditory program in the public schools before she was hired by the Montgomery County Department of Libraries. Therefore, she has an entrée into that program and goes to the schools on request for story hours and book talks. Whenever she visits there, she distributes a handout suggesting ways in which the school and the library can work together. (See Appendix C). (During the 1987-88 school year she planned to take the classes she would visit to the public library nearest the school. She wrote early in 1988 to say that this had not worked too well because of transportation problems.) Parents have been requesting interpreters for their children at story hours in different libraries and Ms. Cohen arranges this. The library has made funds available for interpreters for all county agencies through a contract with Deaf Pride, Inc., an interpreter network agency. All listings of library programs state that deaf or hard of hearing individuals may request a cued speech, sign or an oral interpreter five working days in advance of any library program by calling the special needs library.

THE COLLECTION

The library has a circulating collection of books on handicapping conditions that is probably the largest in the county. The collection covers treatment as well as educational and social aspects. There are many books on learning disabilities, and increasingly the center is buying books about blindness, Alzheimer's disease, schizophrenia, learning disabilities, deafness, and technology for disabled people. A display of books on the disabled sits on a table near the information desk. The library has many biographies and autobiographies about people with disabilities.

The library has a large collection of videocassettes and has general reference books such as *Books in Print, Large Print Books in Print*, and the *Physicians' Desk Reference.* Other reference books are more specific to their target population (the *Handicapped Requirements Yearbook, Gallaudet Encyclopedia of Deaf People and Deafness, Information Resources for the Handicapped,* and *Exceptional Children Educational Resources).* The library receives more than fifty periodicals and categorizes them by topic in a listing near where they are shelved. All but the two latest issues circulate, and the library will make free photocopies of articles requested in noncirculating issues. The library has the *Concise Heritage Dictionary* in fifty-six cassettes, a Visualtek, and a display of magnifying lenses donated by a local dealer. The magnifying lenses will eventually be lent to readers.

Prominently displayed near the entrance to the center are giveaway brochures about a wide variety of services for disabled people in the Washington, D.C., area. An exhibit case that contains a display of toys has the following sign on it: "The department endorses the Library Bill of Rights: 'Libraries that make exhibit space and meeting rooms available to the public they serve should make such facilities available on an equitable basis regardless of the belief or affiliation of groups representing their use.'" This sign appears at other places in both the Davis Community Library and the special needs library.

COMMUNITY RELATIONS

How does the library publicize its services? Most often it does so by word of mouth. Ms. Nichols said the children's librarians she knew when she worked in a branch often refer patrons to her. Ms. Cohen does outreach in the deaf community. Organizational contacts help bring people into the library. Ms. Wygant reported that she received referrals to homebound service when a relative would inquire at the library. Patrons and service providers spread the word. Each library has information folders on the desk next to the computer terminal where books are checked out, including information about special services. An article about homebound service in a local newspaper with Ms. Wygant's picture on the front page has produced calls about the service and has attracted volunteers.

Montgomery County has a Provider's Council, an organization of public and private agencies providing human services. Ms. Wygant used to attend these meetings, but now other staff members also go. People attending the meetings introduce themselves, take turns making formal presentations, and learn about each other's services. Referrals go in all directions as a result of these contacts. When I visited, Ms. Cohen was promoting the publication of a newsletter similar to *First Dibs* (see Chapter 7) that would make staff and the community more aware of library services. (The first issue of the *Communicator* was published in October 1987.)

Even before it was established, the special needs library had an advisory council with representatives from the groups it serves: deaf people, hard-of-hearing people, blind people, mentally ill people, physically handicapped people, and parents of the learning disabled.

STAFF

Professional librarians are in charge of each area of special services. Competition is intense; as many as forty people apply for a single job. Those best qualified are interviewed by a panel of peers. For a recent job opening this panel consisted of the personnel office's equal opportunity representative, the librarian for deaf and hard-of-hearing individuals, and another staff member sensitive to the needs of disabled persons. Twice a year the special needs library staff gives new staff in the Montgomery County Department of Public Libraries a special orientation on handicap sensitivity and communication with the deaf community. Special needs staff members are trained for their duties by coaching.

SENIOR BOOKMOBILE

Montgomery County's senior bookmobile operates out of mobile services in the library's central office in Rockville on a monthly schedule. It has a hydraulic lift by which loaded book trucks can be dropped onto the ground and then wheeled into nutrition sites or residential centers for older adults. This service has replaced some of the bookmobile sites where older people are not able to climb in or out of the community bookmobile. The senior bookmobile librarian does some programming, using BiFolkal kits occasionally.

FRIENDS OF THE LIBRARY

Friends of the library are a vital part of the Montgomery County libraries. A recruitment flyer reports that in March 1987 the Friends and the Arts Council of Montgomery County cosponsored a mime program targeted for children with disabilities at the Wheaton library. One-third of the 100 children attending were handicapped. Also in March the Friends sponsored a program at the Gaithersburg library called "Signs of Jazz," which included signed songs and dances from the fifties to the eighties.

The special needs library is a showplace for the county as government agencies seek to meet the requirements of federal, state, and local laws to provide equal access for people with disabilities. The library administration is also attuned to the mainstreaming philosophy of providing service to disabled people, wherever they are. A schedule of service hours indicates the access features of each library in the system: TDDs in six libraries, audio-loops in four libraries, and wheelchair accessibility in six. The Department of Public Libraries, encouraged by its advisory group, plans to renovate many of its buildings to make them increasingly accessible. Large print books are in all the public libraries in the system, and many of the books in the special needs library are duplicated at other locations.

Note

1. Susan F. Cohen, "United but Accessible System Meets Library Needs of Deaf and Hard-of-Hearing Individuals," *Illinois Libraries* 68 (November 1986): 556.

References

Brandehoff, Susan E. "'Rehabilitation Community' Focus of Computer Literacy Project." *American Libraries* 13 (December 1982): 711.

Cohen, Susan F. "United but Accessible System Meets Library Needs of Deaf and Hard-of-Hearing Individuals." *Illinois Libraries* 68 (November 1986): 555-59.

"Montgomery Co. Brings Computer to the Disabled Population." *Library Journal* 108 (January 1, 1983): 11-12.

Chapter 10

Duluth Public Library, Duluth, Minnesota

Duluth Public Library, with its four branches, is by far the largest of the fifteen public libraries in St. Louis County.

The main library building was opened in November 1980. Director Janet Schroeder says: "We worked hard to make the building totally accessible to handicapped and elderly customers. However, making a building accessible only solves a small part of the problem. The greater challenge is making the library's collections and programs accessible to these two groups of customers."

HANDICAPPED ACCESS CENTER

One vehicle for meeting this greater challenge was the handicapped access center, which was part of the new library. An LSCA grant from the Minnesota Office of Library Development enabled the library to purchase a Kurzweil Reading Machine (KRM). Randy Vogt, who has an M.S. degree in vocational rehabilitation counseling, was employed as coordinator of the center. His position was originally funded through the city of Duluth's 100-day program for employing handicapped persons. Following that period the library received a four-month grant from the Edward Congdon Trust of Duluth to fund the position. During the next two years the locally based Ordean Foundation made two one-year grants so that the library could continue to hire Mr. Vogt and purchase equipment. In 1983 his position was made a permanent, city-funded library position.

Beginning with the KRM the handicapped access center has added equipment to meet the special needs of visually and physically handicapped people: an Apollo viewing system, which enlarges print up to sixty times; a *Talking World Book*, which contains the 1980 *World Book Encyclopedia* on 219 cassettes; and a TDD with an automatic answering service. Other aids in the center are machines for demonstrating the talking book program available from the Minnesota Regional Library for the Blind and Physically Handicapped; a radio reading service receiver for broadcasts from Minnesota Radio Talking Book Service; and adaptive telecommunications equipment to demonstrate how people with hearing, speech, vision, or motor impairments can overcome problems in using a telephone. This latter equipment was lent to the library by Northwest Bell.

All of this is featured in a brochure that bears the center's logo (see Appendix C) and an eight-minute slide-tape presentation that Mr. Vogt shows to community groups. Both emphasize the accessibility features of the library: pressure release doors; accessible telephone, water fountain, and restrooms; designated parking spaces near the main entrance of the library; and convenience of the library to public transportation. They point out that the library has two wheelchairs for users' convenience, cassettes and large print books for persons with visual impairments, and toys for children with disabilities. The slide-tape shows the library's on-line catalog, which responds to touch. The brochure points out that interpreters for library programs can be obtained through the mayor's information and complaint office.

The center has a small reference collection and a pamphlet file on topics of interest to people with disabilities. These supplement the materials in the general library collection. Near Mr. Vogt's desk is a large holder with multiple copies of brochures from agencies with programs for disabled people.

COMPUTERS FOR PERSONS WITH DISABILITIES

In 1983 Mr. Vogt became conscious of the growing interest in computers for persons with disabilities and attended a workshop on this subject conducted by Closing the Gap in Henderson, Minnesota. Delores Hagan, a presenter at the conference, has advised the library about computer hardware since then. It has purchased an Apple IIe microcomputer with two disk drives, a color monitor, two printers, and a Power Pad graphics tablet. It has also purchased specialized equipment such as the adaptive firmware card that permits a person unable to use the keyboard to enter data into the computer by sixteen different routines. Other adaptations are a table that can be adjusted to the height needed by the user, a variety of switches, and an Echo Plus speech, music, and sound synthesizer. The center has software for graphics, word processing, and databases, and tutorials for all equipment. Mr. Vogt also trains people to use the computer through the Duluth Community Schools' Project Access.

The handicapped access center has been used primarily by people with physical disabilities, especially by those with cerebral palsy. The Lighthouse for the Blind, a rehabilitation facility in Duluth, has brought people to the center, but they have rarely come back to use the KRM or the Apple microcomputer.

In 1986 the library expanded the concept of handicap to include illiteracy and applied for and received one of the first LSCA literacy grants. Five more Apple computers were purchased in 1987, and the handicapped access center combined with the computer assisted learning center (CALC), which emphasizes adult literacy training. A new brochure states that CALC serves: (1) adults who wish to brush up on reading, writing, and math skills, (2) handicapped persons who need adaptive equipment to use microcomputers and the full range of the library's collection, and (3) adult microcomputer users. While I was visiting Mr. Vogt, a GED class (students studying to pass a high school equivalency exam) came for a one-hour session. Mr. Vogt schedules users for one-hour periods, but if no one is waiting to use the computer when the hour is up, time can be extended. Because the role of the center has expanded, a half-time literacy coordinator and a librarian III staff the center.

NEW SERVICES

The adapted toy project is a new part of this expanding service. In 1986 the library received $2,439 from the Minnesota Library Foundation; it matched this amount to establish a collection of toys, games, and recreational equipment designed or adapted for use by children with disabilities. The collection is housed in the center, where Mr. Vogt administers and supervises it. An advisory group of parents and professionals and the local chapter of Telephone Pioneers are working with Mr. Vogt on the project.

The newest part of the library's services for people with disabilities is a collection of sign language videocassettes, established with a grant from the Eddy Foundation. The cassettes are selected by a special user committee because no one on the library staff knows sign language. This collection was established in response to a request from the deaf and hearing impaired community.

Today the handicapped access center is on the second floor of the library, near the elevator and steps and adjacent to the reference department. It moved from a less visible location at the west end of the second floor when it took on additional responsibilities as the computer assisted learning center. Mr. Vogt reports to the head of the reference department, but he says this may change because the literacy program is administered by the extension department.

COMMUNITY INVOLVEMENT

Early in the center's history Mr. Vogt was heavily involved in planning workshops. In April 1981 an all-day workshop, "Attitudes--the Invisible Barriers," was open to the public and library staff. In June 1981 Mr. Vogt presented the first of a series of four workshops for staff, "Serving the Physically Disabled at Duluth Public Library," with the help of the G. Polinsky Rehabilitation Center. This was followed by "Deaf Awareness" in September 1981, with a deaf student as a resource person; "Library Service for the Blind and Physically Handicapped" in November 1981, with speakers from the Minnesota Regional Library for the Blind and Physically

Handicapped; and "Survival Sign Language" in December 1981, presented by the Regional Service Center for the Hearing Impaired.

Mr. Vogt is well-known in the community. He is a member of the Governor's Advisory Council on Technology for People with Disabilities. In February 1985 he received a Sister Kenny Institute Certification of Recognition for "employees with disabilities who have successfully contributed to the quality of work and community life and for outstanding work performance and individual accomplishment." That year the Duluth Public Library also received a certificate of recognition for "continuing commitment to the employment of qualified workers with disabilities and in appreciation for providing meaningful and challenging work opportunities for all employees" from the Sister Kenny Institute and a certificate of appreciation from the Duluth School District's Program of Community Work Skills for Students with Handicaps in recognition of the library's assistance. Mr. Vogt wrote a sensitive article on attitudes and the disabled, which was published in the October 1985 issue of the *Duluthian.*[1]

In its initial years the center had an advisory group, but Mr. Vogt says it is no longer needed because he knows people he can go to directly for advice. He issues press releases to publicize any new aspect of the service but feels that he should be out in the community promoting the service, especially the KRM. Until 1987 he worked alone. It has been difficult for him to be in the center and in the community at once. The new half-time staff member has relieved that situation somewhat. Mr. Vogt is working on a policy and procedures manual for the center.

HOMEBOUND SERVICE

For disabled people who cannot come to the library, the library goes to them. Mr. Vogt arranged for me to talk to Beth Kelly, head of adult services, who is responsible for the homebound service. Four professional librarians in adult services keep in telephone contact with and select books for 80-100 homebound people. Four teams of two volunteers each deliver the books. Each librarian spends a maximum of thirteen hours per week selecting materials. They keep no record of what each person has read but may pencil the reader's initials in the back of a book if it is the only copy so they won't send the same book a second time. Readers generally request best-sellers or books about a particular subject. About half the readers want large print. Clerical staff check out the books, put them in library bags, and attach name and address tags and sometimes directions to the person's home. Once a month a team of volunteers picks up the bags and spends a minimum of three hours delivering materials to an average of twenty people. The four routes are clustered geographically, and volunteers can use a city vehicle; most prefer their own cars.

As of my own visits, the Duluth Public Library was not publicizing this service because of a vacancy in one of the four professional librarian positions in adult services. However, they continued to serve readers already getting books. The Friends of the Library provide money for mailing requests, which come to the library between regular visits. Volunteers pick up these books on their next visit because the postal employees in Duluth do not pick up the packages. A half-time volunteer coordinator recruits new volunteers when they are needed. Orientation to their responsibilities is informal. The library provides a collection of books for one nursing home that has a volunteer librarian. This collection is changed every six weeks. It seems to me that this library has been successful in integrating disabled people by providing special equipment and assistance when it is needed but keeping the service essentially mainstreamed.

Note

1. Randall Vogt, "Attitudes and the Disabled," *Duluthian* 20 (September-October 1985):44-45.

Chapter 11

Broward County Library, Fort Lauderdale, Florida

Broward County's main library in downtown Fort Lauderdale is the biggest public library I have ever seen. A massive eight stories of glass and steel, it fills a city block and is connected to a parking garage across the street by a glass-enclosed bridge on the second floor. The popular library, a 300-seat auditorium, and a gift shop are on the first floor. Large print books are in the popular library. At the time of my visit, no signs pointed out their location. (Since then, signs have been made.) A sign near the entrance says that wheelchairs are available at the second-floor information desk. Readers can go by escalator or elevator to the second floor where they will find the information desk, the children's department, and a restaurant. There are eight floors in all, with administrative offices located on the eighth floor. The main library and all but one of the twenty-three branches are totally accessible.

TALKING BOOK LIBRARY

The talking book library (Broward subregional) moved from its previous home in a library branch to Broward County's main library in September 1983 while the new building was still under construction. In 1978 the Broward County Library System, the Florida State Library, and the Florida Division of Blind Services' Regional Library for the Blind and Physically Handicapped worked together to create the seventh subregional library for the blind and physically handicapped in the state. The Broward subregional was to be an outreach model.

The talking book library, located in the northeast corner of the main library, is headed by Joanne Block. This library within a library is at a very visible location on the ground floor. It has sliding glass doors, making it quite accessible, and is enclosed by glass on three sides, making it light and airy. Thousands of cassette tapes, records, and braille books, along with the talking book equipment, are housed there. Work areas for staff and volunteers are tucked against the room's solid wall. The large room is decorated with crafts and artwork created by talking book patrons. Most notable is a large abstract piece made of discarded flexible discs by Esphyr Slobodkina, author of the children's book *Caps for Sale.* Racks of information about services and a display collection of aids and appliances for people to try out contribute to the library's inviting atmosphere. The circulation desk is just inside the entrance, and help is immediately available.

Even though the Broward subregional initially had a collection of talking books, its purpose was limited to recruiting readers, who then received their talking books from the regional library at Daytona Beach. Only the walk-in patrons could borrow books from the talking book library. As requests for local service grew to 2,600 registered talking book patrons in Broward County, the subregional library began to circulate books. It serves approximately 1,000 people, and the regional library serves the rest. When readers choose books from *Talking Book Topics,* however, they usually send their lists to Daytona Beach.

Readers either come to the talking book library for books or staff mails the books to them. Staff members know the readers personally and so can help them choose books they will enjoy. The Broward patrons either leave the selection to the staff or call in author, title, or subject requests. Many of the readers served by the subregional library are experiencing the trauma of becoming blind and discover that through the library they can read again. Staff also refer readers to other agencies, such as the local radio reading service, the Florida Division of Blind Services, and the Broward Center for the Blind.

When readers apply for the service, they receive four books. Then they are asked how many books they can read in a month. There is no official limit to the number they can have, and no date due is stamped in the books. The library contacts a reader if someone else wants a book he or she has had for a while. Ms. Block said that hers was one of two subregional libraries in Florida that was keeping a manual circulation file, but this would change when the library began using READS, the computerized circulation system developed by the National Library Service for the Blind and Physically Handicapped. (The system was installed in December 1987.)

Many talking book readers in Broward County are temporary residents. The talking book library gives them temporary service; they are transferred to the Florida regional library only when they move to the state permanently. Some people are temporary users for years.

FUNDING

For several years LSCA funds were used to support subregional libraries in Florida. Now these federal funds are used only for establishing new subregionals and for extending service through special projects such as READS. Ms. Block has been successful in raising money for special projects. The Delta Gamma sorority has given money for six small commercial cassette players that play talking books. Readers can try them out before they buy one or borrow them to use when they travel. At the time of my visit, Delta Gamma was raising $500 to purchase games to circulate to users (e.g., braille Monopoly and large print Scrabble). These were to be introduced at the library's tenth anniversary party in 1988. The library is constantly receiving donations from readers and their families, and gift money is used to purchase aids and appliances for examination and loan.

WORK WITH COMMUNITY GROUPS

Ms. Block works closely with many community groups. Three years ago and again in November 1987 she was one of two key people organizing a vendors' fair, at which company representatives show the latest modified and adaptive equipment and materials for helping people with disabilities in academic and vocational programs. This one-day event has been held on the eighth floor of the main library. Special education and vocational education teachers and administrators, parents, and the community are invited. Ms. Block is also treasurer of the committee that holds the three-day Broward County Expo for the Handicapped each fall at a local shopping mall. She participates in planning Barrier Awareness Day at the Broward County Community College. She is secretary of the board for the local radio reading service, where she has a monthly radio program, "The Loquacious Librarian," on which she discusses library news and subjects of general interest. She is a member of the Disabled Persons Action Committee and the Broward chapters of the American Council of the Blind and the National Federation of the Blind. Through her involvement in these organizations she stays abreast of community efforts on behalf of people with disabilities. She speaks to groups by invitation and frequently gives tours of the talking book library. A flyer, "The News about Talking Books," which explains the service, is distributed at fairs and through library branches and departments. The talking book library has developed a new brochure, with very basic information and pictures, to be used for mass mailings.

Ms. Block prepares a newsletter, *For Your Ears Only,* when something triggers a need. The September 1987 issue highlighted the expo and the vendors' fair. She includes other information as well. The county printing department will print the newsletter, or the regional library at Daytona Beach will reproduce and mail it. If it is mailed from Fort Lauderdale, a volunteer folds and labels 2,600 copies.

STAFF

Besides Ms. Block, there are six other people on the staff: a librarian I, a data entry operator I, three clerks (one blind), and the head of the books-by-bail service, which is housed on the second floor of the main library. (The librarian I, the data entry operator, and one clerk were added through a Library Enhancement grant from monies budgeted for library service for blind and physically handicapped people by the Florida legislature.) To acquaint library staff with talking book library and books-by-mail staff, Ms. Block photocopied their pictures and wrote a brief description of the library. She sent copies to main library and branch staff. Ms. Block looks for staff who are flexible, public service oriented, pleasant, friendly, and caring. Knowledge about disabilities is not required; that is learned on the job. Because the Broward subregional is a resource center, visitors stop in with all kinds of questions. A great deal of staff time is spent explaining talking books to nonusers and demonstrating aids and appliances.

Cecil Beach has been director of the Broward County Library since 1976. He is service oriented and receptive to new ideas, but cannot always approve the hiring of new staff. (The county government, which funds the library, is reluctant to add staff. The talking book library has been fortunate in having three positions funded with state money.) Ms. Block works directly under the supervision of the assistant director for special projects.

VOLUNTEERS

Ms. Block has been very successful in working with volunteers and has used them to implement many of her ideas. She started a book discussion group when one of her patrons said he had no friends since he lost his sight. The group met at the south regional branch in Pembroke Pines when the talking book library was located there. When it moved, Ms. Block turned her job over to two volunteers who lead book discussions every other week. The National Library Service for the Blind and Physically Handicapped provides cards with brief annotations for new talking books, and Ms. Block sends these to the leaders who read the information from them to the group and take orders. Other talking book discussion groups are ready to go as soon as Ms. Block can find volunteers to lead them.

Another volunteer is in charge of the "talking book express," a new service in a branch close to a high concentration of senior citizens. About fifty cassettes are available for people to borrow when the mail service doesn't keep up with their needs. The volunteer has the freedom to promote the service as she wishes. Ms.

Block's goal is to have a talking book express in all the branches in five years. The size of the collection and the services provided depend on the branch, its staff, and volunteers. A volunteer has already designed a logo for this new program.

Volunteers do some taping in their homes if materials are not available elsewhere and if the readers need the material right away. Other people who volunteer to be talking book buddies are paired with users of talking books. They read *Talking Book Topics* to users and help prepare request forms. Members of Anchor Club, a high school affiliate of Pilot Club, give time to the library each week. They inspect tapes, sort cards, and enter books on the Visifile. They have also guided people at the vendors' fair. Volunteers are recruited through the library's community relations department, which prepares newspaper publicity about the talking book library and advertises for volunteers, and through the talking book library itself. The main library's volunteer coordinator gives the library access to probationers doing 50-100 volunteer hours of community service. While there is a major countywide program to recognize volunteers, Ms. Block has a Let's Start the New Year Off Right party for her volunteers each year.

BOOKS-BY-MAIL

The library's books-by-mail program was initiated with LSCA money and is now operated from the second floor of the library by one library assistant under Ms. Block's supervision. Readers can receive large print or regular print. A separate application for large print requires certification of eligibility by a doctor, social worker, or other authority. This certification process makes it possible for the library to mail books as free matter for the blind and handicapped. Regular print readers must pay the return postage. Books are mailed in nylon zippered bags. The library budgets $2,500 a year for large print for this collection and subscribes to a McNaughton plan to meet the needs of regular print readers. Six hundred people who can't get to a Broward County library or a bookmobile use this service. Like the talking book service, it is highly personalized and books are sent out by request or as books are returned.

OTHER SERVICES

When the talking book library began, it had a collection of books about disabilities. Because the talking book library is open only forty hours a week, Ms. Block decided it was better for these books to be transferred to the subject department where they belong. (The rest of the library is open much longer hours.)

At one time Ms. Block was head of the system's bookmobile service. As more and more branches opened, bookmobile service has been cut back. There is no special service to nursing homes, but many get talking books and books-by-mail for their residents.

DEAF SERVICES

On the suggestion of a staff member, the south regional branch of the Broward County Library System, located on the Broward Community College south campus, has developed a deaf services program for its community. The program has a collection of books, magazines, pamphlets, and directories for and about the hearing impaired; captioned videocassettes for loan or viewing at the library; and captioned feature film showings. Interpreters are provided for programs on request. The branch has a TTY, and public phones with amplified volume control. These services are publicized in a brochure. Captioned film programs are offered at two other branches as well, and captioned videocassettes are also on loan from the main, east, and west regional libraries. The main library has a TTY. These resources are publicized by a bookmark with the hand-spelled alphabet on one side. The talking book library has a TDD with its display of aids and appliances, and a file of materials on deafness. Ms. Block is in the process of developing a request for a grant to create a countywide deaf services program. It will make services now offered at the south regional branch available at a number of branches.

The library system planned to initiate a "decoder club" program beginning in January 1988. Through it closed captioned videocassettes can be borrowed by hearing impaired or deaf patrons who have registered by mail or in person at the main library's fine arts/audiovisual department. Most deaf people live in other parts of the county so they can request the videocassettes by TDD and have the videocassettes delivered to the nearest branch. This service will be publicized through deaf clubs and services for the deaf and hearing impaired.

Ms. Block is viewed as the person in the Broward County Library System who is primarily responsible for library service to people with disabilities. While she recognizes that statistics do count with library administrators, she feels service is successful if anyone benefits from it.

PART 4

MAINSTREAMED SERVICE

Mainstreaming is a term that gained popularity following passage of P.L. 94-142--The Education of All Handicapped Children Act--in 1975, legislation that has been called the Mainstreaming Act. Actually, the law mandated a free public education for every child in the "least restrictive environment" where his or her needs could be met. Only when the handicap was so severe that children could not be educated with the use of supplementary aids and services were they to be placed in separate classes.

The goal of mainstreaming in a library setting has been to integrate services for disabled people with existing services rather than to create "special services." As public schools have discovered, this may require modifications of the facilities, and it certainly calls for special training of the staff.

Writing in *Accessible Library Services*, Lienne Sorenson gives an accurate picture of the decisions a library faces when it decides to mainstream people with disabilities:

> From the beginning it has been our intention to develop a mainstreamed model of library services to persons with disabilities. That is, we planned to serve the disabled person side-by-side with other library clients. We adopted a concept of viewing physical disabilities as on a continuum of slight to severe, and felt we could reasonably expect, with the help of new technology, special format materials, and other resources, to mainstream most disabled persons who were able to get to the library. Since many disabilities are moderate enough to be hardly noticed, and many materials and other resources are readily

accessible, we assumed that clients could help themselves and the matter of the disability need not even be an issue.

The reality proved to be more complicated when a number of more severely handicapped individuals, attracted by the publicity given the SALS program, began to come to the library. One group from a special recreation center expressed interest in making regular visits. These people could not be easily mainstreamed. In order to benefit from their visits to the library they needed more help in staff and time than the library could appropriately devote to them. Questions arose that went beyond the opportunity to provide material resources in the library. What is the library's responsibility in giving physical assistance to the individual? What is the responsibility of the service institution? Finally, what responsibility does the disabled patron assume? The concept of mainstreaming had to be more clearly defined.[1]

Each of the six libraries in this section has determined when it can mainstream patrons and when it must provide special services. In each library a single person is responsible for assessing the need for new services, developing them, and evaluating their success. Job titles indicate the librarian's overall responsibilities: director at the Monroe County Library System in Michigan, coordinator of children's and extension services in the Fitchburg Public Library in Massachusetts, Coordinator of extension and special services in the Prince George's County Memorial Library in Maryland, librarian for services to persons with disabilities in the Queens Borough Public Library in New York, manager of Skokie accessible library services (SALS) at the Skokie Public Library in Illinois, and coordinator of special services at the Memphis-Shelby County public library and information service center in Tennessee. It is interesting to note that even with emphasis on mainstreaming, it has been hard to let go of the term *special services.*

While these librarians are responsible for work in other areas as well--library administration, jail service, literacy programs, children's services, older adult services, reference, information and referral-- they are actively involved with disability groups in the community. Consumer advisory groups have been giving input to all the mainstreamed programs. Because the library administration is committed to mainstreaming, training of other library staff is part of these librarians' jobs, and they do this in cooperation with other areas of the library through workshops, manuals, displays, and personal contacts.

Several services at the Memphis Public Library make it unique among the libraries described in this book: it operates a radio reading service and has a television station that produces some programs for people with disabilities and their families. The Skokie Public Library is unique because it is committed to training librarians throughout Illinois to serve people with disabilities.

Mainstreaming is a concept that can be applied in libraries of any size, in rural as well as metropolitan areas, as these portraits will demonstrate.

Note

1. Lienne Sorenson, *Accessible Library Services: A Brief Guide to Serving Persons with Disabilities in the Public Library* (Skokie, Ill.: Skokie Public Library, 1987), 1.

Chapter 12

Monroe County Library System,
Monroe, Michigan

In the spring of 1980 Bernard Margolis, director of the Monroe County Library System in Michigan, came to Ohio to speak at two of four workshops on public library services to people with developmental disabilities. The series, supported by LSCA funds and coordinated by the state library of Ohio, was called "We Are Not Children." I was the state library consultant for services to the handicapped at the time. A member of the state library's Outreach Advisory Committee had sent me an article entitled "Library Serves Developmentally Disabled" that described the Monroe program.1 The article convinced us that Mr. Margolis should be a presenter.

THE LIBRARY SERVICE TO THE DEVELOPMENTALLY DISABLED PROJECT

The Monroe County Library System had thousands of books to be repaired and rebound. It contracted with a local sheltered workshop, MORE (Monroe Opportunity for Rehabilitation and Education), to do the work, and the 3-M Company contributed the materials, machinery, and training. Thus the library administration became aware of people in the community who were not receiving library service.

The administration formed an advisory group consisting of developmentally disabled people and of staff from the agencies serving them. Out of this relationship grew a proposal for a project called Library Service to the Developmentally Disabled. From 1977

131

to 1980 the Monroe County Library System received funds for the project from the Developmental Disabilities Act, first through the Michigan Department of Public Health and then through the Michigan Department of Mental Health.

The project had three components:

1. *Staff training was intensive with two-day workshops for two successive weeks, followed by one-day workshops for the next three weeks.* Developmentally disabled people were involved as both planners and participants. They dramatized the need for service as they told about their experiences in libraries. Much of the staff training was experiential, including values exercises and simulation activities. Emphasis was placed on developing skills in communication.

2. *Jobs in the library were created for developmentally disabled people.* The library received additional funds from the State Bureau of Vocational Rehabilitation and the Association of Retarded Citizens and provided on-the-job training for people recommended by the sheltered workshop. These employees typed, worked in the library's print shop, answered the telephone, staffed the information desk, and planned programs. A total of six people went through this training program during the grant period. The wider community in Monroe County applauded the library's efforts.

3. *The library initiated new services and developed a collection of materials.* While it did not specifically advertise programs for developmentally disabled people, the library encouraged this group to attend a library orientation program, learn to use a film projector, check out materials, pay fines, learn to read with the help of a volunteer tutor, participate in voter education programs, and come to the library for film programs and special events. The only special activities were film programs to teach everyday living skills to people in group homes. The library purchased materials (many of them from local

stores) that could be used by anyone but that were especially valuable as teaching tools for people with developmental disabilities. A catalog of the developmental materials collection lists more than eighty kits and devices (e.g., a shopping list game, graduated boxes, color discovery cards, knobbed puzzles, and book holders).The catalog also lists films about disabilities, filmstrip/cassette sets to teach skills and to entertain, and a bibliography of books and government publications on developmental disabilities.

STRUCTURE OF THE LIBRARY SYSTEM

Monroe County's library system has its headquarters on the western edge of the city of Monroe. Local units of government provide the facilities for sixteen branches, and the county library system staffs the branches and supplies materials and special equipment. An advisory group appointed by the local unit of government for each branch guarantees that the branch reflects the community's desires and advises the system's board of trustees.

The county library system is supported by a county millage levy, which is taken to the voters for renewal every four years. It also receives all court-mandated fines imposed on people found guilty of state crimes and misdemeanors in the county. As a matter of fact the headquarters library is named the Edward D. Ellis Building after the newspaper editor who in the 1830s convinced delegates at the Michigan Constitutional Convention to give the court-levied fines to libraries. The rationale was the libraries would educate people so there would be no more crime. In August 1987 alone the library system received $90,000 in fines paid by overweight trucks at a weigh station on Route I75. The library earns additional revenue through the operation of a printing shop; it contracts for library printing nationwide.

The library has continued to have its books repaired and bound at the sheltered workshop. It has also offered this service to libraries in a seven-county cooperative in lower Michigan, a cooperative for which it is the fiscal agent. The cooperative operates a delivery service between the libraries, making it feasible to have books repaired in Monroe County.

During the period of the Library Service to the Developmentally Disabled project, some staff continued to feel uncomfortable serving people with developmental disabilities in spite of the in-service training they received. Mr. Margolis feels that staff members have matured in the past several years and can work with people from group homes--there is one next to the library headquarters--who come to the library to look at picture books and magazines or read the newspaper. Only one workshop, "Dealing with the Difficult Patron," with a section on persons with developmental disabilities, has been held since 1980.

EMPLOYMENT OF PEOPLE WITH DISABILITIES

The library system has sixty-seven staff members, three of whom are developmentally disabled. The library administration has adapted jobs or changed work sites to accommodate people with disabilities. Two people in the processing department use wheelchairs. A librarian at one of the branches had multiple sclerosis and used a wheelchair. Part of the facility was redesigned so that she could work as long as she was able. During the summer the library employs students from two local work programs, one of which is a program for special education students. In the summer of 1987 one young woman who uses a wheelchair was employed in the processing department. When staff were being scheduled to work at a library exhibit at the county fair, she wanted to help. Mr. Margolis made arrangements for this. The library has not had an advisory group representing disabled persons since the project ended, nor are they represented on any of the advisory groups for the branches.

MATERIALS

The Monroe County Library System experienced some tough financial times in the early eighties and discontinued purchasing materials for the developmental materials collection. The collection was dispersed from headquarters to the branch libraries, and much of it is now in half a dozen group homes. Each home received 16-

mm projectors and some other materials during the project. Some of the materials are now being used in the library's literacy programs. The printed catalog has not been updated but still provides a guide to the collection. Materials move back and forth through the system, aided by telephone and computer contacts and the delivery system.

The headquarters has the largest collection of large print books in the system, and branches borrow from it on a regular basis. It buys everything--good, bad, and indifferent--and has standing orders with all companies that offer such a plan. Videocassettes are very popular; the system circulates 30,000 a month. Collections rotate to the smaller libraries. Records, cassettes, 16-mm films, easy-to-read materials, projectors, screens, and a public address system can all be borrowed from the Monroe County libraries. While the acquisition of materials is centralized, each branch has money for purchasing materials to meet its own needs.

INFORMATION AND REFERRAL

The library system has had an information and referral service called At Your Service since 1974. Although the service still maintains information files and publishes an annual directory at the headquarters library, now branches also provide information and referral service. Mr. Margolis said that the public doesn't differentiate between a reference question and an information and referral question; so why should the library? The *Monroe County Organization and Information Directory,* which sells for $3.00, lists organizations, groups, clubs, and agencies in the county and selected state and national organizations. For each entry the name, address, telephone number, purpose, availability (hours), and eligibility requirements for membership or services are given. The library also publishes the *Monroe County Industrial Directory* and the *Guide to Fun! in Monroe County.*

OUTREACH

A bookmobile operating out of the headquarters provides countywide service with stops at nursing homes and senior centers.

Deposit collections are left at sites that have space to house them and a volunteer to promote use of the materials. Two groups of RSVP (Retired Senior Volunteer Program) volunteers, coordinated by the headquarters library, provide service to homebound people. Other shut-ins receive library materials from volunteers working out of the branches or bookmobile staff on days when they are not scheduled for a bookmobile run. The system does not have talking books or equipment but acts as intermediary between talking book readers and the subregional library for the blind and physically handicapped at Battle Creek, where talking book mail service originates. Homebound readers and bookmobile patrons alike have access to the system's total collection.

PHYSICAL ACCESS

As for physical access the library buildings run the gamut from complete access at the headquarters to no access. The Dorsch Library in Monroe has been renovated and a ramp and elevator added, but access is restricted once you get into the building. Mr. Margolis is most concerned about elderly people and those with heart trouble who can't climb steps and even find it difficult to negotiate a long ramp. The library administration is continuing to address the problem of access.

PUBLIC RELATIONS

With its own printing department the library loses no opportunity to publicize its services. It makes use of the one county daily newspaper, local weeklies, and a county radio station. The library's public relations staff works with them all and publicity is countywide and local. Monroe County has no television station. Residents have access to Toledo and Detroit stations, neither of which has accepted library promotion from Monroe County. At the time of my visit Mr. Margolis had just applied for LSCA money for a direct mailing about library services to all county residents.

When the grant program ended and the library's financial problems began, relatives of disabled people and service providers were concerned. They accepted the inevitable, however, and Mr.

Margolis rarely hears any comments about the service any more. If the library suddenly had money, Mr. Margolis said that he would use it to promote library service to people with special needs.

Note

1. Bernard A. Margolis and Dale Ann Winnie, "Library Serves Developmentally Disabled," *American Rehabilitation* 5 (November-December 1979):30-32.

Chapter 13

Fitchburg Public Library,
Fitchburg, Massachusetts

In 1962 Fitchburg Public Library was the first regional library in a new statewide program in Massachusetts. The library and its bookmobile serve people living in the northern half of Worcester County and people from New Hampshire who work and shop in Fitchburg, a total population of 100,000-150,000.

The library had been recommended as one that effectively mainstreams people with disabilities into its total program. The Massachusetts Board of Library Commissioners has identified it as one of seven access centers in the state. These libraries are "located in barrier free buildings, have staff who are particularly sensitive to the needs of patrons with disabilities, and have a variety of aids to facilitate the use of library resources by patrons with visual, physical, and communication disabilities."[1]

Elizabeth Watson, coordinator of children's and extension services since 1971, has major responsibility for seeing that the following goals are met: (1) to further develop community access to services, materials, and programs and make an earnest effort to overcome the geographical, educational, physical, and psychological barriers that hamper library use; and (2) to plan and carry out programs that appeal not only to the broad cross-section of the community but also to groups within the community that have specific interests and concerns.

COMMUNITY INPUT

Since the mid-seventies, Ms. Watson has had an advisory group made up of local people who are blind, deaf, and physically handicapped. When the library is applying for money for a special project, the group may meet three to five times within a month or so. The library has received LSCA money several times and funds from the Quota, Lions, and Rotary clubs, the Grange, and local banks. The group met weekly when the members were assessing the building's accessibility, and monthly while accessibility features were being added. The library building is now totally accessible to people using wheelchairs and crutches. Shelving is about 80 percent accessible in the youth library, which is attached to the Wallace library (the original building) at a lower level with a ramp connecting the two areas. The advisory group recommended that a railing be installed on the ramp even though the standards did not require it. A restroom for handicapped persons was added because the library was built before that was a requirement.

Ms. Watson may go to an individual member of the advisory group about a special concern. Before the library purchased its third-generation TDD (a Minicom IV), she consulted with the deaf member of the advisory group.

Ms. Watson works on an ongoing basis with the local rehabilitation center, the Massachusetts Rehabilitation Commission, the Council for Deafness, and the local Association for the Blind. Citizens to Remove Architectural Barriers is a regional group that meets monthly. Ms. Watson attends its meetings two or three times a year, as do other members of the library's advisory group. She also serves on the board of Literacy Volunteers. Her finger is constantly on the pulse of the disabled community so she knows when something is happening that requires a response from the library, whether it be developing a special book collection or buying a new device.

A youth library staff member serves on the Council for Children, an organization that includes day-care providers, health personnel, and mental health personnel. The Fitchburg Public Library belongs to CHIRP (Community Health Information Resource Project), a network of public libraries aided by hospital libraries, academic libraries, and health agencies and funded with LSCA monies. Through CHIRP the citizens of the community have access to a wide spectrum of information on health-related topics.

SERVICE TO DEAF PEOPLE

The library provides TDD service to deaf people who want library information or wish to have calls relayed to hearing persons and to hearing persons who need to have calls relayed to deaf persons with a TDD. The TDD is located in the youth library, and there are two TDDs for lending. In the past the library offered introductory classes in sign language to staff and the community. Like other library services these were free. Because the library was not able to provide classes at a more advanced level, people had no place to go for additional training and became frustrated. Fortunately both the local community and state colleges now offer sign language classes. The library has recently ordered an interactive computer program from Microtech Consulting Company to teach American sign language.

The local Association of the Deaf and Hearing Impaired, which includes members of the library's advisory committee, met at the library for four or five years. The library coordinated the showing of films from the Captioned Films for the Deaf for a monthly program restricted to the group of fifteen to thirty deaf persons. At the time this met a need, but now many captioned videocassettes are available. The deaf community is much better served by the regular marketplace. Captioned films are now available through the regional library system; the Fitchburg library has its own captioned videocassettes, so that audiovisual programs can be mainstreamed. The library has a closed-captioned decoder for lending.

Although the library has long had signed storybooks for children, it had its first signed story hour in the summer of 1987. Each summer the library offers a preschool library experience on Wednesday mornings for 85-100 children. One parent, who is an interpreter, asked if Ms. Watson would mind if she signed for a deaf child who wanted to participate. Given the librarian's assent, the parent contacted several parent groups and four to eight deaf children were at every one of the programs. The parent then agreed to interpret several programs that are funded jointly by a Massachusetts Arts and Humanities grant and Friends of the Library. These are given in the library's auditorium and attract 200-300 children. The first row of seats was reserved for deaf children.

In its publicity for a monthly performing arts program for adults--drama, poetry, and music funded by the same groups that support the children's programs--the library has always stated in the brochures that people who require interpretation for the deaf should let the library know a week in advance so that the library can arrange for interpreters. Only a few requests have been made. Now with local talent available and with the positive response to the interpretation of children's programs, Ms. Watson anticipates that there will be more requests. She said that the public address system had been unsatisfactory for the adult programs because many of the programs were musical and the quality of amplification for music was not pleasant to listeners.

SERVICE TO PEOPLE WITH VISUAL IMPAIRMENTS

Adults and children who are blind can use the library's cassette books. There is a great demand for them by both sighted and visually impaired people. Individuals can also register at the library for the talking book service, which is a mail service from the Worcester Subregional Library for the Blind and Physically Handicapped. The Fitchburg library has a small collection of talking books that people can borrow in an emergency and a few braille materials. There is a collection of talking book catalogs and books that are prominently displayed to the back of the library's information desk.

The TRS (telephone reading service) meets a need identified by the advisory group. Each week one of five volunteers makes a recording that gives the library's hours and special events, community events, and selected sales items from the flyers of the two major supermarkets. The library collects the materials, the volunteer puts together a fifteen- to twenty-minute taped message, and the tape is played on a telephone answering service in response to an average of 200 calls a week. The number for this ten-year-old program is listed in the local telephone directory.

People with visual impairments, both adults and children, have access to the library's large print collection, which includes several magazines as well as books. Large type books are labeled LT with a yellow sticker on the spine. Recently the children's large type books were interfiled with others, but those for adults are still kept separate.

A Visualtek is in the reference area. Ms. Watson has a collection of magnifiers and aids to make writing, card playing, and telephoning easier. She lends these to people to try out, displays them at meetings, and takes them along whenever she talks to groups. She also has a collection of catalogs listing aids like these although most can be purchased in Worcester, located twenty-five miles away.

LEARNING CENTER

An area between the youth library and the Wallace library contains the learning center. It houses a collection of materials for adults with limited reading skills. Some were purchased at the request of the Association for Retarded Citizens (ARC), which has a sheltered workshop close to the library. Staff from the workshop used to bring clients to the library twice a week but do so less frequently since their funding has been reduced. ARC has given materials to the library and submits lists of books it would like the library to purchase. The collection includes materials for teaching self-help skills that can be used by house parents, publications developed for use by mentally retarded people, and editions of the classics with controlled vocabulary. Fiction from this collection has recently been integrated with the regular fiction collection--a yellow label identifies it--but nonfiction will stay in the special collection. A Bell and Howell Language Master is also available. These materials can be used by anyone trying to develop reading skills.

The library proper provides office space for the part-time executive director of Literacy Volunteers, space for tutors to work with students, and meeting space in addition to the space used by the learning center. The literacy program was started in 1971 with the library initially sponsoring it. Now, however, the library refers people to Literacy Volunteers as the need arises.

The library has materials about disabilities in the general collection and in the learning center, ordered by the adult services staff and Ms. Watson respectively. The special collection includes filmstrips, pamphlets, and books that can be used as awareness tools with staff and community groups. The center also has a collection of toys to foster the development of prereading skills and to serve as remedial devices. Local special education teachers have lists of the toys and can recommend appropriate toys to parents.

OUTREACH SERVICES

Shut-in service and deposit collections in nursing homes were in place when Ms. Watson came to the library. Both had been established in the sixties as a result of a comprehensive needs assessment for all kinds of outreach. A volunteer selects books for shut-ins, checks them out, and puts them in delivery bags. Some of the books are delivered by a volunteer. The rest are delivered either by the bookmobile supervisor in her own car or by the bookmobile if a home is on its regular route.

The percentage of people over sixty-five in Fitchburg is above the national average. The fact that the city was one of the first communities in the state to build housing for senior citizens may account for this. Now there are five housing units for older people, three of them high-rise buildings, and several other units of congregate housing with an elderly population. The bookmobile stops once a month at all except the two high-rise buildings within walking distance of the library. There are lots of rest homes, the name Massachusetts gives to housing for elderly people who cannot live alone but are not bedridden, and some critical care nursing homes. Once a month the bookmobile provides the homes with deposit collections and specific books for individual readers. The bookmobile supervisor talks to residents, brings back to the library the lists of books they'd like to have, and gives these to the volunteer who fills the requests. Many of these people receive large print and cassette books, and the library can enroll them in the talking book program if they are eligible. Books from the library's general collection are used for these services.

The library also serves FLLAC (Fitchburg, Lunenburg, Leominster, Ayer, Clinton) a five-city collaborative for severely handicapped children through the bookmobile and by individual visits. The children also come to the library.

PUBLICITY

How does the Fitchburg Public Library publicize its materials and services? The advisory group serves a very important role here as do Ms. Watson's contacts with community groups. As children's coordinator she is already involved with the schools. She is in touch with the Title II (special education) coordinator at least once a year.

A display near the information desk publicizes talking books and the newsletter published by the Worcester Subregional Library for the Blind and Physically Handicapped. Large print books are also close to the information desk. A bench nearby gives people the chance to rest while they browse. A 1980 catalog of *Large Print Books in the Central Massachusetts Regional Library System* and a 1984 supplement kept with the large print books list the holdings of the twenty-three libraries in the system.

The local newspaper is generous in publicizing special events and new developments. In the spring of 1987 it did a story with pictures about a special display of books and materials and at least once a year prints an article about the basic service. Ms. Watson arranges exhibits at health fairs and hands out information, such as a brochure describing the library's services for people with disabilities. Information periodically is sent to the Elder Affairs Council. The Visiting Nurses Association and an organization that provides homemaker services make referrals to the shut-in service. Ms. Watson sends information about services to churches for inclusion in their bulletins or public announcements. Because so many ways are used to publicize the services, there is no easy way to determine which are most effective.

STAFF TRAINING

How are staff made aware of services and sensitized to the needs of people with disabilities? Again Ms. Watson draws on all available resources. The librarian at the Worcester Subregional Library for the Blind and Physically Handicapped comes whenever there are three or four new staff members. This person orients them, not just to the needs of people who use talking books, but to the needs of people with other disabilities. The library has a monthly half-day staff meeting, repeated on a second day so all staff can attend. Resource people from local hospitals, rehabilitation centers, and mental health agencies come for thirty- to forty-five minute presentations about some aspect of service to disabled people. Recently the library staff needed help. Several emotionally disturbed people had behaved in a manner unacceptable to the library The library director arranged for a presentation by a mental health worker and a member of a local club for persons with emotional problems. Whenever deaf and blind staff members have been hired, Ms. Watson has invited someone from the Association for the Blind or the Massachusetts Office for Deafness to come to prepare other staff ahead of time.

As for the future of Fitchburg's mainstreamed services, Ms. Watson will make certain that the library remains accessible to all groups as the needs and composition of the community change. Until 1986 the local public schools served no deaf children, who were bused to another city. Now there is a class for deaf children in Fitchburg. This affects library service to the schools because children come to the library for author visits three to five times a year. Adjustments have been made. As children with disabilities are integrated into school programs, the library responds to their needs, just as it has responded to those of other citizens with disabilities.

Note

1. Brochure produced by the Massachusetts Board of Library Commissioners in 1982.

Chapter 14

Prince George's County Memorial Library System, Hyattsville, Maryland

I have heard about Prince George's County Memorial Library System as long as I have known about library service to people with disabilities, so I was not surprised to find that this library was recommended as one I should visit. I was especially eager to talk to Honoré François, coordinator of extension and special services because the focus of her work is to integrate people with disabilities into all library services. Ms. Francois started working in Prince George's County in 1974 in a newly created position.

Prince George's County library has twenty community branches. The administrative offices are in Hyattsville in a building linked with one of the four area libraries in the system. Each area library is responsible for smaller libraries in proximity to it. A community librarian supervises one to three smaller branches.

BUILDING ACCESS

Prince George's County has one of the country's toughest pieces of local legislation on access, Council Bill 49, passed in 1976 as an amendment to the county building code. It addresses the concerns of people with disabilities about assembly seating space, parking, traffic control inside buildings, even library stack areas: "The width between library stacks shall be no less than thirty-six (36) inches and the turning radius at the end of the stacks shall be no less than sixty (60) inches." In the late seventies, all library buildings and other public buildings were surveyed to see whether they met the standards; steps were taken to improve access. Now all of the library buildings are physically accessible, Ms. François says.

HOMEBOUND SERVICE

Homebound service, which has never been large, was already in place when Ms. François joined the library. It was staffed with volunteers then, and still is, although the way it is organized has changed. When customers, as they are called in this system, request homebound service, Ms. François's clerk-typist or someone in the extension/special services office generally interviews them by phone. She explains what library services are available and asks about the individual's reading interests and needs: Do they need large print or talking books? Are they hearing impaired? Do they speak English as a second language? This information is sent to a designee in the branch nearest the customer's home. The branch designee assigns a staff advisor and/or a homebound visitor. Homebound visitors are either volunteers identified through the system's volunteer services specialist or people recruited locally from the community or the library.

The staff advisor orients volunteers to library rules and policies and advises on selection of materials. Many staff are called upon to be staff advisors because fifty-two people in Prince George's County receive this service. (Involving a lot of people helps many become sensitized to the needs of people with disabilities.) Ms. François encourages staff advisors to call each homebound customer and make the first visit with the volunteer. The volunteer establishes a schedule for visits, usually every three to four weeks. The volunteer can deliver any library materials in the system, except videocassettes and 16-mm films, and can also borrow materials through interlibrary loan for the homebound person. When materials are returned, a record of them is kept to ensure that readers will not be given the same books twice.

If a volunteer cannot deliver books as scheduled, the staff advisor finds a substitute, personally delivers the books, or sends them by mail to be picked up on the volunteer's next visit. The staff advisor schedules periodic meetings with the volunteers to discuss and evaluate service. Three months and six months after service is begun, Ms. King calls the homebound customer to see whether the service is satisfactory. In all the years Ms. François has supervised this service, there have been only three complaints.

Homebound readers are all ages, but most are in their seventies and eighties and may be temporarily or permanently homebound. Although they may have physical problems, lack of transportation and age are more often critical factors. In some cases three generations of a family receive library materials. Ms. François says that the homebound people receiving this service would be the library's best readers if they could come to the library.

TALKING BOOK CENTER

Ms. François is responsible for the talking book center, which is located on the lower level of the Hyattsville area branch. In 1979 the Prince George's County library established a subregional library for the blind and physically handicapped after having had a deposit collection of talking books since the early sixties when it had field-tested the subregional concept for the Library of Congress' Division for the Blind and Physically Handicapped (now the National Library Service for the Blind and Physically Handicapped). The Maryland Regional Library for the Blind and Physically Handicapped sent its records for all talking book readers in the county to the library when it became a subregional library, and service has continued directly from the center. It now serves almost 800 readers. There is one full-time librarian who manages day-to-day operations, a full-time circulation assistant, and five part-time clerical aides. The aides check all returned materials and rewind the tapes. As a result the talking book center does not get complaints. Volunteers help with clerical tasks, and they tape materials not available through the National Library Service network or Recordings for the Blind.

Staff members interview all new readers by telephone and give them the option of coming to the library for their machine, picking it up at a nearby branch library, having it sent to them by mail, or having it delivered by library staff. Along with a packet explaining the service, readers receive information about the Washington Ear, the local radio reading service. Readers can come to the library for books or have them sent by mail. After a customer has received service for three months and for ten months, staff make follow-up calls. Once a year they call customers who have not used the service for six months. The talking book center was consulted when the National Library Service developed READS, its computerized circulation system. Ms. François expected to have hardware installed and the system operational in the talking book center no later than June 1988.

The talking book center has braille writers, book holders, handheld magnifiers, and manual and automatic page turners for demonstration and loan. It distributes free white canes provided by the Lions Club. Although the center receives few requests, staff can duplicate braille materials on a Thermaform Braillon. (A maximum of ten pages is done free of charge.)

The center has two kits for parents of preschool children with visual impairments. These contain tactile and audio materials to promote learning skills. Another learning device for loan is a Bell and Howell Language Master, which can be adapted to use with hearing impaired and visually impaired children as well as stroke and aphasia patients.

LARGE PRINT BOOKS

All library branches have large print books. Large print collections are assigned to the area libraries and large branches. Small branches get deposit collections. Large print books, like other materials in the system, are part of the central selection process. Each branch librarian chooses titles from a biweekly list prepared by the selection officer. The talking book center also has a collection of large print books that it mails to readers who receive its mail service. The books are also part of deposit collections for nursing homes, nutrition sites, and senior citizens' housing. Prince George's County Memorial Library has had a large print catalog in the past, but the last annual one was published in 1982. Since then it has issued quarterly author-title lists with annotations. In 1988 Ms. François and the selection officer were planning to convene a staff committee to study large print, develop guidelines for weeding the collection, and perhaps issue a new catalog. The committee was to include the talking book center librarian and representatives from two branches of different sizes.

OUTREACH SERVICES

Ms. François also coordinates library service to nursing homes, housing for older people, and nutrition sites. Each branch provides scheduled on-site visits, deposit collections, or both with volunteers assisting the librarians in the delivery of service. Programs are done on demand (but not so often as activity and recreation directors would like) to capitalize on the audience's interests and to stimulate the use of library materials. The area libraries provide most of this service because they are larger and have more staff. Service is taken to forty-three places, including eighteen nursing homes, fourteen senior citizen facilities, and three nutrition sites. The library has a written facilities agreement that spells out the library's responsibility and expectations of the facility. (See Appendix C.) This agreement was based on a document originally prepared by the Pierce County Public Library in Tacoma, Washington, which appeared in *The Librarian and the Patient: An Introduction to Library Services for Patients in Health Care Institutions,* edited by Eleanor Phinney.[1]

SERVICE TO THE DEAF COMMUNITY

Library service to parents of deaf children began many years ago when Lee Katz, the mother of a deaf child in Prince George's County, helped the library's children's services develop kits for parents and deaf children. The kits contained books, toys, a manual of suggestions for using the contents, and a list of organizations to contact for further information. They were used as models for the kits developed later and sold by the International Association of Parents of the Deaf (now the American Society for Deaf Children). The library still has a series of five kits circulating from eight of its branches.

The library's next move in serving the deaf community was in 1975 when it received LSCA funding for five years for a demonstration project. The project was planned as an integrated service, and TDDs were installed in four area branches. Ms.

François trained staff to use the equipment, but she also taught them about the communication needs of deaf people. *Films for Hearing Impaired Children,* a listing of 16 mm-films that can be used when all or part of the audience is hearing impaired, grew out of this project. The library purchased books, magazines, and pamphlets about deafness, hearing impairments, and sign language for adults and children. Forty hours of sign language instruction were offered to staff, but they learned other ways of communicating with deaf people as well. With the help of an advisory committee of consumers and agency personnel, the library developed policies and procedures relating to deaf services and guidelines for the use of the TDD. These became part of the Prince George's County Memorial Library Policy and Procedures Manual.

Ms. François developed a manual for a continuing program of staff training and turned the training of new staff over to the branch supervisors. Performance standards relating to service to deaf persons were written into position descriptions so staff members would understand what the library was trying to accomplish and how they could contribute. (See Appendix C.) This procedure is followed whenever new services are introduced. The specific standards are removed from the job descriptions once the services are integrated.

TDD numbers are listed in all publicity materials for the seven branches where these devices are presently used to receive requests for library service and to make outgoing calls. Each library with a TDD has one person who promotes the service and gives the users' recommendations to Ms. François.

The library purchases many closed-captioned videos. Interpreters are provided for selected programs that library staff determine to be of particular interest to deaf persons. For example, during the summer of 1987 a house plant clinic and live performances of "Summer Books Alive" were interpreted. If a program is offered at a number of sites, it will be interpreted at one. The monthly calendar of events states, "Interpreters can be provided for book discussions upon request." Ms. François says three days' advance notice is required. The library pays the local rate for interpreters.

In 1985 the library contracted with SURRES, a University of Maryland group, to do a needs assessment of the deaf community.

As part of the library's long-range plan, it wanted to identify what deaf persons perceived as their most pressing information needs, where they went to get answers to their questions, and how successful they were at getting those answers. SURRES used the library's TDD to call 105 deaf adults over age eighteen. The study showed that deaf adults tended to use the library as a first or second choice of resource but often were not able to get answers to their questions there because access to consumer goods and services was their primary information need. Although many organizations and businesses in the metropolitan area have TDDs, there are still not enough.

When the library first installed TDDs, staff and volunteers provided a relay service to community agencies and businesses. When a call came in on the TDD, a hearing person would call the organization that didn't have a TDD and relay messages back and forth between the hearing and deaf persons. Then an all-volunteer agency was created in the community that provided the service almost twenty-four hours a day, even taking the social calls that the library did not handle. Since then the library has not relayed messages except in emergencies. However, the 1985 survey seemed to indicate that the library should take another look at this service. It has an important role in both identifying access points that already exist and articulating the needs of the deaf community to other agencies.

COMMUNITY INFORMATION

The community information part of extension and special services gives the community access to over 1,000 membership organizations in Prince George's County and more than 400 agencies in the larger geographic area that provide direct services to Prince George's County residents. Louise Tankersen is the community information specialist. With the help of Ms. King, clerk-typist, and extra help in the summer, she continually updates the profiles of the 400 agencies listed in the computer and produces a directory of membership organizations. CLIC, the community library information center, is an off-shoot of the Neighborhood Information Project of the early seventies and one of the forerunners of information and referral centers in libraries. Currently the computer file contains 65 percent of the potential listing. The profiles give the name, address, telephone number, hours, services, clients served, fees, application method, and location of sites. The files are reissued each month in microfiche form with a keyword index and many cross references. There are copies in all the branches, and a brochure publicizes CLIC.

The *Directory of Organizations in Prince George's County*, which lists membership organizations from computer clubs to garden clubs to political groups to disability groups is published annually and sells for $5.00. Politicians depend on it, and free copies are given to elected officials at the local, state, and national levels and to government agency and department heads. Each organization listed also receives a free copy but has to come to the library to get it. The library also sells a mailing list (labels) of the organizations and can provide a zip code listing.

OTHER SERVICES

Ms. François is also responsible for service to the County Corrections Center, a new generation jail that opened in the spring of 1987. The library and the county corrections department jointly pay the librarian's salary, but the librarian is on the library staff. When the corrections librarian has scheduled time off, Ms. François can call on librarians in the system who have volunteered to fill in. Ms. François coordinates the workplace (job information centers in thirteen branches) and the library's well-developed literacy programs in the four area branches.

WORKING WITH STAFF AND COMMUNITY

Each of the services that Ms. François initiates in branch libraries has a contact person responsible for day-to-day service, with whom Ms. François stays in close touch. Ms. François also trains people for special assignments. She identifies their needs, knowing that they want to do a good job, and then provides the necessary resources. These may be in-service training, field visits, or personal consultation. Staff members are quite involved in planning and developing new services; at some point a new service will be integrated into the old service. Advisory groups have been used at the planning stage, as when the library received the LSCA grant for its services to deaf people, and Ms. François continues to seek advice from individuals and organizations.

Ms. François promotes library service as a way to mainstream people with disabilities. She attends meetings of community groups – both service providers and consumer groups – and keeps up with the issues. She looks at what the library is doing and should be doing and translates this into service. She plans staff meetings to promote physical, communication, and print accessibility and encourages all kinds of groups to use the library.

Ms. François is pulled in many directions and feels that she should devote full time to each demand. The staff she supervises directly--the talking book center, the community information office, and the new generation jail--have their own well-defined responsibilities. However, she works with and through the entire staff of the Prince George's County Memorial Library to see that the library needs of people with disabilities are met. (Branches deliver most of the services she initiates.) She must deal with changes in staff as well as in staff members' responsibilities. She is constantly educating staff. She is a liaison with agencies in the community, assesses the need for new services, involves staff in planning services, prepares staff for new responsibilities, and evaluates existing services. She is a key person in the system, and the difficulty of her trying to do so many jobs is understandable. When she started working thirteen years ago, her goal was to work herself out of a job. That is not likely to happen soon.

Note

1. Eleanor Phinney, *The Librarian and the Patient: An Introduction to Library Services for Patients in Health Care Institutions* (Chicago: ALA, 1977).

Reference

Cawthorne, Edythe, and Barbara Wolfson. "Library Kits for the Deaf." *Library Journal* 98 (October 15, 1973):3128.

Chapter 15

Queens Borough Public Library, Jamaica, New York

On July 21, 1981, the governor of New York signed a law that authorized Coordinated Outreach Services grants, a program of a magnitude unsurpassed by any other state. Following a five-month period during which the state developed regulations, New York's twenty-two library systems submitted applications for $29,000 each to be used for a four-month period to develop services for persons who were blind, physically handicapped, aged, or confined to institutions. The second grant of $40,000 was for a full year, and the amounts have increased since then.

LIBRARY SERVICES TO PERSONS WITH DISABILITIES

The initial goals of the grant project in the Queens Borough Public Library were: (1) to expand and update the existing services to disabled library users; (2) to establish an advisory council of disabled library users and representatives of agencies serving disabled persons; and (3) to promote awareness of and sensitivity to disabled persons and their need for library service. In January 1982 Emily McCarty came from the Cuyahoga County Public Library in Ohio to head the program as the Queens Borough Public Library's first librarian for the physically impaired.

Service to people with disabilities was not new. The library, along with other library systems in New York State, had received a Kurzweil Reading Machine (KRM) several years earlier, again as the result of the state legislature's authorization of the purchase of

157

KRMs for all library systems. The central library had a TTY. Prior to 1980 the Queens Borough Public Library had received LSCA funding for a program for the hearing impaired. All the libraries in the system had large print books. Mail-a-book service operated out of the Queens Village branch. Ms. McCarty and her successor in 1986, Pauline Lewis, helped by the continued influx of state money, developed a service that is essentially mainstreamed but is "special" when it needs to be.

THE QUEENS BOROUGH PUBLIC LIBRARY SYSTEM

Queens Borough extends from LaGuardia Field on the north to Kennedy International Airport on the south. A fingerlike extension of land beyond Kennedy, which is separated by a cluster of small islands, is also part of the borough. The central library in Jamaica is truly in the center of the borough, with sixty branches located throughout the 109-square-mile area that has a population of nearly two million people. The area is populated by scores of ethnic groups and a steady influx of immigrants, and there is constant movement of the population within the borough, as discussed in "Keeping Current: How the Queens Borough Public Library Adapts Its Services to the Demands of Urban Change" by R. Bryan Roberts.[1]

In 1977 the library contracted for a computerized circulation system and began a new patron registration process that included a detailed questionnaire to be answered on a voluntary basis. A high percentage of the applicants supply information on their ethnic background, age group, preferred language, educational level, and occupational group. These data have helped the library develop its collection and have enabled it to analyze library use. Each branch receives an annual budget from which it can purchase materials for its collection. Very popular fiction and nonfiction are purchased centrally and promoted throughout the system by colorful displays.

I spent a morning with Eileen Gellman, who joined the staff of the library services for the physically impaired division several months after the division was created, and Edith Branman, head of programs and services for the Queens Borough Public Library. Ms. Branman administers this program and other outreach projects, such as the new Americans project and the age-level specialties (e.g., the adult literacy program and the adult learning center). I talked with Ms. Lewis, the librarian for the disabled, by telephone; she provided me with annual reports of the project since its beginning. Before coming to Queens Borough she headed the office of special services at the New York Public Library.

THE COORDINATING OFFICE

The central library is organized by subject departments. A large information desk faces the building's entrance, and the departments surround it like spokes of a wheel. The popular library department is to the immediate left, and the office for library services to persons with disabilities (a change from its original name) is on the left side upon entering the popular library area. The office is small, and a separate room houses the Visualtek and the KRM. A larger area with two desks (one for the part-time secretary and one for the librarian or library assistant on duty) contains a small collection of books for staff use. A bank of files contains application forms for various community services, brochures about disabilities, a growing information and referral file, and equipment for loan or demonstration purposes. The office acts as a service center. More important, it is the headquarters for an active program of reaching out to the 200,000 people with disabilities in Queens Borough and for supporting library staff systemwide who serve them.

Library services to persons with disabilities does much of its work by phone. While I was there, the phone was ringing constantly. Staff throughout the system have been trained to call the office for assistance. New library staff are brought to the office as part of their orientation to the library. At the central library, the information desk refers many patrons to the office where staff members make a point of helping a person even if it means going with him or her to another department.

The office supplies application forms for the talking book service, In Touch (the radio reading service), and Half-Fare (transportation system discounts). It has talking book equipment, records, cassettes, and catalogs. People can come in for a demonstration, or staff will give instructions over the phone. The New York Public Library's library for the blind and physically handicapped in lower Manhattan mails out machines and books to readers once they are registered for the service.

Staff members use *The Red Notebook,* a resource collection on services to deaf people (see Chapter 5), along with other books from the small reference collection to answer patrons' questions and make referrals. They often call a patron to see if their referral to other agencies has been helpful. If someone's talking book machine is not functioning, they advise that person to take the machine to the nearest branch and arrange to have a new machine delivered in exchange for it.

ADVISORY COUNCIL

The New York State Library requires each library system that receives Coordinated Outreach Services grants to have an advisory council. Queens Borough's council meets twice a year and currently has representatives of the Red Cross, the Mayor's Office for the Handicapped, the New York City Board of Education Hearing Education Services, the New York State Office of Parks, Recreation & Historic Preservation, Disabled in Action, LaGuardia Community College Continuing Education Program for Deaf Adults, Jamaica Service Program for older adults, and the New York City Department for the Aging. The author of a sign language dictionary and a blind user are also members. Library staff serving on the council are the assistant head of the central library, the librarian for older adults, the head of the Queens Village branch (out of which mail-a-book operates), Ms. Lewis, and Ms. Branman. At the beginning of each year the staff members present their plans for the year and ask for council input. The council evaluates the program at the end of the year. Frequent contact is maintained between the librarians and the advisory council members between meetings.

Dr. Martin Sternberg from Adelphi University, author of *American Sign Language: A Comprehensive Dictionary* and member of the council, teaches a beginning and intermediate course in sign language twice a year. These hour-and-a-half sessions, which run for ten weeks, are free to library staff and people in the community. The library lends textbooks to the students. The two classes are scheduled in succession in the evening. Sometimes the library holds practice sessions with an interpreter.

Other advisory council members refer their clients to the library service. Under the sponsorship of the New York Board of Education, deaf students attending public schools and the Lexington School for the Deaf do paid and volunteer work in some library branches.

COMMUNITY RELATIONS

The library's public relations department prepares and distributes press releases, public service announcements, brochures, and fact sheets about services to persons with disabilities. Involvement of staff in the community, however, is the key factor in making the program visible. Ms. Lewis is a member of the METRO Committee for the Disabled and the Queens Interagency Council on Aging. Staff members make frequent presentations about library services to agency clients or residents of homes and to professionals working with them. They participate in open houses and resource fairs organized by other agencies, and they speak and demonstrate equipment to college classes (e.g., St. John's University's division of library and information science and LaGuardia Community College's human services department). Branches have mailing lists of people who have attended programs that they use to mail publicity about other programs. The office has its own mailing list of agencies with which it maintains contact and a list of persons who have taken the sign language classes.

PROGRAMS AND WORKSHOPS

Programs may be initiated at the suggestion of the advisory council. One case is free hearing screenings. The mobile van unit operated by the New York League for the Hard of Hearing parks in front of the central library twice a year for half a day to do the screenings. Every time, approximately one-third of the people tested are referred to other hearing clinics because of hearing loss.

Some programs are planned in cooperation with other divisions or departments of the library. A workshop, "Learning Disabled and

Physically Disabled Students in the ESL (English as a Second Language) Classroom: Identification, Teaching, Referral," was part of the new Americans project. A sign and mime program was done in conjunction with the children's room. All programs sponsored by library services to persons with disabilities are interpreted, including the meetings of the advisory council. The New York Society for the Deaf has a pool of interpreters, and the library uses several in Queens Borough on a regular basis.

At the beginning of the project a workshop for library staff on the hard of hearing and one for branch librarians on sensitivity to and services for disabled people were held. Because staff and services change constantly, Ms. Lewis held an update and orientation to library services to persons with disabilities for division heads at the central library and three sensitivity workshops for professional branch staff in March, April, and May 1987. The sensitivity programs provided firsthand experiences with a man in a wheelchair and a blind woman. Every branch library had a representative at these workshops. Ms. Lewis also visits the branches and attends the regional meetings of librarians, taking advantage of further opportunities to educate the entire staff. Young adults' and children's consultants have asked for more help for their staff, and Ms. Lewis was planning to have an in-service program for them in the fall of 1987.

In 1982 the office hosted a series of programs for the public. "Into the Mainstream" featured films from the library's film department and speakers from the community. All programs were interpreted in sign language and held in the accessible central library. The staff of the central library prepared an annotated bibliography/filmography, also called "Into the Mainstream," for distribution.

In 1986-87 library services for the disabled, in cooperation with the New York State Office of Parks, Recreation, and Historic Preservation, presented a monthly series, "Out and About," on Saturday afternoons. These were held in different branches and featured recreational opportunities for older adults and people with disabilities--indoor and outdoor activities, travel, careers in leisure occupations, access to transportation, disabilities and the media, and outdoor gardening. All were interpreted and held in accessible locations. The brochure publicizing these programs listed services for the visually impaired, the hearing impaired, the mobility impaired, and the homebound (see Appendix C).

Other programs have been a class in English as a Second Language, conducted in sign language for non-English-speaking deaf persons; a two-hour demonstration, "How to Use Wheelchair Accessible Buses," that took place outside the central library and gave people time to practice using a wheelchair lift; a program on low vision, cosponsored by the Queens Lighthouse and held in one of the branches; a performance by the Little Theatre of the Deaf; an exhibit of photographs and books on notable deaf persons at the central library during Deaf Heritage Month; and a presentation on vision problems and assistive devices by the executive director of the National Association for the Visually Handicapped. One of the by-products of the programs has been an increase in telephone calls, especially TDD calls, and office walk-ins.

EQUIPMENT

The office's collection of equipment has continued to grow since its first Coordinated Outreach Services grant. New software was added to the KRM to improve its performance. Use of the KRM increased from seventy hours during the first year it was in the library to five hours a week in the summer of 1987. The office is open daily from Monday through Friday, but staff members make evening and Saturday appointments for readers who cannot use the KRM during a weekday. It has been used successfully with learning disabled people who need to both hear and see print to understand it. For that purpose the library supplies two copies of a book. Gift funds enabled the library to buy an answering machine that gives a recorded message for both the voice and TDD phones when the office is not staffed. Other purchases have been an automatic page turner, a Viewscan, a Visualtek, a Perkins brailler, video equipment, an updated TDD, a closed-captioned decoder, handheld magnifiers, and other aids for people with impairments. Staff do not prescribe or suggest but instead demonstrate the equipment to people and refer them to other community agencies for evaluation.

The TDD is the only one in the system, and the office receives an average of twenty calls a month. Beginning in the spring of 1987 staff started relaying calls to other community agencies. Deaf or hearing people can also use the TDD to make local calls. An amplification device was added to the library's phone system for use by staff members with hearing loss. A Com-Tek system of amplification for people with hearing loss is lent to meeting sites that cannot afford their own system, is used for library programs, and is demonstrated at branch open houses. Vision Aids showcases and demonstrations of other equipment have been given throughout the borough in branches, schools, library schools, and other community agencies to publicize library services for people with disabilities.

VOLUNTEERS

A volunteer reader service was established in October 1982. Six volunteers--staff members on their own time or outsiders--record material that is difficult to obtain through the talking books service or Recordings for the Blind. Volunteers record materials at the library or in their own homes. The library provides the tape and the material to be recorded. If a user wants to keep the tape, he or she gives the library a tape in exchange. Volunteers are recruited by the library's volunteer coordinator, and they are asked to read a selection on tape before they are assigned to the volunteer reader service.

COLLECTION

The central library buys at least one copy of every large print book published. Branches also buy large print books, and Coordinated Outreach services funds are used to supplement these collections, especially for the Queens Village branch where mail-a-book operates and the Peninsula branch, which takes book collections to nursing homes in its service area. Large print books are shelved in the popular library section at the central library and are labeled Large Print. In 1982 an author-title catalog of large print books was produced in large type (see Appendix C). Supplements were published in 1983 and 1986. These are sent to all mail-a-book readers who request large print, to all nursing homes, and to anyone else requesting a copy. Throughout the central library are signs: "If small print strains your eyes, ASK FOR LARGE PRINT BOOKS: A BIBLIOGRAPHY."

Close to 3,000 books circulate each month from the mail-a-book service at the Queens Village branch; over 50 percent are large print. Funds are allocated to the branch for the purchase of books selected by mail-a-book staff. Although the service has its own collection of popular materials, a reader may request any book in the system. Books are mailed in jiffy bags with a mailing label and stamps enclosed for their return. Staff keep a manual record of the books readers have had and look forward to the time when they can use a computer for this purpose. Patients in nursing homes that do not have deposit collections are eligible for the mail-a-book service.

BUILDING ACCESS

The first librarian for the physically impaired was made the library's compliance coordinator for Section 504 of the Rehabilitation Act of 1973. Part of that responsibility involved assessing library buildings in the system to see if they were barrier-free. A group of consumers helped in the process. Today, twenty-six libraries are accessible (some only partially), and the library administration is continuing to address this problem. The "Guide to Public Libraries in Queens" cites the accessible branches and the bus and subway lines that can be used to reach each library.

SERVICE TO OLDER ADULTS

Following two years of work by a staff committee on library service to older adults and an open forum to determine the needs of the area's senior citizens, the library created the position of librarian for the older adult, filled by Irene Schaefer in March 1985. Library services for older adults is another component of the Coordinated Outreach Services grant. A survey of nursing homes in the borough showed that the Rockaway Peninsula south of Kennedy International Airport had the largest number of nursing homes in the borough and an older population (28 percent are over sixty-five) that is isolated from the rest of the area.

Sister Mary Ryan, a former teacher, social worker, and hospital administrator, was hired as a full-time staff assistant to Ms. Schaefer, working out of the Peninsula branch. With the help of a part-time clerical assistant, she rotates collections of 50-75 books-- large print, regular print, fiction, nonfiction--to thirty-three skilled nursing homes, health-related facilities, and adult homes every eight weeks. In addition Sister Mary is responsible for programs to challenge, educate, and entertain older people, from art history to book discussions to drawing lessons to ways to stay well. The programs have worked well on the peninsula, and Ms. Branman hopes to try them in other areas.

Films are lent free of charge to senior centers, nursing homes, and nonprofit groups throughout the borough. An attractive brochure, "Growing Better," describes library options for both the active older adult and older adults with disabilities. One activity is a drama club for older adults interested in acting. Performances draw standing-room-only audiences. Workshops for would-be thespians are held periodically in branch libraries.

SERVICE TO CHILDREN

At the other end of the age spectrum exceptional children have been considered in all aspects of children's librarianship. The children's collection has books about and for children with disabilities. Stories and poetry have been introduced in an advanced American Sign Language class and then used for programs with hearing impaired children. The visit of the Little Theatre of the Deaf attracts large numbers of deaf people, young and old. The library welcomes special education classes. Developmentally disabled and emotionally handicapped students visit in small groups with teachers and parents for picture stories, poetry, folk tales, films, and handicraft activities.[2]

OTHER PROGRAMS

In response to my question about the extent to which developmentally disabled people are involved in programs, Ms.

Branman said some were in the library literacy program. The library's philosophy is that it doesn't make any difference why a person can't read. When Ms. Branman worked in social sciences, the department organized a four-week program, one to one and a half hours a week, to teach library and job search skills to people about to return to the community from the Hillside Psychiatric Center and Creedmoor Psychiatric Center. The library tries to work with local agencies whenever needs are identified. A psychodrama group at Creedmoor Psychiatric Center has done programs to help the library staff deal with problem patrons. The library has displayed art created at Jamaica Services, a day treatment center for people released from the institutions, and a client at that center has volunteered at the library. To quote Ms. Branman, "We don't believe in isolating knowledge or skills."

A twenty-hour-a-week job and career counselor is on the staff of the library's adult learning center. This person provides one-on-one counseling to people with disabilities and the general public. Services to persons with disabilities also supports the adult learning center of the Queens House of Detention for Men by providing adult basic education materials and a series of programs on special issues in education. Inmates have access to a copy of the library's "Com-Catalog," and books are delivered through the mail-a-book program. State funds were used to purchase recreational materials for the Queensboro Correctional Facility.

PLANNING

Many people are involved in planning services for disabled people. The outreach services and age-level consultants are under the umbrella of programs and services, making it easy for them to work together. When there is a need for coordination with the branches, the extension services department becomes involved. The support of the administration is strong.

Ms. Lewis has the added stimulation of meeting each quarter with her counterparts in New York City, Brooklyn, Westchester, Nassau, and Suffolk, who are also administering Coordinated Outreach services programs. She also meets once a year with the twenty-two Coordinated Outreach services directors in New York State.

When I visited, Ms. Lewis was planning a series of programs on living skills for people with disabilities, a workshop on parenting skills for parents of children with disabilities, a workshop in cooperation with children's services, a basic reading and writing skills class for adults who are deaf, and sensitivity workshops to include all levels of library staff. And that is only a small part of her three-year plan.

Notes

1. R. Bryan Roberts, "Keeping Current: How the Queens Borough Public Library Adapts Its Services to the Demands of Urban Change," *Bookmark* 38 (Spring 1980): 364-67.

2. Jean St. Clair, "Queens Borough Public Library Adapts Library Service to the Needs and Interests of the 1980s," *Bookmark* 43 (Fall 1984): 36.

Reference

McCarty, Emily H. "Outreach: Total Involvement in Service to People." *Bookmark* 43 (Winter 1985): 81-82.

Chapter 16

Skokie Public Library, Skokie, Illinois

Judging from the number of people I saw at Skokie Public Library, it seems to be an important part of the community. The art exhibits, the prominently displayed flyers about programs, the brochures about services and materials, and the collection itself are evidence that this library is truly a community cultural center. Located in the Chicago area, the library is second only to the Chicago Public Library in size.

SALS

I was in Skokie to learn about SALS--Skokie accessible library services--from Liene Sorenson and Eva Weiner. Ms. Sorenson manages this service, which was begun with an LSCA grant in 1985. It was the brainchild of Ms. Weiner, a library trustee, who had a serendipitous experience at the American Library Association's annual conference in 1982. As she walked by the Kurzweil reading machine, it attracted her attention. She stayed for a demonstration. Later in the conference she attended a program where Dr. David Hartman, a blind psychiatrist, was the speaker. This set her to thinking that if she were blind, the KRM would give her access to the 350,000 volume collection at the Skokie Public Library.

Ms. Weiner was involved every step of the way in bringing reality to her dream of accessible library services in Skokie. She attended a conference on academic library service to disabled students at Florida State University's School of Library and

Information Studies. She visited Monterey Peninsula Community College in Monterey, California where technology was being used to give disabled students access to printed materials. She shared what she had learned with the Skokie library board and its director at that time, Mary Radmacher. The library first tried to get private funding but didn't receive enough from a local company to purchase a KRM. Ms. Radmacher and John Tieberg-Baille, head of circulation, then developed a plan for an integrated program of library services to people with disabilities and submitted it to the Illinois State Library. In July 1985 the library received an LSCA grant of $93,000 to purchase equipment and materials, and to employ a full-time professional librarian to establish SALS. The library received $50,000 in LSCA funds for its second year of operation and $49,000 for the third and final year of LSCA funding.

When Liene Sorenson took on the job of managing SALS, she had the support of her immediate supervisor, Sandra Palmore, community services coordinator, and of the new library director, Carolyn Anthony, who arrived two months after the project began. Ms. Sorenson has accomplished a great deal at Skokie library. For two years she depended on help from the library's administrative secretary and volunteers. In the third year she would work seven and a half hours a week at a public service desk--reference, readers' advisory service, nonfiction--but she would have a full-time secretary for the first time.

The library never intended to establish a one-stop center where people with disabilities could have all of their library needs met. Its goal was to demonstrate that people with disabilities can be mainstreamed in a public library setting. Ms. Sorenson was instrumental in setting that process in motion and guiding its growth. As services were publicized, SALS attracted some people who could not be easily mainstreamed and who required more help than the staff were able to give. After two years of wrestling with this problem, the library came to the conclusion that its role is: "(1) to make the building as accessible as possible; (2) to provide the equipment, materials, services, and programs that best address the information and reading needs of persons with disabilities; and (3) to publicize the foregoing continually and assertively, letting the community know that the library welcomes them and is ready to serve them with sensitivity and respect."1

BUILDING ACCESS

The library has an electronically opened front door, an elevator, and an accessible telephone, water fountain, and restrooms. The accessible door and water fountain were funded by the village of Skokie with Community Development grant funds. To discourage children from using it as a plaything, the door is locked. A push on the button notifies circulation desk staff, who can see the door and activate its opening from a button at the desk. Since SALS was created, the library has made the auditorium accessible to persons using wheelchairs.

EQUIPMENT

To improve access to print and nonprint information, the library purchased a variety of electronic aids. The KRM was the first. Although it is the least used (by July 1987 only four library patrons had been trained to use it), it put SALS in the spotlight because it is newsworthy. Both Ms. Weiner and Ms. Sorenson are convinced that there are people who could use it, if they can only be found. Currently a physician in rehabilitation medicine is helping a young man learn to use the Kurzweil. Once a person can operate it, he or she can teach others. The KRM is kept in the community services office, but Ms. Sorenson is not the only person who can show people how to use it. She has taught twenty other librarians to demonstrate it.

Five Visualteks purchased with project money have been the most popular items for persons with low vision because of their power to magnify text up to sixty times the original. The four circulating instruments have been used constantly, and the library has a waiting list of people anxious to try them. (The two Ednalite magnifiers, which were in the library before the project, are less popular.) A larger Visualtek is kept in the reference area. A speech compressor and a talking calculator are both lent to users, as are two braillers, which are gifts of the Lions Club and the Telephone Pioneers.

The library purchased two TDDs. One is kept at the circulation desk, and the second is in Ms. Sorenson's office where she can make or receive calls or people can use it to make local calls. A portable amplification system (the Williams Sound personal PA system) has been particularly successful. It has been used for film and live programs in several of the library's meeting rooms. The receivers can be adjusted to meet the amplification needs of individuals. It is especially useful for people attending the monthly meetings of the local SHHH (Self Help for Hard of Hearing People) group.

A computer with large print and voice capability to access the library's on-line catalog and execute software programs was listed in the SALS brochure for over a year before it became a reality in the midsummer of 1987. A series of events contributed to the delay in purchasing the hardware and software. An IBM PC/XT computer, with Vista large print capability and a Vert Plus speech synthesizer, was recommended by the Hadley School for the Blind in Winnetka, the Chicago Lighthouse for the Blind, and the Blind Rehabilitation Center at the Hines VA hospital.

In addition to accessing the library's on-line catalog, which includes the holdings of three other libraries in the North Suburban Library System (Morton Grove, Waukegon, and Deerfield), the new computer would give SALS access to the database of the subregional library for the blind and physically handicapped that provides Skokie with talking books. Staff would be able to order talking books through the computer. Several word processing programs and a typing tutorial would be available to blind or low-vision people; they could schedule time at the computer. When I was in Skokie, eight people had already signed up for a formal class on using the computer, to be taught by two library staff members. The library does not intend to develop staff expertise for teaching but will offer the equipment and basic assistance so people can practice the skills they have learned elsewhere (e.g., the Hadley School for the Blind). This means the library must make the right links with the community. The computer adaptations that SALS has now are for people with visual impairments. Ms. Sorenson feels the

172

library should consider purchasing adaptive hardware and software for physically handicapped persons, if there should be a demand.

MATERIALS

Spending money wisely during the first year of the project, especially the $20,000 for new materials, was a challenge. The staff who normally ordered large print materials, books on cassettes, videotapes, and children's books assisted with selection. They ordered several thousand large print books, a thousand cassettes, and several hundred closed-captioned videocassettes. Ms. Sorenson selected 400-500 books about disabilities and subscribed to about thirty periodicals. As someone new to the field, she found it difficult to identify materials for SALS patrons. She used the circulars published by the National Library Service for the Blind and Physically Handicapped but felt it would have been helpful to have had a source that evaluated the books and suggested what groups would find them useful. Ms. Sorenson feels that some of her purchases were mistakes. She bought the *Concise Heritage Dictionary* on tape--fifty-six cassettes--and it has only frustrated blind people because it is so difficult to use.

The library adopted a policy of buying a closed-captioned version of any videotape available in that format. These are used extensively, as are several sign language videotape series, which circulate to agencies and a senior citizen center where sign language classes are held. SALS purchased four closed-captioned decoders; two are on extended loan to group homes and two circulate for three-week periods. The library also bought three videocassette players for loan.

TALKING BOOKS

Prior to SALS the library had a collection of talking books at the circulation desk. It became part of the SALS service when Ms. Sorenson recruited Pat Kretchner as a volunteer in January 1986. Ms. Kretchner is an avid Skokie Public Library user and a former clerical assistant at the New York Public Library. She started working one morning each week and now volunteers there three to four mornings, delivering equipment to new readers, mailing talking books, placing orders, and returning books to the Suburban Audiovisual service, which is one of Illinois' fourteen subregional libraries for the blind and physically handicapped. Seven to ten volunteers contribute more than fifty hours each month to the talking book program.

Another service that predates SALS by three to four years was initiated by the Skokie Women's League. Once a week volunteers record selections from local newspapers and make duplicate copies of the cassettes at Skokie's Office of Human Services. They bring them to the library to be mailed to talking book readers who have signed up for this service.

OTHER SERVICES

In May 1987 the library opened an employment resource center in a small room near the reference desk. Its purpose is to encourage people to use the library's wealth of resources in this area and to go to the reference staff for help. The room is set up by a reference staff member who features a different topic each week. "Employment Opportunities for Disabled People" was featured during the summer, with a special program as well as a display.

Since its beginning SALS has hosted a series of Thursday evening visits to the library by groups of people with disabilities, in cooperation with the Maine-Niles Association for Special Recreation, which provides transportation for the visits. The programs have included demonstrations of equipment, lectures, book talks, films, and videotapes, with guests and staff contributing. The library celebrated Deaf Heritage Week with displays of books, periodicals, videocassettes, and other materials about and of interest to deaf persons. The local chapter of SHHH meets regularly at the library, and Rocky Stone, founder of the national organization, spoke at a joint meeting with another chapter in 1987.

The library encourages special recreation centers and group homes to bring people for preplanned programs, tours, or free library time. The day before I was there, Ms. Sorenson had given a library tour to a group of teenagers from a school for developmentally disabled people. Any librarian could have been called on, but she was free. The purpose of the tour was to generate interest in the library. She showed the group a videotape, large print books, the on-line catalog, and she got the young people involved as they looked at art prints by asking each person which one he or she liked best and why. Five of the eight obtained library cards before they left.

All SALS services are free. Anyone in the Chicago and suburban area can use them. A SALS symbol is put on the borrower's card and entered into the computer. Ordinarily Chicago residents are required to purchase a fee card to borrow materials from the Skokie Public Library.

PUBLICITY

SALS has been well publicized through local newspapers and television. Its brochure and newsletter (*SALSLETTER*) have been sent to 1,500 people in the Chicago area: to talking book users served by the eight area libraries, to persons listed in the TDD directory, to 500 Chicago area agencies serving disabled people, to 100 professional librarians and library schools, to 150 librarians in the North Suburban Library System and neighboring Suburban Library System, and to friends of the librarians and trustees. Five issues were published during the first two years as part of the LSCA-funded project. It was discontinued, but it served its purpose well. It let people with disabilities and those who serve them know of Skokie's accessible library services. It was set in 16-point type and liberally illustrated with photos of special events, librarians, and library visitors. Each issue featured a "success story" about someone using SALS services. Several issues included a supplement for library staff in smaller type. A bimonthly newsletter for public library staff was to be published during the third year of the project and sent to every public library in Illinois.

The supplement to the newsletter was one means by which SALS fostered the involvement of the entire library staff in serving disabled persons. During the first year Ms. Sorenson conducted two staff workshops, one a general program and the second a demonstration class on sign language. However, most of the staff training has been on an individual basis. Ms. Sorenson has prepared a manual for each service desk with copies of pertinent information about the equipment and lists of large type books, closed-captioned films, and cassette tapes. Staff generally refer problems to her, but an effort is underway to make library staff members more self-sufficient and willing to act on their own. SALS celebrated its first anniversary with displays, demonstrations of equipment, and refreshments. Over 100 community leaders, people with disabilities, and librarians attended. Close to its second anniversary, the library and the Skokie Advisory Council on Disabilities, of which Ms. Sorenson is a member, hosted a conference, "Emphasizing the Able--Widening Opportunities for Disabled Persons," with over 200 people attending. U.S. Senator Paul Simon was one of the speakers.

SALS reached the broader library community when it hosted a workshop, "Meeting the Service Needs of Disabled Library Users," in 1986. Librarians in the Chicago area have also been invited to special events such as the anniversary celebrations. In the third year of the project Ms. Sorenson planned to conduct workshops for librarians in three different areas of the state and to send the newsletter to all public libraries in Illinois.

PLANNING

Board members and the library administration have been involved in SALS planning. SALS has also had input, however, from a twelve-member advisory committee made up of representatives of organizations of and for people with disabilities and librarians. There has been informal advice, too, from people in the community. A nationally known advocate for deaf people called Ms. Sorenson on a daily basis once she learned the library had a TDD. Because of the excellent publicity SALS has received, it has not been necessary for Ms. Sorenson to go out into the community to reach concerned people.

At the end of two years SALS outgrew the staff conference room to which it was initially assigned. Now it is part of community services, a section of adult services with which it frequently interacts and shares a suite of offices. Here there is space for the KRM, the computer, the talking book collection, equipment when it is not on loan to clients, and a work area for the volunteers and the new clerical assistant.

OUTREACH SERVICES

Sandra Palmore has been community services librarian since 1974. She is responsible for library service to people who cannot be mainstreamed. Initially Skokie librarians went to nursing homes to provide programs that activity directors could not do. That was in a time when much less was expected from activity directors. The primary purpose of library programs was not to entertain or educate but to advertise library service. Ms. Palmore had to convince the activities directors that nursing home residents would use library service and that the nursing homes would not be charged for lost materials. The library's philosophy was and still is that everyone on the professional staff is involved in programs. No one person should be identified in the community as "the library." Librarians could do anything they wanted--tell stories, dance, give slide shows, talk about astrology, lead meditation--as long as they used or referred to books. In the beginning the librarians visited four nursing homes once a month, but as the activity directors initiated more programs, the library reduced its visits to four times a year. Some of the homes now bring residents to the library. The library supports the work of activity directors or volunteers in the homes by supplying films, books, art prints, and articles. Activity directors move often. If a new one does not continue the home's relationship with the library, the residents often demand library programs and services.

The Skokie library has had active book discussion groups for twenty years. Ms. Palmore developed Senior Literary Circles for mentally alert people in four extended care facilities and one congregate housing residence. Prior to the meeting participants must read or have read to them short stories or poems that are to be discussed. The library reproduces selections in large type for visually limited people. The sessions last half an hour to an hour and are attended by seven to thirty people and the activity director. Residents would like to meet every month, but Ms. Palmore can lead them only every eight weeks.

The homebound delivery program had been a vest pocket operation until 1987. The library had no volunteers until SALS started using them. Ms. Palmore estimated that the cost of delivering books to individuals, if the library staff did it, was $8.00 a book, and it was not fair to the taxpayers to assume that expense. She tried using Meals on Wheels, but it did not work. No one thought reading was important. She sent brochures with the meals but was not able to promote the service personally. When homebound people called the library and said they couldn't get through the weekend without books, the library was able to send books by a Skokie social worker. After the social worker's job was cut from full- to half-time, this was no longer possible. Ms. Palmore solved the problem by keeping, with their permission, written records of what people had read, wanted to read, hated to read. When they called and said, "I need five books," she checked out the books, bundled them, and left them at the circulation desk until someone picked them up. The homebound person made arrangements for the person who ran other errands to pick up the books.

Now the library is beginning to recruit volunteers, and already one is taking books to seven to ten people each month. The service has not yet been advertised; Ms. Palmore is waiting until she gets the volunteer program on a sound footing. Volunteers will be used throughout the library for other jobs the library cannot do with its present staff. Because volunteers have helped SALS accomplish all it has done, volunteers seem to have found a home at the Skokie Public Library.

The impact of SALS on library service in Skokie has been like the ripples created when a rock is tossed in a body of water. Ms. Weiner's comments on SALS reflect the library's service to people with disabilities today: "It was done for the handicapped, but every patron in the library, since we don't limit it to handicapped people, has this big advantage. . . . The average patron has an advantage by the library's having all these wonderful things. . . . These [people with disabilities] are people who really should make use of the library like anybody else, not just get material. They should be part of the whole library."

Note

1. *Accessible Library Services: A Brief Guide to Serving Persons with Disabilities in the Public Library* (Skokie, Ill.: Skokie Public Library, n.d.), 1.

References

Palmore, Sandra. "Nursing Home Services: Skokie Public Library." *Illinois Libraries* 58 (June 1976): 502-4.

_____. "Senior Literacy [Literary] Circles: An Enrichment Program for Extended Care Facilities." *RQ* 26 (Fall 1986): 90-96.

Sorenson, Liene. "Skokie Accessible Library Services: The First Year." *Illinois Libraries* 69 (January 1987): 54-56.

Chapter 17

Memphis-Shelby County Public Library and Information Center, Memphis, Tennessee

If I'd gone to Memphis in June as planned, I would have missed the excitement of a new era of library service to people with disabilities. My original letter of inquiry did not reach Judith Drescher, director of the Memphis-Shelby County Public Library and Information Center. When I wrote again in the fall of 1987, Jean Hofacket, the new coordinator of special services, promptly responded with an invitation to visit her library.

Through a main library that has twenty-two branches and two bookmobiles, the library serves a metropolitan library area ranking fourteenth largest in the United States. Although many services were already being offered to people with disabilities through departments of the main library and the branches before the new director came, Ms. Drescher recognized the need for centralization to ensure that all segments of the population were being served equitably.

Ms. Hofacket's job is a newly created position. Her first assignment was to survey the community and develop logically unified patterns of service. She anticipated that the needs assessment and planning period would take approximately two years, but both the library staff and community were so supportive that she became involved in program development almost immediately. Through the groups she works with, she is still trying to get an overview of what special populations need and want. She has already identified seven areas to target: the aging, disabled, incarcerated, institutionalized, catastrophically ill, homeless, and illiterate. She has already initiated plans for all but the incarcerated.

OUTREACH SERVICES

Departments in the main library, the branches, and the bookmobile have been serving nursing homes, senior centers, and homebound people. The literature department sends collections to retirement homes in the main library's service area. Two staff members are responsible for selecting materials each month, and the retirement home staff pick up the collections and return them to the library. Several branches also provide collections to retirement homes, senior centers, and nursing homes. The head of the branch or department sends a letter, with details of the arrangement, to the head of the agency. The head of the agency must complete and sign an application form and send the library a letter requesting borrowing privileges. Then he or she must go to the library to sign a borrower's card, which is free and good for one year. The agency is responsible for controlling the use of the card and for all materials borrowed against it. Lost materials must be paid for in full along with a processing fee. Materials are considered lost four months after the date the book is due back in the library. No overdue fines are charged.

One of the two bookmobiles, equipped with a hydraulic lift for wheelchairs, makes twenty stops at homes whose residents are about equally divided between people with social disabilities (drug abuse, mental illness, juvenile offenses) and those who are elderly or have physical disabilities. The library also has a written agreement with the homes or agencies the bookmobile serves. Stops are scheduled on a weekly, biweekly, or monthly basis to meet the institution's needs. The bookmobile has a strong collection of books on psychology, psychiatry, health, pregnancy, and child care. It also carries high interest low vocabulary materials, large print books and magazines, and popular music albums. Bookmobile staff present film programs at nursing homes, book talks for all ages, and puppet shows for children.

Because Memphis's public transportation system is inadequate, people who are not independently mobile find it difficult to go to the library. A pilot project was to be initiated in March 1988 to address their need. Five sites were to be chosen by branch librarians to receive deposit collections. The sites to be chosen had to serve at least 300 people a day, being either senior centers or high-rise residences for elderly people. The bookmobile staff were to survey the site and then return to the site with branch library staff to survey clientele. The branch staff would then select collections, to be changed every twenty-eight days. Bookmobile staff would deliver the materials on Mondays and Fridays. This was to run for one year, at which time additional sites would be added.

To be eligible for service to shut-ins, an individual must live in Memphis or Shelby County and be unable to visit the library because of physical disability, extended illness, or advanced age. Requests for service come most frequently through the branches, which forward the information to the literature department at the main library. The literature department contacts the Friends' office, which coordinates a very active Friends group. The Friends find a volunteer who delivers the books selected by staff at the branch nearest to the shut-in's home. Ms. Hofacket anticipates that the literature department may eventually be freed from its responsibility for coordinating this service.

LINC AND QUIC

LINC, the library information center, is one of the library's best services for older people and disabled people because they don't have to go to the library to use it. LINC was established in 1975 during the heyday of library information and referral centers, is one of the few survivors of that era, and is now partially funded by United Way. In addition to responding to the constantly ringing phones--80,000 calls a year--its staff of seven information librarians, many qualified as social service workers, serve as individual liaisons to different community agencies. LINC also publishes a *Directory of Human Services in Memphis and Shelby County,* with monthly updates, *LINC's Latest,* available in every branch, and maintains a card file of community resources. LINC publishes a biannual

Directory of Clubs and Organizations, an *Employment and Training Resources Directory,* a *Directory of Children's Services,* a monthly community calendar, and a *Summer Survival Kit* listing summer activities for children and young adults in the community. When LINC is closed, callers hear a recorded message that gives alternative sources of help. (See Appendix C for a LINC brochure.)

QUIC, the quick information center, which opened April 6, 1987, is a telephone reference department, recommended by library consultants Lowell Martin and Tom Childers to handle subject department overloads. All library calls go to QUIC, which responds to any query that can be answered in five minutes or less. The QUIC public service desk is just inside the entrance to the main library. It handles general information questions but refers walk-ins to the appropriate subject department. QUIC's thirteen staff members answer an average of 700 questions each day from a collection of telephone directories, encyclopedias, a core collection of 250-300 reference titles, and vertical files developed by staff during an eighteen-month planning period. LINC has a TTY number, and QUIC will add a TDD in the future. The library has not kept separate statistics to indicate the amount of use of LINC's TTY.

WTTL

WTTL, the West Tennessee Talking Library, is a radio reading service that has operated as a department of the main library since 1979. There had been a radio reading service at Rhodes College in Memphis in 1977, but listeners couldn't understand why they couldn't get free service of the same high quality as listeners received in Nashville, where the library operated the service. Concerned people came to the Memphis public library and demanded that the library system establish a radio reading service. Steve Terry, WTTL's station manager, formerly with the Nashville radio reading service, established the Memphis service. Mr. Terry argues that radio reading services in libraries differ from services under other umbrellas in that they do not duplicate the National Library Service for the Blind and Physically Handicapped's talking book program. Listeners in the eight-county area the station reaches through its closed-circuit radio channel soon let it be known that they didn't want books broadcast because they preferred to listen to talking books on their own initiative. Furthermore the copyright law and the Federal Communication Commission's profanity law made it difficult to read books on the air. Now WTTL broadcasts only an occasional best-seller, before it is available as a talking book, and books about Tennessee that can be read in twenty-nine-minute segments without continuity being interrupted if segments are missed.

The station is on the air eighteen hours a day, six days a week, as it has been since programming began six months after Mr. Terry arrived. Volunteers read newspapers six hours every day. As a subcarrier of a public radio station, WTTL broadcasts National Public Radio's "Morning Edition" and "All Things Considered." It is basically a news station, and that reflects the desires of its 6,600 listeners who are surveyed by telephone annually. The WTTL brochure states: "Information programming may deal with such topics as adjustment, employment, rehabilitation, hobbies, recreation, consumer information, and home economics. There are many opportunities to share experiences, exchange views, and learn from others with similar needs through telephone call-in programs, interviews, and coverage of legislative news, seminars, and hearings." There are 2,700 people waiting for radio receivers for this service. The library is considering possible changes in the method of service that would eliminate the need for special receivers and thus reduce this backlog. Beginning with the July-September 1987 issue, WTTL publishes a quarterly program guide.

Besides Mr. Terry three other full-time staff--an engineer/announcer, a program producer/announcer, and a coordinator of volunteers--and 250 volunteers are involved in WTTL's operation. Volunteers, most of them over sixty-five, are recruited through television. One hundred and seven of the 250 are active. On the average they volunteer three hours a week, with a total of 140,000 hours volunteered in eight years. Some programs are prerecorded in the station's four studios. Broadcasting is fully automated, enabling the station to operate with minimal staff and to use up to eighteen hours of prerecorded materials. A satellite dish outside the library brings in National Public Radio programs. Mr.

Terry estimates that the production equipment is worth $80,000-$90,000. It has to be kept in excellent condition for automation to work. Staff are able to monitor the station twenty-four hours a day via a computerized alarm system. When Mr. Terry spoke to the Corporation for Public Broadcasting, he recommended that a radio reading service should not get federal funds unless it had an operating budget of $100,000 a year for programs at least eighteen hours a day, six days a week.

WTTL is partially supported with LSCA funds, as it has been since it began. Twenty-five percent of its funding for equipment comes from local contributions raised by civic groups such as the Lions Club, while the remaining 75 percent is from the Public Telecommunications Facilities Program of the National Telecommunications and Information Administration. The studio walls were donated by a local benefactor. Eventually Mr. Terry expects that the station will have to get into corporate fund raising. The community is very supportive. In fact the mayor was scheduled to do promotional announcements for television early in 1988.

In 1982 the American Foundation for the Blind stated that WTTL was the best radio reading service in the country. Mr. Terry and his staff want to continue being trendsetters. The philosophy that permeates the service is this: If they can't provide the best quality service, why do it at all? Their goal is to serve 134,000 people by 1993. Both Mr. Terry and Ms. Hofacket are concerned about reaching nursing home residents. In their area of the state people with disabilities are often placed in nursing homes, regardless of their age, and many potential radio reading service users reside in them.

TELEVISION STATION

The Memphis-Shelby County Public Library and Information Center is one of approximately twenty-five public libraries in the United States with a full-service broadcast television station, operating twenty-four hours a day, seven days a week. Cable channel 9, under station manager Ann McComic's direction, produces twenty to twenty-five half-hour programs a month. From 7 P.M. to 3 A.M. it carries Arts and Entertainment Network programs.

Locally produced programs include *Health Awareness,* a program with easy-to-understand medical information, and *Neighbor Line,* a live biweekly call-in program about neighborhood issues, featuring a local city council member and a representative of the mayor's action center, which handles complaints. Ms. McComic is committed to the needs of people with disabilities and elderly persons. She has done programming with the Gray Panthers occasionally and has had information programs with parents of children with disabilities. She and Ms. Hofacket are planning to produce some captioned programs. They have found through a statistical survey that more people than they had realized own decoders for captioned film. They are also planning a general information series on various disabilities in 1989.

THE IMPACT OF THE NEW COORDINATOR

Ms. Hofacket's presence is felt in the services already in place at the Memphis-Shelby County Public Library and Information Center. But that is only the beginning. In her first five months at the library she had already established liaisons with several community agencies. For example, the Metropolitan Interfaith Association serves as a social service agency, with support from religious groups in the area, United Way, and grants. Ms. Hofacket writes a monthly column, "At Your Library," for the association's *Mid-South Senior,* which goes to 60,000 senior adults in four counties in western Tennessee. The column includes information about the library and book reviews. Beginning in January 1988 she would be working with the association to put book packs in places that temporarily house homeless people. These packs, to be delivered with food packs and linen packs, would include donated magazines, books for children and adults, and information about the library, none of which have to be returned. Many of the homeless are families caught without jobs in the movement of the population through Memphis.

Ms. Hofacket serves on the executive board of the Center for Independent Living, whose goals are to make it possible for the 300,000 people in the area with disabilities to live independently, and to provide information, education, and assisting services. The center is building a collection about disabilities, and the public library will exchange catalog information with it, possibly in the form of compact discs. Ms. Hofacket is also building a professional collection of books and periodical titles in her office to supplement materials in the library's subject departments. Science/business/social sciences has an especially strong collection of materials about disabilities.

Ms. Hofacket is a member of the Board of Day Care for Adults for the Salvation Army and the Board for the Aid to End AIDS Committee. She frequently speaks to groups and appears on radio and television shows. If groups do not have a monthly or weekly meeting she can attend, she invites a representative to join her for lunch or invites him or her to the library to see the resources important to the group. She is teaching members of the planning commission of the county government about library materials that are not in the commission's library and about ways that the library can help the commission plan services for the aging and disabled.

Part of Ms. Hofacket's responsibility is to work with library staff members throughout the system, creating an awareness of segments of the community that have not been served and suggesting what needs to be done and ways to do it. The library director is committed to library service to the total community and believes it is better for the library to be proactive than reactive. Ms. Hofacket has visited all branches at least once and plans to continue this on a quarterly basis. The farthest branch is twenty-five miles away so she dictates notes into her tape recorder as she drives and carries a portable computer that she can use as a word processor wherever she is. She has addressed the issue of sensitivity to special populations at the branch and department heads meetings. In December 1987 she made a presentation on Deaf Heritage Week, prepared a display, and sent packets of relevant materials to the branches. She plans to work through the staff development office in the future, with the emphasis on basic service awareness. Some questions she will answer are: How do you work with a person in a wheelchair? What are the needs of aging patrons? What do buildings need to look like? How do you communicate with deaf people?

In each department or branch is a current awareness person who can create informational memos on local, state, national, and international issues or special events. These memos are distributed to the person's counterparts throughout the system. Ms. Hofacket can create such a memo on her computer or photocopy information from other sources. Sample issues of "FYI . . . Information for Current Awareness Specialists" contain a listing of a weekly series of programs on coping with holiday blues, cosponsored by a hospital, two mental health organizations, and the library and held in the library; the table of contents from *Editorial Research Reports* on AIDS dilemmas; information about a meeting entitled "Dealing with Aging Parents and One's Own Aging." The National-International Committee of this group was creating a voter education packet for the 1988 presidential elections, which would be available in regular print, in large print (to be done with a MacIntosh computer), and on tape (to be done by WTTL volunteers).

In September 1987 Ms. Hofacket started publishing the bimonthly *Special Services Newsletter* that is distributed to staff. Its purpose, as stated in the first issue, is to provide regular communication between all Memphis public library agencies concerning the characteristics and special service needs of special populations. The first issue included a basic bibliography on AIDS. The second issue focused on Deaf Heritage Week, giving background information, suggesting activities for the week, and relating brief information about deaf individuals, local organizations, and titles on deafness from Ms. Hofacket's office collection.

MATERIALS

With one of her target areas being catastrophic illness, Ms. Hofacket is focusing on both Alzheimer's disease and AIDS. Her emphasis is on educating staff about the ramifications of the diseases, especially AIDS, and guaranteeing that the public has access to all available materials. In January 1988 the library will publish a directory of AIDS resources that will enable people with minimal reading skills to find information in city and county agencies as well as in the library. Also in January she will be producing a monthly television program called "Aids Update," jointly hosted by the Red Cross and the Aid to End AIDS Committee.

Ms. Hofacket found that the library had a strong collection of materials about disabilities and for use by people with special needs. Much of the information about disabilities is in the science/business/social sciences department. Branches have purchased materials when there was a community need or when staff were interested. The literature/philosophy/religion department has a portable TDD and captioned decoders for loan, a Visualtek, a browsing collection of popular talking books, and large print books. The library has a large video collection, most of it in the art/music/recreation/film department, but-one half of the branches have videos as well. Cards in the public catalog indicate which videos are closed captioned. The printed catalog of videos published by the art department also states which are captioned.

Since Ms. Hofacket's arrival she has ordered all large print materials for the branches. Formerly they were purchased by the literature department and the individual branches. Then the branches were divided into two territories, each with a purchasing agent who selected large print. Now all large print titles are housed at the main library and are borrowed by the branch heads for three-month periods. The library has standing orders with all the large print publishers, and Ms. Hofacket orders individual copies and duplicates as they are needed.

INTERNAL GRANT SYSTEM

The Memphis public library has an internal grant system; it set aside $40,000 in 1987-88 for this purpose. Branches can apply for a grant of $3,000 for special collections by submitting a brief description and budget for each grant. Ms. Hofacket takes a shopping list of collections she would like to have in the library system when she visits librarians and offers to help them develop proposals. Branch heads are generally anxious to expand their holdings. Highlands branch, where the local chapter of the Alzheimer's Disease and Related Disorders Association meets, used such a grant to establish an Alzheimer's disease information center in November 1987. The branch will publish a bibliography that will be used in the library as well as distributed to medical and social services in the community. This branch is close to several medical centers and has adequate parking. Ms. Hofacket will consider putting more professional materials on disabilities in either the Shelby State Community College branch or the Gill Campus branch. A daily delivery system and a computerized catalog make material easily available throughout the system.

Ms. Hofacket has encouraged the bookmobile staff to use a grant to purchase BiFolkal kits and create a Memphis music kit, with music tapes from blues to Presley, slides, photographs, and rhythm band instruments. There are 300 senior centers and nursing homes in the community. The library staff cannot do programming on that scale, but it has a wealth of materials that nursing home and senior center staff can use. Ms. Hofacket will train library staff as well as home and center staff to use the BiFolkal kits and in 1989 plans to start a newsletter to help senior center and nursing home coordinators with programming. Also in 1989 she plans to develop a kit on Christmas. The kits will be publicized for use by all ages, booked through the branches, and circulated from the special services office.

NEW SERVICES FOR PEOPLE WITH LOW VISION

As part of Ms. Hofacket's five-year plan, she was planning to open a low vision center on the main floor of the library in 1988 in order to bring together the large print books, talking books, popular books on tape, and the Visualtek. The library was planning to purchase an Optacon, magnifiers, and possibly a Kurzweil reading machine, if a survey showed community need and interest. Ms. Hofacket was developing a collection of assisting device catalogs and a braille reference collection. A corps of volunteers would be available to help people schedule time to use library materials. This center was not designed to segregate people with visual disabilities but would make it easier for them to go to one place as a starting point. The traffic pattern to the center would be maintained, even though other areas of the library tend to shift as collections grow. Visually disabled groups who have contact with WTTL; WTTL's program manager, who is blind; and the Center for Independent Living all have had input in the plan for the center, to have been established with a combination of in-house and grant funding.

Ed McBride, automated systems manager, was working with Ms. Hofacket to write specifications for a patron access computer catalog to address the needs of visually handicapped persons. They were considering talking terminals, touch screens, and user access through a home computer. Requests for proposals were sent out in June 1988, and they hope to be in operation in 1990. The system will also be designed for the convenience of twelve or so library staff members with disabilities.

ACCESSIBILITY

An accessibility survey has not been done for the entire system, although all branches built with LSCA funds have accessible entrances. Some are totally accessible; others have problems. The library had bids out in December 1987 and was ready to award a contract for a planning, expansion, and accessibility study for the main library and possibly the system. Ms. Hofacket, with help from individuals and an advisory group from the Center for Independent Living, will utilize *The Guide: Facilities Evaluation and Modification Guide*[1] as they work with the contractor. Ms. Hofacket and this group will also be involved when any new buildings are constructed.

Signage inside the library is good, but out-of-doors signs need to be improved. (As a newcomer Ms. Hofacket has been aware of these shortcomings in her attempts to find the branches.) New signs--four feet high and erected at an angle that can be read at a distance--are being installed at the main library and all the branches.

ADMINISTRATIVE MATTERS

Ms. Hofacket is responsible to Sallie Johnson, the assistant director of the main library. She, along with the coordinators of children's and youth services and the coordinator of branch services (all new positions), serve with the director and four assistant directors as the administrative cabinet responsible for the administration of the library and recommendations to the library board. Ms. Hofacket has a full-time secretary and was hoping to add a work-study position in

1988. In the future she hopes to have an adminstrative assistant, beginning at the professional entry level. The program is funded through the main library's budget. In 1988 some money would come from branch services.

While Ms. Hofacket is still new to her job, she has definite ideas on how she will measure the success of her program. She feels that you get a skewed picture when you compare statistics on library use by special populations with statistics on library use by children. Statistics become meaningful only when you can say x number of the population is handicapped and x number uses the service; both are almost impossible to determine. She prefers to use critical information from agencies and individuals. Once service is established and she has access to users, she will do user surveys, as WTTL has done annually, and broad community surveys. She will also compare her program with other programs in the United States, Canada, and Sweden, picking out five libraries from a range of sizes that she can use as a standard. She did this at other libraries when she evaluated programs.

At the Memphis-Shelby County Public Library and Information Center I had an opportunity to talk to many staff members, the library director, and the director in charge of the main library. This contact supported my early conclusion that enthusiasm on the part of library staff and support of the administration are an unbeatable combination for a successful program of library service to people with disabilities.

Note

1. *The Guide: Facilities Evaluation and Modification Guide* (Raleigh, N.C.: Barrier Free Environments, 1984).

PART 5

REGIONAL LIBRARIES FOR THE BLIND AND PHYSICALLY HANDICAPPED

Regional libraries for the blind and physically handicapped came into being with the passage of the Pratt-Smoot Act in 1931, which authorized an annual appropriation to the Library of Congress for books for blind adults. After consulting with the American Library Association and the American Foundation for the Blind, nineteen libraries were designated as regional distribution centers.

Since 1931 reading materials have been produced in braille, on discs and cassettes, for children as well as adults, and for people with physical disabilities as well as those who are blind or visually impaired. Fifty-six regional libraries, three multistate centers, and more than a hundred subregional libraries are part of the network. All but two states--North Dakota and Wyoming--have a regional library that is generally part of the state library agency. California, Michigan, New York, and Ohio have two regional libraries. In some states subregional libraries have been designated to provide services to readers within specified areas of the regional library's jurisdiction. The Library of Congress National Library Service for the Blind and Physically Handicapped continues to produce and distribute materials and equipment and provide supportive services to the network, some of this being done by contract with multistate centers. The many changes in the first fifty years of the service are described in detail in *That All May Read*, published by the National Library Service for the Blind and Physically Handicapped in 1983.

Besides the two regional libraries described in this section, the Kansas State Library, Division for the Blind and Physically

Handicapped, at Emporia and the Alabama Public Library Service Regional Library for the Blind and Physically Handicapped in Montgomery, regional libraries are part of the services described earlier in the District of Columbia Public Library and the Public Library of Cincinnati and Hamilton County. There are differences in the two services described here, yet their responsibility is basically the same as for all libraries that are part of the network: to provide library materials to persons who are legally blind, who cannot read ordinary print with the aid of corrective glasses because of a visual handicap, who cannot use the standard book format because of a physical handicap, and who cannot read print material in a normal manner because of the severity of an organic dysfunction, such as dyslexia.

Chapter 18

Kansas State Library,
Division for the Blind and Physically Handicapped,
Emporia, Kansas

The Kansas regional library for the blind and physically handicapped has been innovative since it was established in 1970 as the first regional library to operate through a system of subregional libraries. In the mid-sixties, a group of readers, librarians, and representatives of the State Services for the Blind met to plan a strategy for establishing a regional library in Kansas. They took a plan to the 1968-69 session of the state legislature and were turned down. A year later their proposal was approved.

With assistance from LSCA funds during this same period, Kansas set up seven library systems to cover the state. The logic of serving blind and physically handicapped readers through the same system was hard to ignore. When the Kansas regional library opened in 1970 as part of the Kansas State Library in Topeka, it was across the street from the state library. Its main responsibility was to set up subregional libraries to deliver service to readers throughout the state.

Today the Kansas Network consists of the regional library and six subregional libraries. The current configuration of service is as follows:

- Central Kansas Library System (seventeen counties): service from the Great Bend Public Library.

- Northwest Kansas Library System and Southwest Kansas Library System (thirty-three counties, roughly the western

197

third of the state): service from Norton, Kansas--headquarters for the northwest system--with a half-time consultant from the southwest system to assist in serving twenty-one counties in the lower half of the area.

- South Central Kansas Library System (thirteen counties): service from Hutchinson, the headquarters for the system.

- Southeast Kansas Library System (sixteen counties): service from the Wichita Public Library to Sedgwick County and the fifteen counties in the southeast system. A half-time consultant from the southeast system works with the subregional.

- Northeast Kansas Library System (fourteen counties): service from Topeka Public Library.

- North Central Kansas Library System (twelve counties): service from Manhattan Public Library.

The subregionals have been in existence for almost twenty years and they have developed strong collections. A new brochure called "Welcome to Talking Books" emphasizes the network aspects of the service, a concept that needs constant reinforcement.

BRAILLE SERVICE

The most recent development--so recent that it was indicated by a label attached to the library's brochure--is a core collection of braille books located in the Kansas City (Kansas) Public Library, created from gift books donated by Triformation Braille Service, Inc., and books received from the Multistate Center for the South when that facility was closed. New books are sent each month from the National Library Service for the Blind and Physically Handicapped. The collection was formed at the instigation of the Kansas chapter of the National Federation of the Blind. With the help of an LSCA grant the books are placed where the library's interlibrary loan department can circulate them.

The public library is about a mile from the Kansas State School for the Visually Handicapped, and there is daily courier service between the two facilities. Students visit the library, not just to borrow braille, but to use other public library services as well. In the fall of 1987 a work-study student at the school started working with the braille librarian.

Readers request braille through their subregional library or by mail because they do not have toll-free telephone access to the Kansas City Public Library, as they do to the subregionals. Because the state boundary cuts through Kansas City, the State Library of Missouri and the Kansas State Library have agreed that walk-in patrons from Missouri can check out braille books, just as they can printed books.

RELOCATION TO EMPORIA STATE UNIVERSITY

I was interested in the Kansas regional library not necessarily because of its subregional system, but because of its most recent innovation, a move from Topeka to the Emporia State University campus in Emporia. Librarian Caroline Longmoor invited me to visit the library and learn more about this development.

Ms. Longmoor became head of the Kansas State Library's Division for the Blind and Physically Handicapped (the official name of the regional library for the blind and physically handicapped) in 1978, after the original building site had been razed and the division had moved to a storefront building in the business section of Topeka. When Ms. Longmoor read in a local paper in 1981 that the state was going to trade the land on which the storefront was located for a building across the street from the State Capitol, she realized that there would be at least two moves for the library in the offing–one to temporary quarters and a second to a permanent home. About this time the National Library Service for the Blind and Physically Handicapped sent all libraries in its national network a copy of its *Summary Proceedings of a Symposium on Educating Librarians and Information Scientists to Provide Information and Library Services to Blind and Physically Handicapped Individuals*.[1]

This publication caused Ms. Longmoor to start thinking. She knew that Emporia State University had the only school of library science in Kansas. It also had served students with disabilities since the early fifties and had a special education program and a program in rehabilitation. Why shouldn't it become a model of cooperation between academia and library service for the blind and physically handicapped?

Ms. Longmoor talked to her boss, Duane Johnson, the Kansas state librarian. Mr. Johnson and Ms. Longmoor talked to Dean Grover of the School of Library and Information Management at Emporia State University. The dean was interested and so all three met with the president of the university and looked at possible sites.

Change is never easy. People were concerned that the regional library might be swallowed up by the university and lose its identity with the state library and the subregionals. In the fall of 1982 the state library hired Harris C. McClaskey, a library consultant from Minnesota, to meet with the subregional librarians, their library administrators, and the regional library advisory council. An open meeting held in the Emporia State University student union provided an opportunity for people to air their fears and concerns.

On Dr. McClaskey's recommendation, plans went ahead for the move to the basement of the Memorial Student Union, the location that best met the library's needs. Ms. Longmoor negotiated with the Kansas Department of Corrections to supply the manpower for the move. Mr. Johnson negotiated with the Kansas National Guard for the loan of two semitrailers and four drivers. The post office could not supply the sacks needed for packing talking books, but Mr. Johnson and Ms. Longmoor were able to get two barrels of parachute cord at the Surplus Property Warehouse. Prisoners used it to tie up bundles of talking books.

The actual move took one week. Disruption of service was minimal because talking book users are served primarily by the subregional libraries. However, it took a month or two to get things back in order.

The university president had offered the state library its choice of available spaces. Mr. Johnson and Ms. Longmoor chose an area convenient to a loading dock. The dock is not used regularly, however, because the daily mail is brought to the post office in the student union and a regional library staff member picks it up and takes it by elevator to the library. Large shipments, such as a supply of talking book machines, are left at the dock. Ms. Longmoor said that the location of the library is not ideal but it is better than the building they left in Topeka.

RELATIONS WITH UNIVERSITY DEPARTMENTS

As part of the state library's contract with the university, the regional library can use the media center and the university press, which prints its brochures and annual newsletter. Because the library school lost its accreditation the same year the regional library moved to Emporia, and was for two years intent on the task of regaining accreditation (which it did), the relationship between the library school and the regional library developed slowly. Two graduate students are employed half time duplicating tapes, and several students have done practicum studies at the regional library. Two classes in special education visit the library each semester. Ms. Longmoor talks to them about services and equipment. Cooperation with university departments has many possibilities, limited only by Ms. Longmoor's time to initiate and the departments' ability to follow through.

Ms. Longmoor had planned a discussion with the university librarian, the disability services office, and students with disabilities about topics such as helpful accommodations and student adjustment to the university. The meeting had to be canceled, however. A volunteer with a background in journalism is currently surveying disabled students for the same information.

Although there was not enough space in the university library for the regional library to locate there, relations between the two libraries are good. We visited Mr. Stewart, the university library director, who talked about the ways in which his library accommodates students with disabilities. Students in wheelchairs used to have to use the back door, but now the front entrance is accessible. The disability services office conducted an emergency evacuation test on campus, and it dramatically pointed out the need for an evacuation plan. At the beginning of every term several people in each class are assigned the responsibility of getting any student with a disability out of the building in an emergency. Library staff have similar responsibilities.

Students using talking books continue to receive their service from the subregional libraries, but in an emergency, such as the need for a book for an assignment the next day, they can go directly to the regional library. The university library and the regional library can and do use each other as a resource.

Both Mr. Stewart and Ms. Longmoor are interested in developing a collection of automated equipment for blind and physically handicapped people. When I was there, they were making plans to examine a computer service for disabled persons in Lincoln, Nebraska. Ms. Longmoor dreams of having workshops throughout the state showing potential employers, special education teachers, and rehabilitation counselors what people can do if they have the right equipment. This would generate a need for a training program and further coordination with the university.

When the regional library moved to Emporia, a committee was formed to evaluate the success of its working relationship with the library school. The committee included a representative of the state library (not Ms. Longmoor), a representative of the library school (not the dean), and two subregional librarians (two librarians chosen by Ms. Longmoor because their lack of enthusiasm about the move would cause them to give her straight answers). The committee met a year after the move, and Ms. Longmoor feels that it is time to meet again.

STAFF

Ms. Longmoor and one other staff member (the person who duplicated tapes) moved to Emporia with the library. She hired two more people, an office assistant II to handle the fifty magazines circulated through the regional library and an office assistant I to pull and shelve talking books. The person who duplicated tapes has been replaced by two library school students who share that position. During the summer of 1987 two practicum students, assigned to the regional library by the dean of the library school, were plotting subregional library statistics on graphs. This was to be used at a meeting of network librarians.

RELATIONS WITH SUBREGIONALS

As head of the Kansas Network, Ms. Longmoor feels that the regional library can be successful only if the subregionals are successful. She constantly tries to reinforce the idea that they are working together for the same purpose. She meets with them four or five times a year in different parts of the state to discuss common concerns.

The subregional libraries receive collections of talking books from the National Library Service for the Blind and Physically Handicapped. Each subregional library circulates books to the readers in its service area and keeps its own records of what has been sent to individuals and groups. Each library publicizes the program in its area, using the brochures provided by the regional library and the National Library Service, as well as any other means it chooses to reach potential readers. Each regional has a toll-free telephone line by which to stay in touch with its readers and the regional library.

The regional library's role is "to coordinate the services throughout the state, provide magazines directly to users, maintain a back-up interlibrary loan collection of books, make duplicate replacements for damaged tapes, provide reference service, and act as liaison between the Kansas Network and the Library of Congress."[2] It also has a toll-free telephone line.

Part of the regional library's responsibility is to keep accurate statistics that are used as the basis for funding the subregionals. Each subregional library receives a base grant of $5,000 of the funds allocated for all the subregionals (LSCA and State General Fund grants). The remainder is divided among them on a basis of individuals served. Each active reader counts as one person; each active deposit collection in a nursing home or other institution counts as four people. (Although a study in Kansas showed that the average number of people served in institutions is eleven, Kansas uses an average of four, determined by the National Library Service on the basis of a national survey.) Ms. Longmoor and her staff keep records of the readers served by each subregional. The subregionals notify them of new readers and readers no longer using the service. Ms. Longmoor audits the subregional statistics annually to ensure that all are keeping accurate records. This monitoring pinpoints problems in the subregionals' operation, she says.

Since 1985 the Kansas regional library has published an annual newsletter for talking book readers. Again Ms. Longmoor emphasized the theme, "we all work together." She asks the subregionals to submit news items, and she fills in the gaps for those who do not.

When readership appeared to reach a plateau, Ms. Longmoor sent readers a two-part post card evaluation. She has continued this practice for the past four years. The cards are color coded so that each subregional area is easily identified when the forms are returned. The subregional librarians receive results of the survey from their own area and statewide figures but do not receive results from other subregionals. This is an effective way for the regional and the subregionals to monitor their progress. Ms. Longmoor has also sent a questionnaire to the subregional librarians, asking them how the regional library could be improved.

VOLUNTEERS

In the spring of 1981 Ms. Longmoor initiated a networkwide effort to recruit and train volunteers. Freddie Peaco, a staff member at the National Library Service for the Blind and Physically Handicapped, led five workshops across the state in five days. The workshops were publicized in local newspapers, and interested people were asked to place their reservations through the regional library's toll-free number. One hundred potential volunteers attended. People who went to the workshops and agreed to volunteer with a subregional library became a part of VOICE (Volunteer Outreach in Communities Everywhere). They were given name tags to indicate their status. Some have continued as volunteers; others have left. The program has not grown as Ms. Longmoor had hoped it would.

A couple from Emporia who had attended the Topeka workshop joined the group of volunteers about two years later, after the library had moved to Emporia. Ray Polley repairs machines; Jolene Polley helps with mailings. The library paid airfare for Mr. Polley, a radio ham, to go to the National Library Service in Washington, D.C. There he was trained to repair talking book machines.

Subregionals that do not have volunteers to repair their machines send the machines to Emporia, and Mr. Polley repairs them in his home.

Efforts to use volunteers to record materials have not been as successful. The regional library does not have a recording studio so volunteers, working in their own homes, cannot produce material of as high quality as that prepared in a controlled environment. The regional library refers patrons to the Braille Association of Kansas in Wichita for brailling and taping and the Topeka Volunteer Taping Unit for taping. The library circulates newsletters from the Area Agencies on Aging and magazines such as *Kansas!* and *Kansas Wildlife*, which these groups record.

ADVISORY COMMITTEE AND THE FRIENDS PROGRAM

Ms. Longmoor keeps in contact with the Kansas Association of the Blind, the Kansas chapter of the National Federation of the Blind, and the state Lions organization. She believes that in-house services and outreach services are both full-time jobs and that her primary responsibility is to build rapport in the network (outreach). The advisory committee, called the Kansas Council for Library Service for the Visually and Physically Handicapped, is the regional library's outreach link. It grew out of the group that campaigned for a regional library in Kansas in the mid-sixties. When Ms. Longmoor came to the library, the group was meeting infrequently. She helped it to become incorporated and write bylaws. The committee has fifteen members committee, appointed by the state librarian. Five members are regional library users, five are professionals working with users, and five are members-at-large. Each member serves a three-year term. Each year five members are replaced. (Photographs of members past and present are prominently displayed in the entrance area of the library.) The council meets two times a year. The state librarian attends the meetings. Ms. Longmoor is an ex officio member, gives an update at the meetings, and keeps members informed by letter of any new developments between meetings. The members offer both advice and support.

In 1987 the advisory council created a Friends of Kansas Talking Books group. Dues for membership range from $3.00 for students to

$1,000 for life membership. Membership cards make members ambassadors for the service. Ms. Longmoor admits that she borrowed the idea from the Colorado Regional Library, but it works in Kansas, too. Over $1,000 was received the first two weeks after notice of the new group appeared in the library's newsletter. Ms. Longmoor plans to use some of the money to publish a collection of talking book users' stories about how talking books have made a difference in their lives. She has some qualms about the Friends program because she feels that the subregional librarians may look at it as competition for money that might go to them. She hopes they will feel that the purpose for which the money is used will benefit them as well.

WRITING CONTEST

In 1985 Ms. Longmoor initiated an annual writing contest for Kansas high school students. (This was inspired by her fond memory of winning a writing contest in her youth and by a similar program in Oklahoma.) With permission from the State Department of Education, the library sent packets to high schools, inviting juniors and seniors to write a "letter to the editor" about the free talking book service. The project gave students a chance to learn about the program and inform others about it. The entries were judged by Emporia State University English faculty members, and a $100 savings bond was awarded to one winner from each subregional area. The top winner received his or her award from the governor with appropriate fanfare. In the process many people, including the governor, were exposed to the program. Although fewer students entered the contest the second year, the advisory council recommended that it be continued. The contest has been supported by gifts to the regional library (later to be formalized by the formation of the Friends group discussed above).

FUNDING

The regional library's budget is a line item in the state library budget. Each year Ms. Longmoor develops three budgets at an A, B, and C level. The A budget is the least the library could get by with.

The C budget is what it really needs. For three years she asked for computer hardware so the library could use READS software developed by the National Library Service. For two years she was turned down. She applied to Kansas foundations for $183,000 for the same purpose and got $1,000! In 1987 she got half of the $200,000 requested from the state and achieved the beginning of a system of recordkeeping for the Kansas Network. One of Ms. Longmoor's dreams for the future is coming true.

A look at the Kansas regional library shows that good things can happen when an enthusiastic program head (the regional librarian) who respects the people through whom the library must accomplish its objectives is matched with a supportive administration (the state librarian). As Carolyn Longmoor says, "If the regional library is doing its job right, the subregionals are, too." Her analysis of statistics from six other states of approximately the same size shows that Kansas is the only one serving as many as 37 percent of the eligible readers.

Notes

1. *Summary Proceedings of a Symposium on Educating Librarians and Information Scientists to Provide Information and Library Services to Blind and Physically Handicapped Individuals* (Washington, D.C.: Library of Congress National Library Service for the Blind and Physically Handicapped, 1982).

2. "Welcome to Talking Books" (Emporia: Kansas State Library for the Blind and Physically Handicapped, n.d.).

References

Longmoor, Caroline. "Kansas Regional Library Moves to University," National Library Service for the Blind and Physically Handicapped *News* 14, no. 2 (April-June 1983): 1-2.

"Workers Recruit, Train Volunteers." National Library Service for the Blind and Physically Handicapped *Update* 5, no. 1 (September-October 1981): 1-2.

Chapter 19

Alabama Public Library Service, Regional Library for the Blind and Physically Handicapped, Birmingham, Alabama

My first surprise when I visited the Alabama Regional Library for the Blind and Physically Handicapped was to learn that it was housed with the state library agency. I had known that organizationally it was a division of the Alabama Public Library Service, but not until I was in the building and directed to a lower level was I aware of the physical connection.

In 1976 the Alabama Public Library Service moved from its downtown site into a beautiful new modern building, approximately eight miles east of the center of Montgomery. Soon after that Governor George Wallace issued an executive order transferring responsibility for the regional library for the blind and physically handicapped from the Alabama Institute for the Deaf and Blind to the state library agency. Early in 1978 the collection and Jimmy Gibson, the braille librarian, moved from the E. H. Gentry Special Technical Facility for the blind in Talladega into space designed to be a barrier-free prototype structure occupying 50,000 square feet on two floors.

BARRIER-FREE DESIGN

The addition to the Alabama Public Library Service building was designed by Birmingham Architects Moss, Garikes and Associates and was constructed with Public Works and Capital Development funds totalling $1,213,040. Architect Charles A. Moss, Jr., who had also designed the new state library building, and his partner, Arthur Garikes, had experience with hospitals and libraries, but designing a barrier-free library for blind and physically handicapped individuals was a new concept. They called upon many people for advice, including people with disabilities and the state library's LSCA Advisory Committee and its Executive Board. The work, titled *Planning Barrier Free Libraries,*[1] represents the experiences Mr. Moss encountered in the planning and design stages. Miriam Pace, a consultant at the Alabama Public Library Service at the time, worked closely with its director, Anthony Miele, to find money to buy furnishings and equipment that would be appropriate for the barrier-free library and to get funding from the state legislature for staff. Ms. Pace served as the first regional librarian in Montgomery.

I entered the regional library through the main entrance to the Alabama Public Library Service so I never felt the full impact of the separate entrance on the east side of the building, with its automatically opening doors and the sculpture of Helen Keller gracing the entrance lobby.

SUBREGIONALS

My second surprise at the Alabama regional library was learning that two of the subregional libraries had been discontinued. Seven subregional libraries were created in Alabama long before the regional library moved from Talladega to Montgomery. When the Alabama Public Library Service's Executive Board made the decision in 1981 to use LSCA monies for other programs instead of staff for the subregionals, two dropped out of the picture. Now there are five subregional libraries serving readers in seven counties. The regional library serves the remainder of Alabama's blind and physically handicapped population in sixty counties.

STAFF

Fara Zaleski is the third person to head the regional library in Montgomery. She has been acting head since October 1, 1987. Ms.

Zaleski came with fifteen years of experience in public, state, school, and church libraries. Because she has worked at all levels of service, she is credible to staff members of every rank. With the support of a new Alabama Public Library Service director, Blane Dessy, who came to Alabama from Ohio in September 1986, Ms. Zaleski is trying to open up communication among her staff, the regional library, other divisions within the state library, the subregionals, and the users.

Ms. Zaleski is attempting to familiarize staff members with the operation of the library so that each one will know how the entire organization is dependent on him or her. Because of the nature of the work--an average of 12,000 items a month is sent to 3,300 Alabamians, following procedures prescribed by the National Library Service for the Blind and Physically Handicapped--there is little opportunity to exercise creativity. That has made it difficult to retain the professional library staff that fill the two reader advisor positions and the position of assistant to the head/reader advisor.

Every morning before the library is officially open for business, staff members gather informally in the staff room. Ms. Zaleski holds impromptu meetings with staff or with small groups at other hours, but her real management style was identified at a recent Library Administration and Management Association (MBWA) workshop entitled "Management by Walking Around." That is also the style of Director Dessy, who works closely with Ms. Zaleski and generally checks in each morning. Ms. Zaleski is one of three division heads in the Alabama Public Library Service who attends administrative staff meetings with the director, support services head, and business manager. This gives her a strong position in the organizational structure.

Except for warehouse personnel--the staff who sort the mail, pack and unpack shipments of books and machines, and shelve returned books--all staff members must be selected from the State Personnel Office's register of jobs. Because much of the work in the regional library is routine, many applicants view jobs there as steppingstones to employment in other Alabama Public Library Service divisions.

READER ADVISORS

The reader advisors, Susan Clements and Mike Coleman, hired at a librarian I level but with previous library experience, are responsible for readers in assigned Alabama counties. Their work involves responding to readers' mail and telephone requests and choosing books when the readers indicate interests rather than specific titles. A computerized circulation system, designed for the regional library and connected with the state's Honeywell computer, has been in place since 1979. Each morning the reader advisors get computer-produced status reports on all books checked in the previous day and a list of patrons needing books but having submitted no requests. Every three months the reader advisors remind patrons to send request lists to the library. To improve relations with patrons, Ms. Zaleski has rewritten the form letters that welcome new readers, request information missing on the application form, and remind them of overdue books. Overdue letters are sent to check on the mail service. Readers are asked to contact the library by the toll-free line to say if they received the book in question, sent it back, or still wanted it. In 1987 the library froze book service to anyone who had not responded to an overdue letter in over a year and resumed service only when the reader called the library. That procedure cleared out 70 percent of the overdue books. Some readers check out books once and are never heard from again.

Ms. Zaleski is attempting to make work more interesting by giving staff responsibilities beyond their primary duties. One of the reader advisors handles mail from the readers, a task Ms. Zaleski had when she was assistant to the head (this position has not yet been filled) , and the other works with the state library's reference staff to answer reference questions, a service that is relatively new at the regional library. One reader advisor does the in-house cataloging. The other initiates outgoing telephone contacts with Ms. Zaleski's patrons as needed. The reader advisors are also trained in recording and warehouse procedures because everything is interrelated.

OTHER STAFF

Mr. Gibson, the braille librarian, his wife, and one of the reader advisors are regional library users. (Mr. Gibson agreed to move from Talladega to Montgomery on the condition that his wife be employed.) As the person who handles snags, she has become an invaluable part of the service. An Apollo closed-circuit magnification system has been ordered for her use. Mr. Gibson, who handles the circulation of all braille to 220 readers, will soon have the use of a VersaBraille, an Apple computer, an Apple Imagewriter printer, a Romeo printer, and an Echo talk system (a speech synthesizer). When this equipment arrives, he will be able to make braille or print copies of correspondence and materials; a sighted person can do the same. One immediate use will be to produce braille materials for a state legislator who is blind. Mr. Gibson's secretary (who also handles the records for talking book machines and equipment) reads his correspondence to him, but he is able to do most of his work independently. The Gibsons are a hit with school groups who come for tours of the library, and they ably represent the library to the sighted community. When I was there, Ms. Gibson had just retired from a term as president of the Montgomery chapter of the Alabama Council of the Blind.

Tim Mooneyham is the periodicals librarian, but he also checks in all materials returned to the library. This process has not been automated to the extent of using bar codes and a wand. Mr. Mooneyham is also secretary to the assistant to the head of the library when there is a person in that position. The two reader advisors share a secretary, who mails catalogs and handles correspondence to their patrons. The regional librarian's secretary, hired just two days before my visit, is also the receptionist for the library.

COMPUTERIZATION

The computer has enabled the regional library to continue operating with the same number of staff, sixteen people, that it had eight years ago even though circulation has increased from 3,500 titles a month to 12,000 titles a month. The computer will hold up to 200 requests for each reader. Additional requests are kept in the patrons' folders. The computer limits readers to fifteen books at any one time, but this can be overridden for special situations such as walk-in patrons. Some updating of the program needs to be done (e.g., there is currently no way to cancel institutional service), but the state library's computer staff have not had time to write an updated program. Ms. Zaleski planned to inventory the collection in 1988 so that the computer would include all the materials returned from the two subregionals that were closed. Within a month of so of my visit, the library was to receive a computer from the National Library Service for the Blind and Physically Handicapped. It would allow direct access to BRS and the total records of the National Library Service. Although the library already has access to BRS through the Alabama Public Library Service, this will be much more convenient.

RECORDING PROGRAM

Jim Cooper works with the recording program. The library has four recording booths and duplication equipment for talking books. Volunteers are kept busy recording books of special interest to Alabama readers. Two of the magazines they record, *Grand National Illustrated* and *Grand National Scene* are about auto racing. Late in 1986 the library published Volume 1 of *Regional's Bookshelf,* an annotated listing of the 132 titles--fiction, nonfiction, and children's books--recorded up to that year. Volume 2 was to be published in 1988, bringing the list of titles almost up to date. The materials meet the National Library Service specifications for recording. A narrator review board, made up of two library users who are blind, a voice teacher, and a radio/television person, review a tape prepared by each volunteer applying to be a narrator and must approve the application. Monitors operate the tape recorders for the narrators, and other volunteers review the quality of the completed tapes. One of the narrators is eighty-three years old and has many more books she wants to record. The lieutenant governor's wife is a narrator, and most of the staff have passed the narrator's test so that they can record materials in an emergency, such as when state officials need materials. Mr. Cooper also has volunteers make copies of books, both nationally and locally produced, and periodicals to be sent to readers.

VOLUNTEERS

Richard Grant is volunteer coordinator; editor of *What's Line*, the regional library's quarterly newsletter; and the person who handles public relations and community outreach. He recruits volunteers through social service organizations, sororities, churches, and newspaper publicity. There is a local pretrial diversion program for first offenders, with requirements that they go to school, get a job, and do volunteer service on a weekly basis. Mr. Grant has three people under this program and has had several others in the past. The Eagle Scouts, parochial school honor groups, Junior League, and Telephone Pioneers all give time to the regional library. The Telephone Pioneers and their wives--six to ten of them--repair talking book equipment on Mondays from midafternoon until 9:00 P.M. Staff speak with pride of a former judge who is part of that corps. One Telephone Pioneer was hired permanently two months before I was there to catch up on the backlog of machine repair, and he still volunteers his time on Monday nights. Other volunteers shelve master copies of tapes for books or help where they are needed most.

Nearly 200 volunteers worked 2,108 hours in 1987. On December 7 the regional library staff honored them with a dinner party in the library, music by a local country and western band, and special recognition to the volunteer of year, the volunteer organization of the year, and volunteers who had worked five years. Users and Alabama Public Library Service staff were also invited, and one of the volunteers played Santa. This annual event is financed through the library's sale of newspapers and aluminum cans contributed by staff and patrons.

PUBLIC RELATIONS

What's Line is sent to people who receive service directly from the regional library, to heads of the subregionals, to regional librarians in other states, to all the public libraries in Alabama, and to 600 groups and individuals who provide services for people with disabilities. Ms. Zaleski is attempting to personalize it by featuring users and staff. It is available in recorded and braille versions as well as large print. Books produced at the regional library are featured, and issue no. 4 in 1987 had an article about the braille edition of John Bartlett's *Familiar Quotations*, which the National Library Service for the Blind and Physically Handicapped had given to forty-three regional libraries for their reference collections.

Mr. Grant has been almost exclusively responsible for the regional library's public relations effort, but Ms. Zaleski hopes to involve more staff. He attends local health fairs, meets people there and at other places outside the library, and invites them to come for a tour. He schedules and plans these visits, which usually begin with an orientation film about people with disabilities. Jimmy and Deborah Gibson talk about blindness, and Jim Cooper speaks about the recording program. When Ms. Zaleski stops to say hello, she reminds people that the library needs volunteers and the audience can help recruit readers. Some groups come each year. In 1987, 616 people in thirty groups, from kindergartners to consumer groups, attended these programs.

The regional library keeps a supply of current catalogs and handouts in the lobby for visitors. People attending meetings in the state library often come downstairs to the regional library during their break times. Thus the service gains additional visibility. Library staff mail appropriate information statewide to rehabilitation teachers, teachers of children with learning disabilities, nursing homes directors, and ophthalmologists. Members of the advisory committee help in publicizing the service throughout the state. The regional library uses the National Library Service's application form and sends out copies through the mail as people request them. It also publicizes the radio reading services in Montgomery and Birmingham and has sent out surveys to assess interest in such a service in the Mobile area. The Alabama Public Library Service director is planning a new brochure and slide presentation about its services. Both will include segments on the regional library, which can be used separately. An effort is now being made to represent the regional library as part of the state library agency rather than as a separate agency.

ACCESS TODAY

Although the physical facilities of the regional library are only 95 percent barrier free now because of expansion in the work area, the library is still considered a prototype of a barrier-free library. Handrails guide patrons to the automatic sliding doors at the entrance. The restroom doors also open with a push-plate activator. Curving walls were intended to make it less hazardous for blind people, but Mr. Gibson says even round walls hurt when you run into them. By virtue of being in the suburbs, the library has ample parking. A large canopied entrance protects people who arrive at the front door. The lobby is large enough to accommodate people in wheelchairs, and the reception desk is just inside the main entrance. A bronze sculpture of Helen Keller reading Charles Lamb's *Tales from Shakespeare* was created for the library by Clydetta Fulmer, a native of Montgomery, and dedicated in 1981. It is a joy for both sighted and blind visitors. Ms. Zaleski encourages people to touch it and often holds Helen's hand as she talks to groups. This representation of a native Alabamian was funded by the Kiwanis Clubs of Alabama.

The conference room just off the lobby houses a large collection of books about disabilities, both reference and circulating copies, large print books (older titles because the Alabama Public Library Service no longer purchases and seldom circulates these), and print/braille books on display. Books are selected by the state library's acquisitions department. If a book on disabilities is of general interest, it is sent to the regional library; if it is medically oriented, it stays in the reference department of the state library. The general public can check out these books through the Alabama Public Library Service desk; regional library patrons, parents, children, students of local university special education classes, and members of associations can check them out directly from the regional library. The books are listed in the state library's microfiche catalog. A copy of the dictionary on cassettes is used for demonstration purposes.

Library orientation sessions begin in the conference room. The regional library's advisory committee meets there, and it, like the two meeting rooms in the main part of the building, is used for meetings sponsored by other state agencies. A glass wall at one end of the conference room opens onto an atrium with a waterfall. Although the waterfall was designed so that blind people could hear the splash of falling water and deaf people could watch the scenic area, the library attracts few casual visitors. Some new patrons visit the library, but only six patrons come regularly, primarily because there is no public bus service.

Early in its history the regional library received a grant for a series of twelve captioned film programs. Generally three people attended, with a high of five. The regional library has a TDD that is more likely to be called by deaf people who are not using their local public library. The library has a collection of games and equipment that can be used by blind and physically handicapped people. These are on display to show parents and people with disabilities what is available.

CHANGES WITH NEW ADMINISTRATION

The consumer advisory committee has had a spotty history, with the group periodically becoming dormant and then being resurrected by the regional library. Currently it consists of fifteen members, with a core group of patrons, presidents of the National Federation of the Blind and the American Council of the Blind in Alabama, and a representative of the Alabama Institute for the Deaf and Blind at Talladega. This group then chooses other members. The chairperson develops the agenda for the quarterly meetings, and the regional librarian and the director of the Alabama Public Library Service have input only as the president solicits it. The regional library tapes and brailles the minutes and agenda for the meetings.

For the first time, in 1987 the regional library promoted the state library's statewide summer reading program. Children receiving the regional library service were encouraged to participate in the program through their local library or through the regional library. The regional library selected materials it already had from the statewide bibliography and suggested related titles. Eight children participated and received certificates at the end of the ten-week period. Ms. Zaleski is involved in the Alabama Public Library

Service's Committee on the Year of the Young Reader and is debating whether to have a story hour at the regional library.

Relations between the regional library and the subregionals have been strained in the past, and Ms. Zaleski has taken the first steps to improve communications. The subregionals were created by the National Library Service for the Blind and Physically Handicapped before the regional library moved to Montgomery. They have never felt a part of the state system. They have been funded separately and operate autonomously. Although they request talking books (900 in 1987) and order machines and equipment from Montgomery, they tend to call the National Library Service when they have questions. Ms. Zaleski has scheduled quarterly meetings to be rotated among the subregionals and will prepare an agenda for each one. At the December 1987 meeting the Alabama Public Library Service's long-range plan was discussed. The National Library Service recommends that regional library staff visit subregionals annually, and Ms. Zaleski plans to send pairs of staff members.

The regional library supplies 160-170 agencies, most of them nursing homes, with deposit collections of talking books. Ms. Zaleski is encouraging these groups to select their own materials. Twenty-seven sites with deposit collections and one subregional library circulate braille and talking books. There appears to be an unusually high rate of braille readers in Alabama.

Although Ms. Zaleski had been acting head only a few months when I talked to her, she had been assistant to the head for a year and a half and had definite opinions about how she would judge the success of the regional library: fewer complaints from patrons about the service, fewer broken and mismatched books sent to readers, an increase in the use of the reference service, good feedback from the subregional librarians (an invitation to attend anything), and improved relations with the Alabama Public Library Service staff.

Note

1. *Planning Barrier Free Libraries* (Washington, D.C., Library of Congress National Library Service for the Blind and Physically Handicapped, 1981).

Chapter 20

Conclusion

Some years ago a new librarian commented to me that life would be much easier if library schools would teach one standard way of doing things, which could then be followed by all the libraries in the country. This book will disappoint readers with any such expectations. It does not suggest a single program model. I hope instead that something can be learned from the experience of each library portrayed here. The librarians I visited used a variety of methods to serve people with disabilities. There is evidence that they have sampled the wealth of literature mentioned in the introduction to this book, have been stimulated by attending library conferences and workshops, and have conferred with their consumers. Although my personal preference is for mainstreamed services, with special services offered to the person who cannot be mainstreamed, I cannot conclude that it is the only way or even the best way to meet the needs of a particular community. The effectiveness of each service must be judged through user feedback such as user surveys, demands by user groups, and statistics on use.

Readers who are looking for equivalent information about each library will also be disappointed. Jean Hofacket at the Memphis-Shelby County Public Library and Information Center spoke of the problem of comparing apples and oranges. I faced the same dilemma. If I had attempted to give identical information for every library I visited, I do not believe that a clearer picture of service would have emerged or that this process would have enabled me to develop a model library program.

Portraits of Library Service to People with Disabilities has been written with the intention of giving persons with disabilities some insight into the services librarians offer them and of giving librarians and other concerned persons the kind of experience they would have at a professional meeting when the formal sessions are over and participants share their down-to-earth experiences. They don't often talk of goals and objectives, but planning is a vital part of their programs. (The exercise of developing goals and objectives is valid only if it is meaningful to the persons involved and is not done solely to meet the requirements of the funding agency.)

As professionals, librarians are willing to share their mistakes on a personal basis but much less likely to do so in print. I had evidence of this when I sent typed drafts of chapters to be reviewed by the librarians I had interviewed. They had been quite honest with me, but seeing their honesty reflected in unblinking print was intimidating. However, I believe that more willingness to share beyond the informal level would benefit other librarians and consequently users. Librarians are responsive to internal and external pressures, and services to people with disabilities are changing constantly as administrators seek to balance needs and resources. (Changes in the purchase and distribution of large print books at the Tampa-Hillsborough County Public Library Service in Florida illustrates this. Another example from the same library is the case of librarians backing away from something they enjoyed doing--programming in nursing homes--because another more basic part of the service was suffering.)

Staff and administrators change, too. The portraits of service can be viewed only as a picture of service during my visits from June through December 1987. By the time I had sent drafts of the chapters to the libraries, the service had already changed, in some cases quite drastically. By the time this book is published, there will be many more changes.

If someone were to ask me to name the single feature that contributes to a successful program, I would have to say an able and enthusiastic person in charge of services to people with disabilities who has the support of the library administration. *Check This Out,* which contains descriptions of discrete programs rather than complete libraries, states, "It is necessary to know that the program has a real impact, and that the impact is not simply the result of the efforts of a talented individual or a unique staff who would make any program a success."[1] The talented individual is important. I find it hard to imagine the programs described here working without the energy and enthusiasm of the talented individuals I met. But the person in charge cannot do it all alone. There has to be that appreciation, trust, willingness to listen, encouragement, stimulation, and help in finding the necessary resources on the part of library administration.

The strong areas in some libraries were the weak ones in others. Some librarians were active in community groups, and the services were vigorously promoted. In others there was the fear that a public relations effort would deluge staff with more requests for service than they could handle so people learned about the library's offerings only by word of mouth. Some publicity efforts did not produce results, most notably those directed to churches and hospitals. (This is not unusual and may be explained by the fact that these organizations have their own busy agenda, which they consider to be more important.) When TDD service is not vigorously promoted in the deaf community, its use appears to be minimal. A newspaper announcement or listing in a directory is inadequate.

I was impressed by the variety of sources tapped by libraries for funding services to people with disabilities. The ideal is to designate a percentage of the library's budget for this purpose, but this is not a perfect world. While the most common source was LSCA funds, libraries also received money through other federal programs (the Developmental Disabilities Act, Community Development Funds, the National Endowment for the Humanities, and the Public Telecommunications Facilities Program) and from service clubs, foundations, businesses, and Friends of the Library.

Libraries that emphasized mainstreamed service were more likely to have consumer advisory groups. The regional libraries for the blind and physically handicapped are exceptions because standards specify that they should have such a group (*Standards of Service for the Library of Congress Network of Libraries for the Blind and Physically Handicapped*).[2] Often an advisory council is part of a service while it is federally funded and so perhaps a requirement by the agency dispersing funds, but it is discontinued later. An advisory council with representation from consumers is a mechanism for getting user input and would strengthen services, I feel.

Many of the librarians I talked to said that their buildings were physically accessible, but only a few of them had asked users to assess this. Having people with disabilities survey libraries and determine what should be done to make them accessible is an excellent way to involve them and make them library-conscious.

I may not have learned the full extent to which the libraries employed persons with disabilities, but recent technology is opening up careers in library service to them. Many libraries for the blind and physically handicapped have made a special effort to employ persons with visual impairments. This has seemed to sensitize other libraries to the need to open employment opportunities and perhaps has stimulated client confidence in the service.

It has been my observation that many people are involved in library service to people with disabilities because of a personal experience with someone having a handicap. This is still true to some extent, but it is good to see people attracted to this service who do not have prior commitments to it. Perhaps attitudinal barriers are being overcome.

Librarians are creative people and will continue to develop services to meet the needs of their users. However, I fear that each new generation serving people with disabilities will feel obligated to rediscover the wheel unless they know something about the achievements of the past. This book provides a foundation on which they can build, just as it makes people with disabilities aware of library services that may be available to them.

Notes

1. U.S. Department of Education, *Check This Out: Library Program Models* (Washington, D.C.: GPO, July 1987), 1.

2. *Standards of Service for the Library of Congress Network of Libraries for the Blind and Physically Handicapped* (Chicago: ALA, 1984).

Appendix A

ALA Decade of Disabled Persons Committee Checklist

BARRIER-FREE DESIGNS

- Curb cuts.

- Oversize parking areas.

- Gradually sloping ramps.

- Doors at least 32" wide.

- Essential switches and controls within reach of people in wheelchairs.

- Restrooms with grab bars, stalls and fixtures that accommodate wheelchairs.

- Raised letters and numbers.

- Oversized carrels and turnstiles.

- Furniture that accommodates wheelchairs.

PROGRAM ACCESS

Print

- Braillers.

- Magnifiers.

- Kurzweil Reading Machine.

- Large print books.

- Books in braille.

- Talking Books.

- Playback equipment and accessories for disks and cassettes.

- Radio Reading Service.

- Visual Tek.

Information and Referral

- Collections concerning people with disabilities.

- Information on community organizations.

- Collections of important resources in books, journals, newsletters (e.g., basic rights, financial benefits, adapted home interiors, travel and transportation, sexuality).

- Directories of products and services.

Hearing

- Films/videotapes with open and closed captioning.

- TDD (Telecommunications Device for the Deaf).

- Amplifier for the telephone.

- Interpreters at programs.

- Sound amplification in meeting rooms.

- Deaf culture and sign language enlightenment.

Other

- Computer software accessibility.

- Books by mail.

- Materials and equipment circulated free by mail or by walk-in services.

- Services to homebound persons.

- Positive staff attitude through education.

Appendix B

Glossary and Resource Directory

Adaptive equipment: A wide range of devices, aids, tools, and equipment that can be used by persons with disabilities to enable them to function more efficiently.

ALA (American Library Association): A national association of libraries, librarians, library trustees, and other persons interested in library and information services. For more information write to:

American Library Association
50 East Huron St.
Chicago, IL 60611

American Council of the Blind: A national membership organization composed primarily of blind and visually impaired persons. For more information write to:

American Council of the Blind
1010 Vermont Ave., NW, Suite 1100
Washington, DC 20005

American Foundation for the Blind: An organization that publishes extensive material on blindness, serves as a clearinghouse for information on the subject, offers consultant services to government and private agencies serving blind persons, and sells consumer products. For more information write to:

American Foundation for the Blind
15 West 16th St.
New York, NY 10011

American Society for Deaf Children (formerly International Association of Parents of the Deaf): A membership organization providing information and support to parents and families with children who are deaf or hard of hearing. For more information write to:

American Society for Deaf Children
814 Thayer Ave.
Silver Spring, MD 20910

Amplification device: A device that increases the volume of sound on a telephone, radio, record player, public address system, or other equipment. For more information write to:

National Information Center on Deafness
Gallaudet University
800 Florida Ave., NE
Washington, DC 20002

Apollo CCTV: *See* Closed-circuit television (CCTV) reading machine.

Audio-loops: An amplification system where a length of wire connected with the public address system encircles a room or a part of it and emits a signal that is picked up by a hearing aid with an induction coil or by a wireless receiver and a headset worn by individuals needing amplification. For more information write to:

Self Help for Hard of Hearing People
7800 Wisconsin Ave.
Bethesda, MD 20817

Automatic page turners: *See* Page turners.

Barrier free environments, Inc: A research, design, and consulting firm that specializes in designing homes and commercial buildings to be used by everyone, including disabled and older people. For more information write to:

Barrier Free Environments, Inc.
P.O. Box 30634
Raleigh, NC 27622

Bell and Howell Language Master: A system for individual instruction that uses cards with magnetic sound recordings and a built-in microphone. For more information write to:

Bell and Howell
27882 Camino Capistrano
Laguna Niguel, CA 92677

BEX: A multimedia word processing program for Apple computers with options of print, large print, voice, or braille output. Can be used by persons with vision impairments and by sighted persons. For more information write to:

Raised Dot Computing
408 S. Baldwin St.
Madison, WI 53703

BiFolkal Kits: Packages of materials designed to trigger memories and encourage groups of older adults to share their stories. The kits include slide/tape sets (or videotapes), tapes of music, skits in large print with props, scratch-and-sniff cards, realia, and a manual of program suggestions. For more information write to:

BiFolkal Productions, Inc.
911 Williamson St.
Madison, WI 53703

Book holder: An aid for individuals whose strength or grasp may not be sufficient to support the weight of reading material. For more information write to:

National Library Service for the Blind and Physically Handicapped
The Library of Congress
1291 Taylor St., NW
Washington, DC 20542

Book leasing plan: A plan by which a library can rent books for temporary use. For more information write to:

McNaughton Book Services
500 Arch St.
Williamsport, PA 17705

Baker & Taylor Co.
652 E. Main St.
Bridgewater, NJ 08807

Bookmobile: A truck or semitrailer that serves as a traveling library. For more information write to the state library agency in your state.

Bookmobile Conference: An annual conference conducted by the State Library of Ohio to give bookmobile staff and administrators a chance to upgrade their skills, analyze programs, and exchange ideas. For more information write to:

Bookmobile Conference
The State Library of Ohio
65 South Front St.
Columbus, OH 43266-0334

Braille: A system of raised dots that blind persons can use for touch reading and writing. For more information write to:

American Foundation for the Blind
15 West 16th St.
New York, NY 10011

Braille-Edit: A microcomputer word processing program written for blind persons. It has been superseded by BEX. For more information write to:

Raised Dot Computing
408 South Baldwin St.
Madison, WI 53703

Braille writers, or Braillers: Devices for the manual production of braille (e.g., Perkins brailler, braille typewriter). For more information write to:

American Printing House for the Blind
1839 Frankfort Ave.
Louisville, KY 40206

Brooklyn Public Library: *See* SAGE Program.

BRS (Bibliographic Retrieval Service): A vendor offering computer access to a broad selection of data bases consisting of bibliographic citations and abstracts, some of which have been developed specifically for people with disabilities. Includes records of the holdings of the National Library Service for the Blind and Physically Handicapped. For more information write to:

Bibliographic Retrieval Service
1200 Route 7
Latham, NY 12110

Captioned films (or video): Films or videos with dialogue, narration, and sound effects printed on the screen. Similar to subtitles in foreign language films.

Captioned Films for the Deaf: A federally funded program with a network of libraries that distribute films to deaf schools and classes for the deaf as well as to groups of deaf adults. For more information write to:

Captioned Film/Video Program
Modern Talking Picture Service
5000 Park St., North
St. Petersburg, FL 33709

A Chance to Grow: A parent self-help group dedicated to the rehabilitation of brain-injured children and adults; founders of the Josephine Kretsch Library on Brain Injury. For more information write to:

A Chance to Grow
5034 Oliver Ave., North
Minneapolis, MN 55430

Closed captioning: Dialogue, narration, and sound effects printed on the screen but "closed" because they can be seen only when a decoder, called a TeleCaption, is connected to the television set. For more information write to:

National Captioning Institute, Inc.
5203 Leesburg Pike
Falls Church, VA 22041

Closed-circuit television (CCTV) reading machine: A reading device that magnifies printed material electronically on a television screen. Magnification can be varied up to 60 times the original and allows people with exceedingly poor vision to read print. Images on the screen can be reversed to show white print on a dark background. For more information write to:

Telesensory Systems
455 North Bernado Ave.
Mountain View, CA 94043 (Apollo and Viewscan)

Visualtek
1610 26th St.
Santa Monica, CA 90404 (Visualtek and Voyager)

Closing the Gap: A periodical dedicated to exploring the use of computers by disabled children and adults. Closing the Gap also provides hands-on training in the use of computers, and workshops and presentations on developed software and adaptive devices that benefit physically, mentally, and educationally disabled persons. For more information write to:

Closing the Gap
P.O. Box 68
Henderson, MN 56044

Community Development Funds (also known as Block Grant Funds): Federal funds administered by the Department of Housing and Urban Development to develop viable urban communities, such as decent housing and a suitable living environment and to expand economic opportunities for persons of low and medium income. For more information write to:

Department of Housing and Urban Development
451 7th St., SW
Washington, DC 20410

CompuServe: A computer service that gives subscribers access to a wide range of general information, financial data, games, newspapers, and a travel bureau. It also offers a data base specially designed for handicapped computer users. For more information write to:

CompuServe Consumer Information Service
5000 Arlington Centre Blvd.
Columbus, OH 43220

Com-Tek: Manufacturers of wireless listening systems that retransmit the audio from the sound system to hearing impaired persons through individual receivers and headphones. For more information write to:

Com-Tek
375 West Lemel Circle
Salt Lake City, UT 84115

The Concise Heritage Dictionary: Originally published by Houghton-Mifflin in 1976, the 820-page dictionary has been recorded and voice-indexed and is available in fifty-six cassettes. For more information write to:

American Printing House for the Blind
1839 Frankfort Ave.
Louisville, KY 40206

Cranmer Modified Perkins brailler: A Perkins brailler to which sophisticated electronics, circuitry, and a microprocessor have been added. It can function as a standard braille writer, a computer terminal, a braille printer, a text editor, and a tactile graphics printer. Information can be stored on or retrieved from cassette tapes. For more information write to:

Maryland Computer Services
2010 Rock Spring Rd.
Forest Hill, MD 21050

Echo speech synthesizer: A device that converts digital information to spoken words and letters. With appropriate software it can be connected to a computer. For more information write to:

Street Electronics Corp.
1140 Mark Ave.
Carpinteria, CA 93013

Ednalite magnifiers: *See* MasterLens.

ERIC (Educational Resources Information Center): A decentralized nationwide network providing educational information through various clearinghouses. Its bibliographic database lists articles and publications with abstracts. Microfiche and print copies of many documents are available for purchase. For more information write to:

ERIC
Office of Educational Research and Improvement
U.S. Department of Education
Washington, DC 20208-1235

Federal Programs Advisory Service: An agency that publishes information about federal programs. A looseleaf format permits its subscription services, such as the *Handicapped Requirements Handbook,* to be updated continually. For more information write to:

Federal Programs Advisory Service
Thompson Publishing Group
1725 K St., NW, Suite 200
Washington, DC 20006

First DIBS: A disability information network that publishes a bimonthly newsletter by the same name. For more information write to:

First DIBS
P.O. Box 1285
Tucson, AZ 85702-1285

Flannel board story: Story told with the aid of pieces illustrating the setting, characters, and action. These are constructed to adhere to a flannel backing. For more information read Paul Anderson's *Storytelling with the Flannel Board,* volumes 1 and 2, published by:

T. S. Dennison & Co.
9601 Newton Ave., South
Minneapolis, MN 55431

FOCUS: Library Service for Older Adults, People with Disabilities: A monthly newsletter for librarians and others interested in initiating or expanding services. For more information write to:

FOCUS
2255 Pine Dr.
Prescott, AZ 86301

Friends of Libraries for Deaf Action (FOLDA): An organization of volunteers whose goal is to improve library service to the deaf community and improve communications between deaf and hearing people. For more information write to:

FOLDA
P.O. Box 50045
Washington, DC 20004-0045

Gaylord boxes: File boxes that hold book cards or can be used for other library purposes; distributed by library suppliers. For more information write to:

Gaylord Bros.
Box 4901
Syracuse, NY 13221-4901

Gaylord MasterLens: *See* MasterLens.

Hal's Pals: Dolls with disabilities. For more information write to:

Mattel, Inc.
5959 Triumph St.
City of Commerce, CA 90040

HEATH (Higher Education and the Handicapped) Resource Center: A national clearinghouse on postsecondary education for handicapped individuals, a program of the American Council on Education funded by the U.S. Department of Education. For more information write to:

HEATH Resource Center
One Dupont Circle, NW, Suite 670
Washington, DC 20036-1193

Information Development Corporation: An organization providing technical assistance for making facilities accessible to handicapped people. For more information write to:

Compliance Assistance Service
Information Development Corporation
360 St. Alban Ct.
Winston-Salem, NC 27104

Kids on the Block: Large puppets created by Barbara Aiello, a special education teacher, to teach children about disabilities, differences, and other areas of social concern. These have been purchased by many community groups, including libraries. Ms. Aiello provides scripts and training for puppeteers. For more information write to:

Kids on the Block, Inc.
9385-C Gerwig Lane
Columbia, MD 21046

KRM (Kurzweil Reading Machine): A reading machine that uses a computer to convert printed text directly into synthetic speech. For more information write to:

Kurzweil Computer Products
185 Albany St.
Cambridge, MA 02139

Large type (large print): Type that is taller than that used in most adult books (10-12 point type); 14 point is the minimum size for large type materials, with the most common sizes being 16 and 18 point. For more information write to:

National Library Service for the Blind and Physically
Handicapped
The Library of Congress
1291 Taylor St., NW
Washington, DC 20542

Library Outreach Reporter: A bimonthly library publication devoted
to areas such as service to the disabled, programs for the aging,
literacy programs, and ethnic library services. For more
information write to:

LOR
1671 East 16th St., Suite 226
Brooklyn, NY 11229

Library Video Network: A network of Maryland libraries that
provides staff and facilities for developing information,
educational, promotional, or other video programming. For
more information write to:

Library Video Network
1811 Woodlawn Dr.
Baltimore, MD 21207

LSCA (Library Services and Construction Act): Federal legislation
authorizing funds to assist state libraries in establishing or
improving services. For more information write to your state
library agency.

Machine Lending Agency: An agency designated by the National
Library Service for the Blind and Physically Handicapped to
receive, issue, and control the inventory of talking book
equipment. For more information write to:

National Library Service for the Blind and Physically
Handicapped
The Library of Congress
1291 Taylor St., NW
Washington, DC 20541

McNaughton plan: *See* Book leasing plan.

Magnifiers: Lens to increase the size of print, available in various powers of magnification, handheld and on stands, illuminated or nonilluminated. For more information write to:

National Library Service for the Blind and Physically Handicapped
The Library of Congress
1291 Taylor St., NW
Washington, DC 20541

Maryland Computer Services: A company that engineers personal computers and software for people with disabilities. For more information write to:

Maryland Computer Services
2010 Rock Spring Rd.
Forest Hill, MD 21050

MasterLens: Stand magnifiers with their own fluorescent light source. For more information write to:

Contact East, Inc.
P.O. Box 786
North Andover, MA 01845

Microtech Consulting Company: A company that makes sign language software for almost all makes of computers. For more information write to:

Microtech Consulting Co., Inc.
909 West 23rd St.
Cedar Falls, IA 50613

Minicom: One of many telecommunication devices for the deaf: *See also* TDD/TTY. For information on Minicom write to:

Ultratech, Inc.
6442 Normandy Lane
Madison, WI 53719

Multistate Center: An agency operating under contractual agreement with the National Library Service for the Blind and Physically Handicapped to provide material support services to regional libraries and machine lending agencies in an assigned part of the service's network. For more information write to:

National Library Service for the Blind and Physically Handicapped
The Library of Congress
1291 Taylor St., NW
Washington, DC 20541

National Federation of the Blind: An organization with state and local chapters that works for the complete integration of blind persons into society. For more information write to:

National Federation of the Blind
1800 Johnson St.
Baltimore, MD 21230

National Library Service for the Blind and Physically Handicapped: A federal agency established by an act of Congress as part of the Library of Congress to administer a free national library program of braille and recorded materials for blind and physically handicapped persons. For more information write to:

National Library Service for the Blind and Physically Handicapped
The Library of Congress
1291 Taylor St., NW
Washington, DC 20541

Optacon: A reading machine that converts a visual image into tactile forms that can be felt and identified with one finger. For more information write to:

Telesensory Systems
455 North Bernado Ave.
Mountain View, CA 94043

Page turners: Manual or mechanical devices that enable persons with limited or no use of their hands to read printed material. For more information write to:

National Library Service for the Blind and Physically Handicapped
The Library of Congress
1291 Taylor St., NW
Washington, DC 20541

Perkins brailler: A device for the manual production of braille. For more information write to:

American Printing House for the Blind
1839 Frankfort Ave.
Louisville, KY 40206

Pop-up books: Children's books with sections that pop up and create three-dimensional illustrations.

Portable amplification system: A sound system for hard-of-hearing persons that can be easily carried from one meeting room to another.

Power Pad graphics tablet: A 12-by-12-inch touch-sensitive board that turns an Apple computer into a drawing pad, a communications tool, or an educational tool. For more information write to:

The Handicapped's Source
ComputAbility
101 Route 46 East
Pine Brook, NJ 07058

Print/braille books: Books that combine the complete print book with accompanying braille text embossed on either clear acetate interleaves or directly on the printed page. For more information write to:

National Library Service for the Blind and Physically Handicapped
The Library of Congress
1291 Taylor St., NW
Washington, DC 20542

Pro Term talking terminal program: A talking telecommunication program that runs on the Apple II family of computers and uses

From the original sources we learn that the woodwinds and horns were organized in three groups as "Harmonie" 1, 2, and 3 respectively, of which the first group (of one pair each) was presumably the solo group, the other two groups joining for tutti passages, which in at least one of the original parts are carefully marked to this effect. Solo and tutti passages are distinguished even for the timpani, implying at least two players.

This brings us to the question of the sources. Haydn's autograph does not survive, but three copyists' scores are extant that Brown with good reason characterizes as "authentic" because one of them ("Tonkünstler") was Haydn's conducting score and contains autograph cues. This is the score with solo-tutti indications. A second score ("Estate") contains numerous corrections in Haydn's hand, and a third served as the engraver's copy for the first edition of the full score, published by Haydn himself in 1800. There are, in addition, three sets of parts, which Brown for similar reasons also considers to be authentic.

The original print served as the basis for the Mandyczewski edition, published by Breitkopf & Härtel (1920) and widely used in modern performances. I am in no position to judge how closely this edition agrees with the original print. However, in at least one instance—the articulation of a few passages in No. 3, where Brown (pp. 64–66) shows discrepant patterns in the first edition and in six other authentic sources—we see that Mandyczewski altered the bowing patterns of the original print in order, so it seems, to make them conform to Riemann's theories of upbeat phrasing. This one example makes one wonder in how many other instances the modern editor may have tried to "improve" on Haydn's text.

Interestingly, Haydn did not use the original print for his performances, but rather parts and scores that had undergone a number of emendations. These changes mostly involve refinements of orchestration, such as the addition of bass trombone and contrabassoon in certain passages (listed by Brown, p. 26) or the reorchestration of the famous sunrise passage in the accompanied recitative of No. 13. The listing of a few other such discrepancies is scattered within the chapter. It would have been helpful to have a complete tabulation of those instances where, as Brown puts it, Haydn "kept tinkering with the music" in the course of the early performances.

One of these discrepancies is found in an unusual notation in the parts written by Haydn's personal copyist (and servant) Elssler in measures 4–7 from the "Chaos," as shown below (ex. 16.1). According to Landon, these were the original performance parts, and Brown considers this notation of slur, dynamic *messa di voce* and an apparent staccato mark as "the most vexing interpretive question found in any of the authentic sources."

Example 16.1.   F. J. Haydn, *Creation*, "Chaos," mm. 4–7

Landon interprets this sign as an attempt to fix the exact middle point of the hairpin symbol for a crescendo-decrescendo combination. He speculates that Haydn did not include it in the first edition for fear it might be misunderstood. Brown thinks it might represent a kind of *Luftpause* before the beginning of the diminuendo (p. 32). Neither of these explanations is very convincing. A *Luftpause* within a legato slur is highly unlikely; and as to the middle point of a *messa de voce*, it is rarely a problem and its exactness hardly ever essential. I would like to suggest another answer: the vertical dash was used throughout the eighteenth century, from Bach to Haydn and Mozart, frequently in accentual meaning (to take the place of the > sign that was not yet available until Haydn used it in the last decade of the century). In our example it probably meant a short and sharp accent at the divide between the hairpins. A *sforzando* would have been too violent and too broad; the vertical dash stood for a quick accentuation, produced by a sudden increase of bow pressure followed by its immediate release.

Concerning ornamentation, Brown offers interesting testimonials about Haydn's aversion to unnecessary ornamental additions. Among them is a statement by Albert Christoph Dies (in his *Biographische Nachrichten von Joseph Haydn*, [Vienna, 1810]) relating Haydn's personal report that Mademoiselle Fischer "sang her part with the greatest delicacy and so accurately, that she did not permit herself the least unsuitable addition." And Therese Saal, who sang the soprano part of the *Creation* many times under Haydn's direction, was praised in a journal for her "simple, sincere, and appropriate delivery" and her judicious abstention from runs and embellishments so often interpolated by others.

Some additions are of course needed, such as cadential fermata embellishments. Two of the sets of parts include a few such embellishments penciled in, and they are appropriately brief. Their design is sometimes perfectly fine, but in at least two of the reproduced instances from the "Tonkünstler" parts, they are inelegant and un-Haydnish (in No. 30, mm. 115 and 218, reproduced in Brown, pp. 50 and 51). Brown cautions that these specific parts were used for performances throughout the nineteenth century; the interpolations could have been written at any time during that period. These two, whenever written, are quite certainly not exemplary.

Regarding bowing and articulation, our current concern with consistency and uniformity of bowing was unknown at the time. In fact, prior to World War

II few European orchestras practiced such uniformity until Toscanini enforced it at La Scala. Some conductors actively opposed it, among them Richard Strauss, who believed that better tonal results were achieved when the choice of bowing was left to individual preferences of players. With that in mind, we must not be surprised to hear that "careful editing of the bowings was of little concern to Haydn" (p. 62). Brown tabulates different bowing patterns in seven sources for two passages in No. 3 (referred to above). In view of this lack of uniformity we should realize that exactness of articulation can be important in certain cases and relatively unimportant in others. In a basic legato context, for instance, the exact disposition of the bowings can be a minor matter. Consequently we find in the *Creation,* as in many other classical works, inconsistencies where consistency is immaterial.

Brown's attempts to provide guidelines for such inconsistencies, however, seem neither clear nor convincing. In discussing the discrepant bowings of No. 3 he says, *inter alia:* "Articulatory irregularities with regard to large-dimension repetitions in the case of a more generalized articulation are usually parallel, and if the articulation is more detailed, it must be carefully considered." I have read this sentence several times and still do not understand it.

Another principle formulated, "The repetition of the same pitch in values of a quarter note or larger when occurring over a bar line is often meant to be tied," is questionable and dangerous. While composers, Haydn among them, may often have been nonchalant about the niceties of consistency regarding slurs, ties are another matter altogether: they affect not only melody but also rhythm and are an essential structural element. I cannot remember having seen a case in, say, Bach or Mozart, where a presumably intended tie was not so marked. Naturally, even a genius can stumble, but I would think that one would need telling evidence from either parallel spots or simultaneous parts before introducing an unmarked tie.

Regarding tempo, Brown holds that Haydn's preferences were overall on the fast side. This is perfectly possible, but the evidence Brown cites does not seem to be sufficiently substantive for such a generalized statement. Landon criticizes modern conductors for taking Haydn allegros too fast, and he may have a case. But then there is hardly an aspect of performance practice more difficult to pin down than tempo.

The tempo indications in the *Creation* are remarkably consistent—so Brown affirms—in all sources (a few exceptions are listed on p. 72). He makes a good point about the tempo of the "Representation of the Chaos." Marked Largo ₵, it is usually taken at an extremely dragging pace. Modern conductors are bewildered by the frequent combination in the Classical period of largo or adagio and ₵. It seems incongruous, since many of these adagios cannot reasonably be beaten in two (like, say, the introduction to Mozart's great E♭ Symphony), and consequently the sign is ignored as meaningless. The sign must not be ignored. It did not mean to beat in two, but rather that the piece should be rendered at the fast end of what is still within the character of an adagio or largo (which can be less slow than an adagio). The "Chaos" should be beaten in four, paced as in an andante con moto to give the triplet arpeggio figures a *leggiero* character. The *alla breve* sign thus finds a sensible interpretation.

Brown's monograph contains within its small size a wealth of often fascinating material. It vividly depicts the complexity of the source situation, given the intricate relationship between several sets of parts and several manuscript scores as well as the first printed score, all of which were closely linked to the early performances of the oratorio under Haydn's direction. Considering that some emendations by Haydn, and others of uncertain origin, were entered into certain but not other sources, some before, some after the publication of the first edition, we have the unusually confusing situation of several "authentic" sources that do not agree with one another. We cannot therefore speak of a definitive version. To have analyzed these intricate relationships and laid them out with insightful clarity is the considerable merit of this book, which should be studied by every conductor of this work and by every musicologist engaged in source studies of any kind.

17

Anthony Newman: *Bach and the Baroque*

A review of Anthony Newman's Bach and the Baroque: A Performing Guide to Baroque Music with Special Emphasis on the Music of J. S. Bach *(New York, 1985).*

Anthony Newman is well known as a splendid keyboard performer who can dazzle his audiences with brilliant virtuosic feats. He can, and often does, play faster than perhaps any of his colleagues, and shows occasionally other signs of eccentricity. Yet he is a fine and sensitive musician who has unquestionably a great deal to offer his students. Wishing to share his experience, knowledge and insights with performers at large, he wrote a guidebook to Baroque, and more specifically, Bach performance. As anybody knows, the subject is eminently topical in this age where the search for "authenticity"—whatever that may mean—has become an obsessive pursuit. The subject is also a thicket of controversy and unanswered questions where any new reliable guide would deserve to be enthusiastically welcomed. I regret to say that those who expect this latest entry into the thorny field to provide such reliable guidance will be disappointed.

Not that the book is without merit. A man with Newman's keen intellect and rich performance experience can be expected to have some valuable observations to impart. He does live up to this expectation and we have reason to applaud some helpful contributions. There is, however, a negative side to the picture that, alas, seems to outweigh its positive counterpart. The negative side has various aspects, many of which can be gathered under the label of careless scholarship.

To start on a positive note: at the very outset of the book Newman has some astute things to say about the danger of biases formed by hearing a work,

---

This article originally appeared in *The American Organist* (April 1987): 40–43. Reprinted by permission of the publisher.

or a passage, played in a certain manner and about the ensuing resistance to a performance that deviates from the familiar.

Valuable, too, is the reprint on pages 30–36 of an extended passage from Kirnberger, Bach's student, about the relationship of meter and tempo, including his discussion of circumstances where an alternation of heaviness and lightness applies not just to beats but to whole measures. Newman asks how strong and weak measures can be recognized. In a thought-provoking chapter he expounds a theory that makes some good points and illustrates them with Bach's *Italian Concerto*.

Interesting and valuable is the chapter on the dance, dance music and the suite, written "with Richard Troeger." The chapter deals with the actual steps and movements involved in the various dances. The information is interesting but only of relative pertinence to instrumental dances. Mattheson had already pointed to the considerable differences between actual dances, and "play-dances" and "song-dances." Still, though Bach's dance pieces were often highly stylized and removed from the actual dance, an awareness of the latter's origin is of help in grasping its basic character. The table of dance tempi (derived from metronome-like devices) was taken from the modern studies by Borrel and Sachs. Most of the tempi shown are surprisingly fast.

The chapter on symbolism, written "with Marion Shepp," gives a good summary of the findings of previous writers on both melodic symbolism and on Bach's fascinating, mysterious involvement with the medieval mysticism of number symbolism. Some new items were added to those previously discussed.

The chapter on organ, harpsichord, and clavichord, written with the help of Laurette Goldberg, pleads for tracker-action instruments, discusses specific problems of American organs, and, very interestingly, contrasts the two main types of German Baroque organs, the Schnitger and Silbermann types. It contains helpful remarks on the harpsichord and on lute playing.

Newman takes a very reasonable and courageous stance about playing Bach on the modern piano which, he says, "can bring out lines in a way that the harpsichord cannot" (p. 202). One could add in support of this thought that what matters for Bach is line and not tone color. Had he been concerned about tone color, he would have prescribed registrations for the organ which, as every organist knows, he hardly ever did.

When we turn to the main subject of the book, the problems of performance, there is, unhappily, hardly a chapter that does not invite criticism. So much is questionable that it is impossible to deal with all of it short of writing a whole book. Not that anybody has or will ever have all the answers; and whoever might claim to know how exactly Bach or any other master of the period intended to be interpreted is either touchingly naive or is a charlatan. But it is possible to look at theories on performance and recognize that they are wrongly argued or based on faulty assumptions. And that is where the many weaknesses of this book can be found. For reasons of space alone, I shall limit my comments to a few important subjects.

The chapter on "Tactus, Pulse, Beat and Time Signatures" that contains the mentioned extensive quote from Kirnberger is marred by a near-total confusion of terms and concepts. The introduction of the term "tactus" for Bach and his contemporaries is pointless. It referred, in mensural notation, to a basic beat, a "normal" beat of about M.M. = 70 that was presumably valid as a solid guide-post around 1500 but began to lose its solidity in the course of the sixteenth century, when directors chose and changed the beat according to their sense of the music. In the eighteenth century, the term was long since forgotten. Worse still, Newman first equates "tactus" with pulse and beat: "Tactus, sometimes called pulse or beat" (p. 24), when later in example 22 or 25 he clearly distinguishes between them by explaining the beat as "tactus and a half." Here he meant a faster beat than 70, namely 90–120 (p. 35); hence, I would think, a smaller (minus one-third), not a larger tactus. See also the tabulation of meters, beats and tactus on pages 40–41. It is all totally confusing. A $\frac{3}{4}$ signature with sixteenths as the fastest notes is not necessarily "fast, to very fast" (p. 40). Not to speak of those works where an adagio or largo is marked, there are many unmarked ones in $\frac{3}{4}$ that surely are not lively, such as the organ Passacaglia, the violin Chaconne, the E-Minor Prelude preceding the "Wedge Fugue," the Chorale Prelude *Wir danken dir, Herr Jesu Christ* (BWV 623) and many others.

The ideas expressed in the chapter on "Irregular Beat Alternations" are highly suspect. When Bach divides a virtuoso passage between the two hands and indicates the division by patterns of beaming, as for instance in measures 65–67 of the *Chromatic Fantasy* (see Newman's ex. 83) Newman sees in these beaming patterns a clue to phrasing and accentuation when in fact they were a sort of silent fingering that served to facilitate the execution, but were not meant to be heard. In fact, the suggested execution that phrases according to recurring melodic designs weakens the passages by making ordinary what is extraordinary: the power of passages like these lies in their very irregularity, in the very conflict of melodic design and rhythmic disposition that gives the repeated melodic figure each time a new physiognomy. This is true of example 82 from the D-Minor Concerto, and more so of example 83 from the *Chromatic Fantasy*. To melodically regularize such passages amounts to a triumph of pedantry over poetic imagination.

When we come to questions of inequality, of fingerings, of overdotting, the so-called French overture style and of ornamentation, I have to overcome my repugnance to tooting my own horn. I have written at length on these matters and have taken issue with the very authorities that Newman relies on. I believe that without undue arrogance I can say that an author dealing with these questions with a scholarly pretense ought to have acquainted himself with my pertinent writings on these subjects as well as with David Fuller's articles in the *The*

New Grove. In 1985 it was not sufficient any more to see in Sol Babitz, Michael Collins and John O'Donnell the ultimate authorities without being guilty of incomplete research. (For several years my main writings on matters of rhythm have been conveniently available in *Essays in Performance Practice*.)

In the chapter on "Inequality and Note Holding," Newman offers a variation on Babitz's theme song that the old keyboard fingerings produced an involuntary unevenness and that therefore such unevenness must have been intended by the composer. The argument is fallacious since any involuntary unevenness is due to technical defect, not to artistic intent. (I have dealt with this question in *Essays*, pages 42–48, and plan in the near future to return to the subject in greater detail.) Newman contends that fast playing of a string of notes on the piano produces dynamic, but not rhythmic inequality; on the harpsichord, by contrast, "rhythmic unevenness of adjacent notes . . . independent of the technical proficiency of the performer" (p. 104). This does not have to be so. Such unintended inequality is, here too, simply a matter of defective skill and Newman would be the first to be able to play fast notes with perfect equality. Also it makes little sense that a performer who can play fast notes on the piano with rhythmic equality should be unable to do so on the organ or harpsichord. The very idea that virtuoso passages like, say, the grandiose sweep of measures 3–8 in the G-Minor Fantasia and Fugue are to be rendered as a series of uneven pairs of notes is nothing short of grotesque.

Newman further confuses matters by mixing five different kinds of inequality under one heading. Apart from unevenness caused by technical incompetence (the would-be "Scotch snaps") he lists four more: as second type he presents Caccini's famous illustration of rubato singing (from 1602), whereby equally written notes are rhythmically manipulated in various manners, while remaining within the beat. There is neither any regularity nor any convention involved; the rhythmic freedoms are arbitrarily chosen by artistic judgment.

Third is the genuine convention of the French *notes inégales* which regularizes inequality according to meter—note-value relationships (e.g., eighth notes in 3-meter, sixteenth notes in C meter for passages that move predominantly stepwise). In such contexts the long-short, generally mild unevenness came close to a stylistic requirement. Incidentally, Newman's example 121 from "Dom Bedos" (the actual writer was Père Engramelle) is incorrect: the second pair of eighth notes is played like the first, not at half its duration. Incorrect too is his statement that sixteenths or eighths are uneven in C meter: after Nivers in 1665, all following writers insist that eighths in C are always strictly even. Moreover it is not true that "Bedos" and Couperin specifically state that dissonant pairs on a "good" beat should be played short-long (p. 107). Neither says anything to that effect. Couperin simply has a notational symbol: a dot over the second of two notes under a slur that indicates its emphasis. (He quit using it after the second book of clavecin pieces.) It does not apply to notes not so marked and Engramelle (including "Bedos") makes no mention of short-long inequality.

Fourth, Newman refers to several writers who suggest that the first note under a slur is to be slightly lengthened. He is mistaken in saying that Leopold Mozart excepted from this rule notes that are in a rhythmically weak position. On the contrary, among the illustrations of contexts for this rule Mozart shows (chap. 7, pt. 2, par. 5) no fewer than nine where the respective notes fall on a subdivision of the beat, the weakest possible placement in the measure.

Fifth, the author offers up a whole series of alleged proofs for inequality in Bach that have been presented by others several times before but are by now damaged goods: I am confident to have disposed of their evidence value many years ago. There is no point in repeating all the arguments, and I shall limit myself to declaring that the would-be evidence of example 123 from the B-Minor Mass (Domine Deus), example 125 from the *Trauerode*, example 134 from the Magnificat and example 135 from the D-Minor Clavier Concerto is strictly chimerical, while referring to my *Essays,* pages 48–53 and 61–64. Readers interested in the matter of uneven notes might wish to read my whole chapters 3, 4 and 5. My advice would be not to apply inequality to Bach, Handel, the German organists, nor to the Italians. Limit a mild long-short inequality in its proper context to French masters only.

The chapters on dotted notes and the overture style suffer from the same failure to keep abreast of scholarly developments. As main proof for what is commonly called the French overture style Newman adduces again a piece of shopworn evidence: the comparison of the two versions of Bach's French Over-ture in C Minor and in B Minor (Newman, exx. 140 and 143). Some fine scholars had fallen into the trap before by seeing in the later, rhythmically sharpened B-minor version an "orthographic variant" of the C-minor that is supposed to sound exactly the same. The theory is untenable. B minor is, after all, not an "orthographic variant" of C minor and Bach, who revised countless of his works, had a perfect right to choose another rhythm along with another key. A careful measure-by-measure analysis of the two versions reveals the utter absurdity of the theory of identity. The B-minor version is as little an "orthogra-phic variant" of the C-minor one as the *Leonora* Overture No. 3 is of *Leonora* No. 2. With it this "proof" for the "overture style" vanishes into thin air. (For a thorough discussion of the overture style see in my *Essays,* chaps. 6–10 and especially 10.) *Do not overdot the E-flat Prelude of* Clavierübung *III!*

The chapter of triplets is perhaps the most misleading of all. It starts inauspiciously with a quote from a Mr. Banner, an obscure Paduan organist about whose musical competence nothing is known. Michael Collins discovered a manuscript treatise of his in which he delivers himself of the opinion that two notes against three is "one of the most forbidden musical situations." Like Collins before him, Newman accepts Banner as supreme arbiter of musical taste for his age, and his stern verdict as binding law. Thus Newman writes (p. 125) that "two against three ... did not belong to the musical vocabulary of the period." The statement is simply not true. Binary-ternary conflicts never ceased to occur, and to be intended, in the music of the last four or five hundred years. However, the question of both triplets and rhythmic conflicts is complicated and certainly not answerable with the help of Banner's Law. Triplets were always meant to be rendered literally, though at all times to the present performers, including some famous virtuosi, often squared them when it was easier to do so. As to rhythmic conflicts, they were often meant to be rendered as written, but in Bach's time, due mostly to notational deficiencies, there were instances where an assimilation was sometimes certainly, sometimes probably, intended. Such assimilation took place always from binary to ternary rhythms, not the other way around. In an attempt to sort out these complexities I have written an essay that by now has come out in the sixth volume of the *Music Forum* and is reprinted here as chapter 3. For cases of intended conflict I can refer here only to one irrefutable example, the Chorale from Bach's Cantata No. 105. Here no master juggler, no magician can resolve the magnificent clash of twos against threes. There are many more instances of such intended clashes; Bach clearly did not bow to the authority of Banner's Law.

Newman, leaning on Collins, affirms that under certain circumstances triplets, dactyls and anapests can be used interchangeably, meaning that Bach often wrote a triplet when he meant a dactyl or anapest and vice versa, even where no rhythmic clash might serve as pretext for such manipulation. Are we truly to assume that Bach played witless teasing games with his performers, expecting to get a good laugh at those who did not see through such masquerade? Newman does not limit such masquerades to three-note figures. In his examples 145 and 146 he demonstrates how Bach's binary gigues from the first French Suite and the fifth Partita and even the horn call at the opening of the first Brandenburg Concerto are to be ternarized. All these suggestions are misjudgments. Binary gigues are minorities in the eighteenth century, but they have a venerable ancestry, going back to English virginalists, French lutenists (the Gautiers among others), masters like Froberger, Schmelzer, Biber, Georg Muffat, Poglietti, and many others who used binary next to ternary designs. Why should not Bach do so, he who took great freedoms with dances, many of which are much more "in the spirit of ... " or "in the tempo of ..." than in conformance with the textbook types. There is no need to sanitize his binary gigues by pressing them with clumsy force into a ternary mold. Bach knew what he wanted and wrote it out accordingly.

Then in order, maybe, to compensate the binary realm for its losses to ternary aggression, Newman allows the reverse operation: in the fifth Brandenburg Concerto at the first entrance of the soloists (ex. 148), the triplets in the right hand of the clavier set in measure 10 against binary sixteenth notes in the left should be played as anapests, and so no doubt the analogous triplets in violin and flute in measures 14–16—all this in order to comply with Banner's Law! So far I have luckily been spared in concert such an all-binary treat.

There are many more statements and discussions in the book that invite critical comment but I think I have made my point; the book contains some valuable sections but those parts that deal with interpretation are severely flawed by incomplete research and careless documentation. It cannot be recommended as a guide to historical performance.

18

Raymond H. Haggh: Translation of Türk's
Klavierschule

A review of the School of Clavier Playing (Klavierschule) *by Daniel Gottlob Türk. Translated and with introduction and notes by Raymond H. Haggh (Lincoln and London: University of Nebraska Press, 1982).*

One of the many manifestations of the current intense interest in historical performance is the growing list of old treatises that are available in English translation. Türk's voluminous (over 400 pages in the original) *Klavierschule* in its first edition of 1789 is a valuable addition to this list, but should be viewed from the perspective of what it is and what it is not. Basically, the book is a review of North German mid-eighteenth-century theoretical thought on performance and keyboard technique, extended to encyclopedic length by two factors: 1) Türk's compulsive urge to pursue every question to the last detail (even Professor Haggh admits to a pedantic streak in his author), and 2) his remarkable and quite innovative referral to, and discussion of, what previous writers have said on a subject. In this respect it is certainly the most scholarly of all the major eighteenth-century tracts on performance.

Concerning his own ideas, his indebtedness is greatest to C. P. E. Bach and Marpurg, but mostly to the former. Notably the chapters on fingering and the "essential ornaments" are by and large elaborations of what these two authors had to say. As to fingerings, he admits—as does C. P. E. Bach—besides the modern scale pattern, the older manner of crossing over of fingers other than the thumb. In matters of ornaments Türk is, if possible, more severe still about their regimentation than Philipp Emanuel (though he does follow Marpurg in admitting *Nachschläge*).

The most valuable, least derivative, and least dated chapters are the last

This article originally appeared in *The American Recorder* (November 1983). Reprinted by permission of the publisher.

two, on extemporaneous ornamentation and execution. There we find very fine discussions of fermata embellishments and cadenzas, and valuable remarks on the problems of phrasing. But for the rest, this is a retrospective work, a fact made apparent almost immediately by the focus not on the fortepiano, not even the harpsichord, but the *clavichord,* which at the time of publication was on the verge of extinction.

From all this we can gather what the book, its date notwithstanding, is emphatically not: it is not a guide to Mozart and Haydn performance (with the possible exception of the last two chapters). If we accept this limitation, its availability in English is to be warmly welcomed.

The translation was a true labor of love. It was done over a period of twelve years, during which Professor Haggh, besides grappling with an old-fashioned vocabulary, did a huge amount of research to provide the text with a thorough underpinning of references to both old and new writers. Embodied in back notes that are intermingled with—but clearly distinguished from—Türk's own, these annotations offer helpful amplifications as well as frequent résumés of theoretical thought on various problems discussed in the text. They greatly enhance the value and usefulness of the publication.

The prose translation is, on the whole, very satisfactory and reads well. I do not claim to have made a word-by-word comparison; I limited myself to some spot checks whenever a passage seemed questionable. In a few of these cases I found minor lapses, where the translator tripped over a hurdle of antiquated German. A single example will have to do. At the beginning of chapter 3, Türk explains why he devotes a whole chapter to the appoggiatura. He writes: "Da es aber Vorschläge von sehr verschiedener Dauer etc. giebt, so dass eine etwas ausführliche Anzeige erfordert wird," which is rendered: "But since appoggiaturas are of very differing durations and require a very detailed notation. . . ." I checked this sentence because I found it confusing. A more precise rendition would be: "But since appoggiaturas are of very differing durations, etc. [the 'etc.' implying additional problems], they call for a somewhat detailed explanation . . ." (hence the devotion of a whole chapter).

Such are minor flaws within a frame of overall competence. What I found more disturbing are infelicitous translations of certain terms. One that bothered me (and maybe should not have) is the unorthodox subdivision of chapters into "parts" (Türk's *Abschnitte*), when traditionally parts are the larger, chapters the smaller units of a book. "Section" would have been a better, and more literal, rendition.

"Termination" for *Nachschlag* is not a happy choice, because the term so pointedly implies an ending, whereas in the overwhelming majority of cases a *Nachschlag* is a connective grace that does not end a phrase but leads into another melody note. Haggh derived the term from Edward Reilly's splendid translation of Quantz, where it is used to denote the suffix of a trill. In that case it is not an ideal choice either, but it is less confusing because the focus is on the way a trill is ended; such focus is absent in all other applications, as shown, for instance, in every example in chapter 3, part 4 of Türk. The reader is advised to substitute mentally the term *Nachschlag* for all occurrences of "termination." (Walter Emery, in his book on Bach's ornaments, naturalized the term, using "nachschlags" as plural, because he found no proper equivalent for it.)

Infelicitous, too, is the rendition of *Vorhalt* as "suspension." Following the example of other theorists (among them Petri), Türk uses this term to designate the long appoggiatura (*veränderliche Vorschlag*). Now a long appoggiatura *that is prepared* and resolves stepwise has the harmonic function of a suspension (though a suspension in the narrower sense is tied over the beat), hence the term would be acceptable in such contexts. But often the appoggiatura enters unprepared (see the start of the example on p. 205 in chap. 15), in which case the term is improper and misleading. "Long appoggiatura" or, to stay with Türk's (and C. P. E. Bach's) terminology, "variable appoggiatura," would have been the better choice.

In another instance, what would seem to be the obvious translation is not an advisable one. Following the example of Kirnberger and his student Schulz, Türk, in his discussion of phrasing, uses the term "Rhythmus" to designate a not clearly specified subdivision of a melody (see on this Haggh's notes 19 and 21 on pp. 506ff.). Understandably, Haggh renders "Rhythmus" as "rhythm." But the concept of rhythm, as it is commonly applied today, is complicated enough that it is ill-advised to introduce a new meaning foreign to its present usage. "Melodic unit" or "phrase subdivision" might have been preferable.

Professor Haggh gives good reasons why he used the first edition, and not the enlarged second one of 1802, for his translation. Still, those who value Türk as theorist would have welcomed an appendix containing some of the more important additions of the later version, in which he makes a number of new references to Haydn and Mozart.

The index, like Türk's, is limited to terms and common expressions. In view of the many theorists mentioned in the notes of both Türk and Professor Haggh, an index of names would have been useful.

The book is well produced (though, surprisingly, with a ragged right margin), and the music examples are well printed. Of the few misprints I found, I want to mention only one because it is misleading. In music example (e) on page 275 the turn is printed with four equal, small thirty-second notes, when the first three should have four, and the fourth note only two, beams.

I do not wish the reservations expressed in this review to obscure the undeniable fact that this translation represents a major scholarly achievement, and that the book belongs in the libraries of all graduate schools.

Index

Academy of Ancient Music, 12
Academy of St.-Martin-in-the Fields, 12
Accent, 215, 218. *See also* Grace note; *Nach-schlag; Port de voix; Vorschlag*
Acciaccatura, 218
Accompaniment, interpretation of, 19, 222–23
Adlung, Jacob: on the history of music, 4
Agogic accents, and *notes inégales*, 66, 69, 74, 75
Agricola, Johann Friedrich: and *galant* style, 20; and J. S. Bach's obituary, 196; on parallels in ornaments, 132; on synchronizing triplets with dotted notes, 45; theoretical writings applied to other composers, 20
Agricola, Martin: on sesquialtera, 40
Aldrich, Putnam: and J. S. Bach's keyboard ornaments, 125; and ornament tables, 127; and performance practice, 22
American Society of Ancient Instruments, 14
Amsterdam Baroque Orchestra, 13
Anglebert, Jean Henri d': Dolmetsch on, 20; keyboard works of, 27; ornamentation, 130, 131, 137; ornament tables, 129, 134
Appoggiatura, 127, 132–33, 139, 151, 202, 204, 244, 245; beat placement, 126–27, 130; improvisation of, 178; in Mozart, 150–51, 166, 184–91; in Vivaldi, 180–81, 183; length of, 139–43, 147–50, 180–81, 184–86, 244; symbolized, 140, 181; written out, 140, 166, 183. *See also Vorschlag*
Appoggiatura trill, 114, 127, 179–81, 183, 184–86, 188–90, 216
Aria, history of the term, 205
Arpeggio: and articulation, 107, 108–9; beat placement, 95, 107, 108–9, 114, 118, 127, 163–64; and harmony, 127; and neighbor note principle, 126; symbolized, 130, 164; written out, 107, 164

Articulation: and dotted rhythms, 74; and historical performance techniques, 29; idiomatic considerations, 80; in early music, 23–24, 26, 29, 170, 233; and *notes inégales*, 74; and ornamentation, 105–10, 126, 127–28, 136–37; and phrasing, 112–13; relative importance of, 26, 78, 79, 232–33
Aston Magna Foundtion, 15
Authenticity (in architecture), 8–9
Authenticity (in musical performance): 3–4, 5, 7–16, 25–26, 169–70; and historical vs. musical factors, 28–30; nature of, 17–24, 169–70, 229; and numbers of performers, 170, 230–31; and ornamentation, 123–25; and scholarship, 17–18, 19–24, 170–71, 229, 235–36, 243; and seating arrangements of performers, 239–31; and use of vibrato, 169–170, 171–73. *See also* Articulation; Early music; Expression; Historical instruments; Ornamentation; Performance practice; Phrasing; Rhythm; Tempo
Azaïs, Pierre-Hyacinthe: and slide notation, 138

Babitz, Sol: on *notes inégales*, 65, 68; on uneven notes and keyboard fingerings, 238
Bach, Anna Magdalena, notebook for, 205–6, 208n.6
Bach, C. P. E.: appoggiatura, 133, 139, 141, 245; and *galant* style, 20, 133 and J. S. Bach's obituary, 196; and ornamentation, 94–95, 98–99, 104, 132, 184; and parallels, 132; slide, 138; theoretical writings applied to other composers, 20–21, 94–95, 141, 151, 184–85; trill, 134; turn, 110
Bach, Johann Sebastian: and Agricola, 20; appoggiatura, 130–31, 132–33, 137, 202, 204; articulation, 23–24, 79, 80, 83n.4,

137, 233–34; and Baroque style, 195, 197, 203, 206–7, 221; binary rhythms, 18, 45–57, 58–60, 62n.13, 239–41; compared to Handel, 221; and concerto style, 196–97, 198–99, 223; dance pieces, 236; dotted rhythms, 18, 45, 56–60, 86, 238–39; dynamics, 19; editions and transcriptions of, 7, 9; expression, 19; and feminine cadences, 201, 202; French influences, 129–30, 137, 202; and French overture style, 239; and *galant* style, 195, 197–205, 206–7; German influences, 129–30, 135–36, 196–97; instrumentation, 19; interpretation of accompaniment, 19, 222–23, 225; Italian influences, 129–30, 196, 198, 222–23; keyboard works, 15, 27, 78, 128–30, 136–37, 236; and Leipzig Collegium Musicum, 10; Lombard rhythms, 203; meter, 237; mordent, 130, 204; *Nachschlag*, 244–45; notation inconsistencies, 77–79, 83n.4; *notes inégales*, 21, 65, 68, 74, 75; and numbers of performers, 170; obituary of, 196; organ works, 27, 236; ornament table, 124, 133–34, 151; ornamentation, 19, 94, 124–26, 128–30, 132, 204–5, 244–45; parallels in, 132, 200–201, 202, 204; performed by early music organizations, 12–14; phrasing, 19, 237; pitch, 26; playing the fortepiano in 1733, 27; *port de voix*, 204; and Quantz, 20, 139; revival of interest in, 7; rhythmic clash vs. assimilation, 38, 44–61, 62n.13, 90n.6, 224, 239–40; slide, 129–30, 137–38; style of, 195–205, 206–7; symbolism in, 236; tempo, 18–19, 236, 237; tone color, 27, 170, 236; trill, 113, 118, 129, 133–34, 135–37, 204; triplets, 37, 45–60, 62n.13, 201, 202, 239–41; uneven notes, 238–39; and variation form, 205; *Vorschlag*, 127, 129, 130–33, 137

Works
—*Art of the Fugue*, 132, 197
—Brandenburg Concertos: No. 1, 48, 49, 240; No. 2, 199; No. 5, 57, 58, 79, 83n.4, 240–41
—Canonic Variations, 197
—Cantatas: No. 4, 201; No. 21, 199; No. 51, 198–99; No. 75, 47, 48; No. 80, 201; No. 84, 80; No. 91, 86; No. 105, 45–47, 240; No. 107, 83n.4; No. 110, 58–59; No. 119, 90n.6; No. 140, 198; No. 147, 56–57; No. 172, 199; No. 210, 200; No. 211 ("Coffee"), 200; No. 212 ("Peasant"), 200

—"Cappriccio sopra la lontananza," 202
—*Chromatic Fantasy*, 9, 199, 237
—Clavier Concertos: D Minor, 237, 239; E Major, 47–48
—*Clavierbüchlein für Anna Magdalena Bach*, 59
—*Clavierübung* III: E♭ Prelude, 239
—Easter Oratorio, 47–48
—Fantasia and Fugue, G Minor, 238
—French Overtures: B Minor, 239; C Minor, 239
—French Suites: No. 1, 240
—Goldberg Variations, 195, 197, 203–4, 205–6
—*Italian Concerto*, 236
—Magnificat, 239
—Mass in B Minor, 26, 197, 198, 200–202, 203, 239
—*Musical Offering*, 51, 197, 206–7
—Organ Chorale, *Christ lag in Todes Banden*, 52
—Organ Sonata in D Minor, 51
—*Orgelbüchlein: Herr Gott, nun schleuss den Himmel auf*, 52; *In dulci jubilo*, 53–56; *Jesus Christus, unser Heiland*, 59; *O Mensch, bewein' dein Sünde gross*, 136–37
—Partitas: No. 5, G Major, 240; No. 6, E Minor, 59–60
—*St. Matthew Passion*, 224
—*Trauerode*, 239
—Violin and Harpsichord Sonatas, 221, 222; No. 1, B Minor, 223; No. 2, A Major, 223–24; No. 3, E Major, 49–50, 224; No. 4, C Minor, 57, 224; No. 5, F Minor, 224–25; No. 6, G Major, 225
—*The Well-Tempered Clavier*, 6, 7, 26, 37
Bach, Wilhelm Friedemann: 124; notebook for, 205
Bach Ensemble, 15
Bacilly, Bénigne de: and *notes inégales*, 71
Badura-Skoda, Eva, 22, 27, 150, 151, 158–59
Badura-Skoda, Paul, 22, 150, 151, 158–59
Balancement, 172
Banchetto Musicale, 15
Banchieri, Adriano: cited by Collins, 39; on sesquialtera, 52, 61; on triplets, 37
Banner, Giannantonio: on binary-ternary conflicts, 239–40
Barnett, Dene: on inconsistencies in notation, 77–78, 79
Baroque style, 195–97, 203, 206–7
Bassoon music, interpretation of ornamentation in, 175–92
Battishill, Jonathan: and keyboard transcriptions of Handel's overtures, 81–82

BBC, 12
Becker, Carl Ferdinand, 4
Beethoven, Ludwig van: 73, 89–90n.5; and application of French overture style, 22; inclusion in early music movement, 3; ornamentation, 121; playing Bach, 7; performed by early music organizations, 12–14; trill, 113, 166; and variation form, 208n.7
  Works
    —Diabelli Variations, 204
    —*Leonora* Overtures Nos. 2–3, 239
    —"Spring" Sonata, 73
    —Symphony No. 7, 89–90n.5
Belesta, Mercadier de: on *notes inégales*, 72
Bene, Adriana Ferrarese del. *See* Ferrarese del Bene, Adriana
Beringer, Maternus, 42
Berlioz, Hector, 3, 12
Bernhard, Christoph, 135
Berwald, Johan, 230
Beyer, Johann Samuel, 135
Biber, Heinrich Ignaz Franz, 203, 240
Binary rhythms: notation for: 18, 35; performance problems, 36; vs. ternary rhythms, *See* Hemiol(i)a; Rhythmic clash vs. assimilation; Sesquialtera proportion; Triplets
Binkley, Thomas, 13
Bodky, Erwin, 15
Boehm, Georg, 129, 136
Bordes, Charles, 9
Bordoni, Faustina, 203
Borrel, Eugène, 236
Boston Camerata, 15
Boston Handel and Haydn Society, 14
Boston Society of Ancient Instruments, 14–15
Bourgeois, Loys, and evolution of *notes inégales*, 67–68, 69, 70
Bowing patterns, 231, 232–33. *See also* Articulation
Brahms, Johannes, 208n.7
Brijon, C. R., 135
Britten, Benjamin, 208n.7
Brown, A. Peter: on performing Haydn's *Creation*, 229–34; on tempo in Haydn, 233–34
Brown, Howard M., 6, 11
Brüggen, Frans, 13, 28
Bruhns, Nicolaus, 129, 196
Buelow, George J., 202
Buelow, Hans von, 9
Bull, John, 44
Bustard, Clarke, 16n.3
Buxtehude, Dietrich, 129, 136, 196
Byrt, John: on *notes inégales*, 65

Caccini, Giulio: 5; and Lombard rhythms, 203; and rhythmic freedom, 70; and rubato singing, 238
Cadenzas: 175, 184, 191, 244; and improvisation, 122, 155–56, 160
Calvisius, Sethus, 43–44
Cape, Safford, 11
Capella Antiqua (Munich), 13
Capella Coloniensis, 13
Capirola, Vicenzo: trill symbols, 123
Carissimi, Giacomo, 8; on hemiolia, 43; on triplets, 37; use of "L'Homme armé," 5
Casadesus, Henri, 9
Cavalieri, Emilio de, 5
Chaconne, vs. passacaglia, 212
Chambonnières, Jacques Champion de, 134
La Chapelle Royale, 13
Chaumont, Lambert, 131, 135
Chopin, Frédéric, 3, 208n.7
Choquel, Henri-Louis: on *notes inégales*, 71–72
Chrysander, Friedrich, 7–8
Circolo mezzo, 217
Clavichord, 10, 69, 236, 244
Clocks, musical. *See* Musical clocks
Collegium Aureum, 13–14
Collegium Musicum: 3, 15; in Chicago, 14; in Freiburg, 11; in Leipzig, 10; at Yale, 14
Collegium Vocale (Ghent), 13
Collins, Michael: 22, 238; application of theoretical treatises, 37–38, 39–41, 42, 61–62; on blackened notes, 39, 40; on hemiolia, 38–39, 44, 61; and *notes inégales*, 65, 68; on sesquialtera proportion, 38–39, 61; on triplets, 37, 61–62, 62n.13, 239
Coloraturas. *See* Ornamentation, melismatic
Concentus Musicus, 14
Concerto Amsterdam, 13
Conducting, 209, 212–13, 229–31
Corelli, Arcangelo: 8; Christmas Concerto, 202; influence on Handel, 222; and variation form, 205
Couperin, François: 124; Allemande *La majestueuse*, 134; articulation, 23; Dolmetsch on, 8; editions of, 8; mordent, 134; and *notes inégales*, 71; ornament tables of, 129, 134–35; and ornamentation, 128, 129; slide, 138; trill, 116, 134; use of the harpsichord, 27, 29
Crappius, Andreas, 43–44
Crüger, Johann; on hemiolia, 43; on sesquialtera proportions, 43; on triplets, 43
Crusius, Johannes, 43–44
Czerny, Carl, 7

Dadelsen, Georg von, 205–6
D'Agincourt, François, 138
Dandrieu, François, 135
Dart, Thurston: 11, 12, 23; on French overture style, 22, 80–81; and historical instruments, 11; and interpretation of early music, 12, 22; on pitch-levels, 22, 23
Davis, Colin, 12
Dechaume, Antoine Geoffroy-. *See* Geoffroy-Dechaume, Antoine
del Bene, Adriana Ferrarese. *See* Ferrarese del Bene, Adriana
Denis, Pierre, 138
Denkmäler der Tonkunst, 8
Des Prez, Josquin, 6, 196
Deutsche Vereinigung für alte Musik, 10
Diction, and rhythmic interpretation, 86–87, 142–43
Dies, Albert Christoph, 232
Dieupart, Charles, 129, 130, 134
D'Indy, Vincent, 9
Döbereiner, Christoph, 10
Dolmetsch, Arnold: 11, 12, 23; and historical instruments, 10, 19–20; and interpretation of early music, 10, 19–22; on *notes inégales,* 21, 68; on over-dotted rhythms, 21; use of historical treatises, 20–21; use of ornament tables, 21
Donington, Robert: and common practice, 22, 80–81; on French overture style, 22; and interpretation of early music, 12, 22; and J. S. Bach's keyboard ornaments, 125; on *notes inégales,* 22, 65, 68, 73, 74; use of ornament tables, 22; on vibrato, 23
Dotted rhythms: French use of, 74–75; interpretation of, 18, 21, 82–83, 85–86, 238–39; and *notes inégales,* 66, 69–75; synchronized with triplets, 45, 57–60; and tempo, 86. *See also* French overture style; *Pointer*
Dufay, Guillaume, 6
Durchang, 218. *See also Nachschlag*
Duval, L'Abbé: on *notes inégales,* 71
Dynamics: in early music, 19, 24; and fortepiano, 211; and ornamentation, 95–96, 105–6, 107, 110; relative importance of, 26, 78

Early music: expanding definition of, 3–4; interpretation of, 10, 12, 18, 30; performance of, 3–4, 169–71, 223–24; revival of interest in, 3–4, 6–16, 19, 30, 243; and scholarship, 3–4, 7–8, 10–12, 18–22, 29–30, 229, 243. *See also* Authenticity

(in music performance); Historical instruments; Performance practice; names of individual countries and performers of early music
Eingänge, 122, 158–59, 184, 187, 191–92
Elsmann, Heinrich, 42
Elssler, Johann, 231
Emery, Walter, 133, 245
English Baroque Soloists, 12
English Concert, 12
Engramelle, Marie-Dominique-Joseph: on *notes inégales,* 72, 238–39; on trill, 135
L'Estro Armonico, 12

Faber, Gregorius, 40
Faber, Heinrich, 42
Falck, Georg, 135
Farncomb, Charles, 12
Faustina. *See* Bordoni, Faustina
Feder, Georg: and Haydn ornament, 97
Ferguson, Faye, 125, 139–53; on appoggiaturas in Mozart, 139–44, 147–51, 166; and parallels, 150; on synchronization of voice and accompaniment in Mozart, 141–44, 151; on turns in Mozart, 146–48; and Mozart's autograph Index, 145; and Mozart's ornament symbols, 145–46, 152–53n.16
Fermata embellishments, 158–59, 160–63, 232, 244
Ferrarese del Bene, Adriana, 161
Feyertag, Moritz, 135
Figured bass, 221–22
Finck, Hermann: on sesquialtera, 41, 42; on ornamentation, 215; on parallels, 132, 150; on triplets, 42
Fingerings, keyboard: 238, 243; and phrasing, 237; and uneven notes, 69, 238
Fischer, Johann Kaspar, 129
Fischer, Therese, 232
Fitzwilliam Virginal Book, 44
Flute, 23
Fortepiano, 211
France: and interest in historical music, 6–7
French overture style: 14, 22, 77, 81, 85, 237, 239; applied to Baroque performance practice, 21, 22; and overdotting, 77, 85; and synchronization, 77, 80, 85, 88, 89; and upbeat contraction, 77, 80, 85–87. *See also* Dotted rhythms
Frescobaldi, Girolamo: binary-ternary cross-rhythms, 44; influence on J. S. Bach, 197; and Lombard rhythms, 203; and rhythmic freedom, 70; Toccatas (1637), 44; transcribed by J. S. Bach, 129; trill, 136

Friderici, Daniel: on sesquialtera proportions, 43; on triplets, 37
Froberger, Johann Jacob, 129, 136, 240
Fuhrmann, Martin Heinrich, 135
Fuller, Albert, 15
Fuller, David: 237; on *notes inégales,* 65–66, 67–69, 72, 74–75

Gaffurius, Franchinus, 39
Galant style: 20–21, 195–204, 206–7; and Italian *opera buffa,* 195, 198, 297
Galilei, Vincenzo, 5
Galpin Society Journal, 11
Ganassi, Silvestro: and Lombard rhythms, 203; on parallels, 132; trill symbols, 123
Gardiner, John Eliot, 12
Gasparini, Francesco, 218
Gastoldi, Giovanni Giacomo, 196
Gautier (also Gaultier), Ennemond ("Le Vieux") and Denis ("Le Jeune"), 240
Gengenbach, Nicolaus, 42
Geoffroy-Dechaume, Antoine: on ornament tables, 124; and performance practice, 22
Gerber, Heinrich Nicolaus, 131
Gerlach, Sonja, 115
Germany, early music performance in, 3, 10–11, 13–14
Gesius, Bartholomäus, 43
Gibbons, John, 28
Gigault, Nicolas, 131
Glareanus, Henricus, 39
Gluck, Christoph Willibald, 7
Göbel, Reinhard, 14
Goldberg, Laurette, 236
Goodman, Roy, 12, 13
Grace note: 122, 151; improvisation of, 178; in Mozart, 150–51, 166, 186, 187–88, 189; in Vivaldi, 180–82. *See also Nachschlag, Vorschlag, Zwischenschlag*
Grace-note trill, 134–35
Grassi, Bartolomeo, 44
Graun, Carl Heinrich: ornamentation, 130
Graun, Johann Gottlieb: ornamentation, 130
Graupner, Christoph: ornamentaton, 130, 212
Greenberg, Noah, 14–15
Grigny, Nicolas de, 129, 131, 135, 138
Groppo, 217
Gurlitt, Wilibald, 11

Haas, Karl, 12
Hagen, Oskar, 13
Haggh, Raymond H.: translation of Türk, 243–45
Handel, George Frideric: and Baroque style, 195, 221; compared to J. S. Bach, 221; and diction, 86–87; and Dolmetsch, 20,

21; dotted rhythms, 81–83, 85–89; editions and transcriptions of, 7–8, 82, 85, 89, 222; French overture style, 80–81, 85; and improvisation, 128, 222; instrumental works, 6; Italian influence, 222; notation inconsistencies, 77–78, 81–82; *notes inégales,* 21, 68, 73, 75; operas, 6, 12, 13; oratorios, 6, 8, 12; overtures, 81–82, 85; performed by early music organizations, 8, 12; rhythmic alterations, 81–82, 85; and tone color, 27
Works
—*Alexander's Feast,* 8
—*Messiah,* 8, 21, 82, 85, 86–89
—*Ode to St. Cecilia,* 8
—*Riccardo I,* 82
—Sonata, op. 1, no. 1, 73
—Violin and Harpsichord Sonatas: 221–22; No. 1, A Major, 222; No. 6, D Major, 222
Handel Opera Society, 12
Handschin, Jacques, 25
Hanover Band, 12, 13
Harnoncourt, Nikolaus, 14, 24, 170
Harpsichord, 9–10, 15, 27, 29, 212, 236, 238
Hase, Wolfgang, 42
Haydn, Joseph, 7, 12, 68: accent marks, 232; arpeggio, 95–97, 107–9, 114, 118; articulation markings, 105–10, 112–13, 232–33; and C. P. E. Bach, 20–21, 94–95; bowing patterns in, 231, 232–33; cadenzas, 122; as conductor, 229–30, 234; dynamic markings, 95–96, 105–6, 107, 110; editions of, 115, 231–33, 234; *Eingänge,* 122; fermata embellishments, 232; and Haydn ornament, 94, 97–104, 118; and improvisation, 122; inclusion in early music movement, 3; little notes, 97, 99–100, 106–11, 116–17; mordent, 97, 99, 101, 103, 105, 114, 115–16, 118, 119; and musical clocks, 105, 114–19; notation inconsistencies, 77–78, 231–33, 234; ornamentatoin, 93–105, 113–19, 122, 232; performance conditions of, 229–31; performed by early music organizatoins, 12; phrasing, 112–13; portamento, 95–96; *Schneller,* 103; slide, 95–96, 114, 118; tempos in, 233–34; and Türk, 20–21, 245; trill, 93, 100–103, 105–6, 113–19; turn, 94, 97–100, 105, 109–19; *Vorschlag,* 94, 95, 105–6, 118, 179
Works
—*L'Anima del Filosofo:* 97
—Cello Concerto in D Major, 98–99, 101, 103

—*Creation,* 229–34
—*Missa brevis,* B♭ Major, 97–98
—Piano Sonatas: A Major, 97–98; B Minor, 101; D Major, 110; E♭ Major, 107, 108, 112; F Major, 107, 108
—Piano Trios: D Minor, 110, 111; E♭ Major, 110, 111; F♯, 110, 111
—String Quartets: op. 17, no. 1, 101–2; op. 17, no. 2, 102; op. 20, no. 4, 102; op. 64, no. 1, 110, 111; op. 64, no. 2, 95, 105, 106; op. 64, no. 4, 105, 106; op. 71, no. 1, 103, 107, 109; op. 71, no. 3, 99–100; op. 74, no. 1, 107, 109; op. 74, no. 2, 114; op. 77, no. 1, 94, 100; op. 77, no. 2, 94
—*Stücke für das Laufwerk:* 115; No. I.4, 116–17; No. II.1, 117; No. II.4, 117; No. II.7, 115, 116, 117, 118–19
—Symphonies: No. 45, 102; No. 50, 102–3; No. 90, 99; No. 95, 96; No. 99, 96; No. 101, 95–96; No. 102, 100; No. 103, 105, 106
—Trumpet Concerto, 101
—Variations: F Minor *(Un piccolo divertimento),* 98–99, 100
Heinichen, Johann David: ornamentation, 130, 215, 218
Hemiol(i)a: 41; indicated by blackened notation, 37, 38–40, 42–44. *See also* Sesquialtera proportion
Herreweghe, Philipp, 13
Hill, George R., 115
Hindemith, Paul, 14
Hirsch, E. D., 20
Historical instruments, 3, 4, 9–11, 12–13, 14, 19, 25–28, 29–30, 170; and performance techniques, 3, 10, 11, 12, 19, 23–24, 29; vs. modern instruments, 25, 27–30. *See also* names of individual instruments
Historical Performance (journal), 15
Hochreiter, Karl, 22
Hogwood, Christopher, 12, 14
Hotteterre, Jacques: and *notes inégales,* 70; and *pointer,* 71
Hubbard, Frank, 15
Hummel, Johann Nepomuk: and edition of Mozart, 9; trill, 113

Improvisation, and ornamentation, 93, 121–22, 128–29, 155–61, 163, 175–76, 192, 222
Inégalité. See Notes inégales
Instruments, historical. *See* Historical instruments
Isaac, Heinrich, rhythmic complexities, 36
Italian mordent, 181

Josquin des Prez. *See* Des Prez, Josquin

Kerll, Johann Kaspar, 44, 129, 136
Kirkendale, Ursula, 206–7
Kirkendale, Warren, 205
Kirnberger, Johann Philipp, 236, 237, 245
Klotz, Hans: 22, 125; on Bach's ornamentation, 125–34, 135–38; and detachment principle, 127–28; and dissonance principle, 127; on metric freedom of ornaments, 125–27; and on-beat principle, 126–27, 133–34; and ornament tables, 126–27, 130–31, 133, 136, 138, 151; on parallels, 132; and slide, 137–38; on symbolized vs. improvised ornaments, 128–29; on symbolized vs. written out ornaments, 136; and trill, 133–34, 135–37; and turn, 126, 127; and *Vorschlag,* 130–33, 137
Koopman, Ton, 13
Kreutz, Alfred, 131, 133
Kuhnau, Johann, 212
Kuijken brothers, 13

L'Abbé le Fils, 135
Lacassagne, L'Abbé Joseph, 135
La Chapelle, Jacques Alexandre de: on *notes inégales,* 70; and slide, 138
L'Affilard, Michel, 138
Landon, H. C. Robbins, 230, 231–32, 233
Landowska, Wanda, 9–10, 11
Lasso, Orlando, 36, 37, 196
Lasso, Rudolph, 37
Le Bègue, Nicholas Antoine, 134
Leech-Wilkinson, Daniel, 169–70
Leonhardt, Gustav, 13
Leonhardt Consort, 13
Leppard, Raymond, 12
Le Roux, Gaspard, 130, 134
Levarie, Siegmund, 14
Levin, Robert: 155–67; alternatives for execution of ornaments, 165; appoggiatura vs. grace note in Mozart, 166; and *Eingänge* in Mozart, 158–59; and embellishment of solo recapitulations in Mozart, 156; and fermata embellishments in Mozart, 158–59, 160–63; on improvisation in Mozart, 155–61, 163; on parallels, 157; and performer-as-composer approach to Mozart, 155–56, 157, 159, 163; and rubato in Mozart, 164; and subjectivity vs. objectivity in music interpretation, 159
Loeillet, Jean Baptiste, 135
Löhlein, Georg Simon, 45
Lombard rhythms, 203

London Baroque Ensemble, 12
London Classical Players, 13
Lossius, Lucas, 41
Loulié, Etienne: and *notes inégales*, 71; and slide, 138; and symbolized graces, 131; and *Vorschlag* anticipation, 138
Lübeck, Vincent, 136
Lully, Jean-Baptiste: articulation, 23; operas of, 6
Lute, 10, 236

Maffei, Marchese Scipio, 211
Maier, Franzjoseph, 13
Mandyczewski, Eusebius: edition of Haydn, 231
Mann, Alfred, 87
Mannheim school, 10
Marcello, Alessandro, transcribed by J. S. Bach, 129
Marchand, Louis, 131
Marchand, Luc, 138
Marcus Fabius Quintilianus. *See* Quintilianus (Marcus Fabius)
Marenzio, Luca, 7, 196
Marpurg, Friedrich Wilhelm: on the role of performers, 18, 30n.1; trill, 134
Marriner, Neville, 12
Marshall, Robert L., on J. S. Bach's style, 195–96, 198–201, 202–4, 207
Martini, Padre: on the history of music, 4–5
Mattheson, Johann J.: on *Accent*, 215, 218; on *acciaccatura*, 218; on the application of rules, 210, 215, 218–19; on *circolo mezzo*, 217; on conducting, 209, 212–13; on *Durchgang*, 218; on dynamics, 211–12; on the fortepiano, 211–12; on *groppo*, 217; influence on German music, 209; on meters, 211–12; on musical forms, 211, 212; on ornamentation, 130, 209, 210, 214–18; on performance practice, 209–10, 211–15, 218–19; on recitative performance, 211–12; on rhythms derived from poetic meters, 81; on the role of church organists, 214; theoretical works, 209; on *tirata*, 217; on trill, 216, 218; on vibrato, 216; on vocal performance techniques, 214–16, 218–19; on vocal vs. instrumental music, 209–12, 214
McGegan, Nicolas, 15
Mei, Girolamo, 5
Meissner, Joseph Nikolaus, 172–73
Melkus, Eduard, 146
Mendel, Arthur, 23, 208n.5
Mensural notation, and binary vs. ternary rhythms, 35–37, 41–42
Messa di voce, 24, 231–32

Meter: and note values, 211; and recitative performance, 211–12; and tempo, 233–34, 236–37
Monody, 5, 122
Montéclair, Michel Pignolet de: and *notes inégales*, 70, 71
Monteverdi, Claudio: 22; and use of *trillo*, 172
   Works
   —"Ohimè se tanto amato," 202
   —*Orfeo*, 12
Mordent: 114, 115, 116, 118, 119, 134, 204; and articulation, 128; beat placement, 105, 114, 115, 116, 118, 119, 127; and Haydn ornament, 97, 99, 101, 103, 118; and harmony, 127; improvisation of, 178; and neighbor note principle, 126; symbolized, 130, 147, 152–53n.16; vocal, 218. *See also* Italian mordent
Morgan, Robert P., 24
Morgenstern, Christian, 152n.4
Morley, Thomas, 39
Moscheles, Ignaz, 9
Mozart, Leopold: appoggiatura, 147, 185; on articulation, 24; and mordent, 99; and phrasing, 113
Mozart, Wolfgang Amadeus: 3, 12, 68; appoggiatura, 139–44, 147–51, 166, 184–90; arpeggio, 163–64; articulation, 78–79, 83n.3, 233; autograph Index discrepancies, 145; and C. P. E. Bach, 20–21, 141, 151, 184; cadenzas, 122, 155–56, 158–60, 184, 191; and common practice, 124–25; concessions to singers, 161; dynamic marks, 147, 151; editions and transcriptions of, 9, 160–61, 185; *Eingänge*, 122, 158–59, 184, 187, 191–92; embellishments in solo recapitulations, 156, 163; fermata embellishments, 158–59, 160–63; grace notes, 150–51, 166, 184–89, 190–91; and "gusto," 192; and improvisation, 122, 155–61, 163; influence of J. S. Bach, 6, 7; little notes, 141, 142–43; mordent, 147, 152–53n.16; notation inconsistencies, 77–79, 144–47; and numbers of performers, 170, 230; and ornamentation, 93–94, 95, 104, 122, 141, 156–58, 163–64, 184–85; parallels in, 158; personal life and music, 198; reorchestrations of Handel's works, 8; rubato vs. caesura in, 163; synchronization of voice and accompaniment, 141–44, 151; tempo, 145, 233; and tone color, 170; and Türk, 20–21, 151; trill, 113, 118, 147, 152–53n.16, 166, 180–92, 245; turn, 145–48, 152–53n.16, 164–65; use of the piano, 28;

on vibrato, 172–73; and variation form, 208n.7; *Vorschlag,* 141–45, 148–50, 151, 179, 183–85, 187, 189
Works
—*Al desio di chi t'adora* (K. 577), 161
—Bassoon works: Concerto in B♭ Major (K. 191[186e]), 185–91; Sonata in B♭ Major (for bassoon and cello) (K. 292[196c]), 184, 191–92
—*Così fan tutte,* 157, 161–63
—*Don Giovanni,* 83n.3
—*Die Entführung aus dem Serail,* 162
—*Eine kleine Nachtmusik,* 166
—*Mitridate,* 161
—*Ein musikalischer Spass,* 200
—*Le nozze di Figaro,* 83n.3, 145, 161
—Piano Concertos: G Major (K. 453), 147–48; F Major (K. 459), 83n.3, 148–50, 166; D Minor (K. 466), 160; C Major (K. 467), 83n.3, 159; C Minor (K. 491), 28, 83n.3
—Piano Sonatas: A Major (K. 331 [300i]), 157; B♭ Major (K. 454), 145–47
—Rondo in F (K. 494), 156
—String Quartets: D Major (K. 575), 83n.3, 143–44; F Major (K. 590), 83n.3, 145
—String Quintet, D. Major (K. 593), 83n.3
—Symphony in E♭ Major (K. 543), 78–79, 230
—Variations, G Major *(La bergère Célimène)* (K. 359 [374a]), 158; F Major (K. 613), 159; "Come un agnello" (K. 460), 159
—*Das Veilchen,* 83n.3, 141, 145
—Violin Concerto, D Major (K. 218), 160
—Violin Sonata, G Major (K. 379[373a]), 152–53n.16, 163–64
—*Die Zauberflöte,* 140–41, 142–43
Mozart pitch, 23
Muffat, Georg: on *notes inégales,* 69, 70, 240
Murschhauser, Franz Xaver Anton, 43, 135
Music publishing: scholarly methods in, 7–8
Musica Antiqua (Cologne), 14
Musical clocks, 105, 114–19
Mylius, Wolfgang Michael: hemiola, 43; trill, 135; triplets, 37

Nachschlag: 215–16, 244–45; and articulation, 128; and harmony, 127. *See also Accent; Durchang*
Newman, Anthony: on performance of J. S. Bach, 235–41
New York Pro Musica, 14–15
Niemecz, Joseph, 114–15, 118

Nivers, Guillaume Gabriel: mordent, 131, and *notes inégales,* 71, 238; and ornament tables, 129; *port de voix,* 131; trill, 131
Norrington, Roger, 12
Notation: and problems of interpreting early music, 18–19, 121, 175–76; and rhythmic imprecision, 35–36, 69–71
Notes inégales: 21–22, 65–76, 81, 88–89, 171, 211, 238–39; and agogic accents, 66, 69, 74, 75; and articulation, 74; and dotted notes, 66, 69–75; evolution of, 67–68; as a French convention, 65–71, 75, 90n.7; and keyboard fingering, 69; and meter, 66–69; mildness of, 68, 71–72, 74, 90n.7; and notational discrepancies, 73; and note values, 65–68, 75; ornamental function of, 67–68; and rubato, 66, 69, 74, 75; and stepwise motion, 66–67, 74, 75

Obrecht, Jacob, 6
O'Donnell, John, 238
Orchestra of the 18th Century, 13, 28
Orchestra of the Age of Enlightenment, 13
Organ, 4, 11, 27, 236
Organist, role of in church services, 214
Ornament tables: 126, 129, 130–31, 134, 135–36, 139; dangers of, 21, 93, 123–24, 127, 151; history of, 122–23; role of, 123–24
Ornamentation: and articulation, 105–10, 126, 127–28, 137; and beat placement, 93–101, 105–12, 114, 117–19, 126–29, 163–64, 166; dated nature of, 210, 215; and diction, 142–43; and dynamic markings, 95–96, 105–6, 107, 110; and expression, 122; for the keyboard, 125–26, 128, 129, 131, 135, 136, 204–5; functions of, 93–95, 121–23, 175; and harmony, 106, 122, 126–27; history of, 121–22, 128–29, 175; and improvisation, 121–22, 128–29, 155–61, 163, 175–76, 178, 192, 214, 218, 222; interpretation of notation, 19, 93–94, 95–104, 121–25, 164–65, 176–77; and little notes, 97, 99–100, 106–11, 116–17, 122, 129, 141, 176; melismatic, 122, 128–29, 158, 176, 178, 214, 215; metric freedom of, 125–27, 178, 192; and note denominations, 176; and ornament tables, 21, 22, 93, 122–25; and parallels, 132, 138, 150–51, 157; and performance of early music, 170, 171; and phrasing, 112–13; relative importance of, 78–79; scholarly interest in, 10, 121, 237–38;

and skeletal notation, 176, 222; subjectivity vs. objectivity in interpretation, 159, 165; symbolized, 121–24, 128–30, 136, 139, 151, 175–76, 178–79, 184–85, 192, 215, 218; and tempo, 176–78; written out, 121–22, 128–29, 136, 176–77. *See also* Appoggiatura; Arpeggio; Cadenzas; *Eingänge;* Fermata embellishments; Grace note; Mordent; *Nachschlag; Port de voix;* Portamento; *Schneller;* Slide; Trill; Turn; *Vorschlag; Zwischenschlag*
Ortiz, Diego: on parallels, 132, 150

Pachelbel, Johann, 129, 136
Paganini, Niccolò, 199
Palestrina, Giovanni Pierluigi da: 8, 36, 44, 196; influence on J. S. Bach, 197; transcribed by J. S. Bach, 129; use of "L'Homme armé," 6, 44
Parallels: and accompaniment, 132; and ornamentation, 132, 138, 150–51, 157; and tempo, 132
Passacaglia, vs. chaconne, 212
Passaggi. See Ornamentation: melismatic
Patronage in music, 6–7
Performance practice: as a scholarly discipline, 18, 29–23, 155; early writings on, 209–10, 211–16, 218–19, 243
Performance Practice Review, 15
Performers: numbers of in early music, 170, 230; role in interpreting early music, 18, 25, 192; seating arrangements of in early music, 230–31
Pergolesi, Giovanni Battista: 124; transcribed by J. S. Bach, 129
Peri, Jacopo, 5
Perlman, Martin, 15
La Petite Bande, 13
Philharmonic Baroque Orchestra (San Francisco), 15
Philomusica of London, 11
Phrasing: and articulation in Haydn, 112–13; interpretation of, 19, 24, 26, 170, 244, 245; and ornamentation, 112–13
Piano, 23, 27–29, 236, 238. *See also* Fortepiano
Picerli, Silvero, 61–62
Pinnock, Trevor, 12
Pirrotta, Nino, 205
Pitches: level of in early music, 19, 22, 23, 24, 26–27, 28, 29
Pleyel (piano firm), 9
Poglietti, Alessandro, 240
Pointer, 71. *See also* Dotted rhythms; *Notes inégales*

Pont, Graham: on French overture style, 77–78; and inconsistent rhythmic interpretation, 77–79, 80–82, 85
Port de voix, 129, 131, 138, 152n.6, 204, 218. *See also* Accent; *Vorschlag*
Portamento, 95, 96–97
Praetorius, Ernst: on triplets, 37
Praetorius, Michael: 11; on the history of music, 4; on musical instruments, 4; on the organ, 4; on sesquialtera proportion, 41–42; trill, 135; triplets, 37; on vibrato, 172
Printz, Wolfgang Caspar: on the history of music, 4; trill, 135–36, 219n.2
Pro Musica Antiqua (Brussels), 11
Pruitt, W., 72
Purcell, Henry: and *notes inégales,* 75

Quantz, Johann Joachim: and appoggiatura, 139; and anticipated *Vorschlag,* 131, 133; on dotted rhythms, 20, 21, 86; on *notes inégales,* 21, 69, 75; on parallels in ornaments, 132; and symbolized graces, 131; theoretical writings applied to other composers, 20–21; on triplets synchronized with dotted notes, 45
Quintilianus (Marcus Fabius), 207
Quitschreiber, Georg, 42

Radio stations, and the early music movement, 12, 13
Raison, André: ornament tables, 129, 131, 134
Rameau, Jean-Philippe, 13; and articulation, 23; Dolmetsch on, 20; keyboard works of, 27; ornament tables of, 130, 134
Ramm, Andrea von, 13
Recitative, 5, 211–12
Recorder, 10, 23
Reger, Max, 208n.7
Reicha, Anton, and *notes inégales,* 75
Reiche, Gottfried, 199
Reilly, Edward, 24
Reinken, Johann Adam, 129, 196
Rhythmic clash vs. assimilation, 35, 37–38, 44–62, 72–73, 88–89, 224, 239–41; and polyphony, 87; and solo vs. ensemble performance, 87; and tempo, 57–59, 60, 86
Rhythms: derived from poetic meters, 81; and diction, 86–87; ornamental use of, 79; and performance of early music, 170, 171, 238; solo vs. ensemble performance of, 82, 87. *See also* Binary rhythms; Dotted rhythms; Hemiol(i)a; Lombard rhythms; *Notes inégales;* Sesquialtera; Syncopation
Riemann, Hugo, 10, 231

Rifkin, Joshua, 15, 16n.3
Rognioni, Francesco, 203
Romanticism, and the early music movement, 7
Rousseau, Jean: on interpretation, 212
Rousseau, Jean-Jacques: 122; on *notes inégales*, 72
Rubato: and *notes inégales*, 66, 69, 74–75; vs. caesura in Mozart, 164; and uneven notes, 238
Ruhland, Konrad, 13
Rust, Wilhelm, 7

Saal, Therese, 232
Sachs, Curt, 236
Saint Lambert, Michel de: and articulation, 23; ornament tables of, 129, 130–31, 134; ornamentation, 128, 129, 130–31, 138; on parallels, 132
Saint-Saëns, Camille, 9
Salieri, Antonio, 230
Salomon, Johann Peter, 230
Santa Maria, Tomás de, and rhythmic unevenness, 69, 70
Sarti, Giuseppe: Mozart's Variations on "Come un agnello," 159
Scheibe, Johann Adolf, 197, 198
Scherer, Sebastian Anton, 136
Schering, Arnold, 204, 206
Schmelzer, Johann Heinrich, 240
Schneller, 103
Schola Cantorum (Basel), 11
Schola Cantorum (Paris), 9
Schubert, Franz: inclusion in the early music movement, 3; ornamentation, 121; Piano Trio in B♭ Major, 62n.1; trill, 113
Schulz, Johann Abraham Peter, 245
Schumann, Robert: inclusion in the early music movement, 3
Schütz, Heinrich, 8
Schwärmer, 172
Senfl, Ludwig, 41
Sesquialtera proportion, 38–40, 41–44, 61. *See also* Hemiol(i)a
Shaw, Watkins: edition of Handel's *Messiah*, 86, 89
Shepp, Marion, 236
Siret, Nicolas, 138
Slide: and articulation, 127–28; beat placement, 95–96, 114, 118, 127, 129, 137–38; and harmony, 127; improvisation of, 178; and neighbor note principle, 126; symbolized, 129–30
Slide trill, 187, 188
Smith, John Christopher: and rhythhmic alignment in Handel scores, 82
Société des Instruments Anciens, 9

Solomons, Derek, 12
Somfai, László: on Haydn's ornamentation, 93–94, 111, 112, 114
Speth, Johann, 136
Spitta, Philipp, 8
Stavenhagen, Bernhard, 10
Stein, Maria Anna, 164
Stierlein, Johann Christoph, 135
Strauss, Richard, 233
Strinasacchi, Regina, 146
Strunck, Nikolaus Adam, 129
Studio der frühen Musik, 13
Style galant. See Galant style
Swieten, Gottfried Bernhard van, 6, 8
Symbolism, in music, 236
Syncopation, indicated by coloration, 39, 199

Tactus, 237
Tagliavini, Luigi Ferdinando, 161
Tartini, Giuseppe: grace notes, 166; mordent, 99
Taruskin, Richard, 25, 29, 169–70
Telemann, Georg Philipp, 10
Temperley, Nicholas, 169–70
Tempo: and dance, 236; in early music, 18–19, 24, 170, 233–34; and meter, 233–34, 236–37; and rhythmic clash, 56–61, 86; and ornamentation, 176–78
Ternary vs. binary rhythms. *See* Hemiol(i)a; Rhythmic clash vs. assimilation; Sesquialtera proportion; Triplets
Tierces coulées: and use of grace notes, 181–82
Tigrini, Orazio, 39, 61
Tirata, 217
Tone color, in early music, 26–27, 28, 170
Toscanini, Arturo, 233
Tremolo, 172, 219
Trill: and articulation, 128, 137; auxiliary start of, 106, 113–14, 116–18, 129, 131, 133–34, 135–37, 166, 179–81, 184–86, 189–90; beat placement, 93, 106, 113–14, 126–27, 133–35, 166, 179–81, 184–86, 187; cadential, 122, 179–80, 181, 183, 185–87; compound, 204; and harmony, 127; and Haydn ornament, 100–103, 118; improvisation of, 178; in Mozart, 184–92; in Vivaldi, 178–81; length of, 133, 136, 216; main note start of, 113–19, 135–36, 137, 179, 181, 184–85, 186–88, 189–90, 216; and neighbor note principle, 126; symbolized, 122, 129, 136, 147, 152–53n.16, 178–79, 184, 218; trill chains, 216. *See also* Appoggiatura trill, Grace note trill; *Schneller;* Slide trill; *Trillo; Tremolo*
Trillo, 172, 219n.2
Triplets: and blackened notation, 37; notation

in binary meter, 35–43, 239–41; synchronized with dotted notes, 45, 57–60; vs. binary rhythms, 36, 41–42, 44, 45–57, 58–60, 61–62, 62n.13, 239–40
Troeger, Richard, 236
Trümper, Michael, 42
Türk, Daniel Gottlob, 151; application of writings to Haydn and Mozart, 20–21, 244; and appoggiatura, 244, 245; editions of, 245; influence of C. P. E. Bach, 243; and examples from Haydn and Mozart, 245; influence of Marpurg, 243; on keyboard technique, 243; on ornamentation, 132, 163–64, 243; on phrasing, 245; theoretical writings of, 243; translation of, 243–45; and turn, 147
Turn: 127, 134–35, 139; and artiulation, 110; beat placement, 93–94, 105, 109–13, 127, 164–65; and dynamics, 110; and harmony, 127; and Haydn ornament, 97–104, 109, 118; and neighbor note principle, 126; and phrasing, 112–13; symbolized, 93, 94, 109–12, 145–48, 151, 152–53n.16; written out, 94, 109, 110, 111–12, 117–18

Uneven notes: application of, 238–39; and keyboard fingerings, 238; kinds of, 69–71, 238–39. *See also Notes inégales;* Rubato
Urio, Francesco Antonio, 8

Van Helmont, Charles-Joseph, 135
Vanneo, Stefano: and ternary rhythms, 39–40
Van Swieten, Gottfried Bernhard. *See* Swieten, Gottfried Bernhard van
Variations, 205, 208n.7
Veilhan, Jean-Claude, 22
Vibrato, in early music, 23, 24, 26, 169–70, 171–73, 216. *See also Balancement; Schwärmer; Tremolo; Trillo*
Victoria, Tomás Luis de, 7
Villeneuve, Alexandre de: on *notes inégales,* 71; and slide, 138
Viollet-le-Duc, Eugène Emmanuel, 9
Vivaldi, Antonio: 68, 75; appoggiatura, 179–81, 183; concerto style, 223; grace note, 178–79, 181–82, 183; inconsistencies in

notation, 176; influence on J. S. Bach, 223; and ornamentation, 176, 181, 184; slide, 178; tempo in, 178; transcribed by J. S. Bach, 129; trill, 178–81; *Vorschlag,* 179, 183–83
Works
—Bassoon Concertos: A Minor (F. VIII, no. 2), 179, 180; D Minor (F. VIII, no. 5), 181, 182, 183; E Minor (F. VIII, no. 6), 181; C Major (F. VIII, no. 13), 179–80; F Major (F. VIII, no. 20), 181, 182–83; B♭ Major (F. VIII, no. 36), 178; E♭ Major (F. VIII, no. 27), 183
Vocal performance techniques, 214–15, 218
Vocal vs. instrumental music, 210–12, 214
Von Buelow, Hans. *See* Buelow, Hans von
Von Dadelsen, Georg. *See* Dadelsen, Georg von
Von Ramm, Andrea. *See* Ramm, Andrea von
Vorhalt. See Appoggiatura
Vorschlag: and articulation, 106–7, 107–8, 127, 137; beat placement, 94–95, 106–8, 118, 127, 130–33, 151, 179–85, 187; definition of, 130; and dynamics, 113–14; and harmony, 106, 127, 132; in Mozart, 183–85, 187–89; in Vivaldi, 179–83; and neighbor note principle, 126; and note denominations, 147–50, 181, 185; symbolized, 130–32, 179–85, 192. *See also Accent;* Appoggiatura; Grace note; *Port de voix*
Vulpius, Melchior, 42

Walliser, Christoph Thomas, 43–44
Walther, Johann Gottfried, 138
Wenzinger, August, 11, 13
Werckmeister, Andreas, 132, 210
Wolff, Christoph, 197, 206

Zacconi, Lodovico: cited by Collins, 39; on binary vs. ternary rhythms, 40–41; on sesquialtera proportion, 44; on triplets, 37, 40–41
Zarlino, Giuseffo: cited by Collins, 39–40; on sesquialtera proportion, 40; on triplets, 37
Zwischenschlag: and articulation, 128; and harmony, 127

:ones were thrown with terrific force. The stone that went through the ipstairs window made it all the way to the middle of the upper hallway.

When the police left I remembered standing in the shadows upstairs with the .22. It was loaded, but so what? It was nearly a toy, a slow-firing, ight-load weapon. What if the crazies I imagined earlier actually had come charging through the shattered windows? The windows had gone out so ast I had been sure they were firing an automatic weapon.

I thought about buying a large-caliber pistol. Tomorrow, as soon as the stores opened, I'd go buy a pistol. Perhaps a Browning automatic with a fourteen-shot magazine, like the one Al Pacino had in *Serpico*. It would go into the cabinet next to the bed, its slide locked back. At the first sign of trouble I would ram a magazine into the butt and the slide would slam forward, carrying a round into the chamber and leaving the hammer cocked and ready. Come on, you goon, I'm ready for you this time.

Well: not tomorrow. This is New York, not Utah or Texas or Florida. You don't just walk up to the counter and pick up a handgun here. You have to go downtown and be fingerprinted and have a good justification for the judge and you have to prove you're of good character. All these things take time. I wanted that automatic now.

"Your honor, I am of good character and people throw rocks through my window so would you let me buy that pistol in the window?"

And what if the judge said yes? What would I *do* with a gun if I had it? Have a shoot-out on the lawn? Have a manly movie-type face-off with some moron who gets his jollies shattering glass after a boozy night out? The dialogue has been scripted in a thousand B-movies: "Drop that rock, you sonofabitch, I've got you covered!" Or: "Okay, buddy, I'm ready for you this time. Holster that rock and get ready to draw!" Glass-breaking is very scary and potentially dangerous, but it isn't and shouldn't be a capital crime.

I remember someone asking Clint Eastwood once about violence in one of his movies. "That was *him*, the guy I played in the movie who did that," Eastwood said, "it wasn't *me*." The person didn't understand or accept the answer, or didn't like to think that the real-life Clint Eastwood just didn't walk about the one street that is most of downtown Carmel with an enormous sidearm ready to dysfunction forever any hostiles who approached.

I'd grown up with movies and television dramas in which Mr. Colt's Equalizers solved problems of terror. ("God may have created men equal," went the cliché, "but it took Mr. Colt to make it a fact.") The bad guy appears and the solution lies in the gentlefolk finding a champion who would, with all modesty and grace and hesitancy, blow him away forever.

Well, you don't blow away someone with an early morning rock in his hand and a late-night load of booze in his belly. Conflict in real life isn't solved that easily, fear isn't neutralized that simply. I know a lot of

I told the lieutenant what had happened, that Diane had been sleeping and I had been reading and our windows had been shot out in rapid succession.

"Rocks," the patrolman said from the other side of the room.

"What?"

"Rocks. They threw rocks through your windows." He lifted up one of the curtains and I saw on the floor a baseball-sized white stone.

There was a moment of wonderful relief. I associate rocks with vandals, people doing something hostile for the hell of it. Like the people who decorate New York City subways and walls with spray paint and aren't artist enough to spray anything interesting. Guns I associate with people who have a purpose. That is probably a result of watching too much television.

"Oh," I said, more than a little embarrassed. "I thought the windows had been *shot* out."

"Sure," the lieutenant said. "Makes the same noise from this side. A big bang and a lot of glass. Reasonable thing to think." I was liking him better.

"Scared hell out of me."

"Would me too," he said.

"So we just ran out of the room."

"Damned right," he said.

They looked around for a few minutes, but there was nothing for them to do. There was no victim to rush to the hospital, no perpetrator to restrain with chrome cuffs, no missing objects to list in black notebooks.

"We're going up the block for a while," the lieutenant said. "We'll come back."

"Why are you going up the block?" Diane asked.

"Guy up there had his windows busted up too."

They returned in twenty minutes. The lieutenant carried three rocks. He took one of mine. "Same kind of rocks," he said. I nodded. "You know what those windows of yours cost?" I said I had no idea. "The guy up the block, he said his windows cost $500 each. They're bigger than yours and they're thermopane. Yours thermopane?" I admitted they weren't. "They got four of his windows and the glass on his front door."

"You got any vendettas with anyone?" the patrolman asked.

Vendettas! I had a vision of the Corsican Brothers. Diane and I shook our heads.

"Sometimes something like this is a vendetta," the lieutenant said.

"Then why would they garbage the other house too?" I asked.

"Cover. It's great cover. That way you don't know it's them."

But that way, I thought, you don't get the satisfaction of knowing your victim knows it was *you*. Few people can manage secret revenge. The only people I remember who manage secret revenge are characters in Jerzy Kosinski novels.

"Maybe they got the wrong house," the patrolman said.

"They broke our windows by mistake?" Diane said, getting really angry now.

"We don't know that. Maybe they broke *his* windows by mistake. Your houses are similar colors. Maybe they were told what color house to hit, they hit one, then they noticed the other one so they hit that one too just to be sure."

"So they wouldn't have to come back," the lieutenant said. "That makes a lot of sense." The patrolman nodded modestly. Both policemen were very tall. They stood by the door. The patrolman now held one of the stones in his right hand. The stone rested partly in his palm and partly on the third joint of his first and second fingers. With his thumb, he rotated the stone as if he were looking for the stitching.

"What about fingerprints?" Diane asked. She watches a lot of television and believes in fingerprints.

"Nope. These rocks are too porous to hold prints. Anyway, even if they had prints, they're not much good. Prints are good only if you have somebody, a suspect. Then maybe you can match them up. Otherwise, it's too hard. If it was a homicide they might try to do something, but not for this sort of thing. Not for petty violence."

In the economics of urban hostility, homicide gets a measure of techno-logical inspection not earned by shattered glass. The discrimination seemed reasonable enough, but secretly I, like Diane, would have preferred to have seen the forces of Law Enforcement humming through the dawn finding the evil perpetrators: *All right, Rodney, we've matched the chemical composition of these stones and have found they could have come only from the private quarry behind your laboratory. And we found your pinkie prints on a smooth concave surface.*

"Good grief, Inspector. How did you find me out so quickly?"

"Police work, Rodney. Modern police work."

It doesn't work like that. If you don't see them or if they don't call up to tell the police or you who they were, then you can forget it. Murders have the highest rate of crime solution, which everybody who watches television knows, but the reason for the success rate is most murders are done by friends or relatives who hang around after it's over. Many of them call 911 themselves to say, "Hey, you guys should come over here because I just did something I maybe shouldn't have. I mean, Gloria's not moving and there's a *lot* of blood."

Pre-dawn rock-throwers don't call. Ours didn't, anyway.

The lieutenant was now the one fondling a rock in his right hand. He

had placed the other two from his set on our hall table. "It this sort of thing."

"I would think so," I said.

"Drunks from the bars, they're usually done with this stu And it's raining tonight. Most drunks don't go out throwing at four-thirty."

I had thought the same thing. I had always thought this ti safest. Even the dedicated creeps were usually home in bec ones set on violence had usually done it by this quiet hour home resting up for the next time. When I lived in Boston and San Francisco I regularly used to walk five A.M. stree midnight. I didn't know if those streets were in fact so much they seemed that way. Nothing ever happened, anyway.

I told the policemen I was relieved to know it hadn't Bullets could have come through the curtains. My head had with the curtains. I thought it would have been awful for D waked up to all that gore.

I was holding one of the stones now; I didn't remember pic having it handed to me. "There aren't any stones like this aro said. The cops nodded. "That means they planned to do it."

"But it doesn't mean they planned this house," the patroln only means they planned to do it to somebody. Anybody."

"Some people," the lieutenant said, "don't have things and th want other people to have them either."

"It's just petty violence, sir," the patrolman said.

I was sure it had been at least two people. The rocks came and too accurately for it to have been one person with a load one arm, firing them in sequence with great power and good very late and it was raining, the time of night when you want co your mischief just so you'll be sure later you really did it.

Two people, perhaps more. No: just two. More would have coordination, intelligence, planning. This seemed the sort of young men would do. A little planning, but not enough to involve

That was as far as I could get. I couldn't visualize faces. In the d of night, not long before the sky will crack with dawn, there are two men standing on the pavement in front of my house with a doz stones they have brought from somewhere far away. They don't k and I don't know them; they don't know whether or not someone beyond the curtains, they don't know whether the upstairs middle they smash looks upon an empty room or a baby's crib. They don' care.

I wonder if the faces were angry. If they were, at what and at who people doing long prison terms who fell prey to that simplistic and idiotic notion.

And, theory and speculation about intruders aside, what if one of our kids or one of their friends happened to find this wonderful 14-shot weapon? What if it accidentally went off and maimed or killed someone who was merely idly curious? Most people killed with handguns kept in the house for protection are people who live in the house—not strangers in the night.

No help there, I decided.

So what was I going to do—get some rocks of my own to throw back next time?

Later that morning a detective came by. He was very polite, though we all knew he couldn't do much. He asked if we could think of anyone who had a grudge. Diane and I said no.

"You both teach at the university?"

"Yes."

"Perhaps someone there?"

We couldn't think of anyone there. (Well: there was Prof. _____ in the English department with whom I'd argued in several recent faculty meetings. But I couldn't picture him standing in the road firing stones into my French windows. Academics write about each other; the only things they throw are insults.)

"Maybe someone you gave a low grade?"

"No."

Students who get low grades aren't likely to respond in these terms, we decided. If they're too lazy to do the work necessary to get an adequate grade they'd be too lazy to lurk in the bushes with rocks until 4:30 in the morning.

We didn't know anybody around Buffalo who responded to the world in those terms, but it was clear that someone had been reacting to something that night. The detective took one of our remaining stones. He said it was a kind of stone not found in the park across the street and we said we had noted that fact.

Sunday night, the night after the raid, we had dinner with a couple down the street, a surgeon and his wife. They had invited their back-fence neighbors, Ed and Martha, who live on the street paralleling ours. Ed announced that they had been burglarized twice, both times during the day, both times by professionals.

I told them that our insurance agent had told us when we moved to this neighborhood that we would no longer have to worry about clumsy junkie burglars trying to score for a television set to peddle.

"Wonderful," I had said.

"Nope," the insurance agent replied. "In this neighborhood you get professionals. They don't *bother* with television sets."

"Oh. Wonderful"—a different tone of voice.

He reproved me for the tone. "Professionals are better at finding really valuable stuff but they're far less likely to hurt anybody. It's the amateurs who are dangerous."

Martha concurred. She said their most recent burglary had occurred only moments after she left the house for an hour. "Those guys," Ed said, "they knew exactly what they were doing. Everything was very neat when we got home. The drawers were all closed. The only thing was, everything valuable was gone. They left all the junk jewelry."

I told them I found their story reassuring. I was afraid of incompetents who didn't know how to competently check out a house for vacancy.

"You get those creeps too," Martha said. She told us that a few days after the second burglary she got out of the shower and heard sounds from the first floor. Ed was at work, the cleaning lady had gone for the day. She went to the top of the stairs and saw a man standing at the bottom step, looking up at her with glee. She reached just inside the bedroom door, got Ed's shotgun, and jacked a round into the chamber.

If you're not hunting or shooting skeet, few sounds in the world are quite as ominous as the sound of a shell slamming home into a pump shotgun's chamber. I told them how once in a prison yard in Arkansas I had seen a guard freeze into position two hundred men when he did that.

"I did more," Martha said. "I told him, 'If you don't get out of here right now, I'm going to shoot your balls off.' He left immediately."

"That's terrific," our host, the surgeon, said. "But I would have said, 'I'll blow your head off.'"

"I knew what was on that creep's mind," Martha said.

"It wasn't so terrific," Ed said. "She didn't tell me when I got home that the safety was off and that there was a round in the chamber. I went to put the gun away and I blew a big hole in the floor."

Monday morning I was doing something in the back of the house. I noticed the heavy metal grill covering one of the cellar window walls had been lifted off. The grill weighs about a hundred pounds, not the kind of thing to lift up by itself or to be moved by the wind.

It could have happened any time over the weekend. While we were at a concert Sunday afternoon, while we were having dinner with the neighbors Sunday night, while we were watching television, while we were sleeping.

I dialed the number the detective had left. He had written in very neat small letters on a tiny piece of tan paper his name, his district, and his phone number. "You think of anything I ought to know," he had said. "You call me at this number night or day."

"He's not here today," the man who answered said. "He's on nights this week."

I identified myself and said the detective had told us to call if we had further information or problems after the weekend's window vandalism.

"I'll tell him you called," the man said. "I'll leave a note for him."

"He'll call us?"

"Sure he will. But he's off for two days now. He won't call until Wednesday. I'll leave the note for him." The man hung up.

What if the grill-lifter came back tonight? First busted windows before dawn, now heavy iron grills pried up in the dark of night. What next?

I dialed 911 and they sent a car immediately.

The two patrolmen were very polite, though once again it was clear they could do nothing to help. Once again fingerprints were out; it had been raining off and on for three days and nights. While they looked at the heavy grill I again went through my pistol acquisition scenario in my mind.

The larger of the two policemen pointed through Diane's study window to the dog, a medium-sized Samoyed. "He probably scared them away. He'd scare me away. I tell you. I wouldn't go in there with that dog running around. Best protection you can have."

I didn't say, "But officer, that dog has never been tested in combat. The thing she's best at is bringing her bone or ball and frolicking with the kids. She barks at the mailman's jeep or strangers in the driveway but we have no idea how she'd handle an intruder once inside."

He knew what I was thinking. "The dog looks nice to you, but I sure wouldn't take a chance. Too damned big."

The nice thing about a dog is you don't have to worry about one of the kids finding it and accidentally setting it off. The bad thing about a dog is unless it is a well-trained beast, you don't know if it will go off at all.

After the policemen left, Diane and I took Polaroid pictures of the uplifted iron grill, just as two mornings earlier we had taken Polaroids of all the broken windows. I'm not sure why: maybe as evidence for later; more likely as souvenirs we felt obligated to acquire, just as tourists feel obligated to take pictures of the Eiffel Tower or Vatican or White House even though cheap picture postcards provide perfectly adequate images of those structures. The personal photographs, however bad they are and however much better the cheap postcards are, don't serve to document the building; they prove that the traveler was really there, that it really happened. In a world of tiny transistorized sound and video recorders and instant cameras, one documents everything: birthday parties, Christmas with the family, a pried-up heavy iron grill. We put the camera away and huffed and puffed and jammed the heavy grill back into place against the coaxial cable belonging to the Cablescope people.

Late that night we watched a movie. The picture was dismal. We changed channels: all the pictures were dismal.

"I just thought of something," Diane said.

"What?"

"The Cablescope man was working around the corner of the house Friday. Maybe *he* left that corner of the grill off."

We went out and looked and sure enough, that was where the wire made its entry to the house. He had lifted the grill and slipped his wire through the cellar window. He hadn't bothered to set the grill back because he knew it would squash his cable. He should have run the cable through the grill in the first place but he'd probably run it in, hooked it up, realized his error, and decided to let it slide in the expectation no one would ever notice. So that explained the uplifted grill and the dismal picture.

I wondered if every object out of place on the property would now precipitate panic. I was certain that if it hadn't been for the smashed windows we would have thought about the Cablescope installer earlier.

Tuesday morning the mailman rang the doorbell, which he rarely does. The dog went berserk in the vain hope that the mailman would actually come into the house and she would finally get the chance she fantasized about every Monday through Saturday morning between eleven A.M. and noon. We went outside, the dog continued attacking the window, and the mailman handed us the usual bundle of letters, bills and periodicals. He said the man at the corner who had been victim to the same vandals wanted me to call him. "He says you're not in the phone book. He said to tell you he is in the phone book."

I called. The man talked about the damage to his house, said the insurance would cover his loss, but that didn't really matter. "I've lived here twenty-seven years," he said, "and until two years ago nothing bad ever happened. Two years ago, a Saturday afternoon, someone shot through one of my windows. The windows on the other street." Since his house was on the corner, he was doubly vulnerable. "The cops said it was probably just kids."

"There's no such thing as 'just kids' when they're shooting," I said.

"Exactly," he said. "I don't know what else to do now. Put up a metal fence? That would look awful. Put up hedges? The reason I like it here is this is a pretty street. Who wants to live behind a fence and hedges? Maybe I'll get bulletproof windows. I have to replace the thermopane anyway."

The policemen this time had asked him the same questions they had asked us. "Vendettas they asked me about. They asked me if I'd fired anybody who might carry a grudge. I told them I've never fired anybody. People have quit, but I never fired them. People who quit don't come and throw rocks through your windows at four or five in the morning. Crazy people do that."

He told me that many years ago the people in the neighborhood had gotten together and hired a retired cop to patrol the street at night. "It cost us $20 a month each and it seemed worth it." I asked if they had been having problems. "No," he said. "But some other neighborhoods were and we just decided we'd spend a little money to stop trouble from getting started."

"Why did you stop having him patrol?"

"We didn't. One Saturday morning they found him dead around the corner. In his car." I thought of sinister things, but they didn't apply. "Heart attack. He just died of a heart attack. We never got it going again because nothing ever happened here. This was a nice neighborhood. Maybe we should hire another cop for the nighttime."

It seemed crazy and reasonable, both at once. Here we were in a modern city, paying huge taxes, and we were talking about hiring our own armed marshal like characters in *Warlock* or some other western movie. And if that didn't work, then what? Vigilante parties rousting strangers?

Tuesday morning about one A.M.: a terrific boom, a deep and lengthy boom, no cherry bomb or M-80. I was upstairs in my study writing an article about Homer; Diane was downstairs in her study writing about Blake. We met on the stairs. "What the hell was *that?*" she said.

"I don't know. Maybe they're back with artillery."

Once again we looked into the night from the windows of the darkened bedroom. Nothing was moving save a few cars on the road the far side of the park. We couldn't see the cars but we could see their moving lights.

The telephone rang. It was the surgeon down the block. "What the hell was that?" I told him that was exactly what Diane had just said. "So what was it?"

"I don't know. Wake you up?"

"No. I just got into bed. You don't know what it was?"

"No. Maybe they were blowing up somebody's house."

"I don't hear any sirens," he said. "But it was too loud to be a firecracker or shotgun or backfire."

"Well, it's your turn to call the cops. I've done it twice this week."

"No point in it. What can they do?"

"Find the guys with the cannon."

"Not likely. I talked to my cousin today." His cousin was a detective working a different part of the city. "He said they'd cut the force by nearly a third and they're talking about cutting more. He said there were only two detective units assigned to the busiest crime section of the city now and that's all they've got. And he said they're all angry because they didn't get raises again this year. They'll come out and do something if it's serious, but otherwise you can forget it."

"You want me to call you if I find out anything interesting?"

"No. I've got two gall bladders first thing in the morning."

It was impossible to go back to the problems of Achilleus. I turned on the TV and went through the channels. *Three Days of the Condor* was finishing on one of the Toronto stations. I watched as Robert Redford told Cliff Robertson he had given the *New York Times* the Story. Robertson's last line, as I remember it, was "And what if they don't print it?" Every time I had seen that movie I had not the slightest doubt in the world that the *Times* would print the story.

The great thing about movies and television is everyone eventually does exactly what he or she ought to do. Those programs make the bizarre and conspirational seem perfectly reasonable. In those stories, bad guys go around logically plotting against specific parts of the world. The stories don't prepare you at all for the random, the idiotic, the frivolous. They teach us well about the calculating robber, the lustful or greedy or vengeful murderer, all of whom leave whatever clues are necessary for eventual capture. They tell us nothing about the nutto in the alley who doesn't really care if we have a pocketful of money or not, who wants only to bop someone on the head and who is using the robbery as an excuse, an occasion, the same way a wife beater or child beater uses the fact of being drunk as an occasion for the brutality he really wants to do anyway.

When the movie ended, Diane said, "I'm still nervous. What *was* that noise?"

"If it was an explosion," I said, using the voice meant to imply I knew exactly what I was talking about, "it had to be far away. At least a half-mile. Anything that loud would have rattled the house if it had been nearer. We just got the tail end of the noise."

"How do you know that?"

"It seems reasonable."

"To you it seems reasonable."

"Maybe it was a sonic boom."

"That rattles windows. Breaks them."

"Not if you're on the weak end of the wave."

I told her about a segment on the U-2 reconnaissance plane I'd seen once on the *Today* show. The information was public because the government has another plane that flies higher and faster and because most of the U-2's work is now done by satellites anyway. "It could have been something like that flying very far away," I said. "The wave travels. Maybe it was some SAC game." I told Diane that *Today* had told me we monitored ground activity during one middle-east war with reconnaissance planes based in Georgia. "That's fast-moving if the work area is six thousand miles away and you're to be home for dinner. The U-2 flies at 70,000 feet. The sky is black up there. You see stars all day long. You see Los Angeles and San Francisco and Seattle and the Rockies all at once. The planes have cameras that can resolve objects on the ground one foot across."

"One foot across? From seventy thousand feet they can make out objects only one foot across?"

"From higher. That's just what the U-2 can do. The other plane can do it. Satellites can do it."

"Then why can't they find out who broke our goddamned windows?"

The house of a civil rights worker I knew in Kentucky was bombed one night. No one was hurt, but the baby and his wife were terrified and the house was reduced to rubble. He had just gotten back from a hard organizing trip and was sound asleep when it happened. His wife had been next to him in bed, still awake. She heard the car slow down, but cars had slowed on their street before. This time, the car slowed and the house exploded around them. After that night, she told me, she never again heard cars change their motion outside without experiencing again that crazy terror. "I knew I was all right," she said, "but I didn't know if anyone else was. And I didn't know if they were coming back to finish the job."

People I know who have been physically assaulted have several times told me that the worst part of the experience was what came after the encounter with the person who brutalized them. The sense of defilement passed, the wounds healed, but what remained was an unshakable mistrust of people casually encountered on the street, in the elevator, at the doorway. The violence had rearranged their relationship with the world and unidentified noises forever ceased being free and innocent and without meaning.

I don't think I will ever again in real comfort sit by an open window listening to records or letting the TV perform while I read and wait for the sky to go through its morning display. We were, I know, very lucky. It was only rocks, after all. Diane cut her leg, but not seriously. Nothing was destroyed that couldn't be replaced easily. The insurance company paid for the smashed windows, the broken lamp and table. (That's not free: it only means a lot of people had to share with us the expense of the damage. When you're not the one collecting an insurance settlement, you're helping pay the checks sent to those who are.)

The real cost is in our radically altered relationship to the night and to the darkened street. Sounds are no longer just interesting: they are now signals of potentially dangerous movements in the dark. When the curtains are open at night I look harder at the dark places than I ever did before. The cars of lovers making out or high school kids downing a sixpack are no longer dismissed from consciousness. When Diane sleeps on the couch and I read, she is more likely than before to leap up at the sound of a car changing gears outside or when the dogs (we have two of them now; the newer one is *really* big) move suddenly on the rug. If I know a car is out there and people are in it, concentrating on my reading is more difficult than it should be. It has been a good while since those windows came crashing in, we are on better terms with the night than we were those first few months, but we will never be on the terms we were with it before the stones were thrown.

A friend who was raped near her house told me of the moment in the middle of it all when she realized the man wasn't after sex, that it was the rude violation he wanted most. When he was done he punched her a few times in the face and in the abdomen, then he left, taking his time. "It didn't matter who I was," she said.

That, I think, is the scariest kind of violence—the kind that doesn't care who you are, the kind that just happens, that someone does for reasons having nothing to do with who or what you are. For a bank teller, a robbery is frightening and unpleasant but it makes perfect sense; banks, as Willie Sutton said, are where the money is. It is the dry assault of a rape or sudden crack on the skull by someone who doesn't even bother to lift your wallet that leaves the residue of terror from which you are never again totally free. I am sure I would feel better about this whole thing if I knew it was done by someone with a vendetta. I don't think it was.

The guys who threw the white rocks through our French windows didn't know who or what was on the other side of the glass and they didn't care. The lesson they had to teach us was an important one: the walls of a nice house do not keep away the world outside, and the nicely filmed fantasies of television and film belie the crude triviality and gratuitousness of the real violence that may at any moment crash into the lives of any of us. The reason television violence is so beloved is because it is, no matter how realistically it is portrayed, finally an artificial violence. The television lie isn't merely the absence of real gore and the foreshortening of real pain; the lie is in the foolish notion that everything makes sense. The bookish clerk in *Three Days of the Condor* who returns with the sandwiches to find everyone in his office murdered comes to learn it was all part of a logical malfunction within the CIA: the killers are always caught by our prime-time television cops and detectives, witty men and women who Figure it Out; McCloud on late night reruns gets the bad guy time and time again while his choleric supervisor sputters and misses the point.

Television heroes are seen giving and taking hard punches to the head, and the next day all of them are seen using their hands and perhaps even eating food that must be chewed before it can be swallowed. In real life, it is a long time before the punched jaw functions easily again, before the damaged eye can tolerate even overcast daylight without pain, before the swollen knuckles can do anything but hang like meat at one's side. The violence on television always lets you know who the actors are and what they are doing; it is deliciously logical and orderly and our only problem is following the heroes as they unravel the secret structures that make sense of it all.

In the fictions, when the bad guys are caught the troubles and the story are over; it is the exact equivalent of wedding bells in romances. In fiction books and films everything has to make sense. The reviewers nail you for loose ends every time; it's the one rule they won't let you break. Real life has no such rule. Real life is full of loose ends. Real violence rarely makes much sense; it rarely has a point. Little is gained, the satisfactions are abrasive and they burn, the injuries last a very long time. There is no secret structure on the street or when the street comes crashing through your early morning windows. It's only some faceless man with an anger the terms of which you will never know, a kindly cop whose anguished impotence you will never fully appreciate. No nice resolution, no final commercial just before the white credits let you know that all things are back in their proper places and order truly does reign in this world.

There is only the sure knowledge that it could happen tomorrow as easily as it happened yesterday, that it might be the same persons or new persons, that you'll never find strange eyes as easy to focus on again as you did before, the dark before the dawn as friendly a place as before, and that there is not a thing you or anyone else can do about it.

The Indians of Attica:
A Taste of White Man's Justice

(The Nation, 1975)

The shooting in Attica's D yard stopped at 9:52 A.M. on Monday, 13 September 1971. Bullets from the guns of state police troopers and Attica correctional officers killed 10 hostages and 29 inmates and wounded 3 hostages, 85 inmates, and 1 trooper. Many more inmates were injured when guards and troopers took over the yard and set up a gauntlet in which naked inmates were beaten with clubs as they were herded back into the cellblocks.

It was America's bloodiest prison uprising and it had been a long time coming. Inmates had several times petitioned New York Corrections Commissioner Russell G. Oswald to alleviate the overcrowding that had the prison operating at near double its designed capacity; their requests went unanswered. The uprising itself doesn't seem to have been planned, but once it started it was embraced by a convict population desperate for change.

Shortly after 9 A.M. on Thursday, 9 September 1971, Attica prison inmates took control of "Times Square," the confluence of passageways connecting the prison's four main cellblocks. Slightly over an hour later, nearly 1,300 inmates and 43 hostages were in D yard, one of the prison's four enclosed exercise areas. By the middle of the afternoon, guards had regained control of everything except two cellblocks, the four exercise yards, and the connecting tunnels and catwalks. Commissioner Oswald arrived from Albany at 2:00 P.M. Over the next several days an observer team was assembled, negotiations went on, and media attention grew exponentially. Correctional Officer William Quinn, injured in the initial violence at Times Square, died Saturday afternoon. Negotiations with prisoners continued over the weekend.

When the observer team arrived at the prison Monday morning, its members were herded into a room with no windows and told to wait. At 9:46 A.M., state police helicopters dropped teargas on D yard. As soon as the helicopters moved off there was an orgy of gunfire from troopers and correctional officers firing from high points surrounding the yard.

Prison officials told reporters that hostages had died because their throats had been slit by the inmates and that several hostages had been found with their genitals stuffed in their mouths. Several days later the Rochester medical examiner told reporters that, except for Quinn, all the dead guards had been killed by police and guard bullets; none had their throats cut, and none had their genitals removed and stuffed in their mouths.

The State of New York continued to deny any responsibility for the deaths in D yard, but in 1983 settlements were made with the families of the guards who had been shot to death. The state still denies any liability for any inmate deaths. In October 1991, after seventeen years of legal motions, the liability trial for the inmate deaths began.

Prosecutions of Attica inmates for taking part in the uprising didn't go well. Only two prisoners got extra time for their involvement in it: John B. Hill and Charles Pernasilice, the subjects of this article, who were convicted for their involvement in the death of prison guard William Quinn. The few other convictions and guilty pleas were so iffy the defendants got only concurrent time for sentences already in progress or credit for time served. Most of the prosecutions resulted in dismissals or acquittals.

Three books bracket what happened at Attica that grim weekend: Tom Wicker's *A Time to Die* (1975), Russell G. Oswald's *Attica: My Story* (1972), and the McKay Commission's *Attica: The Official Report of the New York State Special Commission on Attica* (1972). Wicker, a highly regarded *New York Times* reporter and columnist, was a member of the observer team attempting to effect a peaceful solution to the uprising. Although the McKay Commission had a large staff and the power of the state at its disposal and Oswald could report on private conversations with Governor Rockefeller, Wicker's book is, nonetheless, far closer to the heart of the matter than the other two.

One happy note: the "subjunctive" murder I predicted in this essay never happened. John B. Hill and Charles Pernasilice finished their sentences without physical harm.

THE FIRST OF THE ATTICA murder trials ended at 9:17 P.M. on Saturday, April 5, when, after three days of deliberation, an Erie County jury announced that it had found 23-year-old John B. Hill guilty of the 1971 murder of Attica guard William Quinn, and 22-year-old Charles Pernasilice guilty of second-degree attempted assault on Quinn.

The only evidence against Pernasilice came from one witness who claimed he had seen Pernasilice strike Quinn across the back, but medical testimony showed that Quinn's back was unbruised. Pernasilice had originally been charged with murder, but State Supreme Court Justice Gilbert King reduced that charge because of lack of evidence; King didn't explain why that didn't warrant a complete dismissal. Most observers thought Pernasilice had been put on trial with Hill only so that the jury could have someone it could acquit to ease the burden of convicting Hill.

The state didn't want to try Hill alone because the evidence against him was particularly weak for a murder indictment. There was no evidence of premeditation; the inmate witnesses didn't make their identifications until long after the 1971 rebellion, and in exchange for their testimony they received early release from prison and some got police protection when they were charged with subsequent offenses; one of the two guard witnesses admitted he had lied in his identification of a third potential defendant because he knew that he would be rewarded with transfer to a prison closer to his home; the other guard witness not only gave different testimony at different times but had been employed by the foreman of the Wyoming County grand jury which brought the forty-two separate indictments naming sixty-two former and present inmates. (That same grand jury refused to bring any charges against troopers or guards for torture or wanton killing of inmates, as documented by the state's official McKay Commission.) The defense expected outright acquittal for Pernasilice and either conviction for manslaughter or a hung jury for Hill. One judge not connected with the case agreed: "With that testimony," he said, "I can't see them getting a murder conviction."

Perhaps the most important factors in the trial were the attitude of Justice King and the political orientation of Buffalo, the Erie County seat. The state agreed not to have the Attica trials held in Wyoming County, which is where the prison is located, but that was only because the major industry in Wyoming County is the prison—most people there work in the prison, work in service industries connected with the prison, or are related to the white rural guards who staffed the prison at the time of the rebellion. So the trials were moved to Erie County, 30 miles away. The defense had attempted to get the trials held in New York City, where the ethnic balance of the population more closely approximated the population of the prison, but they failed. Erie County is a place of tight-knit ethnic enclaves and comfortable white suburbs; the area is politically conservative. During the prison rebellion, local papers ran full-page stories about guards who had their throats cut and torn genitals stuffed into their mouths. The stories were later proven false, but the idea that the violence had been precipitated by a number of downstate violent "niggers" never lost currency.

Justice King had little experience in criminal cases and he was terrified of coming off as another foolish and bumbling Julius Hoffman. He ran a tight, almost paranoid court, complete with a caged-in entryway and heavily armed deputies in constant attendance. He was so afraid of reversal that, in the early days of the trial, he met regularly with another Supreme Court justice to go over his decisions; he several times without explanation reversed himself the following morning. King refused to permit the defense to discuss the political or social situation at Attica; he allowed no testimony about anything before or after the first day of the riot. It would be hard to prove his rulings were prejudiced, but most courtroom observers felt he regularly sided with the prosecution and reacted to objections from Hill's lawyer, William M. Kunstler, from his cocounsel Margaret Ratner, and from Ramsey Clark (who, with Edward Koren and Herman Schwartz represented Pernasilice), with an animosity not generated by anything that had happened in his courtroom. After the verdict, for example, Kunstler and Clark asked that both defendants be allowed to stay on bail until sentencing and appeal; King refused and immediately remanded both to the county jail. The attorneys argued that the defendants had always appeared whenever anyone asked for them during the past two years, and that Pernasilice's offense was only a Class E felony (maximum of four years). The judge remained adamant. Kunstler said he was worried that Hill and Pernasilice would be murdered in jail. "If they die in jail you know who put them there," he said. "You did," the judge replied. Reporters in the courtroom got the sense that the judge was speaking of Kunstler's politics, not his defense.

Kunstler's concern was not irrelevant. Hill and Pernasilice had been convicted for killing and assaulting a prison guard. Ironically, neither should have been in Attica in the first place, since they had been sent to prison as youthful offenders, not felons. Hill now faces a life sentence; Pernasilice faces one to four years. The great danger, while the appeal drags on, is that both will be murdered in prison. The guards won't do it, but it is easy enough in those places for the guards to influence inmates to do such work for them. Pernasilice, who will be in prison for only a short time even if his appeal fails, is in a more dangerous situation than Hill; the guards will want to make their point before he is set loose.

From the guards' position, making the point is important. These two young Indians are the first Attica inmates to be convicted in a case involving the death of a guard. If they were to do easy time or go free after only a year or two, then the guards will feel that their own lives are in greater danger. It isn't likely they will allow that. The killings will occur as the murders of Becket and Jock Yablonski probably occurred, in the subjunctive: Would that someone would rid me of this rude servant. . . . And someone will—someone always does.

After the jury was polled, Kunstler and Clark rushed to the county jail, their concern being for the immediate safety of Hill and Pernasilice. Kunstler was stopped by reporters on his way out. "This is an utter miscarriage of justice," he told them. "These are two innocent men who have been convicted after a trial in which perjured and fabricated testimony was offered. . . . I know that if John Hill is in jail for having killed a corrections officer, he will be killed or molested or injured or harmed in jail. . . . " (Kunstler had some grounds for fearing the kind of protection the deputy sheriffs in the jail would give his client. One deputy told the jury that Margaret Ratner was "a prick," and a day after being reported for that told a row of spectators in the courtroom that the defense staff and defendants were "faggots, all of them—faggots." A policeman called Kunstler a "fucking Jew." Most important: during an early stage of the trial the deputies had themselves beaten Pernasilice.

The sequence of trials has been carefully planned by the prosecution: the first had to do with the presumed rape by blacks of a white; that was thrown out for lack of corroborating evidence. The Hill-Pernasilice case had to do with the presumed killing of a white guard by a pair of young Indians. The next case will involve the killing of one inmate by other inmates. The various cases dealing with kidnapping and felony murder come late in the series. The state wants convictions on the easy ones before it goes on to the others.

Shortly after the end of the Hill-Pernasilice trial, two public revelations threatened to make a judicial shambles of the entire Attica prosecution sequence. First was the discovery of a 140-page report by former Assistant Atty. Gen. Malcolm H. Bell on irregularities in the Attica prosecutions that had been given to New York Governor Carey the first week in January. Bell had been in charge of much of the grand jury phase of the Attica prosecution. He claimed that his boss, chief Attica prosecutor Anthony G. Simonetti, had kept him from presenting to the Wyoming County grand jury information about slaughter by prison guards and state troopers during the taking of the prison and about torture of inmates after the institution was secured. When in mid-April Bell began talking to the press about his report, Carey agreed to have an investigation of the charges, but he didn't explain why the report had been kept secret until the Hill-Pernasilice trial had been completed. One National Guard doctor told reporters that he had told officials about tortures he had seen immediately after the takeover, but he wasn't formally questioned until two and a half years later, by which time he could no longer identify the people involved. No one in the Attorney General's office explained why such evidence was ignored for so long or why Bell's investigations were limited.

Defense attorneys in various Attica cases immediately began filing motions for dismissal on the ground of selective prosecution: some inmates who were only in the yard during the rebellion have been charged with kidnapping, while police and guards who, against orders, shot down unarmed men (the prison guards weren't supposed to take part in the invasion) were not even subject to serious attention by the investigators. It was long assumed that the Wyoming County grand jury brought in no guard and police indictments because its members identified closely with prison authorities, but now it appears that they were supported in that point of view by state officials who wanted the trials limited to inmates and former inmates.

Before the force of Bell's disclosure was fully appreciated by defense staffs, there came another disclosure that may be even more explosive: a young woman named Mary Jo Cook admitted that she had spied on the Attica defense team for some months and had transmitted that information to the FBI. Although FBI representatives insisted her work was not connected with Attica (she was hired to spy on the Vietnam Veterans Against the War and on welfare rights groups), she pointed out that her monthly informer fee increased after she started transmitting Attica defense information. The FBI did admit she was paid from June 1, 1973, through October 22, 1974, "at which time she was discontinued." They did not say why she was discontinued or what was done with the Attica information she supplied.

There is still no way to evaluate how much that information helped the prosecution in the Hill-Pernasilice case, but New York sociologist Jay Schulman, who worked on the jury selection project, said he was amazed at the state prosecutors' "unfailing correctness" in rejecting jurors the defense wanted to have sit on the trial. He said that in none of the many other political trials he worked on in the past several years had the prosecutors' rejections so accurately frustrated the defense attorneys' desires. Unless one assumes that the prosecution in this case was untypically astute, then Ms. Cook's information seems to have played a vital part in the prosecution of John Hill and Charles Pernasilice.

It is hard to take seriously FBI claims that they didn't seek Attica information and that they didn't work with the state prosecutors. Recent revelations about FBI perjury and deception in the Wounded Knee trial indicate that the agency is quite willing to lie to judges about how it acquires information and how it rewards spies and informants it places in defense organizations. It will take far more than press questions to establish the truth of what the FBI did in the Attica trials and to evaluate how much the chances for a fair trial were reduced by FBI transmittal of privileged conversations and defense strategies. Nor do we know how many other paid informants the FBI has currently spread among the defense teams working on the other Attica trials. Kunstler and Clark moved to have the convictions of Hill and Pernasilice set aside because these revelations indicate the prosecution was so contaminated that the defendants had little chance at a fair trial. State attorneys have made it clear that they will fight these motions.

Someone said recently that Attica is the only public horror of recent years that never made it into the pop culture. Unlike the Kennedy assassinations, the war in Vietnam, the Chicago 7 trial and the Nixon fiasco, Attica was just too awful to be absorbed, too gratuitous to make sense in the glittery scene of late-night talk shows, amusing posters and easy books. A secret social ulcer was revealed during those horrible days in the Attica yard, and the main spokesmen were gunned down in an explosive orgy by troopers and prison guards who indiscriminately slaughtered their own along with the convicts. The conversation started in the Attica yard was drowned in the blasts of rifles and shotguns. The man who ordered that silence—Nelson Rockefeller—is now Vice President of the United States.

In this sequence of trials, the state of New York is desperately trying to make it all sensible. It is trying to say that the blacks and their friends were responsible. That is a lie, and the million-dollar conviction of two Indians who at the time of the rebellion were teenagers who shouldn't even have been in Attica, and the desperate attempt to squelch awareness of the significance of selective prosecution and illegal spying on the defense, are only the most recent steps in making that lie a commodious and acceptable public truth.

Exiles from
the American Dream

(Atlantic Monthly, 1967)

The most significant change in the street drug world since this piece was written has been the AIDS epidemic among intravenous drug users. AIDS kills more drug addicts than overdose and infectious myocarditis, hepatitis, and all other diseases transmitted by dirty needles. The other changes in the drug world are minor, almost cosmetic. Crack replaced amphetamines as the illicit accelerator of choice; the steamy rhetoric of the federal war against crack was adopted from the 1960s federal war against amphetamines. The apparently recent decline in use of crack seems to have come about for the same reasons as the decline in amphetamine use: education and fashion, not arrests and imprisonments. In the 1960s the Federal Bureau of Narcotics (FBN) handled opiate and marijuana cases, the Food and Drug Administration (FDA) handled non-narcotic pharmaceutical cases (barbiturates, amphetamines), and Customs and the Border Patrol got involved in shipments into the country. After a succession of notable failures and scandals, FBN was absorbed into the Bureau of Drug Abuse Control, and that agency eventually gave way to the Drug Enforcement Agency (DEA). Not long after his election, President George Bush created the Office of National Drug Control Policy (ONDCP), whose first director was William J. Bennett, who had previously served as director of the National Endowment for the Humanities and secretary of education. The ONDCP office was a coordinating agency without any operational authority of its own. Bennett announced that his first major coordinating project would result in a significant alleviation of the drug problem in Washington, D.C. The effort failed.

Law enforcement remains not only the most expensive, but also the least successful, form of drug abuse control. The very nature of the lower-level drug economy is such that if local dealers are arrested, new dealers spring up to take their places even before they're out on bail. There is a never-ending stream of replacements for users who are arrested and institutionalized in jails or hospitals because the conditions that make patterned drug use attractive are not changed one bit by incarcerating users and dealers. Drugs are a symptom of a problem, not a cause of it, and the drug economy is profoundly elastic. So, ironically, the primary effect of efficient law enforcement as the key method of drug control is a consistent increase in the price of the drugs being controlled—which, as any market analyst knows, means that selling them becomes even *more* attractive. According to Harvard researcher Mark A. R. Kleiman, federal expenditures for enforcement of marijuana laws in the 1980s grew from $526 million to $968 million, but those expenditures changed neither the drug's availability nor its rate of use. Instead, the federal efforts stimulated the production of domestic marijuana, much of which was far more potent than what had been imported previously ("Policy on Marijuana Has Failed, Study Says," 1989). In the same period, the street price of a kilogram of cocaine dropped from $65,000 to $16,000 (Morganthau, 1989:47), suggesting greater availability than ever.

The Cambridge research organization I mention at the beginning of this article was the Arthur D. Little Company (ADL), a major consultant firm. Somewhere in the middle of the project several of us on the field team realized that a vice president of the company was rewriting our reports each night so Treasury Department officials wouldn't see what we were writing about federal narcotics policies. When we complained, we were told that it was important to keep the *really* critical points about practice and policy out of the formal reports because those would only antagonize a potential client. "If the government accepts what we have to say here, they're going to have to do a lot of retooling, so there's no point pissing off the people in Treasury we'll have to deal with later," was how it was explained to me. I argued that if the tough stuff were taken out of our reports there would be no reason for the Feds to make any changes. "Don't worry," the ADL vice president said, "I'll be having discussions with a representative from Treasury and I'll communicate our major concerns orally. That will save them embarrassment." One member of our team said that if all communications about what mattered was to be limited to oral argument, it might be better if some members of the research and field teams joined in the discussions; the ADL vice president, after all, knew nothing about the study except what he read in our reports. "No," the ADL vice president replied, "this is above your level, and we don't want to antagonize them." It was clear that he thought any or all of us would antagonize the Feds and he knew how to stroke them properly.

Then the project was over and I was back at Harvard for the fall term. One October morning I went to ADL to pick up my copy of the final report. "I can't give you one," the secretary said. I asked why not. "I've been told not to give copies to any of the consultants on the field team," she said. Copies of the report, she said, were restricted to ADL executives, Treasury Department and FBN officials, and the Crime Commission liaison officer. Someone in ADL gave me a copy of the report anyway and I saw why we'd been omitted from the distribution list: many of our most critical points had been chopped out by an executive who'd had nothing to do with the research except approving our expenditures and collating our data. Most notably absent was all our discussion exploring the likelihood that narcotics law enforcement incurred greater social and economic costs than narcotics law abuse.

The ploy didn't work: the Crime Commission (so I heard) thought the ADL report was so pusillanimous that there were no further contracts. And the man to whom the ADL vice president presumably recited all our key points: he left Treasury shortly thereafter and took a job as counsel for ComSat, and not long after that he was killed in a plane crash.

IN THE SUMMER OF 1966 I traveled around the country for a Cambridge research organization that had contracted with the President's Commission on Law Enforcement and Administration of Justice to study certain problems having to do with drug abuse and control in this country. The main part of my job was talking with and observing at work a spectrum of participants: police, judges, doctors, administrators, addicts, pushers, ex-addicts, rehabilitation personnel, and so on. We found early in the study that none of the sets of figures purporting to tell the numbers of drug abusers and their relationship to the economy were much good, and that almost everyone had The Answer. We spent the summer getting as many points of view as we could, then tried to make sense of those that were sufficiently rational and to evaluate those that seemed worth it.

After the report was written, I realized that many of my blacks and whites had gone to problematical gray, the burden of increased knowledge. I realized also that part of that knowledge was of a kind outside the numbers and specifics that fill government reports and sociological journal articles; it is composed of pieces of information that do not array themselves in nice neat patterns; they do not form pretty theses or admit nice tabular or verbal conclusions—but somehow I cannot help feeling that they are in many ways more important, more germane, than the figures and the charts. Art and science go around constructing and projecting coherences; the street does not think in coherences, it is just there.

An example: unlike police who deal with homicide or other major crimes, who have onetime or rare contact with their customers, the police who handle problems of morality rather than injury, crimes like prostitution and drug addiction, tend to develop a peculiar rapport with the people with whom they war. They do not deal in terms of single events, but in continuing relationships, some of which they must maintain in order to obtain information, others because there is no reason not to. This varies from city to city, but there is a clear level of consistency. The narcotics detective must live in the junkie's world, know his language, appreciate his pain; he may be—and often is—antagonistic to all of these, but he is rarely independent of them.

The sections that follow are from notes scribbled in police cars, in bars, on planes, on a beach, sitting in a park; they are some of those other pieces.

New York

Ray Viera is the larger, more volatile of the two. His hair is wavy with streaks of gray, and he tends to tap your shoulder when he is involved in a statement. Burt Alvins is smaller, wiry; most of his head is a short gray-flecked crew cut. Burt negotiates the green Lark around some construction on F.D.R. Drive; it doesn't feel much like a police car.

"Everybody lives outside the city now," one of them says.

"Not everybody," I say.

"I mean all the cops and firemen I know. Except for a couple of young single guys. Everybody else is out on the Island or up in Westchester. It's going to be just the poor and the illegal left in New York. People are moving out in droves. They're not doing it to escape the taxes. Taxes are just as high out there. They're doing it to keep their children together."

They complain about court decisions. "We've become robots. We can't think, we're mechanical men."

"Everybody I know quits at twenty years to the day. It's not the job he dislikes, it's the handcuffing."

"A thing a normal person would consider suspicious a policeman can't consider suspicious because we're robots."

"I'd give a month's pay to bring Earl Warren here and give him the tour I'm giving you."

"There's legitimate people here. They're suffering, they're in jail."

I ask how to break through the hostility, what you do about the reputation for brutality.

"You just count the days you have left."

We drive along 118th Street. The area crawls with big-city specialties: numbers, junk, whores. Garbage piles up in back, between the houses. The garbage men can't get in there because the backs are locked, so the stuff mounts and mounts, and every once in a while they make an assault and get some of it out, chasing away rats as big and careless as dogs.

"We have to go see somebody."

"One of our informers," Ray says. "This guy's not stupid. He's intelligent. He's a nice guy. Wait till you see him though."

We enter a building just above Central Park. Someone lives on the first floor. The second, up the narrow dark stairway that is even darker after the bright sun, is vacant. All the doors are open; one is unhinged and lies flat in the room, as if something walked right in without bothering to stop. Another door hangs at a grotesque angle, the top hinge ripped off. More rubbish in there. A few empty bottles. We go up another flight, and Ray goes to Elmer's door. It is unlocked, and he eases it open slowly. Elmer is sitting on the bed, a blanket over his knees. "Anybody here?" Ray asks.

"No. I'm alone."

Ray waves us in. The room is about twelve by twelve. A big, old TV is on a bureau by the wall. A new Sony is on another bureau, turned on to a talk show. Elmer tells us a prostitute friend bought it for him as a present.

"How are your legs, Elmer?" Ray asks.

Elmer moves the blanket from his thighs. On both are long running sores, about four or five inches long and a half inch or so wide; they look deep; something oozes.

"Jesus Christ," Burt says. "Why don't you let us get you in the hospital for a while?"

"Maybe next week."

"Those sores don't look so good."

"I can't go in this week. You know."

"How are your arms?"

"Feel a little better." He holds his forearms out and moves the fingers. A Popeye caricature: from the elbows up, the arms are the thin sticks of an old man; below the elbow, they are swollen like thighs. The fingers all look like oversize thumbs. Like his thighs, Elmer's arms are covered with scars that look like strip photos of the surface of the moon. There are too many of the dime- and quarter-size craters to count.

"This is Bruce, Elmer. He's a new man, and we're breaking him in."

Elmer looks up, noticing or acknowledging me for the first time. He nods and shrugs. They make a date to meet somewhere later in the week.

"You sure you don't want us to get you in a hospital, Elmer?" Ray asks.

Elmer says no.

For me, Ray asks, "Elmer, what you shooting now?"

"About eight bags."

"When did you start?"

"1955."

"And how old are you now?"

"Forty-eight."

There's a silence, directed to me. Elmer looks sixty-five or seventy, and they all know I'd thought him an old man. He folds the blanket over his thighs, and we go out. On the way, Burt gives Elmer a few bucks and says get some cigarettes.

Going down the stairs, Ray says, "If he tells you he's shooting eight bags, that means he's shooting twelve. That's sixty bucks a day. Seven days a week. Four hundred and twenty dollars a week. Almost what I make a month." Elmer, obviously, is in some business activities about which the police prefer not to ask.

Most New York addicts, I know, spend less than twenty dollars a day for narcotics. Few look as grim as Elmer. But enough do. And enough wind up dead because of infection or accidental overdose; many have TB. The physiological debilitation and destruction result from concomitants of drug taking: the junkie spends his money for drugs instead of food, his drugs are cut with quinine and other chemicals that often do him considerable damage, and worst of all, the material he injects and the instruments he uses are so unsanitary that he constantly risks the kinds of infection that have scarred Elmer. The junk itself, so long as it does not exceed the addict's tolerance, is not really as physiologically harmful as cigarettes or alcohol, but the life-style is vicious.

"Some of these guys," Burt says, "they get worse than Elmer. Ruin all the veins in the arms and legs, burn them out, and they shoot in the mouth. And when that goes, in the penis. Hurts like hell, they say, but they can find the vein."

I ask them if their visiting Elmer's apartment in daylight might not get him into trouble with other addicts. They say no, they spend a lot of time questioning addicts, most of whom are not informers, standard procedure.

"These people around here—they know who you are?"

"Sure, they know us. Even if they'd never seen us before, they'd know us. If you're white around here, you're either a bill collector or the Man. They maybe don't know which Man you are, but you're one of them."

"Or a trick looking for a whore," Burt says.

"You still get white tricks coming up here?"

"They'll always be coming up here."

We drive past a crap game. There are about fifty men standing around. Some of them yell.

They talk about Elmer. "I'm worried about him, Burt. Can't we get him into some hospital?"

"He doesn't want to go. We can't force him."

"Well, how about we get him some antibiotics for those sores? They're just awful."

"You have to have a prescription for that stuff."

"Maybe I can get somebody to let me have some."

"Heroin you can get; for penicillin you need a prescription."

We stop for a traffic light. A kid about five years old looks in the car, at me, says, "Fuck you, cop," and walks away.

We sit in the car by the 125th Street New York Central station. Two junkies they know hustle down 125th, counting money. We know where they are going, but there isn't sufficient cause to follow and arrest.

"I know what the courts are trying to do—protect the honest citizens. But you know something: in all the years we've been in this business, we've never hit one guy that was a square."

"The trouble with this job," Burt says, "is you take it home with you. We get together, and our wives say, why don't you talk about something else. They don't understand."

"You can't put if off at night," Ray says.

I look through their report book. They get two days off per week, but I notice that they work at least one, and sometimes both of them, either going out with an undercover agent or appearing in court. Many of the workdays run twelve to sixteen hours. I ask why they stick with it.

"I think it's a challenge," Burt says. "I like the work. But as my partner and I have told you a number of times, our hands are tied. To do this kind of a job I guess you have to have some dedication in you. It's a losing battle: for every one you arrest, there's five to take their place. But when you do make a good arrest, it can make the whole thing worthwhile."

I say something about Elmer.

"They ought to put a picture of him in the papers," Ray said. "Show some of these people."

"You could show them a picture of Elmer," Ray says. "Tomorrow they pick up a paper to see what the Giants did. That's it. As far as it goes."

Driving downtown we pass through Central Park. "It's like reverse shock treatment," Ray says. We see a spreading plume of black smoke over on the East Side, somewhere in the Eighties.

Burt: "Probably a junkie cooking up."

Ray: "Good-sized cooker."

And Burt: "You come back after a day off and hope maybe things are going to be a little different. Then it's not. There's still glass in the street. The same people."

Houston

Morning in the Narcotics Squad room. Captain Jack Renois and Don McMannes are the only ones in. Hooker, the secretary, does things and fetches coffee. The detectives come in around 11:00 or 11:30 and wait for the phone calls from informers. Things come alive around noon, after the addicts get up. One of the detectives is selling a shotgun; it is passed around and admired.

A phone rings. An addict snitching on another addict. For money, for a break on a case. Or maybe just talking for a while. I begin to appreciate the odd symbiosis. The addicts and the cops move in the same world, live the same hours, wait for deals to happen on the same streets. One addict had said something to me the week before, complaining about the hassles he was always in, and one police official had complained to me this morning about the difficulty he had getting adequate funds and equipment. Both used exactly the same sentence: "We got to scuffle for every fucking thing."

Don comes back into the room; he had been on the phone for about thirty minutes. "He just wanted to talk for a while," he tells me. "Somebody I arrested once." The addicts sometimes call up officers, not to snitch or bitch, but just to talk to someone who understands. For them, no one appreciates their hassles and their world better than the cop, who is so close they don't even consider him a square.

On Lieutenant Kennedy's desk: *"FIAT JUSTITIA, RUAT CAELUM."* And under it, in small letters, "Let justice be done, though the heavens may fall." "I saw it a long time ago and I liked it and it's been on my desk ever since," he says. "A reminder, I guess."

With one of the detectives, I go out to visit an informer. She is a slight pretty girl with dark eyes. Two children are in the house, and she says she can't stay in the car talking for very long. She talks about Joey, with whom she lives, currently in jail needing bond. "They say that county farm's a bad place. I don't know. Maybe I'll get him out."

She used to be a good booster, but no more. Shoplifting has become too dangerous: "I got too many children now. Nobody to take care of them if I go to the joint." A new connection had come by a few days ago and given her fifty dollars' worth of narcotics without asking for money.

"How come?" asks the detective. "He want some trim?"

"I don't know. Maybe. If Joey wasn't there." She tells us where the connection lives and who is with him, and the phone number.

"You hooked again?"

"No. I can't afford it. I shoot all the dope I can get, though."

"You high now?"

"No. I had two caps this morning. That's all."

Later the same day: riding with Mike Chavez and his partner, Charley. While Mike is at a phone booth, Charley tells me he has just been transferred into Narcotics from Vice. He says about every whore he knows is on some kind of drugs, that whenever they broke into a prostitute's apartment they found narcotics or pills.

"Did you ever file?"

"No."

"Why not?"

"Wouldn't stand up. Almost everything we would do is illegal. They know it, and we know it. Our job was mainly harassment. Make them uncomfortable enough to move on." Later he tells me it is as hard to make a prostitution case as a narcotics case. A few weeks earlier in Harlem, a New York policeman had told me the same thing.

Mike comes back. "Anything?" Charley asks.

"No."

Chavez has never taken the test for sergeant. Only one sergeant is permitted in the Narcotics unit, and if Chavez were promoted, he would be forced to change assignments. He likes the work and is very good at it.

He tells me that the talk and newspaper articles about violent addicts are nonsense; what bothers him is the crime associated with addiction. I mention the six million or so alcoholics, and all the damage they do. Chavez pulls up to a booth to make another call. While he is gone, Charley tells me what I said is irrelevant. Chavez comes back and says, "Funny, what you were saying. They have a bar in that store, and I could see that every stool was occupied." He says he would like to find some other way of handling the problem, but he doesn't know one that would work. He shrugs and says it bothers him sometimes. "But I'm a policeman, you know." He turns to Charley, sitting in the back, and says, "You got your gun?"

"Yeah."

I turn and see on the seat a .38 automatic. He tells me you need a holster for a revolver and everything bulges, but an automatic can be just tucked in the belt. I ask Mike if he has his.

"In the trunk."

Later that night, Donny tells me they almost never need weapons. No

Houston addict would draw on a detective because the addicts know the detectives aren't going to shoot without a good reason. "Only time any of them ever does anything with a gun is to say, 'I got a gun.' I say, 'Where?' and he points, and I say, 'Put it on the table,' and he does. Or if he has one in his hand when we bust in, he just swings it around and hands it over. We all know each other."

Austin

I was in the homicide room of the police station waiting for Lieutenant Harvey Gann, the detective in charge of the Vice and Narcotics Squad. According to friends of mine in Houston and Huntsville, he is a very good policeman. Gann came in, laughing. He and his partner had just been out on a narcotics watch that didn't work out. They were using an old pickup truck and had stopped for a red light when two women walked over, and one said, "You want to have a good time?"

"How much?"

"Ten and three."

"What's the three for?"

"The room, baby."

Gann asked if the same applied for her friend and his friend. The other woman said yes. Gann noticed a tall Negro standing in a nearby doorway, and said, "Who's he?"

"Just an old nothing sonofabitch that hangs around."

Gann and his partner got out of the truck, took off their LBJ hats and lensless glasses.

"Goddamn, Lieutenant! It's you again!" The woman began laughing.

"You see," he told me, "I had arrested her four times before. And I put those hat and glasses right back on because we couldn't all fit in front, and I had to ride with them in the back of the pickup, and I'd be damned if I'd have anybody I know see me riding around town in a pickup truck with two old whores like that."

New York

The undercover man is late.

The two detectives, Al Koch and Ray Imp, lean against the phone booth they use for an office. The phone has an "Out of Order" sign on it that is phony. The two men are easily identifiable (one is about 6 feet 3 inches and has shocking red hair; the other is about 5 feet 10 inches and is shaped like a triangle but gives the feeling of a tank), and when they appear on the street, the dealers disappear, so they hover outside the Village perimeter, wait for a call from someone telling them a person they want to arrest is at a specific location, then go in and come out quickly.

The undercover man arrives at eight, an hour late. His name is Sam, and even though I know he is a police officer, I can't quite believe it—the first qualification of an undercover agent.

Al tells me it will be boring waiting with them. He suggests I go with Sam.

"But I know people in the Village."

"Do they know what you're doing in town?"

"No."

"OK. You go with him. They'll think he's just some beatnik friend of yours. We'll just be standing here until he calls anyhow. But take that notebook and cigar and pen out of your pocket."

I hand over my things and go away with Sam.

We walk to the Rienzi, where we are to meet someone named Wilson, his informer. Wilson isn't there, and Sam curses him, saying he can't stand an unpunctual man. He tells me the statistics reporting 60,000 addicts in the United States are all wrong, there are hundreds of thousands of them. I must have looked incredulous because he says, "Yeah, man, I'm serious. Look around you. Half these people smoke weed."

"You don't get addicted to marijuana. They're not addicts."

"Goddamn right they are."

We walk down the street. Someone says hello to me, and I nod. Sam says, "I'll tell you who uses weed all the time: those folk singers. Bunch of addicts."

"Oh."

"You know any of those folk singers?"

"A few."

"They use weed."

We pass one place just as a four-man singing group is going in with their guitars. They pass in front of us. One of them sees me and waves; another says, "Hi, Bruce." I wave back. Sam looks at me queerly, then shrugs it off.

We go back to the Rienzi and talk about Court decisions.

"Those bastards. What this country needs is a Hitler for a while. Get these people off the streets. Should have elected Goldwater; he'd have straightened that Court out. You know why I hate addicts?" I shake my head. "I'll tell you why: I got a nice wife, over on Staten Island. She never heard a dirty word in her life. A nice girl." He says it with finality. I don't make the connection, but I decide to let it ride; it is too early in the evening to reveal my opacity.

We watch the teenage girls in their carefully considered outfits.

We go into a bar, and over a beer he talks about his work. "Shouldn't we talk about something else? Someone might be listening."

"Nah. Nobody's listening. Nobody listens here." I don't tell him that when I go into bars like this, I always eavesdrop. Constitutional.

We go up the street to get something to eat, but on the way meet Wilson, the informer. With him is another man, who wears khakis, a white T-shirt, and a yellow sport shirt open all the way except for the bottom button. Wilson, the informer, goes off to talk with Sam.

The man in the yellow shirt says to me, "Who you with?"

"Huh?"

"I said who you with?"

"What are you talking about?"

"It's OK, man, I'm undercover too."

"A city cop?"

"No," he says, shaking his head.

"FBN?"

"No."

"Who?"

"FDA." He pauses, maybe to see if I'm going to make a wisecrack. When I don't, he says, "You city?"

I shake my head.

"Federal?"

I shake my head.

"Then who are you undercover for?"

"I'm not a cop."

"Come *on,* man."

A thin effeminate man in his twenties lopes up the street, walking sine waves. "My consciousness has expanded, expanded!"

"Man, is he drunk," the FDA man says.

"It might be something else." The thin guy weaves back. "What you on, man?" I ask.

"Five days on, five days off."

"Off and on what?"

"LSD, psilocybin off days. Little junk to keep the heebies away." He bumps into the FDA man and pats the shoulder of his yellow shirt. "Ain't it a bitch when your family's square?"

"Your family square?"

"You don't *know.* My father is —— [he names someone in city government whose name we know], and he is *square.* "

On an off chance there's another celebrity with the same name, I ask, "Which——?"

"You know which one."

"Come on."

He pulls out his wallet and shows us his collection of identification cards, credit cards, and licenses; they all say——, Jr. Sam joins us. I look for Wilson, the informer, but he has disappeared. Thin says his family is down on him because he uses drugs.

"What else?"

"Drugs and because of the homosexual business."

"Are you queer?"

"Maybe a little."

He says he can get, in quantity, marijuana and pills. Sam and the FDA man try to stare one another down: if Thin produces grass, he is Sam's; if he produces pills, he is FDA's. Thin weaves in and out of the street. He goes to peer in a car window.

"I thought he'd pat my gun when he was tapping my shoulder just now," FDA says.

"You wearing a gun?" Sam says.

"Yeah. You?"

"I got a little .25."

"Ah. I got my .38 service."

"That cannon. You're crazy. If you ask me, you're better off with nothing."

Thin swings back to the sidewalk. Wilson, the informer, returns and points at someone, and Sam says, "Oh, oh, there's my man," and goes off down Bleeker. FDA wanders away with Thin, talking hippy.

"Come on," Wilson, the informer, says. "We got to stick with Sam."

"Where is he?"

"I don't know. Maybe he went into the park." We walk toward the park. "You new on the squad?"

"I'm not on the squad."

"Oho. A fed, huh?"

"What makes you think I'm a cop?"

"C'mon, man, it's OK. I'm an informer. We're all in this together. It's like I'm a half-cop, you know."

"Oh, all right, I'm working for the feds. But I'm not a cop. I'm a schoolteacher, and I'm doing a study."

"Hey, that's good. Say, what's your undercover name?"

"Bruce."

"What's your real name?"

"Bruce."

"You can't do that. You got to have an undercover name."

"I always use Bruce."

"OK, man, it's your *schtik*. We might meet someone, and I might have to introduce you or something. Where do you say you come from?"

"Cambridge."

"Come on, man, the Village is crawling with people from Cambridge."

"I *am* from Cambridge."

"Jesus Christ, man!"

We walk into Washington Square Park.

(Wilson stopped and talked with some characters he knew, and I stayed out of the light, which he seemed to appreciate. I knew several undercover agents had been exposed, "burned" in the argot, and badly beaten recently. I wondered what this nut was leading me into. I wondered what they were all leading themselves into. These people were so different from the cops uptown, the serious and competent Alvins and Viera, with whom I'd sat that afternoon in a car in the west Eighties, talking with an informer while pretty polished women and expensive fat ladies passed us by, seeing only four men in a car; that informer knew he was dead if he should be seen with us, and the conversation was serious. Here it seemed they'd adjusted to the madcap crowd, not only in appearance but in procedure, in thought. A crazy game world on both sides again, like Houston. But different.)

We walk on toward the arch. Wilson tells me he'd like to work for the FBI as an undercover man in the Communist Party. "They ever use people for anything like that?"

"I believe they have, on occasion."

"You think they'd hire me? It's not like I'm inexperienced. And I hate this amateur crap."

"I don't know."

"They wouldn't take me in the army. I would have been good in the army, but they wouldn't take me."

"Why not?"

"'Cause I'm an addict. Got a record. All that crap." He shrugs. "But I'd sure like to be an undercover man working on Commies. Man, I'm a natural. Who'd ever suspect."

We spot Sam. Wilson and I sit next to him on the bench. Sam tells us where the suspect is sitting. Wilson gets up, grabs my arm, and says, "Come on, man."

"Where we going?"

We walk behind the public toilets to a phone booth, and I wonder again about the setups. If even the police, who should know better, want to think I'm a cop, surely the other side would be willing to make the assumption. He calls the phone booth where Al and Ray wait. Wilson describes the suspect. "In the park, man, on Junkies' Row. Junkies' Row, I said." He hangs up, and we go back to watch the bust go down, but neither Sam nor the suspect is there. We rush out of the park, but see neither of them.

"You sit on that rail over there, and when Al comes by, you say, 'I don't know where the sonofabitch is.' Keep your head turned away. That way, if anyone is nearby, they'll think he asked you about someone and you wouldn't tell him anything; if no one is near, it won't look like you're talking to him at all. Everybody in the Village knows Al and Ray."

I sit on the rail, watching out of the corner of my eye for the two detectives to appear. I see them coming. As they near, I coolly turn away, waiting subtly to deliver my code message.

Several shoes stop in front of me, toes pointing my way. "Hey, Bruce," Al says. "Where'd they all go?"

"Shhh! We'll be spotted."

"Ah. Where'd they go?"

"Down McDougal."

They go down McDougal. I wait a tactful time, then follow. I see Al standing on the sidewalk across the street from Minetta's. I sit on a stoop about four doors away. Al comes over and sits next to me.

"Go away, Al. We'll be seen together." I feel as paranoid as a pusher.

"Ah, it's just the school kids. Nobody will notice."

A policeman with a walkie-talkie strapped to his body tells us to move on.

"In just a minute, officer," Al says. The policeman says make sure it's just a minute, and Al says we certainly will and thank you officer.

We watch the girls in their carefully considered outfits and the boys in their pageboys. "Bunch of kids," Al says. "Let's go back to the car."

"What if I get noticed walking with you?"

"Nah. Don't worry about it."

We walk back to the car.

After a while Ray comes with another detective, and we go back to the phone booth. It rings, and Ray answers. He listens for a moment, then sticks his head out. "Hey, Bruce: you're burned."

"I'm what?"

"You're burned. They saw you with Al, and they all know you're a cop."

"I'm not a cop."

"Tell *them.*"

They all laugh. "Way it goes," one of them says.

It is almost 1 A.M., and the street is thinning as the action moves indoors and only the desperate are left. No business here. They adjust the "Out of Order" sign and decide to quit early for a change.

Los Angeles

Bill Sanderson and Jack White look like TV actors who are supposed to look like L.A. detectives: both are good-looking, young, bright detective sergeants; both have been attending college part-time and expect a degree this year; both have been on the police force for eight years, in narcotics for less than one year.

Like police everywhere, they complain about some of the Supreme Court decisions, but they do not seem to feel as hamstrung. It takes more work and more men, but still the jobs seem to get done. "I think the Supreme Court is trying to force the problems back on the community that created the problems," one of them says.

"I can see why some people go to heroin," the other says. "It is the ultimate: it puts you to sleep and keeps you awake."

In Watts, we stop at the intersection of Central and Vernon. Where a large drugstore used to be there is now a tremendous tent and a hand-painted sign: *You must see and hear Rev. Eugene Lewis. Evangelist who ministers like Christ.* Like the topless joints in San Francisco, Watts is one of those places visitors must see; one gets the same feeling of futility in both. White and Sanderson point out locations where they made interesting drug arrests, locations where they hope to make others, places where they were during the riot. We are supposed to be discussing narcotics, but during the early part of the afternoon it is the riot. They still do not understand it; no one seems to. The houses are a surprise to me: in the East it would be a lower-middle-class neighborhood in a residential town. Parks, lawns, some cars. If you don't have a car, I find out, it takes an impossible amount of time to get around out here. Still, it is so unlike Harlem. Had so overwhelming a riot occurred first in swelling and wretched Harlem, we might have dismissed what Watts said: a man could want and need more than a house.

Later, we have dinner in a Mexican restaurant around the corner from the temple Aimee Semple McPherson built; then we ride over to Hollywood. The radio gives Jack White a woman's phone number. The first phone booth cheats him out of two dimes, the second booth works.

White makes a date to meet her, and we race back to headquarters to pick up another car and some buy money. A lieutenant comes with us. We follow Jack to the bar, then drive down half a block and park in the shadows of a closed garage.

The lieutenant, just off vacation, says, "It gets harder and harder to generate enthusiasm for this kind of mess."

"Vacations do that," Bill says.

"It's not the vacation. Just getting a little tired of it."

After a while, Jack comes out of the bar with two women. One of them gets into the car with him, the other goes away. He U-turns and goes up the street, and we follow him at a distance.

Jack parks in front of an apartment house, and we park under a streetlamp fifty yards behind. There are three cars between us. With the light directly overhead, our car is not so suspicious: you can't see anyone inside unless you are quite close. I can't see anything in the other car, but Bill says Jack and the woman are still in it. He tells me they are probably

I told the lieutenant what had happened, that Diane had been sleeping and I had been reading and our windows had been shot out in rapid succession.

"Rocks," the patrolman said from the other side of the room.

"What?"

"Rocks. They threw rocks through your windows." He lifted up one of the curtains and I saw on the floor a baseball-sized white stone.

There was a moment of wonderful relief. I associate rocks with vandals, people doing something hostile for the hell of it. Like the people who decorate New York City subways and walls with spray paint and aren't artist enough to spray anything interesting. Guns I associate with people who have a purpose. That is probably a result of watching too much television.

"Oh," I said, more than a little embarrassed. "I thought the windows had been *shot* out."

"Sure," the lieutenant said. "Makes the same noise from this side. A big bang and a lot of glass. Reasonable thing to think." I was liking him better.

"Scared hell out of me."

"Would me too," he said.

"So we just ran out of the room."

"Damned right," he said.

They looked around for a few minutes, but there was nothing for them to do. There was no victim to rush to the hospital, no perpetrator to restrain with chrome cuffs, no missing objects to list in black notebooks.

"We're going up the block for a while," the lieutenant said. "We'll come back."

"Why are you going up the block?" Diane asked.

"Guy up there had his windows busted up too."

They returned in twenty minutes. The lieutenant carried three rocks. He took one of mine. "Same kind of rocks," he said. I nodded. "You know what those windows of yours cost?" I said I had no idea. "The guy up the block, he said his windows cost $500 each. They're bigger than yours and they're thermopane. Yours thermopane?" I admitted they weren't. "They got four of his windows and the glass on his front door."

"You got any vendettas with anyone?" the patrolman asked.

Vendettas! I had a vision of the Corsican Brothers. Diane and I shook our heads.

"Sometimes something like this is a vendetta," the lieutenant said.

"Then why would they garbage the other house too?" I asked.

"Cover. It's great cover. That way you don't know it's them."

But that way, I thought, you don't get the satisfaction of knowing your victim knows it was *you*. Few people can manage secret revenge. The only people I remember who manage secret revenge are characters in Jerzy Kosinski novels.

"Maybe they got the wrong house," the patrolman said.

"They broke our windows by mistake?" Diane said, getting really angry now.

"We don't know that. Maybe they broke *his* windows by mistake. Your houses are similar colors. Maybe they were told what color house to hit, they hit one, then they noticed the other one so they hit that one too just to be sure."

"So they wouldn't have to come back," the lieutenant said. "That makes a lot of sense." The patrolman nodded modestly. Both policemen were very tall. They stood by the door. The patrolman now held one of the stones in his right hand. The stone rested partly in his palm and partly on the third joint of his first and second fingers. With his thumb, he rotated the stone as if he were looking for the stitching.

"What about fingerprints?" Diane asked. She watches a lot of television and believes in fingerprints.

"Nope. These rocks are too porous to hold prints. Anyway, even if they had prints, they're not much good. Prints are good only if you have somebody, a suspect. Then maybe you can match them up. Otherwise, it's too hard. If it was a homicide they might try to do something, but not for this sort of thing. Not for petty violence."

In the economics of urban hostility, homicide gets a measure of technological inspection not earned by shattered glass. The discrimination seemed reasonable enough, but secretly I, like Diane, would have preferred to have seen the forces of Law Enforcement humming through the dawn finding the evil perpetrators: *"All right, Rodney, we've matched the chemical composition of these stones and have found they could have come only from the private quarry behind your laboratory. And we found your pinkie prints on a smooth concave surface."*

"Good grief, Inspector. How did you find me out so quickly?"

"Police work, Rodney. Modern police work."

It doesn't work like that. If you don't see them or if they don't call up to tell the police or you who they were, then you can forget it. Murders have the highest rate of crime solution, which everybody who watches television knows, but the reason for the success rate is most murders are done by friends or relatives who hang around after it's over. Many of them call 911 themselves to say, "Hey, you guys should come over here because I just did something I maybe shouldn't have. I mean, Gloria's not moving and there's a *lot* of blood."

Pre-dawn rock-throwers don't call. Ours didn't, anyway.

The lieutenant was now the one fondling a rock in his right hand. He had placed the other two from his set on our hall table. "It's kind of late for this sort of thing."

"I would think so," I said.

"Drunks from the bars, they're usually done with this stuff before three. And it's raining tonight. Most drunks don't go out throwing rocks in the rain at four-thirty."

I had thought the same thing. I had always thought this time of night the safest. Even the dedicated creeps were usually home in bed by dawn. The ones set on violence had usually done it by this quiet hour and they were home resting up for the next time. When I lived in Boston and New York and San Francisco I regularly used to walk five A.M. streets I feared at midnight. I didn't know if those streets were in fact so much safer then, but they seemed that way. Nothing ever happened, anyway.

I told the policemen I was relieved to know it hadn't been bullets. Bullets could have come through the curtains. My head had been in line with the curtains. I thought it would have been awful for Diane to have waked up to all that gore.

I was holding one of the stones now; I didn't remember picking it up or having it handed to me. "There aren't any stones like this around here," I said. The cops nodded. "That means they planned to do it."

"But it doesn't mean they planned this house," the patrolman said. "It only means they planned to do it to somebody. Anybody."

"Some people," the lieutenant said, "don't have things and they just don't want other people to have them either."

"It's just petty violence, sir," the patrolman said.

I was sure it had been at least two people. The rocks came too rapidly and too accurately for it to have been one person with a load of rocks in one arm, firing them in sequence with great power and good aim. It was very late and it was raining, the time of night when you want company for your mischief just so you'll be sure later you really did it.

Two people, perhaps more. No: just two. More would have required coordination, intelligence, planning. This seemed the sort of thing two young men would do. A little planning, but not enough to involve a squad.

That was as far as I could get. I couldn't visualize faces. In the deep dark of night, not long before the sky will crack with dawn, there are two faceless men standing on the pavement in front of my house with a dozen large stones they have brought from somewhere far away. They don't know me and I don't know them; they don't know whether or not someone sits just beyond the curtains, they don't know whether the upstairs middle window they smash looks upon an empty room or a baby's crib. They don't ask or care.

I wonder if the faces were angry. If they were, at what and at whom? The stones were thrown with terrific force. The stone that went through the upstairs window made it all the way to the middle of the upper hallway.

When the police left I remembered standing in the shadows upstairs with the .22. It was loaded, but so what? It was nearly a toy, a slow-firing, light-load weapon. What if the crazies I imagined earlier actually had come charging through the shattered windows? The windows had gone out so fast I had been sure they were firing an automatic weapon.

I thought about buying a large-caliber pistol. Tomorrow, as soon as the stores opened, I'd go buy a pistol. Perhaps a Browning automatic with a fourteen-shot magazine, like the one Al Pacino had in *Serpico*. It would go into the cabinet next to the bed, its slide locked back. At the first sign of trouble I would ram a magazine into the butt and the slide would slam forward, carrying a round into the chamber and leaving the hammer cocked and ready. Come on, you goon, I'm ready for you this time.

Well: not tomorrow. This is New York, not Utah or Texas or Florida. You don't just walk up to the counter and pick up a handgun here. You have to go downtown and be fingerprinted and have a good justification for the judge and you have to prove you're of good character. All these things take time. I wanted that automatic now.

"Your honor, I am of good character and people throw rocks through my window so would you let me buy that pistol in the window?"

And what if the judge said yes? What would I *do* with a gun if I had it? Have a shoot-out on the lawn? Have a manly movie-type face-off with some moron who gets his jollies shattering glass after a boozy night out? The dialogue has been scripted in a thousand B-movies: "Drop that rock, you sonofabitch, I've got you covered!" Or: "Okay, buddy, I'm ready for you this time. Holster that rock and get ready to draw!" Glass-breaking is very scary and potentially dangerous, but it isn't and shouldn't be a capital crime.

I remember someone asking Clint Eastwood once about violence in one of his movies. "That was *him*, the guy I played in the movie who did that," Eastwood said, "it wasn't *me.*" The person didn't understand or accept the answer, or didn't like to think that the real-life Clint Eastwood just didn't walk about the one street that is most of downtown Carmel with an enormous sidearm ready to dysfunction forever any hostiles who approached.

I'd grown up with movies and television dramas in which Mr. Colt's Equalizers solved problems of terror. ("God may have created men equal," went the cliché, "but it took Mr. Colt to make it a fact.") The bad guy appears and the solution lies in the gentlefolk finding a champion who would, with all modesty and grace and hesitancy, blow him away forever.

Well, you don't blow away someone with an early morning rock in his hand and a late-night load of booze in his belly. Conflict in real life isn't solved that easily, fear isn't neutralized that simply. I know a lot of arguing about whether or not Jack will be allowed to go inside with her. Jack isn't going to give her a chance to go out a back door with the money, and he wants to find out what apartment the man with the stash is in so we can move in later—if there is a man inside; it might be a phony deal.

It gets tense. If there is someone inside, there may be trouble: if Jack is recognized, he is unarmed and might not be near enough a window to call for help. We wait. Nothing moves in the car ahead, and after a while Bill wonders too. He gets out of our car, strolls down the block away from both cars, crosses in the dark somewhere below, walks up a side street, comes back down the opposite side, then retraces his steps. He gets back in. "They're still there."

Footsteps from down the block. A man approaches, reading a magazine in the dark. He slows down when he's under streetlamps, speeds up in the dark places between. He crosses directly in front of our car, his face buried in the magazine. "Now isn't that something," the lieutenant says. The man is reading *Startling Detective*.

More time passes. Jack's car lights up and U-turns, going back toward the bar. We duck, let it go a little bit, then do the same, going pretty fast. We come out of the U-turn, run a red light, and zip past a patrol car.

"Uh," I say.

"I guess they recognized me. Or the car," Bill says.

Jack is stopped at a red light a block ahead. He turns right, then stops in front of the bar. After a while the woman gets out and Jack drives away. We follow him and park both cars in a dark place.

He tells us the woman wouldn't let him come inside, and he refused to trust her with the money. "C'mon baby, take a chance," she said. "Everybody gets screwed sometimes in this business."

"Not me," he told her.

They tell me they've been having trouble nailing a couple of Cuban traffickers. The lieutenant says he liked the old days better. "I'd rather work a nice clean old Mexican dope peddler. You go boot his door in, take him down, and that's all there is to it."

I'll tell you something: it is not *just* a nitty-gritty world out there; it is a thing more unreal sometimes than the one we academics are usually accused of maintaining. You discover after a while that no one wears a white hat except the man who is talking to you right now; everyone spouts dogma except that single voice under that single white Stetson. Little Pavlovian mechanisms set junkies and cops in the same motions, day after day after day. The élan varies with the jurisdiction: in New York it is cold and faithless antagonism with exceptions, part of the general *Weltanschauung;* in Texas, where everyone has a gun, the policeman and criminal feel closer to one another.

It is little people, little, little people, playing out an ugly little game among themselves and taking it with precious and desperate seriousness, positing some lovely and fragile élan because both sides know that no one else in the world is willing to love them. Exiled from our American dream where everyman has his soporific and his weapon, the junkie and the cop find themselves bound to one another in one agonizing coil, and like Burton and Taylor in *Virginia Woolf,* they've learned the visceral lesson: people who bleed each other need each other.

Blackballing the Fiedlers

(New Republic, 1967)

In the fall of 1965 Leslie A. Fiedler, perhaps America's best-known literary critic, left the University of Montana, where he had taught for more than two decades, and joined the faculty of the University of Buffalo, which had only a few years earlier become part of the rapidly expanding State University of New York (UB was never, as I snidely assert in this essay, an "innocuous diploma mill"). In early June 1967, Fiedler and his wife Margaret were arrested on the misdemeanor health code violation of maintaining premises on which narcotic drugs were used. Fiedler had not been accused of using drugs himself, but he was an outspoken proponent of individual freedom in a conservative town still not comfortable with what many perceived as a takeover of its local university by Jewish outsiders. He was an attractive and accessible target for the politically ambitious police narcotics captain, Michael Amico.

A police undercover informant working for Amico befriended the Fiedler children and through them got regular access to the house. She wore a radio transmitter with the microphone hidden in her brassiere. One evening she radioed the stakeout car that a piece of hashish was on a third-floor bathroom sink. The police raided the house immediately, arrested the Fiedler children on a drug possession charge, and arrested the Fiedlers on the misdemeanor health charge. It was a grand scandal, with one of the two local papers reporting the affair as if it had involved massive quantities of illicit chemicals and unprintable sensual activities. In point of fact, it was one kid on the third floor with one small piece of hash, one informant talking to her left breast, and a large household unaware of the hash or the electronic cleavage. Leslie and Margaret Fiedler were, at the time the police burst into the house, reading books in the first-floor living room.

There never was ever any question who Amico and the prosecutors were really after. "I actually stood trial," Fiedler told me recently, "and a long, exhausting trial it turned out to be. In the end I was sentenced to six months in jail. Margaret was also tried with me. We simply made a deal beforehand that if they were willing to drop the charges against the kids, we would be willing to take the heat and give them the publicity they were after."

Five years and an enormous number of dollars later, Fiedler's conviction was thrown out by the New York Court of Appeals, which ruled that Fiedler hadn't done anything illegal or been aware of anyone else doing anything illegal, hence there hadn't been any misdemeanor to plead guilty to. In essence, the Court ruled that the whole procedure had been a sham.

In the article, I describe the attempt to drive Fiedler from his home and the withdrawal of his Fulbright invitation to Holland. There was more to come: Fiedler's appointment to an endowed chair at the university, scheduled for the following September, was rescinded when heirs of the family that had provided the funds complained to university president Martin Meyerson about Fiedler's character. Meyerson later used other university funds to provide Fiedler some of the support he had been promised when he'd left Montana.

In the tradition of *Animal House,* here's what happened to some of the major players later:

—Mike Amico, the Buffalo city policeman who engineered the Fiedler arrest, was subsequently elected to two terms as county sheriff. He ran for office on his success as a police narcotics captain, basically the Fiedler case and a long string of minor cases against students for possession of marijuana.

—Joe Tuttolomondo, Amico's deputy sheriff in charge of narcotics cases, was given a fifteen-year prison sentence for felony sales of heroin.

—Buffalonians become more comfortable with the changed character of their university and less frenetic about people who happen to be in proximity to other people engaging in casual cannabis use. Fiedler is now one of the attractions Buffalonians brag about when they tell outsiders about their town. One of the papers that excoriated him in 1967 recently devoted most of a Sunday page to an article celebrating his wisdom and accomplishments.

—One of the detectives who had executed the search warrant on Fiedler's house that night saw me in a Buffalo restaurant a few years ago. "You know Fiedler, right?" he asked. I said I did. "You want to do us both a favor, Fiedler and me?" I said I'd be happy to do that. He asked me when I was coming to that restaurant again. I told him. "Okay," he said, "I'll see you then." He turned up a few minutes after I got a table the next time I was there. He took a large white envelope from his jacket pocket. "I've had this for twenty years," he said. "It's something we took that night, and I took it out of the stuff they had at headquarters because I knew they were going to garbage a lot of personal things and I thought he'd want this back." I asked why he hadn't just given it back to Fiedler himself. "Me? One of the guys who busted him? He doesn't want anything to do with me. You give it to him. And don't tell him where you got it, okay?" Okay, I said. "I never wanted to go in there," he said. "The whole thing was stupid from the beginning. We should have been out chasing bad guys and there we were, getting headlines for the captain." The envelope contained family photos: the Fiedler kids, small, smiling at the camera, playing with toys, the things kids do.

It was sad, this decent cop for twenty years trying to find a way to undo for Leslie Fiedler some of the damage he had unwillingly and unhappily helped inflict, never being able to just go up to Fiedler's house and say, "Here, this is yours, we fucked up, I never wanted any part of it."

When I gave Fiedler the envelope I started explaining why I thought the cop had held on to the envelope for so long and why he wanted to remain anonymous now. Fiedler stopped me with a raised hand, the palm forward, like a Buddha. "I know why. Tell him it's okay. Tell him I said thank you."

I'll tell you one other sad thing about the Fiedler bust story: people in positions of public trust are still using the hoked-up horror of drugs for personal political advantage. For a particularly egregious example, read the next article.

SHORTLY AFTER HIS ARREST on a misdemeanor narcotics charge (the rarely enforced statute against anyone who "opens or maintains a place or places where any narcotic drug is unlawfully used"), Leslie A. Fiedler, who doesn't use, sell or donate marijuana, was notified by the Traveler's Indemnity Company that his homeowner's policy was being cancelled. There was no explanation, just the simple statement that his account was not wanted, along with another statement informing him that should he fail to get another policy within ten days, the Manufacturers and Traders Trust Company might foreclose his mortgage. Fiedler reinsured the house with the United States Fidelity and Guaranty Company, which, a few weeks later, also cancelled out without explanation.

The Fiedlers realized the first cancellation was perhaps not so gratuitous as they had thought, so they went to an independent insurance agent and requested that he get them a policy with a company that knew the facts—that Fiedler, professor of English at the State University of New York at Buffalo, had been accused of a misdemeanor—and that would insure. The agent was encouraging and the Fiedlers relaxed a bit. On the ninth day of the ten-day period, Margaret Fiedler tried to find out what the agent had accomplished, but each time she called, the agent's secretary told her he had just stepped out and would call back in a few minutes. He never called and, in desperation, Margaret phoned the mortgage department at the bank to explain. The bank did the explaining: the agent had called the *bank* the day *before* and said he hadn't obtained the policy, so the next move was up to the bank. Late in the tenth day Margaret was given a binder by Allstate, the insurance firm owned by Sears. Two weeks later (August 16), the Fiedlers received a refund from the Rochester regional Allstate office, and a note that said, "All insurance companies have certain qualifying standards which, together with our judgment and experience, tell us whether we can provide insurance in each individual case. Risks that can be insured by one company might not meet the standards of another company.

"Sometimes, because of these standards, we must give up business we would otherwise like to have. This happens only after thorough consideration is given each case.

"We're sorry we won't be able to accept your application for insurance protection. . . .

"As you see, a period of time remains before your protection stops. This will allow you time to apply for similar insurance elsewhere. We urge you to do so. Then you won't run the risk of being without protection.

"Thank you for your friendly interest in Allstate."

The Allstate agent knew quite well the Fiedlers did not want to "run the risk of being without protection" (which is why they applied in the first place) and that without such insurance they would lose their house (Congress has guaranteed most veterans the right to a home loan, but it has left the veto power in the hands of the insurance companies); he knew also that they had been blackballed and *no* regular American insurance company would handle their account. This is like Boston's Louise Day Hicks telling Roxbury Negroes that education will solve their problems while her school committee maintains in Roxbury the worst schools in the state.

Who rolled the blackball? Conversation around the university focused on three possibilities: (1) the Buffalo Police Department resorted to extralegal pressures in the hope of running Fiedler out of town; (2) Fiedler's bank, perhaps pressured by some outraged local Brahmin, requested each insurance company in turn to reject Fiedler's policy; or (3) some of Fiedler's neighbors in Buffalo's comfortable Central Park section ($25,000–$50,000 homes, only recently invaded by professors) complained to their own insurance companies, and through them effected the blackball. Investigation by friends of the university has pretty much ruled out the second possibility: the bank seems sincerely interested in getting the Fiedlers insured and the problem settled; the first and third possibilities, neither mutually exclusive, are both still talked about.

There did not, until very recently, seem to be any recourse. Household insurance agreements are terminable at the will of either party and, as with moving companies, there is little government protection for the consumer except in cases of demonstrable fraud. It has been reported that a few days ago the home office of Allstate, when queried about its acceptance of the blackball, agreed to instruct its local agents to reinstate the policy.

But even if the insurance problem is resolved there are other, continuing aspects to the campaign that is being waged against the Fiedlers. The arrest has broad connotations for a town that still cannot accept the major university that now occupies the buildings and land which only a few years ago housed a homey, familiar, socially and intellectually innocuous diploma mill, and also cannot accept the strange clothes, the occasional beards, the iconoclastic entertainments (the San Francisco Mime Troupe, Ginsberg, *MacBird,* etc.), the out-of-town accents.

The puzzlement and outrage manifest themselves most directly in hate mail. Last year, university president Martin Meyerson was the object of much of it; this year Fiedler is the target. Like the following: "Having read the expansive article concerning you and your activities, 'On Being Busted at Fifty,' which appeared first in the *New York Review of Books* and was reprinted by the Buffalo *Evening News* there seems one logical avenue—*Return to the land of your ancestors,* taking Dr. Myerson [*sic*] for moral support, as well as Leary. Our taxes might then be diverted into *sounder areas of need.* [Signed] Concerned Tax-Payer, Logical Parent, Clear minded individual able to 'get along' without hallucinations in a busy world." Or this one (printed in block letters and unsigned): " . . . You [*i.e.,* the UB faculty] are a bunch of the hated Jewish and commie rat nest. Its the 2nd best in the US after the Red nest—U of Cal at Berkeley. And its hero Meyerson when he was thrown out there. Who in hell got him here? . . . How come that leftie rats and poisoners of young minds remain at UB. Why don't you all go to stinking Russia. Or the damned hated Israel?"

A few of Fiedler's respectable middle-class neighbors have joined the assault. A friend of mine was walking by the Fiedler house and noticed a group of neighborhood children, who ranged in age from about eight to ten, standing before the house shouting and throwing papers and bottles on the lawn. She was at first surprised (she lives in the neighborhood and knew the children to be generally well behaved), then shocked when she realized the parents of the children were standing across the street, calmly watching. "Those kids don't read newspapers," she said to me, "and I know they didn't think up that lawn littering by themselves." A few neighbors have remained friendly, or at least civil (one became friendly for the first time only after the harassment began), but others now refuse to say hello or even nod when they pass the Fiedlers on the street.

It isn't only the police, the cranks, the neighbors and the insurance cartel. Someone persuaded the University of Amsterdam, where Fiedler was supposed to go next month on a Fulbright, to withdraw its previously confirmed invitation. Fiedler was not even accorded the courtesy of a direct letter from that university, but instead was informed thirdhand by an official in the American Fulbright Commission (which disagreed with the Dutch action and has tried, without success, to set things aright). Fiedler wrote the rector of the University of Amsterdam, inquiring about the report he received and asking why they reneged on his appointment. In his reply the rector vaguely alluded to proceedings "in progress" and said, "Personally I may add that I read one of your articles on the narcotic problem and personal freedom, which impressed me very much and which I thought straight-forward. I certainly will welcome an opportunity to meet you personally." He knows that it is now probably too late for the Fulbright Commission to get Fiedler an appointment elsewhere in Europe for this fall, and, the academic world working the way it does, this means Fiedler may have several months without a position. The rector never communicated with any official of this university about Fiedler's status (which is unchanged, since he is not convicted of any crime). There is a movement beginning to boycott the Netherlands as a Fulbright location.

The financial burden on the Fiedlers is considerable (some contributions have arrived for the defense fund, but not nearly enough), but at least there is a mechanism for defense against the legal charge. But against the other attacks there is no defense. Neighbors and strangers, bigots and xenophobes, a Dutch university and several of the unassailable American insurance companies have proclaimed Fiedler guilty, whether he is guilty or not.

The Drug Czar's Ideas Are a Bust: Going through These Things Twice

(*New York Times*, 1989)

A few months after this op-ed piece was published, William J. Bennett, George Bush's first director of the Office of National Drug Control Policy, urged massive increases in prison and law enforcement appropriations at both state and federal levels; he made no demands for similar increases in appropriations for job, education, or drug prevention and treatment programs. He told a *McNeil-Lehrer Report* interviewer (9 August 1989) that the massive Reagan administration cutbacks in aid to education, job, health, urban renewal, and other programs were *not* a contributing factor in the increase in crack use and sales. The black community, Bennett said, had long suffered major problems, so the cutbacks of the past several years were nothing special. What really matters, he said, is the family; if the family is healthy, drug use will decline. That's like saying if we have eternal life, we needn't worry about death.

Bennett said nothing about what is done to family health when the kids are in understaffed schools, parents can't get work, job retraining centers and neighborhood health clinics are shut down because of lack of funds, and nearly all other public services are reduced. His rhetoric reminded me of General William Westmoreland during the Vietnam War: always confident that with just one more major escalation of armaments and one more increase in the ranks of warriors on the ground the battle would be won. The war in Vietnam wasn't won by American firepower and the war on drugs won't be won with increased arrests and packed prisons.

I was appalled by Bennett's indifference to the history of drug control in this country and his assumption that force could fix everything. In the 1960s New York's governor Nelson Rockefeller convinced the state legislature to vastly increase prison terms for drug possession and sale and to impose mandatory minimum prison terms. The result was twofold: the prison population developed a troublesome convict base (drug offenders had no incentive to behave well because they were ineligible for parole) coupled with a halving of the conviction rate. People who went to prison for drugs stayed far longer than those who went before, but far more of those brought to trial went free. Restrictions on plea bargaining resulted in a vast increase in the number of cases actually going to trial, leading to a tenfold increase in the amount of time before trial. Because the jails were so crowded, judges began letting drug defendants out on lower bail than they'd been demanding under the older, less punitive laws (Shribman 1989). The net effect was exactly the opposite of what the laws were supposed to have achieved.

In recent years, a number of prominent conservatives (among them author and editor William F. Buckley, economics Nobel laureate Milton Friedman, and former secretary of state George Shultz) have advocated drug legalization. Their reasons have been primarily pragmatic: the social and economic costs of drug control were greater than the costs of drug abuse.

Friedman, for example, in "An Open Letter to Bill Bennett" published in the *Wall Street Journal* (7 September 1989), charged that the "major source of the evils you deplore" was law enforcement itself and that they were occasioned by "demand that must operate through repressed and illegal channels." Friedman quoted from his 1972 column in *Newsweek* arguing for legalization at the beginning of Nixon's drug war, then wrote:

> The major problem then was heroin from Marseilles; today, it is cocaine from Latin America. Today, also, the problem is far more serious than it was 17 years ago: more addictions, more innocent victims; more drug pushers, more law enforcement officials; more money spent to enforce prohibition, more money spent to circumvent prohibition.
>
> Had drugs been decriminalized 17 years ago, "crack" would never have been invented (it was invented because the high cost of illegal drugs made it profitable to provide a cheaper version) and there would today be far fewer addicts. The lives of thousands, perhaps hundreds of thousands of innocent victims would have been saved, and not only in the U.S. The ghettos of our major cities would not be drug-and-crime-infested no-man's lands. Fewer people would be in jails, and fewer jails would have been built.
>
> Columbia, Bolivia and Peru would not be suffering from narco-terror, and

we would not be distorting our foreign policy because of narco-terror. Hell would not, in the words with which Billy Sunday welcomed Prohibition, "be forever for rent," but it would be a lot emptier.

Decriminalizing drugs is even more urgent now than in 1972, but we must recognize that the harm done in the interim cannot be wiped out, certainly not immediately. Postponing decriminalization will only make matters worse, and make the problem appear even more intractable.

Alcohol and tobacco cause many more deaths in users than do drugs. Decriminalization would not prevent us from treating drugs as we now treat alcohol and tobacco: prohibiting sales of drugs to minors, outlawing the advertising of drugs and similar measures. Such measures could be enforced, while outright prohibition cannot be. Moreover, if even a small fraction of the money we now spend on trying to enforce drug prohibition were devoted to treatment and rehabilitation, in an atmosphere of compassion not punishment, the reduction in drug usage and in the harm done to the users could be dramatic. [Friedman, 1989]

Bennett rejected Friedman's argument primarily because it wasn't new and because it had been advocated or endorsed by classes of people Bennett didn't like: "As the excerpt from your 1972 article made clear," Bennett wrote, "the legalization argument is an old and familiar one, which has recently been revived by a small number of journalists and academics who insist that the only solution to the drug problem is no solution at all." Then his reply became moralistic, jingoistic, and ad hominem: "I remain an ardent defender of our nation's drug laws against illegal drug use and our attempts to enforce them because I believe drug use is wrong. A true friend of freedom understands that government has a responsibility to craft and uphold laws that help educate citizens about right and wrong.... Today this view is much ridiculed by liberal elites and entirely neglected by you. So while I cannot doubt the sincerity of your opinion on drug legalization, I find it difficult to respect. The moral cost of legalizing drugs is great, but it is a cost that apparently lies outside the narrow scope of libertarian policy prescriptions" ("A Response to Milton Friedman," *Wall Street Journal*, 19 September 1989).

Not long after that exchange, Bennett resigned his job as director of the Office of National Drug Control Policy. President Bush announced that Bennett would become the new chairman of the Republican National Party, but somewhere between his resignation from the drug czar job and acceptance of the party job Bennett had a change of mind. He told reporters that his several years in government service made it necessary for him to spend time making real money, so he was abandoning politics for a while and was going off on the lecture circuit. (He was replaced in the ONDCP director job by Bob Martinez, the former governor of Florida, described by one senator as being qualified for the job only because he lost his most recent election campaign to a Democrat.)

Bennett's confidence in law enforcement as the primary solution to the drug problem was endorsed by his boss, President George Bush, in a nationally televised speech on drug control (6 September 1989). "This is the first time since taking the oath of office," Bush began, "that I felt an issue was so important, so threatening, that it warranted talking directly with you, the American people. All of us agree that the gravest domestic threat facing our nation today is drugs."

Well, "all of us" *didn't* agree with that. Some of us thought that the national debt, continuing economic disparity on racial grounds, collapse of the infrastructure, corporate and political greed, our dependence on petrochemicals, and the long-term costs of the savings and loan failure were at least equally major threats to our social well-being. And we agreed with Milton Friedman that drug law *enforcement* continued to do far greater social damage than drug abuse.

Bush went on to say that, "Drugs have strained our faith in our system of justice. Our courts, our prisons, our legal system are stretched to the breaking point. The social costs of drugs are mounting, in short, drugs are sapping our strength as a nation." Bush, like Bennett, argued on grounds of morality and distaste: drug use is bad and unpleasant. He announced that in his new budget he would request an additional $2.2 billion for the war against drugs, bringing the 1990 drug budget to nearly $8 billion. At least three-quarters of the increase was for law enforcement.

The fallacy of the punitive approach to illicit drug use is its assumption that a quick-fix cure—arrest, trial, incarceration—can solve the problem. Movies work like that; real life is more complex and more long-term. In social matters, quick fixes are rarely good economics: they may be easy to talk about in speeches (they seem so simple and neat), they often get good press (they make for great sound bites), but they don't change much of anything.

No one thing turns a person into a crook or a drug addict; no one thing turns another person into a successful researcher or business person. We're the product of a wide range of forces; we respond to a wide range of opportunities. Instead of addressing with force the personal careers that seem to have failed, we'd do far better to address with help the personal careers that haven't yet developed. This involves a complex range of services, opportunities, programs, and options. It involves time—if we think locking someone away for ten or twenty years is necessary to provide proper punishment and deterrence, why not give community development and educational programs the same life expectancy?

Putting our resources into expanded prisons and larger police departments commits us to accepting the state of affairs; addressing the problem early on in terms of the community says we're dedicated to changing the set of conditions that made those increasing deviance and injury rates a fact of our lives. It's like that commercial in which the mechanic says "Pay me now or pay me later": it's cheaper, more convenient, and safer to opt for prevention instead of dealing with disaster. Fix a community and everybody benefits; lock up more people and tune up the prisons and you've got a large number of people in well-tuned prisons. Politicians tend to opt for short-term solutions because they're looking forward to the next election and they want numbers they can display when they start making speeches on the next campaign trail. That makes for snappy politics, but it doesn't make our streets one bit safer, nor does it redeem any of those squandered lives.

THE DRUG CZAR, William Bennett, recently told Meet the Press that one of his interesting new policy ideas was to focus a major portion of law enforcement attention on the casual users of drugs. We have been thus far unable to do much about the large-scale drug dealers, he said, so it's time to go after the consumers.

He also said that the Bush Administration was considering advocacy of mandatory prison sentences, confiscation of vehicles in which drugs were found and publication of the casual users' pictures in newspapers.

Mr. Bennett's ideas are hardly new. They comprised our basic policy of narcotics law enforcement during the 1950s and 1960s—and they were a major flop.

In 1966, I worked on the task force research group appointed by President Lyndon B. Johnson's crime commission to study Federal, state and city narcotics law enforcement policy and effectiveness. At all three levels, department heads told us that their primary interest was big dealers.

But when we worked with field agents, we found exactly the opposite policy was in effect. "They say they want big shots," one agent said, "but we're rated on the box score—how many busts we make each week. Check the blackboard. It doesn't say anything about the size of the dealer; it just totes up the number of them."

The blackboard was on the wall of the main office of New York City's special narcotics squad. It listed arrests week by week and compared them with the same weeks in the previous year. Any week in which this year's arrests dropped below last year's resulted in pressure from superiors.

We saw similar blackboards in drug enforcement offices in New York, Houston, Los Angeles, San Francisco, Washington and elsewhere. "We'd all like to do quality cases," a Federal agent said, "but we wind up going for quantity. Anybody who tells you different is lying or doesn't know what's going on."

How do you prove you're doing a good job on the narcotics watch? You can't measure how much is being bought, sold or used. If it takes a year to arrest a big dealer and two days to set up a user-dealer—well, there's nothing wrong with arresting the little guy, is there?

Mr. Bennet's other two ideas are even less compelling. Cars used in drug offenses have been seized for years. In the 1960s, agents of the Federal Bureau of Narcotics were the envy of other law enforcement agents because they drove confiscated Cadillacs, Lincolns and Toronados while FBI and other agents went around in Government-issue Chevys, Fords and Dodges.

Then the dealers began using rental cars. The narcs weren't going to go head to head with Hertz and Avis, so the policy atrophied. Large quantities of drugs are still delivered in rented or stolen planes, boats and cars. Surely we're not going to have a Federal policy that seizes the personal car of a casual user while we're not seizing the car rented from Hertz used to deliver a half-million dollars worth of crack.

And I doubt that the rogues' gallery in the papers will do much good. A few years ago, there was a movement to publish in newspapers the names of men caught by police decoys posing as prostitutes. The idea was the same: Humiliate the user and the market will go away. It didn't work.

Newspapers rarely print photos of people convicted of vehicular manslaughter, rape, armed robbery or driving while intoxicated. Why should we expect them to give up space to print photos of the thousands of people arrested on minor drug charges, many of them for the fourth or fifth time?

Consumption has to be reduced, surely, but cops aren't going to do it by increasing arrests at the bottom of the drug industry. Making cases against big dealers is difficult and making cases against foreign exporters is nearly impossible. But difficulty is no reason to adopt policies that are achievable but pointless. If all drug czar Bennett can come up with is a return to the failed policies of 25 years ago, we'll get about the same results.

How do you "get out of going through all these things twice?" Bob Dylan asks in a song. One answer is to remember what you did the first time and try to do it differently the next time around.

Deviance as Success: The Double Inversion of Stigmatized Roles

(*The Reversible World,* ed. Barbara Babcock, 1978)

In this essay I tried to explore some reasons people defined as criminal or deviant act the way they do. People not tagged as deviant may have very good ideas why they are unhappy about the presence of deviants in their communities, but no viable change or accommodation is likely to occur unless there is some understanding of what deviance looks like from the other side. It's not enough to know what people do; we also have to appreciate the payoff that makes the behavior attractive or necessary.

Most political discourse on criminal and deviant behavior reads as if the participants were inanimate objects: *this is what crooks/addicts/perverts do and this is how we'll discourage them from doing it again* isn't much different from *this is the way the Niagara River flows at this point and this is what we're going to do to divert it twenty-seven feet.* Human behavior can sometimes be described in group terms, but it always occurs in individuals. Any attempt to understand why people behave the way they do that doesn't take individual locus into account is likely to miss the point, and any attempt to influence behavior that focuses only on the desires of the person or agency wanting the change to happen is likely to fail.

Had William J. Bennett understood this, he might have been far more successful as drug czar. People, as any psychologist knows, engage in behaviors because, among the options presenting themselves, those behaviors seem to offer the most pleasure or the least pain. If we try to deal with people only in terms of *our* comfort or discomfort, our only weapons are force and guilt, and as soon as those forces are relaxed or deployed elsewhere the problems emerge all over again.

"Deviance as Success" is the most academic piece in this book and I apologize for some of the diction. I like the argument I was making here, though I'd make it in different terms now. It was written for a symposium on symbolic inversion chaired by Barbara Babcock at the American Anthropological Association meeting in Toronto in 1975.

Il boit, mais il était fait pour l'opium: on se trompe aussi de vice; beaucoup d'hommes ne recontrent pas celui qui les sauverait. Dommage, car il est loin d'être sans valeur. [He drinks, but he was made for opium: one can also be mistaken in one's vices, and many men never find the one that could save them. Too bad, for it is far from being without value.]

André Malraux, *La condition humaine*

THIS ARTICLE IN PART derives from a conversation I had one afternoon several years ago with a person I thought was a habitual burglar. We had been talking about his criminal career and I realized early in the conversation that his working criminal career was very short, but his convict career was depressingly long, that he evinced far more animation when talking about his convict role than when talking about his criminal role, and that he perceived his criminal acts as discrete and his convict role as continuous, even though the latter was gapped temporally (he'd stayed out several years a couple of times) and geographically (he'd done time in California, Texas, Kansas, and other states). The last time he'd been free he stole a bright red jeep, held up a finance company with the jeep double-parked directly in front of the finance company's large and clear plate-glass window, then drove two blocks away where he again double-parked, this time in front of a bar. The robber then went inside and set the cashbox and his pistol on the bar and ordered drinks for the house. He was arrested a few minutes later. When he told me the story he cursed his luck and omitted most of the details. Others later filled me in on the twice double-parked jeep and the drinks-for-the-house gambit; my friend simply said he'd had the misfortune to be picked up right after a clever daylight robbery.

But he was always very good at escaping from prison: he'd escaped from two state prisons in California, one federal institution, and several others. Shortly after the last time I saw him he escaped from a Texas prison, stole a car, and took off along the nearby interstate highway and headed toward

Dallas—a couple of hundred miles north. The only problem was, the car he stole was a state car, and all Texas state cars—as he must have known—have large block numbers painted on their roofs. The state police helicopters spotted him in minutes.

It was clear to me—and to him too—that he was basically happy as a convict, though he hated prison, and basically unhappy in the free world, though he very much liked its options. He didn't keep coming back to prison because he couldn't keep from stealing, but rather because he didn't know how to live anyplace else.

Sometime later, when I was doing a study of prison sex roles, I recognized a similar pattern with a number of informants.[1] It seemed clear that many of those occupying the role of "punk" (insertee, in present sociological jargon) *needed* the prison community. Their words didn't say that directly, and most wouldn't agree to it if asked, but many got themselves into prison for the most trivial reasons, and many violated parole in the most absurd ways. The same applied, though to a far less significant extent, to some of the men occupying the "stud" (insertor) role. The only sex role actors who seemed consistently outside this pattern were those who had been acting-out homosexuals in the outside world, "free-world queens" in the prison argot.

The queens seemed to hate prison, but they managed and coped. According to other inmates, prison was for them "the promised land," for they were needed there in ways they were not needed outside, and, in the prison value system, it was common to hear them described with some respect by men who in the free world held homosexuals in contempt. The logic was, "At least they're man enough to admit what they are." The punks were lowest on the status ladder, and the other inmates generally assumed that the punks allowed themselves to be used sexually because they were "weak," because they wanted protection or extra food. Most studs maintained that they were homosexual in prison only because of the absence of women, that they used punks in preference to masturbation. The particularly aggressive studs were often described by other inmates as "punks out for revenge," in other words, individuals who presumably had been punks in reformatories and were now getting even. In conversation, most of the punks and studs said they filled those roles only because they "had to." Almost none admitted homosexual behavior in the free world—the queens did that, not they—and only a few admitted knowing any homosexuals outside of prison.

I finally understood this: many—not all, but many—of those argot-role actors, especially punks and some of the studs, would very much like to be homosexual outside, but they just *didn't know how.* Because of their ethnic or geocultural backgrounds or situations, they never learned—and they were now too old to learn—how to be competent homosexuals. They could not ever admit that to themselves, surely; if one suggested it to them, one risked violence. So they were discharged from the institutions, went back to "normal" but transitory and apparently unsatisfactory relationships with women (the unsatisfactory part of the relationships rarely, in their accounts, had to do with specifically sexual matters; rather they had to do with problems the women presented—dishonesty, adultery, and so on), lived a "normal" life, then were busted again, and again sent back to prison, where they immediately assumed the sex roles they had occupied previously.

For them—and I must stress they comprise only some of the argot-role actors—prison was the only place they had a moral structure that permitted them to be acting-out homosexuals, a place where there was a grand body of folk culture that legitimized their behavior. There was some stigma, but it was quite another kind: for the social agencies dealing with these men, the problem was criminal—theft, burglary, forgery, and the like. But in fact these individuals used the criminal behavior only as a vehicle for admission to a place where their real deviance could for them be legitimately enacted.

The prison dealt with them in terms of the wrong stigma, which is why they kept coming back and back again. The only way their cycle might have been stopped would have been for them to be located on a comfortable heterosexual track or for them to be taught how to be competent homosexuals. For all of them, these ambiguous prison sex-role actors, the stigma of convict was far less troublesome than the problem of homosexuality, and by adopting the convict stigma they were enabled to act out the homosexual roles without any of the attendant stigma they would have suffered (and self-applied) in the free world. Even the punks, so much disrespected and disliked in prison, had clear and accepted roles in prison. These were roles the actors could often claim were thrust upon them—either by necessity or by force—rather than being roles of choice.

The problem with a stigma, as Erving Goffman several times points out in his book on the subject (1963), is that it becomes a focus for identity; most of the other characteristics of the individual are subsumed to it. A dwarf who is a skilled brain surgeon and concert pianist is certain to be forever regarded as a dwarf who happens to have those skills, not as a surgeon or pianist who happens to be notably smaller than everyone else. A deviance stigma produces what Everett C. Hughes calls a "master status" (1945), a status that overrides all others and provides a continuing focus for identification, however unfair or inappropriate.

But that focus may, and often does, work in just the opposite direction: those who, for whatever reason, *need* such a status, may take it on more or less voluntarily, more or less consciously, and they may rest in it. The stigma may block perception of another stigma far more awful or terrifying or difficult to negotiate (in which case the assumption works exactly as "screen memories"), but it is the stigmatized and deviant role that is in fact selected and enacted and informed.

For Goffman, it is the stigma that spoils identity (p. 4), and his subtitle— *Notes on the Management of Spoiled Identity*—properly indicates his concern with how people negotiate the stigma itself. He describes how it is perceived by "normals" and how the stigmatized persons negotiate their own and others' perception of the stigma. My concern here is quite the opposite: I am interested in persons who *adopt* a stigmatized role as an accommodation, and I am suggesting that many individuals label *themselves* deviants and that the affirmation of stigma is what ratifies identity in a manageable way.

I have for some time been concerned with techniques used to rationalize or legitimize extraordinary violence, such as using nonhuman names for the "enemy" (gook, slope, kike, nigger, savage, and so forth), thereby removing him from the area of moral concern; or by ritualizing the event (by having a priest be an integral actor in criminal execution, for example), thereby removing the event from the area of moral responsibility; or by chemically altering one's own state (by excessive consumption of alcohol before beating up one's children, for example), thereby removing oneself from moral responsibility.

These legitimizations involve a process of making a nonperson of the one who is to be harmed or of making a nonperson of the one doing the harm ("I was crazy . . . " "I was drunk . . . " "I was tripping . . . " "The state has determined . . . " "It was only a gook . . . "). This process becomes problematic only when the device of other-making or depersonalization is only partial or fails, and the other is still partially like or among us, in which case the violence becomes something like eating a pet duck—legitimate in theory, but terrifically distasteful.

A similar process goes on (consciously or unconsciously) among many who choose deviant careers. The only difference is, in the deviance situation the person who is made the *other* (what, as my colleague Theodore Mills points out, Melanie Klein calls the "not-me") is oneself, and that otherness is selected because it offers a kind of identity not available in the boundaries of "straight" or "square" society. Many modes of deviance— which to us in the square world almost always represent some significant failure of energy, will, character, or morality—actually represent a careful management of strengths, and the process is not at all unlike the normal process of occupational selection. People select the deviance that is most appropriate to them, or at least try to.

The quotation from *La condition humaine* with which I prefaced this essay expresses that notion most concisely. Old Gisors, the retired sociology professor, is talking with his son, Kyo, about Baron de Clappique, the frenetic hustler who has just left the room. Gisors, himself an opium addict, discusses Clappique's alcoholism and suggests that it's the wrong vice, that Clappique would suffer far less if he found one better suited to his needs. Gisors' problem is an inability to act: he is the frozen intellectual, so immobilized by theory that he is capable only of considering options. His opium addiction gives a form or name to his impotence (just as the prison situation gives a form and tolerable name to the role actors I discussed in the first section of this essay), and he ascribes Clappique's constant disequilibrium to the latter's inability to find the drug or vice that would fit his own psychic configuration, that would explain himself to himself.

It is impossible to adopt fully a deviant life-style and identity without also assuming the symbol pattern associated with them. Since both the style and the identity are negatively perceived and frequently negatively sanctioned by the larger society, we have a symbolic inversion given full articulation: instead of taking on the role of transvestite or the mode of amorality only for a transient ceremony the individual adopts it as a basic life-style, for only with that life-style can some degree of comfort be achieved or can suffering be substantially reduced, and only with exclusion or exile from the larger society may the perceived disorder be made orderly.

Howard S. Becker has written about deviance as more a function of a labeling process than an inherent quality of an actor—the deviant person is one who has been labeled as such by others. This identification, Becker writes, engenders a master status:

> The question is raised: "What kind of person would break such an important rule?" And the answer is given: "One who is different from the rest of us, who cannot or will not act as a moral human being and therefore might break other important rules." The deviant identification becomes the controlling one.
>
> Treating a person as though he were generally rather than specifically deviant produces a self-fulfilling prophecy. It sets in motion several mechanisms which conspire to shape the person in the image people have of him. In the first place, one tends to be cut off, after being identified as deviant, from participation in more conventional groups, even though the specific consequences of the particular deviant activity might never of themselves have caused the isolation had there not also been the public knowledge and reaction to it. [1963:33–34]

But once the labeling process occurs with any frequency, the deviance acquires a public form, and specific behavior is deviant whether or not one goes through a formal labeling process. People usually know when they are acting in those behaviors, but as they know when they are acting in most other roles that have acquired a public label and a public definition. Some behaviors are of course ambiguous and some are of course not recognized as such by the actor, but even if he has never been arrested, a middle-aged man who "hustles" young men in public restrooms knows he is deviant, as does a young man who sticks a needle in his arm four times a day and pumps heroin into his veins.

The form is there and it has a name. As much as a social agency can affix it to any actor or any agent, any actor or any agent has the option of affixing it to himself. If society doesn't confer the label, an individual can assume it. Becker notes that the group has an identity and offers worked-out justifications for the deviant behavior, which is why deviant individuals may join such groups (p. 38). But conversely, what is important for us is that the group offers a readymade identity that one can assume totally.

The inversion here is twofold: one part is the assumption of the deviant role, and the other has to do with the role actor's relation to it. We usually assume that the latter is negative and loathsome, but frequently exactly the opposite is the case. What seems to be happening is that *the deviance makes tolerable, or explains acceptably, something awful for the actor.* That process of making tolerable or explaining acceptably may simply consist of giving a name to what was nameless or a form to what seemed formless. Heroin becomes the reason, speed becomes the reason, the prison situation is the reason. . . . But since even masochists seek comfort, the problem is finding what is most comfortable; much deviance selection is in fact comfort-seeking behavior.

A critical step is the enunciation and annunciation of stigma: "I am this other." This is not the same as Melanie Klein's dichotomized "me" and "not-me," for the statement "I am this other" is one of identification of the self when no such identification was previously possible or adequate, not a setting off of someone else or something else. The enunciation and annunciation "normalize" the actor's otherness, make him a member of a stigmatized group, hence someone now *based,* rather than a problematic member of a larger society in which he is a stigmatized other (perhaps secretly stigmatized, but that is no less real for anyone who perceives his own stigma—*he* knows it is there). There is a shift from a shame-guilt status in which the individual must cope with the consequences of his "problem," to an occupational status in which the individual copes with the needs of his stigma, and identifies and is concerned with problem-solving rather than truth-hiding.

Once inside the deviant structure, as many observers have pointed out, one is deviant only in regard to normals (who are now "those squares" or some equivalent); that is perhaps only partial comfort, but it is comfort nevertheless. That one is a convict causes no shame within the prison community (though other things may); it is only outside, with squares, that the historical role may become a problem. Many ex-convicts without firm social or family supports seek out other ex-convicts for association, not because they have something in common to "talk about," but rather because the things that are present but *unspoken* with squares are nonexistent with other ex-convicts.

There are two discrete aspects to this process:

1. Some selection of deviant community membership is deliberate and serves to focus a constellation of personality problems that previously lacked focus. The stigma attendant upon deviant-group membership is less onerous than were the constellation of problems, and in fact that stigma seems to explain if not actually legitimize these problems.

2. Some selection of deviant community membership functions exactly as the screen memory functions in excluding from consciousness memory of an event too painful to negotiate directly. Just as the victim of an awful assault may remember only the exact and trivial details of an insignificant event that occurred some while before it all happened, the deviant in this mode says, "*This* is my problem," and for him, acting in terms of that assertion is far less anguishing than confronting another alignment or constellation with identical contributing elements. He selects the most comfortable master status: "dope fiend" is more comfortable than "useless" or "impotent"; "speed freak" is more comfortable than "purposeless"; "convict" is more comfortable than "catamite." The first status in each of these sets is socialized, which means it has the social and moral support that comes with membership in any group, the legitimizing power of culture; the latter status of each pair is solitary and isolated from the general community. Part of the function of asserting a deviant role is disasserting other roles: "I am this thing, so I am not that other one." All sorts of translations are possible, depending on what is selected, and all sorts of roles are excluded: "I've never hurt a woman, child, cripple; I've never shot dope, been a drunk, robbed the blind; I've never snitched on a pal; I've never done it for money...."

Becker has adequately described the labeling of actors as deviants, but my concern here is with the individuals whose private situations are such that they select for themselves deviant patterns and communities which name and explain their site and locus. Many actors use nominally negative social slots to maximize their options and reduce suffering in the most fruitful and tolerable ways. Their inversion, as I noted above, is twofold: in the *fact* of being deviant (that is, being in the deviant role rather than no role at all), and in the *selection* of what we usually consider an eschewed role. I think of the following: heroin addicts who lament how dope acquisition takes all their time and how heroin addiction destroys their sexual drive;

speed freaks who complain about not being able to do anything useful because amphetamine lets them do trivial things for hours on end (such as picking the lint out of a rug by hand) as if these things were important; prison catamites who complain about being sexually used and scorned; prison pederasts who complain about prison catamites; prostitutes who hate social sex because their workaday trade poisons their attitude toward heterosexual intercourse.

After a lot of time doing fieldwork I learned what most people in the Life knew all along: many of those junkies had a lousy sex life before heroin or at least had consistently unsatisfactory relationships with the people with whom they had those sexual affairs; that a lot of the speed freaks were barely functional anyway and began taking speed in the hope of functioning better; that a lot of prison catamites and pederasts seemed to work very hard getting back into prison; that a lot of the prostitutes hated intercourse even when it was done for free and with a friend.

Not all; none of this applied to all. Not all; but enough so that I wondered about people who adopt a form of deviance that makes tolerable or explains acceptably something awful in themselves. I described above the situation of convicts who would like to be homosexual in the free world but simply do not know how, and who therefore get themselves thrown into prison again and again. There are amphetamine addicts who use the great busywork drug as a rationale for dysfunction. There are alcoholics who thus acquire a vehicle for the rage they must otherwise suppress and with which they cannot quite live. And there are addicts who find addiction less disturbing than the psychosexual hang-ups that have no explanation without dope, and who find the pattern of drug acquisition and use so full of success that it matches nothing in a previous career of failure.

John William Rawlin, of the Delinquency Study Center of Southern Illinois University, reported to me an addiction pattern in the St. Louis area in the mid-1960s that I found puzzling for some time. According to Rawlin, heroin became very hard to get at that time. The normal traffic pattern of New York to Chicago to St. Louis produced a very dilute product anyway, and when the New York concentrations in that period decreased, the quality of dope declined all along the market route. St. Louis junkies were mostly buying nickel bags of mannite, milk sugar, or hydroquinone. One would expect they would either abandon their habits (since pharmacologically most of them were nearly clean anyway, however much of the supposed junk they injected) or start robbing drugstores. Neither happened. Instead, many of the former heroin addicts began shooting methamphetamine hydrochloride (which they called "splash" and "spliven"; elsewhere it is called "crystal"). St. Louis narcotics squad detectives told me Rawlin was correct, and said they didn't understand it at all. The pharmacological effects of opiates and amphetamines are polar: opiates numb, close, shrink; amphetamines sharpen senses, stimulate movement, make time comfortable. Opiates produce quietude, amphetamines produce busyness. Opiate overdose produces coma, amphetamine overdose produces toxic psychosis that often manifests itself in severe paranoia and violence.

But the St. Louis junkies didn't seem to care: they went to the same shooting galleries to shoot up, scored from the same connections, and bought the magic white powder (methamphetamine instead of heroin) in the same little glassine envelopes they knew so well. The addicts maintained the heroin subculture on a methamphetamine metabolism; obviously the subculture had had powerful and spectacular magic working for it.

From the security and legitimacy of the square world, we perceive the descent into junk, into heroin addiction, as a shutting off; the decision to nod in the corner, as the penultimate cop-out (the ultimate is suicide, and much addiction is a courting of that). But this is an oversimplification. A junkie spends only a small portion of his day nodding; most of his time is spent having little, but significant, successes: he must hustle money by stealing, by turning tricks, by peddling something stolen previously, by passing a check, by tapping a till, etc., and he sometimes must do this under the pressure of oncoming withdrawal. He must score for some dope, sometimes with the withdrawal symptoms already manifesting themselves; he must find a dealer, find a safe place for a transaction, and enact the transaction. He must find a place to cook up his dope, a place where some other junkie won't take it away from him and where a passing policeman won't take him away from it, a place safe enough that he can nod off—if the dope is decent—for a little while. He must, four or so hours later, begin the process all over again.

Little successes every day. Dozens of them. Failures are immediate, success is absolute. Most street junkies have a career of failures—failure in school, in jobs, in marriage. But junk, however it is regarded by the anti-junk world, is not simply the ultimate failure. Quite the contrary: it is a continual reaffirmation of the fact and efficacy of success.

Little wonder then that the St. Louis addicts were unwilling to abandon their world of success, that they were willing to substitute another chemical even though it was a pharmacological opposite; little wonder that so many junkies are so hard to cure, that so many spend two to five years in prison, are released, spend a frustrating week or two on the streets, and then go find a connection who can make them smile again.

I wondered about the applicability of all this to the soldier addicts returning from Vietnam, but recent federal reports seem to support my theory. Most of these addicts—who were getting a grade of dope of better quality than any United States mainland addicts except physicians—kicked the habit on their own, most of them very soon after their return to the U.S. If chemical effects were the dominant mechanism of opiate addiction, this group should have been the most difficult to cure. The apparent ease with which they seem to have kicked indicates the relative insignificance of chemical dependence outside a social situation that makes the chemical dependence useful. For these soldiers, kicking heroin, the best heroin around, was easy once they were out of the war situation. The government claims that only about 3,000 serious addicts remain of the Vietnam group; even if this is off by a factor of three, the abandonment is extraordinary and can be explained only by a lack of subcultural supports and a change in intrapersonal needs.[2]

I am not attempting here an ontogenetic explanation of deviance or deviation. This essay does not try to establish why a certain person should become deviant in the first place, nor does it try to describe the personal or social pathologies operating. One of my concerns, however, is to view deviance in a manner other than the traditional pathological model. My focus is on adaptive behavior: given a set of circumstances, what might an individual do with them? My essay picks up the scenario of the role actor *after* he is fully developed as a character and at the point where he is seeking or has already discovered the proper play to act within. When I use the words "choice" and "choose" I don't always mean that the individual sat down and rationally selected a pattern of action. I use choice in the Sartrean sense: every yes or no, every decision one makes, has a normative component; every decision is itself an act, every act reflects a decision. One is responsible for one's acts if only because one may eventually be called to account for them—for punishment *or* reward. That accounting may be internal or external, but the process is there; it is there even when one escapes it, for we all know when we've gotten away with something. Things matter, acts matter, decisions matter. The sum of one's choices, the sum of one's acts, define position, role, pattern, locus. These little choices generate larger ones; those smaller resolutions produce larger definitions.

When I say that some deviants select the form and style and scenario most suited to them, the one most likely to permit some success or shield some intolerable perception or pain or relieve some general suffering, I don't mean to imply that they're happy about it. Some may be, but many are not. I don't know many really happy heroin addicts; after a long hook the drug gives little pleasure and the work is very hard. But given their situation in life at that point, it may be that addiction offers less unpleasantness than any other options open, for the forces working for it are so strong that ignoring them will give more pain than acquiescing. That applies equally to job selection in the square world, where the job for which one is most suited by temperament may not be the job for which one is most suited by training, and it often happens that at a particular time some compromise is necessary to find work at all; one may not be particularly happy in the work, but one is less unhappy than one might be doing something else, or doing nothing at all. Few persons are fortunate enough to have temperament and training coincide perfectly with general opportunity; the question is how satisfactory a compromise one can manage and what the ultimate costs of that compromise are.

We make assumptions about those we label as deviant. One is that they act out of weakness, in distinction from the successful people of the world, who act out of strength. They are what they are because they failed into it; the successful—us—are what they are because they've worked to get there, be there, live there.

But is the process really so different? In a way, many of those deviants also act out of strength: they select, from the range of behaviors and roles apparently open to them, a set they can do. And they don't kill themselves. The savagery with which they sometimes pursue those behaviors and roles reveals a ragged resistance that suggests an irreducible pride of self, sense of self, demand to live.

"Healthy" people act as much from their weakness as their strength—it's only that they find the appropriate place to locate that weakness, and place it so it doesn't appear as weakness at all (and we should regard this notion of "weakness" as an illegitimate category for discussing behavior—we should talk only of appropriate and inappropriate, adequate and inadequate, successful and unsuccessful). Ira Cohen said to me, "You take somebody who's compulsive and suspicious and he's a meticulous good researcher. Or take somebody who's narcissistic enough and he's a good stand-up comedian—*if* he's narcissistic enough. If he isn't, he gets in trouble—like Lenny Bruce."

The losers of this world, those we label as losers, we say have chosen out of weakness: we see their choices as reflecting inadequacy or impotence or inability to achieve. And we like to think that we, on the other hand, choose out of freedom and from vast possibility, that our choice is out of strength rather than weakness. The difference between them and us has to be very great, we need that difference and so many of our labels depend on it: sanity, socialization, success. We claim lucidity, and we need to deny it to them. But the process of occupation selection is in fact exactly the same.

Order, we know well enough, always seems preferable to chaos. That is because within order, however uncomfortable one's position, one at least knows what the position is, while chaos, by definition, admits of no easy or constant definitions about anything. The labels *convict, addict, homosexual, alcoholic* all have attendant stigma, but the taint is often preferable to the chaotic disorder of a life without the label. Some of those labels define socialized roles, they need complex cooperation of others, but all of them, once recognized as a role, define a locus.

There is a need for study of what happens in this peculiar world somewhere between game and theater: almost a scripted drama with clear and unambiguous roles, roles that have prerogatives and limits. The advantage of having everyone cast in a role isn't only that the role defines oneself, but that it limits everyone else.

But this isn't a game. The enactment of these patterns lacks one essential element of game or theater: adequate closure. Time runs out on a game, curtains ring down on the players. These outsiders, like you and me, go on and on. There is no point at which the teams go off to some private place to shed their bulky uniforms and don street clothes, no place where the actors go to wash off the grease and paint, no point at which the audience packs up and goes home. There is no audience for this play, and other than death, the third act rarely seems to end. That's because this is, ultimately, real life, and real life is, however much our simplifying theorizings suggest otherwise, neither game nor play.

I think of William Faulkner talking about Joe Christmas: "He didn't know who he was, and so he was nothing. He deliberately evicted himself from the human race because he didn't know which he was. That was his tragedy, that to me was the tragic, central idea of the story—that he didn't know what he was, and there was no way possible in life for him to find out. Which to me is the most tragic condition a man could find himself in—not to know what he is and to know that he will never know" (Gwynn and Blotner 1959:72). I have suggested in this essay that some of our outsiders have found something that gives their outsiderness a name, and that naming permits them to survive.

NOTES

1. See the interviews about, and my comments on, prison sex in Jackson 1972: 353–412.

2. This pattern was reported to me by T. D. Hutto, former Arkansas Commissioner of Corrections. I think it deserves serious study because it is the first time since the passage of the Harrison Act over fifty years ago that a large addict population has given up drugs because of a simple change in situation. Back in 1916, all those "old lady addicts" the government worried about so much quietly gave up their laudanum compounds; they never did go howling through the streets

in search of a fix. That the New York heroin was much weaker than the Vietnamese heroin isn't enough to explain the mass abandonment of addiction: New York has many drugstores and doctor's offices. Since the majority of line infantrymen were from the same socioeconomic groups as the majority of stateside addicts, the abandonment is even more significant.

Who Goes to Prison:
Caste and Careerism in Crime

(Atlantic Monthly, 1966)

Our prison population has more than tripled since this article was written: at the end of 1989 state prisons held 610,000 men and women, and county jails and federal prisons held at least 200,000 more. According to many workers in the criminal justice industry, prison populations have gotten nastier over the past twenty-five years: as the rate of prison commitments accelerated, the less violent offenders were more likely to receive probation or short sentences to make room for the violent criminals coming down in increasing numbers and with longer sentences. Because of plea and charge bargaining and changing styles in the maintenance of criminal justice statistics, there's no way to know if this is fact or mere impression. But even if the perception is accurate, nothing in this article is changed: with rare exceptions the rich and famous don't go to prison and when they do go they don't go for very long. Unless their case involves the kind of civil rights issues important to a William Kunstler or the kind of publicity attractive to an Alan Dershowitz, poor people get marginal legal representation.

The ancient Japanese called ours "the Floating World" because of its instability relative to the eternal. I was reminded of this when I saw abortionists in my list of "people who commit crimes which could send them to prison [but] who do not go" at the beginning of this article. When "Who Goes to Prison" was first published in 1966, abortion was illegal in most of the country, and capital punishment was on the way out; in 1972 the U.S. Supreme Court found the current practice of execution unconstitutional (*Furman v. Georgia*). In the years since, thirty-seven states have rewritten their capital punishment laws to make them acceptable to the terms of the seven separate and not entirely compatible opinions in *Furman,* and more than 1,700 individuals are now awaiting execution in the United States. In the same period a woman's right to a safe abortion was legalized in *Roe v. Wade* (1973) and then placed into jeopardy in *Webster v. Reproductive Health Services* (1989). How might you explain to a Martian or even a rational Englishman why, in slightly over two decades, we went from being unwilling to terminate pregnancies or execute murderers to being unwilling to terminate murderers but willing to terminate pregnancies, and then to being willing to terminate murderers and unwilling to terminate unwanted pregnancies?

UNLESS YOU HAVE led an abnormally isolated adulthood, the chances are excellent that you know many people who have at one time or another committed an act, or consorted with someone who was committing an act, for which they might have been sent to prison. We do not consider most of these people, or ourselves, criminals; the act is one thing, the criminality of it quite something else. Homicide, for example, is in our law not a crime; murder only is proscribed. The difference between the two is the intention, or to be more accurate, society's decision about the nature of that intention.

Most prisons are organized nominally to handle the personalities who fit the public's image of the Criminal—that nefarious deviant who supplies such fine copy for scandal sheets and television scriptwriters—but only rarely do prison staffs have an opportunity to deal with that sort of offender. Largely, a state prison is populated by people who are not too bright; impulse criminals (whose offending act reflects not a life pattern but a set of extreme circumstances—most murderers are in this category); chronic convicts (a large group of men who stay out for short periods only because they don't know how to get along anywhere *but* in prison, and who seem to spend their criminal hours out of prison seeking not profit so much as prestigious reincarceration); some habitual offenders (those who can't manage to stay out of trouble but who still base their value systems in the world outside); and a very small number of professionals who had a run of bad luck or a moment of carelessness.

The men who become prisoners are the most obvious criminals: clumsy, stupid, impulsive, hung up. Some have gotten what they deserve, some are oversentenced, some belong in mental institutions, some shouldn't be in any institution.

Most of the people who commit crimes which could send them to prison do not go. Consider, for example, the large number of criminals who go unpunished simply because the general public insists on cooperating with them. Call girls, bookies, loan sharks, abortionists, and bootleggers know quite well that their customers are as anxious to keep their activities from the attention of the police as they are themselves, that even if an arrest does occur, most honest citizens will do whatever they can to avoid involvement. Like the distributors of narcotics, these offenders are protected by members of the society against which they supposedly offend, by otherwise honest men and women who would no more think of turning them over to the police than of admitting they had visited an abortionist or consorted with a whore or blown a week's pay on a bum tip and had to borrow at an exorbitant rate to pay the bookie.

Other crimes go unreported, and there is no way to document their number. No one knows how many public officials take graft in any single year, but surely there are many more than those who make the headlines. Many business firms will not prosecute shoplifters, embezzlers, or pilferers, because they believe the damage to their reputation will be more costly than the satisfaction that might result from a conviction. Many rapes, for exactly the same reason, go unreported: victims think there will be no apprehension or conviction of the criminal and they will suffer embarrassment in addition to their humiliation (not without some cause: there were convictions of adults on the original charge in only 16.7 percent of the rapes reported to the police in 1963).

The late Edwin H. Sutherland, a well-known criminologist, devoted considerable study to what he termed "white-collar crime"—offenses committed in the course of their business activities by persons in relatively high positions. Among these offenders are persons who file fraudulent tax reports, businessmen who misrepresent the facts in a transaction, and lawyers who resort to illegal methods in order to secure acquittals for their clients.

In collaboration with Donald R. Cressey, Professor Sutherland once wrote that "crime is found in most occupations and is very prevalent. The people of the business world are probably more criminalistic in this sense than are the people of the slums. The crimes of the slums are direct physical actions—a blow, a physical grasping and carrying away of the property of others. The victim identifies the criminal definitely or indefinitely as a particular individual or group of individuals. The crimes of the business world, on the other hand, are indirect, devious, anonymous, and impersonal. A vague resentment against the entire system may be felt, but when particular individuals cannot be identified, the antagonism is futile. The perpetrators thus do not feel the resentment of their victims and the criminal practices continue and spread."

The deliberate and intelligent offenders—the professional killer, the high-level narcotics distributor, the fraudulent corporation executive, the thoughtful burglar, the physician salting away money which ought to be paid to the IRS—go to prison so rarely they hardly affect the statistics. And when they do go, they do not stay very long. Prison population reflects only that part of the criminal world that isn't smart, rich, dishonest, or lucky enough to stay out of jail. To this point, the Honorable Charles E. Wyzanski, Jr., Chief Judge, U.S. District Court, Massachusetts, remarked recently, "Unfortunately the whole system is one in which the hydra heads are plucked and not the trunk."

While the rich and professional obtain competent and expensive legal aid, the poor, despite recent Supreme Court decisions regarding procedure and representation (*Gideon, Escobedo, Douglas, Pointer,* and so on), are at an appalling disadvantage. Even if they are innocent, they cannot afford to hire a top-notch lawyer; a court-appointed attorney may take a sincere interest in their case, but it is more likely he will not. The poor defendant cannot put up bail, and regardless of the facts of the case, the man not out on bail is more likely to be convicted than the man who enters the courtroom through the front door. If there is a delay between his arrest, trial, and acquittal, he finds himself saddled with debts accumulated during the period, and perhaps he has lost his job. The bail system, observed Ronald Goldfarb in the *New Republic,* "plays into the hands of the organized criminal while it discriminates against the poor one or the one who commits an isolated criminal act; it is a vehicle for discrimination; it can and does subvert the judicial process; and it is frequently applied improperly as a form of punishment." The accused without money for bail "is punished before he is tried, and whether or not the ultimate verdict is guilty or not guilty. The defendant is also handicapped in assisting his defense. His chance of obtaining acquittal is lessened." The great success of the Vera Foundation's Manhattan Bail Project, arranging for many defendants to be released on their own recognizance, has clearly shown, in the words of Herbert J. Sturz, the project's director, "that verified information about a defendant is a more reliable criterion upon which to base release than ability to buy a bail bond."

One particularly repugnant illustration of the kind of inequity fostered by our bail system occurred in New York last April. On a tip, it was claimed, police arrested on a narcotics charge a woman who had a bottle of pills in her purse. Because she did not have the $25 bail money, she spent twenty days in the House of Detention. The woman could not get the police to telephone the physician who had issued the prescription found with the pills; the police, apparently, were too busy to bother. Five days after her arrest the police laboratory verified her story: chemical analysis revealed that the pills were for her thyroid condition. But it was another fifteen days before anyone bothered to unlock the door to her cell. Would the police have dared act in so cavalier a fashion with anyone they thought had any power or influence at all? Nobodies don't count; no one cares about them: they don't file lawsuits.

The amateur gets arrested first. The man who does in his wife or an acquaintance is easily apprehended and convicted, but the professional killer, who has little or no connection with his victim and no apparent motive, is hard to find. None of the gunmen responsible for Boston's 30 gangland slayings in the last twenty months has been convicted; there were only 17 convictions resulting from 926 known gangland slayings in Chicago in the period 1919 to 1957. In a 1964 FBI sampling of 2,951 murders in 1,658 cities, it was found that of the 2,162 persons formally charged, only 984 were found guilty as charged, 431 were found guilty of a lesser charge, 175 were referred to juvenile court, and 572 were acquitted or dismissed. Even if every one of the juvenile suspects was found guilty, the conviction rate would still be under 50 percent. And that tells us nothing about the many murders that are undetected.

Like the Boy Scout, the professional goes prepared. Preparedness, more than anything else, is enough to distinguish him from the merely habitual offender, who can commit crimes well enough but isn't sufficiently adaptable to handle the occasional problems that may occur in their wake. Some professionals consider the possibility of imprisonment much the same way an investor considers the possibility of a bad turn in the market:

"We got together and talked it over and decided that to get the amount of money we wanted in the shortest time, that crime was the way to get it. Now crime, we feel, is just like any other business. In other words, there's setbacks in crime and there's deficits. Just as if you run a business, there's always a chance it might burn down or you might go bankrupt or your employee might embezzle every dime you've got without the insurance to cover it. It's the same with crime. Of course the penalty for going bankrupt in crime is much stiffer than—but at the same time your material gain is much greater than—in a regular business."

But most professionals do carry insurance. One Texas thief always let his lawyer know where he was working and kept him on a regular retainer: "We were giving him $500 every two weeks. This $500 was to make any bonds. Fees—that was all extra. The $500 was for him to get there and keep us from getting killed. Now they have a law that they can't whip a confession out of you, they won't accept it in court anymore. It has to be given with counsel present. Well, son, when they got confessions in the past it didn't make any difference how they got them: they were good."

The amateur and clumsy thief gets to prison so frequently not only because he doesn't know how to steal well but also because he doesn't know how to handle a decent "score" when he does happen to hit. An inmate of Indiana State Prison told with scorn the story of another inmate who had been one of three men on a smoothly executed $30,000 payroll holdup:

"This guy had changed suits once a week, normally on the weekend like any other working joe. He had a car leaning sideways. But then he started walking into the crap tables, playing $500, saying, 'Let 'em roll.' He'd throw craps and say, 'Hell, there's plenty more where that come from.' Changing suits two and three times a day. Throwing parties. . . . So the minute the pop comes he's offered a ten flat [a sentence having a maximum of ten years]. I think it was for two or three thousand dollars. He couldn't afford it. His buddies could hand the detectives a few dollars and let 'em water it down a little and they came up with a ten flat. He had enough nerve to say, 'Some dirty rotten sonofabitch must of ratted us out!' I said, 'Man, you *sick!*' Now he got a ten-to-twenty-five and his buddies got a ten flat apiece because they had a little money to pay off."

The professional finds his referents, his values, in the outside world. For some, the incentive is purely acquisitive: they want things or the status things seem to represent. Other values are subsumed in the quest, sometimes quite consciously. "In my walk of life," one killer told me, "you've got to use a certain amount of cold calculation, at times animal cunning, and brute force to survive. And in doing so, you leave a certain amount of your feelings buried deep and you keep them that way. . . . I'm not interested in being tough. Every act I have committed to an extent has been made on the basis of the buck. 'Cause I've learned that . . . the buck is what makes you an American citizen as well as a person [that] can [be] respected. A broke man is like a dead man. No one wants to hear what he got to say, 'cause what the hell, he must not be of any value if he's not using it for his own benefit. . . . I see no sense in walking around with my collar turned up and talking out the side of my mouth. That's backwards. I want to look like anything except what I actually have lived the life of being."

Once one has met a number of professionals in situations in which rapport may be established, one discovers they are frequently middle-class in background and quite articulate. These are two qualifications that open the standard channels of economic advancement in the noncriminal world. Many of the pros are agile enough to make as much money legally. And they often know it. One said to me, only half-joking, "I bet you wonder why a bright clean-cut kid like me from a good family turned to crime." I said I had indeed wondered about that. "I like the life," he said, meaning the romantic business of spending big, carrying an automatic in a special shoulder holster, moving in two worlds at once. For others, the money is sometimes secondary to a feeling about the criminal act that is almost sexual. The following statement was made by a Southwestern burglar highly respected by his colleagues:

"Now after I get inside, all my fear more or less is gone. And you concentrate on the safe, and you can look at it and—of course you always know what kind of safe it is before you make your entrance and everything. You go in, you got your tools and everything, and you can estimate what's in the safe. If it's a place that has delivery trucks, you can figure $500 per truck for every truck they got and they'll have that much in the safe. I mean that's the average for any kind of business whether it be a beer truck or a dry cleaning place. But still in all, that jewel might be the one. It just might be the guy that's beating the income tax, or it might be the guy that's booking all the big football payoff or layoff or something. And there's no charge in the world, man, like when you see that smoke. . . . For instance, if you're punching it and you hear that pin hit the back of the safe: *clinggg!* You know you're home free. Or if you're peeling it you see that smoke come out—whenever you pop that door and see the smoke you know that you've cracked the rivets and it's all yours. And when you see that safe door open, it is a *charge.* I think the most safes I ever made was six of them in one night. But that was four of them in one building—you just go from safe to safe. But, man, it never became less. You know, it's not like screwing. The first time it's pretty wild, then each time it tapers off; you get part of the same drive, you know, the same action, but it's not like the first. A safe's not like that. Each time it's more so because you figure the odds are more in your favor of it being the big score."

Since the professionals are the most articulate and agile members of the criminal population, it is not surprising to find that on the rare occasions when they have to do some time, they rise quickly to positions of power in the prison society. Even though they are few in number, their influence is often extensive. In Texas, the professional is called a "character," and one of them explained at some length just what the qualifications were and how one's status in the world outside affected one's inmate career:

"Crimewise you have a differentiation. First of all, you've got your rapos and you've got your women beaters and your women killers and your incests and all of these crimes against another person that is more or less unprotected. Now those people are looked way down on. Because we know that they will do it to my wife or your wife or our children just like they'll do it to anybody else. And don't ever forget one thing: characters think a lot of their families; that's about the only thing they have. They're the people that, whenever we get in jail, well, they're the ones that send us money to have something to smoke and so forth, and they're the only ones that you can depend on. And actually they really know what a family means, more than anyone else who probably never had to call on their family. They're pretty conscious about their families. Now, you got your intelligents. Some pretty intelligent people in the penitentiary that are not characters but foul-ups. A lot of your checkwriters, lot of 'em are college graduates. They're not a 'rum'; you can't consider them a idiot or a rum, and you can't consider them a character. So they're just some of the people, just part of the people that make up the population of the prison system. They don't have any definite place in a prison system.

"Your real characters are ones that go out and use the underworld as a means of livelihood and go about it in a professional way, in a professional manner.... I think that a character is somebody that makes his living completely outside the law but yet has some principle about it. And you'd be surprised at the difference in the way the police treat us.... Hell, they talk as much character talk as you and I can. They get their point over and you can get your point over to them. 'Course, sometimes it don't do you too much good....

"The penitentiary officials, they recognize this. They recognize the class distinctions, and they operate accordingly. Now you take all the key positions in the prison, they're either given to the intelligent person I was talking about—like the checkwriter or somebody like that, that gets off in a storm—or they're given to the characters. Now if it's handling other convicts, if it's down to where you're gonna tell another convict what to do and dictate his policies to him, they always get a character to do that.... It's on your record. They know that I'm a character. I've never been taken into the captain's office and asked to cop out [inform] on somebody. He knows I'm not gonna do it. And he respects me enough not to even ask me. So he and I, we get along fine.... The penitentiary knows that there's characters and there's idiots and there's rums. And your characters will always be running the penitentiary. They can't hire enough guards.

"Down here, one a these rums, one a these idiots, he's not gonna get in my face. Because he knows that he can't survive and do it; he knows I'm gonna hurt him.... A character is a professional thief, whereas the rest of them are on-again-off-again, hooligan-mulligan, you know, they're just not professional. I guess we frown on them as much as a doctor would a chiropractor."

This statement offers more than a sample of professional pride. The "rums," the chronic convicts, are frowned upon by the characters for the same reason they are frowned upon by the police: they are failures. They cannot make it in the free world, and the great gap that separates them from successful criminals is carried over into the prison milieu. Dr. David Haughey, former director of psychological research, Massachusetts Department of Correction, said recently that very few successful criminals come to prison, but "those who are taken into the training system and are found to be wanting—they don't profit from their training and are fired or let go in some sense—turn to crime on their own. They tend to be unsuccessful there, too. And it is very frequently these kinds of individuals who come to prison—and come again. Because failure is characteristic of almost every area in which they have tried to perform. They have been failures in school, they have been failures at work if they attempted it. . . . These men are failure types, even in crime."

Ironically enough, it is in prison where the failure type or rum may find the only place he can settle in some comfort. Harvard psychiatrist Norman Zinberg has compared the attitude of the chronic convict with the attitude found among many career military men: both "bitch" about the way of life, the regulations, the officials; both eventually get out, spend a short and tumultuous period at large, then find their way back to the ranks. In inmate parlance, they are "doing life on the installment plan."

A characteristic solipsism about activity outside prison develops when an inmate tries to avoid admitting to himself that he needs prison. One lifer in Texas told me he had been convicted on circumstantial evidence. I asked for details, and he said, "There was a gunfight of three, four plainclothesmen and myself. I wasn't committing any crime—though I was on escape from here. I was armed. There's where I was violating the law. But I wasn't committing any crime, I wasn't trying to commit any crime. I was attending to my own business, but the situation developed to such an extent where there was a gunfight. . . . A chief of detectives was killed." Notice that the facts regarding his actual killing of a policeman are set in passive and impersonal terms. That he was at the time of the gunfight a wanted man, escaped from prison, where he had been serving a life sentence for murder, and was blazing away with a Luger automatic and a .38 caliber revolver doesn't seem to matter very much.

His story is a classic "bum-rap" tale. Except for the professionals and the impulse criminals, it is hard to find inmates who do feel there was adequate cause for their incarceration. Some insist they were railroaded, some that they were tried on the wrong charge, some that they were given an unfair sentence. Some are right, most are not. The outstanding example of the genre in my experience was offered by one triple-murderer who in all sincerity told me he had been "bum-rapped," not because he hadn't killed those people—he admitted that freely—but because there were at least four procedural errors in the course of his trial.

The cry of "bum rap" is particularly important to the chronic convict who often faces parole with mixed feelings. He is anxious to get out, to find a woman, walk down the street, wear a different color outfit; but he knows he won't make it out there because "they" won't let him.

He has to get back inside without letting it appear, to his colleagues or himself, that he wants to come back. One man was released, stole a bright red Jeep, parked in front of a finance company office, held up the finance company, drove down the block and parked in front of the nearest tavern, went inside and set his pistol and the finance company's money box on the bar in full sight of everyone, ordered drinks for the house—and complained about his bad luck when the police walked in a few minutes later. The type is not uncommon. He'll come back screaming, but no matter what gets in his way, he will come back: it's home.

Most of the persistent offenders come from the lower economic levels, and one of the most wasteful and unnecessary sequences of crimes connected with poverty is that resulting from narcotics addiction. Poverty does not *cause* addiction, just as it doesn't cause any other kind of crime. But the two occur together so frequently that we cannot ignore their intimacy: addiction is largely a lower-class disease. And since it is a disease that is handled by a police agency rather than a medical one, the infected tend to be at the same disadvantage before the law that the unempowered always are.

The Federal Bureau of Narcotics has long had its say about narcotics legislation, and the punitive controls now operative are a national scandal. Many observers feel those controls do little to stop addiction, but no one knows for sure—the statistical methods used by the bureau are so unreliable that it is impossible to determine the changes in the addict population effected by the various repressive laws.

A considerable number of responsible students are convinced that the repressive laws do more to increase the spread of crime than stop it. Isidor Chein, professor of psychology at N.Y.U., said recently that "the worst consequences, by far, of addiction are entirely a result of our public policy with regard to addiction." At best one can say that the bureau has failed slowly; at worst, that its attitudes have contributed more to the maintenance of the criminal population than any legal blunder since Prohibition. By law, the American addict is a criminal, although alcoholics, who are far more numerous, far more dangerous, and far less healthy, are quietly tolerated. The addict's greatest problem, other than the fact of his addiction, is getting money to buy drugs. He robs, connives, panders, swindles— anything to get money for that shot. He is a frequent visitor to court and prison; he is easily arrested, easily convicted, easily readdicted when he gets out. He is usually broke. When arrested he is dependent on a court-appointed attorney; he tends to have a poor arrest record, and is likely to go to jail.

The kinds of inequity still latent in our system are perhaps best illustrated by a pair of narcotics trials held a few years ago. One involved an addict, Gilbert Mora Zaragoza, the other the highest-ranking narcotics distributor yet sent to prison, Vito Genovese.

Zaragoza—high-school dropout, epileptic, low IQ, junkie—was the first person convicted under section 107 of the 1956 Narcotics Control Act, which permits sentences as severe as execution or life without parole for adults convicted of selling narcotics to minors. Zaragoza had no previous convictions for peddling, and the minor to whom he sold the narcotics was an old friend who had been set up by the Bureau of Narcotics. Nevertheless, Judge William C. Mathes sentenced him to life without parole.

I asked George H. Gaffney, Acting Commissioner of Narcotics, about this apparently callous entrapment. "The only comment I can make on the conviction of Gilbert Zaragoza," Gaffney wrote, "is that he was afforded a proper trial before a jury in United States District Court and was found guilty upon competent evidence. The method of obtaining evidence by making purchases of narcotics from a person with the requisite predisposition to engage in such activity has been approved many times by various Circuit Courts of Appeals and by the United States Supreme Court." Then God help us all.

Zaragoza's sentence is all the more obscene when we note that Genovese, convicted in 1959 for narcotics conspiracy, was sentenced to fifteen years in prison and ordered to pay a $20,000 fine. With good behavior, Genovese need serve only eight years. The retail take for heroin sales in this country is estimated at $300 million a year, and one doubts that Genovese was forced into poverty by the assessment.

Even if it were not true that the poor and stupid are shortchanged in the police station and courthouse, they surely are after they get to prison. Parole boards are generally composed of reasonable, honest, well-meaning men, and when an inmate comes before them, they consider with as much fairness as they can muster his past record, his conduct while in prison, the likelihood of his success outside. What determines the likelihood of success? The man's economic situation, his associates, his place of habitation. The offender with money or connections can easily demonstrate that he will be able to get along without difficulty; so can most professional criminals. The noncriminal impulse offender and the professional tend to serve time quietly in prison; they're smart enough to stay out of trouble. But the offender whose social and intellectual inadequacies were responsible for his getting into trouble in the first place—where will he go and what will he do?

The answers are obvious: back to the same street, the old crowd, the old routine. It is not surprising that he doesn't find early release. No wonder that he spends a long time behind bars. No wonder, but no fairer. We can understand why the poor go to jail more frequently than the affluent, why the smart spend less time behind bars than the stupid, but we should understand also that this same set of conditions makes the failures more antisocial, more bitter.

David Haughey commented on the effect of this: "From the inside, this certainly is part of what leads the average inmate to feel that he is the victim of a corrupt society, and that everyone on the outside is just as corrupt as he is. It's just that they have more things going for them—friends, money, influence, power. And when you don't have power, then you serve time."

That inside view is, unfortunately, the correct one.

Devil's Island Redux

(Society, 1982)

In early 1982 *Society* editor Irving Louis Horowitz asked five social scientists (James A. Inciardi, Donald R. Cressey, Ernest van den Haag, Isidore Silver, and me) to comment on a brief essay in which Tom J. Farer suggested two devices to deal with what he perceived as the ineffectiveness of the American criminal justice system. Farer proposed a nice Devil's Island for career criminals and an educational and training system with real incentives for younger criminals. The second proposal is eminently laudable, and I thought it unfortunate that government funds for such enterprises have consistently declined over the past decade. The first proposal is deliciously simple in theory, but only if the theory stops short of considering felons as human beings. Once that consideration is made, then it's just one more grand plan that misses the point.

I FIRST THOUGHT Tom J. Farer's statement was merely a parody of all those simplistic speeches by politicians working to fan the flames of discontent. But *Society* would not base a serious symposium on mere parody, so I decided the Farer statement was perhaps a criminologist's "Modest Proposal" —a document that updated Jonathan Swift by the same number of years it backdated prison work. Then I thought back on my ten-year experience with *transAction* and *Society,* tried to remember significant moments of satire, failed to remember any, and had to conclude that Farer is probably serious in his proposal; that it isn't modest at all. It's just absurd.

Any essay loaded (as is Farer's) with such phrases as " ... law-abiding citizen ... citizens yearn ... people are not yet willing ... obviously ... most experts do agree ... most penologists agree ... the men who run prisons agree.... " is suspect. The "boss-words" indicate the article is neither substantial nor expert enough to carry its own argument. The author is not going to persuade by facts or logical argument. It's going to be a matter of faith. Farer's article is based on a set of assumptions (perhaps drawn from those experts and penologists who agree so much or from the list of things for which citizens yearn) that are by no means so simple or unambiguous or tenable as he would have us believe.

He assumes that the amount of violent crime in America can be significantly reduced by giving long sentences to individuals who can be correctly identified by law enforcement officials and dealt with fairly by the judiciary. Little in the available data indicates that this is the case. Farer seems to have based his plan primarily on the suggestions of the cops with whom he is in communication and agreement: "when people so close to the situation have achieved something close to consensus, the validity of their insight ought to be tested," he tells us. (Or, as J. Edgar Hoover put it in his 1936 address to the Daughters of the American Revolution, "The practical, hard-headed, experienced, honest policemen who have shown by their efforts that they, and they alone, know the answer to the crime problem.")

Setting public policy on the basis of line agency perceptions or desires can be extremely dangerous. Our military involvement in Southeast Asia escalated specifically because Lyndon Johnson believed the insights and accepted the recommendations of General William Westmoreland. People in line positions see the world's problems in terms of their own immediate perceptions, their own immediate needs. There is nothing surprising in that; one expects such visions. But what makes sense at the line level may not make sense at the broad policy level; what makes a cop's job appear more logical may not be what makes the community safer. (A colleague just returned from fieldwork in Haiti tells me that persons arrested for felonies there often disappear before any court proceedings begin. "It cuts down on the recidivism rate," he said. I asked what happened when the police disappeared the wrong person. "They don't have to worry about that in Haiti," he said.)

Farer's notions of political history are not comforting. "The prison would be treated," he writes, "as if it were a classic colony or trust territory being prepared for self-determination." Other than being physically distant from the parent country, this proposed institution bears no resemblance at all to classic colonies. Most colonies are settled by volunteers who want to be there, or they are places where the dominant country took power by force and eventually returned self-determination to those who owned it in the first place. British convicts were transported to Australia, but the basis of the community was not the convict society. The model for the community Farer suggests is not Australia at all; it is Devil's Island. (Last year's melodramatic film *Escape from New York* had the criminals isolated on Manhattan island. It was a mess.)

Why should we expect these people to get on well in an unguarded penal colony? The plan of population assumes they are of a kind, that by putting them in a single place we will only be ratifying a preexistent but heretofore unformalized community—like taking several batches of Mormons or East European Jews or Armenians or Navahos and settling them somewhere new. But that is not the case here; these people are *not* all alike. Many of them have nothing in common other than their violent crime and their conviction, and even the terms of those factors differ enormously.

Most prisons are places of criminal predation. There is nothing surprising in that: the population is composed of criminal predators barely controlled by a small group of guards who work out accommodations to keep the predation from getting out of hand. Guards are not in prisons merely to keep inmates from getting out; they are also there to keep the crime that goes on within the walls below whatever limits the particular prison's administrators are willing to tolerate.

What happens in Farer's community? Violent felons have a sufficient degree of freedom to give them practical functioning in a volitional society—a society with *fewer* controls than that from which they were recently exiled. We are using them as guinea pigs for each other's potential failure of decency, putting them at greater risk than they were in prison. Does conviction for a felony warrant that? (There would be pressures to go to the penal colony, even with its greater danger, since residents of the penal colony would obviously have a better shot at early release.)

Consider the matter of sexual activity in the convict colony. Sex remains a problem in traditional prisons because some individuals continue in prison the violent and predatory styles they utilized outside prison: there are rapes, coercions, fights over punks. Will the convict colony merely replicate that, or will the problem be eased somewhat by the presence of women criminals? Where will these women criminals come from? Far fewer women than men commit violent crimes, and their recidivism rates seem to be lower. Shall the convict colony be homosexual by design? That does not seem a particularly bright policy recommendation, even in these enlightened times. Would it be fair to keep out the few women convicts who are qualified by temperament and career? What shall be the permitted rules of competition for the attractive women? What about the convicts who had children in their care in the free world—shall those children be allowed to come along? What about children born in the convict colony? Shall they stay until either parent is freed? What if the other parent wants custody? What if both parents are released at the same time and each wants to return to his and her free-world family—which one gets custody of the colony-born child? What happens if the mother behaves badly and is returned to a traditional prison while the baby is still nursing?

All of which is to suggest that Farer's plan seems lacking in certain practical aspects.

There is also the matter of free-world equity. The colony idea, absent the requirement for a violent felony conviction, is wonderful. There are a number of people who would be happy with a free section of arable land, a $25,000 tax-free stake, and a small annual subsidy to keep them going until the crops came in or the shop got going. How do we justify making such a bounty available only to individuals who have been willing to shoot, stab, rape, or maim?

The plan for treating younger offenders is also, absent the criminal part, nifty. Who wouldn't want to go to a school with "outstanding physical facilities, a faculty second to none, a faculty-student ratio without parallel, and a course of studies leading to employment in the most dynamic sectors of the economy"? That is so nice a plan that if I were a poor kid trying to make it through a crumbling school system (one crumbling all the faster because of the Reagan/Stockman gutting of all nonmilitary budgets), I might even consider shooting one or two strangers just to get into that wonderful program. It would surely offer a better chance of heading into a decent life than anything else on the horizon.

Surely we should do everything possible to straighten out those who are severely bent. But it is topsy-turvy to make such benefits available only to those who so far have been least interested in them or who have profited least from what was available. It is inefficient to offer help only to those who have already failed to profit from help. The plan is directed entirely toward pathological eruptions—toward the transient and specific, toward symptoms; it does not approach causes at all.

Farer tells us nothing we might do about violent crime; he merely suggests something we might do with a small number of violent criminals. His motives are no doubt decent and practical (we have a crime problem, criminals seem not to be well handled now, we need a better model), but his solutions (a penal colony near the equator for adults and intensive education and therapy for adolescents) are silly-putty.

Protecting Society

The criminal law is a body of abstract statements designed to inhibit and punish the behaviors of real people. Its specific end is to set terms for punishing those individuals found guilty of having violated the rules it sets forth; its general end is to discourage people from violating those rules in the first instance. Its overriding goal is to make society safe and predictable.

Legislatures create criminal sanctions only for behaviors they believe rational people might elect. There are, therefore, laws proscribing and punishing torture of persons other than oneself and sexual assaults on domestic animals and unwilling persons; there are no laws (to my knowledge) proscribing and punishing torture of oneself or sexual assaults on elm trees or onions or videodecks.

Legislatures do not usually develop criminal sanctions for things no one is going to do anyway. The criminal law is designed to protect members of society from predation by other members of society; it is also designed to protect society itself from what it perceives as predation by its own members. Criminal sanctions for the latter are directed toward behaviors that disrupt or impede governmental functions (tax fraud, perjury, espionage) or behaviors legislators believe are socially disruptive even though they are likely to involve no complaining citizens (drug use, consensual sexual encounters, abortion, pornography). The latter kind of legislation is most subject to fashion. It was easy for Harry Anslinger to get through Congress punitive regulation of cannabis use in the 1930s, when few people used it; in the 1970s, when cannabis use had become widespread, the laws were eased and, in many jurisdictions, mere possession for personal use ceased to be a criminal offense at all. When it was believed that only perverts engaged in sexual behaviors other than male-female/genital-genital, the laws of most states imposed severe penalties for homosexuality, oral and anal intercourse, and other variants. When it became apparent in the 1970s that millions of otherwise noncriminal adults engaged in some of those behaviors regularly, the courts and legislatures modified those laws to exclude private behavior among consenting adults. The law on "victimless" or "noncomplainant" crimes is always in flux. The law regarding injurious crimes tends to be constant. The rules of trial may change, the terms of punishment may change in accordance with some external goal (e.g., the recent trend toward fixed sentences and flat time introduced to replace the apparent iniquities of indeterminate sentences, or the introduction fifty years ago of indeterminate sentences to replace the apparent iniquities of fixed sentences and flat time), but murder, robbery, forgery, burglary, rape, etc., stay on the books and will continue to stay on the books.

Us and Them

The rules are suspended when the state is at war, a situation which defines the individuals at risk as "the enemy" rather than citizens of some reasonable jurisdiction. That is why it is permissible to kill enemy soldiers in combat but not (in theory) when the opposing soldiers have been taken prisoner. A prisoner of war is part of *our* system, hence in possession of certain rights defined by our laws. Military or criminal prisoners do not have the same rights as the rest of us; their status as prisoners exempts us from according them certain freedoms. But we assume that prisoners must be punished by the rules, while enemy soldiers can be killed without reference to any rules other than those that define them as enemies at that moment. There is a world of difference between killing a soldier from the other side one minute before or one minute after an armistice has gone into effect.

We regularly utilize such rules about status to justify our own killings at home. A possible felon with a gun pointed at a citizen can be legally killed by that citizen or by another citizen or policeman; if the possible felon has put the gun away, then the license to kill is suspended. We can execute someone we define as deserving legal execution, but only after an extensive march through procedures designed to prove and document that he has been condemned and is being killed according to the rules.

In war, our good boys kill their bad guys. Stripping a nice watch from a dead enemy soldier is not a guilty act; stripping a watch from a dead accident victim on the highway at home is an entirely different matter. The accident victim is one of us; the enemy soldier is not.

Except for real crazies and real professionals, both of which are rare, people rarely kill others of their own kind. Under normal circumstances they behave like most other animals. Extreme violence is permissible only when it is done to people who are "not like us." Most homicides that do not occur in a fit of rage involve strangers. In war, we do not kill Joe, Mac, Toby, Louann, and Betty Blue; we kill the krauts, nips, gooks, slopes, kikes, niggers ——. We are human beings; the others are something else. We live in a world of and are protected by the rules; they are outside the rules.

For many of those who engage in rational violent crime, there is a similar we/they dichotomy that controls who may be the legitimate subject of violence. The dichotomy may get its cutoff from a street intersection, a skin pigmentation, a uniform insignia, a language difference. Many of those we identify as violent criminals perceive the area we think of as our city as a war zone, a place with their territory and the others' territories, a place where injuries to the enemy count for nothing at all. We may deplore that logic, we may punish it; but neither our disagreement nor our vengeance can dissolve it.

Defining criminals as being radically different from us in some essential way has traditionally legitimized the scope of criminal punishments. Farer tells us, "These are not ordinary human beings who are inclined toward normal calculations of self-interest. They are people with tragically twisted minds who will always tend to discount the risk of imprisonment." Such an oversimplification is finally not very useful. Some criminals may be crazy; most are not. Some may be stupid, but that doesn't mean they aren't acting in terms of what they think is self-interest. Perhaps they may not understand that certain actions are not as much in their self-interest as those actions seem, perhaps they have not been well trained in delaying gratification, perhaps they do not understand probability. But turning them into something other than "ordinary human beings" prevents us from ever dealing with them rationally. It locks us into a sequence of failure and brutality because it continues their abstraction, the abstraction that lets us deal with them as people who "are not like us."

There are economic differentials that should not be ignored. The rich and even the moderately comfortable do not steal to live, so their crimes lack the reckless urgency characteristic of crimes of the poor. The poor are rarely able to embezzle large sums, cheat on their income tax, develop complex frauds. Their crimes are certainly more frightening than the crimes of the rich, for they are doomed to working at the point of a knife or muzzle of a gun, but that is not necessarily a matter of preference. Many thieves would much prefer embezzling $100,000 from a bank to holding up liquor and grocery stores. That is not meant to justify stealing by the poor or anyone else; most poor people never rob or hurt anybody. But the difference in access is one reason the crimes that frighten us most tend to be perpetrated by portions of the population far away from the comfortable worlds of lawmakers and professors.

A powerful logic legitimizes our criminal sanctions. There are two groups of people the state can legally exile from normal society: the diseased and the criminal. The difference in the two is that those adjudged diseased are assumed to be free of guilt, themselves victims; while those adjudged criminal are assumed to be bearers of guilt, makers of victims. Both have their liberty restricted in part to protect others: barred institutions are meant to keep us safe from the violence of the insane, the contagion of the infected, the predation of the criminal. The diseased are also incarcerated for their own good: so the state can keep them from hurting themselves while it tries to make them well. The criminal are incarcerated because they have not *been* good: so the state can punish them for having hurt others while it tries to make them good. The boundaries between diseased or criminal on one side and everyone else on the other are only partly fixed. They limn the normal, and as accepted definitions of "normal" change, so do the definitions of medical and social pathology.

There is one other important difference: medical service is usually delivered in rational terms (there are specific diseases, and treatments are made available to deal with them), while criminal service is usually delivered in political terms (police go where the pressure sends them or where their own budgetary needs move them; legislators create sentences to answer political pressures; judges and prosecutors are political employees).

Our criminal law assumes those who commit crimes have chosen to do so. Our license for doing them injury is our assumption that they have chosen to do us injury. If someone accused of violating a criminal law can convince the judge and jury that he or she was incapable of controlling his or her behavior at the time and had no intention of doing harm ("The dog bit my leg while I was handing Charlie the gun and it went off"), that is usually the end of the matter. The most rational crimes are most subject to deterrence. People rationally consider and execute frauds and paid murders, corporations elect to contaminate the water and the air; those making the decisions consider the risk and the gain, and they opt for or against the criminal act. Increase the penalties and the enforcement efficiency and those crimes will go down; weaken penalties or enforcement (as has the Environmental Protection Agency recently) and the violations go up. The law functions most efficiently as a deterrent with those who believe they can survive reasonably within it, those for whom its violation appears discretionary rather than necessary.

Law enforcement agencies can do relatively little to control that discretionary margin. They can shift it slightly one way or the other, they can broaden or narrow it slightly, but the factors influencing it are created elsewhere. Even severely repressive police actions cannot compensate for the large social and economic factors that determine the location of that discretionary margin. This was recently documented forcefully by Robert Waite, whose SUNY/Binghamton Ph.D. thesis examined juvenile delinquency in Nazi Germany. Even though Nazi police measures grew more repressive, Waite discovered, juvenile crime increased. As the German social and economic structures disintegrated and the youths felt themselves less and less a part of the society that sought to control them, the crime rates increased. Even the great power of the German civil police could not slow the rate of increase. Neither can our police or our courts or our prisons.

Criminal justice agencies deal with specific cases, with specific individuals; their problems are rarely neat. Practical criminal justice is a world of continuing accommodation. Police, prosecutors, courts, and prisons operate the way they do because of real time and real money constraints and because they are institutions with internal priorities of their own that have little to do with the abstract ends of the criminal law. A robber is sent to prison to be punished for his robbery and to keep him from robbing other free people for a period of time, but the prison rules are set up to make the prison as manageable as possible for the keepers and residents. The specific and general deterrent effects of the criminal law are impossible to measure, so no criminal justice agency ever really defines its *behaviors* in terms of deterrence. The punitive effect of the criminal law results from the simple fact of restriction of liberty, so no agency measures the abstract impact of quantity or quality of punishment. The prophylactic function of criminal law is absolute, since no criminal is preying on free citizens while he or she is locked up (and no one measures the amount of criminal activity and predation *within* prisons; few people outside prison care, since convicts are not part of our world). Only rarely does the disjunction between the reasons for institutional decisions and the reasons those agencies exist (e.g., why courts make the decisions they do as distinct from the goals of the drafters of the laws empowering the courts to act as they do) become apparent, and then it is usually misinterpreted. Prison problems are seen as resulting from inadequate funds or incompetent administrators (which keep the prison from "doing its job"), and lack of staff and space are seen as the source of problems in the judiciary (which keep the courts from "doing their job"). Whether the courts and prisons are in fact doing the job expected by the law is rarely a matter of examination.

Few people are pleased with the way our criminal justice system functions. Police think that prosecutors lose too many good cases, that courts let too many crooks go on technicalities, and that prisons do not keep crooks locked up long enough. Prosecutors complain of sloppy police work, judges who do not pay attention or read the law, defense attorneys who procrastinate, and prisons that do not do their job. Judges complain about cops who lie, incompetent and feckless defense attorneys, DAs who will settle for any deal that keeps their calendars moving, and prisons and parole boards that subvert their sentences. Prison officials complain of discrepant sentences that let prisoners think *they* are the ones wronged, sentences that are too long or short, parole boards that revoke parole for stupid reasons, and legislatures which fault them for riots or escapes but pay no attention to anything else. Defendants and serious defense attorneys complain of the enormous difference in the quality of justice meted out to the rich and to the poor. Members of the general public consider all the money they are paying to keep the criminal justice empire working, they consider how unsafe they feel on their streets or in their homes, and they decide they are not getting their money's worth from any of those agencies.

This is where the politicians come in (along with silly solutions like

Farer's). The "war on crime" mentality erupts every election season like a herpes sore at a time of high anxiety. The "war on crime" mentality assumes a coherent enemy out there, one that can be defeated if we can just take out enough of the opposing soldiers. This is nonsense. There is no coherent enemy out there. Whatever war there is, is more like Vietnam than World War II or Korea: there is no battle line, there is no uniform, there are no serial numbers, the participants change daily.

Punishment and Prevention

Our crime problem is really two problems, and they cannot be joined. Much bad law has resulted from a confusion or amalgamation of the two. One problem is concerned with what to do once a crime has occurred; the other, with what we might do to prevent crimes from occurring.

There are specific eruptions, specific crimes perpetrated by specific individuals. The crimes should be solved, the perpetrators punished. If they have the ability to understand what they are doing and why they are doing it, they should receive progressively more severe punishment, perhaps resulting in total isolation from society. Punishment should be sure and quick and fair. Hardly anyone disagrees with those notions; their solutions are primarily a matter of efficiency.

Should prisons be nice or nasty? Should there be a cutoff in severity of offense after which alternatives to incarceration may not be used? The current answers are always modifications of yesterday's answers. Changing the answers changes the options or situations of some individuals, but it rarely changes the nature of the system itself. As Michel Foucault has pointed out, prison reform has been part of prison design since the invention of the prison.

A more important question is whether the criminal justice mechanism can do anything significant about the incidence of crime, or whether its effect and impact are limited, like the changes in prison, to shifting the margins slightly but not changing the behaviors substantially.

Often, finding a solution to a problem is not a matter of finding answers only; it also entails finding the right questions to ask. Trying to fix the crime problem by fixing the criminals (maiming them, killing them, isolating them, retooling them, punishing them) has been with us for centuries, but we still have criminals in abundance. There is no evidence that suggests doing a better or nicer or more efficient job of handling people who have already developed a willingness to offend violently will change the development rate of new individuals willing to behave violently. Most crimes of violence are committed by people who have not been previously convicted of such a crime; the criminal justice system sees them only after the fact.

Treating symptoms is sometimes necessary. It is surely necessary when there are no other options. Doctors treat symptoms when they have no tools for fighting the disease, or when they have no notion what disease they are really treating, or when the disease is so far along they cannot treat its causes. In those situations, they try to make the patient as comfortable as possible and hope for the best. That same spirit energizes most applications and modifications of our criminal law.

It is presently fashionable to say that the liberal social and economic reforms of the 1960s and 1970s failed. Surely some of the programs did not accomplish all they promised and some were inadequately designed or badly managed. None of that matters so much as the simple fact that the programs were in place for a very short time before dismantling began. How could we expect that ten years of marginal economic experimentation would eradicate massive economic problems and bring about massive social stabilization? We have not even been able to clean up the mess in the Hudson River in fifteen years.

Our society is large and complex. The causes of social problems are not easy to find, and they are rarely single causes anyway. The causes are not easy to fix even when we know what they are. Sometimes all we can do is deal with the mess.

Basic reformation of our society over a long-term period will probably do something about crimes of theft and crimes of violence against strangers. Some violent crimes will still occur; there are some people who *like* to commit violent crimes. But most criminals would really prefer to live well and have the range of options enjoyed by people with a decent income and a stable economic situation. Economic reformation will not occur for many years, if it occurs at all, and it is neither wise nor practical to make short-term policy decisions on the basis of utopian plans. Real economic and social equality of opportunity in America is probably as silly and naive a dream as Farer's plan for a functional penal colony near the equator. The poor and the disenfranchised, the stupid and incompetent, the sick and the lonely will be with us for a long time to come. And so will violent crime.

In the interim, we will have one insignificant modification after the other, one silly suggestion after the other, one new law after the other. "We are always passing laws in America," wrote Robert Ezra Park. "We might as well get up and dance. The laws are largely to relieve emotion, and the legislatures are quite aware of the fact."

Until we stop letting our legislators feed off the hysteria about crime, until we force them to take action that will decrease the likelihood of most crimes occurring in the first place, the killing dance will continue. We may please our aesthetic sensibilities by designing more felicitous penal colonies, but we will not be free of the continuing need to establish more and more of them.

The Black Box of Criminal Bureaucracy

(*Society*, 1985)

This essay is about how bureaucracies work. It began as a policy talk in the Distinguished Lecturer Series at the Criminal Justice Center in Huntsville, Texas, in 1978. The invitation was to discuss "The Bureaucratic Crisis in Public Institutions," with a focus on penal institutions. As soon as I began working on the talk I realized that in terms of management and function, what I had to say about prisons applied to bureaucratic life in general.

The essay in its present form still focuses on criminal justice bureaucracies, but what I say about the pressures for continuity, resistance to change and reform, and the character of individual identity within organizations applies equally well to such other public institutions as hospitals, colleges, the military, IRS, CIA, the Bureau of Indian Affairs, and NASA. From an outsider's point of view, complex institutions are instrumentalities to external ends: people enter a hospital so they can come out well; people enter a college so they can come out educated; Congress funds the CIA so elected officials will have information upon which they can make informed decisions. From the insider's point of view, institutions are organic and dynamic, with specific and compelling internally generated and defined behavioral demands. The discrepancy between the inside and outside perceptions of what really matters explains much of the dissatisfaction outsiders have with institutional performance and the frustration insiders have about outsiders' demands.

I KNOW OF NO PUBLIC INSTITUTION that functions internally the way outsiders assume it should or does function. People within institutions do not make decisions or evaluate one another for the reasons outsiders assume. They rarely share outsiders' goals or indicators of success. The difference results in great frustration, anger, and hurt. It produces grim sequences of reform movements, each of which is designed to make things better and all of which seem merely to make things more complex or muddled. Prisons and schools and welfare departments are reformed regularly. Sometimes—as with the reintroduction of the determinate sentence in American prisons in the 1970s—the brand-new cure is what was once the old-fashioned evil. Changes are too often little more than cosmetic—restrictions on plea bargaining lead to new sophisticated styles of charge bargaining—and within a few years the cycle begins again or continues as always always. As Michel Foucault points out, reform has been part of the penitentiary design since the institution's invention, and so has been the failure of reform.

Outsiders define institutional roles in terms of transient clients and transient issues, and they assume that the institution itself is a fact of life, something there like water or rocks. For outsiders—all the rhetoric notwithstanding—institutions are the buildings. Insiders perceive institutions in quite different terms: they think of roles and relationships, of their own survival, of behaviors, options, powers, and restrictions that make sense within the building. Sometimes it is like the outsider saying, "I want you to ride this horse to town and get the groceries," and the insider responding, "It's not a horse, it's a dog, but he's great with children."

I have many times heard people I considered thoughtful social observers speak of nurses and doctors, of teachers and noncommissioned officers, of academic deans and professors, of policemen and judges, and of prison guards and wardens as people who affect life within certain institutions. Often the conversations were about how or why one public institution or another had failed or betrayed or disappointed us. We shared, in those conversations, a misconception I did not fully appreciate for a long time: those doctors and teachers and guards and wardens and deans and cops and welfare workers are not people who merely affect the life of an institution; they are not peripheral appendages an institution has to bear. They are part of the institution; in many ways they are the institution.

That is a simple enough observation, but an understanding of its implications may help us explain why public institutions nearly always seem to fail the public that pays the bills, why such institutions regularly hurt and infuriate and frustrate the individuals who pass through as transients, and why the long-term residents of the institutions come to regard the larger world outside as a place rather foreign, a place lacking all understanding of how things work, a place that is not very friendly.

The long-termers of most institutions are not the people for whom the institutions are ostensibly built. In a prison most long-termers are not the convicts. Few people sent to a penitentiary stay there more than three years, and very few stay more than four, but most of the staff are around considerably longer than four years. Most staff workers who are still on the job after four years will continue in the institution for some time; they become the long-term residents.

The new employees who quit or are discharged early—most public bureaucracies, but particularly welfare agencies and prisons, have very high turnover rates during the first year—are in a position not unlike the transient clients or convicts who do not come back after an initial involvement, those who are not chronic. Those who leave early are those who learn something they could not or did not determine from outside: they do not belong in the institution. The high turnover means that there is a great discrepancy between outside expectations and inside realities; it is an indicator of the real separation of the institution from the larger society. Survival through that initial period enhances any individual's identification with the institution and his perception of the institution's identity. Because of the high rate of early self-selection as inappropriate, membership in the group of survivors reinforces the apparent institutional isolation from the world outside.

Often we refer to complex public institutions as "bureaucracies," and we tend to deal with them as if they were what scientists call "black boxes." A black box is a mysterious entity: we know what goes in, we know what comes out, but we know precious little about what occurs inside. Generally, we do not really care about institutional black boxes. Except in times of notable riot, few outsiders care about what happens within a penitentiary. (How are guards promoted? What are they paid? Under what circumstances is a warden disciplined? What do convicts do all day? What is the working relationship between a guard and a convict or between a guard and a warden?) From the outside, black-box bureaucracies seem monolithic in structure and coherent in internal organization; they are rarely either. In all such institutions at least four significant roles or classes— politicians, managers, lineworkers, and coerced transients—survive in an uneasy combination of hierarchy and federation.

Politicians are individuals who are professionally within the institution but who are charged with maintaining contacts with the system or world outside: the college president, the chief or commissioner of police, the director of the hospital or prison system. In theory, they supervise the operation of the institution, but they often assign that responsibility to senior assistants and spend their time and energy explaining the institution to and defending it from the world outside. It is they who deal with the budget committees of the legislatures or city councils. All of them are what social scientists call *interface agents*—workers who operate where one system meets or intersects another system and who function in both sectors. They also receive pressure from both sectors: a prison director receives pressure from the courts to liberalize convict management while his wardens press to increase their autonomy. Not surprisingly, the politicians have the greatest lateral mobility.

Managers handle competition within the institution among suborganizations over resources and privileges, and they control the functioning of the suborganizations: the dean, the police captain, the chief of surgery, the warden. Such people are also interface agents in that they mediate between their staffs and their superiors, but their allegiance is correctly perceived as institutional. They develop statistics to make the organization look functional, and they work hard to keep potential scandals from escaping institutional control. Their efforts are directed toward enhancing and protecting the institution, though the effect may be deceiving the world outside or protecting individuals they know are culpable.

Lineworkers mediate between the institution and the transient: the teacher, the correctional officer, the policeman, the floor attendant, the secretary, the assistant district attorney, the caseworker. Like the transients, they are generally subject to policies defined elsewhere, and they are rarely allowed to influence those definitions directly. Their basic mode is one of adjustment and accommodation rather than creativity or innovation. The givens for them are the policies—not the external goal the policies ostensibly serve—and the transients to whom the policies are to be applied.

Transients, the individuals for whom the institutions ostensibly exist, are those who are more or less coercively managed within or by the institution: convicts, students, patients. In criminal justice there are two groups of transients: the people who complain about crime (victims) and those who appear to have committed crimes (criminals). The transients continue as classes—there continue to be criminals and victims of criminals—but the permanent positions continue both as classes and as individuals—the judge on the bench today will be on the same bench next year and the year after. The victims suffer, complain, and witness, and the criminals are arrested, prosecuted, and locked up in unending streams, but the police officers patrolling the streets and investigating the complaints, the prosecutors mediating between the police and the courts, and the wardens and guards setting forth the terms of the convicts' daily life change only once in a while; the cop who takes your call in March may well have been the cop who took your call last July, when you were calling about the visits of different crooks.

Each of the four roles or classes has a different set of definitions of what are legitimate functions, legitimate modes of behavior, and qualities of decent or successful behavior. None of the four responds to the same questions, none of the four deals with the same constituencies in the same ways, and none of the four fears or is at risk from the same dangers. Often, the only thing they share is the case, the root of the institutional connection. From the point of view of the larger society—from out here where we live—each institution has a specific job. The institution is supported because of that official job. A dismal paradox exists: the jobs for which outsiders create and maintain institutions are almost never the jobs by which members of the four insider classes define and legitimize themselves.

That discrepancy—between outside and inside definitions of function and legitimacy—produces much of the bureaucratic evil. To assert that institutions do evil things because individuals within them are evil requires us to assume that these occupations draw and accept and continue in place an extraordinary portion of society's evil and malevolent citizens. That does not seem likely, and empirical observation indicates it is not true. We are forced to examine the nature of public service bureaucracies themselves to understand how and why they behave as they do.

Mobility at the Top

There is virtually no lateral mobility in criminal justice operational work except at the top. Researchers may move from program to program, from government agency to a university and back again; chiefs of police may move from city to city and directors of prison systems from state to state; but workers within the systems almost never move anywhere but up, down, or out. The transients are the most mobile members of all: you can go anywhere and get sick enough to wind up in a hospital or behave criminally enough to get arrested.

The chiefs often move because of occupational necessity. Many of those top jobs are tied to the incumbency of an elected official. A new mayor or governor brings a new chief of police or a new commissioner of corrections. The changes have nothing to do with the quality of work done by the previous appointee. Sometimes the changes occur specifically because the previous appointee was too much identified with the organization he or she directed: the new governor, for example, wants in top state management positions executives who owe their primary job allegiance to him rather than to an organization; a man who identifies with an institution rather than a regime may feel at ease taking the institution's position when it is at odds with the regime's. Such institutional identification may make for good staff morale at the institution, but it makes for lousy politics and few governors let it happen. Especially in volatile institutions, politicians like executives who are their men, their pals, men in their debt, men in their camp.

Occasionally, individuals with interesting reputations acquire a fine mobility because the politician doing the hiring wants to buy a piece of that reputation. San Francisco Sheriff Richard Hongisto, twice elected to office by a coalition of young people, dope dealers, homosexuals, political activists, and several other interest groups, was appointed chief of police by Cleveland's young and ambitious mayor, Dennis Kusinich, in 1977. But Hongisto was too independent for Kusinich's taste and was fired not long after taking the job. He was hired in 1978 by New York's Governor Hugh Carey to run the state's prisons—until the state Senate rejected him. Hongisto's immediate predecessor in the corrections job had resigned because of economic constraints, political pressures from above, and agitation by the guards' union and the convicts, all of which he said made the institutions unmanageable. Before him was Russell G. Oswald, who, before he authorized the Attica slaughter on September 13, 1971, had enjoyed the reputation of being a liberal, reform-minded prison administrator. At the time of the Attica disaster Oswald had been commissioner less than a year. Before that, his career illustrated well the mobility of the chiefs: he had been full-time member (and sometime chairman) of the New York Board of Parole since 1957, after being director of the Massachusetts Department of Corrections, director of the Wisconsin Department of Corrections, and state supervisor of the Wisconsin Bureau of Probation and Parole.

A few top law enforcement and correctional jobs are insulated from changes in government—usually because of special skills of specific incumbents. J. Edgar Hoover used a mixture of willingness to supply presidents with information against opponents and the veiled threat of blackmail to keep his job for over four decades. Lyndon Johnson, who loathed Hoover, was once asked why he didn't fire him. Johnson said, "I'd rather have him inside the tent pissing out than outside the tent pissing in." Sometimes the security derives from a more civil notion of administrative relationships. Some states, for example, have prison boards specifically organized to protect and isolate the commissioners of corrections from gubernatorial whims. Texas prison board terms are staggered, making it unlikely that any governor could appoint a majority of board members. Only the board can hire and fire the commissioner.

Police departments are the least amenable to lateral entry of all criminal justice agencies. "At present," writes Rodney Stark, in *Police Riots: Collective Violence and Law Enforcement,*

all patrolmen are hired for the job of patrolman. Those who show merit (or simply wait for seniority) eventually are promoted to sergeant, detective, and even chief. It has been said with some justice that chiefs of police are simply patrolmen who have been on the force for 25 years. The general weakness of police administration is not very mysterious considering that it is performed by men who were not chosen for their administrative skill or training, but for physical aggressiveness and willingness to pound a beat. (1972:226)

Most professions have lateral entry options at all management and performance levels. The effect of this is that the organizations establish and maintain their own identities independently of the individuals participating at any particular time, and individuals who fit specific organizational needs can be recruited and moved in. Such individuals often bring with them information and attitudes not previously part of the institutions' repertory or configuration, and that contributes an important vitality.

Institutions with no lateral entry repress growth and development among members. To develop ideas of performance at variance with the accepted mode means that one is likely to miss out on advancement (which is a reward for "good" behavior) and that one will get the least-preferred job assignments. Institutions with no lateral entry force individuals to adapt or to quit. Institutional survivors are those whose own ideas are most in line with the institution's or those who are best able to subsume their own intelligence to bureaucratic procedure. New York's Knapp Commission, in 1973, cited the lack of lateral entry options as one of the factors contributing to the extraordinary amount of police corruption it discovered.

A police captain in New York does not join the San Francisco or Kansas City police department as a captain. A warden does not move from New York to Nebraska. A district attorney or judge does not move from Alabama to South Dakota. The usual justification given is that each of these positions requires a great deal of local knowledge to function properly. A working cop needs to know street people and have steady sources of information to be effective, but how many police captains anywhere ever go out on the street? A district attorney (DA) must know the attorneys and prosecutors in order to know what kind of deals can be made and with whom hard bargaining will work well; the DA must know the police well enough to know who can and cannot be trusted. A judge in one place is not familiar with the special legal codes of another place. A warden's power is really based on his channels of information within the prison, the informal channels involving his employee and convict informants.

Without lateral entry, the pressures on any individual to conform to peer pressure are nearly insurmountable. No lateral entry means that the folk culture of management is always more powerful than the formal culture of management. Police recruits spend a few months at an academy, then are assigned to cars with older heads who tell them "how it really is."

To argue that something is not being done by the book, marks a recruit as a fool or a troublemaker; other policemen will not work with him, will not share information with him, and, at an extreme, will not come to his aid if he is in trouble. The cliché is, "You can't beat city hall," but the real opponent is the locker room.

A worker spends twenty or twenty-five years surviving in a system before he or she becomes a ranking administrator. Survival all along the way is predicated on actual or assumed acceptance of the system as it works. The Knapp Commission reported that even so-called "good" police administrators never turned in their colleagues who were on the pad: they were not on the take themselves, but they would never think of blowing the whistle on those who were.

There is almost no lateral mobility at lower levels. A police sergeant or a prison lieutenant in most states is a civil service employee. Even if one should find a job in another department or prison, he does so at great risk, because he gives up his job security and may lose pension benefits. A top management law enforcement or correctional executive moving to another state generally has his moving expenses paid and often moves into living quarters paid for by the new employer. Policemen and guards do not get such subsidies. They cannot afford the move, and most departments and prisons do not want them. Police departments in most places are "good ole boy" networks. Individual policemen depend on knowing how someone will react, not just in situations of danger and violence but in normal situations. Departments have customs about goofing off, petty graft, minor hustles, covering for one another in times of trouble. Outsiders cannot be trusted to behave correctly. In prisons a large part of a line officer's effectiveness depends on knowledge of individual inmates; a large part of a ranking officer's effectiveness depends on knowledge of individual inmates and individual officers. They insist it is not like a hospital, where all operating rooms and all gall bladders present the surgeon or nurse with essentially the same sets of options and problems. Outsiders, they insist, do not know the terms well enough.

Although lateral entry into managerial ranks in criminal justice is rare, lateral mobility within the ranks is common. A warden in a large state prison system may move from prison to prison, a police captain may be assigned to a precinct on the other side of town, a parole supervisor may be moved to a new office. The same lateral mobility exists at the lowest ranks: policemen, guards, parole officers, assistant district attorneys can be moved to any work site. The options these workers have in any of these job situations are so slight that it makes little difference who occupies the job at any particular time. So long as there is minimal competence, anyone who understands the organization's requirements can occupy any position at his or her job level.

Criminal justice bureaucracies each operate on internally defined and generated and ratified goals, and none of the agencies shares goals in any realistic way. All are out to "win the war" against crime, but there are no practical measurements of that, and there are no battlefield maps. A prosecutor does not receive or issue battlefront reports and a judge would not bother reading any if they existed. A prison director is too busy preventing escapes, riots, and gang-bangs in the shower, and cooling down guard unions and organizations, to fret about the ups and downs of the crime rates in the cities. The successful manager in criminal justice agencies is the one who satisfies the bureaucratic demands of the organization. The pressures for such conformity come from both above and below. The lack of lateral entry in most criminal justice areas reinforces the conformistic value pattern and the disjunction from the rest of the system.

Lineworkers struggle to keep things on an even keel. "One reason for the oft-noted tendency of patrolmen to form cliques, factions, and fraternal organizations," says James Q. Wilson, in *Varieties of Police Behavior: The Management of Law and Order in Eight Communities,* "is not so much to celebrate the virtues of ethnic solidarity, though the organizations tend to be along ethnic lines, but to defend officers against what is to them arbitrary authority and 'outside influence.' The power of the administrator is to be checked because the administrator, if he is a strong man, is 'out to get us' and, if he is a weak one, is 'giving away before outside pressure.' "

Changing an individual worker in a complex organization—unless the individual is extremely incompetent or perverse—rarely changes the workings of the organization. Interactions may be smoother or rougher, faster or slower, but they remain essentially the same. That is why a police captain can be moved from precinct to precinct or a warden from prison to prison without difficulty. It is only necessary that the bureaucratic worker be the proper type.

All complex bureaucracies depend on the ability of the organization to handle individuals as interchangeable parts. If the organization is to survive, its procedures must permit whoever fills the slot to make the requisite moves and answer the postulated questions. In order for that to occur, the ability of those individuals to alter the operation of the bureaucracy must be minimal. The "best" bureaucracy is one in which the worker can move into the job and immediately do it perfectly, and one in which the worker cannot, however hard he tries, alter the system itself. In the perfect bureaucracy the worker who tries to do violence to the system or who questions or attempts to alter the institutional goals or measurements of success is himself found wanting and is expelled.

To say that changing bureaucratic functioning is "difficult" misses the point: the bureaucracy is so constituted that internal pressures for real change are read as pathological, and the agent of that pathological reading himself becomes the problem rather than a potential source of the solution of a problem. Bureaucratic workers who attempt to alter the system in which they function are perceived as troublemakers; they do not fare well in institutional life. They are either forced out or they suffer terrible frustration. If they stay and endure that frustration, they often burn out; they become mechanics, going through the routines, handling the cases, maintaining order, preparing reports, accumulating the data, doing the job, and waiting for the end.

Responsibility and Accountability

William G. Nagel, who has long argued for a moratorium on prison construction, said in a paper given at the Congress of Correction in 1976, and published in *Crime and Delinquency* in 1977, that the advances in technical skills and improvements in physical facilities in American prisons had produced changes that were more cosmetic than real, that the nature of the institution imposed roles and processes that transcended the changes of the 1960s and 1970s:

> Warm people entered the system wanting desperately to change it, but the problems they found were so enormous and the tasks so insurmountable that these warm people turned cold. In time they no longer allowed themselves to feel, to love, to care. To survive, they became callous. The prison experience too often corrodes those who guard and those who are guarded. This reality is not essentially the product of good or bad architecture. It is the inevitable product of a process that holds troubled people together in a closed and limited space, depriving them of their freedom, their families, and their humanity.

The same kind of observations can be made about workers in other bureaucracies—not only policemen and judges and prosecutors, but welfare workers, health inspectors, and even schoolteachers. All these individuals work in systems that do not, from the outside, seem to be working well; all the institutions are regularly under attack from one quarter or another. In each the outsiders served or handled or controlled are troubled or troublesome, and in each the new workers (especially the very best) look upon their jobs as working *with* people and *upon* a system. They hope to be effective in a way that makes the system work better.

This is not a problem confronting a worker on the Ford production line, a store sales clerk, a technician in a film processing laboratory. For those workers the problems are mechanical: are the parts coming off your phase of the line within the specified tolerances, are you handling the customers as well and as rapidly as everyone else on the floor, are the negatives and transparencies technically adequate for the customers? The lineworker is not told about and does not much care about the company's profit margin (unless there will be layoffs), the sales clerk does not care why people buy what they buy or the function of the store in the economic configuration of the community, the film technician does not care what is on the film and what function it has after it leaves the cutting table. Such workers may be parts of a system, but they rarely see themselves as having any influence upon it.

Workers in the social agencies often expect their work to matter, to have a significance beyond the moment of application or encounter. Unfortunately, there are no adequate measures for such expectations. The bureaucracies all adopt indicators of success that have little or nothing to do with the needs of the larger community or the aspirations of the workers who enter in the hope of doing something about those community needs. The bureaucracies develop indicators that make the same kind of sense that producing a gear within a specific tolerance makes—the indicators are specific and measurable. The only difference is, there is no whole car at the end to be driven away. Neither is there any profit or loss: performance on the line is measurable, but bureaucratic accountability to external goals is not.

In business institutions, responsibility and accountability apply to the same behaviors, the same interactions, the same functions. That means it is possible to evaluate business workers directly in terms of outside expectations. Ford stockholders expect the corporation to produce cars of reasonable quality and profits of reasonable dimensions. If a specific subcontractor or department produces bad parts or costs too much money, the Ford executives decide whether or not the cost subverts the corporate mission. If it does, they take specific action: the efficiency expert shock force moves in, Group Seven is fired, new subcontractors are found—whatever needs to be done is done. Not so in public institutions.

Consider public colleges. The primary function of all public colleges is the production of educated men and women. I take "education" in this sense to mean the ability to fulfill a certain range of complex job assignments and the ability to enjoy and spiritually profit from the humanities. I have never heard of a single college professor who was evaluated for tenure on the basis of whether or not his or her former students were able to take on complex job assignments or were able to enjoy and spiritually profit from the humanities. That is because presently no way exists to link a student's educational experience within a college class to the quality of that person's life outside of it. Too many variables are involved.

There is a disjunction between what the institution is supposed to be doing and what workers in the institution can be rewarded for doing. Colleges evaluate faculty members on the basis of criteria for which they can be held both accountable and responsible. There are only three such criteria in most colleges: adequate publication, university service, and teaching ability. All three criteria are countable: one can count the students, the committees, the articles and lectures and books. A promotion committee has an easy job when there are many entries, a difficult job when there are few. The professional choices are made on the bases of what can be measured, not what is wanted.

The characteristics of bureaucratic discrepancy we find in criminal justice agencies are found in all service institutions, however benign their mission. All experience the inside/outside disjunction. In each case the disjunction results from a different sense of mission and role and value among the career workers and the external franchisers. Whenever such discrepancy of purpose or disjunction in mission becomes visible, the institution will seem to have failed society and society will seem to have betrayed its institution. At such moments institutional workers often try to find an indicator that will appear to negate the discrepancy and legitimize the work that has been done. So the colleges count the teachers' publications.

The assumption of mere cynicism on the part of bureaucrats is too simplistic. I suspect most people would prefer to do good work, and I think people are sincere as often as not. It does not matter: few people have the energy or skill or intelligence to be truly cynical at work day after day after day. People work very hard at getting things to make sense; even when their work requires them to perform vile acts, they seek—and usually manage to find—an institutional logic that makes the behavior not only reasonable but imperative.

Consider the situation in profit-making institutions. However complex their internal organizations and however Byzantine their corporate relationships, profit-making institutions always have one unambiguous bottom line by which everything is finally evaluated: was money made or lost last year? We need not argue the morality of profits. Making money is the primary responsibility of all corporations except those special few declared non-profit by the Internal Revenue Service. No historical or psychological or sociological argument or explanation can nullify or legitimize a continuing loss for General Motors or Jack Daniels or Polaroid or 3M. Too many pension plans depend on profitable seasons. A stockholder's report offers no line for fine intentions gone wrong. If there is no money in the bank for a year or two, staff people disappear. If there is no money after several years, the entire enterprise disappears: witness Hudson, Packard, DeSoto, Edsel, Abercrombie & Fitch, Design Research, Kresge's.

When things go wrong in profit-making institutions, various techniques help executives work back to determine why and how the problems occurred. People and departments are not only responsible for what goes on, but they are also accountable. In business, accountability and responsibility are joined. If a batch of Jack Daniels tastes and smells like lemon-flavored glue, the Jack Daniels quality control team will trace that batch back and will either isolate the fellow who was sniffing lemon-flavored glue that day and dropped some into the mixing kegs or they will find the quality control inspector who failed to sniff early enough.

Public institutions do not function that way. That is because none of them is defined and legitimized by products or profits; they offer only processes, and process is another matter entirely. There is no bottom line to a process. If a convict finishes his term in the penitentiary, accepts his state suit, a bus ticket back to the town where he was convicted, and $25 or $50, puts on the state suit, uses the ticket, and spends the $25 or $50 on a pistol with which he immediately kills an innocent citizen, it is impossible for anyone to single out a specific correctional officer or psychologist or chaplain or warden and say, "Because of your incompetence or your failure of imagination or your lack of kindness or love, this man is a homicidal maniac."

The tools for such assignment do not exist. Institutional life is too complex and thick for adequate determination of individual accountability for official goals. This inability to hold workers accountable for official goals has vital ramifications, the most obvious of which is this: workers in an institution are held accountable only for things that occur and can be measured within the institution, in ways that make sense within the institution, and for things that can be translated into institutional values. It is always—and usually only—on the basis of institutional priorities that an individual will be promoted or not, fired or not, given a raise or not, given more power or less.

Doing the Job

All serious bureaucratic workers define what their job is and do it, more or less. If that definition is not compatible with the outsiders' definition, it is proof that outsiders understand nothing. The job of the institution's senior politician is to mediate, as much as possible, between inside and outside definitions and, when adequate mediation is not possible, to act as buffer between the two incompatible definitions of vocation. The prison administrator attacked because of high recidivism rates points to institutional security, the prison administrator attacked because of institutional violence talks about outside agitators. The police chief threatened by a citizens' review board talks about the threat to professionalism. Always, the thrust is to deflect the outside question to an inside concern.

Like everyone else, workers within bureaucratic institutions deal as much as possible with issues and problems that make professional life logical, endurable, safe, and meaningful. They work to guarantee their own survival and that of their unit within the institution. All of this is compounded within complex bureaucratic institutions. From the outside, we often elect or are forced to deal with them as if they were monoliths: the Army, Harvard, the New York Public Library, the Los Angeles Police Department; but I do not know of any such institution that behaves internally as if it were at all monolithic. All have within them subunits or subinstitutions that behave in relation to the mother institution exactly as the mother institution behaves in relation to the world outside. The same four discrete institutional roles often exist within each of the subunits. There are black boxes within the black boxes.

Within a university the library takes on institutional behaviors, and so do the English department, the athletic department, the secretarial pool, the purchasing office. Inside a prison system the various units take on institutional behaviors and roles, and within each unit the larger operational modalities do the same thing. It is a rare and quirky institution in which all segments function at peace and harmony. More commonly, the segments mistrust one another and the wagons are always drawn in a tight circle. That is why central office officials are often honestly astounded at revelations from a renegade employee or an investigative reporter: the managers of the subunits regularly keep massive amounts of information from their own supervisors in the administrative centers because in part their job is to defend their units against incursions by all outsiders.

In 1978, for example, while Texas prison administrators were preparing for their defense in a trial, an inmate collapsed from heat prostration one Friday afternoon at Ramsey prison, about 50 miles south of Houston and some 125 miles away from the Texas Department of Corrections' central offices in Huntsville. Investigation by the Ramsey warden revealed that the inmate was a recent admission, just back on a parole violation. The usual policy for new men working in the field was to give them a week on half-days, to let them adjust to the work and the weather. Someone— apparently an inmate clerk—blundered, and the man was improperly sent out to the fields, where he collapsed a few hours later. The Ramsey staff did what they could to make sure such a blunder would not happen again; they were fully aware that in the middle of a highly emotionalized trial, even innocent mistakes could not be tolerated. The following Tuesday a reporter asked the prison director about the condition of the man who had collapsed at Ramsey. "What man are you talking about?" the director said. The reporter told the director the collapsed man's name. The director knew nothing about the incident.

Why had the warden not told the director about the incident? Not to protect himself—it was clear none of the Ramsey administrators would have been blamed. The Ramsey warden thought he had "taken care of the problem" adequately by reprimanding those who were careless and making sure that inmate clerks and official supervisors would be more careful with such inmates in the future. Telling the central office about the incident would gain nothing for Ramsey, and they would look clumsy and inefficient. They thought it better to take a chance that the incident would be forgotten than to involve outsiders—in this case their own superiors in the organization—in a problem they had handled internally.

The disjunction between central command and subunits helps explain why institutional executives who attempt rapid changes are often frustrated and undermined by their own underlings. Robert McNamara had high hopes and fine promises when he attempted to bring big business methods to the sloppy and cumbersome Department of Defense during the Kennedy administration. He was going to end the waste of money, the waste of personnel, the waste of time. In the end, they wasted McNamara. He did not comprehend the critical difference between profit-making and service institutions. The Department of Defense was essentially the same at the beginning and the end of his tenure as secretary of defense, and only some minor procedural changes survived him.

In 1977 Jimmy Carter's CIA director, Admiral Stansfield Turner, summarily fired hundreds of CIA field agents. After the firings were completed, Turner fired the official who carried out the firing procedure. I suspect Turner felt the only way to alter radically the behavior of Covert Operations was to simultaneously discharge all the current operatives and then start over—with agents who subscribed to his model of institutional performance. If the CIA is like most other bureaucracies, Turner probably was disappointed to discover that his new covert agents replicated the styles of the former covert agents, and that his brave attempt to create anew was the organizational equivalent of lopping off a lizard's tail.

Another basic rule of institutional behavior deals with interface agents, the people who mediate between an institution and the world outside or between a segment of the institution and the rest: an interface manager always defines success or failure in terms of data that can be readily captured by staff and easily presented to outsiders. The definitions have nothing to do with function, mission, or public service.

When it comes to numbers, physical scientists have a great luxury: they can examine interactions or behaviors both in their laboratories and in life; they can set up parallel situations in which various elements are added or subtracted; they can select the conditions they will examine. Given enough time and arithmetic and adequate instruments, they can isolate the specific factors determining physical events. Social scientists cannot (usually) do that, nor can people who manage social agencies. They have to make do with what actually happens. For service institutions—all of which are assigned public functions that are unmeasurable—that limitation causes significant problems.

Police and corrections officials have very different population selection options. Anyone, potentially, can be dealt with by the police. The police often make policy decisions that determine who will come into their hands. Crackdowns on vice may result in increased arrests of prostitutes, pimps, dope dealers, and gamblers; they may also result in increased arrests of "square" citizens dealing with vice professionals—the hookers' johns, for example. Public concern about drug use may result in massive harassment and arrests of high school and college students. A particularly horrible series of fatal accidents in which auto drivers were drinking may result in a plethora of drunk driving arrests. The number of these arrests is always limited by the amount of time police have to spend: police departments never arrest more individuals than they can handle. The police may be subject to outside demands for performance, but they always set their own levels of adequate performance.

Prisons have no choice about the members of their transient populations: people are delivered in buses and must be accepted. A warden cannot send an inmate back to a judge in a certain county with a note saying, "We don't like this fellow and we decline the option of accepting him," or "We're full up this month," or "You've exceeded your quota of felons for the season." The prison administrators have no option about access.

Prisons and police adopt arithmetic techniques to describe their handling of the transients; those arithmetic techniques are designed to convince outsiders that a good job is being done. In both cases the arithmetic information is nearly totally irrelevant. It is important that we keep in mind the special problem of all criminal justice evaluation: the real social indicator of success rests in events that do not happen. The difficulties with events that do not happen are twofold: there is no way to count them, and there is no way to be sure what factors forced those uncountable nonevents.

The public presents the police with two basic problems: safe streets and safe homes. People are concerned about bad checks and crooked repairmen, about the whores downtown and the gay bars uptown; they may be distressed when they hear that junkies are nodding off in city parks or that cars speed on Main Street. What people actually worry about is getting hit on the head or raped or stabbed or having the kids come home from school all bloody and hysterical. People fear direct, confrontational crime, and after that they fear crime that violates their personal spaces. Tenderloin deviance may be a matter of interest, but that is other people and another part of town. Few people take white-collar crime very seriously—in part because no one seems to be getting hurt physically and in part because most Americans think some measure of dishonesty is part of normal business.

Effective police work consists of catching crooks and preventing crimes. (I'm excluding from this discussion police jobs appropriate to meter maids and crossing monitors and other noncriminal justice workers.) Crime prevention is more important than crook catching because it occurs before individuals are hurt; but crime prevention is vague and ephemeral, impossible to measure. The measures that do some good—putting high-intensity streetlamps in neighborhoods with a lot of break-ins and vandalism, say—are not part of a police department's budget. That is why public funds for crime prevention programs dribble away to nothing in tight budget times.

How does a community know if its police are doing a good job or not? One possible measure is whether or not citizens can walk with safety through certain neighborhoods at various times of day or night. Another measure might be how likely a family is to come home from a night at the movies and find the family silver and color television set where they left them. The problem is that what is measured is not necessarily the effectiveness of the police. If the police are working very hard but a demographic shift produces more street crime, the annual report will blame the police. Conversely, if the police do a wretched job and people avoid downtown entirely, the end-of-year statistics will suggest that the city is far safer than last year and the police will take the credit. The factors contributing to the drastic increases in urban criminal violence in the fifties, sixties, and seventies, and the decline in that violence in the early eighties, are complex and various; few are factors the police can do anything about. Sophisticated techniques and expensive equipment may help police apprehend more felons or keep track of the felons they have caught by traditional means, but few of the techniques or machines keep the felons home in the first place.

Snow does a better job. Houston has half again as many burglaries as Chicago and about 25 percent more burglaries than Buffalo; New Orleans has a third more burglaries than Chicago; Houston and New Orleans have 50 percent more rapes than Chicago and 60 percent more rapes than Buffalo. We might conclude that New Orleans and Houston have more burglars and rapists running around than do Chicago and Buffalo, or that the police departments of New Orleans and Houston do a far less adequate job of protecting the citizens than do those of Chicago and Buffalo. Nevertheless the most significant factor in those different rates has nothing to do with citizen criminality or police behavior, attitude, or efficiency; it has to do with the differences in climate. Burglary and rape are extremely difficult in Chicago and Buffalo about five months out of every year. Most stranger rapes occur inside buildings after forced pickups in public places; few women spend much time walking streets in those cities in the winter months. Burglary can take place at any time, but it is far more difficult when the storm windows and doors are in place and locked, the streets are slippery, snow makes the neighborhood brighter, and one has to worry if the getaway car will start.

Apparent indicators of police crime prevention effectiveness can be surprisingly deceptive, not because of police mendacity but because of the complexities of social behavior in an urban environment. In the late 1960s and early 1970s, for example, New York City police worked very hard to break up the so-called bopping gangs because of the increasing number of injuries and deaths resulting from their organized gang fights. Sometimes gang members mistook innocent kids for members of other gangs, and a number of murders resulting from such misidentification produced great pressure on the police to break up the gangs. The police were successful: most of the violent gangs disappeared within a few years. Later studies suggested that the violent behavior by former gang members continued, with one significant difference: the violence that was formerly directed against members of competing gangs was now randomly distributed through-out the community. Innocent strangers were getting hurt.

Urban police, challenged by everyone from the press to the city council to citizens' groups and religious organizations to produce results, lament what appear to them to be unreasonable limitations: "If you bleeding hearts didn't tie our hands for political reasons that make no sense out here in the combat zone, we could make the world safe for democracy and the streets safe for your wives and daughters." They define success in terms of what they can measure: the CBA—crimes cleared by arrest. The CBAs reflect police accounting standards—what level of qualification police officials demand for an arrest to get on the books—nothing more. The CBAs measure only police work, even when it is accurate. The figure is not changed by a digit if every arrest results in immediate dismissals by a magistrate furious over dirty procedure, nor is it changed if every arrest leads to a long prison term. Few police departments maintain records of crimes cleared by conviction or guilty plea. "That's not our job," they say. "The prosecutors and courts screw us up. You can't hold us responsible for the lousy deals they're willing to make, or for what they do or do not do."

Given the current political climate, I do not think the police can be blamed for this statistical chicanery. If an agency has a job that cannot be done or that cannot be shown to have been done, then the only viable alternative to mass resignations is development of substitute questions about performance that can be answered: What is our body count? What is your grade-point average? What is the precinct's rate of crimes cleared by arrest? What is the hospital's rate of postsurgery complications? What is your caseload? This suggests another rule of bureaucratic behavior: workers behave in ways likely to enhance or optimize the picture given by the readily capturable data. They avoid risks that may jeopardize those answers; the institution takes more seriously behaviors related to such data than behaviors relating to the official mission imposed from outside.

Agencies empowered to act in certain matters usually will act in those matters whether or not their action is necessary. That is because only by acting can they demonstrate they weren't doing nothing. In New York State agencies, purchasing small pieces of office equipment sometimes takes as long as six months, because many different offices are involved in the purchasing process and each office generates paperwork to demonstrate its business. The problem is not limited to public agencies.

The central internal goal of each agency remains self-validation. All the rewards, inducements, budgets, promotions, bonuses, and honors go to those individuals who can operate the agency with no significant challenge to its self-definition and patterns of operation. Always, the individuals most severely sanctioned are those who challenge the order. It does not matter whether the challenger is an insider or an outsider, a permanent member or a transient. When Frank Serpico told outsiders how much corruption really existed within the New York Police Department, he was set up and shot down. A prison guard who makes trouble by challenging the order of the system will be driven out of it; a convict who makes trouble by challenging the order of the system will be locked more deeply within it. For the prisoner, there is a Catch-22: the man who adjusts least well to the system is the man the system holds onto most tenaciously.

Reform

A Texas prison official—Michael C. Murdock, chief of planning and development of the Research, Planning and Development Division—read an earlier version of some of the preceding remarks about criminal justice bureaucracies and wrote me that he felt "the institutions are functioning in a logical, predictable, and essentially desirable manner." Mr. Murdock's letter utters from the inside some of my perceptions about bureaucracies and also offers an internal rationale for some of the bureaucratic behaviors I still find puzzling: most important, he focuses on process rather than end. The letter suggests one further bureaucratic imperative, one that consistently works to deflect the energy of the system away from external goals: in bureaucracies, means become ends. The ends are almost always ambiguous and distant; often, Mr. Murdock says, they are the result of competing political interests and so they arrive as confused or confusing conflations of concerns.

A common aspect of bureaucratic functioning seems a consistent expansion of required forms and necessary countersignatures and spaces for approval. New York State's elaborate purchasing organization—developed to make sure the state acquired goods at the lowest possible cost, with the least likelihood of purchase agent and seller corruption and connivance, and the greatest likelihood of the state getting the best available goods for the workers' needs—has become a lethargic monster. It adds an enormous cost to the purchase of any item. Extended delays while purchase requisitions make their way through various accounting, approval, bidding, contract granting, standards evaluating, and other organizations mean that prices at time of purchase are frequently much higher than prices at time of order, and goods delivered are frequently totally inadequate. The organization has developed in complexity as it has been attacked for its complexity; it has become expensive in response to attacks on its waste. The reforms are regularly subverted by introduction of new levels of approval, new agencies of oversight, and the reason is that, from within the bureaucracy, the only way to show that more work is being done is by creating more work and more documents that reflect the added work. Most of the processes are tautological: they exist only because the agency requires them.

It may very well be that bureaucracies can never reform themselves, that all they are capable of is more efficient documentation of themselves. When challenged, they hold a mirror up for inspection, and we outsiders are once again frustrated because we were desperately hoping for a pane of clear glass.

The fear bureaucratic workers have of institutional reform is dysfunctional from a social point of view, but it is not always irrational. Outsiders rarely understand insiders' fears because the two rarely share a notion of institutional function. Outsiders impose or engineer change in terms of their external perceptions of function, reward, and organization, and these only occasionally coincide with insiders' perceptions. When such changes produce unpleasant or dysfunctional results, insiders say, "We told you so," and outsiders feel they have been sabotaged.

Criminal justice agencies are like Spencer's piece of metal with the bump: we may perceive a need to flatten the bump, and we may attack the bump directly with a hammer. "Common sense" says that attacking it directly with a hammer will get rid of the bump. "Common sense" is partly right: with adequate hammering on the deviant spot, a flat harmony with the surrounding metal will be achieved, but new bumps will turn up in quite unexpected places. If we attack each of those new bumps, the sheet of metal begins to look like bubbled acrylic. The difficulty is that "common sense" can never appreciate the continuing dynamic of the entire sheet, and only an approach that adequately appreciates that entire dynamic can do anything but worsen the problem. The skilled metal worker, Spencer says, taps the metal in several places, sometimes not touching the deviant spot at all; he engenders a new relationship of the metallic associations and stresses—and winds up with a smooth sheet of metal. That is hard to do with criminal justice agencies because the real relationships among the parts are often not visible until the superfluous bumps are created by attempts to make distant spaces smooth and neat.

Prison administrators suffer a curious problem because of the recent upsurge of alternative correctional programs. As more and more nonviolent offenders are diverted into noncarceral programs (a tendency no prison administrator I know disapproves), the residual population in prisons becomes more and more violent and recidivist. The people who come to prison are those with the worst crimes, the worst records, the least chances for success. In a system in which liberalization of criminal definitions keeps more and more individuals out of the prison, there is a concomitant intensification of prison inmates with long sentences and serious personality problems. Instead of running prisons for the safe and predictable inmate—with some special provisions for the unsafe and the unpredictable inmates—administrators have to focus on the aberrant. Prisons become more—not less—coercive; they become more—not less— dangerous; and inmates become more—not less—likely to recidivate. The immediate effect of diversion programs is to make prisons less manageable than ever.

This problem would not exist if the rhetoric allowed prison administrators to say, "You're sending us greater and greater percentages of losers, so you shouldn't be asking us for greater and greater percentages of successful salvage operations." They cannot say that. They do not know how, and their failed results are too far in time and paperwork from the reason for the increasing failures. If the entire system were perceived systematically, the problem would be reduced, but it is not perceived systematically.

Because liberal reform may lead to increased prison unrest and more repressive prisons is no reason to eschew liberal reform, but it does mean that we cannot view prison unrest now as equivalent to prison unrest twenty or thirty years ago. The rhetoric is the same, but the terms of the equations have changed significantly.

Even simple, obvious reforms can have unforseen unpleasant results. For many years Arkansas's women convicts were housed in an old wood building on a one-acre plot of land in the middle of Cummins, the

12,000-acre prison for men. The women's unit was bounded by a high cyclone fence. The men convicts did not get in and the women convicts never got out—except when they were being sent home. The building consisted of one large dormitory room, a dining room so small the inmates had to eat in shifts, a kitchen, a small library, and a sewing shop. In the early 1970s a couple of housetrailers were brought into the compound to serve as schoolrooms. Near the building office were a couple of rarely used solitary confinement cells. When two women with escape records and convictions for a particularly brutal murder came to the prison in 1974, they were put in those cells. At its maximum the women's unit had about seventy inmates.

In 1974 plans were published in Arkansas newspapers for a new women's prison to be built in Pine Bluff. The new building would have individual cells, pretty dining halls, modular units, schoolrooms, and workshops. It would relieve the overcrowding and humanize the incarceration. The convicts and the officials looked forward to the move. Unfortunately, so did Arkansas judges. It turned out that for years many of them had actively sought diversion schemes for female felons because they thought the old house at Cummins a horrid place. As soon as the plans were published, the rate of incarceration for women increased dramatically and the average sentence length for nonhomicide commitments increased also. Before the new building received its first resident, officials had to commission construction of a new wing to accommodate the 50 percent increase in inmate population that had already arrived. By the time the prison opened in 1976, it was already overcrowded. The inmates were more comfortable than they had been previously, they had more options for mobility within the prison compound, and they had more privacy; but far more of them were doing far more time behind bars. The leap into modernity created a condition of long imprisonment for more prisoners than were originally suffering in the old building. At a time when correctional experts were arguing for reduced sentences and fewer commitments, the construction gave state judges a fine motive for increases in both.

Change is not free. Reform is necessary because of present evils, but since the true system is almost always invisible, even to the participants, the real meaning of the reform enacted is often not apparent until later. The reason so much reform fails is because not until the reform has been made can we see the shape of the body or extensions of the body upon which it was imposed. Each act of significant reform in a bureaucracy creates a new system, a new secret. Reform of public institutions must be continuous because each real reform redefines the institution and all roles within it. The institution often fights to absorb reform without enduring real change, which manifests itself as sabotage or further convolutions. Solutions are often easy to postulate, but it is not until long after the drink has been swallowed that we learn whether it was medicine or poison—or both at once.

What is most depressing about the current wave of reform is not the dimension or the nature of the problem or the scope of the suggested solutions. It is rather how many times the same things have been said before in nearly the same way. For as long as urban police and courts and prisons have aspired to public fairness and responsibilities, the same problems have been defined and concerned citizens have mounted campaigns to get things right. Like all institutions, prison functions in a context: it is locked into a complex system, it is a social being. Ignoring that context, that body, means reform merely deals with symptoms. There is nothing inherently wrong with treating symptoms, especially if it makes the patients think they are getting better and if treating symptoms is all the technology permits. It is naive to mistake such treatment for a frontal assault on the real problems.

The institutions need their reformers. The reformers set the safe boundaries against which the operators of the institutions can react. The reformers have suggestions for a civil police, a fair court, a decent prison. The police commissioner says that, given the situation, his men are as civil as might be expected; the prosecutor and judge say great improvements are being made daily; the prison director says that, given the population problems and his budget, his prison is as decent as is presently possible. The subsequent conversation takes place between these two extremes.

Reformers are, finally, the lifeguard of the system. They say, "You have things wrong, but we shall make you well. Just listen to us." Their advice is always happily ameliorative. For trivial problems they can do great good; for basic issues they are useless, because they operate, as the institutional managers, out of the same ideal. The liberals who would reform prison believe prison has a function that is not being fulfilled; the silent idea is that if only things were done more decently, the place would work. They are always bitter when their suggestions are accepted and things seem as dreadful as before. They assume their designs have been betrayed, sabotaged, misapplied. Betrayal, sabotage, and misapplication are not necessary.

Totally outside the conversation is interrogation of the institutional foundations: what is justice and who is entitled to it and who shall arbitrate its distribution and how do we know when we have found it? Conversations on those questions founder on abstraction, and meanwhile the managers and workers in institutions daily handle their clients, their caseloads, their security perimeters. It is unlikely that our reforms will change their definition of clients. Our world is too far away from the daily flow of drivel and trivia, the sequence of requests for decisions, of power without responsibility, of responsibility without power, of accountability for the wrong things, of blinding commodity. Justice is a gorgeous ideal. Most workers in criminal justice still think about it sometimes, still wonder what it really is and where it might be found.

Living Downstream

(1981)

"Living Downstream" appeared in a tabloid prepared for the Institute of the American West conference, "The American West: Colonies in Revolt," which took place in Ketchum, Idaho, 30 June to 3 July 1981. The conference was part of a series put on by the institute over a seven-year period examining the West in art, economics, and politics. "Colonies in Revolt" was organized by the institute's national council (Alvin M. Josephy, Jr., William K. Everson, William H. Goetzmann, Peter Hassrick, Bud Johns, Annick Smith, and me), and its acting director, Robert Waite.

The basic point of the piece is probably obvious: nothing is free or unrelated in the biosphere; poison created and dumped doesn't go away, it just goes somewhere else for a while, and then it comes back. Lately, I've become convinced that this is a basic law of life on our planet, whether we're talking about personal, social, or ecological matters. Problems aren't solved by flushing the toilet or locking people in jail or blinding ourselves to the pain of those around us; the accounting is never avoided, it's just delayed, and interest accrues always.

There's a kinky story about the lake across the street from my house that I mention in the article, but first here's some background: Not long after the article was written, federal funds were obtained to divert the Cheektowaga sewage away from Delaware Lake, sort of. I write "sort of" because the funds provided for construction of an underground channel that skirts the lake except for the first one hundred yards, where the diversion is an open culvert separated from the lake by a raised path about fifteen feet wide. Normally, the path is about four feet above the water level. It works fine except for periods of heavy rainfall when the underground channel clogs and the culvert feeding it overflows into the lake. That happens two or three times a year and people figure it takes the lake about two or three weeks to clean itself out after the underground channel starts flowing again. The open culvert exists because the people upstream from Delaware Park were happy to have the downstream sewage diverted, but not if that meant it would back up to where it came from. It's a kind of compromise common in American politics. Those of us who use the lake and the park don't think the lake is biologically clean, but it's clean enough so we're not bothered by the old stench, even on warm days—and that's a great improvement over the way things were.

Here's the kinky story: After the Cheektowaga sewage was diverted and the lake was usually clean, people started spending time around it again. Without the rotten smell in the summer, the circumference became a nice area for picnics and walks and bike rides. By the third year of the diversion project, the lake had begun freezing over so it was once again possible for people to walk across it in winter and, if the days before the hard freeze hadn't been too windy, to ice skate. The lake was, for the first time in more than a decade, capable of supporting aquatic life, so it was stocked and after a few summers one could go fishing there without feeling silly. The lake was fulfilling the function Frederick Law Olmstead had in mind when he designed it and the park surrounding it a century ago.

The city had a parks commissioner named Bob Delano. On his job application, Delano had claimed he was a Vietnam veteran and a college graduate, neither of which was true, but apparently no one examined his credentials too closely because of his very close association with Buffalo mayor Jimmy Griffin. Parks Commissioner Delano, according to a recent federal indictment, decided to poison the lake in Delaware Park.

The indictment says that Delano had parks department workers operating a private refreshment stand during hours they were ostensibly working for and getting paid by the city. Some city councilmen objected to this and the stand was closed down. In retaliation, according to the indictment, Delano ordered parks department workers to dump into the lake several fifty-gallon drums of the same salt used to de-ice city streets in winter. The ice on the lake melted and no one could ice skate that year; a good number of fish died as well. When the FBI began investigating the de-icing of the park lake and other curious behaviors, the mayor said that parks department employees who talked to FBI agents were "snitches."

Parks Commissioner Delano was indicted on seven felony counts by the

222 / Disorderly Conduct

federal grand jury. Most of the counts had to do with theft and diversion of services, but one had to do with pouring the chemicals into the lake. Delano thereby became the first public official in America indicted under the Clean Air and Waters Act.

I tell you this parochial story because when I wrote "Living Downstream" I was thinking about the kind of contamination that occurs because of greed and indifference. I hadn't ever encountered contamination out of spite. I was wrong when I wrote that the pollution in the eastern part of the country has "all been done." There's always room for a little more, given adequate motivation and opportunity.

FEW EASTERNERS think much about colonization. That's because there isn't anything to colonize there. The power generated by Niagara Falls isn't enough to supply New York; the massive assault on the offshore waters have trivialized the old fishing industries; the potential gas domes beneath the Atlantic floor are all unproven. The East doesn't share your problem of continually dropping water tables—perhaps because so many Easterners are moving south and west. The East is a place of producers and managers; it is like England and Japan. The time for outrage over the absence of unspoiled space there has been past for a century.

In my part of the country there isn't much land left to pollute. It's all been done. Acid rain kills the fish in the mountain lakes, polluted runoffs kill the fish in the Great Lakes. Local control isn't so much an issue back East as it is in the West—except in matters of social policy. My neighbors organize to keep the halfway houses out; organizing to keep the garbage out hasn't occurred to them.

Which I find curious. Across the street from my house is a large park that has near its middle a big lake. When I first moved to Buffalo fifteen years ago, people boated on that lake in summer and ice-skated on it in winter. Ten years ago, the boats were put away because the water had become so vile no one could dare risk falling in, and the ice skaters had gone elsewhere because so many pollutants were dissolved in the lake water that the freezing point had dropped below ten degrees Fahrenheit.

The pollutants come from chemical factories and sewage treatment plants upstream. We have local control for such matters—so Buffalo cannot fine Cheektowaga when Cheektowaga elects to float turds along the stream that feeds Delaware Lake. These things seem to matter only for the people who are downstream from other people.

The thing is, we're all downstream from someone with chemicals or turds. They're everywhere.

Out West, local control might keep the MX out, just as back where I live it keeps the halfway houses out, but I wonder what it can do for the upstream garbage floating down your way, or the upstream diverters of the water supply.

It is difficult for most Easterners to feel total pity or sorrow for those in the West who complain about outside intrusion and control. We have it too. We've had it longer than you have. We can't keep the next town from dumping its sewage in our water supply. We can't punish adequately the corporation that is willing to pay a fine rather than correct its operation. We can't flee Love Canal or West Valley.

Who isn't colonized by some distant interest? This has become a country of abstract interests. There is no simple bad guy to single out any more. You can't find a Rockefeller or a Carnegie or a Ford or a Frick and say, "That's him. That's the sonofabitch who's exploiting us."

What is "exploitation" anyway? Perhaps it's taking out without putting something back—not feeling the necessity of living symbiotically.

A century ago out West, outsiders came and took things out bodily; they mined the gold and silver and shipped it away. No matter. The stuff was worthless in the rock anyway. The miners spent real money, created towns, built roads; they moved in. Now, the outsiders cart things out, but they leave little behind but garbage. The strip mines poison downstream land and water; the water is ripped off for overpopulated cities a thousand miles away and the land is dessicated; the deep mines are operated by machines that replace hundreds of workers. The government offers to destroy the microecological systems of the desert and replace them with an enormous potential target zone.

Who do you go after to stop it? Those big name, big money individuals aren't there any more. The corporations aren't owned by individuals any more. They are as much owned by the pension plan of a high school teacher or a truck driver or a typist or a steamfitter as by Mr. Mogul Megabucks sucking on a fat cigar and thinking about what he can get away with tomorrow. Sure, the board members remain rich and powerful, but they behave as they are permitted to behave, as they are encouraged to behave. Those people answer to the demand of reasonable profits on investments. The other stuff, from their point of view, is for the philosophers. Can you imagine the fund manager for a massive pension plan accepting vastly reduced profits in the name of being kind to the land?

I realized, while making these notes, that over $100,000 of my money is presently invested in firms about which I know nothing. Someone else handles that portion of my portfolio. Her concern, her job, is only seeing that that portfolio returns as much on investment as possible. She does not, I presume, think in terms of social or ecological or political issues. Her job is perfectly simple: make money on the money I and several thousand other people have entrusted to her. That money belongs to schoolteachers and union members. The family fortune of the Rockefellers and the Kennedys doesn't compare to the present fortune of the Teamsters Pension Plan or TIAA or Harvard University.

There are those in the East who feel that a small number of people in the West have an enormous amount of power. A very small number of people in the Intermountain States control an enormous amount of land; a very small number of people control a large portion of the U.S. Senate. Bill Goetzmann refers to a "micro-provincialism" in the West. I once would have considered that a redundancy, but now I wonder. Has the West ever been (as the romantics would have us believe) a place where democracy really had a stand or has it been, ever since the coming of the white man, a place where the strongest and most powerful, acting in terms of that "micro-provincialism," got their way? Is what seems to be happening here now, this phony "Sagebrush Rebellion," any different from what has been happening here all along? How do you distinguish, in these conversations, between honest pride and arrant arrogance, between legitimate self-interest and venal selfishness?

I worry about the conversation that sees the Federal government as the same kind of exploitative beast as a monolithic corporation. Sometimes the proper response to a machine or process that has failed is to fix it or make it better. Abandoning the relationship isn't necessarily the road to anything better.

All the world, now, is downstream from someone, and lacking perfect conscience in the personal and corporate and governmental worlds, there seems a need for the kind of public conscience (with power) that big government could provide. I would like to be left alone as much as any of you, but I want to be left alone by you, too, and that is one of the jobs of government: making sure we don't damage one another.

My feelings are not unmixed. Government rules and regulations and clerks and officials are a royal pain in the ass. They take a lot of my time. I am creative in finding ways to circumvent them. I would prefer to put those creative energies into some other endeavor.

But in government, I know how to find out how decisions are made and I know how to influence the decision-makers there. Some of them respond only to money, to flat-out bribes, but the Spiro Agnews are rare. Most elected officials I know respond to community pressure—not simply because of an unmitigated desire to come back two or four or six years hence, but because they take seriously the idea that they represent a constituency, that if they're going to vote conscience or greed, they must do it with the full knowledge that the constituency is paying attention and will eventually have an opportunity to comment. The only way I know to influence a corporation that decides raping the land is more profitable than working with the land is by getting a government agency big enough and powerful enough to help intervene.

The question is what level of government shall do that intervening.

I knew an armed robber who worked with a gun for years. He stole from everything except banks. I asked why and he said, "You can beat the states. The states have only so much money to get you. The Feds have all the money they need." When we had that conversation, he was doing five years for 22 armed robberies—that was in a state in which an armed robbery conviction carried a sentence of 15–25 years. I asked how come he was doing only five and he rubbed his thumb and index finger together.

In "Godfather II," Michael Corleone tells one of his associates that one thing living in America has taught them is that anyone can be killed. We could paraphrase that: in America, anything can be bought. The problem is coming up with enough money and finding the right person to pay.

It's harder with the Feds. Not impossible, but harder. They are more bureaucratic than anyone, there are more of them, their records are sloppier, they can't hide things very well.

Do the people of the Intermountain West have the right to full control over the future of their lands? The answer to that isn't quite so simple from the other sides of the ranges. Does anyone have that right anymore? Shall they find a way to abandon partnership or dependency? Can they? Can the rest of us allow it?

The questions aren't neutral. The Civil War was fought over exactly those issues. Is there an interdependence to the Union that gives the other states a real and valid interest in certain carryings-on within any of the states?

Hardin developed for us the metaphor of the Commons: if we don't have rules controlling use of shared areas, there will be those who will violate it, those who will abuse or overuse it. Another metaphor equally appropriate for our time is the one I suggested earlier, that of living downstream. We all live downstream from someone and if that distant someone elects to put sewage in the stream that ambles through his private property, then the water that subsequently passes through my private property will taste like sewage. The theory of the Commons is adequate, perhaps, for the limited space of the East; out West, it's not only a matter of sharing, it's a matter of mutual interdependence.

We cannot leave decisions to the free marketplace. We don't have a free marketplace in this country and haven't had one for more than a century. Few manufacturers or farmers or consumers would want a free marketplace. All most of them want is a marketplace in which the restrictions apply only to everyone else.

A character named Ikkemotubbe appears in several of William Faulkner's novels. Ikkemotubbe, a Chickasaw chief, betrayed his people by selling some of their land. The betrayal wasn't in the making of profit; the tribe didn't care about that. The betrayal was in selling something no individual, not even a chief, had ever before been perceived as owning. Before Ikemotubbe's betrayal, the land belonged to everyone; everyone had equal rights to it, everyone had equal custodial responsibility for it. Ikkemotubbe's legal action said that someone now had the sole right to it and that someone was empowered to abandon custody.

What does it mean to own something that has preceded you and will succeed you too? That you can assign its profits to your heirs? That you can render it uninhabitable forever? Profit is transitory, ephemeral. The destruction—now that we have man-made desertification, PCBs, radiological detritus that takes ten million years to cool off and such—is not ephemeral.

Alvin Josephy says that "the Easterners are hard-put to revolt." Well: who among us isn't? And so what? In a world as interdependent as ours, perhaps revolt is not a rational mode of doing anything anymore. Can Easterners still live on the products of their land? Can Californians still live on the products of their land? Can anyone out West live the lifestyle he or she chooses without steel processed elsewhere, without rubber made elsewhere, without all those things that come in from the great outside? Few of us are even nearly self-sufficient and no portion of this country can make it on its own. The only people who can survive without the complex mutual interdependence of the states and regions and nations are those who live so marginally we consider them eccentrics or candidates for the poverty program.

The argument isn't simply over who shall control—town, county, state, nation—but also whether or not any of those governments can be made to control decently and rationally, whether we can teach them to leave us alone for the things we can and should handle for ourselves, and to help us with the things that greed or parochial interest confuse too greatly. Shall county governments fund cancer research? Shall they mount their own armies of the night? Would Balkanization of the mountains help anyone who needs help, or would it merely simplify and make less expensive the work of the real exploiters?

We desire appropriate action and appropriate inaction. We need destruction of bureaucracy that exists for its own sake and destruction of those agencies that exist only to perpetuate themselves and not to help us. We no more want the predation of corporate greed than we want the predation of bureaucratic arrogance. But there must be a balance that will allow business to function, government to help, and individuals to live with decency.

Who you fight is as important as what you fight about.

Gatekeepers

(September 1988)

This is the prepared text for my presentation at "Editing Reality," a symposium Diane Christian and I organized at SUNY Buffalo in late September 1988. The other participants were anthropologists Dennis and Barbara Tedlock (SUNY Buffalo), Jean Jackson (MIT), and Dan Rose (University of Pennsylvania); ethnomusicologist Steven Feld (University of Texas); filmmakers Frederick Wiseman, Emile de Antonio ("De"), and Diane Christian; sociologists Howard S. Becker (Northwestern University) and Michal McCall (McAllister College); and historians Lawrence Levine (Berkeley) and Michael Frisch (SUNY Buffalo). They were all dealing with ways in which scholars and artists edit their vision, data, and works, so I thought it would be useful to look at some of the outside forces influencing such decisions—particularly the force of money.

I should tell you that I've been well paid for writing some of the articles in this collection, but this was the piece that cost me the most money—$75,000 that I know about, probably a good deal more in the long run.

I published the portion of the talk having to do with the National Endowment for the Humanities (NEH) in the *Journal of American Folklore* (*JAF*) as an editorial titled "The Humanities at Risk." It produced some nice mail and two curious messages. The first message was delivered to me by an official of the National Endowment for the Arts (NEA) when we were taking part in an American Folklife Center board of trustees meeting at the

, "We will or we won't broadcast your film or publish your article or
ook." They say, "Make these changes and you're in; don't make these
anges and you're not."

They're the program editors at PBS. They're the editors of *Harper's* and
merican Anthropologist and the *New York Times* and the CBS "Evening
ews." They're the executives in private research organizations manipulat-
g data upon which public policy is made. They're panelists and program
fficers at such agencies as the National Endowment for the Humanities
nd National Science Foundation.

They are the gatekeepers. Some of those gatekeepers edit our reports of
eality directly; they take our vision of the world and they tinker with it so it
ts their vision of the world. Other gatekeepers define the context so we
dit *ourselves* in ways we otherwise might not. In large measure, these
gatekeepers define what kind of work will be done and what kind of work
will not be done.

People who are successful at the kinds of work done by participants in
this symposium are extremely rational. We may look or act eccentric at
imes, but it's just a pose, I assure you. Designing, shooting, and editing
movies, and formulating, carrying out, and making sense of fieldwork are
extremely complex enterprises. Slobs are incapable of such work. Slobs
may putter at it, but they can't do it. Being extremely rational, we are, in our
work, always trying to get exact answers to three critical questions: *What,*
exactly do we want to do? How, exactly, shall we *pay for* it? And what,
exactly, shall we *do* with it?

At the very moment we're defining our projects we're looking around for
funding and ahead to publication or distribution. We don't hover overlong
on projects that don't get funded, nor do we invest much time in projects
we know will never be finished or published or distributed. Documentary
filmmaking, for example, is extremely expensive and it is physically difficult;
I don't know anyone who does it for private or long-delayed consumption.
Our editing of reality begins with the definition of subject, it is modulated
by our sense of available resources, and the process continues until some
publisher or distributor takes it off our hands.

I'm going to be talking mostly about academics and nonfiction filmmakers,
but I'd ask you to keep in mind that the other presenters of reality are
likewise influenced by the other external editors of reality. Television news,
for example, is, like *National Geographic,* picture-driven: the value of a story
is usually directly proportional to the amount and quality of film footage
accompanying it. The television news editors fear stories without pictures
because they believe their audiences won't tolerate mere words. When
South Africa and Israel banished film cameras from areas of conflict, the
time allotted those subjects on evening news broadcasts shriveled. The

Library of Congress. She said a program officer at NEH was very annoyed at
the piece and would be writing me about it. "Mad at me personally or as
editor of *JAF*?" I asked. "As editor," my interlocutor said. "Fine," I said, "I'll
be happy to publish the letter. The subject needs airing."

I saw the woman who was supposed to be writing me the letter the next
afternoon. She told me that her boss, the head of an NEH division, wanted
me to call him. "I'll call him at the break," I said. "I hear you're going to
write me. What are you going to say?"

"You'll see when you get my letter."

I called her boss. He said, "Some people around here are very upset at
what you wrote."

"Is there anything wrong or untrue in what I wrote?"

"That's not it. That's not what they're upset about."

"Do *you* think there's anything wrong or untrue in what I wrote?"

"Of course not. I agree with you. You're more right than you know. But
articles like yours can have a chilling effect on applications. If people read
that sort of thing, they won't apply, and the fact is that we do manage to get
some of those projects through. If people aren't even applying, then even
more damage is done."

I asked him if he thought that was the best way to handle the problem—to
pretend publicly it didn't exist and to smuggle one or two refugees across the
border when the moon was dark. He said it was all he knew how to do and
it was better than doing nothing. I said that was how I felt about my editorial.
"Well," he said, "You'll be getting a letter on the matter from _____." He
named the same woman I'd been told about by the person at NEA.

The letter never came and I never heard anything more about the
matter from anyone at NEH. At least not directly. I had an application in
process at NEH about that time, one I'd been invited by staff to submit. The
announcement deadline passed and I never heard whether the proposal
had been funded or rejected, so I called the director of the program, a man
I'd never met but with whom I'd talked on the phone a few times. He
seemed very embarrassed. "Your project wasn't funded," he said. I expressed
some regret, but nothing more: in the world of arts and humanities grant
seeking, one expects to fail some or even most of the time; the competition
is high and panels can be directed by one or two people with a particular
orientation. I've had many grants, but I've filed many more grant applications.
Rejection is always disappointing, but the failure of an application to get
funding isn't anything extraordinary.

So I was ready to let this one go, perhaps to apply again the following
year with a revision of the same proposal that took into consideration the
review panel's objections. The director of the program continued talking,
and I realized that the panel's objections probably weren't at issue. A

revised application wasn't likely to have any greater success than the one that had just been rejected.

"You have to understand," he said. "Sometimes everybody thinks a proposal is terrific, the staff likes it and the panel gives it a very high rating, but then it just disappears upstairs. They don't tell us why those projects disappear, but they do. Not all the decisions are made at this level. Do you hear what I'm saying?"

I said I did and I thanked him for his frankness. "You should try us again sometime," he said. "Reapply."

"Really?"

"Well, you know how these things go."

A friend to whom I recounted the conversation said, "Of course, you dope. What did you think they were going to do up there, thank you for having written those things about them?"

No, of course I hadn't expected thanks, I said, but I rather thought they'd have bent over backwards to be fair to a critic, to prove they really weren't political at heart or vindictive in practice.

"You really *are* a dope," my friend said.

One happy note: largely in response to the kind of criticism quoted in the PBS section of this talk, the Corporation for Public Broadcasting (CPB) has set up the Independent Television Project, a program in which independent filmmakers administer production grants for other independent filmmakers. It's too early to know if this will really end the control of CPB funding by the more powerful stations, but it may very well be a minor breakthrough.

HENRI KORN OF INSTITUT PASTEUR in Paris and Don Faber of the University of Buffalo Medical School have spent much of the past twenty years studying the Mathner cell in carp. The Mathner cell is the nerve that gets them all doing the same thing at the same time when they're frightened. The behavior is called *escape response*. Fish that have a good Mathner cell function survive longer than fish that do not. Other fish have Mathner cells and exhibit the escape response, but for technical reasons Henri and Don prefer the carp version. The carp they use is the one we call goldfish. They have learned a great deal about the way nerves function and communicate and adapt through their studies of that goldfish nerve and its dendrites. But that's not why I'm interested in it.

I'm more interested in the apparent miracle of the fish. There they are in the aquarium, perfectly bounded by the bottom, through which they

cannot see; the surface, which they will never transcen[d]
transparent sides, through which they can never go.
though the keeper of the pet shop or the friend whos[e]
you not to) and they all execute that identical escap[e]
instant. If they're facing you, suddenly you're seeing t[he]
facing left, suddenly they're facing right.

The amazing part isn't that when the stimulus happens
it's that they all do the *same* something, and each fish is a[
and perfect independence of every other fish. The only t[
the water in which they are all suspended, has no appare[nt]
of this except as the medium through which the messa[ge]
case the reverberation of the tap on the glass. Each [
message and, like a Marine precision drill team, each fish [
exactly the same way.

You may wonder why I'm telling you this, since our [
editing reality, not aquatic behavior. I mention the carp an[
cells and the taps on the glass because they are depressing[
forces and agencies that control which of those academic an[
realities get edited in the first place and which of those edi[
light of day.

We like to think that we select and execute the proje[
interest to us in some utterly personal fashion, but in fact [
all too often significantly modulated by externals, by taps o[

The participants in this symposium are all scholars a[nd]
gather information from the world and edit it into someth[ing]
others. They do the editorial alchemy of converting field n[otes]
into books and recordings, or editing miles of raw and—t[o]
theirs—inchoate footage into films and videotapes. To the r[e]
editing we have immediate access.

But they're not the only editors of reality. Nor are they the[
of their own vision of it.

There is, in both academic and media contexts, another cla[ss]
entirely who are also central to the process of documenting,[
presenting reality. They are never quoted or cited; their nar[
attached in significant ways to any of the documents of our c[
they bear or accept at most minor public responsibility for the[
failure of those objects. Their names are unknown to the gen[eral]
often their names are inaccessible even to those whose options[
whose work they judge.

They set the terms and conditions under which the scholars[
and journalists perform. They say, "You will or won't have this gr[

Grenadan invasion totally displaced the destruction of the Beirut Marine barracks on television news. One editor said, "People get excited about only one story like this at a time." There's an editor in the mind that is in conversation with those editors out there in the world, real or imagined.

The great power of the gatekeepers isn't merely in the moments they say *yes* or *no;* rather it's in their ability to train *us* to suppose moments where they might say yes or no. They appoint us their assistant editors, and we do the work at our own expense.

The mere fact of great personal wealth may ease the problem posed by noncompliance with the system's terms of order, but it won't transcend them. If your ethnology isn't in a certain style and shape, it won't be published by any "acceptable" journal or press. Private wealth may provide the resources to do the fieldwork and get that ethnology published, but whatever its content, a self-published book will never carry the automatic authority of a book published by Johns Hopkins or Harvard or Oxford. Reviewers and scholars look to the institutional imprimatur before they look to the contents. A book published by one of those presses might be trash, but few reviewers open the covers assuming trash; a self-published book might be ground-breaking and brilliant, but few reviewers open the covers assuming they are so. Wealth may get your film made, but it won't get it shown.

Small groups or even single individuals often wield great power here. Franz Boas set the operating conditions for thirty years of American folklore and anthropology studies by his editing of major journals in those fields and his placing of his students as editors when he grew bored with that work. Major foundations often have one person as their advisor in a particular field or line. Applicants with any sense examine lists of recent publications and grants, infer the desiderata, and cast their manuscripts and proposals in that light.

I hope this doesn't sound paranoid. I don't envision small cabals of malevolent individuals who sit around figuring out ever newer and cleverer ways to get us doing things we don't want to do in ways we wouldn't have chosen. It isn't done like that and it doesn't work like that. The program officers in the endowments and foundations want to help people engage in good projects that work; the editors want their journals to sparkle; the publishers want not only books that sell well but books they can be proud of. Nearly everyone's intentions are good.

But good intentions aren't what's at issue. The program officers who want to help people do their work steer the people for whom they have the highest regard into formulations most likely to find funding. The editors wanting their journals to sparkle select manuscript reviewers and authors whose work they respect, hence whose ideas or models are very close to their own. In both funding and manuscript evaluation, the peer process is infinitely tunable. It is not inherently fair and it is hardly ever objective.

Let me briefly discuss two representative manifestations of this condition: funding at the National Endowment for the Humanities and access to broadcast by the Public Broadcasting Service. The National Endowment for the Humanities changed during the Reagan years. Appointments to the NEH Council (the group that sets policy and has final say on grants) were far more political than they ever had been before, and political appointments to the NEH staff occurred at far lower civil service levels than ever before.

The gradual coagulating of vision at NEH happened slowly and subtly. It was fought by the staff, but battles with the political appointees consumed time and energy that had previously been used to help applicants prepare proposals. So even when staff won they lost. Word filtered down through the various levels of NEH administration that projects from or about ethnics would have a far more difficult time of it, as would projects dealing with anything of a modern political nature. The preference was to go to large established organizations dealing with traditional projects. "The humanities," NEH Chairman William Bennett said, "are in the past." Sure, people could apply for projects not in the past, but, well, who knew what the director and the council would do?

So the NEH program officers, by and large a highly competent nonideological group, began applying subtle pressure on applicants to cast their proposals in ways more likely to ensure funding. This pressure was most likely to be applied to individuals and groups program officers thought most competent, since there was no point in giving that kind of sensitive advice to people whose proposals were likely to fail in any event. Many individuals would, when choosing among possible projects, submit to NEH the one most likely to receive funding under the current conservative regime. Many proposals that might have been funded during the Carter years weren't even submitted in the Reagan years.

There never was any need to say formally and publicly, "These projects and these individuals or groups won't be funded." The system was such that most of the applicants and projects the new policymakers wanted excluded did the excluding themselves.

Not only were program officers aware of and sensitive to the changing policy higher up in NEH, but so were panelists. Panel service is a strategic enterprise. There are only a certain number of proposals you can go all out for. I remember several times seeing panelists back off strong endorsement of projects because they were convinced the proposal would be shot down by one of the political appointees in NEH staff or the politicized NEH Council.

The current chairman of NEH is Lynn Chaney. The text of her recent "Report to the President, the Congress, and the American People" appears in this week's *Chronicle of Higher Education*. It is a document that tells us that the humanities are the canon, and we tinker with that canon at our peril. It is wrong, Chairman Chaney says, to focus on the political and social and economic aspects of "great books"; these books should be studied for their beauty (which she assumes is a constant throughout time) and their value (which she assumes exists external to all social meaning).

The report is an astonishingly ethnocentric and elitist document. The only black writer quoted, Maya Angelou, is brought in to tell us why Shakespeare is a great black poet; the only Spanish-speaking writer mentioned is from South America. No Native American is mentioned at all. Alexis de Tocqueville is quoted at length.

"To counter the excesses of specialization and to strengthen the contributions the academy can make to society," she writes, "those who fund, publish, and evaluate research should encourage work of *general* significance." Chaney points with pride to the "PBS series of conversations with Joseph Campbell [which] recently propelled a book of those conversations and two books of Campbell's writing to the best-seller lists." Best-sellers they may be, but I don't know a competent anthropologist, ethnologist, or folklorist who thinks Campbell's mythology is anything but impressionistic drivel. It is the kind of wonderful generalization Chairman Chaney calls for; it is also intellectual amateurism of the most pretentious and misleading kind.

To go by this document, the primary, if not the sole, function of the humanities presenter or scholar is to deliver down: *we* know what culture really is, *they* don't; we bring it to them so they know more about beauty and the past. There is no sense at all that the information of the humanities is ever-developing, or that humanities scholars have as much to learn as they have to tell and instruct. It is a vision that sets the stuff of the humanities very much in place.

NEH is the principal purveyor of all government grants for humanistic research. If NEH decides that humanities are in the past, what areas of inquiry will scholars and filmmakers decide not to pursue because the funding simply isn't there? Walter Berns, a member of the NEH Council, and chairman of the council's Committee on Research, recently argued *against* funding projects dealing with cultures lacking a written language. Leon Kass, another council member, said that studies of a language without a written literature are of interest only to the linguist, not to the humanist. If NEH decides that languages without literatures are too insignificant for funding, then the kind of work done by Barbara Tedlock among the Zuni and by Dennis and Barbara Tedlock in Guatemala will no longer be fundable by NEH.

There are profound secondary effects to this parochialization of the NEH field of view. NEH is a flagship organization; many state humanities agencies and many private foundations take their cues from NEH. Many foundation directors, in my experience, really don't know what they're doing, but they want to do the right thing—whatever it is. Documents such as Chairman Chaney's will tell them what the right thing is.

This is what chairman Chaney has to say of film and television projects:

—Television can be the friend of the book, and there should be further efforts to use television to encourage reading. Both public and private funders of educational television should continue to support productions that are book-related. Network television programs should present books and learning as an important part of everyday life.

—Television has, in its own right, vast democratic potential for education in the humanities. Scholars and filmmakers working together can create highly original works that encourage thought and *teach us about the past* [italics mine]. Such efforts merit the continued support of those who fund television productions.

That's the entire statement. If you were a filmmaker applying to NEH, how would you cast your proposal? If you were a program director at NEH, how would you advise an applicant trying to decide among potential projects?

It is not difficult to see why Marlon Riggs's excellent proposal for *Ethnic Notions,* a film exploring black stereotypes in American life, was three times turned down by NEH. Riggs was told there was no need to look at things like this: they were nasty, they would just give information to bad people, they would bring up bad things. Riggs finally found his funding elsewhere (part of it came from the far more visionary New York Council for the Humanities), and his film won many prizes. But it didn't fit the vision of humanities inquiry and film function operative at NEH in the Bennett/Chaney years.

Independent filmmakers like Fred, De, Diane, and me are dependent on a very narrow range of outlets for our material. The most powerful outlet is public television, since that puts us in touch immediately with a large audience. Most documentary filmmakers I know tailor their work, at least in part, for public television requirements. Many of us try to edit our stories so they get told in 58 or 86 minutes. Those aren't natural numbers, like pi or c. They're what's in a 60- or 90-minute PBS slot after the promos are run (commercial TV is far more consuming: it works on a 48-minute hour).

Except for filmmakers who specialize in animals, very few independent documentary filmmakers ever get their films shown on public television anyway. If their work deals with a difficult social issue, if their work has any significant political content, if they don't have personal connections, they don't get to say hello. The people who edit what is funded by the Corporation for Public Broadcasting and what is released nationally on the Public Broadcasting Service operate within a very narrow vision of what is permissible and what isn't, what is valuable and what isn't.

There are rare exceptions. Fred gets on. I find his films powerful examinations of the basic institutions of American life, and for that reason I'm astonished that PBS lets them slide through. I don't know how it happens, but I don't want to tell them that they're possibly making a mistake by letting real substance get by, so I'll say no more about it.

But De Antonio doesn't get on PBS, ever. A series called "No Sacred Cows" was supposed to put on films about those subjects PBS had theretofore been afraid to touch. When PBS saw the "No Sacred Cows" lineup, the series was cancelled. I think the best evaluation of the management of public television was offered by Fred Wiseman in his March 1988 testimony before the Senate Communications Subcommittee. "Public television," Fred said, "is like a third-rate university where everyone has tenure."

It's the Public Broadcasting Service and it's funded primarily by public money, but the most important programming person in American public television for nearly a decade has been a man named Herbert Schmertz. Herbert Schmertz never worked for PBS; he is vice president of the Mobil Oil Corporation in charge of public relations. He selected and paid for much of the British programming you've seen. Because of what Schmertz did for Mobil, Exxon began doing the same thing. Schmertz, more than anyone else, was responsible for PBS's name among independent filmmakers: "Petroleum Broadcasting System." For the oil companies, it's very cheap advertising to an upscale audience. (If you think for a moment public TV isn't targeted for that upscale audience, ask why we have "Wall Street Week" and "Nightly Business Report," both of which tell you how to invest your extra cash, but nothing about how to apply for or deal with problems concerning welfare, unemployment, Medicaid, or a landlord who won't turn on the heat when it's so cold your breath makes clouds when you try to get him on the phone.)

A PBS executive said about the change in public TV in the past fifteen years: "The change is that we've gotten, in my opinion, much better. We care a lot more about audience, about being viewed, mainly for two reasons. One is a maturation process. In the early days, all we were concerned with was producing quality programming, and then we began to want people to watch. The second is a straight economic reason. We are increasingly dependent upon viewer support."

" 'Great Performances' is made possible," Jack Hitt wrote in *Harper's*,

" . . . by a grant from the Exxon Corporation. By untethering programmers from the constraints of product advertisement, PBS delivered itself into a more refined bondage: corporate sponsorship. Public Television could never produce a show that risks even so small a joke as *Max Headroom* because a company as stately as Exxon will not sponsor anything that lacks the pomp and majesty of heavy bronze. The occasional good idea for a program, then, is forced to beg. The producers of the acclaimed civil-rights history, *Eyes on the Prize,* suffered through a five-year pilgrimage to more than three dozen underwriters before making it on the air."

For the PBS audience and for the independent filmmaker, the sharp bias toward the upscale and the heavy dependence on corporate funding mean that the hours available for programs that examine critical issues in American life are very few. Filmmakers either tailor their product for the safe avenues apparently open, they don't appear on PBS, or they appear on PBS only after great struggle.

"Frontline," which is, with one minor exception, public television's only nonanimal nonfiction series, is a closed shop. A small stock group of producers receive nearly two-thirds of the "Frontline" production money. The minor exception is the new series "P.O.V.," which was created in response to intensive lobbying in Congress by independents' organizations. "P.O.V." has no production funds, and it was able to offer only twelve programs in its first season. It is uncertain enough about funding for its second season to be holding off announcing how many programs it will buy and what it will pay for them.

Lawrence Daressa, a producer and co-chair of the National Coalition of Independent Public Broadcasting Producers, said in testimony before the House Subcommittee on Telecommunications and Finance, Energy and Commerce Committee, on 10 March 1988:

> Let me cite just one anecdote so you can appreciate the pressures on independents. I recently called an independent producer—some of you would recognize his name—to ask his support for our proposals. He said that while he applauded our efforts, he could not publicly support the proposals because he had two projects pending before the Program Fund (by the way, an indication of the trust independents feel towards that body). I asked him if he really wanted to do either of these projects, and he admitted that both had been designed more with an eye towards the station managers on the CPB panels than from his own interest and convictions. I pointed out that if there were a national independent programming service he would again have the opportunity to do projects which he could believe in. And he replied, "You know, Larry, it's been so long since this system let me think as an independent, that I'm not sure I could do so if I had a chance."
>
> This, I think, indicates the real tragedy and betrayal of the last ten years.

Not only has the system failed to make room for new talent, not only has the system declined to nurture minority producers, it has also silenced the independence and stifled the imagination of a whole generation of established, award-winning film and videomakers. Thousands have left the field; more have been excluded from any funding; some have even had to go to work for the stations. Indeed, the independent community has become so discouraged at the situation at CPB that the number of submissions from independents has declined to roughly half what it was three years ago, while station submissions have skyrocketed. (Daressa 1988)

This week's programming on the public television stations here in Buffalo includes seven hours of animal and travel shows, including nightly reruns of the superannuated "Wide, Wide World of Animals," and a program that dealt with "The birth of golden retriever puppies; a cat condo; tips on dealing with a female dog in heat; and part 1 of a 3-part series on cat behavior"—a repeat. The stations also broadcast ten hours of British fiction programming presented by the petroleum industry. We had "Masterpiece Theatre" ("Hugh Brandon's promotion to the position of castle steward adds to his already unhappy personal life. Part 4 of 7"), 2½ hours of the "Nightly Business Report," thirty minutes of "Adam Smith's Money World," and thirty minutes of "Wall Street Week." For the harsher side of life, the stations offered thirty minutes of "Black Forum," and one hour or so of "P.O.V.," the single scheduled program presenting independent nonfiction films. We also received one hour each of "The Prisoner" and "The Lawrence Welk Show."

I've been talking about some of the forces that influence editing of purpose and editing of design. I should mention before I close that though the specifics are current and timely, the process of artists structuring their narratives so they'll get the funding they need to deal with the reality they pursue is extremely old.

The first notable grant applicant in Western tradition was Odysseus, who spends six of the *Odyssey*'s twenty-four books in Phaiákaia trying to get King Alkínoös and Queen Arêtê to provide a travel grant that will take him back to Ithaka in style. Books 9–12 are Odysseus' grant application, his summary of his great journey thus far. The most spectacular segment of that spectacular tale is the First Nykeia, the journey to the underworld. Many readers notice something very strange about that passage: the first long set of significant characters we meet aren't Greek military heroes; rather it's women. I can think of nowhere else in classical Greek literature where the major moment in the major internal narrative begins with a string of women. Those guys were sexist to the bone.

Even before Odysseus got wound up to tell his tale, King Alkinoös said he was willing to provide the grant-in-aid. Not so the queen, who is far more reserved. Phaiákaia is a kind of fairyland and many things are topsy-turvy in it—and one of those topsy-turvy things seems to be that it's the queen rather than the king who makes the decisions that matter. So Odysseus, the craftiest narrator in antiquity, tailors his application accordingly: he begins the key segment of his key tale with the catalog of good women and bad women, of women who used power well and women who used power badly. It is a narrative string specifically designed to appeal to Arêtê, to win her over. When he finishes the Nykeia, Arêtê announces that she'll fund his further travels.

And there, I think, is the heart of the matter: we have our vision and like do-it-yourselfers we find the resources that will permit us to exercise that vision; we tailor and tune our song so the resources will be ours, and we go and make those books and films and journeys, knowing that we're always compromising the narrative at least a little. And we're hoping all the time that even with such compromise it is yet possible to keep the vision pure. Our edits are made partially in response to those external conditions, real or imagined, but they are also made very much in terms of our perception of and respect for our subject, in our desire to tell the truth.

I think it *is* possible for us to be *not* like the carp in Don Faber's and Henri Korn's fish tank. Those goldfish live in a perpetual present, a now in which the tap is there or it is not there, a now in which there is only reaction and no design.

We have design. We have an uncertain past upon which we hope to improve and an indeterminate future in which we hope our work will have validity. The final responsibility is ours. When the work is done, those funding agents don't matter and those programmers don't matter and those editors don't matter. It's the work that matters.

Diane Christian opened this symposium with theory, with a historical look back to Blake and into the heart of things. I guess I've been terribly mundane this afternoon: money, grants, contracts, hustling, negotiating, wheels and deals. I think that our two discussions bracket something essential in the process: it begins in the abstract and then it becomes the most specific and practical kind of work of all, until finally the floor is littered with the pieces that didn't fit, the bits of words or film or sound we sheared away. And then there is something quite independent and free of us, and if we've done our work well, even with those editorial impediments, it takes on a life and trajectory very much its own. In our own work we *can* transcend what Blake called "mind-forg'd manacles." And there's the real pleasure in it, and the real reason for doing it.

What People Like Us Are Saying When We Say We're Saying the Truth

(Journal of American Folklore, 1988)

I began this book with an essay about the kinds of stories people in ordinary life tell and I'm ending it with an essay on the kinds of stories people who want to document ordinary life tell.

My friend Dan Rose, who teaches anthropology at the University of Pennsylvania, says that one of the basic differences in our approaches to documentary work is that I believe in reality and he doesn't. I *do* believe in reality, so I have trouble understanding what Dan is talking about. Sometimes I think he means that it is never possible to apprehend all the aspects of any given moment or event, so what we always deal with are interpretations and re-visions, and our reports and interpretations are always therefore subjective. They are stories. I wouldn't argue with that.

But *something* happened out there: rain fell, love got made, and a parking space was found; the price of grain went up, certain words were said, and the liquid I spilled on my orange sweater caused a dark stain; the man who stepped on a mine left in the sand after the troops withdrew was killed; the child died before the helicopter with food and medical supplies arrived.

I know that all our attempts to document the infinite complexity and horror and beauty of reality are fated to be partial. Two of us will view the same event and document it in radically different ways. The multiplicity of vision can as much attest to the infinite polyvalence of the world as to the rightness or wrongness of our separate reports. The world offers us many stories worth telling, sometimes within a single moment. I think that's a fine thing because I believe telling stories is splendid and important work, and it is, finally, the work I love most of all.

The man bent over his guitar,
A shearsman of sorts. The day was green.

They said, "You have a blue guitar,
You do not play things as they are."

The man replied, "Things as they are
Are changed upon the blue guitar."

And they said then, "But play, you must
A tune beyond us, yet ourselves,

A tune upon the blue guitar
Of things exactly as they are."

> —Wallace Stevens
> "The Man With the Blue Guitar"
> 1936–37

Something Real

NEWS ISN'T NEWS until the newsmen make something of it. Before that, it's just events, the same inchoate reality the rest of us deal with all the time. It's the same with the data of ethnologists, anthropologists, folklorists, documentarians, and all the other specialists who purport to show you how things really are.

The things we look at happened, but what we present to you isn't ever the things themselves. We offer only recreated and edited versions of them, things seen through our eyes, heard through our voices, recast into our media. What we have to offer comes into existence in the editing, not in the happening.

We edit discrete bits of information and in so doing we make narrative objects that are artifacts of our labor, not elements of the world we attempt to portray or otherwise document (see Bruner 1986:139). But the narratives we make do not float in the world; they are not items of the imagination entirely. When you read a novel, you have it all; there is nothing more to the character on that page than you will find in that book. A literary character may take on resonance for you because of associations based on antecedent knowledge, but that resonance is idiosyncratic with you—it is a function of your experience, not the character's reality. When you see or read a documentary, you are experiencing a manipulated fragment of a much larger reality. As James Agee put it in *Let Us Now Praise Famous Men:*

> In a novel, a house or person has his meaning, his existence, entirely through the writer. Here, a house or a person has only the most limited of his meaning through me: his true meaning is much huger. It is that he *exists,* in actual being, as you do and as I do, and as no character of the imagination can possibly exist. His great weight, mystery, and dignity are in this fact. As for me, I can tell you of him only what I saw, only so accurately as in my terms I know how: and this in turn has its chief stature not in any ability of mine but in the fact that I too exist, not as a work of fiction, but as a human being. Because of his immeasurable weight in actual existence, and because of mine, every word I tell of him has inevitably a kind of immediacy, a kind of meaning, not at all necessarily "superior" to that of the imagination, but of a kind so different that a work of the imagination (however intensely it may draw on "life") can at best only faintly imitate the least of. [Agee and Evans 1980:12]

That's the situation from the writer's side. What about from the other side? Can someone who is neither a maker of the object nor participant in the events or situations that are preconditions of that object sense that the portrayal in fiction represents all there is and that the portrayal of reality in documentary represents only a fragment of what Agee calls the "weight" of the real? Can you ever tell the difference? If you don't have independent knowledge of what we're presenting, are you dependent upon us entirely? What, exactly, are you dependent upon us for?

What people like us are telling you when we say we're telling you the truth is a story. We're storytellers and that's our pleasure in it. Different rules apply. The teller of the fiction story must tell a story that is probable. "In fiction," wrote the novelist John Barth, "the merely true must always yield to the plausible" (1968:93). The teller of the nonfiction story can appear to explain or justify an event from the mere fact that it happened that way. The history of Australia was altered because the prime minister drowned while swimming. There was no known malevolence involved. If that drowning had happened in a novel or a TV soap opera, the cause would have been underwater scuba divers in the employ of the CIA, the KGB, an international industrial cartel, or all three. In the real world, major disasters sometimes happen merely because people made stupid mistakes; in the fictional world, there can be stupidity, but it better have a believable motive as well.

Believability in fiction is always an internal matter. The story generates its own boundaries of acceptable reality. If well enough couched, the most astonishing events become acceptably real. The best-known instance of this belongs to Kafka:

As Gregor Samsa awoke one morning from uneasy dreams he found himself transformed in his bed into a gigantic insect. He was lying on his hard, as it were armor-plated, back and when he lifted his head a little he could see his dome-like brown belly divided into stiff arched segments on top of which the bed quilt could hardly keep in position and was about to slide off completely. His numerous legs, which were pitifully thin compared to the rest of his bulk, waved helplessly before his eyes.

What has happened to me? he thought. It was no dream. [Kafka 1952:19]

No documentation, no folklorist or anthropologist or journalist, could get away with that lead.

What can people get away with? It varies with the time and the territory. *JAF* published nothing of an overtly obscene character before its special erotica issue in 1962 (Number 297); since then, the taboos have rested more in individual editors' sensibilities than in any sense of general community standards. Before *Playboy* made photographs of bare breasts marketable over American counters in 1953, the only ordinary publications in America that showed women naked from the waist up were medical journals, which tended to favor afflicted (hence generally unattractive) models, and *National Geographic,* which got away with the display because the breasts belonged to natives in Africa or Polynesia and the reports were therefore educational, not merely entertaining. Franz Boas felt the need to shift into Latin for the three paragraphs of the vagina dentata episode in "The Salmon," a complex myth in the *Publications of the Jesup North Pacific Expedition* published by the American Museum of Natural History (Boas 1900). The classical language barrier, presumably, protected those involved from charges of appealing to the prurient interest: anybody with the language skill required to read about those misplaced teeth was by definition a person of serious and professional purpose. I encountered a similar eccentricity nearly seven decades later when dealing with America's oldest literary magazine, the *Atlantic Monthly.*

In late December 1967 the novelist John Barth (who was then a member of the SUNY/Buffalo English department) came into my office with the January 1968 issue of *Atlantic.* Barth, a man of even disposition, seemed very exercised. "Did you see this? Did you see this?" he said.

"Sure," I said. "Nice, huh?" I thought he was impressed at my article in that issue. The article was about the October 1967 antiwar demonstration at the Pentagon (Jackson 1968).

"Nice? Nice? It's outrageous!"

What, I asked him, was outrageous.

"There were two 'fucks' in your article!"

Barth was no prude about things in print; this didn't make any sense. "So?" I said.

"So they left your two 'fucks' in and they took my one 'fuck' out, that's what's outrageous." He was referring to his story, "Lost in the Funhouse," which had been published in *Atlantic* two months earlier (Barth 1967).

Barth said he had called Robert Manning, then editor of *Atlantic* and said, "How come you let Bruce's two 'fucks' stay in and you made me cut my one 'fuck' out?"

Manning first told Barth that he was inaccurate by half. *Atlantic* had printed only one of my 'fucks.' It was in a quotation. A sergeant said to a soldier in a line deployed to control demonstrators at the Pentagon: "Jones, get that fucking flower out of your muzzle" (Jackson 1968:37). A second 'fuck' was implied by a dash in the term "mother_____." The dash was substituted for what I had written because that time I was only paraphrasing someone.

Barth said that the explanation was not adequate. There was still that other 'fuck,' down there in black and white.

"We printed that," Barth said Manning said, "because Bruce was writing about something real and yours was just a story."

Implicit in Manning's reply to Barth is a difference in license permitted those purporting to report and those claiming to have created. Reporters, in this scheme, have *greater* license because they are not responsible for the quoted words; they are mediums through which the words reach the magazine, and the magazine, in turn, is a medium through which those words for which the writer is not responsible reach the public. The fact that a specific person really said that word in that time and place, Manning implied, licensed my inclusion of it in my manuscript and *Atlantic*'s publication of it in its pages. The artist, on the other hand, is totally and absolutely responsible for his or her words and the magazine, by publishing those words for which the artist is totally and absolutely responsible, becomes responsible for them as well. For the reporter, the words are central to a depiction of what occurred; for the artist, words are entirely volitional. Little wonder Barth exploded.

Bob Manning was an experienced newsman[1] and I'm sure he knew better. When we do reportage we make an implicit promise that we won't make things up, but we don't say anything about the desiderata for selection of facts or even ordering them, other than that we're trying to be fair. We have an enormous range of things we might quote, cite, paraphrase, describe, or summarize. What determines our selections among those things are, at heart, exactly what determines the selections artists make among the same things: we want to tell a good story well.

Storytelling

Journalists and documentarians and academics aren't the only people who want to tell a good story well. Most people want to tell a good story well. In 26 years of working with stories people tell about themselves I've learned that it isn't only poets and professional writers who can incorporate the most subtle turns of phrase in their narratives. Stories are the way we manage reality for ourselves and our presentation of ourselves to others. Ordinary personal narrative sometimes incorporates the most sophisticated turns of rhetoric; the storytelling event is grounded equally in the words chosen and the performance enacted.

There is a conversation that has troubled me for well over twenty years. It took place on a hot and muggy summer afternoon in the ward for terminally ill convicts on the top floor of the old hospital in the state prison in Huntsville, Texas. Large fans hummed at either end of the ward, but they had little effect.

Lying on the bed near where I stood was a dying old man named Pete McKenzie. He told me that many years earlier he had received a death sentence and had avoided execution for 12 years by being declared legally insane. I asked McKenzie what he got the death penalty for.

"There was a gunfight of three, four plainclothes officers and myself. I wasn't committing any crime, though I was on escape from here. I *was* armed, that's where I violated the law. But I wasn't committing any crime. I wasn't trying to commit any crime. I was attending to my own business, but the situation developed to such an extent where there was a gunfight and the gunfight put wounds in my legs and I started shooting after I had been shot."

"Did you get any of them?" I asked him.

"A chief of detectives was killed."

I asked him why the police had started shooting at him if he wasn't doing anything wrong. It was, he said, because he was at the time an escapee from the penitentiary. "And what," I said, "were you serving time for when you escaped?"

"Murder," he said.

"And what were you carrying when the police came up on you?"

"I had a Luger and a .38."

"So you were carrying two guns, you were escaped from a murder sentence, and you killed one of the cops trying to bring you back to prison."

"That's the way *they* said it was!"

Something in the conversation was skewed. When I began working with the transcript, I realized it wasn't in the substance, it was in the diction: *the situation developed to such an extent where there was a gunfight and the gunfight put wounds in my legs and I started shooting after I had been shot. . . . A chief of detectives was killed.*

It's nearly all in the passive voice. Things happen; no one does them; no one is responsible for them. McKenzie wasn't doing any lying. He wasn't saying he didn't kill anyone or that he was innocent. But neither was he admitting culpability. He was, instead, using the subtlety of language to cast that violent shootout and murder of a policeman into a narrative in which he was merely an agency, a prop. It happened, he got the death penalty for it, but he was no more responsible for the event than the two blazing pistols in his hands. Pete McKenzie was using the storyteller's art to make the past reasonable and bearable and manageable. He wasn't lying, but he wasn't telling the truth, either.[2]

It happened again in early 1988. Not the conversation, but the construction. A woman friend of a killer named Jack Henry Abbott sent me a copy of a document Abbott had sent a New York judge a short time before (Abbott 1988). In the document, Abbott asked the court to set him free.

Jack Henry Abbott spent the nine years before his 18th birthday in Utah reformatories. He was free for six months, then he was sent to the Utah penitentiary to do time for writing bad checks. He got more felony time three years later when he stabbed one inmate to death and injured another in a prison brawl. He robbed a bank during a brief escape in 1971; that earned him a 19-year federal sentence on top of the state time. He was 25 years old.

In 1978 Abbott began a lengthy correspondence with novelist Norman Mailer, who was then writing a fictionalized biography of executed murderer Gary Gilmore. When Abbott came up for parole Mailer wrote a strong letter on his behalf. Mailer got some of Abbott's letters published in the *New York Review of Books,* which led to publication of Abbott's first book, *In the Belly of the Beast* (1981). Abbott was transferred to a New York halfway house in early June of 1981. If he had stayed out of trouble for eight weeks, he would have gone on parole.

He didn't make it. Six weeks after he got to New York, he stabbed a waiter named Richard Adan to death. Abbott fled, was captured in Louisiana ten weeks later, and in April 1982 was convicted of first-degree manslaughter. Because of his previous record, Judge Irving Lang sentenced Abbott to the maximum: 15 years to life.

I was struck by the fact that in the entire document Abbott wrote in the hope his sentence would be set aside, he never refers to Richard Adan by name. He refers only to "the deceased." The part that especially caught my attention consisted of these two sentences:

There was never sufficient evidence presented at my trial to support a finding of intent to kill. The deceased in this case was inflicted a single wound under circumstances which would have demanded the infliction of more wounds, if the single wound had been inflicted with the intent to kill and not merely to repel him.

Two strategies are at work simultaneously in that pair of sentences. First, Abbott is arguing that if he really wanted to kill Adan he wouldn't have stabbed him just once, so, absent any evidence to the contrary, the court should conclude that he didn't intend to kill Adan at all, the whole thing ' was just a mistake. Second, he isn't admitting he killed Adan anyway. There is no first person pronoun in there: *There was never sufficient evidence presented at my trial to support a finding of intent to kill.* (Intent to kill by whom? Not some abstract creature in the world. Jack Henry Abbott. But Abbott isn't putting himself into that sentence.) *The deceased* (why not Richard Adan, the man who was stabbed to death?) *in this case* (what other case is at issue?) *was inflicted* (was inflicted? by whom? this is homicide, not suicide, so why the passive voice?) *a single wound under circumstances which would have demanded the infliction of more wounds* (what situation? demanded from whom?), *if the single wound had been inflicted with the intent to kill and not merely to repel him* (repel? as with mosquitoes?). Jack Henry Abbott could say whether or not he intended to kill Richard Adan when he stabbed him in the heart. He doesn't say. He limits his remarks to the legalistic context of the trial, which he faults for a failure of rhetoric. On that basis he demands freedom.

Jack Henry Abbott's document and Pete McKenzie's statement are both extreme examples of the ability of narrators to skirt the intentional and moral character of events without uttering anything that might be a literal untruth. For a long time, what impressed me about McKenzie's statement was how astutely he had used language so he could talk about what happened without admitting his guilt for what happened. After reading Abbott's statement I understood something more was at work: there was also the desire to say such things without lying overtly about them. Language, I understood, had profound moral power that could transcend the very facts its users purport to present. Diction is a component of substance, not a vehicle for it.

Words alone will not tell you where you are or how true anything is. If the words are well enough wrought, you'll believe them, unless you have enough external data to know the truth on your own. If the words are not well enough wrought, you won't care about them, true or not.

"Words," the poet Robert Creeley said a few years ago, "make incredibly powerful grids of determinate meaning. . . . What's the truth of the words? . . . If the words can lie, you've got to take on that responsibility also. You can't depend upon the truth to get you home. . . . The words have, as they say, a greater truth, which is their own ability to say things, so that if you think you're simply going to use them to tell the truth, you're going to realize that you didn't know what the truth was, again, so you've just made another awful mistake, along with millions of other people.... Words don't care about the truth. They care about the clarity of their relationships and their own system, that's their truth. There is no inherent truth in language, other than the system it is" (in *Creeley,* 1988).

Kinds of Talk

In a discussion about meaning in humanistic and scientific statements with Henri Korn, director of research at Institut Pasteur, I said that I thought we were trying to say different kinds of things, that scientists were seeking facts and ethnologists, documentarians, and other humanists were not only seeking facts of a different order, but we sought to do different things with them. "To be scientific is not to present facts," Korn said. "It is to extract what is meaningful from what is not." In that, he said, our ends are identical.

I think the substantial difference between science and humanities is that scientists seek an extraction that can be absolute and value-free, meaningful absolutely in its own terms, while documentarians and other humanists insist on seeing meaning always in the double context of event and interpretation. The equation $E = mc^2$ possesses a meaning identical to what happens when a certain mass is converted perfectly to energy; neither the observer nor the location has anything to do with the absolute fact inherent in the event and the statement describing it. No humanistic statement can achieve such certitude and I doubt any humanities scholar, let alone artist, would want it. The physical scientist wants the certitude the formula describes;[3] the humanist wants the ambiguity of resonating possibility that all art engenders. The language of art thrives on ambiguity, on polyvalence, on multiplicity, on openness:

> The Chinese communes hum. Two daiquiris
> withdrew into a corner of the gorgeous room
> and one told the other a lie.
> [Berryman 1964:18]

What's John Berryman telling us there? Which daiquiri told the lie and what color was his/her hair? What lie was it? What was her/his response? Did it matter? How do you know?

The language of classical physical science seeks an absence of ambiguity and a perfect attenuation of personality. That's why it specializes in vocabularies as shorn of denotative meaning as possible and why it commits everything that matters to paper. You might get it wrong hearing it in the air, but no one seeing it written on paper will have any doubt that the second letter in $E = IR$ refers to electrical current and not one of two symmetrical organs bracketing the top of the nose. Scientific equations with variables are likewise specific and unambiguous. Those equations describe an absolute condition in which if you know all terms except one, then you know all terms including that one. (What is the voltage in that line? What is the current in that line? What is the resistance of that line? If you know any two, you know the third.)

Uncertainty is at the heart of much that is important in 20th-century physical science—but *uncertainty* and *ambiguity* are very different concepts. Uncertainty refers to the state of our knowledge: quantum physics can make general statements about behaviors, but it cannot tell you where and in what state particle x will be at time t. The problem is not with the behavior of the particle, but rather with the physicist's ability to predict.

Uncertainty has to do with a limitation of our ability to know; ambiguity has to do with a multiplicity of meaning extant at once and without contradiction or cancellation. The humanist assumption—widely accepted albeit nowhere proven—is that even the most astute textual or object criticism will not provide access to all the meaning latent in a work of art. And happily so, for the great power of art lies in resonances that go beyond the merely describable.

The discourse of the humanities is one that permits such incomplete renderings. The discourse of physical science, on the other hand, is dedicated to the creation of closed universes of meaning and fixed contexts of possibility. And it is about situations that are, presumably, replicable. The languages must be adequate to get you there exactly.

Modern social science seems split into two discrete and fully incompatible camps, a quantitative camp that pursues the apparent certainty of the physical scientist, and a qualitative camp that embraces the resonant ambiguity and polyvalence of the humanist. Of all the physical scientists, quantitative social scientists are closest to the quantum physicists, whose field is also one largely grounded in probability. Quantitative social scientists can tell you nothing about the behavior, state, condition, or knowledge of the man or woman approaching you on the street, sitting next to you on the bus, or sitting across from you at dinner; they can only offer probabilities.

The managers of numbers in the social sciences aren't just operating with a different technology than the people who engage in what they disparagingly modify with the adjective *humanistic:* humanistic anthropology, humanistic sociology, and so forth. The adjective implies a massive difference in vision, one I suspect is unbreachable. At the extreme, it is only

historical accident that has those managers of numbers and those docu-
menters of life publishing in the same journals and teaching in the same
departments. They are truly worlds apart.

The reports brought back by the writers and photographers and
filmmakers I'm discussing here are never replicable by you or me. The
information they provide is not equal to or in any way similar to the
information provided by someone who tests the atmosphere for the presence of this or that substance or who asks members of a statistically valid
sample to report on the frequency of their sexual encounters or the
amount of their stock holdings or the number of automobiles in their
possession.

These writers, photographers, painters, and filmmakers have gone places
you and I will never go. The places are too frightening or too far away in
space or time. We may be interested in southern sharecropping, but we
won't spend three months living with sharecroppers—and the sharecroppers Walker Evans photographed and James Agee wrote about are gone
from the face of this earth anyway. We may be interested in Inuit and
walruses, but we're not likely to travel to the Arctic Circle to watch them in
relationship, and if we did we wouldn't do it for as long and at such peril as
Robert Flaherty (*Nanook of the North,* 1922) or Jean Malaurie (1976). We
may be interested in treatment of mental patients and how department
stores work, but if we visit either kind of institution we won't see the same
things, film the same things, or organize things the same way Frederick
Wiseman did (*Titicut Follies,* 1967; *The Store,* 1984).

We judge documentary objects not on how well their makers' hypotheses hold up, but on how well they convince us that the distance between
what the makers saw and what they show us transcends hypothesis. Hypothesis is transient; facts endure. What makes us believe them is a construct, a
thing made, a device no different in shape or form or apparent content
than a thing entirely of the imagination. This is why Frederick Wiseman
tells interviewers who press him for his documentary theory, "I can't answer
that. I'm a novelist." That George Catlin (1844) had what we now (and many
people then) consider an eccentric notion of Mandan origin (he thought
they were Welsh) does not disenfranchise his eye any more than pre-
relativity astronomical observations are invalidated by the assumption of
constant time or rectilinear space. The great works of reportage are outside
of visible interpretation—they appear to be coherent and legitimate objects
in their own right.

That is not to say that no interpretation goes into them. Quite the
contrary: they are infused with interpretation. The collection of this fact
rather than that one is an act of interpretation, as is the decision of what
among the things documented are to be presented to others, and what

order is to be selected for that presentation, and what stress and what enhancement and what stripping down occur (Jackson 1985).

Normally, we don't see the interpretation at work, nor do we sense it controlling the information before us. The character of those interpretive acts is the least accessible fact of all, even to the persons engaged in the interpretation. We see not merely what we want to see, but what we are *able* to see.

Framing the World

In the field, the documentarian is confronted with an infinitude of information. There is, literally, no limit on the number of facts that might be accumulated. The limit comes from us: how much time we have, how much we want to preserve, in how much detail we want to preserve it. Sometimes the record we make is predicated on the devices we have at our disposal. In the past two decades, lightweight and inexpensive portable quality sound and video recorders have changed the options available to all fieldworkers. Some documentarians, like Agee and the Hemingway of *Death in the Afternoon* (1932), stored the world in their notebooks. Others, like Catlin and Evans, were able to make pictures, so they recorded visual things.

People who make pictures see frames around the world. They don't ask themselves what's there so much as what can be shown. The photographer is less interested in an event occurring under perfectly flat and dull lighting than an event occurring in light with some character; things in the dark are merely personal. To the recordist, the quality of ambient sound and the distance of the event from the microphone are critical. And to the user of a notebook, keeping up with the action without losing anything important matters more than either light or sound.

Vision is married to devices as much as ideas to facts. No medium or genre in itself guarantees any more truth than any other. Merely by changing the grade of printing paper a photographer can harshen or soften the lines in a face thereby adding or subtracting years of untroubled or agonizing experience. Does he or she deceive? No more than when the person in question is seen by you under fluorescent or reddish light, the first of which makes all complexions hideous and the second of which makes most epidermal imperfections invisible.

A transcription of a tape recording that shows all the *uhs* and *ahs* and pauses and repetitions will, for a reader unused to such documents, show the speaker as a clod. Neat paragraphs and clean sentences show him or her as intelligent. In a study illustrating his reader response theory, literary critic Norman Holland left the tentativeness in the transcriptions of the reader but smoothed his prose to glass; it was, presumably, his way of asserting his distance from and superiority to his source of information (Holland 1981).[4]

The first documentary film to be a commercial success was Robert Flaherty's *Nanook of the North* (1922). In one of the film's most notable scenes, Nanook and his friends battle an enormous walrus that threatens to pull them into the sea. Briefly, they gesture wildly toward the camera. Eventually they capture the beast. Another famous scene shows Nanook and his family preparing for bed inside their igloo. They undress. One of the women is naked from the waist up. (The *National Geographic* Principle at work again. It continues to this day. In recent months, segments of network news shows covering African famine have frequently shown emaciated bare-breasted women trying to feed small children. On the same networks, segments about breast cancer showed American women who were completely covered when facing the camera, even though several were ostensibly being examined by physicians at the time.)

There are nagging questions about Flaherty's igloo scene. First, where is the camera in this shot? Igloos aren't very large, and we know the exact size of this one because we saw (what we thought was) it being built. The camera couldn't be getting that wide an undistorted shot from so close. Second, why is everything so bright? The film stock Flaherty had at his disposal was extremely slow. Where's the light coming from?

From the sky, and the camera was some distance from the igloo on a tripod. There is no igloo on our side; there is igloo on Nanook's side only. For the scene, Nanook built only half an igloo; he left the other side open so Flaherty could film. The half-igloo in which the action took place was itself a freak. "The average Eskimo igloo, about 12 feet in diameter, was much too small," wrote Flaherty. "On the dimensions I laid out for him, a diameter of 25 feet, Nanook and his companions started to build the biggest igloo of their lives" (Sadoul 1972:236). Then Nanook and his family undressed in the Arctic cold so Flaherty could make his well-lighted and deeply focused pictures.

And the Eskimos who were waving at Flaherty during the walrus hunt? They weren't saying hello. They wanted him to get over there with his rifle to kill that beast that threatened to drag them into the icy sea. Flaherty ignored their request for the modern instrument he preferred not be seen on film.

What are you seeing in the film—truth or lie? Presumably the way they undress and get under the robes in the halved igloo is the same way they undress and get under robes in a full igloo. If we had a camera capable of fitting somewhere in the full igloo and film capable of shooting in the dim light of a full igloo, it would almost certainly show just what Flaherty's camera showed—though there would be considerably more crowding of bodies. And if Flaherty weren't there with his rifle that particular group of Eskimos probably wouldn't have had a rifle with which to dispatch a recalcitrant walrus.

So what's the difference?

Representation and reality. One is representation, people acting out themselves. The other is a presentation on film of what was actually happening. The two filmstrips might seem exactly the same, but the meaning is discrepant. With Flaherty, we haven't moved all the way to fiction—the actors portray only themselves—but this isn't the real thing either. In some measure, the first significant documentary was also the first docudrama.

Death Row (1979) is a film about men trying to stay sane while they wait for other men to find a way to kill them. The last line of the film is spoken by a lunatic, a man who would sometimes send me notes signed "Fantastic Dancer of the Mind." His is a long rant that is at once poetically astute and discursively psychotic. Dancer's last line is: "You got to understand the real language that is being spoken."

And that—understanding the real language that is being spoken—is at the heart of the problem I've been trying to identify here. Without that understanding, even words that look like words you think you know won't help you one iota. The transfer of words spoken to words printed on a page, for example, involves a profound act of modal transformation. We don't usually think about that; it's more convenient to be able to think, "This quotation is what that person said at that time and that place." It isn't. Think of the grand old statement and how it might be stressed and timed:

> I love you.
> *I* love you.
> I *love* you.
> I love *you.*
> I love . . . you.
> I love *you?*

And all of that is without context, without body, without weight. The act of moving a spoken utterance to a page is, as Dennis Tedlock has argued, a major act of translation. Not just transportation, but translation (see Tedlock 1983, 1988).

Artists regularly let us know how we're to take things. That's their job—to present language to us in ways that direct us into the understandings they want us to have, or which maintain ambiguities they want preserved. For every utterance, they have at their disposal all the devices of language. Since they are creating the utterance rather than trying to replicate it, they are in absolute control. Anything said in a novel *was* said in that novel;

there is no arguing the fact of the utterance. Anything not said in a novel was never said anywhere in time or space or print. The world of fiction is absolute, and that is an essential part of its pleasure for both creator and reader.

The world of the documentarian is not absolute. It is at best partial. But it is the artist's kind of control to which the best ethnographers and sociologists and reporters and filmmakers aspire. They are not, and don't see themselves as, purveyors of transparent vessels that provide you what they saw. They know the absolute impossibility of that. You see only what they made. If you want to see what they see, go with them next time.

Telling the Truth

Having taken the vision apart, let me very briefly try to put it back together.

I said earlier that on the basis of the text alone you could not tell the difference between a documentary object and a fictional object. But we don't operate with the text alone. Even if we don't know about the thing being presented, there are things we *do* know, and, for reasons I still do not understand, it is astonishingly difficult to make the feigned seem real. In theory it's possible, but I've rarely seen it accomplished.

I have, for example, seen many attempts by competent filmmakers to reenact political demonstrations of the kind that occurred in the 1960s, but the only such political demonstration in a fiction film that had a modicum of verisimilitude was in Haskell Wexler's *Medium Cool* (1969). The reason the political demonstration footage worked in *Medium Cool* was the events were real: Wexler moved his actors through the street demonstrations during the 1968 Chicago Democratic convention.

Moments can be faked. A famous photograph shows a baby on a Manchurian train station platform circa 1939, crying and presumably abandoned or orphaned after a Japanese bombing; the baby, Edward D. Ives reminds me, was placed on that platform by the photographer after the bombing was over. A photograph by a Farm Security Administration photographer Arthur Rothstein shows a bleached cow skull on a windswept and barren plain; Rothstein had acquired the skull elsewhere and had taken to photographing it in what he thought interesting places. The hoax was revealed because people realized they were seeing the same skull against different backdrops. The lie did not survive extension into a set of images (Stott 1973:61).

I think it is extremely difficult to maintain a documentary lie into large organic structures. Single images and brief scenes can perhaps be faked with marginal effort, but the difficulty of maintaining verisimilitude increases exponentially the more images there are in the series, scenes in the film, or chapters in the book. Reality is cluttered with the irrelevant detritus of other events and its controlling arrow of time goes in one direction only. Those two elements in combination make complex fraud virtually impossible.

Over the years, I've probably seen ten thousand malefactors and a fair number of virtuous folks killed in movies and on television. The three media killings that remain most vivid and present to me, however, are Jack Ruby shooting Lee Harvey Oswald in the basement of the Dallas jail in 1963, Eddie Adams's photograph of Saigon Police Chief Nguyen Ngoc Loan shooting a VC suspect in the head during the 1968 Tet offensive, and police in a western state vigorously shooting a robber to death in the cab of his Ford pickup in January 1988. Something in each of those deaths was absent from every one of the fictive killings I've ever seen. Perhaps it was just that I believed they were real.

The real has power and it confers authority. *Sophie's Choice* (1984) is interesting; *Shoah* (1985) sears the brain. Alain Resnais's *Night and Fog* (1955), composed primarily of captured Nazi footage, narrated by a speaker who never shuts up, and strung upon a lugubrious musical track by Hans Eisler, possesses an authority I find in no fictive film about the camps. Many fiction films have included terrifying scenes in mental institutions, but I know of none that compares to the dreary and relentless horror of Frederick Wiseman's *Titicut Follies* (1967).

Here is what I think is going on. The workers in numbers, whether in anthropology or renology, are always going for abstractions; the heart of their work excludes individuals, it excludes you and me. Probability may get very close, but it never has real skin. Fictive work explores the freedom of infinite possibility: let's try this and let's try that; we all know that when it's over we'll be exactly where and what we were. Nothing changes in the course of a fiction film or book except your mood.

After completing a novel, good or bad, you don't have to think about it ever again if you don't want to. You certainly don't have to deal with any external issue it explores or presents. You *may,* but that consideration is not a condition of the medium. The best documentary work denies you that freedom. The information it presents becomes, in part, your responsibility now too. You can be unconcerned with the legitimacy of John Barth's 'fuck' but you can't ever pretend you don't know what Claude Lanzmann told you or what James Agee and Walker Evans told you or what Jean Malaurie and Frederick Wiseman told you. Someday, somewhere, sometime, a decision will be expected of you—a word in a conversation, a vote, a contribution, a nod of agreement, a voice raised in support or anger—and those documents will provide part of the structure that determines the choice you make.

Early on, I quoted Robert Creeley speaking about the way words create their own validity. They do have such power, and in the control of excellent artists that validity can be moving indeed. But the validity of a thing entirely made and of a thing disclosed *and* made is not the same. The thing disclosed provides the thing made with an authority that I do not believe can be faked or forged.

The value of these objects, then, is not just that they move us. Fiction moves us, music moves us, pictures and sculpture move us. Rather, these articulations of the real move us and put us in touch with realities we can trust that are external to our own. Their information is not just factual and emotional; it is also ethical. And because of that, they empower us: they become part of our authority for making and maintaining moral choice. That is the crux and function of their reality.

The studies grounded in the real and focused on the individual, they have heart, and heart is real. I don't know how to weigh it or count it or mark it, but I know when it's there. Through all Flaherty's manipulation, a real Nanook is there and we know it. Through all Agee's excess and Evans's astringency, real families are there and we know it. It is their art that makes that reality present for us, but it is the reality that makes their art possible—and believable.

In the final scene of *Let Us Now Praise Famous Men,* James Agee and Walker Evans hear a strange new sound which Agee after a while identifies as foxes calling to one another in the night. It is here that Agee lets art shatter for the last time the professional facade of journalism. He acknowledges not that the reality is unrepresentable in prose, but rather that it contains the same ineffable resonance to which art aspires; it has meaning at once embedded in and perfectly free of context. The sound they hear is at one with the world and complete unto itself, and with it I will end:

This calling continued, never repeating a pattern, and always with what seemed infallible art, for perhaps twenty minutes. It was thoroughly as if principals had been set up, enchanted, and left like dim sacks at one side of a stage as enormous as the steadfast tilted deck of the earth, and as if onto this stage, accompanied by the drizzling confabulation of nocturnal-pastoral music, two masked characters, unforetold and perfectly irrelevant to the action, had with catlike aplomb and noiselessness stept and had sung, with sinister casualness, what at length turned out to have been the most significant, but most unfathomable, number in the show; and had then in perfect irony and silence withdrawn.

It was after the ending of this that we began a little to talk. Ordinarily we enjoyed talking and of late, each absorbed throughout most of the day in subtle and painful work that made even the lightest betrayal of our full reactions unwise, we had found the fragments of time we were alone, and able to give voice to them and to compare and analyze them, valuable and necessary beyond comparison of cocaine. But now in this structure of special exaltation it was, though not unpleasant, thoroughly unnecessary, and obstructive of more pleasing usage. Our talk drained rather quickly off into silence and we lay thinking, analyzing, remembering, in the human and artist's sense praying, chiefly over matters of the present and of that immediate past which was a part of the present; and each of these matters had in that time the extreme clearness, and edge, and honor, which I shall now try to give to you; until at length we too fell asleep. [Agee and Evans 1980:470–71]

NOTES

An earlier version of this paper was presented as the 1988 Marshal Dodge Memorial Folklore Lecture at the University of Maine, 17 March 1988. My thanks to Professor Edward D. Ives for his invitation to present that lecture. My further thanks to Professor Ives, Professor Diane Christian, Dr. Henri Korn, and Ms. Roberta Chester for their comments on various aspects of this paper. The matters discussed here are an extension of the argument begun in Jackson 1985.

1. Manning had been assistant secretary of state for public affairs in the Kennedy Administration from March 1962 to September 1964. Before that he'd been a working journalist.

2. Vincent Crapanzano (1986) discusses this mode of personal narrative in an article that is, unfortunately, rendered untenable by what I find an arbitrary academic perverseness. Crapanzano says, for example, that we must mistrust George Catlin's descriptions *because* they are so personal, so detailed, and apparently so accurate. That logic leaves room for nothing other than being one's own eyewitness.

3. This applies equally to physicists, biologists, and other physical scientists. Quantum mechanics developed in part because of the failure of hypotheses in classical mechanics to "yield complete agreement with experiment (as, for example, the spectrum of helium" (Considine 1976:1855). That discrepancy was not measurable before the existence of sophisticated spectrographic devices, so there was no way for theorists to suspect a new explanation of physical behavior was even necessary. In neurobiology, linear models of brain theory predominated until the late 1980s, when the availability of extremely fast parallel processing computers permitted the emulation and exploration of very different models. This technology consisted not only of large and very expensive parallel processors, such as the Cray, but also of desktop microcomputers able to perform at 24 times the speed of a VAX and costing less than $150,000. For scientists doing such work, computations that previously took six months now take fifteen minutes. One immediate result was an explosion in the complexity of the kinds of questions asked about brain behavior.

4. In a private communication, the pseudonymous subject of the chapter titled "Why Ellen Laughed" (Holland 1981:143–71) said: "He cleaned up his prose, but he left mine just as it was on the tape. That's not fair. Do you think that's fair?"

References Cited

Abbott, Jack Henry. 1981. *In the Belly of the Beast: Letters from Prison.* New York: Random House.

———. 1988. Indictment No. 5267/81: Affidavit in Support of Motion to Vacate Judgement [*sic*] under C.P.L. Sec. 44.10 (Xerox copy.)

Agee, James, and Walker Evans. 1980 [1941]. *Let Us Now Praise Famous Men.* Boston: Houghton Mifflin.

Barth, John. 1967. Lost in the Funhouse. *Atlantic Monthly* 220(11):73–82.

———. 1968. *Lost in the Funhouse.* Garden City, N.Y.: Doubleday.

Becker, Howard S. 1963. *Outsiders: Studies in the Sociology of Deviance.* New York: Free Press.

Bennett, William J. 1989. A Response to Milton Friedman. *Wall Street Journal.* 19 September.

Berryman, John. 1964. *Dream Songs.* New York: Farrar, Straus.

Boas, Franz, ed. 1900. *Publications of the Jesup North Pacific Expedition,* vol. 1, *1898–1900.* New York: American Museum of Natural History.

Brammer, William [Billy Lee]. 1961. *The Gay Place.* Boston: Houghton Mifflin.

Bruner, Edward M. 1986. Ethnography as Narrative. In *The Anthropology of Experience,* ed. Victor W. Turner and Edward M. Bruner, pp. 139–55. Urbana: University of Illinois Press.

Burrough, Bryan. 1990. Self-Made Man: Top Deal Maker Leaves A Trail of Deception in Wall Street Rise. *Wall Street Journal,* 22 January, A1, A6.

Bush, George. 1989. Text of President's Speech on National Drug Control. *New York Times,* 6 September.

Catlin, George. 1844. *Letters and Notes on the Manners, Customs, and Conditions of the North American Indians: Written during Eight Years' Travel (1832–1839) amongst the Wildest Tribes of Indians in North America.* London.

Chaney, Lynn. 1988. Report to the President, the Congress, and the American People. *Chronicle of Higher Education,* 21 September, pp. A17–23.

Considine, Douglas M., ed. 1976. *Van Nostrand's Scientific Encyclopedia,* 5th ed. New York: Van Nostrand Reinhold.

Crapanzano, Vincent. 1986. Hermes' Dilemma: The Masking of Subversion in Ethnographic Description. In *Writing Culture: The Poetics and Politics of Ethnography,* ed. James Clifford and George E. Marcus, pp. 51–76. Berkeley: University of California Press.

Daressa, Lawrence. 1988. Testimony before the House Subcommittee on Telecommunications and Finance, Energy and Commerce Committee, 10 March 1988. *The Independent.* June, pp. 31–33.

Dead "War Hero" Unmasked: A Life of Lies to Hide Failures. 1989. *New York Times,* 10 October.

Friedman, Milton. 1989. An Open Letter to Bill Bennett. *Wall Street Journal,* 7 September.

Goffman, Erving. 1963. *Stigma: Notes on the Management of Spoiled Identity.* Englewood Cliffs, N.J. Prentice-Hall.

Gwynn, Frederick L., and Joseph L. Blotner, eds. 1959. *Faulkner in the University.* New York: Vintage.

Hemingway, Ernest. 1932. *Death in the Afternoon.* New York: Charles Scribner's Sons.

Herr, Michael. 1977. *Dispatches.* New York: Knopf.

Holland, Norman. 1981. *Laughing: A Psychology of Humor.* Ithaca, N.Y.: Cornell University Press.

Hughes, Everett C. 1945. Dilemmas and Contradictions of Status. *American Journal of Sociology* 1:353–59.

Jackson, Bruce. 1968. The Battle of the Pentagon. *Atlantic Monthly* 221(1):35–42.

———. 1972. *In the Life: Versions of the Criminal Experience.* New York: Holt, Rinehart & Winston.

Jackson, Bruce. 1977. *Killing Time: Life in the Arkansas Penitentiary.* Ithaca, N.Y.: Cornell University Press.

———. *A Thief's Primer.* 1972. New York: Macmillan.

———. 1984. Things That From a Long Way Off Look Like Flies. *Journal of American Folklore* 98:131–47.

Jackson, Michael, and Bruce Jackson. 1983. *Doing Drugs.* New York: St Martin's/Marek.

Kafka, Franz. 1952. The Metamorphosis. In *Selected Stories of Franz Kafka.* Translated by Willa and Edwin Muir. New York: Modern Library.

Kilborn, Peter T. 1991. Scraping By, Illegally, Mining Kentucky Coal. *New York Times.* 3 March.

Langan, Patrick A. 1991. America's Soaring Prison Population. *Science* 251 (29 March):1568–73.

Mailer, Norman. 1968. *The Armies of the Night: History as a Novel, the Novel as History.* New York: New American Library.

[The McKay Commission]. *Attica: The Official Report of the New York State Special Commission on Attica.* 1972. New York: Bantam.

Malaurie, Jean. 1976. *Les derniers rois de Thulé.* Paris: Plon.

Morganthau, Tom, with Mark Miller. 1989. Taking on the Legalizers. *Newsweek.* 25 December, pp. 46–48.

Mydans, Seth. 1991. Videotape of Beating by Officers Puts Full Glare on Brutality Issue. *New York Times,* 18 March.

Nagel, William G. 1977. On Behalf of a Moratorium on Prison Construction. *Crime and Delinquency* 23:154–72.

Oswald, Russell G. 1972. *Attica: My Story.* Garden City, N.Y.: Doubleday.

Policy on Marijuana Has Failed, Study Says. 1989. *New York Times,* 23 August.

Reavis, Dick J. 1985. How They Ruined Our Prisons. *Texas Monthly* 13:5 (May), pp. 152–59, 232–46.

Sadoul, Georges. 1972. *Dictionary of Films.* Translated, edited, and updated by Peter Morris. Berkeley: University of California Press.

Shribman, David. 1989. Bush's Get-Tough Drug Plan Shares Philosophy That Didn't Work for Rockefeller 20 Years Ago. *Wall Street Journal,* 7 September.

Stark, Rodney. 1972. *Police Riots: Collective Violence and Law Enforcement.* Belmont, Calif.: Focus Books.

Stott, William. 1973. *Documentary Expression and Thirties America.* New York: Oxford University Press.

Tedlock, Dennis. 1983. *The Spoken Word and the Work of Interpretation.* Philadelphia: University of Pennsylvania Press.

———. 1988. "The Witches Were Saved": A Zuni Origin Story. *Journal of American Folklore* 101:312–20.

Westmoreland, General William C. 1972. *A Soldier Reports.* Garden City, N.Y.: Doubleday.

Wicker, Tom. 1975. *A Time to Die.* New York: Quadrangle/The New York Times.

Wilson, James Q. 1970. *Varieties of Police Behavior: The Management of Law and Order in Eight Communities.* New York. Atheneum.

FILMS

Creeley. 1988. Bruce Jackson and Diane Christian.

Death Row. 1979. Bruce Jackson.

Medium Cool. 1969. Haskell Wexler.

Nanook of the North. 1922. Alain Resnais.

Night and Fog. 1955. Alain Resnais.

Shoah. 1985. Claude Lanzmann.

Sophie's Choice. 1984. Alan J. Pakula.

The Store. 1984. Frederick Wiseman.

Titicut Follies. 1967. Frederick Wiseman.

A Note on the Author

BRUCE JACKSON is Distinguished Professor and director, Center for Studies in American Culture, State University of New York at Buffalo. He is the author of *Law and Disorder: Criminal Justice in America* and *Fieldwork* and numerous scholarly and trade books, as well as a diverse array of popular and scholarly articles. His documentary films, made in collaboration with Diane Christian, have been broadcast on public television stations in the United States and Europe.